EKTEK

Victoria Osborne

First published in 2016 by Victoria Osborne

Copyright © 2016 Victoria Osborne

National Library of Australia Cataloguing-in-Publication entry

Creator: Osborne, Victoria, 1959- author.
Title: EKTEK / Victoria Osborne.
ISBN: 978-0-9942181-3-1 (paperback)
ISBN: 978-0-9942181-2-4 (ebook)
Target Audience: For young adults
Subjects: Animal rights activists
Fiction. Endangered species—Fiction. Fantasy fiction
Dewey Number: A823.4

Victoria Osborne
www.ourrelationshipwithnature.com

Book layout by www.ebooklaunch.com

There are no passengers on Spaceship Earth.
Everybody's crew.

Marshall McLuhan

(Quote used by permission from Michael McLuhan 2013)

EKTEK001

Last Chance to Eat

Prologue

It was high noon. A lone crocodile lay basking on the riverside mud. Heat smashed onto her rocky skin. Her eyes burned with danger even as she rested. She opened her claw-toothed mouth in slow motion, for air-conditioning.

An elegant brolga drifted in to land beside her on the riverbank. He looked like an ornate grey umbrella as he folded and came to stand. Shining Teeth had just eaten a rotten fish and had no desire to move. The tall bird had no idea how lucky he was.

—*Ah, stuff it.* Quick as a snake's tongue flick, Shining Teeth lunged at the bird, catching him easily mid thigh. The suddenly not-so-lucky brolga stretched his huge wings wide, flapping, scooping air for power, thrashing, as Shining Teeth grappled, chomped and sank her teeth higher up into the feathered torso. The brolga arched his neck backwards, opening and shutting his beak. Perhaps he was gasping for air. Perhaps he was trying to scream.

Shining Teeth plunged into the water, rolling the brolga down into the murky depths. There, tucked under a crevasse in the river's edge, she kept a slimy larder. As she swam back to the surface, the crocodile thought—*How marvellous not having to worry about tomorrow's dinner.*

Shining Teeth settled into the baking sunshine again and half closed her eyes. The river resumed the quiet life once more until a swirl of clay-coloured water heralded the arrival of another crocodile. Grater waded out of the water and ploughed over the top of Shining Teeth who could not have cared less about wet feet stamping on her head. The backs of the two crocs turned pale under the hot sun as Grater fought for air after her sprint and then, when she could speak, announced—*Hardback is trapped.*

Shining Teeth stared at Grater, calculating the implications of their mate's capture. She turned and headed into the water. Grater sucked in lungfuls of air and joined her in the brown soup.

Word travelled fast and Hardback's harem gathered to witness his entrapment. He'd followed the scent of live-goat bait into an unguarded ambush and now there was no way out, certainly not for the goat and, clearly, not for the crocodile.

Hardback lunged at the net, scrabbling and falling. He arched his back, flashing his pale underbelly. His breathing came in rasping barks. His feet flailed and his tail walloped the sides of the soft cage.

When they arrived, Shining Teeth and Grater climbed the riverbank and approached the trap. The other three crocodiles surged helplessly in the surrounding water. Shining Teeth tried to bite through the net but found the cord impossible to grip. She could only avoid entanglement by backing away.

Hardback was delirious. Shining Teeth looked at him through the criss-cross netting. Then they heard the approaching whine of a two-stroke outboard motor—*We'll find you.*

The humans were coming to check their trap. The harem slid into the river without as much as a droplet splash. They remained there, invisible, watching from just under the surface of the water, their legs dangling in the current.

Hardback tried to escape from the only predators known to crocs. The sound of the motor infuriated him. He strained against the net. The humans were practised and impersonal. They tied his mouth and overcame his struggles. They moved swiftly. They knew he would die if he became stressed. They wanted him alive.

Under the muddy surface of the water, five pairs of eyes watched as Hardback was dumped into the bottom of the boat. The two-stroke coughed into life and the humans whined back down the river.

The harem: Shining Teeth, Grater, Asunder, Jata and Damura, needed no discussion and moved off after their male. They followed the boat to where the river met the railway tracks.

At the wharf, Hardback was unloaded from the tinnie and packed into a crate. The crate was then lifted by crane onto the train carriage. The humans moved purposefully, tall and powerful. Finally, satisfied that their charge was secure, the men disappeared from view.

The harem stayed in the river; watching, waiting…

With any luck the train would remain long enough for them to work out a plan. How could they rescue Hardback? What could they do?

Losing patience, the crocodiles swirled around each other, jostling to keep sight of their husband. They snorted and blew water. They clapped their jaws together in frustration—*We must get him back!*

—*Without him we are unprotected!*

—*Get him!*

Asunder took it upon herself to climb out of the water and up on-to the riverbank. She headed straight for the train.

With a mighty sideways lunge, Shining Teeth corralled her back into the swill—*Are you insane?*

—*We must do something!* Asunder sank back into the river—*We need Ektek!*

—*What can Ektek do here that we can't?* growled Shining Teeth.

Asunder looked to Jata, seeking an ally—*What can we do?*

—*We need help*, Jata agreed. She asked Shining Teeth—*Why shouldn't we get help?*

Damura swirled round in front of Shining Teeth—*Ektek has skills.*

—*They've got technology*, Asunder added—*They can fly.*

—*Fly. Nonsense*, spat Shining Teeth— *Flying's for the birds.*

Damura stared hard at Shining Teeth—*What can we do?*

—*Wait!* said Shining Teeth and she slapped her tail on the surface of the water with vehemence—*We wait. That's what we can do. An opportunity will present itself if we are patient and observant. We don't need other creatures interfering in our business. We help ourselves! We are crocodiles!*

The crocodile harem despaired as they waited in the river. They watched for a sign that Hardback might escape. They wished the humans would change their minds and let their giant male go free but neither thing happened. Instead, suddenly, the diesel engine roared into life with a blast of acrid black smoke. All five floating crocs swung towards the noise. Slowly the train began to move along the glinting metal ribbons implanted into the land. It seemed to take forever to get up to speed but then, in no time at all, the roaring monster was gone. The crocodiles watched from the water until there was no more movement at the train station. They clambered up through the sludge to the dry. It was hopeless. Unable to follow over land at any speed, the harem had no way of knowing where Hardback would be taken. Each crocodile walked in a different direction, then, changing their minds, changing bearings, trudged in another, looking for some clue, hoping for some inspiration, but nothing came to help them.

Grater continued in a straight line up the road. As she crossed the train station to follow in her mate's tracks the ground began to shake. There was a distant growling and then roaring as a new train crashed over the lines, slowing as it neared the station. Grater disappeared under the flying wheels of the carriages strobing past.

Shining Teeth ran beside the train. She shook her great lizard head and bellowed to all living things—*Ektek!* She cried out with all her might over the booming train—*Ektek! Ektek!*

A beetle, only incidentally within hearing, needed no further encouragement. He rose groggily into the dusk, as beetles do, and buzzed crazily out of sight.

The train ground to a halt at the station.

Shining Teeth clambered up to Grater, lying physically unharmed between the train tracks—*Are you alive?*

Grater shook her head. She could not hear a thing. Her skull was still thundering. The two crocs shared such a look through the wheels of the train…

The beetle flew, zig-zag-zig, into the darkening sky and came to rest by another beetle. The two coleopterons, strangers to each other, danced and touched briefly, transferring directional information. Then the second beetle bowed and muttered—*Two,* and took off in the same direction, south by southeast.

The second train had left the station by now and Grater crawled, still shaking, away from the tracks. The crocodile harem slid slowly back into the river to wait for Ektek to arrive.

Some distance away, yet another beetle edged up the stalk of a drying plant. Its serrated legs clung impossibly to the stem while its skinny feet could find no purchase and skated over the surface of a leaf.

Flying high above in the evening, that second beetle came into view. It approached, just a speck arriving from out of the blood-coloured sky. It came in to land beside the stalk climber. These two beetles touched for a moment, danced up and down the stalk before the third beetle in the relay squeaked—*Three.* Then it, too, took off, flying as far as it could before seeking the next in the number team, and became no more than an imagined dot in the fiery troposphere.

Chapter One

To a flying Christmas beetle, Bedlam Zoo looked like a prison, a formidable collection of brick buildings and wire enclosures. The perimeter wall was built of large rough-hewn stones and lanced with heavy wrought-iron spikes. The zoo's exterior impression was of strength, permanence and fortitude.

The zigzagging beetle was Spark. As he got closer, Spark thought Bedlam Zoo looked less like a gaol and more like a fortress. He puzzled about it as he flew closer and closer to his assignment. Was the wall keeping inmates in or intruders out?

Bedlam Zoo was in a city. Three sides of the zoo faced different busy urban roads, one with a train line. There was even a zoo railway station, to simplify travel for human visitors who wished to enjoy a fun family day out staring at imprisoned creatures. At the apex of the triangle was a small area of steep bushland that dipped down towards a river. It was fenced with a heap of rusty cars and piled up old whitegoods (now more rusty than white). This area remained untouched by the zoo's maintenance staff because they never received any instructions about it. For an Ektek spider, with their ears and eyes trained to the world-wide-cobweb, it was easy to make any computer communiqué disappear. Ektek made much of the saying, 'Out of sight, out of mind.'

Spark continued his uneven flight towards the zoo. Sounds of exotic animals from various countries grew closer as the beetle approached. The stench of trapped beasts was also increasing. Spark tried to work out if he was feeling excited or terrified. He couldn't decide which as he went over the wire and flew into the zoo. He had made it into Bedlam.

Aging statues of megafauna decorated the well-kept public pathways. As Spark flittered past a real, and really bored, elephant, she used him for target practice. The elephant, whose name was Anna, flung a fountain of dust from her trunk directly into his erratic path. She laughed in that bizarre way of slightly mad elephants. Soon she turned to scratch her backside on a large old tree trunk cemented into her cage. Then she resumed her regime of swaying back and forth and forth and back and back again over her allotted four-metre walkway; her own personal invisible constraint system.

Spark coughed, spluttered uncontrollably and zagged when he should have zigged before coming in to land, only narrowly missing some sharp barbed wire on a railing. He scuttled down a neglected pathway hung with a sign that said 'Staff Only'. The sign was also clearly marked by a line of beetle footprints for those who knew how to see. Past dense shrubbery, he went through a tunnel into the bush, and then rounded a corner. He didn't notice the airship tethered high above him as he entered the foyer of an enormous cave. Who bothers to look up when everything right in front of them is astounding?

Spark's beetle mandibles hung open in amazement as he stared around him at this fabled place. All his life he had heard legends about Ektek. He had finally made it. Wow. He, Spark, Christmas beetle, had arrived in the huge garage area of Ektek. Pulling himself together, Spark nervously approached a large old darkling beetle that appeared to be guarding the entrance to the hangar—*Is this Ektek?*

The darkling nodded. He was a particularly elongated beetle with ridged sheaths over his wings. Not only were they ridged but his elytra also very shiny. His antennae were wider at the tip than they were by his head and they swayed when he added, without any curiosity or pleasantries—*State your business.*

Spark replied—*Urgent. Number five hundred and seventeen.* He thought he'd better say the urgent bit again but, remembering his mother's words when he was just a grub, kept his mouth shut. He'd do what he was told. At least, he'd try to.

—*Follow. Remember your number. That's your mission, now. You are that number.* The darkling beetle led Spark further inside the cool of the cavern—*And keep up, for Zed's sake.*

The two beetles moved past the light reflectors into the repair section of the workshop. Spark stared around him in wonder—*How does it stay light in here?*

—*Solar tubes, contain mirrors,* the darkling beetle kept marching as he explained—*Sunlight reflects down the tubes. Adjusted to get maximum light into the cavern. Obviously.*

Spark was overcome as he gazed around the cave—*It's huge. How...?*

The darkling beetle, secretly pleased to stop and catch his breath, agreed—*Ants and termites. Dug it out. Series of caves linked to each other. Under and round the zoo, kilometres of caverns. Come on, through here…*

Spark couldn't help himself. He found himself stopping again to examine a bank of various shaped containers, grouped under a wide funnel, leading to some sort of ducting—*What's all this?*

The darkling beetle sighed again but provided the information, proud enough of Ektek to want to boast—*Batteries. Charging. Ektek has solar panels on the zoo's buildings. Maintenance staff think they're part of the zoo's grid. Once recharged, those batteries'll be ready for our vehicles. Build up of hydrogen round the batteries gets collected for the airship.*

A collection of sturdy bottles and some tubular apparatus lined the walls. Spark sniffed. He was sure he could smell the distinct odour of overcooked… —*Chips?*

—*Chips. That's right. Chips. Do you have to stick your nose into everything? This isn't the time!* The darkling beetle stopped and barked at the young tourist, possibly reminding himself that he, too, had a job to do—*Get a move on!*

—*Sorry, darkling,* said Spark as he hurried on—*But, chips?*

—*Don't call me darkling!* growled the beetle—*Name's Torque.*

—*Torque?*

—*Yes. Torque. It's biodiesel.*

—*Bio-what?*

—*Biodiesel. Fuel. Recycled chip oil. Powers the tank.* Torque pointed towards a shiny armoured vehicle about the size of a small human car. It was shaped like a stag beetle and carried all sorts of equipment; ladders, cranes and hoses—*Zoo's kiosk puts out used oil for the recycling firm. Twice a week. We take it once a week. No one asks any questions, we don't make a fuss. Simple process involving caustic soda. Bit dangerous but we're careful.*

—*Brilliant place to live,* said Spark—*A zoo.*

Torque agreed—*Got that right, young larva. Find us a lot of useful rubbish. Now then, march. Don't want to lose you. We've got important business to attend. Or you wouldn't be here, remember?*

Torque was head of Ektek security. He believed he was indispensable in the caverns of Ektek and he may well have been right. He certainly did know everything and everyone and what he didn't know was simply not worth knowing.

As Spark followed the old beetle, he couldn't help himself. He gazed about him astonished, not only by the collection of vehicles, but also by the industry with which the mechanics attended them. The reflected sunlight beamed into a group of engineer beetles crawling diligently over the tank's engine. Spark could hear a metallic knocking and a frenetic hissing and then there was a clang as something heavy dropped onto the hard dirt ground. Spark could almost taste the endeavour and purpose in the air as he absorbed the sounds and smells and lights reflecting from polished metal and burnished elytra of beetles hurrying here and dashing there and standing quietly in a corner talking to an attractive...

Oh, there was simply too much to see!

Among the craft parked in the cave, a graceful wingship was just visible in another dock area of the workshop. This craft looked almost like a swan cradling its young under its wide and gently downward curving wings. It was engineered to fit two creatures comfortably in the front, about five metres wide and three metres long. Spark stared at the much smaller plane parked on top of the wingship.

— *The mini-plane,* said Torque, when he saw what had lately captured Spark's attention—*Manoeuvrable, versatile, she can keep in easy reach of the airship, or in this case, the wingship. Lock in the communication channel; they become one flexible craft.*

—*There's so many of them!*

—*Vehicles? Yup, and what's more, fleet is ready at all times.*

—*What if one of them has just been somewhere?*

—*Don't matter; twenty-four hour roster of mechanics to check and double-check each mechanism, each fuel system, communications, everything.*

—*Why doesn't everyone just escape?*

—*Escape what?*

—*Well, here.* Spark looked around—*The zoo?*

—*Too much to do, 'in't there. Who else is going to look after all them poor animals, then?*

—*Er, Torque?* Spark whispered, overcome and overwhelmed by this great cathedral to ecology and technology—*Got any apprenticeships going?*

Torque straightened his hairy exoskeleton—*Let's get on with the job in hand and see how we go after that, shall we? No use getting ahead of ourselves, is there, young collie?*

Spark snapped to attention. He not only remembered his mum's words (keep your mouth shut and do what you're told) but also the grim message he carried. He meekly followed Torque through a tunnel in the stone and dirt to a dimly lit hole in the wall. Torque turned to him—*Wait here,* and disappeared inside.

Spark stared at a tiny shell embedded in the wall and wondered who, or what, he was about to meet. What sort of creatures would these Ektek animals be? What would they ask of him? How would he measure up? There was light at the end of the tunnel and, oh, it was the way out. It started to look attractive. He even took a step towards it; the way home, but he stopped himself. Of course he would go on into the inner chambers of Ektek. Spark was way too intrigued by this adventure to back out now.

Then Torque was at his side again—*They'll see you.*

Spark, filled with trepidation, followed the darkling beetle towards the door and entered a cave filled with blue stars, electronic screen light and lots of strange blinking equipment. The space seemed smaller than it was because it was so crowded with its tangle of machinery. This was the Ektek communications centre. Spark saw there were three creatures in the space and none of them looked particularly fierce or strange. He did, however, feel painfully self conscious as he realised they were waiting for him, their work apparently interrupted.

The biggest one stood with his taloned feet gripped into the dirt making him look, for all the world, like a dinosaur. He was a cassowary with a thick black coat of feathers covering his body, a shapely blue neck hung with red wattles like pirate jewellery, a bony cap on his head and searingly intelligent eyes.

A yellow-footed rock wallaby was also present. His fluffy ears appeared too big for his head and they twitched and flicked, alert. He was covered in luxurious white and brown fur and he stood, leaning back slightly on his glamorous yellow-striped fur tail, with his long legs planted onto the floor and his little arms waiting, en garde.

The last animal was the smallest. She was sitting up, with straight back, balanced on her hindquarters. She was in front of a phalanx of screens and a panel of switches, buttons and track balls. She had short, stiff, red-brown hair. She looked as if she was wearing a distinct punk mask that reflected in the black monitor screen directly opposite her. The dark stripe, underlined and accentuated by a white stripe, covered her eyes like Zorro camouflage. Under it, her black determined eyes glinted. She was interested. Interesting, too. Her long pointed nose twitched as she watched the two beetles enter the control centre. She was a numbat. She flicked out a long worm-like tongue and slurped at a small dish on the control panel, apparently containing the remains of her breakfast. Spark was impressed and just a tiny bit disgusted; that was one heck of a long tongue!

All three animals waited expectantly as the two beetles approached. Torque went straight to the numbat and growled—*Here's the new number. He's called Spark.* To the nervous Spark he said—*Come on,*

9

they won't bite you. As all three creatures chuckled politely, Spark could only hope Torque was telling the truth and followed obediently. They came close to the scaly legs of the cassowary and Torque turned to Spark—*This cassowary is Helmut. He's the pilot of the airship. You'll have seen it on the way in.*

Spark, who of course hadn't looked up to see anything at all of the airship because he'd been so engrossed in everything he could see down at his eye level when he'd arrived, bowed to the giant bird and said nothing of his ignorance.

Torque moved on to the white-and-brown wallaby and said—*This is Hod, one of our engineers,* and Spark bowed again, this time to the yellow-footed rock wallaby.

Finally, Torque moved to the numbat seated in front of the computers and said—*This is Antenna. She looks after our communications systems. She'll take care of you.* Then Torque backed away respectfully, waiting until he was next called upon.

Antenna turned to Spark—*Looks like you've come a long way. Spark, is it?* Torque nodded from the corner, just in case Spark was paralysed with fear; which he was. Antenna acknowledged Torque as well before continuing—*What is your number, Spark?* She stepped from her rock seat and stood on four feet, looking down at him and bending closer to hear the smaller creature speak.

Young Spark watched Antenna as he said—*Five hundred and seventeen. Crocodiles.* And then the two creatures began to dance together. This particular dance had been repeated five hundred and seventeen times between the beetles on their journey towards the zoo. This was anything but an ordinary funky get-to-know-you dance. This was an educational dance. Through Spark and Antenna's movements details were communicated through gestures, scents and sounds. It was the dance of the honeybee, only in a broad accent. Over the years of increasing threats animals had learned several languages to understand each other and for space and direction there was simply nothing better than the bee ballet.

Once Antenna had a clear idea of Shining Teeth's predicament she said—*Considerable distance. Okay.* She turned to the cassowary— *We'll need to think about this, Helmut.* To beetle Spark she asked—*Salties, I presume?*

Spark nodded—*Think so.*

Antenna turned to Hod and Helmut—*One's been trapped. The male. His family want him freed.* Antenna continued her mental computations—*Could get ugly. Helmut? What do you think?*

—*We're about to commence an action.* The cassowary considered for a moment and then spoke—*We can't alter our plans. The restaurant must take precedence. It's taken months to set this up.*

—*Of course,* said Antenna—*There's too much at stake.*

—*If we had unlimited resources,* Helmut, the cassowary, continued, thinking aloud—*The obvious choice would be the airship together with the wingship.*

—*With the sort of territory crocs inhabit we'd need to give ourselves options,* said Antenna—*But it's impossible, given today.*

—*Could the crocs wait?* asked the wallaby.

—*Not sure. Probably no. Given they are crocodiles.*

—*I wouldn't want to stereotype any species here but crocodiles can be patient,* said Helmut—*For a time. Then, of course, they act and speedily. Taking into account they have already delayed any retaliation so far and we can't respond immediately, if we can do something to alleviate their troubles, I think we should.*

Antenna thought for a moment before she spoke—*My father always said, decisions made in haste lead to poor outcomes.*

—*True,* said Helmut—*And we do need to get to that restaurant. So we've got to decide and then get on with it.*

—*Because of the proximity to the river, what do you think? Is the boat possible?* said Antenna, as she weighed the options.

—*Intek is in action currently, isn't it?* asked Helmut.

—*What's Inket?* said Spark in an aside to Torque. He was beginning to relax and enjoy himself, just a little bit.

—*Intek. Tek! Technology. It's the watery side of Ektek.* Torque may have rolled his eyes but in reality he loved having to explain the finer details of Ektek to a lesser, more ignorant beetle—*We've got Uptek in the air, Ontek on the ground and Intek in the water. Learning about problems for endangered animals. In this case…*

—*Illegal fishing,* said Antenna, nodding. She turned to the wallaby—*What do you think, Hod?*

—*The wingship and the mini-plane?* asked the yellow-footed rock wallaby—*Are they available?*

—*Good thinking, Hod.* The cassowary gleamed his bright thoughtful eyes between the wallaby and the numbat—*I don't think Bash or Crawf are engaged at the moment.*

—*That's so,* said Antenna—*Plane and wingship it is. Helmut? Can you get Bash and Crawf organised as soon as possible? Take Spark with you so he can show them.*

—*Absolutely,* said Helmut—*Hod? I'll meet you at the airship. Spark?*

—*Sir?*

—*Let's go.* Helmut indicated the young beetle should accompany him. Torque nodded permission for Spark to leave with Helmut, and the cassowary had to slow as the beetle gathered wing-speed and flew across the control centre. Before they'd even left the room, Hod resumed his previous discussion as though the beetle had never even been there—*We planned to be in place well before opening time and I've still got no way of speaking to you.*

—*We haven't time to fix it,* Antenna agreed—*We'll be receiving your pictures and hopefully you can get in and out of the kitchen without needing any further instructions.*

—*From me or to me?*

—*Funny. Will you cope?*

Hod became defensive—*Don't talk that much.*

—*That's not what your girlfriend says.*

—*Which one?*

—*Oh, Hod! You're so irresponsible!*

—*They love me and so do you.*

—*Can we please get back to the real world?* Antenna turned her attention back to the computer monitor in front of her and began to flick switches with her numbat paws. She focussed on the monitors—*Lucky that little beetle... What was his name again, Torque?*

—*Spark,* replied the darkling beetle from the corner where he waited for further orders.

—*Right. Spark,* said Antenna—*Lucky he turned up just after the zoo had closed. Would have been difficult if we'd had to take animals off duty. Hey, speaking about closing time, where are Min and Wilkinson? They must have been shut down by now? What's keeping them? Torque? Could you get them to hurry along, please?*

—*Of course, Antenna.* Torque disappeared into the tunnel as Antenna turned back to her work. She seemed to move effortlessly around the maze of switches but then, she'd been in training for years.

The Ektek control panel was a patchwork of metal, bone, plant and plastic. Wire, pipe, cord and shell worked around and through six different-sized video monitors. The crowded console included counters, switches, faders, buttons and keyboards designed to be used by different animals of different sizes with differently shaped hands and feet. It existed as part of Bedlam Zoo's technical network. Only the human staff knew nothing about it.

Hod fiddled with the edge of the control desk and started twiddling a button. He jumped when Antenna slapped him on the wrist of his little fluffy arm—*Get off!*

He jumped backwards and then sniggered at her—*You're worse than your dad!*

—*Well, don't go sticking your great hairy paws in where you don't want to go! Unless, you've changed your mind and you'd like a lesson?*

—*If you ever catch me wanting to learn all that geeky techo stuff… You'll know I'm on my last legs.*

—*You could easily do it.*

—*You easily do it. I'd rather chop off my own tail.*

—*You'd never lose your tail, Hoddy. You're so vain,* Antenna smiled at him as he checked the fluffy glory that was his stripy tail and turned her attention back to the screen—*We've got too much to do.*

There was much to do. After the recent death of her father, Antenna took the weight of the Ektek control desk very seriously. Assisted by Hod, Min and Wilkinson, Antenna worked as the spider in the web, paws on the interwoven threads, determining any vibrations out at the Ektek edges. With their help she had been able to pick up the controller skills devised and perfected by her elders. Now, she knew where each Ektek operative was, what their planned action might be and how best to get that information out to the waiting world.

—*Antenna?* said Hod—*I'd better head.*

—*Hang on, haven't checked everything. Look,* Antenna turned to the monitors—*I've got the homepage open here, right?* There was the bright Ektek logo over the question: '*Who will save the animals?*'

—*Great work, Antenna, but I've got to…*

—*Then, there's the vid insert in the main page…*' Antenna turned to another monitor showing a square of fizzing snow bounded by a surround of eco-ads.

—*Wow. How'd you get so much advertising?* said Hod, leaning forward over Antenna's shoulder. She looked up at him, pleased he was so obviously impressed.

—*Got to keep the site up somehow. So, when we get your footage in, I'll stream it into that and finally…* She turned to the next computer monitor which displayed a page opened to an outmail box. A letter entitled 'Media Release' was addressed to 'Commerce News Division Service' and a considerable list of newspapers and television stations appeared in the address box—*I'll have the mail page open so we can notify the media as soon as we get content.*

—*They have to see this Last Chance to Eat place,* said Hod—*With their own eyes.*

—Journos can download any info or photos they want, no credit or by-line necessary. Now we've got income, Ektek can provide images for free.

—I better go, Hod moved back from the screen—*Helmut'll be waiting...*

—Can we just go over it? One more time? For my benefit?

—Uh, if you really have to...

—Okay. Grabbing hold of his faint interest, Antenna increased the speed of her delivery even more—*Helmut transports you and Zip, gets you into the restaurant before they open tonight. You're on head-cam, Zip's with telescopic arm on her vehicle. Zip has sound. We can't communicate...*

Hod struck a soap opera pose—*Don't say that, babe...*

—Hoddy... Antenna needed his attention and couldn't help just a small warning 'teacher' growl creeping in to her voice.

—Yeah, yeah, go on, I'm listening. Communicating, see?

Antenna shook out her irritation—*Your footage, both you in the kitchen and Zip in the dining room, transmits back in here, we edit and then stream out into the web.*

—What do the cod have to say? asked Hod.

—They know everything we've discovered so far about the illegal fishing. We know the Department admitted to losing at least three of their transmitters over the past year but they call it 'natural attrition'. They reckon predation or 'act of God' got 'em.

—Predation. Well. They're sort of right, eh.

—No, they're not. The Department doesn't like to talk about illegal fishing.

—Funding?

—Lack of.

—They call it an acceptable risk.

—How did you find out?

—Email. Here's the screen. Got the whole Murray Cod story... Antenna opened another page in the Ektek website. Again a border of eco-ads framed well-designed images and grabs of information about the big river fish—*It explains how we watched the cod...*

—But not 'who'.

—Obviously, and how we followed the fishers with their catch into Last Chance to Eat. Then, how the Murray cod containing the transmitters were worth a fortune on the plate. If the human nibbling the cod found the transmitter, then that lucky human won the door prize.

—Some treasure hunt! said Hod.

—We've got images from the surveillance operation but it's unclear what happens in the place. Like, why are the animals still alive when they get there?

—*Last Chance to Eat,* said Hod, squeezing overt meaning into the words—*Gives you a clue, don't it.*

—*We have to find out,* said Antenna—*Once and for all.*

—*Can't help the cod but we might be able to help someone else,* said Hod.

—*Yeah, well. Hopefully. Last Chance to Eat has to be stopped, that's for sure. Basically the action is a trespass and exposure. Simple really.* She looked up at Hod, suddenly nervous—*You think? Is it going to work?*

—*Relax, Anti-freeze. Wouldn't change a thing.*

—*Don't call me Anti-freeze! I'm not the big cuddly one, now, am I. Look at your tail!* Then, as Antenna realised she was keeping him from his duty and Helmut would be waiting for him, she straightened up. There was a glint of humour in her eye though as she shouted at him—*Get to work! You're late!*

—*Whose fault is that?* laughed Hod as he turned to go.

—*Get out of here!* Antenna laughed back—*And, thanks, Hoddy.*

Hod gave her a cheeky wave as he left the control centre. She didn't see it. She was already focussed on her screens and keyboards, absorbed, typing, sorting and planning. This action would go smoothly. As if her life depended on it.

.

Chapter Two

A yellow-spotted bombardier beetle crawled over the surface of the wingship, antennae twitching and swishing over the metal. She had a narrow head fused into her body. Her legs were the same red colour as her head. Her elytra were a shiny blue with yellow spots. She was a perfectionist. She stopped briefly to examine a small scratch on the wingship's exterior. She considered the depth and the length of the dent and her red antennae trembled as she thought. She decided it was a mere surface issue and continued her safety sweep.

The other mechanical beetles on duty understood what was required and had already moved into emergency mode. Each had particular tasks to prepare the wingship and plane and each were trained and efficient in their duties.

Helmut and Spark stood to one side, waiting for the wingship's captain and navigator to appear. Helmut bent down to speak to the beetle at his feet—*You'll like Bash. He's not much bigger than you, probably about the same age. He's a corroboree frog.*

—*And, Crawf?*

—*Ah. Crawf is a rather different kettle of beast. He's bigger…*

—*Oh.*

—*No need for alarm. He's a cockatoo. Big, certainly, but you don't want to let him worry you.*

—*Okay.*

—*Look, no, really, don't think anything about Crawf. He can be a bit… Well. You'll see. Just, don't let him concern you.* Helmut turned to the wingship and shouted up at the mechanic beetle—*Excuse me, Manifold?*

The bombardier beetle looked down to the cassowary on the ground—*Yup?*

—*Did you say you'd sent someone to find Crawf and Bash?*

—*Yup.*

—*Okay. Shouldn't they be here by now?*

—*Yup.*

—*Well. Perhaps I'll go and look for them myself? Good idea?*

—*Yup.* Manifold turned back to her work, tightening a bolt near the wing tip.

—*Thanks for that informative chat, Manifold.* Helmut bent down towards Spark—*I'll just see if I can find them. You stay here, right?*

Spark nodded. He was stunned. He felt as if he were floating. Everything was happening around him and yet he was feeling detached, surreal. The smells and sounds of the hangar were so thrilling he felt as though his little beetle eyes had been opened to the possibilities of life—*Yes, Helmut, I'll stay here,* he echoed thoughtlessly, his synapses overloaded to the point of daftness.

Helmut strode off on his gnarly cassowary legs towards the dark entrance to the tunnel, leaving Spark craning his head up over the wheels to see if he could climb up onto the wingship. His courage grew and he clambered, with great difficulty, onto the surface of the tyre. It felt good to be seeing the Ektek world from this vantage point.

Suddenly, Spark was almost blasted away over the hard dirt floor by a series of growls—*Hullo? What do you think you are doing?* A palm cockatoo looked like a thunder cloud with his headdress feathers fully extended as he lowered his head and marched towards Spark, swaying from side to side, rumbling as he came. The bird was dark grey and the bare skin patch on his face was vibrant dark red.

Spark stared in horror at the approaching threat. This must be Crawf and he was getting closer… Just as Spark was about to turn tail and take flight, Helmut reappeared around the side of the wingship— *Ah, Crawf. See you've met Spark. He's your number today.*

—*Not a terrorist? You're sure?*

—*His name's Spark. He's a Christmas beetle. I don't believe they do terrorism.*

—*No, no we don't…* said Spark—*Absolutely not. No way. Not us.*

—*Can't be too sure,* said Crawf as he straightened up and gave himself a little shake—*Hullo? Spark. Didn't know what you were up to on that wheel. Could have been tampering. Can't have anyone tampering with the machine before we take off, can we?*

—*This is Crawf. He's harmless. He might look frightening but he's not. Don't worry.* As Helmut reassured the beetle, a tiny black-and-yellow frog ambled into Spark's view just behind the cassowary. This, presumably, was Bash. His yellow stripes looked like a glossy maze painted over a shiny black pebble. Helmut continued his conversation, seemingly unaware of Spark's thundering heart—*Found Bash. He was under the mistaken impression he was heading out on the airship. Don't know where he got that. Bash, this is Spark. He'll inform you about those crocs. Do you want to get started? I'll head out on the airship. See you.*

Bash and Crawf both nodded as Helmut left them to it. Crawf's crest was now flatter and much less threatening. Spark noticed his giant beak was hooked and looked very, very sharp—*S'pose so,* said Crawf—*Sooner we get the info, sooner we can go see what a bunch of crocs do for fun out on the river banks.*

The three creatures; frog, cockatoo, beetle, came close together and bowed. Spark began his circular dance. He stepped out the shape of infinity again and then again and shook in some variations. These variations provided the information codes: a shake and a nod in one direction meant one thing, a shimmy and a shiver towards another direction meant something else. Soon the frog and cockatoo joined in and followed the beetle's moves. The dance was serious but still gracious. Each creature was careful to place their feet in exactly the right spot and to shake their limbs or wings in exactly the right way. These were their directions to find the croc harem. Any mistake could mean life or death for the pilot and the navigator.

Manifold continued her check prior to lift off without even glancing at the dance. She shouted at a couple of bombardier beetles down in the engine—*Oi! Watch for the plugs! Don't want them fouled again.*

The dance slowed and stopped and the wingship crew became focussed on leaving. Bash and Crawf climbed up into the cockpit.

—*Good luck,* said Manifold.

—*We're going to need it,* said Crawf.

—*Oh, yeah,* said Manifold with considerable emphasis. Crawf raised his head-feathers at her tone but Manifold had gone before he could comment.

Back on the ground, Spark felt himself sway. He shook his head to try to wake up. The long flight, the coming to life of a fable, everything about Ektek; it was all a bit much for his tiny coleopteran brain.

Spark had to lean his shiny carapace up against the wall. Beetles ran past him, one saying to him—*Can't stay there, mate. They're about to roll out the wingship.* So Spark moved to another spot where he could see Bash and Crawf on duty in the cockpit of the wingship. The small plane was secure on the roof and a team of beetles swarmed over the wheels and joints of both craft, performing final checks.

Another beetle scurried past, bumping into Spark—*Crumbs, mate! Out of the way, would you?*

—*Sorry.*

—*Watch it, collie!* snarled another beetle.

—Sorry.

—Get out of here! yelled someone else. Spark was bumped and jostled until he found a place where no one shoved him and he could watch the take off procedure in peace; at least, in physical calm. Inside, he was all turmoil.

Manifold shouted to the beetles leaving the wingship—*Completed your before and after entering checks?*

The beetles chorused—*Affirmative.* Some of the beetles ran out behind the wingship, some to the front and stood ready as Manifold continued her checklist. Presumably, on board, Crawf and Bash were practising some similar procedure that Spark couldn't hear. He was too mesmerised by the beetles. Beetles like him, but these appeared to be strong, purposeful beetles. These were skilled beetles with a mission.

When the engines started, Spark almost wet himself. From a stuttering splurt the small engines rose into a warm hum, then rose again into a sort of humming buzz.

Manifold continued shouting, louder now—*Static vent plugs?*

—Removed.

—Flying controls?

—Free.

—Throttles?

—Primed and set.

—All clear above and astern?

—Clear.

—Standing by chocks.

—Chocks away, the beetles chorused as they heaved at the heavy chocks and ran, pushing the carved wooden blocks to the side wall of the hangar, well out of the way and right in Spark's direction. He managed to duck them and watched as Manifold cried out—*And they're off!*

—Chocks away... muttered Spark and he dodged and wove and ran to follow the little plane out of the hangar, sniffing the smell of burnt chips as if it were the most appetising of perfumes. As he came to the mouth of the hangar, beetles were coming in again and he tried very hard to avoid bumping in to them but it was difficult when his mouth was hanging open and he'd fallen in love with a vehicle that was abuzz with life.

The wingship's high humming increased in volume as it soared out into the sky and buzzed round past the airship which floated into the distance. Pilot Crawf tipped the wing towards the airship in acknowledgement of their shared airspace. The watching beetles on the ground cheered. Then both craft faded into the vibrant blue of the sky.

Spark stood, transfixed, at the great open mouth of the hangar cave. He started to hum in a high buzzing kind of way. His eyes were almost rolling in his head. His brain was full of the glory of ignition and preparation. He slid down the wall at the outside of the hangar, humming to himself—*This is the life,* he thought—*This... Is... The... Life.*

The sky emptied and the trees and shrubbery seemed to embrace him as he lay humming in the afternoon sun. Gradually his eyes closed and his legs became limp. Then his hum sputtered and ceased. Spark gave a tiny beetle grunt and rolled over.

Then, into the silence of the afternoon, came the sound of a tiny, beetle snore.

Chapter Three

I

—Anyone there? Over. Antenna's voice was insistent. She'd been calling for attention for some time now with no result. She hunched over a slender microphone rising out of the computer array like some weird flower bud—*Talk to me, someone! Anyone? Zip? Are you hearing me? Over.*

The light from the control panel flickered over her pointed face. She was frustrated. Something had gone wrong. She'd lost the communication link with the airship and with Zip. Nothing was functioning properly and there was still no sign of Min or Wilkinson. She typed urgently, trying diagnostic tests to assess the problem. There was no explanation for it. The system had collapsed. Deliberately she stood and went around the control desk to kick the side of the computer. It hurt her but made no appreciable difference to the system. She returned to her rock seat and leaned her head onto the keyboard and sighed.

Torque entered the cave and crept close to Antenna. Thinking she was asleep he whispered—*Antenna?*

Antenna, put into a bad mood by the technology failure, sat up and snapped at the beetle—*What?*

Torque hated to be the bearer of bad news and braced himself for a reaction even before he spoke. He looked round to see who might be listening. Even though he established there was no one else there, he whispered—*It's Wilkinson.*

—What about her?

—She's been cleared.

—What!

—Cleared. The old guard. Gone.

—Oh no, Antenna stared in horror at Torque, the news sinking in—*Thanks, Torque. I'll go now.*

Torque followed Antenna as she left her seat and went out into the dirt tunnel. The passageway led to every entrance of the various enclosures of the Ektek animals - mostly from the Australian section but there were others involved. Ektek was a global operation.

The old guard had consisted of Antenna's father and Min's mother, Wilkinson. This unlikely pair, a numbat and a Leadbeater's possum, together with a team of termites, ants and beetles, had set up the computer system that ran the spine of Ektek. Antenna's dad had been cleared recently and now that Wilkinson was gone, Min would be the only Leadbeater's possum left in the zoo.

Her brother, Rawlinson, had been sent out to another facility for breeding. Split up the families; clear the elders, that was the way of the zoo. The old guard had accepted that. It suited them. They knew sooner or later they'd be cleared and they'd be spared the indignity of old age. Everyone had to die sooner or later. If you were no longer bringing in an audience then you were no longer profitable to feed and then, well, your useful days were over.

Although everyone dreaded being cleared, everyone knew death was a fact of life. They also knew that there was a measure of protection from human encroachment in a zoo. Predators, feral competition, starvation and even disease were removed from the equation when you were housed in a dry, maintained enclosure with round the clock veterinary service. Both numbat and possum were wild caught, some of their progeny captive born. It was all they knew and now more of the old guard had been cleared.

That made Helmut the last surviving Ektek elder.

II

Antenna marched down the tunnel towards the nocturnal house. The long coarse hairs on her tail bristled, making her look far more hostile than she actually felt. She muttered to herself as she strode through the corridors. Her stripes flashed on her back as though she were a tiger in a bamboo forest. She thought to herself that Min was being unreasonable. Min had to accept the way of the zoo. She had to learn to think about other animals beside herself. Everyone lost his or her parents. It was natural. Some creatures never knew their parents at all. Min was just being selfish; how dare she. Stubborn and selfish. Someone had to tell her. That someone was going to have to be Antenna. She tightened her lips. All this bolstering wasn't convincing her. She didn't have a clue what she would say to Min. What could you say to someone who had just lost their mother?

III

The nocturnal house was cool and dark in daytime and the lights came on at night so that nocturnal animals would be awake in the pseudo night when paying customers came to visit. It was still dark as Antenna came through the camouflaged entrance from the tunnels and she could smell the drying eucalyptus that decorated the possum enclosure.

Antenna found Min scrunched down into a tiny ball in her bedding. Antenna called to her softly as she approached.

Min opened one eye and scrunched down further—*I could smell death. All day. The vet's been busy.*

Antenna nodded—*You're not the only one, then.*

—*I didn't get a chance to say goodbye. They just came and took her before I even knew.*

—*You mum knew she meant the earth to you.*

—*Did she?*

—*Yes, she did. You know that.*

—*Do I?*

—*Parents are supposed to die. The young take over.*

—*But not yet, Anti.* Min shrank down even smaller—*Not yet.*

Antenna huddled in beside her. Min was cold. Leadbeater's possums came from the mountains. They liked to be cold. They were also known as fairy possums because they were small and exquisite. The two creatures stayed huddled together in the dark, breathing in the smell of dried eucalyptus, sharing sadness. Then, suddenly, with an electronic thud, the lights snapped on and the entire nocturnal habitat was flooded in bright daylight.

—*You're right,* said Antenna—*Let's all give up. Let's forget about Zip and Hod and Helmut. Let's forget all about Ektek. Let's forget about those animals trapped in the kitchen. It's all way too hard.*

—*It is.*

—*We can't give up, Min. It's too important. There's too many needing help. You've got to get up and get going.* Antenna shook her head in frustration—*It's what our parents wanted, Min.* She tightened her lips and whispered to the shocked creature nestled beside her—*I need you to help me. Please.*

A silence frosted between the two mammals before Min sighed—*Can't argue, Anti.* Then Min stood and shook off her bedding.

Antenna followed her out of the nocturnal house and they went back to work.

IV

Zip's voice fizzed through the satellite connection—*Ektek? Can you hear me? Over.*

—*All right!* Antenna was jubilant—*Thank you, Min!*

—*But...?* Min sounded puzzled—*I didn't do anything!* She barely looked up from the wiring as her tiny fingers traced a circuit.

—*You must have.* Antenna seized the mic—*Zip! Am I glad to hear you! What's happening? Over.*

Zip's voice was not quite swallowed by interference—*I've parked the car under the waiters' table. Last Chance to Eat is open for business. Over.*

—*Okay,* Min nodded and turned her attention back to the circuitry.

Antenna spoke into the mic—*What do you mean, waiters' table? What's that mean? Over.*

—*You know, the table where they uncork drink bottles and put serving trays and stuff*—Zip's voice splintered into the speakers—*You know. Collection and sorting. Over.*

—*I do not know.* Antenna shook her head and frowned—*Why's she expect me to know anything about human restaurants?*

—*Because you know everything,* muttered Min.

Antenna glanced up, not sure if Min had attempted a joke in her present emotional state, and she let it pass. Of course she didn't know everything. However, she did understand that this waiters' table would be a perfect vantage point for Zip in the dining room. There would be no people kicking her under the table and she would hopefully be able to operate the camera unnoticed. She spoke again into the mic—*Zip? Can you pan 'round the restaurant, please? Over.*

Immediately, one of the blank screens flickered into life. Min and Antenna watched as Zip's footage was beamed from the car's micro camera to the Ektek headquarters via the airship and the satellite. All systems go. Min and Antenna exchanged a glance. Phew. So far. This was their first look inside the famed Last Chance to Eat.

The place was huge, formal and obviously expensive. The furniture appeared antique. There were white tablecloths. There were ornate stands bearing monster flower decorations that speared the air between the tables. Serious-faced waiting staff wore slick hair and long black aprons over their crisp white shirts, printed with a cunning design of flying passenger pigeons. They flitted from table to table straightening the silver salt and peppershakers fashioned like bulbous sea-cows. They polished up the moa embossed knives and forks on their aprons, preparing for their dinner guests.

Antenna and Min could see Zip was strategically placed under the table against a wall facing the entrance. The kitchen doorway was to her left. The camera was set into a telescopic arm. The pictures shook as the camera changed angles.

Last Chance to Eat was a themed restaurant with attitude, a life and death attitude. In the centre of the restaurant, three skinny creatures, looking a bit like antelope from a distance, huddled together on the top of a set made to look like a mountaintop. One creature turned her head, her eye coruscating in panic. They skittered together to the top of a plateau. The whole mountain picture was surrounded by a moat that the gentle terrified beasts would never be able to cross.

Back in the control centre, Min looked at the helpless beings—*Who are they?*

Antenna breathed in and said—*Chiru.*

—*Chir-who?*

—*You know. Chiru.* Antenna watched the screen with her pointed nose twitching angrily—*Humans make shatoosh out of their hair.*

—*Sha-what?*

—*Shatoosh. Fancy shawls fine enough to pass through a wedding ring. Warm enough to hatch a pigeon's egg. Takes three chiru pelts to make one shawl. Humans love 'em. Wonder who'll win the shawl tonight.*

—*Oh, don't.*

—*What else are they there for?*

—*Hang on,* said Min, leaning forward to see the screen better—*What's that?*

—*Go back, Zip,* said Antenna into the mic—*To the corner. Over.*

The Ektek camera was so small the footage tended to be shaky. Any slight floor movement could disturb it. Zip moved the camera back to focus on a shadowy corner. When the images settled, Min and Antenna leaned in to see a human camera crew setting up their outlandish equipment.

Antenna narrowed her eyes—*Now, you tell me,* she said to Min— *Why would they want footage of three petrified chiru?*

There appeared to be a crew of three people, possibly director, lighting operator and camera operator, clustered together around a large camera. They were unpacking more equipment out of metallic road cases and setting up a veritable phalanx of technology. The human crew were inconspicuous, given the size of their retro gear.

They fitted in, they were expected, and there was a place for them in this restaurant.

—*This is new. Keep your eye on them, Zip. Over,* Antenna said into the mic. What did it mean? Why would Last Chance to Eat need a recording of an evening's custom?

The patrons began to arrive in twos and threes. As a collective group of customers they were impeccably groomed. A staff member greeted the clientele as they arrived. Waiting minions took their coats away to be hung in the wardrobe by the exit. That wardrobe was beautifully carved with a prancing Przewalski's horse rearing up across both ornate doors.

A waiter bearing a bottle of a dark red drink called Carson's Spring dated 1962 approached the waiters' table. Zip snapped the camera down to escape detection. Back in the control room, Min and Antenna suddenly had a great view of a waiter's leg and the tablecloth. From underneath. The camera spun round and in the central screen of the console, Min and Antenna got a full close-up of a furry puppy-like face with a great big nose staring right at them.

Zip was a bare-backed fruit bat and this weird angle was not at all flattering. Zip didn't seem to care. She made some dreadful faces at them and grinned. She whispered—*Go on, dare me...* She grimaced even wider as she reached out her wing tip as if to tickle the waiter's knee.

Antenna whispered into the mic—*Zip! Stop clowning around! Over.* Then Antenna turned to Min by her side—*As if she'd listen to me.*

—*She'll listen. She's all right.*

—*'Course she is. Let's check out Hoddy.*

Antenna turned to a different screen and switched channels until a new picture became clear. This camera was steady and revealed a stainless steel kitchen from above. Min and Antenna watched as kitchen staff moved rapidly through the gleaming temple. It was a magnificently equipped and designed kitchen. Clearly the food prepared here would be of the highest order. Hod was a larger animal than the bare-backed fruit bat and the view was from his taller perspective. Hod was wearing a miniature camera mounted on his head and he must have been standing on something outside the window. Rock wallabies could climb anything.

Antenna switched the vision through to the webpage frame already prepared for it. She typed in commands and ran the program. The image was now part of a web-cast. Ektek was netcasting live footage just as the old guard had envisaged years ago when they held those first meetings with the beetles.

Min moved to the email screen and pushed 'send now'. The screen shut and the Media Release was out.

Antenna turned back to the monitor as Hod's camera captured the face of a small monkey. It was a tiny golden-lion tamarin, staring out from the bars of a roughly formed wooden cage. The tamarin was still alive but beyond shock, beyond hope. Antenna recognised dull despair when she saw it. She hit a series of commands and took a screen shot of the once glorious creature. As Hod continued his tour of the kitchen in the background, Antenna pasted the tamarin's image into a separate page, typing in the caption; 'Char-grilled bush meat'.

In the kitchen again, Hod's head-cam found a leopard, or what was left of it. The leopard's mournful eyes burned into the screen. It was barely alive. Its legs were bent back in a strange way. The leopard's mind was lost. The journey to the kitchen had broken it.

Antenna took a screen shot of the leopard staring into the past and transferred it to the website. She added the caption, 'Vulnerability - a piquant sauce indeed'.

Min was watching the dining room footage streaming in from Zip. More customers arrived and were chattering excitedly as they read the menu and watched the chiru clump together on the faux mountain.

Light drum and bass filtered through the Ektek speakers. Min and Antenna watched as the waiter swung a blackboard towards a glamorous couple seated directly in front of Zip's waiters' table. The board was covered in bold chalk writing in a style favoured by architects. Min nudged Antenna—*Can you get her to zoom in?*

Antenna switched on the mic again—*Zip? Can you zoom in on the menu? Over.*

Zip made no verbal reply but the lens refocussed. Right at the top of the board was chalked a heading: Nemesis Night Specials.

—*Nemesis Night?* Min looked to Antenna—*What's that?*

—*Got me,* said Antenna—*No idea.*

The blackboard list continued:

Japanese Crane
Folded into handmade origami paper
& parched
With cassoulet of wood bison
& maidenhair tree greens

Slivers of roast leopard
Crammed with golden lion tamarin
& celeriac puree
Bombarded with gold leaf flecks

Warm salad of chiru stuffed komodo
With sizzled snake beans
Quince and blue cheese jus
Beleaguered with parmigiana reggiano shrapnel

In the steel-and-white kitchen, Hod's camera had found a caged and muzzled komodo dragon. It was an image straight from a reptilian horror flick. This one was a youngster, the yellow spots clear on its brown scaly skin. It was about two metres long with a powerful head and strong shoulders.

—*They like their komodo fresh*, said Min.

—*And their chiru and tamarin. How do they kill them?*

—*Do you really want to know?* Min was right.

Antenna didn't really want to know.

Hod moved in for a close-up. The muzzled komodo shook his head impatiently. A gleam of other worlds and prehistoric times shone from his eyes.

Antenna froze a screen shot of the komodo with that glint of ancient intelligence captured in the flare of the lens. She processed the image into the webpage, together with the menu description. It made a striking graphic and Min nodded her approval. At the other keyboard, Min entered an editing program and highlighted the video frame in a random flash. It made a dramatic effect.

—*Hey*, Antenna looked at her—*We make a good team. They'd be proud.*

—*We're not supposed to be the team.* Min's eyes filled with tears—*Not yet.*

—*But we are. That's our duty.*

—*Duty?* Min jumped up from the panel and paced across the floor, her long tail flashing out behind her—*What's that mean?*

Antenna turned to watch her surreptitiously, not without sympathy, but still needing Min to focus on their work rather than what Antenna saw as self pity—*Min?*

—*I can't help it, Anti. I keep expecting her. She should be here and she's not and then I remember again and she's gone, gone forever, never will be again and it's so, so unfair.*

Antenna stood up but Min just kept pacing, kept flicking her tail, marching across the cave, kept talking to herself. Antenna realised this grief was real, of course, and new and raw but still... They were working. It was not the time for self-indulgence.

—*I didn't know it would hurt like this. I know when your dad died you just kept on going. I don't know how you did.*

—*Are you saying I'm heartless?*

Min really did look like a fairy then. Frail and petite with a faint glow surrounding her fur like a halo. She opened and shut her mouth a couple of times, not knowing how to reply to her friend. She knew Antenna kept her emotions in check but obviously she must have feelings. Eventually the little possum straightened her spine and spoke through her tears—*Don't look so worried, Antenna. I will keep going. For them.*

Antenna wasn't concentrating. She had been sucked back into her own memory bank. She was suddenly younger, with her dad grinning at her. He was standing backlit in the cavern of Antenna's mind and he said to her—*Your soft heart, Anti! Trouble with you, kitten, is you feel too much. You don't think enough. You got to think, numbat baby. Think. That's the only way forward. Keep thinking with that sharp mind of yours and I guarantee, you'll work it out.*

Antenna shook her head free of sentiment, free of cloying emotions and thought. She thought of all the animals that had been cleared. Then she thought of all the other animals that were being hunted, farmed, culled and vivisected at that very moment—*I'm doing it for the living, Min.*

—*Yes, yes,* shivered Min—*Of course. So am I.*

Antenna nodded and pulled down a new email message screen. This was for all politicians, State and Federal, informing them of the netcast and encouraging them to log on and see the Last Chance to Eat story at the Ektek website. She pressed 'send now'.

Min said—*The Department of Flora and Fauna can't ignore that.*

Antenna sneered—*Especially the ones who aren't dining at Last Chance to Eat tonight.*

Back on screen, in the unedited footage, Hod's camera jerked back crazily, painting an impressionistic blur of the kitchen. It came back into focus on the komodo's face, now released from the muzzle. The komodo opened and shut its mouth experimentally. Long strands of saliva coated its jaws. It looked down the barrel of the camera and opened and shut its mouth.

In the control room, Min leaned forward intently—*What's he saying?*

—*Uh oh,* Antenna couldn't believe it.

Min stared at the screen—*Sorry?*

—*Can't you see?*

—*What?*

—*Hod's set him free.*

—*How did he get into the kitchen? I thought he was using a telephoto from outside?*

—*So did I.* Antenna grabbed the mic—*Hod!* Then she remembered he couldn't hear her. Hod had no sound. She sat back from the mic, remembering their stupid joking about not being able to communicate. This wasn't a joke—*Hoddy,* she murmured—*Hod. What are you doing? Shut it in!* She jumped to her feet and shouted at the screen—*Lock it up again! Before it's too late!*

They watched in silence as the camera backed away, the komodo in frame as he pushed on the door of the cage and it opened, ever so slightly. The komodo froze and looked around the stainless temple where the rituals of victuals absorbed the staff. No one had noticed and the komodo pushed again, softly, and the door swung open just a little further. The komodo hesitated, gathering strength and then he rushed out of his prison, running pell-mell to the nearest open door; unfortunately, it was the fridge.

The kitchen staff swung around in attitudes of terror, their mouths opening and shutting furiously. They must have been squawking like mad. Ektek creatures couldn't understand the sound of humans in any kind of language sense - but most creatures could work out what they meant from their tone - even in this silent movie. People ran to get away from the komodo. It was a human stampede.

On the screen, the images blurred while Hod plunged to safety. When the pictures refocussed the komodo had heaved back out of the fridge. One enterprising chef grabbed a hatchet and hurled it. It glinted as it spun in the bright kitchen light at the frustrated beast. It missed and cracked into the shiny white tile wall. It juddered with the impact and then slid to the floor.

The dragon took off in the opposite direction, this time straight at a horrified young kitchen hand that waved a broom wildly in the general vicinity of the reptile. The komodo wasn't impressed by being swept on the head with a broom and took a good bite of human leg in response. He dragged the spotty youth several metres. The komodo let go just before he reached the restaurant door. The kitchen-hand scrambled to his feet, dragging his injured leg and opening and shutting his mouth frantically as he scurried away from the beast.

In the control room, Min and Antenna were powerless to do anything as they watched the komodo's onslaught continue through the swinging doors leading to the sedate dining room.

—*Zip! Get out of there!* Antenna shouted into the mic—*Instantly! NOW! Over.*

The diners were unaware of the impending komodo. There must have been very good soundproofing between kitchen and dining room. They murmured contentedly as they attended to the rare morsels displayed before them and drum and bass simpered through the air.

That was until the kitchen doors smashed open, resulting in a crazy tumult of panic as humans leapt to their feet, then onto the tables, then the tables tilted, fell, went flying, the disorder ruffled the waiter's hairstyles and they too joined their patrons, running, barking, yowling, screeching and baying…

Then, suddenly, awfully, snowy static hit the displays.

Zip's connection was severed.

At the same time, Hod's footage disappeared.

The only sound in the Ektek control room was the hissing of screens.

Chapter Four

Antenna typed fast. She opened the same diagnostic programs she had run before, checked exactly the same systems as rapidly as she could— *Uptek? Come in please? Over.* There was no reply on any channel. The airwaves were dead. It was just like the earlier outage only this time she had Min working beside her. Min looked in disbelief at both fizzing monitors and shook her head. She went to the computer and removed the carapace again. She took her toolkit from her pouch and sifted through the wires and silicon chips embedded into the patchwork. Part of the computer looked like grey matter and part was based on plant cellulose structures. Min's tiny hands could sense any problems through faint electronic impulses. After diagnosing a slight imbalance she employed an intricately shaped tool into the computer's depths but she knew it was not causing the main problem—*I wish we knew what that crazy scientist did up there*, she muttered as she worked—*Half the time we're working in the dark.*

—*Yeah*, said Antenna—*It's all very well dedicating a satellite to endangered animals but if it drops out...*

—*What good is it?*

—*Maybe that mob of extinct animals up there is having a party and broke something.*

For the first time since Wilkinson's clearing Min and Antenna looked at each other and smiled, chuckled even. It was an absurd mental picture. The satellite was part of a famous rumour. When the scientist sent the satellite up, it was said he'd filled it with endangered animals to make a kind of orbiting ark. It was only a rumour but there was certainly a satellite, for how else would Ektek's communications work?

As for the endangered animals in orbit around the earth, how would they live? The satellite would have to be enormous. It was just an amusing story to tell the youngsters.

As suddenly as they had gone, both Hod and Zip's vision and Zip's sound filled the Ektek office again. Screaming people and crashing furniture blended discordantly with drum and bass.

—*And we're back.* Antenna watched the footage—*Thanks to you, Min.*

—*It wasn't me,* Min frowned as she examined the screens—*It seems to have come back on line by itself. There's definitely something out of order. I'll have to check out that airship when they get back. I don't understand it...*

Antenna managed not to say it out loud but, as she watched the chaos unfolding on the screens, she thought to herself: if they get back.

It appeared that Zip's camera was now lying on the ground with only limited view. Antenna's black eyes glistened in the band across her sharp face as she twisted her head to make sense of the pictures— *There's something on Zip's camera.*

Min gasped—*Not the komodo?*

Another screen showed a blur, going up and down. Hod must have been leaping. The light had changed so Min and Antenna assumed he was moving outside the restaurant. But where was Zip?

Forgetting that Hod had no sound again, Antenna shouted into the mic—*Hod! Where's Zip? Over!* And then, to herself when she realised—*What have you done?* Impossibly, as though he had heard her, Hod's bounding footage on the screen came to a careering halt then spun and returned to the restaurant. People were spilling out onto the footpath and moving well away from the entrance. They were crying and wheezing and falling over. The human camera operator had bundled her bulky camera under her arm and carefully moved away from the building as though she were carrying her own precious baby.

Hod leapt through the milling throng, back into the dining room. The komodo was menacing the waiters' station in the far corner. Zip was trapped. The komodo's huge tail thrashed backwards and forwards.

Hod's camera paused only momentarily. Then he zoomed in to the komodo. As with all Ektek's actions, the quality of the photography varied according to the mental and physical state of the photographer. Here, Hod was shaking so only some of his vision was in focus. And even then clarity was intermittent.

Zip's camera was framed on one side by the underside of komodo foot, and now fluffy brown-and-yellow striped fur filled the rest of the picture. Hod's tail was directly in front.

Min and Antenna struggled to make sense of what they were seeing on the screens. They could hear Hod's voice through Zip's equipment—*Not us, you dumb dragon! Get the humans! You do know what humans are? The tall ones with two legs?*

Then, from Hod's point of view, his own yellow paws entered frame and twitched away the tablecloth to reveal Zip. She was trying in vain to drive her car around the great lizard. One side of the car had been damaged, apparently by komodo bite. The komodo didn't hesitate now, either. He opened his saliva-coated mouth and leered towards Zip. Suddenly the camera snapped and leapt away. Through the blur, the car was just in frame; Hod must have been carrying it. Together with the fleeing humans, the camera was lurching out of the doorway and into the street.

Min and Antenna both jumped as the speaker hummed and Zip's voice came through. She sounded angry, her voice resounding—*We're supposed to be a team,* she shouted—*I'm relying on you for my life! How do you expect anyone to work with you if they can't trust you?*

Antenna let out a sigh of relief—*I suspect Hod will understand Zip's feelings by the time they get back to the zoo.*

—*Loud and clear,* agreed Min.

Antenna switched channels and called in to Helmut. This time there was no problem getting through to the airship—*Uptek, come in please? Over.*

—*Yes, Antenna. Over.*

—*They're on their way back, in a bit of a hurry. You'll need to get moving.*

—*Affirmative. Over.*

—*We need to solve this communications failure. Any ideas? Over.*

—*Sorry, Antenna. Just dropped out. Over.*

—*See you when you get back. Over.*

—*Over and out.*

—*Thank goodness for that.* Min returned the computer's carapace and set to work restoring order in the signal centre—*Antenna? When did you last check the email?*

—*Will now.* Antenna went to the inbox. There were three new messages. Two were from journalists regarding the evening's events in the restaurant. The third was from an opposition politician wanting to congratulate Ektek on blowing the whistle on Last Chance to Eat. He was preparing a speech to denounce the restaurant in the House of Representatives. He would be asking the Department of Flora and Fauna directly what they intended to do about it.

—*Immediate results!* Antenna couldn't have been more thrilled— *Can't ask for more than that, can we? She turned to share her excitement and saw that Min was sombre.*

—*Can you please check the Leadbeater's possum page? He might have left a message there.* Min wanted to check on her brother, Rawlinson, and his safe arrival at the new zoo.

—*Rawlinson? Of course we can do that,* said Antenna, full of optimistic belief in Ektek's powers as she typed in the homepage address and pressed return—*We can do anything!*

—*It's too early for him to have an email address but he might have managed something.*

The first thing they saw when the page downloaded was a bright red lightening bolt across the screen. The Friends of the Leadbeater's Possum had put out a newsflash. It stated that Rawlinson had died in transit, as had the other male. Several other Leadbeater's possums had succumbed to a virus at two zoos. It was now believed that there were no surviving Leadbeater's possums in the mountain ash forests. The last known Leadbeater's possum was incarcerated in Bedlam Zoo.

The last known Leadbeater's possum was Min. Min sighed like a deflating balloon and folded up into a tiny little bundle on the floor. Antenna joined her on the ground and huddled in close. She tried to think of ways to comfort her but what could she say? Never mind? Try to look on the bright side? At least now you're the only Leadbeater's possum left in the world, you're going to be very, very valuable? Somehow, nothing seemed fitting. Silence would have to suffice.

They lay together on the dirt floor. After a while Antenna heard a faint drumming. As she lay there, turning cold and hard, something soft landed on her face. She could feel a faint tickling on her fur. She opened her eyes to see a blanket of ants had arrived, all carrying young green leaves. The ants had brought little leaves to cover Antenna and Min as they rested. The leaves smelled of eucalyptus. They smelled disinfecting and health giving. Eventually the ants left them, warm and cared for on the outside, even if they felt they were turning to stone from the inside.

Torque watched from the shadows, in a glow of approval as the ants passed. He was surprised that the ants could make such a generous gesture of forgiveness after all this time. The ants normally avoided both Min and Antenna because of a silly youthful incident. They had dared each other to eat a regiment of ants before they were old enough to understand what they were doing to the foundations of Ektek. It's difficult for creatures to go against their instincts but they had had to learn and accept that Ektek creatures don't eat ants (even if you are an anteater). They would have to do with the zoo's custard preparation like all the rest. It was part of growing up and it was part of being endangered. It was part of Ektek.

Spark stood beside the darkling beetle—*Will they be okay?*

—*We've done all we can,* Torque nodded—*Now it's up to them to recover.*

—*Will they?*

—*Of course. They have no choice. They're Ektek.*

Chapter Five

Stars pinpricked through the velvet night. The moon was almost full. It had already traversed across of the sky. A plane flew over a silver ribbon of river that spooled out over the undulating land. The compact vehicle banked and turned to follow the shining curve of the waterway.

To the casual observer, the little plane, barely half a metre long, could have been an escapee from the model flying club. In fact, this was no toy. It was a sophisticated machine, in shape almost like a stealth fighter blended with an ultralight. Small fins jutted forward from the bulbous nose of the craft. An aerofoil curved over the powerful fan turbine motor at the rear. It zipped through the air at surprising speed, the ground moving fast beneath.

Bash sat behind the controls of the mini-aircraft. He was a confident and skilled pilot, the controls having been tailored ergonomically to fit the small frog's clinging hands and feet.

From high in the air, the light of the moon etched out a crocodile farm. Neat pens tessellated the property and most enclosures were filled with sinuous patterns made from the twisting and interweaving of croc bodies.

Bash faced a complicated panel of lights and instruments in the cockpit of the small plane. He reached for his radio controls—*Crawf! Over.*

The radio crackled in reply—*Hullo? Don't believe it. Haven't found him already, have you? Can't have. Impossible. Over.*

Bash snickered as he surveyed the crowd below him—*You know crocs. They all look the same to me. Hang on. Wait a minute... I'll get back to you. Over and out.*

Through the night gloom, Bash had seen a crocodile penned by himself. He was still tied up and he was a big one. It could very well be the male they were looking for. Bash pushed a button on his console to zoom in on his night vision display. He watched the croc as he manoeuvred around the property.

Hardback glanced up at the insect-like craft that circled above him. Still exhausted after the capture, he had no energy to ponder the meaning of it. He felt tired and helpless and trapped. He slumped back into the mud, desolate.

Bash reached for his radio again—*Crawf? Can you read me? I think we've got him. Over.*

The radio hissed as Bash continued to fly over the farm and Crawf asked—*Bringing him in single-handed? In the dark? Like to see that. Over.*

Bash took one more look at the layout of the farm as he swung over it—*Very funny. Coming in, ready or not. Over and out.* He turned the radio off and the plane zoomed up the river.

Away from the croc farm, further up river, Crawf waited in the larger wingship for Bash to return from his reccie. To conserve energy he was parked at the end of a runway, waiting until the small plane returned to dock. He looked up as he heard the plane approaching.

Bash landed perfectly on the very small space provided on the wingship roof. He expected nothing less of himself. From a distance it might have looked as if a dragonfly had landed on top of a bird.

Crawf couldn't help ducking involuntarily as the tiny craft bumped onto the roof. This was a difficult procedure but the locking systems clicked into place without difficulty and the little plane was once more affixed to the wingship roof.

Wearing his harness, Bash clambered through the plane's trapdoor and swung himself into the cockpit of the wingship. He unclipped and got comfortable alongside the controls; a tiny amphibian figure nestled at the operating panel.

Crawf commenced flight procedures and adjusted the throttle as the turbines whirred aggressively—*What do you think? Can we get him out?* He looked over to Bash, his large feathered comb rising slightly—*Oh, and one more question; what do we do with him when we do get him out?*

—*Haven't a clue*, said Bash.

—*Well, we can't give up, can we?* Crawf shrugged—*We've got to spring him. Though, what they're thinking sending you and me, I don't know. What the heck can we do?*

—*We've got time on our side*, said Bash—*That load of old croc's not going anywhere in a hurry.*

Crawf leaned forward, easing the swan-like wingship up into the air. At about three metres long, the wingship was able to travel at speed over flat terrain at very low altitudes. It was the Ektek vehicle of choice for middle distances, especially over water. The craft zoomed away over the river, skimming barely a metre from the surface. The stubby wings banked and the craft turned, steadied, then regained position speeding low over the scrub.

They moved inland, out of sight.

Shining Teeth and the rest of the harem had returned to their backwater home to await news. They floated quietly, waiting, just a snout out of the water here and a pair of marble eyes there. They lifted their heads as a distinctive hum announced the approach of the Ektek wingship. The craft slowed and landed gracefully, like a swan gliding onto the surface of a lake, scooping the air before it in curved braking wings.

When the wingship had come to rest, Crawf looked at Bash—*Ready?*

Bash said—*No. And I don't think I ever will be.*

Crawf patted the frog on the head with a wing tip—*They're in trouble.*

Bash stared out of the cockpit at the assembly of reptiles—*They're crocodiles.*

—*Don't act like a snack,* said Crawf—*And you won't be one.*

—*Thanks for that titbit,* said Bash—*You're making me feel crunchy talking about it.*

—*Just get out on the wing!*

The two creatures climbed out of the cockpit and stood on the wing, waiting to greet their troubled animal comrades. As Shining Teeth approached the wingship, Crawf and Bash both backed away a little. But not too far, the wingship wasn't very stable. Bash managed to sneak in behind Crawf. Not that Bash was a coward. He was just very small.

The rest of the harem came, one by one, to join Shining Teeth. The crocodiles were so big and seemed so threatening it was difficult to see how a cockatoo and a frog could even communicate with them. In the end, Crawf jumped right in and shouted to Shining Teeth—*There's a large male at the crocodile farm upstream. Even though it was dark we could make out an old scar on the left flank— recent cut to the tail?*

Shining Teeth turned to her harem—*He's alive.*

Jata breathed in—*At least we know where he is.*

—*And he's staying put,* said Crawf.

Shining Teeth nodded and turned back to the Ektek representative. Oh, wait, she could see there was a frog as well. That made two creatures that couldn't be less impressive. She sighed and asked—*When will you get him out?*

Bash and Crawf looked at each other. Bash swallowed and muttered towards the ground—*Not going to be easy.*

Shining Teeth didn't hear him and didn't think much of him anyway—*What?*

Crawf looked at the approaching crocodiles in the dawn light—*We can't do it by ourselves.*

Shining Teeth growled—*You have all the help you require right here. We have many skills.*

Crawf was unconvinced—*The farmers are armed. There are dogs and fences. It's difficult to see how to get him out at this stage. We need to prepare a plan with our team. We will return.*

—*Oh, that's rich, isn't it,* Shining Teeth turned round to look at the harem—*You thought they could help.*

—*To be fair, Shining Teeth,* said Asunder—*They did say they'd come back with a plan.*

—*They lie. Ektek is a bird and a frog. They are weak.*

—*Hang on a tick, there,* said Crawf—*Shining Teeth, is it? Look, Shining Teeth, it's a big farm. We will need to set up surveillance and see how they operate before we go rushing in.*

Bash chimed in—*Don't worry. There's more to Ektek than just little old us!*

—*We can't bust him out without a plan. He'd die and so would we.*

—*So, we'll be back,* said Bash and both creatures turned to climb into the cockpit.

—*Don't leave us now!* said Damura.

—*Get him out!* shouted Grater.

—*Why can't we raid the place right now?* said Asunder—*They wouldn't be expecting us.*

—*We need to consult our strategists,* shouted Bash—*We will return. Ektek will always do their best to assist an endangered creature.*

—*Or die trying,* said Crawf.

The crocodiles moved closer to the wingship, slowly, and with definite menace. Crawf and Bash grew nervous and scrambled back into their cockpit. Bash muttered—*I wish you hadn't said that. I really, really wish you hadn't said that.*

—*Couldn't help it, Bash. Had to give them something…*

—*Our lives?*

—*Can't see any way out of this one, can you?*

Again the turbines whirred as the craft came to speed and started to move away from the riverbank.

—*Just one way. Just go up,* said Bash, relieved to get away from those prehistoric monsters—*And step on it.*

The crocodiles couldn't believe Ektek was leaving them with nothing. They had put all their hope into an effective force arriving and rescuing Hardback immediately. With a sharp order of command from Shining Teeth, they sprinted after the wingship. Shining Teeth leapt straight up out of the water and snapped her jaws wide around a wing.

Asunder also shot out of the river and grabbed hold of the other side of the little vehicle. The crocodiles grappled with the wingship and finally dragged it, revving hopelessly, and at a dreadful angle, to shore.

Shining Teeth muttered through her clenched jaw—*We need to have a little chat about priorities, don't we, froggy?*

Chapter Six

Several glow-worm colonies had been persuaded to live in the caves under Bedlam Zoo. Fuel, and the power stored from solar energy in batteries, was precious and Ektek only used it when absolutely necessary. Glow-worms were clustered together over a small area in the hangar. Other than their blue fairy stars stretched out across the ceiling of the cave, it was dark, very dark.

Min, Zip and Antenna, together with a small group of assorted mechanic beetles, concentrated on the little red car. Min held a small battery-powered torch, focussed on the bitten side. The damaged vehicle had brought home to the team just how close Zip had been to injury, or worse. The driver's side was completely gone. It would need careful rebuilding.

—*I can't understand how you managed to dodge him,* said Antenna.

—*I don't know what I would have done if Hod hadn't turned up,* said Zip—*Another stunt like that one...*

—*Someone could really get hurt,* said Antenna.

—*Maybe even Hod. Then again, maybe that wouldn't be so bad...*

—*As I see it,* Min was quick to change the subject—*Zip was in the wrong vehicle at the wrong time. The steam engine just takes too long to get going. By the time she'd hit the ignition after the boiler reached pressure, the komodo was already there.*

Zip agreed—*Unfortunately, we thought it was going to be a safe surveillance operation. No one ever imagined we'd have to make such a quick getaway.*

—*That's my fault,* Antenna said—*I should have seen it coming...*

—*It's all Hod's fault,* said Zip—*and I think he should have to face the consequences. Don't you take this on, Antenna. It's not yours.*

—*I still feel...*

—*Not guilty? What are you? A fortune teller?*

As they argued, the hydraulic supports on one side of the vehicle gave way and a wheel fell off, toppling onto the ground. The crash resonated through the cavern. The mechanics all leapt backwards, looked at each other and laughed.

—*Needs work?* sniggered Zip.

Antenna reached out to pat Min—*I can deal with this if you'd rather take some time out?*

—*Oh, for Zed's sake,* Min turned away—*Let's get on with it.* A bombardier beetle climbed onto the fallen wheel—*Hang on,* Min picked her up with her hand—*Let's make sure it's stable before we rush in fixing it.*

Torque and Spark flew into the hangar from the tunnels. They stopped at the car when they saw Min there—*Min! Quick,* said Torque, still trying to get his breath back—*People! Searching your habitat. Now. Go. Fast.*

—*My...?* said Min.

—*Yes, yours. In uniforms. Not our staff. Some others.*

Antenna was surprised too—*But it's still dark.*

—*Can't tell you any more than that,* said Torque—*You'd better get up there, quick.*

Min handed the torch over to Antenna and turned to go.

—*Are you okay?* asked Antenna.

Min replied—*Yes, yes, good, fine. See you at the meeting.*

—*Very sorry for your loss,* Torque flew beside Min as she ran down the passageway—*Going to miss your mum like my own...* he said in a low voice, and then, embarrassed, turned on his darkling wings before she had time to even nod an acknowledgement of his concern. She felt grim but she continued to run. What was happening in her home?

Back at the little red car, Zip looked at Antenna—*What was that about?* Antenna breathed in and said—*You're not the only one with bad news.* And she told Zip about the clearing.

It took no time for the story of Min's awful change in status to spread through the tunnels of Ektek and the enclosures of Bedlam Zoo. It was always greeted with sympathy. No one could imagine a worse plight than to be the last of your kind. It was a nightmare to be an endling.

Helmut was already in the office when Antenna and Zip got there. He sat at the controller's seat in front of the computer console. He was backlit by the changing colours displayed on the screens. He was staring into the middle distance, apparently meditating. He was bent and dusty. He looked wrinkled, his cassowary skin looking too big for his bones.

Antenna, Zip, Torque and Spark all came into the control centre at once. Antenna took a step towards the bird but stopped—*Helmut?*

—Haven't managed to talk to Min yet. The cassowary looked down at Antenna. She could see there was nothing wrong with the flair of intelligence in his eyes—*Too young to cope with losing parents, far too young.*

—Happens to all of us.

—You were too young, Antenna, far too young, when your father went. There was still much for him to teach you. When I heard what Hod had done, leaving Zip like that, in the middle of an operation, his inexperience hit me. Really rocked me. Can we keep demanding so much from you all? Such untried youngsters, running such haphazard undertakings? It's madness. Puts us all in danger and to what end? What do we achieve?

Antenna looked at him—*We're already in danger, Helmut.*

—You know what I mean.

—What else can we do?

—Stop. Wait. Take more time to plan. Train more creatures. Look further afield.

—Helmut?

—Yes?

—She'll be okay. Min. We'll go on as before, as Ektek must. We have no choice.

The cassowary sighed. The weight of seniority was heavy on him. How came he to be the last founding member? He wanted so much to believe that Ektek could continue indefinitely—*I hope so, Antenna. I truly hope so.*

Torque, as head of security, said—*I'll go and see what's happening in the nocturnal house.* He left the control centre, a short dark beetle moving slowly. It would have been quicker to send Spark by himself but that young larva still had much to learn, so Torque merely inclined his head and Spark followed, keeping his head down, trying to be useful, hoping he might be offered permanent Ektek status. He went wherever Torque went, figuring that being obliging was the best strategy when you're after a job.

Helmut, Antenna and Zip, together with assorted beetles and ants, huddled around the light emanating from the computer monitors. They waited silently. Waiting for the one who must be admonished. Finally he came.

When he entered the control cave, Hod's white chest and belly glowed in the blue luminosity. He looked around the group with his head held high. He was defiant.

—Ah, there you are, Hod. Sit down, sit down, Hoddy. Make yourself comfortable. Helmut, the cassowary, looked around the group calmly—*Let's begin the meeting,* he said, his eyes bright in the gloom—*Min can catch up.*

—First things first, then. I think Hod should receive a reprimand, said Zip.

—A reprimand? For doing what I did? For helping a creature that was suffering? About to die? Isn't that what we're supposed to do?

—Maybe we could hear his side of the story before we dole out the punishment, Zip? said Antenna.

—Hod. You endangered one of our own team, said Helmut—*Did you not think of Zip?*

Hod looked down and shook his head before taking in a deep breath and looking back at the group. Some of his insolence had dissipated and he spoke with sincerity—*I just couldn't bear it,* he said— *We do all these actions but they're not really actions, are they? They're just watching, observing, recording, and not doing anything, not real action. Nothing ever seems to change. Things get worse, if anything. So when I saw that komodo, it was like, suddenly, here was something I could do, something that could maybe even save a life for a change. I wasn't helpless any more. For once, I felt like I was doing something. I helped him, for Zed's sake.*

—You were reckless! You were! Zip talked to Hod as though she were explaining basic mathematics to an egg—*You were stupid. You broke into the kitchen, freed a dangerous animal…*

—You weren't there. You didn't see him.

—Not until he tried to eat me!

—You didn't see him squashed into the cage. You didn't hear him. Begging. I had to help him. You would have too.

Antenna leaned forward to catch Hod's attention and focussed her gaze on him. She spoke quietly—*But you can't just act like that, without thinking.*

—I couldn't ignore him! He needed my help.

—But you upset the whole place, continued Antenna, urgently—*Can't you see that? You single-handedly bungled the entire action…*

—And can't you see, no one got hurt? There weren't any big consequences at all.

—That depends on what you mean by big. Did he get away? The komodo?

—They shot him.

There was a pause as they took this in, each Ektek member thinking of the futile waste of life and Hod's attempts to save him. It wasn't fair and each creature present knew they had to be cleverer than this to achieve their ends. Antenna spoke first—*Hod. I'm so sorry.*

—You're sorry. He's sorry. I'm sorry. I know it was an extreme thing to do. I am sincerely sorry I stuffed up with Zip but don't you ever feel like that? Frustrated? Powerless? Do you know? How we make things change?

—It's difficult to get past the fact you left Zip, said Helmut.

—I went back for her! I rescued her. I saved her life. What about that? Seems to me I deserve praise, not a bleeding reprimand!

—You shouldn't have left her in the first place, said Antenna.

—Aren't we supposed to look after our own? said Zip.

Helmut looked at Hod—*You do know you are free to leave Ektek at any time?*

This was an extraordinary question. No animal had ever left Ektek. Antenna and Zip looked at each other while Helmut apparently waited for the answer.

Hod became quiet. It was unusual behaviour for this particular yellow-footed rock wallaby and Helmut, Antenna and Zip shared worried glances in the serious blue radiance. Hod looked down. His shoulders began to shake. Antenna got up and went to him, to pat him sympathetically. As she looked up into his face she jumped backwards. He wasn't crying, filled with remorse and sorrow, as she had expected.

Hod was laughing.

Antenna pushed him hard and returned to her seat, her hair stuck out in anger, puffing out her rusty striped body.

Hod flung his head back, releasing his pent up emotion in a huge guffaw. The rest of the animals gaped in amazement. What was to be done with Hod? They looked at each other but no one had an answer. Hod continued to laugh. Helmut and Antenna glanced at each other. Helmut shook his head slightly and opened his eyes wider, as if to say, see what I mean?

Antenna rose onto her four feet and went to look up at Hod. Then she sat up on her hindquarters, which brought her closer to his height, and looked into his rigid face—*Hod?* He finished laughing and looked at her without any expectation—*You do know Wilkinson was cleared last night? Min's mum died,* said Antenna—*Yes, that's right. She's gone. Min is the endling, now. So, while it's important to do something to help endangered animals individually; we are all, in fact, endangered here. We have to look after each other or we can't do anything to help anyone. We have to work together. Hoddy, please, I need you to help me.*

Hod looked at Antenna. He quietly reached out and made as if to pat her - he was certainly reaching out to her - when Min's arrival broke the tension. She'd been running—*Sorry I'm late. Something's odd...*

—Yes, said Torque, who flew into the cave immediately followed by Spark. He was still a bit puffed when he said—*Had to climb the camera. Make sure it wasn't recording anymore...*

—Camera? What camera? said Antenna—*Recording what?*

—Me, replied Min—*Some sort of video camera. So, I'm asking myself, what for? Why would they want footage of me, sleeping in the false day of the nocturnal house?*

—It's not rocket surgery, is it? Let's see, said Hod—*Do you think it could be, um, because you're an endling?*

—Thanks for that, Hod. Antenna glared at him—*Why are you doing this?*

Hod just shook his head. He looked down and then said—*Okay. Okay. I'm sorry. I'm with you.*

Min watched him curiously and then, back on track, said—*More than that. It's a weird camera and there's something familiar about it. I know I've seen one before but I can't think where.*

—I'm always being filmed, said Zip—*Hey, now you come to mention it, there was a camera in my enclosure yesterday.*

—You didn't say anything? asked Antenna.

—Didn't seem out of the ordinary.

—Of course, sneered Hod—*Just a paparazzi magnet, you are.*

—Thanks, Hod, said Zip with only the merest trace of sarcasm hardening her gratitude—*Though, Min, it was big, wasn't it. Bigger than a normal vid camera? And, yeah, I've seen one too. But where?*

—Let us know when you remember, said Helmut—*But right now we must resolve Hod's discipline issues.*

—It's true, said Zip—*I for one will not work with him again.*

—Right, said Hod—*Consider me reprimanded, then. Can we move on?*

Antenna frowned at him but Hod avoided her gaze. Antenna couldn't work him out. Helmut looked around the small group of creatures, assessing their mood. He nodded, giving implicit permission.

—The difference is, the camera was inside your enclosure, not outside the wire? asked Min.

—Hey, you're right, said Zip—*I never noticed.*

—So it's not just about being the last Leadbeater's possum. I think we need to find out if anyone else is being filmed.

—Right, said Zip.

—I think we should follow them when they pick up the footage, said Min.

—Sounds like we've got a plan, said Helmut.

—What if they've discovered Ektek? said Min.

—How? asked Helmut.

Zip looked at Hod and spoke deliberately—*It is possible that someone followed us after Hod's little intervention yesterday.*

—Listen, Zip. I'm beginning to think I should have just left you to the komodo, said Hod—*I've been reprimanded so just leave it alone, will you?*

—The films aren't our only problem, Antenna changed the subject— *We still haven't talked about Bash and Crawf. They're being held to ransom by the crocs.*

—Safe? asked Helmut.

—For the moment, said Antenna—*The beetles tell me they've found Hardback but the harem want action now. What do we do?*

Helmut looked round the group—*We need to know regular staff movements around Hardback. We'll also need a map of the area. Bash and Crawf have to be freed for reconnaissance. You think the crocs'll buy it?*

—No! said Hod—*This is exactly what I'm talking about, isn't it! More surveillance. More observations. More nothing. They're crocs. They want action! And I know how they feel.*

—Hod… breathed Antenna.

—I'm sorry for Bash and Crawf but if we explain to the crocs we need the information first, we can have the airship on the way by evening, said Helmut.

—That means they'll have to fend off crocodiles for another two days, said Zip

—When they were recording me, said Min, still thinking of her enclosure and photography experiences—*All the crickets were alive and really fresh.*

—Is that unusual? said Zip—*I mean, I wouldn't know. I tend to prefer my fruit not skipping around, you know?*

—The group doing the filming was called The Really Free Wildlife Company. It was on the technician's overalls, said Min—*It felt as if they were trying to recreate a totally realistic environment. With fresh branches and those live crickets.*

—Catchy name. Really Free. Nice idea, said Zip—*Impossible dream.*

—What about you, Zip? Notice anything unusual while you were being filmed?

—Now that you come to mention it, I thought I heard… Nah… Silly…

—What?

—Well, I was almost sure I heard a…

—What?

—You'll laugh at me. Male fruit bat.

—No male fruit bats around here!

—You're telling me! Zip chuckled and looked around the rest of the group. There were all amused by her outburst—*Okay, so maybe I'm just a little bit desperate.*

—You think they're trying to make you feel like you're back in the wild? I mean, they are called the Really Free Wildlife Company, said Min.

—We'll find out tomorrow. After Operation Emancipation.

—We'll take the airship, said Helmut—*With Min, Zip and Hod.*

—*Not Hod,* said Zip.

Hod was exasperated—*Oh, for Zed's sake.*

—*No. Not Hod,* said Helmut—*He can follow in the trike.*

—*And there won't be the extra surveillance equipment; you do know that, don't you?* said Antenna. She could feel their annoyance and at the same time their resignation. This was Ektek. They had limited resources. Nothing would be straightforward.

—*Because?*

—*Intek's searching for illegal drum and mesh nets in the river system,* said Zip—*They need it. What if they had to report an incident?*

—*They've been working on this indig fish operation for a very long time,* said Antenna—*I'll be monitoring them but you'll always be able to…*

—*Permission to speak?* growled Torque.

—*Not you, too,* said Hod. Antenna glanced at him, almost ready to be sympathetic, but not quite.

—*Granted,* said Helmut.

—*This here grub's called Spark. The number from the crocs. Wants an apprenticeship. More than my job's worth to have an assistant without your say so but there's a heck of a lot of security work that needs doing 'round here. More than an old beetle such as meself can get 'round. I'd certainly appreciate the help.*

As a group, Ektek turned to Spark, a somewhat larger beetle than Torque, albeit younger. They had no problem with the idea. It was enough that a creature wanted to join Ektek. As much as a Christmas beetle could, Spark grinned obligingly at them all. Antenna, Min, Helmut and Zip nodded and smiled in return. Hod did not allow any expression over his face.

—*Welcome aboard, Spark,* said Helmut.

—*Looking forward to working with you,* said Antenna.

—*Congratulations,* said Zip.

—*Welcome to Ektek,* said Min.

—*Brilliant,* said Spark.

—*Good luck, mate,* said Hod—*You're going to need every last scrap of it around here.*

Chapter Seven

I

That afternoon, following closing time, Helmut and Zip climbed into the airship; accompanied by a small team of engineer beetles. The airship headquarters, known as Uptek, was a zeppelin-like craft approximately twenty metres long. Ektek could launch and monitor missions by audio links between Uptek - the airship - and Ontek vehicles.

A maglev track was positioned on the top surface of the ship to launch smaller vehicles. If required, the pilot could launch the smaller planes while comfortably sitting in the cockpit of the airship. Magnetic levitation was a system constructed of a series of magnets that could be activated one at a time very quickly. The plane catapulted forward to each new magnet, and then the next and the next, efficiently building enough speed to fling the plane off the airship. The vehicle also carried a variety of surveillance equipment, aerials, a satellite dish and a solar panel array for additional power.

Ektek usually took the airship into the hangar at night. Now, refuelled and refurbished with food and water by the ants and beetles, it was tethered by the emergency Ektek exit ready for Operation Emancipation to begin. Helmut, Zip and the beetles did their last minute inspections before they waited for Min to join them.

Helmut sat heavily in the pilot's seat. He'd checked fuel, electrics and then, with trepidation, turned to the communications system. He had cause for concern. He knew only too well that the radio had failed him during the last action. He was frightened that something he had done had caused the problem and he desperately did not want that to happen again—*Ektek? Can you hear me? Over.*

Antenna's voice answered him promptly—*Thanks, Uptek. Loud and clear. Over.*

—*That's a relief. Any problems I should be aware of? Over.*

—*Manifold tells me they examined every circuit. Nothing. No more thoughts since we last spoke? Two complete communication breakdowns can't happen again. Over,* said Antenna.

Helmut sat in the pilot's seat, pondering—*I shall do my best, Antenna. On that you may rest assured. Over.*

—*Never had any doubts, Helmut. Over.*

Helmut hung his head miserably as he switched off the mic. He had doubts. Serious doubts. He had a dreadful feeling those communication breakdowns were something to do with him. Only, he had no idea what the problem was and he had absolutely no idea how to solve it.

II

Zip was in the hold with Manifold doing last minute checks. They finished tightening the stowage on the little red steam car—*Looking good, here, thanks, Manifold. Amazed your team managed to get it going again,* said Zip.

Manifold gave her a cheery wave as she left the airship with her beetle team—*No worries, Zip. That's what we do.*

—*Thanks, Manifold,* said Zip—*See you when we get back.*

III

In her nocturnal house enclosure in the Australian animal section of the Zoo, where the lights were still off, pretending it was night, Min whispered to Torque—*How much longer's he going to be?*

They watched a man wearing overalls printed with the logo of the Really Free Wildlife Company as he dismantled the camera and put tapes and devices into a sturdy road case. There were several other tapes already packed.

Torque said—*Sssh.*

Min feigned sleep as the researcher warbled amiably with Min's keeper and then, finally, both humans left. The lights snapped on and it was again broad bright sunshine in the nocturnal house. Blinking, Torque thought to himself about manipulating environment—*I'll never get used to that.* When Torque gave her the all clear—*They've gone,* Min jumped up to run through the tunnels, through the cavern and up the rope ladder to the airship. Torque turned to Spark—*Off you go, pip-squeak. Tell Antenna she's on her way.*

Spark nodded and snapped his wings with a click—*Yes, sir!* He flew ahead to relay the information to Antenna in the control centre.

Torque shook his head as he followed the Christmas beetle wavering in the dim hallways—And don't you get lost, you young buzzer!

IV

The Really Free Wildlife Company researcher marched through the zoo and got into a white car in the parking area. The car moved out. Hod waited by the gate inside his trike, fully covered with a sleek fairing designed to cut down wind resistance. The cover made the wallaby-powered vehicle look more like a baby racing car. The trike was low to the ground and the fairing was an all weather cover that also cut down wind resistance. He took off after the car. Fast. The trike was stable and quick, propelled at speed by his mighty wallaby legs.

V

Min clambered aboard the airship and entered the bridge. She sat next to Helmut who immediately commenced launch procedures—*Clear for take off. Over.*

Beetles and ants ran about down below, casting off and shouting encouragements—*All clear above and astern...*

In the hold, Zip hunkered down in her little red car.

—*And we're off. Over,* said Helmut into his radio mic.

—*Travel safe. Over,* said Antenna from the control centre cave. Antenna, and her father in the past, had hacked into the zoo's bureaucracy so the airship could move through any airspace unimpeded. The Ektek administrative activities managed to slip by humans because nothing disrupted the zoo's business; if there was no problem with their communications systems then there was no reason for humans to pay attention to Ektek at all.

The airship was quick to lift off and proceed in its stately manner following Hod on his trike. The skin over the airship envelope was clearly marked 'Bedlam Zoo' and painted brightly with images of animals. From an air traffic point of view, the airship belonged to the zoo but only Ektek used it. From the zoo staff's point of view, someone must be operating it, however, if it was not their department, it was not their business.

The bright skin was an example of the other side of Ektek's survival strategy; the more blatant, the more it was overlooked. Similarly, Hod's trike also used the bold-is-invisible theory. Easily able to keep up with the car through the stop-start of urban traffic, Hod's trike was a sight for sore eyes; or rather, a sight to make eyes sore. The fairing was painted bright orange, decorated with cats' eyes, flashing lights and emblazoned with several large stickers that read, 'A donation a day keeps the whalers away' and 'Our planet is for life'. A large orange flag printed with 'Save the Animals Give Money Now' flapped above his head, making the whereabouts of the recumbent even more obvious to the surrounding traffic. Thank goodness for do-gooder humans and their brazen, weird publicity stunts. It didn't matter what colour the camouflage took, just so long as it was ignored.

The researcher's car turned into the parking lot in a suburban office area. The researcher stopped the vehicle and got out. He strode across the bitumen carrying the road case towards a small nondescript building, much the same as all the other office blocks in the suburb.

Hod spun into the car park - coming almost face to face with the researcher—and kept right on going as if he had some urgent purpose. The researcher gave neither wallaby nor gaudy craft a second glance. Hod paused behind a wall and watched as the man entered the building. He picked up his radio—*Uptek. Come in please. Over.*

The radio hissed with Helmut's voice—*Yes, Hod. Over.*

—*He's just entered a building; corner of Chevron and er... Haliburton Streets. Over.*

—*Thanks, we're right above you. Could you notify as to roof suitability? Over.*

—*I'm going in. Over.* Hod's voice sounded determined even through the radio speakers. Perhaps he wanted to redeem himself after the restaurant. Perhaps he was just surging forward on his adrenalin. In the airship cockpit, Min and Helmut looked anxiously at each other and Min asked—*Hod isn't going to do anything stupid, is he?*

Helmut thought for a moment. Then he looked back to Min. Both nodded. Yup. He could. The mood that wallaby was in anything stupid was entirely possible.

—*Hod! Take it easy! Over.* Helmut wasn't sure if Hod would still have his radio on. He could only assume that Hod and his trike were in the lift. Going up.

VI

Helmut navigated the airship around the office block. Then he said quietly to Min—*Look.*

The airship glided by a billboard erected over the smart foyer area of the building. It featured a large photograph of a simpering Zip. Bold letters proclaimed: 'The Virtual Zoo. See the wonders of the past!'

Helmut shook his head—*I don't think Zip is going to like this.*

—*Are you kidding?* Min laughed—*She's going to love it! Her portrait? On a gigantic billboard for everyone to see? What more could she want?*

Helmut pointed out—*It says, she's a wonder of the past.*

—Oh, right. The past? said Min—*What's going on?*

Hod's voice came through the speakers—*All clear, Uptek. The roof is free of obstructions for landing. Over and out.*

The floating airship hovered over the office block roof. Helmut commenced landing procedures.

Hod, waiting on the roof, took the landing ropes and tied them onto the metal steps of the lift well. Then Hod's voice crackled through the radio—*Leaving the trike on the roof. Going for a reccie. Over.*

Helmut finished shutting down the airship's landing systems—*Thanks, Hod. Over and out.*

In the hold, Zip waited; a keen young fruit bat in need of action. A speaker in the car hissed briefly with Min's voice—*Hold doors now opening. Good luck, Zip. Over.*

—*Over and out.* Zip zoomed out of the hold in the steam-powered sports car—*Yeeeeeeeeee haaaaaaaaa!*

Even Helmut and Min could hear her in the cockpit as they caught sight of her speedy dash across the roof—*At least she enjoys her work,* said Helmut.

The sports car fitted easily into a normal lift. Zip was headed straight for the electrical centre of the building, checking for computer placements. She intended to search for and download any relevant material to the Ektek memory sticks she had tucked into her back pocket hidden beneath her wings.

Sitting still in the cockpit, Min and Helmut heard Hod's voice spitting through the speakers—*Uptek? Our friend is about to leave the building. Over.*

—*At least he's still in radio contact, Helmut,* said Min.

Helmut nodded and replied into the mic—*Any other occupants? Over.*

Hod's voice came through the radio again—*He's taking the only other one I can see with him. Building appears to be otherwise empty. Over.*

—*Be careful,* said Helmut—*There will probably be others still there. Take nothing for granted, Hod. Over and out.*

—*Yeah, yeah, yeah.* Hod turned his little radio off and put it away in his messenger bag—*Tell me something I don't know.* He watched the lift's indicators go down to the ground floor before he walked down the corridor to enter the offices. He found himself in a large open-plan space with short room partitions in pale green fabric. He looked around the humdrum area and smiled. This ought to keep him busy for a while. He began to nose through some paper work and bookshelves.

VII

Zip found herself in a strange kind of studio. The walls were padded with geometric shaped grey foam. The air was still and pressed strangely on her ears. It was very, very quiet. In the centre of the space a brightly lit animal slowly turned around and posed as if for an audience. Zip could walk right round her, and did so, marvelling at the creature. Zip stopped and stared at this vision of light and said—*Hi, there. Fancy seeing you here.*

It was a Leadbeater's possum. She looked a lot like Min. There was no response to Zip's greeting and the lights and projectors that surrounded the tiny possum were undaunted as Zip waved her hands through the illusion. It appeared that images of Min had been made into a hologram.

Zip pressed a button by the sign that read 'The Last Leadbeater's Possum' activating a sound grab. A gravely senior human's voice, someone used to being listened to, someone with power, growled out words authoritatively. His tone was grinding, grim and final. Zip shuddered in horror. Whatever it meant, it didn't sound good for the Leadbeater's possum.

In Uptek's cockpit, Zip's voice came through the radio—*Where's Min? Over.*

Min bent to the mic in the airship—*Right here, Zip. What's up? Over.*

Zip said—*I'm looking at you, kid. Here. Over.*

Min looked around the cabin and out of the windows. Not seeing Zip, she took it to be some kind of joke—*How do I seem? Over.*

—*You 'seem' to be in two places at once. I just waved my hand right through you. You'd better get down here. Take a good long hard look at yourself. Over.*

Min sucked her chin back into her neck, frowned and shook her head—*What's Zip talking about?* She looked back at Helmut—*Did you get that?*

Helmut stared at her blankly and Min could see he was not listening to her. More than that, he was not even conscious of her. Then he turned his head to stare out of the window. He sat bolt upright. He appeared to be listening to something that only he could hear. His eyes became glazed and he twitched—*No!* He shook his head, as if trying to dislodge something, a memory or a figment or a ghost…

Min watched him intently—*Helmut?*

Suddenly he banged his beak into the control panel. Then he lifted his head, shook his bony cap and stared some more. Frightened, Min wondered where Helmut had gone. Physically he was here, but certainly not mentally. She flicked the switch to call Antenna—*Ektek. Come in, please. Over.*

Nothing. Not a hiss, not a static soup, nothing at all. She thought, sighing, what a time for the communications to go down again and spoke into the mic—*Ektek. Come in, please. Can you hear me, Antenna? Please? Antenna? Over.* She switched channels and tried again—*Zip? Can you hear me? Hod? Anyone? Can anyone hear me? At all? Over.*

Silence. Except for the large bird breathing erratically. Apparently, Helmut was lost in his own mind. Min had never seen him act like this. What could she do? She looked at the control panel and at the doors. She was trapped. Nothing. She could do nothing—*Helmut? Stop it. Please.*

Helmut just stared.

VIII

In the well-lit office, Hod discovered advertising for a set of holograms; all endangered animals. There was a stunning poster of a dugong gliding through deep water in green filtered light. The bold headline read: Amazing! Astounding! 3D dugong! Swims like a mermaid! Get close enough to almost touch it!

Here was a beautiful picture of a platypus crouching near the entrance of her tunnel, on the banks of a creek. 'Experience the last faunal emblem up close in extraordinary 3D audio visual technology!'

And here was a tiny Leadbeater's possum peeking down from a mountain ash, 'Stunning Hologram Virtuosity! An emblem, a Leadbeater's possum so real, you'll swear it's looking right at you.'

And, thought Hod, it was.

And, thought Hod, it looked an awful lot like Min.

And, thought Hod, that didn't bode very well at all.

IX

In Uptek, Helmut's battle with his inner demons was slowing down. His twitches lessened as the interference faded from his mind.

Min spoke again—*Helmut?*

Helmut jumped. He looked over at Min in confusion—*Was it you?*

Min examined him—*What?*

—*Talking?*
—*Yes.*
—*What did you say?*
—*Um*, said Min—*Helmut.*
—*What?* said Helmut.
—*That's what I said*, said Min—*I said your name. I said, Helmut.*
Helmut thought about this seriously—*Let me know if you say anything else.*

Min took time to consider this puzzle. She looked askance at Helmut. Was he back to normal? Helmut stretched out his glossy wings and bent his blue neck this way and that. Then he closed his eyes, taking a moment of recovery. Suddenly Min didn't like this mission at all. Why was she bracing herself for danger on a simple surveillance? She leaned over the radio mic—*Ektek? Come in, please. Over.*

Antenna's voice came through clearly—*What's happening, Uptek? Over.*

A flood of relief went through Min and she bent to the mic—*We had another black out. You okay there? Over.* She waited for Antenna's response. Strange. There was none. Min bent to the mic again—*Ektek? Come in please.* That's when Helmut woke up and started banging the side of his head against the window shouting—*You can't make me!*

—*Helmut! Stop it!* said Min. She tried to get between him and the window but he couldn't see her and he was moving with considerable force. She backed down, fearing her small size would make her vulnerable to crushing, and said—*Helmut? Can't make you what?*

—*I must not! I am responsible for more lives than just mine! Others would be at risk!* Helmut became more and more agitated, flinging his head and shouting—*No! It's impossible!*

Through his distress Min heard the buzzer sound which meant someone wanted to enter the airship—*Uptek?* It was Zip speaking through the coms, a blare of reason and sanity into the rarefied atmosphere of the cockpit—*Requesting clearance for steam car, please.*

Min watched Helmut in amazement. He'd always been so in control and so stalwart. Here he was crumpling before her very eyes! Min had no idea what he might do next. She was only a small animal and he was a large armed bird. Was he losing his reason? Could he become dangerous? She looked over at the instrument panel. There was no way of knowing how to open the hold door. There were no labels and she could see no manual override. Helmut continued to argue with himself. He muttered—*I must stay here.*

Min said—*Helmut?*

Helmut looked at her; rather, he looked through her. She reached over to him—*Helmut? It's me, Min. I'm talking to you.*

Helmut didn't give any sign of hearing. He simply said—*I'm not leaving.*

Min said—*That's good to know.* Then she took hold of one of his wings and shook him as hard as she could. She shouted—*How do I open the hold? Helmut?*

The buzzer went once more. Min shook the wing again—*Zip needs to get in? Helmut! Wake up!*

At last Helmut shook his head as if to clear it. He looked at his wing and back to Min. She dropped her hold on his wing. Hod moved to press a blue button—*Under control,* he said.

Min had serious doubts about that.

The radio hissed with Antenna's voice—*Uptek? Can you hear me? Come in please. Over.*

Helmut answered—*Ektek. Hearing you loud and clear. Over.*

Antenna said—*Everything okay up there? Over.*

Helmut didn't even look at Min—*No worries, Antenna. Over and out.*

That wasn't true for Min. She had plenty of worries. Then Zip entered the cockpit at the same time as the coms buzzed and Hod's voice filled the space—*Uptek? Trike clearance requested. Over.*

Helmut reached for the handpiece and said into the mic—*Go ahead, Hod. Over.*

Apparently now fully composed, Helmut activated the hold door to let Hod pedal his trike up the ramp. Hod's voice coming through the speakers held just a hint of urgency—*Coming in, guys. I've untied the ropes. We've got to get out of here. Right now. Over and out.*

—*This place is full on,* Zip started talking the instant she had an audience—*The Really Free Wildlife Company is selling holograms to zoos to replace live animals.*

Min stared at her—*What?*

—*It's true. Zoos won't need real animals any more,* said Zip.

—*What's going to happen to us?* said Min.

Hod entered the cockpit, wiping his paws with satisfaction—*That ought to stop them in their tracks. He brought with him a distinct smell of...*

Zip looked at him suspiciously, sniffing—*What?*

—*Oh, nothing to worry about.* Hod smiled—*Just a little surgical strike.* He flicked a dead match at the group and rattled the rest of the packet he held in his paw.

Helmut was immediately alert—*What have you done?*

Min looked from Hod to Helmut. She couldn't decide who was the biggest problem.

Chapter Eight

I

Up on the airship bridge, Hod tossed the box of matches into his messenger bag and stretched carelessly—*Just taking care of business. Come on, time we went.*

Helmut, Zip and Min jostled round the window. They could see a thin strand of grey smoke escaping from the Really Free Wildlife Company building beneath them.

Helmut snapped into action saying—*Firetek. Urgent.* He pushed a button on the console and immediately a siren sounded, high and loud and a red light on the panel began to flash—*I've unlocked the fire-fighting equipment. Zip. Min. Go.*

—*No, no, no!* said Hod—*You're not listening!* He scuttled forward to the console and stared at the different buttons and switches as he tried to work out how to stop the siren—*We just leave.*

Helmut repeated—*Go.*

As Zip and Min hurried back towards the hold to prepare the tank and equipment, Min said—*Are we sure about this, Zip? Our gear is for bushfires.*

—*Fire in a concrete jungle,* said Zip—*...is still a fire.*

Back on the bridge, Helmut moved in front of Hod, preventing him from touching the console—*Over my dead body.*

—*You should be thanking me, not putting fire fighting into action! You're all mad.*

—*Hod. Tell me. Is an airship with the Bedlam Zoo logo currently parked on top of this building? Is it?*

—*Yes, but...*

—*Is there any chance someone might see it and then connect us with the fire? Is there? Any chance at all?*

—*It's a well-aimed pre-emptive strike. All we do is leave. Simple. We just go away. Right now.*

—*Ektek is completely ignorant of this company's motivations, Hod.* Helmut struggled to maintain his composure, so recently regained—*It*

60

may be that the Really Free Wildlife Company is a threat to animals and we do need to find an effective way to destroy it but then again, it may be that their activities are to help animals and we should encourage them. How are we to know?

—*You always want to think the best of everyone,* Hod sneered—*It's obvious what they're up to.*

—*Is it? How can we find out if we destroy the evidence? Before we get a chance to examine it?*

—*By then it might be too late.*

Young wallaby against old cassowary; big legs versus horny headpiece. Helmut braced himself against the console and shouted into Hod's face—*You remind me of my son. He had no idea either! Just wanted to rush into the fray and beat the bastards. Well. He forgot he could lose.*

—*Forgot?*

—*Over the years I've lost so many: friends, family, creatures with talent, energy, devoted to the cause… Just because you fell over a packet of matches some careless fool left… And it seemed to solve all your problems…*

—*I brought the matches with me.*

There was a distinct odour in the air. It was the smell of danger. Hod and Helmut stared at each other in loathing as dark smoke billowed from the Really Free Wildlife Company building.

II

Min drove the tank down the airship ramp onto the roof. She parked as close as possible to the window from where the smoke was rising. The tank contained rescue equipment and could be used as an all-purpose emergency machine.

Zip and Min braced the tank into place. Zip took the end of the cherry picker attachment, manoeuvring the hose into position above the window while Min primed the generator to run the pump. The airship held water both as ballast and for fire fighting. Most fire fighting happened during animal rescue in the wild. Ektek was capable of hosing down a pathway for creatures caught in fire devastation. However, they weren't used to such delicate operations as putting out office fires in the middle of a city.

Min monitored the water pressure and flow control feeds. Water ran from the ballast containers in the airship, through the tank's pump and out to the end of the cherry picker. Zip could then guide the hose into the building and down to the fire-front. They had established Hod had thrown his lit match into a rubbish bin filled with screwed-up paper. It was now well ablaze and the heat was spreading.

Min raced back to the generator and switched on the pump. Water stiffened the hose as it flowed down to the building. Zip struggled with it, trying to direct water onto the fire. She raced back up the hosepipe to shout at Min—*You've got to get down here. I can't hold it much longer.*

Min yelled back—*Hang on, I'll try to come in closer.*

—*Can you cut down the volume of water?*

—*I'll try.*

Zip struggled to keep the hose pointing at the rubbish bin. The fire seemed to be taking hold. A desk next to the bin had caught alight. The smoke was getting thicker and darker. The two small creatures were fighting a losing battle. And they knew it.

III

In the airship cockpit, Hod continued to argue with Helmut—*Let it burn! We can never make a difference if we're always just creeping around the edges, taking neat little measurements and tidy little observations!*

—*I don't think you have any understanding as to what Ektek does. Do you? Ektek is about communication, pure and simple, and we don't need to be discovered as a group of idiot terrorists. We can't afford to lose the support base we do have and we can't afford to endanger any more lives. Get down there and help them get that fire out, for Zed's sake!*

IV

Min gingerly manipulated the controls to angle the cherry picker's cage towards the window. There was a safety bracket she imagined she might be able to clip around the hose at the end of the cherry picker. She stretched out to assist Zip but could not reach—*Push it towards me, Zip! See if you can get it into that bracket...*

Zip backed towards the window. She tried in vain to get the hose back up to the cherry picker but it was just too heavy for her. She could feel herself weakening but she struggled on, trying to find the strength. She let herself relax, trying to build up for a forceful shove. She counted herself in. One, two, three and heaved with all her might...

The hose refused to lock into the bracket. She almost wept. The fire seemed to be an angry beast, much worse than an attacking komodo. It had come to life and there was nothing she could do to stop it.

V

Up on the bridge, Hod shoved Helmut aside. Helmut stumbled and Hod pushed himself into Helmut's place at the control panel of the airship. Without warning, Hod pressed a red handle forwards, hoping to achieve something - only he knew what. The airship lurched violently as it fought against the anchor of hose and tank and began to rise into the air.

—*You fool! You stupid fool!* Helmut braced himself against the window of the airship and just managed to stay on his feet—*Put it down! Put it down!*

Hod, however, lost his footing and fell over. Helmut made his way to the control panel as the floor tilted—*You could kill someone!*

Hod slid to the other side of the bridge and smacked into the wall.

Helmut fought with the controls, attempting to land the airship and restore balance to the craft—*What are you thinking?*

Right then, nothing. Hod had lost consciousness. He lay still.

VI

The jolt shook the tank on the roof, jerking the hose out of the airship. Water sprayed out of the hose in a spectacular arc as it fell. The hose attachment flew down past the cherry picker cage and crashed into the side of the building.

The impact catapulted Min off the hose. She plummeted, flailing her tiny limbs, her long tail sailing out behind her as she fell.

She fell like a rhinoceros.

Zip heaved herself out of the window above with a massive effort, leaving the rapidly emptying hose dangling and flew straight down after Min. The airship's sudden movement had wrenched the connection to the ballast tanks free. The water gushed out of a hole in the ballast of the airship, splattered uselessly onto the roof and trickled down to the car park.

Zip swooped and caught Min onto her back less than a metre from the ground. She did not land but swerved straight back up into the air. Min clung to Zip's bare back and looked down.

—*Don't you wish you'd been born a sugar glider?* shouted Zip as she flapped upwards in the air.

—*All the time*, said Min. She buried her face in Zip's fruit-bat bareback and wished she'd never been born at all.

An alarm rang from the ballast area in the airship, clashing horribly with the Firetek siren shrieking in the bridge. Back at the controls,

Helmut turned off both alarm and siren and attempted to restabilise the now light-headed airship. He shouted to Hod who had woken and was standing staring out of the window at the roof—*Can you see them?*

—*No. I can't.* In the jagged silence Hod leaned to the windows and looked out at the tank—*What have we done?*

—*You, Hod,* said Helmut—*It was just you.*

The noise of a helicopter came closer and closer to the window. Hod and Helmut both stepped away from the glass. It was Zip's wings beating that extraordinary sound as she flew up to stare into the windows of the airship. As she hovered outside, Min still clinging to her back, Zip kicked the windscreen hard, making both Hod and Helmut jump.

Through the window, Hod signalled it was all his fault. He shouted—*Really sorry, man. I never meant anyone to get hurt.*

Zip snarled back, saying something unflattering and unprintable that Hod luckily could not hear. He understood her meaning clear enough, though. She shrugged and turned, with Min on her back, to dive down to the tank. Zip and Min reached the cherry picker extension just in time to see the building's automatic sprinkler system turn on and begin to spray everywhere in neat rows of water daisies.

—*About time,* said Zip.

Min said nothing, still clinging wide-eyed to Zip's back. They watched the spray slowly dampen down the fire.

VII

Hod turned to Helmut—*Is there anything I can do?*

—*Get down there and help them,* Helmut grunted—*And make her fast.* Helmut had his own work cut out trying to keep the bulky airship steady. The unbalanced ship was now more difficult to manoeuvre than it had ever been.

Hod rubbed his head with his yellow paws and went down to face the team.

VIII

Min and Zip hauled the hose up to the roof of the building. Hod clambered down the airship ramp to the rooftop—*Hey, you guys, I am so sorry…*

Shoulder to shoulder, working silently, and both very tired, Min and Zip had no spare chitchat for the creature who had almost turned

Min into Leadbeater possum street pizza. Min was still in shock and Zip couldn't trust herself to speak.

Hod watched them both for a moment or two, understanding and ashamed. Then he went to tie the ropes back on to the lift well steps. They hit the automatic rewind to get the hose back into the tank, an arduous job as the hose was wet and dirty.

—*Look at the muck we're leaving,* said Min.

Zip said—*Do you think they'll notice?*

—*What?* said Hod.

—*Oh, you're right,* said Zip—*No one will notice a thing.*

—*Some covert operation,* said Min.

It was almost funny but for everyone's heavy heart. Between the three of them they managed to get the tank ready to winch back into the airship's hold. Hod signalled to Helmut to start the crane system and the tank was cranked back with Hod checking the lines as it went.

Zip and Min climbed back down to the Really Free Wildlife Company office through the window, thinking they might be able to put the place back into some sort of order. It was hopeless. It stank. There was water and smoke damage everywhere. The sprinkler system was sputtering and spurting unevenly in haphazard directions. Zip picked up a fallen half-burnt chair. Min pushed in a drawer. Zip shuffled through some sodden papers but anything they could attempt would have little effect on the chaos.

—*Min! Zip! Hey!* Hod's voice shouted down from the roof—*Time to go. Car's back.*

—*Quick,* said Zip as she grabbed some DVDs to take with her. Min picked up a couple of brochures about the Virtual Zoo and they got away.

IX

As soon as Zip and Min appeared on board the airship, Helmut commenced take off formalities—*Uptek taking off. Prepare for all occurrences.*

—*All clear above and astern. Standing by booster pumps,* said Min.

—*Standing by jettison pipes, said Zip.*

—*Throttles?* asked Helmut.

—*Primed and set to maximum,* replied Min.

Helmut pushed forward on the throttle. The airship slowly rose. They could hear water raining out onto the roof as the airship lifted what remained of the ballast tanks.

They floated above the car park to see the researcher walking into the building. Just as he was about to enter the foyer a shadow passed over his head and he looked up.

The animals on board the airship argued about it. Did he see the Bedlam Zoo airship puttering out of sight? There was nothing to be done.

Chapter Nine

—Looks like you were right, Zip. They want to replace all endangered species with holograms and the real animals are to be taken off public display, said Antenna as she dropped a DVD onto a pile of Really Free Wildlife Company brochures with a clatter—*And set free.*

—Set free? asked Min.

—Yup. Released back into the wild, in the interests of conservation. So they say.

Back in the dimly lit garage, Ektek had gathered to debate the findings from their latest flawed action.

—Conservation, said Hod—*That's rich.*

Torque and Spark, the security beetles, were posted by the door—*Hologram?* whispered Spark—*What's a hologram?*

—Sort of a 3D photograph movie lightshow thing. A projection. Electronic stuff.

—It's bizarre, said Zip—*Wonderful but bizarre all the same.* She picked up a poster featuring her very own cheerful self and grinned as she held it up to her face.

—Too good to be true, said Hod. He flicked through a brochure extolling the virtues of an electronic Leadbeater's possum (solar panels optional).

—But why are we to be taken off display? asked Min.

—Yeah, aren't they killing the geese that laid the golden eggs? said Zip.

—Putting the so-called main environmental reason for zoos to exist out of sight and out of mind, do you mean? said Helmut.

—Departmentally approved, said Antenna.

—Out to some dark weedy pasture, said Hod—*Where no one will notice us disappearing.*

—We'll probably have to breed more, said Zip.

—No. That's not it, said Antenna—*They want to release us into suitable fenced reserves in our own habitats. Really. We don't have to breed. We don't have to do anything. It's like we're being let off early for good behaviour.*

—*Darn. I'd like to get some good breeding in,* Zip smiled at her friends and they knew she was only half joking.

—*Is there any independent review on the internet?* said Helmut—*Any published papers or commentary?*

—*There's an article on the web about their attempts to train animals for future freedom.*

—*Who wrote the article?* said Helmut.

—*No way of knowing their connections. Can I suggest requesting a report from the beetle surveillance team at Really Free Wildlife Company office immediately?*

Torque and Spark both snapped to attention the moment the word beetle was spoken. Torque said—*I'll get on to that right away, Antenna. Right away.*

—*Thanks, Torque.*

Torque turned to Spark—*Off you go.*

—*Me?* Spark couldn't have been more surprised.

—*Yes, you. Go on, get going. Organise a relay team and get them over to the Really Free Wildlife Company pronto. We need to know what's going on and we need to know now. What are you waiting for? Get on with it.*

With excitement polishing his elytra, Spark vanished down the corridor. This was real responsibility. He was up to it. He could do it. He'd show them.

Torque shook his head but stayed where he was by the door. It was always tricky letting the babies work on their own but he had to trust them sooner or later. He thought Spark might make something of himself in the security field; after just a bit more training.

Back at the Ektek meeting, Min remained unconvinced—*If they think live crickets and male bat impersonations in Zip's enclosure were life experience then someone's got a lot of explaining ahead of them.*

—*There'll be plenty more to come, I'm sure,* said Antenna—*They'll teach survival skills, you know, like training you to be afraid of predators. When they're schooling numbats, the release team instruct the young ones to be frightened of the shape of hawks and eagles so that kittens run away when they see a bird of prey.*

—*As far as I understand it,* said Helmut—*There's no point in having the last of any species languishing in prison - they might as well go back to wilderness parks and see if we can find a way to survive without human intervention. I must say, I find it hard to believe they mean what they say.*

—*Maybe teach those scientists a thing or two, you know?* said Zip.

—*As if they care about individual animals!* said Hod.

—*Come on, Hod. You know there are some humans who are animals. They* care, said Antenna—*And yes, Helmut. It looks like those guys mean what they say.*

—*Preposterous.* Hod threw back his head and laughed—*No food bills. No vet bills. Let's save money and let them all die quicker so we don't have to worry about the poor little endangered creatures any more. They'll just write sad books with nice photos about what used to be. Are those our best interests?*

—*Does it matter, Hod?* Zip fluffed her fur and wriggled her shoulders in irritation—*The fact remains, they're going to free us! They've already taped Min and me. We'll go first for sure. We're going to be free! You're just jealous.*

—*You'll be laughing all the way to the mountains,* Antenna said to Min. Min couldn't quite bring herself to be excited. The loss of Rawlinson and Wilkinson still weighed heavy. She couldn't see any joy in running around a forest alone.

—*How will we know who's to be released first? said Zip.*

—*They'll choose,* said Antenna—*According to their market research.*

—*We could, of course, make their decision for them,* Helmut said—*Electronically.*

—*It should be you, Antenna,* said Min—*You never think about yourself. You deserve freedom.*

—*Min! I do so think about myself! All the time! And I haven't even been filmed yet. So it's got to be one of you.*

—*You don't know that. They might have hidden cameras. I bet they've got footage of every threatened creature in this zoo.*

Zip agreed with Antenna—*This should be for you, Min. You've been through too much. You deserve to hear the wind through the ash trees before you die.*

—*I'll hack into their system straight after the meeting,* said Antenna—*Now. Hod.*

—*Yes?*

—*Let it be understood that Ektek are not in the business of setting fires. Ektek does not damage property. Ektek does not put team members in direct danger. Let it be understood that, at this meeting, there is formal disapproval of your behaviour.*

Hod tipped his head and pursed his lips. It was a bad pose and Antenna knew it. It was a mockery of polite concern. It appeared that Hod could not have cared less what she said.

—*Oh, come on. It's got to be more than that. He should be banished!* said Zip.

Antenna was astonished. She shot Zip a startled glance. Banishing was a bit much, wasn't it?

—*We can only hope you haven't endangered our chance of release*, said Helmut—*Any of our chances.*

—*That'd be ironic, wouldn't it. Endangering your chances. Endangered ones.*

—*Hod!*

—*Oh, listen. My actions were completely justified!*

—*Whoa! How do you reckon that?* said Zip.

—*If that company wanted to free us for the sake of our health and happiness, they could have done it long before now. Ask yourself. Why not? It's got to be about profit. Somewhere some greedy entrepreneur is going to make money or it wouldn't be a company and it wouldn't be happening. As usual. Can you really believe this is about fancy ideals and rights of nature to exist?*

—*What was going through your mind when you tried to lift off from the roof-top?* said Zip—*Anything?*

Hod looked up to the ceiling, littered with blue glow-worm stars like neon full stops—*I'm sorry about that. I didn't mean to. I wanted to…*

—*Whatever you were thinking, the effect was to immediately endanger Min and Zip. They could have died*, said Helmut—*That behaviour, in the face of your extreme actions only two days ago in the restaurant, is inexcusable. You have broken the basic tenet of non-violence. It is bad enough you've been careless and thoughtless but it's far worse, isn't it. You've been deliberate and devious. You had destructive intentions even as we planned the action. You have gone too far.*

—*Oh, yeah?*

—*Yes, Hod. Please, don't be flippant. Where do you stand with Ektek? You must decide. Then Ektek will decide what is to be done about you.*

Hod glared at Helmut then stared angrily around the circle: a beetle, a cassowary, a numbat, a bare-backed fruit bat and a possum. Creatures he had known all his life. His friends. Then he said—*You want to lie down and die? Just accept it? Oblivion? Oh, good. Well done. That seems optimal to me.*

—*You can't do it by yourself, Hod*, said Helmut.

—*Look at Min. Look at her family. She's the endling. The very last of her kind. What does that mean to you?*

—*Hod*, said Antenna—*Leave her alone.*

—*Her life doesn't just mean her as an individual. It means extinction for her whole species. Extinction. Do you know what that means?*

—*Of course we do, Hod*, said Antenna—*Now is not the time…*

—*The end of her genetic code; the destruction of one of Zed's weird little creatures. Unless they've got one in a jar in a lab somewhere and some helpful scientist decides to bring them back!*

—*Hod*, said Antenna—*Shut up!* She turned away from him, helpless because of the tears welling up in her eyes.

—Look at us. All of us. We're all facing annihilation. The end. Finito. There is no coming back from extinction.

—We know, Hod, said Helmut.

—Don't you think we've got to help ourselves? When? When do we fight back? When we're dead?

Zip felt herself swelling with fury. She jumped up and flew at the wallaby, pushing him in the chest with her feet, and shouting—*Shut up! Shut up! You stupid wallaby, carrying round a dumb shoulder bag because you don't have a pouch. Should have been born a girl, then you might have been worth something!*

—Zip! said Helmut. He ran to help her as she flapped backwards, almost fell and tried to regain her footing. Antenna turned to join them and they settled again, watching Hod warily. The emotional vibration in the cave was intense and the creatures breathed heavily, looking to each other, wondering where they could go from here.

Min sighed, breathed in to give herself strength and then stood. She looked up at Hod and everyone strained forward in the blue shadows to hear what she had to say—*I wish I wasn't the only known Leadbeater's possum left. Of course I do. I wish my family could have survived. But, in the end, what difference will it make? It's not like there aren't plenty of strange little animals left. There are. Heaps. Most humans can't tell us apart anyway. We could be rattus rattus to most of them.*

—No offence to the rats, said Zip.

—No, no, of course not. But what else can we do? We have to keep going, as best we can. Death comes to us all. We know that. That's why we're all mortals. In the end it doesn't matter if we're part of a species or not. We're just individuals breathing in and breathing out. Then Min sat down again. The other animals regrouped and felt calmer then, even though no decision had been made. Min had given them a way forward without an answer.

—Hod. Are you Ektek? When Hod did not reply, Antenna continued—*We have to find a different way. We can't stoop to their level.*

—No one was hurt. Hod was sullen.

—But they could have been, said Antenna—*Not just human bystanders but your own squad. If you were in our place, would you trust you?*

—You caused considerable property damage, said Helmut—*How do you imagine that company will react?*

Hod stretched up to his full wallaby height and looked at everyone in the small circle before he spoke—*When all comes to all, I am Ektek. I do believe animals have a right to roam in safety across the world. I am prepared to die to bring the actions of the unscrupulous to the attentions of the media. Okay, sometimes I get impatient and I want to take a few of them with me. I have to work on that. But I am Ektek. Believe me. You can trust me.*

Just then, Spark arrived at the entrance to the cave and peeked around the corner. Torque stopped him from coming in with a wave of his darkling antenna. Spark waited while the Ektek animals struggled to accept Hod's regret.

—*Is that an apology?* Zip asked Antenna.

—*Look, I'm trying, eh.*

—*Who here is perfect?* asked Helmut.

—*Hod. This has to be your last warning. The next time you go out on your own, even think about taking a shortcut from Ektek's main path, then you will no longer be able to call yourself Ektek,* said Antenna and then she whispered—*And you'll have to leave.*

—*This has never happened before, Hod,* said Helmut—*You're the first Ektek member who has required discipline. Is that how you want to be remembered?*

—*Please, Hod,* said Min—*We don't want you to go.*

At the doorway, Torque had been waiting for a pause in the furore before sending Spark in. He judged there was enough calm - maybe it was the eye of the storm, maybe the end - to let him go.

—*Now?* Spark still hung back.

—*When were you thinking?* whispered Torque—*Sometime next week? Yes. Now. Go.*

Spark crept into the cave and went to Antenna. When he had attracted her attention he said—*The beetle surveillance team have reported.*

—*Yes?*

—*From the Really Free Wildlife Company.*

—*Oh, of course. Here. Tell everyone. Climb up on the panel. Go ahead.*

—*What? Me?*

—*Yes, you. Haven't got time to waste repeating information. Speak.*

Spark flew up to the control desk and looked nervously around at the gathered animals. He looked back to Torque who nodded sternly. Then Spark took in a deep breath—*Um, excuse me, everyone...*

—*You all know Spark,* said Antenna, by way of introduction. She nodded encouragingly at him.

—*Yes.* They looked expectantly at the young beetle. Spark gulped—*Um. Well...*

—*You've heard back from the surveillance team...* Antenna prompted.

—*Go ahead, Spark,* said Zip.

—*Speak up, grub,* shouted Torque from the entrance—*Get on with it!*

—*Right,* said Spark—*The Virtual Zoo team is worried. The translators say they're using words like sabotage and espionage.*

—*Have they connected the zoo to the fire?*

—*No, they have no idea what caused it but they're talking about moving their plans forward. The Really Free Wildlife Company are going to stage two. Straight away.*

—*What's stage two?*

Spark didn't have an answer to that. All the Ektek animals looked at each other.

—*Better get moving then,* said Antenna.

—*Free at last,* said Zip.

Chapter Ten

On the banks of a muddy river, Bash and Crawf sheltered from the sun under the curving shadow of the wingship. The craft had been dropped by the crocs just where Shining Teeth had stopped them. It was mostly out of the water but would not be able to take off from that difficult angle. The two Ektek representatives were, literally, stuck in the mud, trapped at the behest of five of the meanest creatures they'd ever met.

In the shade, Crawf was colourless. His headdress feathers were flat against his head and his cheek patches were pale, almost white. He was listless, leaning his mud-stained head against the wheel of the plane.

—*I don't get these crocs,* said Bash—*Why haven't they killed us?* He'd found his way into a puddle where the wing met the river and soaked his thin skin with relief—*What are they waiting for? What do you reckon? Are they going to? When? Is this some kind of torture? Waiting? Crawf? What can we do? Are we just going to sit here, all day? For how long? How many days?*

Crawf was in no hurry to answer these questions because, as far as he was concerned, there were no answers. He had troubles of his own to ponder. After a time he groaned and said—*I've got to get back. She'll never forgive me this time. It's been too long.*

—*She'll understand,* said Bash—*She'll be glad to see you back when she knows...*

—*Don't think so, not any more.*

—*She's your partner. Of course she wants you back.*

—*I'm no good for her.*

—*Of course you are.*

—*She needs someone who can give her live eggs. And I'm never there.*

—*That's not your fault.*

—*Isn't it?*

—*You work for Ektek. She's got to understand that.*

—She doesn't. She doesn't at all. All she wants is a baby. And I can't give it to her. She'd be better off if the crocs did eat me. Then she'd get a new mate. Have a better chance.

—You don't reckon the vets would have worked this out?

—I don't know. We've both been tested. Don't know what they're waiting for. If I were them I would have cleared me long ago.

Both frog and palm cockatoo watched the crocs, sunning themselves on the mud bank as the river trundled along in its muddy way. They both knew that even though the crocs appeared to be asleep, they could wake at the blink of a little frog's eye or the flick of a little palm cockatoo feather and, quick as a flash, have their little legs off.

—If they were going to let us go, then why don't they? Are they going to knock us off, or are we going free? They'd get a decent feed out of you, at least.

—Shut up, Bash.

—Seriously. We've got a chance. We must do. I reckon we should...

—Hullo? Do you hear that?

It appeared the crocodiles had. They came to life, twisting and turning over one another to face the opposite bank. There was noise approaching. More than mere noise, it was vibration, almost thundering, through the ground. There was smell, too, of farmyard and ordure and there, in the air, was a melodic kind of low horn or hooting. Mooing.

Bash jumped up onto Crawf's lap, or where he would have had a lap if a palm cockatoo had one, and said—*Is it an earthquake?*

Suddenly, a crowd of black-and-white bovines splashed over the hill to the river's edge and lowered their heads into the water.

—What the hell?

Their hooves sank into the mud as they tried to vacuum some drink into their hairy cow gobs. The crocodiles were alert now and on the move. Asunder and Grater looked at each other and slid into the water in unison. Before she too went into the drink, Shining Teeth glanced over at the crazy tilted plane. She saw Crawf and Bash and said—*Okay, you two. Go get Hardback. Do whatever you can. I want him here. Unharmed. Or else.*

She too, sank into the water then. Jata and Damura moved, ready to follow but Bash yelled out as loud as he could—*Hey! Can you give us a hand here?*

Crawf muttered—*They don't have hands.*

—You going to do it by yourself, smarty? Bash glared at the bird—*No? Well. We need the crocs.* Bash shouted to the two crocs again—*You heard what she said. We need to get out of here. Or else.*

Jata and Damura looked at each other and over to the cows clustering one by one at the opposite bank. Knowing Shining Teeth wouldn't have much patience for their absence, the two crocs took a wing each in their jaws and straightened the plane. With a heave they moved the wingship to higher, flatter ground, further away from the water's edge and, without a word, headed back into the river.

All five crocs disappeared into the increasing turbulence. The cows suspected nothing as they meandered into the water and innocently chewed their cuds, sucked up drink and lifted their tails to shit with flood bursts of manure.

Crawf's hair feathers flipped upwards and he flew through the window and onto the pilot's perch as fast as he could. A slight blush of pink flooded his face patches. He examined the instrument panel and flicked some switches. They would have to get by without a full preflight. He needed to get out of there as fast as he could—*Come on, Zed, help us out here...*

Bash, too, had leapt into the cockpit. From this relative safety he stared out the window at the milling cattle—*Should we tell them?*

—*The cows?*

—*Yeah. Warn 'em.*

Crawf was busy trying to get the engines going. The sparks were firing but nothing was catching. Had water got into the electrics when the crocs dragged them back down to earth? He dismissed the frog's concerns—*Bash. They're cows. Aren't you more interested in knowing if we can get into the air?*

—*But they're going to get eaten.*

—*Hullo? Beef? That's what they're for? They're going to get eaten by someone, sooner or later...*

—*Yeah, but not like...*

—*Just like.*

Apparently the five crocs had managed to get themselves into an attack formation for, without any kind of visible signal, two crocs leapt straight out of the water, baring their yellow fangs at the throat of a calf. Almost at the same time, the other three had surrounded an elderly cow that had wandered too far and was now stuck in the mud. There was panic among the cows.

The water boiled with roars and bellows. Eyes rolled in horror and legs flashed into lacey waves of coffee-coloured water. The calf sank to its knees, dissolved into its terror and disappeared into the muddy froth while the older cow struggled with the slashing jaws of her predator and gaping fear.

Finally the wingship's engines fired, sputtered and then roared when Crawf revved the engines. It would have been impossible to hear the gunning aircraft over the still agonising bawling and pounding of hooves. As soon as they ascertained that most instruments were working, Crawf set the vehicle to drive along the river's edge before lifting into the air. Soon they were hovering over the dust that covered the patchwork of stampede down below. The howls faded under the buzz of the engine. Feeling the safety that being airborne provided, Bash looked down at the melee—*What do you reckon about the crocs? Can we help them?*

The river wound through the landscape like a curved knife in the sun.

—*Why not?* said Crawf—*Let's take a look at that Hardback before heading back to the zoo.*

—*Not too close?*

—*What makes the heart grow fonder?*

—*What?*

—*Distance, Bash. Distance.*

Chapter Eleven

I

A good hour before normal opening time, the Really Free Wildlife Company team arrived at Bedlam Zoo. The media entourage, the crews of television outside-broadcast vans, radio presenters and photographers, all grappled with gear. They set up wiring, lights and shots.

Zoo management ran their fingers through their hair, bared their teeth, shook hands and squawked about the nature of emancipation and sponsorships.

Freedom: a word without boundaries... Freedom: use it or lose it. Freedom: if you love someone, open the cage door...

II

Footage beamed into the control centre from the Ektek camera mounted by the entrance. Antenna watched the crowd perform, dumbfounded. Spark sat next to her and recounted information as it came in from beetles stationed all around the car park.

—Zoo's preparing for a press conference. They're going to officially hand Min over to the Really Free Wildlife Company, said Spark.

III

Outside, members of the zoo staff were almost unrecognisable in their best outfits. They puffed up as they went from mic to mic, camera to camera, like pollinating bees. They spouted shiny phrases explaining that this partnership with the Really Free Wildlife Company showed the zoo's thinking was truly progressive and the reporters lapped it up, relaying it all faithfully to their public. This was more than lip service. This was evolution!

Representatives from the sporting company, Anything Goes, the investment company, Future Building, and the confectionary corporation, Sweet Life, were all there, shaking hands and expounding on the value of freedom of choice.

IV

In the Ektek hangar, Min's friends had gathered to say goodbye to her. She farewelled them each in turn, with her eyes brimming with sadness.

—*Perhaps,* said Helmut—*You will be able to find other Leadbeater's possums where humans have failed?*

—*That's right,* said Zip—*Everyone knows fairy possums are shy and elusive.*

—*Humans assumed Leadbeater's possums were extinct once before,* said Helmut—*Erroneously.*

—*They assumed fairies were extinct,* said Zip—*And that's true.*

When Min got to Hod they stood nose to nose, mingling their breath and concentrating on each other in a deep slice of time. Hod opened his eyes first and said very quietly—*Goodbye, Min. I'll miss you.*

Min's dark eyes filled with tears and she nodded, unable to speak for the moment, and turned lastly to Antenna. They embraced and Min tried valiantly to laugh—*Don't go eating any ants,* she whispered and the tears overflowed and began to roll down her fur.

Antenna attempted to put on a brave face and said—*Min, are you sure about this? You could reconsider. It's not too late. What about Ektek? Did you ever think of staying and being the controller? If you really wanted to, you could. You do know that, don't you? Think about it. It must tempt you at least. Be honest...*

—*Antenna. You are your father's daughter. Ektek trusts you. They need you. It's time for us both to grow up.*

—*Is it? Sorry I mentioned it.* They both tried to laugh but it was an effort—*Watch out for low-flying yellow-footed rock wallabies.*

—*None of those where I'm going.*

—*Lucky you.*

An eavesdropping wallaby heard no good of himself—*Hey, watch it...*

—*Shut it, Hoddy!*

—*Walk with me.* Antenna marched Min down the tunnel, away from the rest of the group. Min made sure no one had followed them before she turned urgently to Antenna—*I have to tell you. There hasn't been an opportunity before now. It's Helmut.*

—*Helmut?*

—*Min,* interrupted Manifold—*You have to go.*

—*I'm going.*

Antenna stopped her—*Min? Tell me. What about Helmut?*

—*When the communications dropped out from the airship. It was him.*

—*What?*

—*It affected him in some way. Like, he went off in his mind. I don't know, Anti, it was like… You had to be there. Weird.*
—*Min, they're looking for you.*
—*Okay, Manifold. Sorry, Antenna. Look after Ektek. And Helmut.*
—*I will. Cherish the freedom.*

Min ran through the tunnel to her enclosure for the very last time. Antenna watched her go, her heart heavy with what she perceived as selfish emotion, her thoughts of loneliness without her best friend. Then, exerting her self-discipline, she turned her thoughts to Helmut. How could he be affecting the communication system? There couldn't be anything wrong with him? Could there?

IV

Spark and Torque were also travelling on this day. The security team left the safety of the Ektek garage to fly across the zoo. Once in the car park, they clambered on board the Really Free Wildlife Company van before it left. They carried a tiny radio system. They would file reports whenever possible. Ektek wanted to know where Min was going to be set free. The zoo might be keen to let her go but Ektek was a different matter. Ektek animals stuck together.

V

Antenna and the others watched the television stream live on the internet. Min was ceremoniously plucked from her nest into the media limelight and celebrated, justly, as the first endangered species to be liberated by the Really Free Wildlife Company.

The cameras whirred. The lights beamed her into another life as she was packed lovingly into an elaborate carry case. Human legs marched with her into the Really Free Wildlife Company van.

The van drove out of the Bedlam Zoo carpark. The sponsors shook hands with the zoo staff. Very successful branding all round. Sensational pictures. The television crews packed up their Outside Broadcast vans and the radio people and the photographers zoomed away in their paparazzi style.

VI

Helmut, Zip, Hod and Antenna sat quietly in the control room. They were overwhelmed as they watched the netcast. However much her heart ached with Min's loss, Antenna still had enough analytical thought attuned to consider Ektek's future. She surreptitiously watched Helmut.

He seemed tired and bowed but he was still her teacher and her elder. She needed him to be strong. What had Min said? His mind? Antenna watched him, wondering.

Then, surprising everyone, the radio blared into life and Bash's voice crashed through the stratosphere—*Ektek? Can you hear me? Over.*

There was a rousing chorus of replies as Antenna bent to the mic— *We sure can, Bash! Over.*

—*Welcome back!*

—*Great to hear from you!*

—*Hi, Bash. Crawf there? Over.*

—*Yup, he's here, both safe. Over.*

—*Gidday, Crawf!*

Hod, Zip and Helmut continued to offer helpful comments in the background while Antenna expressed their relief in re-establishing contact. Then they got down to business and Antenna asked—*What's with the croc? Over.*

—*What's not with this croc! We're on the move, following him. Over.*

—*He's still captive? Over.*

—*Sure is. Dunno where they're taking him. Seems to be heading home. Got us puzzled, that's for sure. Over.*

—*Give us a yell when you get somewhere. Over.*

—*There's one more thing you might be able to help us with. Over.*

—*Go ahead. Over.*

—*They washed him. Over.*

—*So? Over.*

—*In a bubble bath. They cleaned his teeth and varnished his toenails. Over.*

The creatures in the control room; Antenna, Hod, Zip and Helmut all glanced at each other. Huh? No one had ever heard of anything like that before. Varnished toenails? On a croc? Antenna shook her head and leaned in to the mic—*What's your thinking? Over.*

—*Some sort of ritual? Only, we don't think it's a wedding. Over.*

—*He's already married? Over.*

—*Too bloody right he's already married and you don't want to meet his wives. Ever. Over.*

—*What other rituals are there? Over.*

—*Think about it. We'll let you know when we find out more. Over and out.*

Antenna closed the radio link and looked up at Helmut, Hod and Zip—*Are you thinking what I'm thinking?*

—*You don't want to know,* said Zip.

—*That's what I was thinking,* said Antenna

—*You're thinking,* Hod agreed—*It's his funeral?*

Chapter Twelve

I

Together with Hod, Zip and Helmut, Antenna sat in the control cave watching dining room footage streaming in from Bash's miniscule camera. They were waiting for Uptek to be refuelled before they could leave. They were going to try to get Hardback out of Last Chance to Eat.

Zip and Helmut looked at each other before Helmut said—*How do we get the croc into the airship?*

—*Can we tow him in with the tank?*

—*He's going to have to want to go, Anti,* said Hod—*We can't fight him.*

—*Oh, I imagine he'll want to go, don't you?* Antenna was setting up video links preparing to netcast whatever was going to happen to Hardback—*Given his options...* She found the relevant electronic address list of journalists, lobby groups and politicians and typed in information regarding Last Chance to Eat and their new swimming pool. Apparently the place had had to undergo extensive renovations after the komodo dragon riot. The affray had resulted in considerable publicity for the business and, of course, any publicity is good publicity. Last Chance to Eat could command high prices for today's crocodile event, whatever shape that might take. She clicked the video into the frame inset in the webpage and set the instructions to broadcast. She looked up at her team and added—*Wouldn't you?*

II

Bash had bumped in all his gear to Last Chance to Eat and was now broadcasting his footage from the restaurant dining room. The tiny yellow and black patterned frog hid in a tower of bamboo, ginger flowers, birds of paradise and rare wild orchids. He settled back into a bloom, satisfied that no one would notice him in the garish floral decoration and then panned smoothly around the room.

Crawf waited on the roof of the eatery. The wingship relayed Bash's footage data to the satellite and thence to Ektek headquarters where the team watched. Everything was in place, all systems checked and working well.

The waiters opened the front doors and the early diners hullaba-looed into the foyer. All became excitement and greeting of stylish folk à la mode: muted champagne pops, lounge music from a louche band and twinkles from designer frocks.

III

Antenna could see it all. The footage was coming in clear as a bellbird into the control computer monitors. Then Antenna heard a whirring sound over the hectic babble of the restaurant patrons. It was the familiar sound of beetle wings. She looked up from her typing just in time to see Spark and Torque fly past the frame.

Bash said—*What are you doing here?*

—*Didn't get as far as any highlands*, said Spark, referring to their journey in the van that had carried Min from the zoo.

Torque stared down the barrel of the camera, looking as serious as a beetle could, and spoke directly to Antenna—*This 'in't that bloomin' komodo café, is it?*

When Antenna gasped, Hod, Zip and Helmut all focussed on the screen, straining forward to get a better view. Antenna turned on the mic and spoke—*What's Spark doing there? And Torque? They shouldn't be in there! Min's one of the most highly profiled threatened creatures in the world! She'd be worth a fortune on a plate! Over.*

Bash couldn't explain it—*She's been brought in. That's all they know. Over.*

—*Find her. Go. Go! Go!!! Over and out!*

Spark and Torque immediately flew off and crashed, smack, into each other. After they'd regained their senses they pulled themselves together and started out again in different directions.

Their audience, back in the control cave, silently willed them on. The feeling of urgency was palpable. The pace quickened. This was not how Ektek had imagined Min's freedom. Antenna spun to face Hod—*We've got to get her out.*

Zip said—*What can we do?*

Antenna frowned—*Where's Crawf?*

—*Is Uptek ready?* asked Helmut.

—*I'll call Manifold*, said Zip and she ran out to find the head of mechanics.

Antenna changed the radio frequency channel—*Crawf? Come in, please. Over.*

—*Uptek 2. Over.*

—*Crawf. They've taken Min to the restaurant. We've got to get her out. Now. Where exactly are you? Over.*

—*In position on the roof, by the stairwell. Over.*

—*Have you got vision? Over.*

—*Bash's on the only camera here. Over.*

—*Forgot. The fishing nets. Right. Any ideas? How we're going to get Min and the croc out? Over.*

—*I can't carry the croc. Over.*

—*No, we're getting the airship ready for him. Over.*

—*Do you have time? Over.*

There was a pause. Reality sank in, cold, hard, horrible reality. What if they didn't get Min out in time? What if Hardback was to be killed today? What if Min…? Antenna stared in turn at Hod and finally at Helmut—*How much time do we need?*

Helmut answered—*How much do we have?*

No one knew the answer and no one wanted to guess.

The screens showed Bash's footage as he continued to pan around the rapidly filling dining room. The lighting was dim but focussed on a huge tree to one side of the room. The upper branches were on a level with people dining. The trunk and root system appeared to go down into the depths of the building. It was a mountain ash.

When the overhead lights lowered, each table glowed faintly with a candle in a holder, cut in the shape of gum leaves. Mottled forest leaf shadows were thrown over the gloomy walls and ceiling. Aroma burners cast a eucalyptus tinge into the air.

It was dusk in the Australian bush at the Last Chance to Eat theatre restaurant. Only, Antenna hoped without hope, it wasn't Nemesis Night again. Was it? She found herself muttering—*Please say it's not Nemesis Night. It's not Nemesis Night. It just can't be.*

Hod and Helmut didn't know what to say. Both had the disgusting feeling it very probably was Nemesis Night and that didn't bode well for Min at all. Zip and Manifold came into the control cave, alerted by Antenna's urgent tones. Zip stood by Antenna's shoulders—*The airship is ready for departure as soon as you say the word.*

—*Good. Get going.*

—*That's it,* said Hod, appealing to Helmut—*She said the word.*

—*Hod's staying here,* said Zip.

—*I can't stay here. I have to help. I can help. I can speak crocodile.*

—*Zip, we've got to work together here,* said Antenna—*We've got to get both of them out. They're going to die. They will get cooked. There's no time to argue. We're Ektek. Like it or lump it, get going and get Min.*

Helmut didn't need to hear any more. He ran to the cave entrance and shouted over his shoulder as he went—*Zip. Manifold. Uptek, now. And Hod. Get moving.*

—*Thanks, Helmut. Thanks, Antenna,* said Hod, pausing.

—*Go!* said Antenna.

Hod followed Zip and Manifold as they ran out. Antenna couldn't help herself. As he went past she said—*Hod?*

—*Yup?*

—*I swear, if you do anything...*

—*It's okay, man...*

—*Don't you dare call me 'man'!*

After they had run out, Antenna sat up even straighter, even more nervous, as she stared at Bash's shaky footage—*Hang on, Min. We're coming!*

IV

Back in the fevered restaurant, Bash focussed on the Really Free Wildlife Company's film crew. They had turned on a large, expensive, retro looking camera and concentrated on their work. The music faded to an end, slowly quieting an audience of diners, waiters and even the chefs and kitchen hands who had come out into the restaurant auditorium to watch.

Watch what?

A dazzling cone of spotlight etched through the smoke to pick out a trumpet player wearing a spangly dress. She lifted her yellow instrument to her painted red lips and musically raised the roof. A blare of brassy fanfare and then a human voice over the public address system brayed some announcement. Then, at the height of the fanfare, the researcher from the Really Free Wildlife Company entered the room with an ornate carrier bag. He ceremoniously opened it to reveal a perfect example of the State faunal emblem: the Leadbeater's possum.

The spotlight found Min. The last known fairy possum in the world looked frozen, her huge dark eyes were pools of fear and her long tail hung limply beside the researcher's arm. The trumpeter's horn coruscated with reflections of candle-light and then the soul-filled melody soared above the forest shadows. The researcher placed Min into the leafy arms of the mountain ash growing to the side of the dining room. The trumpet ceased. There was an expectant silence.

Min stayed exactly where she had been put.

Initially.

In the control cave, Antenna screamed—RUN!!

In the restaurant, the diners applauded, appreciatively. Min shivered as she looked into the hungry eyes of the audience. Then, she ran.

Only, where could she run?

She ran along the branches looking for an escape. The way down was deep and treacherous. The way out along the branches just leaned over the diners. The diners with big shiny teeth smiled their big shiny grimaces and applauded as she came nearer to their tables. The noise only sent her off to another table and so each table across the room had a close-up experience of her terror. The humans appeared to enjoy every moment.

V

Antenna looked up to find she was alone in the control cave. She rubbed her eyes and spoke out loud—*What can we do? How can we get her out of there?* She got up onto her four feet and paced around the cave. She was drawn inevitably back to the screen. It was hard to see the dim picture while the restaurant was clearly enjoying the nocturnal theme of their possum prowl.

Antenna turned the mic back on—*We've got to get her out, Bash. Over.*

—*I know. I know. But how? Over.*

—*Think of something. Over.*

Antenna got up again, strode the floor again and came back to her control desk once more. She tried not to look at the screen. What were they going to do? What was Really Free Wildlife really all about? Antenna hit the mic—*Is Torque there? Over.*

There was a pause before Bash's camera swung around and found Torque. His gravely voice said—*Torque here. What can I do, Antenna? Over.*

—*Could you do it, Torque? Fly over there and guide her out? She could get out into the tops of the leaves and Crawf could come in and fly her out, couldn't he? You could help her. Couldn't you? Over.*

There was another pause as Torque considered the idea and then, strangely, Antenna heard the sound of laughter. Someone was laughing in the dining room. Only, it wasn't a human laugh. It was an eerie laugh.

—*What was that? Over.*

—*We don't know,* replied Bash through the speakers—*Spark's over there with Min right now. We're stuck with a net below and there appears to be some kind of plexiglass above the tree. There's ants tunnelling now but that depends on how long we're going to be here. Over.*

—*Just do something, Torque. Get her up onto the roof. Crawf can pick her up. Over.*

And then there was that laugh again. The diners became silent, almost as if they were waiting for it; a strange kind of laugh, like an eerie birdcall.

The audience gave a horrible echo of mirth, and then simmered down to wait again. The whole restaurant, staff and diners alike, were holding their breath. Waiting for something.

The radio fizzed again, this time it was Bash—*Antenna? Have you seen it? Over.*

Antenna dragged her attention back to the pictures. Bash's camera was pointed up to the ceiling at the far end of the dining room. Faintly, she could see a flitter of movement at the top of the screen.

—*Can you get in closer?* she said into the mic—*Over.*

The camera zoomed in. The dark patch shifted and Antenna looked straight into the eyes of an owl. She sat back onto her hindquarters, a cold menace dowsing her guts. She was well aware that owls were the natural predators of Leadbeater's possums in their mountain forest habitat. She wondered what sort of owl would hunt a furry nibblet in a room full of human beings waiting for the owl to do just what came naturally? What's the bet that some of the humans even had money on the outcome? Perhaps they'd be betting on the length of time it would take for the owl to get the possum. Perhaps some of them were grasping stopwatches even as they watched, impatient for the result. How many of those people wanted that owl to go and get Antenna's best friend right now?

—*Get her out of there!* Antenna shouted to all radio frequencies—*Torque! Spark! Go negotiate with the owl! Someone! Do something! Oh, Min...*

No one replied.

Antenna shuddered as she remembered that numbats are trained to have a necessary response to any bird of prey. Run away! Hide! But Min hadn't been trained. Min was a Leadbeater's possum born in captivity. She knew nothing of instinctual behaviour in the wild. Min was alone with her natural predator in a crowded room. Surely some-one...?

A clipped human voice sang out over the restaurant PA. The voice dripped with sarcasm and venom. The Ektek creatures couldn't tell the details of the words - creatures can't understand the curdled monotone of human speech - but they knew it wasn't pleasant, all the animals listening understood that. Not pleasant at all.

The human audience laughed. They laughed and clapped their hands and Antenna held her head in her paws. The people simmered down until they were quiet again. They were all watching and waiting. Waiting for their bloodlust to be sated. Waiting for their humanity and their civilisation to blossom into dominion over every living thing that moved upon the earth.

The owl laughed again.

Then he moved.

The owl moved so fast Bash had trouble keeping him in frame as he swooped across the dining room. The owl went straight to the mountain ash and grabbed Min in his claws and flew to the very top of the tree. Min was limp. Perhaps she'd fainted. The owl held Min in his foot. He looked around the room. Then, with gusto, the owl bit Min's head off.

Chapter Thirteen

Babble bubbled up from the audience seated at the restaurant tables. The hubbub bloomed near the kitchen among the staff. The boiling volume amplified as delight swelled. Oh, the ballooning glee of this particular restaurant on Nemesis Night. A magnificence of triumph poured out of the voluble diners as they gibbered excitedly at their tables. This was a night to remember. This would be one to tell the grandchildren. There was no doubt this was why people came again and again, at enormous cost, to Last Chance to Eat; oh, the memories.

The sparkly trumpet player raised her horn again and blew to the four corners of the world while she sashayed to the centre of the room. Lights flashed on, revealing the superb new centrepiece of Last Chance to Eat, a huge, Romanesque bath. The audience thrilled and applauded again.

There was a high fence around the pool made of heavy-duty clear material, perhaps Perspex or even bulletproof glass. All the diners had a good view of the proceedings and the glass would need to be sturdy to hold in the present occupant - Hardback, polished and shiny - visible in about a metre of clean water.

The pool was strewn with flowers. It was tiled with detailed mosaics depicting endangered wildlife; a blue whale's tail dominated the bottom of the pool. A rhino, a seal, a panda, an Iberian lynx and a bison rose along the sides in precise detail. There, at the edge, frogs, lizards and turtles scuttled towards various birds: albatross, egrets, storks and a large condor. The big picture was superb.

Hardback lay in all this majesty, listless. His eyes were glazed. Was he drugged or just despairing?

A fountain, in the shape of a thylacine, vomited water from its mouth in the centre of the pool. Nearby, a chilling ice sculpture of a dodo was melting under the lights.

The stunning trumpet player with red, red lips didn't even stop playing as she stretched out her hand with red painted fingernails to the dodo's beak. There, embedded in the ice, was a yellow card. The dazzling woman wrenched the card from the ice, breaking off the dodo's head in the process. Hilarity erupted through the audience as the ice clattered down the sculptural plinth and splashed into the pool. It just missed Hardback's nose.

The woman stopped playing to the gods, turned to the audience, beamed her red, red grimace, looked at the yellow card and trilled to the audience.

The spotlight snapped onto a balding, lardy man doing up his tight jacket as he rose from his table. He put down his huge white napkin and kissed his companion. The applause seemed to carry him, laughing, grinning and waving, up to the stage. The man was overjoyed and appeared to be thanking the trumpet player. She gave him a congratulatory kiss and guided him over to an exercise bike. Even Antenna could understand his extravagant gestures as he feigned outrage that he would have to work for his prize. The audience was almost falling out of their seats with mirth. The man was a jolly good sport and he hopped on to the cycle. Off he went, pedalling slowly at first, the trumpet player apparently calling out instructions and even, cheeky minx, theatrically patting his shiny head with a table napkin. All good clean fun.

As he cycled, the audience, including Antenna, became aware there was a shot of light emanating from the base of the stationary bike. An optic fibre thread carried the light, glittering through the branches of the tree. As the man pedalled, the thread wound into a spool attached to the bike. The illuminated thread became brighter and tighter and stretched, and the very act of cycling became reeling something in.

The house lights began to rise until they revealed the laughing owl sitting at the top of the tree, still chewing on a bloody rag of brown grey fluff. The owl soon forgot any idea of laughing as the thread tightened further. The owl was tethered by his ankle.

The owl looked up sharply and turned his head more than one hundred and eighty degrees when he was tugged off the perch and dropped several metres before it started flapping. The owl was flapping, flapping, flapping for his life now. He rose on the glittering string, the audience hooted and the man pedalled for all he was worth.

The trumpet player worked the audience, howling out, encouraging the man to cycle slower, go faster, go backwards and the owl was played out and flapped and flew and sank and was dragged according to the pleasure of the crowd. Soon the owl flailed over the surface of the pool and still the man pedalled, forwards and backwards and still the owl battled to get away.

Hardback, floating just under the surface, saw the struggle. His eyes locked on the hysterical movement. He could not know the tempting bird was bait. All he knew was that he was hungry. He was untied, he was capable and he was ready. He was half mad from capture and homesickness. He forgot all agreements made in the wild that animals have made among themselves to protect endangered species. He swirled in the water and then shot up two metres into the air to grab the bird, his monstrous jaws wide. His huge teeth cracked and the bird disappeared leaving only a flutter of feathers drifting in the air...

Antenna gasped as she watched the screens in the Ektek cave. Her eyes were dry and her mouth was dry. She felt so brittle she thought she might snap. Frustration, anger and sickness raged through her like electricity but she couldn't stop watching as Hardback splashed back into the water.

In the restaurant, some of the closest diners were splattered with wet and limp flower petals. They screeched with excitement and wonder and turned to see what might happen next.

Hardback's leap gave him energy and he attempted to scrabble out of the tank, his movements erratic as he grappled and scraped and slid down the plate glass walls. Feathers continued to glide through the air, this way and that, slowly joining the flowers floating on the surface of the pool.

The trumpet player, applauding heartily, went to the cyclist and assisted him from the bike. She encouraged the audience to acknowledge his sweaty efforts and he grinned in the heat of applause as he made his way back to the table and sat down.

Two cherubic waiters with long blond curly hair, possibly identical twins, made their lithe way over to the exercise bike and swiftly unlocked the cable of optic fibres at the base.

The trumpet player went to one side of the pool and picked up a long, fantastically decorated didgeridoo. She began to play, softly, hardly moving her shoulders, as the wonders of circular breathing took her over and she blew into the didge. The eerie vibrations filled the room.

One of the waiters went to the other side of the pool while the other threw the spool of optic fibre high into the air and over a sturdy beam. The first waiter caught it and placed it over a winch. Together, the waiters wound the cable in until it tightened in the throat of Hardback and he began to rise in the water. The waiters managed to spin him in such a way they wrapped more of the glittering cable around his neck. They hung Hardback over the mosaic bath and he thrashed. He flung himself from side to side in the pool, cracking against its hard walls and the audience laughed and clapped to see his pathetic little feet clawing the air. He spun, helplessly. Antenna imagined what the audience might have been thinking. Perhaps they were measuring him up for handbags - no, shoes - no, belts - oh, his skin was extensive and varied in texture. There would be plenty for any kind of dream accessory.

Bash continued to record as Hardback in his turn, faced death. A grand chef, wearing his distinctive passenger pigeon Last Chance to Eat apron, checked white-and-black trousers and a high white hat, was picked out of the crowd by the roaming spotlight.

Chef waved and smiled to his appreciative fans. The diners drooled and clapped. He reached for his ceremonial taiaha, held high on a long red velvet cushion by a charming young waitress. Chef lifted the ornately carved weapon, about his own height, gleaming in slender wood. He hefted its weight, lifted its gentle balance over his head and showed it to the audience. It was an object of supremacy.

Then, with extraordinary power, chef spun the taiaha around him. Threatening, advancing, with such strength of intention the audience grew cowed and was silenced.

Chef moved forward, surrounded by his aura, a whirlwind of taiaha force, and struck. He drove the spearhead of the taiaha into the pale thin throat of the crocodile and thrust, thrust hard and thrust again. He let go and the handle of the taiaha smacked around, the blade still stuck in Hardback, clattering the sides of the pool.

The waiters unlocked the capstan and the crocodile convulsed back into the sumptuously tiled bath. The taiaha tilted and slid to the side of the pool, pointing the bone at a mosaic white-headed langur like an awful game of spin-the-bottle. The water slowly stained red. Hardback swayed slowly in the moving stream and grew quiet.

A thunderstorm of applause erupted from the hungry audience. What a prelude to a feast! What a show! What a chef! The chef bowed, grinning and, as if by magic, plucked an owl feather, wafting down in front of him in the air, to wear jauntily in his hair. It stuck out in the side of his chef's hat like a warrior's memento.

In the Ektek control room, Antenna could no longer focus on the screen before her. She lay down on her desk and cracked open. Acrid tears rolled down her face. She sobbed as if she would never stop.

Chapter Fourteen

Hod was the first one out of the airship. He bounded down the tunnel from the garage to the control room as if he would fly. He was panting when he checked in at the computer area. Initially he couldn't see anyone and he entered the space uncertainly. He was by the control desk when he saw Spark waiting by the doorway—*Where is she?* asked Hod.

—*Gone.*

—*Gone? Where?*

—*Torque's with her.*

Hod stood and looked over the console. His eyes narrowed as he tried to remember what he'd been told about the operation of the computers. He sat down in Antenna's place at the control desk and then stood up again. His paws hovered over one switch and then a button and he whistled quietly under his breath. Then he looked at Spark again—*Do you know how to work this thing?*

Spark looked at the wallaby uncertainly—*I'd better go get Torque.*

—*I'll go.* Hod leapt up and through the cave tunnels until he came to the numbat enclosure entrance. He stood in the doorway and bellowed—*Antenna! Where are you?*

—*Oi!* Torque scuttled out of the opening—*What you about? Can't you give her some time?*

—*Do you know how to search the internet? No? Well? We've got no choice. Get Antenna back to work.*

By the time Antenna made her way into the control centre, Crawf, Helmut, Zip and Hod were standing in a rough semi circle around the computer monitors. Bash was seated on the console, looking like an ebony ornament inlaid with slices of buttercup petals.

Torque and Spark stood a little way off, ready to help Antenna if need be. As if they could.

Antenna's dark face fur was wet. She looked at the animals sadly, as if she didn't really know them at all—*You're back.*

—*Yes, all safe and sound,* said Hod in a robust, cheering up manner.

—Not all. Not safe.

—Come on, Antenna. We're alive. We need you.

Antenna closed her eyes and she went to sit down at the desk. Once there, she took in a deep breath and said—*Okay. This was the email I sent out last night.* She searched for and opened a sent email. There was an attached picture of an owl, head turned to face the camera, eyes knowing and powerful. Antenna read the text in a voice cold as a glacier—*It was the last New Zealand laughing owl. The restaurant had been keeping her on a farm, far away from curiosity seekers for years.*

—Waiting for a suitably dramatic occasion? said Helmut.

—Some of the richest people in the world had flown in for the World Bank extravaganza. They were celebrating a new joint currency for New Zealand and Australia.

—Currency?

—Money.

—Do they never think of anything else?

Helmut said—*Go on, Antenna.*

—Crocodile medallions stuffed with laughing owl and Leadbeater's possum, poached in a stock made from boiling a moa bone sent over from the Auckland museum. The stuffing was as light as fairy possum foam. They served the medallions on a victory wreath of New Zealand spinach drenched in quandong coulis, garnished with a pohutukawa flower and stabbed with a shard of wattle-seed waffle. It was as if the words themselves were choking her. Antenna finished reading. A tear plopped down onto the keyboard. Bash involuntarily jerked in horror as the splash hit him, his thin frog skin easily permeated by harmful chemicals such as salt.

—I'm so sorry, Anti, said Zip.

—We all are, said Helmut.

—Yeah, we are, said Crawf.

—Yeah, said Bash—*There was just nothing we could do.*

—Yeah, said Hod—*But we can't just stand round here and moan. We got to pay them back, don't we? We've got to do something. Now.*

There was a silence before Antenna nodded and spoke very quietly—*Yes.*

—Yes? said Hod, surprised.

—Yes. She paused and then spoke—*I never thought I'd say this but you're right. We have to get them back,* said Antenna, spitting out the words as if they were sharp metal tacks—*It's gone too far. I want them to feel like I do. I want them to feel devastated.*

—You want vengeance?

—Yes. Vengeance.

The Ektek animals looked at each other. Hod was burning, on fire, with the desire to act. Zip was uneasy. She could see Antenna's reasoning was caught in an emotional net and she wasn't sure how long it could survive. Crawf was looking at Antenna with his head to one side, puzzled. Bash, too, was frowning and Helmut was looking worried.

—*We can't sit back and let this happen again.* Antenna went on—*They've got to be stopped. Don't you see? Min mustn't die for nothing. She must be avenged.*

—*Avenged?* Helmut muttered under his breath. He shook his head and exhaled heavily through his beak.

The creatures looked at each other again. If Antenna thought it had to happen, well, then. So did they. All, except Helmut, agreed silently by their looks and nods. They were deadly serious. They had had enough. Something had to change.

—*You're right,* said Zip.

—*We're going to destroy the restaurant?* said Hod.

—*Kill them?* said Bash—*The whole lousy lot?*

—*It has to end,* said Antenna—*It is the only way.*

Helmut stood up. He looked miserable and he glanced at each creature before he took his next step. Then he paced the floor, walking up and down as he said—*I feel sick that you can let the Ektek purpose drain away from your hearts. How can you forego so easily the memory of your parents?* He stopped and drew himself up to his full height. He shuffled his feather cloak before he spoke like the elder statesman he was—*Do you really think Min would want another death, more death, in payment for her life? Is that how she would be remembered? Ektek is for life. Ektek is for saving, for rescue and for helping other creatures.*

—*Maybe our best way to help is to clear the way. So many of our elders have been cleared. Maybe it's our turn to take control,* said Crawf.

—*We need a plan,* said Zip—*A good plan: one that will work; one that others will join.*

—*But not of death,* said Helmut—*Please, Ektek. Think what you do, Antenna. Zip. Crawf. Bash. Hod. Please. I beseech you. Do not fall into this morass. We will never be able to redeem ourselves. We need the high moral ground. If we lose that, we have lost everything. You will be destroying Ektek.*

Antenna took in a deep breath. Somehow Helmut's words had managed to penetrate her madness—*Of course.* She stopped, hung her head and waited for the anger to begin to leave her body—*You're right, Helmut.* She raised her head and then looked at Hod. She spoke slowly with no expression, the need for vengeance seemingly gone from her—*It's so easy when you say it. Vengeance. Retribution. Kill. Destroy. But it would be different if we actually had to do it, wouldn't it?*

—*It would be straightforward,* said the wallaby—*It would be easier each time.*

—*Really, Hod? Really? You could really kill people? Possibly lose other creatures in the face of a war that we could never ever win? And you would have no concerns about that?* Antenna looked at Hod and her eyes filled with tears again—*I don't believe you. You're not a soldier. You have compassion, whatever you say. Helmut's right. That way Min would have died for nothing. Ektek does not kill.*

The animals shifted again. As a group their resolve was scattered. Hod felt frustration build up in him—*What are we going to do then?*

Pulling herself together, Antenna loaded another website onto the screen—*This is what the Really Free Wildlife Company are up to right now.* The monitors showed an ad for a short educational film: Extinction of a Species; the death of the very last Leadbeater's possum. There was footage of Min, scampering through the branches of a mountain ash. A bright purple star framed bold print explaining that: our cameras just happened to be there as the last fairy possum met her final fate. A trailer played the opening credits and then, if you desired to view the entire film, payment was requested through a secure payment system of your choice.

The animals in the control cave watched in shock—*It seems the Really Free Wildlife Company have turned their talents to making snuff movies,* said Helmut.

—*What do you mean?* said Zip—*As in candles?*

—*Of course, they hope to profit by the animals' extinction. If their hologram is in fact the last example of a now known extinct creature, then it becomes virtually priceless.*

—*They can't get away with it,* said Zip—*Can they?*

—*Won't human conservation groups do something?* asked Bash.

—*Even if we could find evidence to prove the company was acting illegally, how could we make sure they'd get prosecuted?* said Helmut—*And how could we make sure that prosecution was successful? If we did manage to get them into court, they'd happily pay through the nose for legal defence.*

Hod agreed—*I bet it's already in their budget.*

Helmut continued—*There's only the slimmest of chances they'd be found guilty and punished. Even then, they'd appeal, keep the case clogging up the system for years and still be selling their wares.*

The creatures sat in the blue glow, cold and numb.

—*The Really Free Wildlife Company will release the footage showing nature at its most unsentimental, you know, red in tooth and claw and all that. People pay to keep their expectations upheld. Keeps them feeling righteous,* said Antenna.

—*That's right. Keeping dirty, nasty wild nature under control,* said Zip.

—*But what about the customers?* said Bash—*Won't the audience realise they're watching a restaurant?*

—*They can alter the images any way they want. Special effects to change the background, advanced software to alter the foreground… You can see from the trailer. It was easy to make that look like it was shot in a forest using a green screen and a fancy editing program.*

—*Dead easy,* said Hod.

—*What about the zoo?* asked Crawf—*Do you think the zoo could be in on it?*

—*What?* asked Zip, shock visible on her bat face.

—*They must have been tricked,* said Bash—*Like us.*

—*We don't know that. Why shouldn't the zoo be involved? They'd get a tidy sum for a clearing. It makes perfect economical sense.*

—*Hod! Don't even think it!* said Bash—*It couldn't be true. Could it?*

—*Where do you think your next meal is coming from, Bash? It costs money to care for us prisoners. Public exhibition is one way; fancy new enclosures sorry, habitats, eye-catching graphics detailing threats against our survival, all the trappings of a modern zoo, everything, is expensive. Is it possible that turnstile income is not enough? Why are they always advertising for sponsors?*

—*I can't believe the zoo would publicly champion threatened species and then so blatantly profit by their deaths,* said Helmut.

—*Not intentionally,* said Antenna—*The Really Free Wildlife Company must at least have accomplices in the zoo. How else can they gain access and maintain cover-ups of the deaths?*

—*What about me?* said Zip in a small voice—*I was taped. I must be next.*

—*That's right, Zip,* said Helmut—*Anyone else?*

—*Ana the elephant and Charles, one of the Galapagos tortoises, were both filmed,* said Antenna—*We'd better get them under surveillance.*

Spark nodded and followed Torque as they moved away, preparing to request beetle surveillance for Zip, Ana and Charles at once.

—*I think another visit to the Really Free Wildlife Company might be in order,* said Helmut.

—*Okay,* said Antenna—*Take the airship with Zip and Bash. There's something Crawf and I have to do.*

—*What are we looking for, exactly?* said Bash.

—*Anything that might help dissolve the company,* said Helmut.

—You had your chance, said Hod.

—They would have come back from a fire like a phoenix, Hod. They'd be insured. Place like that, said Helmut—*We need something that will finish them.*

—You mean firebombing.

—I mean economic death, said Helmut—*If their shareholders suffer then even anyone who might consider emulating them...*

Crawf's feathered headpiece was flat against his head, showing his distress but even so, he uttered a short alert cry—*Hullo?* he said—*I've got an idea. Why don't we infiltrate the company?*

The rest of the Ektek animals greeted his suggestion with outright derision and sneers, glad of an opportunity to laugh. Zip thought it funny—*How do you think we're going to do that? Dress up in a human suit and eat roast lamb?*

—We're animals. They're humans, said Hod—*In case you hadn't noticed.*

Crawf continued—*What about the hologram in the office, Zip? Didn't you think it was Min?*

—True.

—Well, then. I could pretend to be a hologram.

—That's just crazy enough to work, said Antenna.

—Thanks, Crawf but if I'm the one on the hit list, then it would have to be me, said Zip.

—We can't make ourselves any more vulnerable... Helmut was saying when Spark entered the room and flew straight to Antenna. The beetle looked worried—*You'd better see this for yourself.*

—Can't you just tell us?

In response, Spark turned and left. The other Ektek creatures trailed behind Antenna and the beetle, as they dodged in procession through the secret passageways. Then Spark led them all out into the public area. It was after hours but they still kept to the shadows and out of the security human's line of sight. Torque waited for them, balanced on a large sign outside the numbat enclosure. It showed an attractive image of Antenna. The sign said, 'Why keep her in prison when we can let our only numbat go free?' 'Coming Soon' was an 'Unbelievable 3D hologram numbat. So real you can reach out and touch her. Almost.' There was a Really Free Wildlife Company logo in the corner.

Antenna turned to look at her team and shrugged. 'How could it be so?' her eyes seemed to ask them.

—There were hidden cameras, said Bash.

—Must have been, said Helmut.

—Unbelievable is right, said Zip.

—*Sorry it's not you?* said Hod.

—*That's just the disgusting sort of thing you would say,* said Zip.

—*Shut up, you two. Anyone else?*

—*No, Anti,* said Spark—*Just you.*

Antenna stared at her image with her dark glinting eyes. She contemplated her options and their inevitable consequences. Here was a bitter-sweet offer: liberty or death.

Surely freedom must be more than annihilation?

Chapter Fifteen

The engine hummed as Crawf flew the wingship into a darkening sky. He looked down as he sighted the coiling river and began to bring the plane down—*We're here.*

—*So soon?*

He glanced over to his passenger—*It might rain.*

—*Is that safe?*

—*Least of your worries.*

Crawf glided through an easy landing and the plane stopped. Antenna looked out of the window. She'd never travelled in the wingship before and was glad to have reached the ground at last—*Thanks, Crawf. I just couldn't ask Bash to do this. It was my job.*

—*Don't worry about Bash.* The sound of wild, free frogs and crickets rose in the evening light, replacing the thrum of the engines—*Believe me, nothing would have induced him to be here now. I'll go first.* Crawf opened his window and looked over at Antenna—*They know me.*

—*Okay.* She opened her window anyway and started to make her way out.

Crawf flew out onto the wing. He held a small stick with his foot and hit the side of the wing rhythmically. He called out—*Hullo? Crocodiles? Is Shining Teeth there?*

In the dim light, a stir of low branches and log-like figures came to life. It was the crocodile's harem and they crawled towards the plane.

Crawf and Antenna stood one on each wing. They would go no further. Crawf ceased drumming. They watched as the crocodiles milled under the wingship with heavy reptilian movements. One of the crocs crawled forward and lifted her head—*I am Shining Teeth. What news?*

—*Hullo? I am Crawf, the palm cockatoo you met before.*

—*Did you bring Hardback?* The harem all started forward, muttering questions, eager to see their mate, scrambling over each other— *Where is he? Is he here? Let him out…*

Instead of answering their questions, Crawf said—*We must have your word that you will let us go unharmed, no matter what.*

—*Where is our husband?* asked Shining Teeth.

—*You must give us your word,* Crawf insisted—*We are honourable creatures wishing you no harm; you must respect that and give us peace in return.*

The crocodiles grumbled and paced under the wingship. They were not happy. Where was Hardback? Was he in the aircraft somewhere? Why did Ektek not let him out? What was the hold up?

Then Antenna stepped forward, still balanced on the wing and said—*Excuse me, Shining Teeth, may I speak?*

—*Be careful, Antenna,* said Crawf, under his breath—*Don't trust them.*

—*Who are you?* called out Shining Teeth.

—*I am Antenna. Numbat. It is true I have bad tidings from Ektek.*

—*That is all Ektek is to us. Bad news. We should never have called you.*

—*Ektek worked rigorously for Hardback but there were greater forces at play here. We have all lost much.*

—*You?* Shining Teeth shook her head in disbelief—*What have you lost, numbat?* She sneered.

—*My parents. My best friend. My place in the world; my home, my everything.*

—*Then you know how we feel.*

—*That is why I wanted to be the one to tell you what happened to Hardback.*

—*He is dead then.*

—*Yes.*

There was a collective gasp from the crocodile harem. They breathed out a sigh that might have been a farewell. They had always believed he would come back to them. Now their hopes were dead, along with their mate.

—*He died bravely, with dignity. I wanted you to know.*

—*Then there is no hope,* said Jata.

—*Not for him,* said Antenna—*But there is for you.*

—*What difference can that make?* said Grater.

—*You can now lay him to rest in your hearts and minds…*

—*But you can never give him back,* said Shining Teeth. She turned and shouted to her harem sisters—*We should have taken him when we had the chance.*

—*What chance? We had no chance,* shouted Crawf—*Hardback was lost from the moment he walked into that trap and you know it.*

—*No!* shouted Asunder.

—*He spent days at that prison farm,* said Jata.

—*Being groomed for sacrifice,* said Crawf—*Under armed guard!*

—*We could have got him out,* said Jata—*But we didn't.*

—*Because Ektek told us not to,* said Shining Teeth.

—*You could not have got him out. We couldn't have got past dogs and men with guns and neither could you,* said Crawf—*What do you expect of Ektek?*

The crocodiles began to move closer, examining the wheels, raising up to see if they could climb up to the wings. Crawf made a move to the cockpit—*Time to go,* Antenna, he muttered as he climbed in to the plane.

—*Help. We expected help,* said Damura—*Was that too much to ask?* Jata said—*We thought that was what Ektek was for.*

—*We were wrong,* said Damura.

—*Dead wrong,* said Grater.

Antenna continued to stand on the wing of the aircraft even as Crawf started the engines—*All I can say,* she shouted—*Is that we tried. We really did try and I don't know how to make it better for you. We wanted you to know, it's not over.*

—*Get in,* shouted Crawf through the cockpit window, over the noise of the engines—*Antenna! Get in now. We're going.*

—*Is that it?* cried out Shining Teeth—*Is that all you have to say about the death of my husband? Our husband? Is that what you leave for us?*

—*I'm sorry,* said Antenna and she turned to climb in the window. Once safely inside the cockpit, she looked out at the crocodiles, tottering, running, scurrying behind the moving machine, their heads raised, their eyes burning in the dark as the wingship rose into the night.

—*It's okay.* Crawf glanced over at Antenna, still staring out the window at the darkness below—*We made it out. Live to fight another day. That's the main thing.*

Antenna wasn't so sure. As she peered grimly into the black beneath them, Antenna whispered to the crocodiles, knowing they could not hear and would never understand her if they could—*It's not over.*

Chapter Sixteen

In the half-light of the Ektek garage, several beetles, together with Zip and Crawf, worked on the tank. The patchwork surface of the vehicle gleamed where, over time, thousands of beetles had burnished the metal. Zip moved the lamp, a long, flexible pipe, closer to the driver's door. The pipe was connected to thin tunnels, in which embedded mirrors were angled to reflect surface sunlight strategically onto the working area. She tightened the locking device she was altering in the door.

They had just about finished modifying the tank, allowing it to be driven by a larger animal, now that Min was dead. The entire cabin had had to be greatly enlarged. The controls and seat had to be replaced. The door had to be changed to a much larger one.

A team of several beetles had been working through the night. They were getting weary and the work had been going too slowly. They were expecting their replacements to arrive soon and the fresh team would be able to continue with renewed vigour while the tired ones slept.

Out of the corner of her eye, Zip could see movement. She looked up to see Antenna meandering past on her way to the exit. She called out—*Hey, Anti! How's it going?*

Crawf also looked up and nodded—*Hullo?* before returning to his work.

—*Yo! Antenna,* said a beetle and another added for good measure—*Gidday, Antenna...*

Antenna didn't reply and just kept marching on. Zip shrugged and continued with her work, thinking the numbat must be too distracted by heavy thoughts of her personal predicament for light-hearted chit-chat. The numbat came to the light-pipe stretched out along the floor and, without pausing, tried but failed to negotiate it. Suddenly the numbat spluttered and fell over, landing on her side.

Zip and Crawf looked up from their work on the tank. Immediate concern caused Crawf to leap up into the air and fly over to the mammal's feet. Zip, also alarmed, hurriedly flew to the numbat's assistance—*Antenna!*

Crawf's wingtip patted Antenna's pointed, furred face, trying to restore her. Her legs kept on kicking in a strange repetitive action. Zip frowned as she watched and tried to touch them but the movement seemed involuntary and constant and her legs were stiff, unable to stop. She looked up to Crawf, full of worry—*Is she having some kind of fit?*

—*Antenna!* Crawf renewed his patting and asked the fallen numbat—*Are you okay?*

—*I'm fine, thanks, but I don't think that's doing so well.* The real Antenna emerged from of the shadows holding a small box. It was a remote control.

Zip and Crawf jumped back from the false numbat and stared at real Antenna. She was laughing as she flicked the controls. The controls were having absolutely no effect on the puppet numbat. There was a metallic clicking noise coming from the active legs—*Still needs work, hmmm?*

The mechanical creature clicked and kicked. Manifold rushed forwards and climbed up the body and into the pretend numbat's armpit. Soon the motors stopped and the kicking was over. Silence spread over the cave once more.

Gobsmacked, Crawf and Zip stared at Antenna and then back to the model as if watching an invisible tennis match. Antenna walked forward and bent down to check the false numbat's leg wasn't falling off. She moved it, backwards and forwards, checking the clicky action—*We can smooth that out, can't we, Manifold?* Manifold, muffled from within the techno creature, squeaked out an affirmative. Antenna thought aloud—*It'll get past those researchers long enough. I hope.*

Crawf came forward to inspect the mechanical toy—*Won't they feel the weight of the mechanics when they pick it up?*

—*Hopefully they won't ever touch it.*

—*You're sure about that?* Zip could see the risks and she didn't like them. Antenna was going to be taken by the Really Free Wildlife Company and they could transport her literally anywhere. Once in Really Free's clutches, Ektek could only hope Antenna would stay within reach. They had to hope the Really Free Wildlife Company would stay predictable. That was, if Antenna wanted to stay alive. Antenna's future rested precariously on a hope. Antenna continued, apparently unperturbed—*I knew they'd do a good job.*

—Thanks, I'll tell the team when they wake up, squeaked Manifold—*I'll start her again, if you like.*

Antenna indicated that Manifold should hold her fire and turned to look at the other animals—*I've got something important to ask. Who's going to take over in the control room? Someone has to. Zip?*

Zip didn't want this discussion and brushed over Antenna's suggestion—*Get it up on its feet first.*

—Crawf?

Crawf also grabbed the opportunity to shift the topic of conversation. He moved forward straight away to grab the remote controlled numbat with his beak and Antenna helped Zip and Crawf push the puppet upright.

Antenna had to admit these two didn't want to talk about the control centre. She gave in for the moment and instead drove the fake beast past Crawf and Zip for a more formal demonstration. This time they watched more carefully as the replica moved. Antenna's paws didn't have the flexibility required to get the most out of the remote control and the fake faltered as it moved.

—Walks funny.

—You don't have to whisper, Zip. Crawf said—*It can't hear you.*

—The model's not too bad. I think we can blame the operator here but you don't have to worry. Crawf'll be the one doing it on the day.

Crawf looked at Antenna. He knew this was a matter of life and death but then, life and death were breakfast and lunch to an Ektek creature.

—Perhaps, Zip, you should consider meeting with me in the control room. Someone has to know how to run the website and you're more familiar than…

—But I'll be out in the action and you're coming back anyway.

—What if I'm not?

—You have to be. Have you shown Crawf how that contraption works?

Antenna could see she was fighting a losing battle expecting these two would take over the computer operation. Although she was flattered they thought so highly of her invincibility, she knew she had to convince someone to take up the reigns or the future of Ektek was at risk—*Here, Crawf, you have a go.* Crawf took the control with his scaly bird foot and looked at it carefully from side to side.

—You push there to go ahead, left, right and reverse. Okay?

—Think so. Crawf tentatively sent the false numbat stumbling forwards.

As Zip exclaimed over Crawf's ungainly first attempts to drive the puppet, Antenna noticed Helmut and Hod arriving into the garage from different directions. Hod was on duty next, to replace Crawf and Zip. Helmut was on his way to the airship. He needed to complete his pilot's pre-flight check. Antenna watched, worried there might be trouble between them.

In an attempt to give Hod more responsibility, and therefore ground his flights of irrational rebellion, Ektek had chosen him as the new tank driver in Min's place.

Helmut took Hod aside before they reached the tank and said— *Please, Hod. Don't try any funny stuff today.*

Hod pulled away from him—*What about you?*

—*Think of Min. Think of Antenna.* Helmut considered Hod—*Just, please, do your job safely.*

Hod had grown up respecting Helmut but, now that Helmut was getting older, Hod was seeing a different side to the elder, a more fallible side—*Do you really think Ektek can make any difference at all? With our careful little actions? Our prim little dobs to the authorities who are probably already well aware of the reprobates and who are so slow and lumbering to change anything?*

—*I don't like to think of the alternative. We're not angry monkeys chucking rocks at cars. We have purpose. We have strategy. We have honour. Perhaps Ektek can help slow the extinction rate a little. Maybe we can inform enough people to make a difference. I don't know. But at least I can sleep at night.*

—*You don't think angry monkeys sleep well?*

—*We've got a chance to communicate with humans. Maybe even get them to think, to realise we're all in the same boat.*

—*I never have a problem sleeping; and there's only one species I'd like to see extinct.*

—*Even they are necessary in the web of life.*

—*That's debateable,* Hod laughed—*Tell you what. Let's have our own Nemesis Night. Lions versus homo sapiens.*

Helmut could see the funny side of Hod's idea too. It was only a small moment between them but they did share a laugh.

—*Don't worry, Helmut. Not a single soul is going to get hurt tonight.* Because he'd turned to go, Helmut didn't hear the very quiet addition Hod muttered under his breath as he leapt past Antenna—*Unless absolutely necessary.*

Chapter Seventeen

I

Antenna walked through the cavernous hangar. Would she ever see Ektek again? As she travelled, she saw the paths of her life so far, in a different, more poignant light. She nodded and waved to beetles of her acquaintance and quietly said her farewells to the vehicles, the machines and the systems of her youth, her life and her family. Finally, she rounded a corner and saw the yellow-footed rock wallaby she'd been looking for.

Hod was working on something in the machine cage with his back to her. This was a lockable part of the hangar where heavy tools were stored to prevent fire and accidents. She opened the door; it squeaked from rust and disuse and she didn't notice Hod's reaction. He was jumpy. He wasn't expecting visitors and didn't want them. He covered his work with a rag as he turned to see her.

Antenna was feeling too emotional to question him or what he might be doing. She wanted to say goodbye and ask him a question— *Hod?*

—*Anti,* he smiled at her in greeting, old friends together.

—*Busy?*

—*Nothing much,* he said and he turned to move her out of the cage—*'Sup?*

—*Got a moment?*

—*Sure.*

—*Come to the control centre and I'll teach you the panel operation.*

—*Me?*

—*Yeah, you.*

—*Sure.* Hod was only too pleased to get Antenna headed out to the main hangar area—*But you'll be back.*

—*'Course.* Antenna, taken aback by the ease of this win with Hod, was thrilled someone was prepared to take on the control mantle. She thought she'd finally been able to find a successor and didn't want to question it too closely—*But you know there's a risk and someone has to be able to keep the place going. It's not going to be that difficult. I made a document that has all the basic instructions and information and it's saved on the main drive...*

Hod looked at her doubtfully as she talked and they walked through the corridors. Although it had served his immediate purpose to get her out of the machine cage, he was not at all convinced that the computer job should be his. In fact, he had his own, entirely different, plans for the future. He followed her into the control cave and stood before the phalanx of monitors and blinking lights. He became increasingly awkward.

—*Okay,* said Antenna—*Make yourself comfortable...*

—*You know, Anti,* said Hod, not coming forward into the space— *That's one thing I don't think I ever will be 'round here. Tech stuff. It's... Just not me.*

—*But you said...*

—*I thought I could. Just for a moment. But now, it's not real, is it? Come on, Anti. You didn't really think I would?*

—*Who then? Zip plain refuses. Bash won't. Crawf won't. It has to be you. You and I are the ones, Hod. We've been trained for this all our lives. You can't give up now.*

—*I'm not giving up. I'm just saying it's not my area. And if there's a chance you're not coming back, then, same stands for me.*

—*What?*

—*Antenna. I wouldn't let anything happen to you. You must know that. But. If you're not here, then I won't be either.*

Still refusing to approach the computers, Hod stood away from the control desk and watched her. Antenna realised he would not sit down with her and he was leaving. She stood also and they stared at each other for a while. He bent down to her and gently held his nose to hers. They let their breath mingle. Hod and Antenna stood quietly forehead to forehead before he broke away and abruptly left the control space.

Antenna stared after him. She had felt his yearning but didn't understand it. She missed the old Hod who had been like a brother. He seemed more like a stranger to her now. Where had that old friend gone and who was this new, tough rebel muscling into his place?

Antenna came back to earth and switched the video monitors on. This was her business. She'd already set up the web pages. The headline read: Is the Really Free Wildlife Company Really for Real? The screens played continual footage of Min's death; both Ektek's version and the Really Free Wildlife Company's edited promotional footage from their website; together with all the relevant links.

She removed the console's carapace and started testing the connection to the satellite. Ektek could only use the satellite for ten hours a day. It restricted the immediacy of some of their internet broadcasts but, on the plus side, it meant Ektek's footage could receive more editorial attention before the public saw it.

She skimmed through her emails and found various new comments on her blog. Most assured her they were expecting the Last Chance to Eat rescue footage, if it were to come to that, to have a large international audience. Internet technology was equal to most challenges and, with the satellite; Ektek had links covering the entire world. Threatened extinction was a global problem and there were many interested groups and individuals online, some of them even human, who would be watching to see a numbat rescued from a theatre restaurant.

Antenna leaned forward to the mic—*Helmut? Can you commence connection, please? Over.*

From the airship, Helmut acknowledged her—*Over and out.*

Antenna had just enough time to set up the netcast camera relay from the airship straight to the web. She pushed send on the media release. There was a special notification to the Department of Flora and Fauna and one to the zoo marked urgent. It was paramount that the zoo understood the connection between the Really Free Wildlife Company and Last Chance to Eat. No one in Ektek believed the zoo could condone what went on in the restaurant but a bit of media attention might boost their outrage.

There would be no one at the control desk to edit. The pictures from the restaurant came in clearly and colourfully, if not always the best quality colour. They would be netcast, sixteen frames every second, while the link was maintained. Antenna nodded. All systems go.

II

It was a grey, misty day. The clouds were low. The air was cold. The ground was wet and shiny. The airship hovered over the zoo car park. From the Ektek security camera at the gate, Antenna could see the Really Free Wildlife Company's van and several media cars had arrived, setting up their OB and loading gear, waiting for the press conference to begin.

Manifold popped her head into the control room—*They're here.*

Antenna left the office area, taking a last look at Min's image huddled among the leaves in the computer generated highland forest. Min's huge eyes glinted on the screen. Antenna felt a terrible sense of loss as she lifted her paw in farewell.

In the hangar, her waiting friends surrounded her. Antenna didn't like to say goodbye at the best of times and this was one of the worst. She didn't want to hurt her friends by dwelling on the possibility of death. Come to that, she didn't want to dwell on the possibility of her own death either. She hugged each of her friends in turn.

—*Good luck*, growled Torque.

—*See you later.*

—*No doubt*, said Torque—*No doubt at all, Antenna. None at all. We'll see you later, that's right. You keep your chin up. That's the way.*

Crawf gestured impatiently—*Come on, Antenna. They're trying to find you.*

—*You'd better take care,* Zip hugged Antenna and whispered—*I don't want to lose another friend.*

—*Neither do I.*

—*When I get back*... Antenna gave her bat friend a wry look.

Manifold ran down the tunnel and called—*Hurry, Antenna! They're getting worried.*

—*You don't have to go,* whispered Zip—*You could run away.*

—*Where?*

—*Stay here! You could!*

—*They'd look for me.* Antenna smiled at her friend and gently pulled away—*They might find Ektek. Can't risk that. No choice. Got to go. Be good.*

Leaving Zip, Antenna ran up to her enclosure and raced into the hollow log just as her keeper, Sanjit, looked in the other end and found her. He tipped the log and looked surprised when he saw her there. Sanjit had looked after Antenna since she had been a baby. He picked her up and looked into her eyes. He could feel her heart racing and he laughed with the media. Who knew what he was thinking? Antenna wished she could speak human. She could have told him a few things he didn't know. She also knew, whatever happened with the Really Free Wildlife Company, what ever happened in Last Chance to Eat, win or lose, she could not come back to this enclosure.

Sanjit patted Antenna and then gave her over to the Really Free Wildlife Researcher. The cameras flashed then, and reporters cackled, seemed to quack some happy questions, clucked and flapped some more. Antenna dangled from the researcher's hands. She was overcome with dread.

A politician grinned nervously into the cameras as Antenna began to climb her arm. A tall thin man, who looked like a scientist, took hold of Antenna and ritualistically placed her into a small animal transfer case. He shut the lid. Antenna made herself comfortable. It sounded like a lot of important speeches were going on, presumably about what it meant to be a numbat living in the civilised world, the important role of zoos and releasing captives born into the wild. She sat, squashed into her little travel cage, and thought to herself maybe this publicity might be good for the animals' cause. She hoped there was a positive side to this experience. It just felt like sacrifice to her.

Then, because she'd been reading the media releases, she allowed herself a little fantasy time. Perhaps they really were intending to fly her to her natural habitat. Perhaps the area really had been feral fenced and pest baited. Perhaps she really was going to be released into the forest. Antenna imagined she could be very happy in a community of newly released numbats. She started to look forward to it. Perhaps she could raise a family of her own. See her grandchildren cavorting in the sun, carelessly eating ants and termites… As the travel case was lifted into the air, she was jolted into reality. She'd believe it when she saw it.

Chapter Eighteen

I

Helmut piloted the airship, Bash sitting beside him. They floated through the grey, misty sky. They would track the movements of the van and act as a relay station between the recording gear and the satellite.

The Really Free Wildlife Company van, closely followed, above and astern, by the airship, drove into the peak afternoon traffic. They drove for some time. Antenna had never been in a human's car before. She didn't like it. She learned to stay lying down, but even then she was thrown against the side of the case far too often for comfort. She wondered they hadn't considered if bruising would hurt the meat. Then she remembered the concept of tenderising.

II

Crawf and Zip were travelling in the red sports car with the fake numbat. They were not actually driving. They were parked in the tank. It would be their job to enter wherever Antenna was to be held, leaving the tank outside, to perpetrate a swap of numbats, if possible. Perhaps they would just wave to Antenna as she explored the forest of her newly found freedom and community. Maybe. Maybe not. They wouldn't take any unnecessary chances.

III

Hod was also ready in the tank, not yet driving. The tank was parked in the belly of the airship. He was in communication with Zip in the car. The tank was to be deployed mainly as a transport vehicle. Unless, thought Hod, it became necessary to ramp up the action. And the way Hod was thinking, it probably would.

IV

Outside, on the roadway, the Really Free Wildlife Company van stopped. Antenna's heart was thumping like a huge road-building hammer. She could feel her ribs being beaten. She didn't like it. It didn't feel like freedom should. It felt far more like meat tenderising.

Silence.

Then humans barked at each other before the van door slid open, people got out and the carry case was hefted, somewhat carelessly, into the air. Then Antenna realised she was inside a building and, as she'd known all along in her tenderised heart, there would be no such thing as freedom for this little rust-coloured numbat.

She could smell tantalising smells of sauces and stocks. Only, to her, the heavy aromas were cloying. She felt sick. There was a low-level hum of business. They were no longer pretending to hold her carry case steady. She fell to one side and scrabbled to regain balance. Finally, they put her down on the ground. Antenna rose groggily to her feet, swayed and then vomited a little in a corner of the case. She didn't think travel suited her.

They cleaned her up when they transferred her to a smaller cage. At least she could see through the bars. She could breathe better too, but she didn't want to because of the smell of sauce.

As expected, she was in Last Chance to Eat. There were no patrons here yet. Most of the dining room was dark and shadowed. Antenna was off to one side, still in her cage. She'd been given fresh water and food, some of that custard stuff from the zoo. She could only sit tight and wait for her chance - either to be rescued or not - whichever came first.

The central section of the room was bathed in bright hot light. A large holographic camera was pointing at a stage set in the middle of the restaurant. The stage was sandy. There was a large termite's nest with a log artistically arranged across the front.

So, this was to be the scene of Antenna's very own Nemesis Night. She was much closer to the human film crew than Ektek had been before. A man Antenna surmised might be a director stared intently into a monitor on the right side of the camera. What might have been a producer watched over the director's shoulder, a mobile phone pressed to the side of her head as she buzzed on and on in snorty human talk. What could they be planning? Was there any chance at all they might be talking about something that might benefit the natural world in even the smallest way?

Antenna thought not.

Antenna watched as the grip adjusted the tracks preparing for the camera move. The boom operator swung a large hairy mic in and out across the set. After watching the boom operator for a while, trying to puzzle out what the heck she was doing, Antenna surmised she was checking for shadows across the bright set.

There was a soft flutter and the nearly black Crawf appeared out of the darkness beside her. He had cloaked his pink face patch with his feathers. He spoke very quietly—*Hullo?* He melted back into the dark. Antenna almost fainted with relief. Then she could hear the clicking of her cage door as he attempted to undo the lock with his beak. It seemed to be taking a ridiculous time and making an awful noise. There were people everywhere. Any minute now, one of them would come to investigate…

—*What's the problem?* she whispered.

—*My beak.*

—*What's with the beak?*

—*It's hollow.*

—*Hollow?*

—*I've got to be careful.*

—*I see.* Antenna didn't see and she couldn't think how she could help him with his fragile beak so she waited, fairly screaming inside. She watched the people going about their business, back-lit from the dazzling light of the stage, not paying her any attention at all. There were people operating machines - cameras, lights and sound - everywhere. Even in the ceiling. Antenna watched them all, trying to stay calm and distracted, as Crawf tinkered away with his lock.

Up in the lighting grid, Antenna saw a small movement in the shadows. She focussed on the place and sure enough saw the twinkle of a tiny frog's eye in the glare of the stage lighting. It was Bash. He was preparing to broadcast proceedings to headquarters. He placed his camera on a strategic strut and watched. He panned across the space with his tiny viewfinder. Antenna hoped his footage was beaming to the website. She almost waved but figured she didn't want to be attracting attention to Crawf so abstained from any irregular movements.

Crawf continued his struggles with the cage. He used more and more force until the cage began to shake.

—*Careful, Crawf…* Antenna didn't think he could have heard her; he was making so much noise with the lock. He kept on and on, making more and more of a racket, until he finally knocked the whole cage over. It crashed onto the floor and rolled.

—*Run!* screeched Crawf —*Run for your life!*

—*Oh, well done, Crawf,* Antenna muttered. She was thrown about in the cage as it tumbled across the floor. She wondered what the humans would make of that loud cockatoo screech. Did they have parrot on the menu that night? When the cage came to a stop she lay on the ground and realised she was still alive and even more tender. She was now under a table that was covered by a draping tablecloth. She knew she wouldn't have long before the humans raced over to see what had happened. Amazingly, the restaurant staff chose that very moment to turn on their funky bossa nova vibes and no greasy tune had ever been more welcome to any creature's ear. It would help to cover any further noise she might have to make to get out of the cage.

Luckily the door was above her and the lock had been broken. Antenna wasn't sure if it had been the weak beak or the smashing across the floor that had done the trick but she wasn't going to hang around and try and work it out forensically. Not when she needed to get the heck out of there. She clambered out of the cage and ran to another table, and then another until she felt relatively safe under a table near the wall and then she stayed very still. Crawf would have to look after himself.

There was consternation among the film crew as they yelped and bleated to each other, bustling to and fro searching for her cage, but they only seemed to succeed in getting in each other's way.

After Antenna had calmed down enough to breathe, she had to find out where she'd landed. She peered out from under the tablecloth and, just as they had planned, there was the trusty replacement numbat, skittering across the floor. It was so well manipulated by old 'weak beak' Crawf that it looked almost real.

A woman with a clipboard ran over. Another assistant appeared from the other angle. They both put their clipboards down. One ran to the numbat puppet and bleated nervously. Evidently she was too scared to pick it up. Antenna wondered if the woman thought it might bite. She only wished it could. They could have built a bite mechanism into the faux numbat. If only! That would have given those humans a fright. Then Antenna was ashamed of herself, remembering Helmut's words. Ektek wasn't for biting people.

The other woman picked up the cage and examined it. It seemed undamaged to her. She lowered the cage over the numbat replica, as though trapping a spider in her bathroom. She tapped the creature over to one side and flicked the door shut. Then she placed the cage, together with the pseudo numbat, onto a table in plain view. Everyone picked up their clipboards and left. No one made a fuss. Everyone kept their heads down, concentrating.

The switch had been made.

Antenna thought it must be nearly time, although she did wonder to herself, time for what?

The dark restaurant was becoming busier. Waiters were showing customers to their tables. Down near the staging area, a sound engineer frowned and adjusted a lever. A gaffer adjusted a lamp high up in the lighting grid. Footsteps came nearer to Antenna. The assistants met and flapped their clipboard notes at each other and yabbered in human gibberish.

Antenna could see the false numbat was turning around inside the cage. It looked as though it were chasing its tail. What a time to have fun. Crawf must have been practising, shoving those controls around with his hollow beak, just as hard as he could go.

All Antenna had to do was find Zip, who was hopefully waiting nearby in the red sports car but Antenna couldn't see her. Her eyes probed the shadows, seeking hidden traces of her friend in vain.

The Really Free Wildlife Company's production team signalled they were ready. A green screen was set in place and various habitats were projected behind the set. A harried man in a black tee-shirt opened the slightly dented cage and took the compliant numbat to the set. As soon as the fake numbat was placed onto the rocks it immediately started to climb to the termite's nest. Crawf was concentrating on getting a lifelike gait and the model numbat did look convincing, even to Antenna. Personally, Antenna thought she would have been much more wooden than that. She thought she would be unable to move at all. She'd be terrified. What was going to happen to that little pretend beast? What would be its Nemesis?

The restaurant was still filling with clients. An excited hum blended with the oily lounge music. The waiters marched speedily to take orders and fill drinks. Elaborately dressed women relaxed, their shatoosh protecting them from the cool of the evening. Antenna wondered about the chiru they'd seen only a few days before. When they'd shot the komodo, did they kill the chiru, too? Make their fancy recipes without the show or did they conjure up some fantasy hunting sequence to make it all worthwhile?

The imitation numbat was filmed as the technicians ran their tests on various backgrounds for the benefit of the producer and the director. They watched their little monitor very seriously as they compared the numbat against computer-generated backgrounds of a snowfield, a dense forest, a beach… There were sounds of arguments from the crew. The director hooted.

The technicians replaced the sandy vista with a forest floor. On screen, the model looked right at home. As the real, breathing Antenna watched, she realised all this effort had to be worth a packet to the humans. A holo numbat in every zoo, because there was no way to see a real one, must lead to healthy royalties and acclaim. But, Antenna knew, and the Really Free Wildlife Company must have known, that she was not the last numbat. There were at least two healthy surviving communities in the wild. She began to realise the Really Free Wildlife Company hadn't made much of a song and dance about her. She realised she must be there as background; no, she was there as bait, for some other creature.

There was a conference going on at the monitor and an assistant was dispatched to deliberate with a waiter. The director spoke to the Director Of Photography, perhaps checking to see if they had enough useable footage. The producer gave him the nod. It was time for the assassination.

Antenna felt panicked. Who would be the star of Nemesis Night tonight?

There was a small pause while the waiter passed on the message to the person in charge of production for this evening and then the music changed subtly and faded away to silence.

Deliberate footsteps trod slowly past Antenna. Very slowly. Ceremoniously. Then she heard a rusty squeak that sent shivers down her spine, down to the deepest echoes of her ancestral memories.

A human's sardonic tones snarled an announcement over the public address system. A scattering of polite applause rose in response. Then the spotlights swung over to a man slow-marching through the room. The man had a large bird on his arm. The bird was wearing a tight-fitting leather hood. This was the bird that squeaked like a rusty door hinge. The flinty voice on the PA barked on and on and the audience reacted and clapped and roared. The man removed the bird's hood with a flourish. The watching creatures could see it was a peregrine falcon. One of the rarest birds in the world.

The customers, waiters and kitchen staff applauded.

Antenna slunk back under the tablecloth and shook miserably. She was thankful she had already vomited. She felt empty. She almost felt sorry for the peregrine. She was pretty slim pickings. Lucky for Antenna, she was still hidden. For the time being. However thin Antenna was, the peregrine would know the difference between a nylon-fur covered radio-controlled puppet and a real live numbat. That was for sure.

The man let loose the powerful bird. It took to the air, its squeaky voice serrating the silence. Antenna cowered under the table.

The peregrine's wings fanned the air so forcefully one guest had to run to save his toupee from falling into the mosaic pool.

The peregrine spotted the model numbat and circled in the air above it. The audience laughed and clapped lightly. There they all were, wishing, taking bets and hoping… Would it be sooner? Or later?

Oh, sooner!

The falcon swooped down to the artificial numbat. It was so fast; so unbelievably fast. The bird's claws ripped into the numbat's back. It shook the animal until its mechanics were exposed. A spring and a bolt clattered onto the floor, as the peregrine hefted the model and carried it up to the ceiling.

As the audience roared its approval, the peregrine realised the puppet was inedible. Without pausing in its flight, it dropped the flopping, broken thing. The puppet smashed into a table of portly men and X-ray women. They pushed back their seats as metal cogs and triggers flew towards them. There were screams, flailing arms and overturned wine glasses.

The peregrine, wheeling around above of the dining room, looked directly at Antenna. The vivid beam of hunter and hunted connected between them. Antenna, filled with terror, ripped her vision away from it. She ducked down behind the tablecloth and knew it was only a matter of seconds before the great bird sought her out.

Then, Antenna heard the familiar hiss of the little steam car. Zip drove straight under the table. Antenna leapt into the passenger seat and ducked her head as they drove out crazily from under the cloth and careered between the tables. The hubbub of a shocked restaurant easily covered the hiss and purr of the steam powered car's engine.

The peregrine now had Antenna in his sights. He soared, following the red car with his eagle eye.

Then there was a huge crash.

The rear restaurant doors flew from their hinges as the tank lurched forward into the room.

Hod drove the metallic car, shaped like a giant stag beetle, straight into the middle of the set and then into the most expensive looking camera and sound gear. The tracks of the tank crunched into video recorders and the mixing board. But still the tank rolled on through the restaurant, crushing tables and chairs like twigs, people blowing like leaves around it.

Antenna was horrified at the destruction but was powerless to stop the tank. There was nothing to do except cringe in her seat, as the car zoomed towards the exit, and watch Hod on the rampage.

Zip shook her head at the damage and worried that there were too many people who could get hurt. She reached into her back pocket and pulled out a tiny digital sound system. She stuck it onto the front of the car and turned the volume up. A blare of emergency bells shattered the air and an electronic voice, that Ektek had produced, hoping the translation was correct, yawped sternly: Warning. Evacuate. Evacuate. You will be evacuated. Please move away. Please move away from the building. Evacuate. Evacuate. You will be evacuated.

Most of the customers had already left by this time, running and screaming in undignified haste, shatoosh waving behind them like flags. The film crew stood en guarde, ready to protect their precious equipment with their lives.

Although Zip was driving fast, Antenna was still out in the open and she knew that the falcon could just pluck her out of her seat any time it liked. She watched as another bird streaked up to the ceiling. It was Crawf. The palm cockatoo confronted the Nemesis as they flew fast around the room, performing an extraordinary aerial display.

Crawf screeched at the peregrine—*Flee! Flee!* Or it could have been—*Free! Free!* Or even—*Fee! Fee!* Whatever it was, the bird of prey heard him and swooped down to the level of humans and out of the door into the real world.

Back on the ground, Hod did a completely unnecessary and very wide three-point turn. The staff and camera crew's concern for property faded as interest in their own safety took over and they scattered in panic. Seeing the humans dive for cover, Zip screeched to a halt next to the camera. She jumped out of the car and struggled with the holographic equipment, trying to tip it over. Antenna jumped out to help her and they managed to heave the whole thing, tripod and all, into the back of the car.

Zip disengaged the blaring speaker and mp3 player from the top of the bonnet. She placed it next to the fallen control desk, which took up the announcement. It blared, even louder than before: Evacuate! Evacuate! You will be evacuated!

As they jumped back into the car and drove off, Zip chuckled— *This is good, very good. With that hologram I never need to be in my enclosure again!*

Antenna thought about this, knowing she didn't have the choice. She could never go back to her enclosure. She felt homeless and out of place. She looked over at Zip—*It is a freedom of a sort, isn't it.*

—*Good as we're going to get today.*

Hod continued his mad parade, driving over tables and smashing the termite nest into a pulp of painted polystyrene. Leaving the bio-diesel engine running, he stopped the tank in the middle of the now empty room and jumped down from the driver's seat. He rushed over to a corner of the restaurant and fiddled with something.

Bash had made his way down from the lighting grid above and was getting into the tank by the time Hod got back. Crawf was already inside. Zip drove the car through the tank door and heaved on the handbrake. She and Antenna slammed the tank door shut and shouted out to Hod they were ready to go. Hod revved the engine. They took off out of the empty restaurant, driving over everything in their way. It was a bumpy ride.

Mission accomplished.

The tank had not been built to be a speed machine. So Hod drove it to the rear of the building where Helmut was ready in the airship; the winch lines lowered and prepared. The tank drove into place in the airship's shadow. Hod hopped around the outside of the tank, attaching the wires to the frame before re-entering. Zip followed him, checking each connection was fast before she too climbed aboard. From the tank's controls Hod radioed to the airship—*Uptek? We're ready. Over.*

Helmut's voice replied through the radio fuzz—*Commence tank lift. Over.*

The tank rose slowly to the airship's docking and cargo area. Once the winching was complete and the tank was secure, the creatures came out of the cargo hold and went up to the bridge where Helmut piloted the craft.

—*Thanks, driver,* said Zip.

Helmut didn't appear to hear her. He was concentrating attentively as he activated the airship's forward movement. Beads of sweat had gathered around his bony headpiece.

The airship rose and turned away from the city centre. Crawf said—*I went into the kitchens to see if I could help any of the animals in there and they'd all gone.*

—*Yeah, I set them free. Before I drove into the dining room.*

Antenna turned her full attention to Hod—*What did you think you were doing?*

—Saving you.

—Snap, said Zip who had been the one to pack Antenna into her little car and who had driven Antenna to the exit at the very time Hod made his smashing entrance.

Hod wasn't bothered—*I know that now.*

—But why? asked Antenna—*You were supposed to wait until Helmut signalled you.*

—I only had vision. I didn't know. I was worried.

—Did you have to drive all over tables like that?

—I thought he'd got you.

—Even so, you didn't need to destroy everything, did you?

—Didn't I?

—Oh, Hoddy. Considerate to a fault.

As they floated away in the airship, Ektek watched the restaurant building recede. A group of humans stood some distance away, apparently still obeying the evacuation order.

Safely in the bridge, Bash asked—*Is the video going to be enough? To convince the Zoo? They're going to have to be a lot more vigilant, aren't they?*

—Hullo? Until someone else comes along, greedier and with another atrocious idea, said Crawf—*Sure they will.*

Hod held out a small device in his little paw for their inspection. The creatures looked at it. They looked at him questioningly. He smiled and said—*Here's a little something I prepared earlier.*

—What for?

—Glad you asked, Bash. Hod pressed a button on the device. There was a dull boom from far off. Hod said—*Good, isn't it?*

The airship seemed to shift a bit, drifting away from the force of the explosion. The creatures looked out of the window as a pall of smoke billowed from the crushed restaurant. There was a stunned silence. Hod had firebombed Last Chance to Eat, just as he'd been threatening all along.

Bash burst into tears, which is never good for a frog. Salty water really stings that fragile skin.

—Hoddy. Antenna said. She nearly cried too but instead, clenched her jaw and said—*Hod. You are no longer Ektek.*

—You said. You, Antenna, said Hod—*You said you wanted to pay them back. For Min.*

—That was only in the heat of the moment. I wanted to stop them, but not this, this wanton destruction, this waste, this…

—No-one was in the building.

—But Hod, we can't keep fighting on this level. There are too many humans. They have all the power.

—Not all the time, they don't.

—Their whole purpose is to conquer. They have conquered all of nature. They have conquered all of us.

—Not me, they haven't.

—Hod. The only thing we can do is try to educate them.

—Is that right?

—Yes! Educate and win them over. We're all together in this.

—That's the only way we can survive, surely? said Crawf.

—That's the only way for any of us, said Zip.

—Are you saying that all creatures could live together with homo sapiens in a tolerant and understanding global community?

—Yes. I am. Antenna gestured to the rest of the team—*We all are. What else is there?*

Hod threw back his head and laughed. He laughed and laughed and his guffaws were fuelled by grief.

Helmut alone paid no attention to the renegade. The cassowary was caught up in his own turmoil as he secretly struggled with his inner voices. Was he breaking into internal pieces? Was he hearing voices from another dimension? He had become aware that Ektek was one reality and these sounds and words he heard were another. It was beginning to frighten him. More than frighten. He was distraught as he piloted the airship into the Zoo grounds but he did an excellent job of hiding his anxiety from his fellow squad members.

V

The other Ektek creatures were troubled as they tied up outside the cavern. As he was leaving through the cargo hold, Hod turned to shout at his erstwhile team—*You can keep going with your cute little actions and reports to the Department, expecting things to change. Me? I'm going to make things happen. I'm going to make those humans sit up and take notice. You just watch me.*

His dramatic exit was spoiled when he pushed past Antenna intending to climb down the rope ladder to the ground. He paused when he saw the distress in her face—*I'm sorry, Antenna. I know I let you down but I have to go.*

—You don't have to…

—Anti, I feel so hemmed in, so powerless, in this damn zoo. Maybe I'll be able to spread my wings, make a difference…

—You don't have wings.

—*Oh, shut up.* His manner changed abruptly and he asked her— *Why don't you come with me?*

—*I can't do that!*

—*Why not? You can't live in the zoo anymore. You're free. You can go anywhere you like.*

—*I know you think Ektek is a waste of time but I don't. We can help. I don't know how many and I don't know for how long… If I can help just one then there's still hope for all us weird furry creatures…*

—*All creatures great and small…*

—*Go ahead and smirk all you like. I can't save the entire planet from being overrun by cows and sheep but I might be able to make someone think…*

—*Fine. I'll go my way and you'll go yours and we'll agree to differ and we'll never see each other again.*

—*Good.*

—*Remember, Anti. I'm the one who chose freedom. You didn't. You're a prisoner as much as ever. Ektek possesses you and you've made Ektek into a dungeon.* He took off, climbing down the ladder, bounding onto the ground and away from the zoo.

—*Bye, Hoddy. Survive!* Antenna came to stand next to Zip at the hold entrance. They watched him leaping crazily toward the city streets

—*Good riddance,* said Zip.

Antenna glanced sideways at her.

A tear rolled down Zip's face. She roughly brushed it away—*Old wally shit head.*

VI

Bash had hung back in the cockpit and watched the bent cassowary with concern—*Are you okay, Helmut?*

Helmut managed to nod and spoke with great difficulty—*I'll just get on with a few things here. Go on ahead.*

—*More hands and all that,* offered Bash—*After all, I'm the one with the hands…*

—*Go on, mate. I'll be fine.*

—*Are you sure?*

—*Sure. See you in a minute.*

Bash left the bridge uncertainly. He was still worried about Helmut when he saw Antenna and Zip just about to climb down the ladder. He hopped up to the numbat—*Antenna? It's Helmut.*

Antenna, remembering Min's warning, was instantly concerned— *Where is he?*

124

—*The bridge.* As she turned to go back into the airship, Bash added—*Antenna? He's not in a good way.*

—*Like what?*

—*Like, he's disturbed. When we were travelling, it was as though there was some kind of interruption in his head.*

—*Thanks, Bash. I'll go.*

—*I don't think he wants a lot of attention.*

—*That's okay, I'll come with you, Bash,* said Zip—*You go, Antenna. He'll talk to you.*

Antenna turned back towards the bridge as the frog and the fruit-bat left the airship.

Helmut held himself together until he was sure all the crew had left the craft. Then he crumpled and broke down, crying at the controls in the airship—*Why can't you leave me alone?* He shouted to no one, to some kind of invisible tormenter. There was no reply and the cassowary drooped, desperate, in the pilot's seat.

Antenna quietly sat down in the co-pilot's chair and watched him struggle with himself. After a time, sensing someone was there, Helmut lifted his head to look at her—*Antenna. We made it.*

—*Thanks to you.*

—*Luck. Sheer luck.*

—*Helmut. I'm going to have to relieve you of flying duties.*

—*I'm the one with the experience. Who else can do it? You rely on me.*

—*I do. There's no one else with your knowledge but you can't pilot the airship until we find out what is wrong with it.*

—*With me, you mean.*

—*Helmut. You are Ektek's greatest asset, our wisest warrior. You've seen it all before.*

—*You mean, I'm past it.*

—*No. I mean you deserve a rest while we sort this out.*

—*Foolish young kids. I told them not to go. They didn't listen to me. I knew what would happen. That Hod. He's just the same. He's going to get himself killed, just like my son. You need me, Antenna. You can't retire me like this…*

—*I'm not retiring you, Helmut. Just taking your advice. We need some time to recover. Take stock. We all do.*

—*Without Ektek, I am nothing,* said Helmut, slumped and muttering—*I've got nothing to live for. Nothing.*

—*Helmut, please don't say that.*

—*Then you tell me, young numbat. What is the point, then? What's the damn point of being alive?*

Antenna watched the horizon out of the airship window. She watched the shroud of smoke wisp across the densely crowded city-scape. Was that a peregrine falcon flying off into the distance?

Ektek was in the business of saving lives. Well, they'd just saved Antenna's life. That gave her something to live for, didn't it?

Didn't it?

VII

In a clearing, near a river, mud was churned into a circle. Grater, Asunder, Jata, Damura and Shining Teeth marched slowly, closely following each other, round and round and round, their scaly legs and feet pounding, sinking, dragging, clawing into the sludge.

The reptiles continued their march of grief long into the night. Their eyes glowed with crocodile intensity.

Jata stumbled. They were all tired.

Asunder tripped and fell. The rest of the harem continued to move over her, shakily. They were exhausted. Each stumbled in her turn and finally, collapsed to the ground.

Knowing they could go no further, they opened their mouths and sang out long eerie wails from the very base of their beings. They were keening for their lost husband.

The keening sailed through the air, lying like smoke over the river. The noise was incredible. The land shuddered in sympathy. The tiny creatures of the riverbed listened. It was an age-old tale of farewell.

Grater's voice began to shake.

Damura coughed.

Slowly the crocodiles could sound out no more. Their grief was spent, the keening choked and they slept where they fell.

Shining Teeth was the last to close her marble eyes.

VIII

The next day by the river a brolga pair danced in the rising sun. They flew their ballet high into the yellow dawn. The sun gleamed hot over the brown mud and sparse vegetation. The agitated sounds of river life wound through the humidity.

The crocodiles stirred and shook their heads from side to side. They dragged themselves to the river's edge to drink.

Shining Teeth rose to her feet. She knew she must lead them to find food. Then she must lead them to find a new mate, someone who would be capable of protecting them all. There was something else, too. Something even more fundamental. She joined the rest of the harem by the water. She raised her strength to croak—*We will avenge his death.*

—*Yes*, murmured the harem together—*Yes, yes, yes…*

Their familiar lives were lost now. Everything had changed. There was no male in their river. They must seek elsewhere. This river was bordered by cleared and fertile farmland. There was no place without homo sapiens. They must travel and they must encounter humans. But this was mere irritation in their plans. They were focused on their main purpose. It was time the crocodiles fought back.

—*We must destroy them*, said Shining Teeth.

—*Yes, yes, yes…*

The sun rose higher and grew more dazzling. The heat pressed down on the earth. The five females moved inexorably across farms, factories and roads. They intended to find Ektek and they intended to punish: maim, hurt and kill. Their group mind had decided. The crocodile harem intended to obliterate Ektek.

EKTEK002

Out of Spite Out of Mind

Chapter Nineteen

His mouth clenched open. His lips curled back. His aching diaphragm shoved down and sucked the next hot breath into his lungs. He fled.

The dark background blurred as he hurtled past. A scattering of fallen leaves shuddered aside. Air and dust puffed out as his long feet thudded onto the ground. His striped tail jerked erratically behind him. His hair was matted and damp. He'd fallen at the edge of a dam escaping a dogfight a few hours ago and the mud had dried into awkward clumps in his fur.

He was a yellow-footed rock wallaby but that was irrelevant. Nothing mattered except staying alive. He pounded down the road. When they picked him up in their yellow headlights, cars blasted their horns at him but he just kept going. Hod surmised the drivers might have thought they were being helpful. He almost jumped out of his skin when a loud blare dopplered past. It was as if they were warning him to stay off the road. Bloody brilliant. He'd tried to avoid the tarmac because he had a brain, not because air-conditioned humans had a streak of kindness towards endangered wildlife and wanted to go toot-toot-tooty at him.

As far as the throbbing blood in his veins and the searing of air rushing into his lungs allowed him to think, he began to feel just a little bit sorry for himself. It was only a matter of days since his breakout and he felt like he'd been running for months.

When he'd deserted the zoo, he'd thought he could just wander into a handy forest or wilderness and live out his life leaping up rocks with all the other happy little rock wallabies. That was as much of a plan as this furry fugitive could afford.

However, there seemed to be a problem with this idyllic vision; he'd been having difficulty trying to find the entrance to the wilderness. He'd seen many huge, colourful buildings surrounded by parking areas for cars, manicured parkland with runways leading up to emerald-green curved lawns with little flags poking out of them and fenced places for human young to run and scream in. There'd been extensive places where just one type of plant grew behind fences but they'd had dogs. He'd become an expert in jumping barriers of all kinds and he'd even gone for an unexpected bath in a swimming pool more heavily chemically treated than the seal pool. In all his travels he hadn't seen anything remotely like the dreamtime bush of his imagination where a bunch of animals could roam happily ever after.

It had become clear to him that those who were wild-caught and living back in the zoo might have been telling the truth. He'd always thought their stupid stories about humans being everywhere and roads being everywhere and houses being everywhere and smoking factories being everywhere and damned illogical dogs being everywhere were just that—stupid stories to keep zoo-born creatures like him nice and comfy and shut up, mindless, ridiculous and gawked at in the safe-house confines of the zoo. As he gasped for breath, Hod started to imagine that being shut up in a comfy little zoo might have some merits. Only, how the hell could he get back there?

He could hear the cracking of sticks and the crashing of swerving bodies as the dogs came closer. The time for negotiations had passed. They weren't interested in sharing information. They wanted flesh. His flesh. He could almost smell their hunger and their elemental need for blood.

The dog in the lead was glossy black except for the white flare across his chest. Even his eyes were black. His open mouth displayed a blood-red ribbon of tongue flapping beside its mountain range of glinting teeth. Hod imagined he could hear him slavering over the zoom and zaat of traffic.

Hod, used to riding a trike on roads, had more experience with timing and dodging drivers than your average yellow-footed rock wallaby. He also knew he was running out of choices. He couldn't afford to lose time by slowing. He would have to cross the road. Fast.

He'd have to fling himself into the middle of the road—that ridiculously thin strip of white stripe between oncoming vehicles—and hope for the best.

The black dog came so close that Hod had no choice left. He had to go. He aimed for the middle white lines and moved. He landed and stayed put, frozen, as vehicles zipped past on either side of him with their horns blaring, and watched the oncoming traffic for a break.

The black dog, with eyes only for Hod, raced after him and pelted headlong, and audibly, THWACK, into a purple people mover. The dog spun up, up, round, over into the air. He flew onwards and down and landed, splat, head cracking into the hot road as the people mover screeched to a halt.

Hod didn't look back. He waited for a reasonable gap between a truck and a motorcycle before sprinting across the other lane and into the cover of a clump of scrubby acacias. He didn't stop there. He kept going.

He paused in a driveway further up the road to watch two more dogs see their mashed leader being dragged off the road by the tip of one leg. The humans cawed to each other, and to the dogs, making warning sounds and waving their arms but Hod watched in horror as a brown dog, a kind of pointy, spikey looking creature with a pale belly and a yellow arrow on her nose, skidded into the driveway right beside him.

Hod spun round and realised he was at some kind of fuel depot. The pointed dog had dropped to a low hunting approach, flattened ears, crouched, ready to spring...

Hod reached up to the bowser, grabbed the handle from a petrol pump and held it like a gun. The spikey dog kept low and kept on coming; the yellow arrow on her nose pointed straight at Hod.

Suddenly, she rushed him. The other dog across the road, a spotty, insipid grey being, shouted and yelled and dashed from side to side along the edge and the traffic went narrrl narrrl past. The purple people-mover people tried to fend the dog off with a dead branch from the roadside, all the time yelping and yowling out of their pink human mouths.

Hod watched as the arrow dog came at him, seemingly in slow motion. He raised the gun of the pump handle and, squeezing with both paws, sprayed out stinking liquid. The dog slumped to one side, overcome and revolted at the stench.

This gave boyscout Hod the time he needed to fish inside his shoulder satchel for a box of matches. A good rock wallaby is always prepared for a surgical strike—*Hey, little doggie. Wanna go woof?*

The first match didn't catch but the second did. The dog had recovered from her chemical dousing and was getting to her feet. She seemed determined to carry on with her plan to exterminate Hod, the creature she must have imagined to be poor helpless wildlife. So Hod flicked another match against the box. It burned. Hod threw it and the match soared, spinning yellow-orange in the darkness, into the brown fur of the hungry dog. The dog screamed and ran. Flames burned bright. Not so helpless wildlife after all.

Hod, warm enough already, didn't bother to stay by the fire. He disappeared into the trees. He ran again. There was no time to lose. He had to find somewhere to rest. Soon. He dashed from tree to tree to rock. He hugged the rock, something solid at last.

He laid his face into the cold stone. Trying to get more air. Trying to breathe. Trying to be quiet. Trying to quiet his drumming heart. Trying. To. Be. Quiet.

He could see no way out of this endless chase. It was hopeless. Hod rubbed his head on the rock. He leaned hard on the stone as his eyes focussed. He was looking at a floodlit sign. Animal. Yes. He could read that. Animal he was. Knew about animals. The next word was trickier. Sanctuary. Animal sanctuary.

His blood slowed to a mere boil and his lungs stopped making a whooping sound. Sanctuary. That meant something good, didn't it? Didn't it mean safety? Hod was in dire need of safety, a rest and some food. He didn't have a choice. The last dog would figure out how to cross the road sooner or later and he suspected there was a good chance there'd be dogs, or foxes, or bloody dragons for all he knew, on this side of the road anyway. What about the sanctuary itself? Who would put a dog in a sanctuary? He had to risk it.

He soon discovered the entire place was similar, at least in theory, to his ex-home, Bedlam Zoo. It meant to keep invaders out or inmates in. Either way, lighting picked out a towering fence around the perimeter. The Sanctuary was covered in vibrant purple and red flowers. Unfortunately for Hod's already sore paws, the masses of colour hid sharp needle spikes and Hod looked around him, knowing it was just a matter of time before some creature or other happened upon his scent.

He had to get in to the sanctuary. There were no cars in the well-lit car park, meaning it was still early, or maybe it was just after closing time. Hod had no idea. He'd been living in a panic for too long now. He thought maybe it was early. He'd tended to travel by night, but right now, his mind was salt-ridden thirsty. His tail was grazed. His feet were bleeding. He kept moving around the perimeter. His eyes searched the fence line for a weakness. His glance bleached the horizon for canine hunters. The main door was locked. He passed again round the parking spaces, the back fence, down the side and then he saw the gap.

Someone with two left hands and no thumbs had, apparently, shoved a break in the wire back into place. Hod surmised it would be reasonably easy for a rock wallaby to unwind but his vision started to blur. He was running out of time. He wrenched off his shoulder bag, left it on the outside, leapt up and pushed at the line of cut wires. He pressed and twanged his way into the scratchy mess.

It was impossible. He hung in the middle of the fence, limp, help-less and weak. He had to find the strength to push on. He couldn't be discovered like this and he couldn't die here. It would be embarrassing. He closed down into something small, trying to focus his strength. If he could just rest here a moment, he could gather some forces togeth-er and maybe find the power to stretch out and break through. Spikes from the plant were scratching him everywhere. Hod ignored them and focussed on finding his inner explosion. He counted slowly to himself, rock wallaby style, and then shot through with every last morsel of fibre he could muster.

He landed on soft, watered lawn and the repetitive sound of sprinklers. He pressed his head into the dampness and breathed. He sucked in moisture from the ground. Then he turned back to the fence to close it up behind him. He surely didn't need a surprise visit from any mystery predators. He wound round the wires as best he could and made the fence at least look smooth to the eye again. Then, he dropped to the ground and sat, panting, trying to find his equilibrium. He turned to see where he had landed. And immediately wished he hadn't.

He was nose to nose with a huge crocodile. She smiled at him— *Why, hullo, there*, said the croc—*Who have we here? Oh, how rude I am. I'm forgetting myself. Let me introduce myself. I'm Shining Teeth. And you are?*

Hod bit back his first retort, something impudent about smiling at a crocodile, and shook himself into some semblance of politeness. What were the chances he'd heard about this crocodile before? Rea-sonably good, it seemed, because he had. He'd heard a lot about Shining Teeth. None of it was nice.

He wanted to be careful here; very, very careful. And, come to think of it, he wouldn't even smile. Not at this particular crocodile.

Chapter Twenty

Antenna slept at her desk. Her thin face squashed into her paws and dribble pooled by her cheek. The dark stripe under her eyes didn't show the tear tracks.

The computer desk hummed on with only one monitor operating. Bedlam Zoo's media page was open at a recent story:

> After the release of our very last numbat into the wild, Bedlam Zoo is proud to announce our exciting new consortium. Seven international zoos will work togeth-er to rebuild numbat populations. Bedlam Zoo will provide the latest in high-technology breeding facilities. Experts hope the innovative program will extend the gene pool beyond the environmental bottleneck faced by Australia's current wild numbat population and al-low visitors to comprehend the conservation efforts of modern zoos.

Antenna woke up. She sucked in a thread of drool and snorted. Her eyes flickered and blinked open. She shook her head in discomfort and tried to stretch out the crick in her neck. When she focussed on the screen in front of her she couldn't help reading it again and her eyes welled with fresh tears.

Antenna was a numbat. In fact, Antenna was the very last numbat to whom Bedlam Zoo had offered the taste of freedom. Antenna wouldn't be able to take part in that lovely media story. To her, that is what it was: a delicious, tempting, fairy story. Freedom? For Antenna, freedom had sunk. Antenna snapped out of the Zoo's website and shook herself into consciousness.

Her own chance at freedom had been a lie and her release had been into the very jaws (or rather, predatory beak) of gourmand death. Humans had controlled her bedtime right up until Hod's funny little fire-bomb had finished Last Chance to Eat, a restaurant Ektek had discovered profiting from the fragrant sauce of vulnerability. Last Chance to Eat had, finally, been barbecued by a rock wallaby.

Now, she might well be free from the demands of public display, but Antenna was still caught in a trap. Her family were dead. Her best friend was gone, killed in Last Chance to Eat. Antenna couldn't feel more alone. She was an outcast. She had no home, no enclosure, no keeper, no place in the zoo. She couldn't expect the ants to keep stealing food for her. One day soon, she would have to take responsibility for herself; she would have to leave the zoo, forever. Until then, however, she was shut in a cave system under a zoo that would soon feature a nest of incommunicable consortium numbats she would never even see. She shook her head. She had to snap out of it.

Antenna's personal desktop featured an image of a possum with a long furry tail, large eyes and a white neck. This was Min, a Leadbeater's possum. Min's huge luminous eyes gleamed back at Antenna, willing her on, giving her strength to work. Antenna nodded at her. Today would be a day for Min. For Min's memory.

This morning at sunrise, before the zoo's human workers arrived, many of the zoo's animals would escape. They wouldn't go far. They would find their way through the intricate tunnels under the zoo to meet in the hangar cave. These were the animals that worked for Ektek. There was to be a memorial service for Min, an entomological tattoo, with massed beetles flying overhead and marching ants demonstrating their military precision.

Antenna dreaded this kind of formality but it did mean that the animals would have a chance to talk about Min. They would remember her achievements and why she had given her life. The Ektek community would reflect on why they were fighting and what every animal on the planet had to lose.

A darkling beetle quietly entered the room. He cleared his throat and coughed—*Antenna?*

—*I'm awake.*

The beetle flew up to the control desk. It was Torque, senior security officer, in charge of the memorial service—*Sun's coming up, Antenna. Beetles are ready. Just need the word.*

Antenna moved away from the desk and stood up—*Thanks Torque, I'm ready now. Have you seen Helmut?*

—*Could try the airship?*

—*Right. Thanks.*

Torque flew beside Antenna as she strode out of her office and into the hangar.

—Didn't mean to sleep so long, said Antenna.

—Sorry. Should have woken you earlier but...

—Not your fault.

—Thanks, Antenna. Won't happen again. Not if everything goes according to plan, according to the way things ought to be...

Outside, the sky was brightening. Trees and shrubs were beginning to define as more than mere silhouettes. Antenna looked around at the already assembled animals and nodded. She glanced up at the tethered airship. It would be a good viewing platform for the tattoo and she needed to talk to her elder: her mentor, and her friend, Helmut. He would know what had to be done for Ektek and for her own sake. He had known her father and he had known Min. Helmut would be sure to offer good advice.

—I'll watch from up there. Give me a minnie. Antenna made her way up the ladder to the airship.

Torque nodded and flew back to give the word to the beetles. Show time.

In the airship, Antenna found Helmut slumped in the pilot's seat, muttering to himself—*Helmut?* She reached out to touch his feathered back—*Helmut?*

The cassowary registered neither her touch nor that she'd spoken to him. Helmut seemed further away each day. He appeared to be aging by the hour. His normally shiny, black feather cloak was grey and dusty. The blue skin on his neck seemed baggy, stretched and scaly. His eyes flicked in all directions, restless, never stopping for a moment. His chef's cap of bone seemed taller and thinner too, as if it were growing gaunt with the rest of him—*Where are the flowers of space? What do they look like? How many meteors does a living being need to survive?*

—Meteors? What are you talking about? Helmut? It's time. The beetles are flying over for Min's memorial service. Did you remember? Antenna listened to his quiet muttering, tensed her lips and shook her head. She could make sense of some of his words but much was said quietly, under his breath, a continual seamless rant—*... see the Milky Way? See Jupiter? See Mars? I hear you, my angel, I hear you and I shall save you and together we will be saved. Glorious will be the day we can be together, when we shall walk hand in hand through heaven...*

—Helmut?

—... with me, my love. Oh, Zed, I long to be with you. My heart is aching with longing. Now that I've heard you I cannot wait to meet you. Zed is my light, my life and my hope. I give my all to Zed.

—Helmut. Look. The beetles...

The tattoo commenced. Antenna watched the solemn flyby with hundreds of Ektek beetles arranging in and out of formation. Ovals of glittering colour flashed into an avalanche of concentric stars that in turn transformed into a spiral that became a kind of tornado. It was an early morning firework display.

—... *through the bent space, I hear you, oh most beautiful of voices, I hear you, my angel and my heartbeat. We will amble together by the rivers of Heaven, through the forests of wonderment. I will be with you, by Zed, and we shall journey through life and save the sick and the suffering and teach the high and low to love each other and care for each other and have eternal compassion...*

—*Helmut? I need your help.* Antenna tried to break through Helmut's bizarre meditation—*Please?*

More coleopterons than had names flew this day for Ektek; long bodied darkling beetles, scarab beetles, harlequin beetles, whirlygig beetles, jewel beetles with their lustrous metallic colours, and cumbersome dung beetles with their bulbous bodies and shovel noses all swirled; beside, in and out, through, making kaleidoscope patterns in the sky outside the window.

Tilting his head from side to side, seeing nothing, Helmut continued muttering—*... wouldn't I give if I had anything to give then I would because I'm dreaming of life in the air again when I can be with Zed. The righteous will be with Zed and the evil and thoughtless will drown in their own selfishness...*

A rapid volley of explosions shot across the sky; flat beetles with coppery red forequarters and metallic blue rears performed, firing off their own personal explosive discharges. These were bombardier beetles and they arched their stems and shot out hot mushroom clouds of white peroxide propulsion juice from their rear ends, one per beetle, in a synchronised pattern of both sound and vision.

At different times, brightly coloured click beetles fell to the ground. Then, clowning around, kicking and rocking on their backs, they began to spring upwards, spin and finally land on their feet, each accompanied by a clicking sound; a cacophony of clicking beetle fun.

—*Helmut?* Antenna stared ahead at the sky, knowing Helmut couldn't hear her but determined to speak her mind, determined to make her feelings real, heard by someone, even if not understood— *Did you hear, they're bringing a new family of numbats into the zoo? What do you reckon? Numbats. That's me. My kind and I'll never be able to see them. I'll never be able to talk to them.* Antenna stared at him. Did he hear her at all? —*I need to talk to you. You're the only one, except that I don't know where you've gone. Helmut? Please? Can you hear me?*

On the ground, masses of ants wheeled in marching patterns. Their little feet drummed on the dirt, creating a vibrating rhythm; the atmosphere pumped, energising and alerting all to the drill.

—*Helmut?* Antenna watched the ants and glanced at Helmut every now and then, shocked by the deterioration in his condition; it seemed both his physical and mental processes were damaged now. She wondered when he had last eaten. She realised he would not hear her; he could not hear her—*Oh, Helmut.* She tried to shake off her selfish need for his advice and turned to face the music.

As the sunrise tinted the sky, the beetles outside the airship rose and fell in circular formations. Watching their work made Antenna remember Min and her own father, Calaby. She so wished they both could have been there. She felt her father would have burst with pride.

Calaby had named Ektek after the twin tenets of ecology and technology. Min's mother had also been a part of the founding creatures. Together with the ants and the beetles, the founders had created technology that gave them the power of communication, not only with other animals but also, anonymously, with the one animal that denied its very animalism, human beings.

Min, Antenna's childhood friend, was the last Leadbeater's possum in captivity, and probably the very last of her species. Everyone at Bedlam Zoo had been devastated when she had died so horribly in the restaurant. Especially Antenna. Antenna and Min had grown up together and, with a certain absconded yellow-footed rock wallaby, had been expected to take over the running of Ektek when the time came. Now, all the responsibility was up to Antenna and she didn't even formally live in the Zoo anymore.

Antenna looked over at the confused cassowary sitting in the pilot's seat of the airship. Helmut, too, was one of the founders, a friend of Calaby and Antenna's last connection to her father. Now, it seemed that he too had made his choice to leave, at least mentally.

—*Helmut? I have to go but I'll be back. Can you wait here?*

—*...white asteroids fling themselves into infinity. How can I reach you, Zed? I only want to be with you. She's in my dreams. She's all one, she's the only one...*

—*Helmut? Stay.* Antenna turned to leave. She paused when she got to the door and looked back at Helmut, wondering. How could she help him? She had no idea. She left him, still muttering, and went down to meet the other creatures who had been watching the tattoo. She saw Zip first. Antenna stood next to the bare-backed fruit bat who nodded a greeting and asked—*Helmut?*

—*Not available.*

Zip looked at her—*Still sitting in the pilot's seat, crying?*
—*We have to get him to the vet.*
—*'Course.*
—*I must congratulate the beetles first.*
—*Go. I'll be here.*
—*Thank Zed for that!*

They grinned at each other as they moved off separately to join the performers. A susurration of applause smattered across the landing area as the ants and beetles reached the hangar cave. They broke ranks and moved haphazardly, full of adrenalin, looking for friends and chatting heartily about successful manoeuvres and near misses. There was no doubt. The invertebrate tattoo was a spectacular success.

Chapter Twenty-one

Water sprinklers continued their rhythmic arcs of flashing silver in the dawn as the crocodile smiled at her guest—*Nice of you to drop in; Hod, is it? Hod. Lovely name.* Shining Teeth smiled at Hod, still nose to nose.

Hod made a slight movement backwards but she was too quick for him. She edged her snout even closer, pressing into his nose—*Oh, no, no, no. Surely you're not thinking of going? Not when you've only just arrived? Do stay. We're about to find ourselves a volunteer. Hang on, just need to check something.* Shining Teeth swung away from Hod and shouted—*Is everyone here clear on the role of volunteer?*

Hod assessed his position. He already knew he'd left the frying pan. Well, then. This must be the fire.

He took in a deep breath and shook his head as if waking himself up. He was in parkland. It did not, however, feel at all peaceful. A warning tinge of red blushed in the sky.

He could see expansive lawns and lush leaves like great wide welcoming fans on the surrounding embracing trees. But the atmosphere itself, framed and charged by four more crocodiles, was not welcoming. They poised, like weird, knotted log benches, around the edge of a motley and quivering group of native Australian animals.

Wallabies of assorted extraction, lizards and wombats clustered up close together. Everyone looked very, very nervous. It seemed many of the cages of the sanctuary had been emptied for the assembly. The crocs, for the main, remained still and quiet but when they moved so much as a toenail, so much as an eyelid, so much as the tip of a tail, the kangaroos flinched, the possums cringed and the horseshoe bats squashed in just that bit tighter to their neighbours. No one wanted to be on the edge of this particular gathering.

Shining Teeth ambled in, too close, to the pack and sauntered around some more. She looked them over in a friendly, concerned sort of way. Sardines in a can had more gaps between them than had this bunch of survivors in a sanctuary—*I see I'm going to have to repeat myself, given our new visitor.* She smiled graciously at Hod—*That's right, Hod.*

Come right on in. Make yourself at home. Listen, friends, and I'll go through it one more time. We're on a mission, my lovely sisters and I. We're trying to find a group of animals that owe us for... well, let's just say they... owe us. Our search has not been straightforward, however. We've found in the last couple of weeks it's been a bit difficult getting around town in a group. People tend to notice us, especially when we're chewing on their leg. Sadly, it's just not safe for us. Not for any of us crocs. So, we thought, hey, why not send a messenger. Find out where Ektek is, and then we can sneak in and visit them under the radar, if you get my drift. See what I mean? That's where the volunteer comes in. The volunteer is one of you; a nice, unobtrusive creature, who can travel without much attention, find Ektek's headquarters and then tell us the address. That's not much to ask, is it? Got that? Shining Teeth scanned the crowd with her gleaming orange eyes— *Who's up for a bit of infiltration?*

Silence.

The creatures shivered collectively. Without warning, Shining Teeth opened her mouth and snapped up a skinny little water dragon, not biting but holding him between her teeth. He immediately fainted. The lizard was unconscious and drooping when Shining Teeth spat him out—*I hate to talk with my mouth full. I really do. Jata? Could you take over?*

Shining Teeth paused to see Jata nod, then she scooped the water dragon back up into her mouth. The creature flopped like a wet tea towel in her picket-fence maw. Shining Teeth flicked her head and spat the little dragon up, up, up, into the rising sunglare. As the water dragon curved and turned in a slow arc back downwards, she opened her mouth. The dragon fell with a soft sound into her waiting gob. Shining Teeth snapped her jaw shut and chewed.

The assembled creatures drew in a shocked gasp and shrank even more closely together.

Shining Teeth finished chomping and gulped; water dragon all gone—*Nice. Appetiser. Tasty.* She smiled and, without a warning, grabbed again, a little round bandicoot. It was clear one of its forearms was bent, deformed in some way. The bandicoot yelled with alarm. It wriggled and jumped as best it could while Shining Teeth maintained her smile, keeping a light hold on her little morsel. Muffled hooting continued from between her teeth as Jata beamed round at the group—*I think what Shining Teeth is trying to say, is that, if we don't get a volunteer, each creature will get to be a meal. Is that right, Shining Teeth? Yup. She's nodding. That's right.*

Hod slowly came forward as the rest of the animals digested what she'd said. Hod could see the animals all thinking the same thoughts.

Not *have* a meal? No. *Be* a meal. Right. That's not good. No. Don't want to be a meal. Want to *have* a meal. Definitely. That's what most of those creatures were thinking. That's what Hod was thinking, too.

Hod went straight to Shining Teeth—*Put the bandicoot down.*

Shining Teeth said—*Mmmmfff?* and looked at Jata.

Jata said—*I think she means 'I beg your pardon?' Is that it? Did you say, 'I beg your pardon?'*

Shining Teeth growled and shook her head.

—*Too polite?* Jata said—*You mean, you just said, 'What?' Like that? Rudely? 'What?'*

Shining Teeth said—*Mmmmmfff,* and swung her mouthful up and down in an agreeable way.

—*This is a sanctuary. Put down the bandicoot,* said Hod—*I'll volunteer.*

Shining Teeth spat out the little stripy creature. There wasn't a cut on him but he was slimy with spit. He lay on the ground momentarily disorientated before he jumped up, honking—*Crikey! Let me at 'em, I'll give her what-for!*

Hod looked down at him and pushed him none too gently with his great big wallaby foot—*Take a rest, honker.*

The bandicoot shut up, squeezed in with the others and curled into a ball next to a wombat, only occasionally snuffling in outrage. Then Hod turned away, left the huddled animals and went over to a nearby low brick wall. He sat down and leaned back on the wall, clearly expecting the croc to follow him.

Shining Teeth looked over at Jata and then to the other members of the croc harem. She had some reluctance to deal with someone as arrogant as this wallaby. Didn't he have any idea who they were? What they were? Why wasn't he as scared of them as the others?

Shining Teeth dragged her huge hulk over to Hod and lowered her long frame to the ground beside him with a bump—*I suppose I should thank you, volunteer, but I don't know how.*

Hod had no intention of making it easy for her. He looked into the distance. After a decent pause he added, carelessly—*Doesn't surprise me.*

—*You're a cheeky bastard, aren't you? You might want to mind your manners.* Shining Teeth replied—*No time to waste. Down to business. Ever heard of Ektek?*

Hod apparently still had not a care in the world. He took his time answering—*Everyone's heard of Ektek.*

—*Have they, now?*

—*Everyone's born knowing those stories. Ecology, technology, great legends...*

—You'll be surprised to know they actually exist, said Shining Teeth.

—Is that right?

—Yes. And I've met them.

—All of them?

—Just a couple. Came in a plane.

—What were they like?

—Big bird. Cockatoo maybe. Black. Pale black. What's that called?

—Grey?

—Is it? Shining Teeth wasn't used to accepting knowledge from others—*Grey?* She looked at the fluffy creature sideways. He confused her. Why wasn't he scared of her?

—Sure. Pale black is grey, said Hod.

—Grey bird and a frog. Tiny, tiny frog. Activists. Joke, eh?

—Eh.

—Yeah. Who'd'a' thought? Shining Teeth couldn't work this fluffy renegade out at all. Was he being sarcastic? She stared at Hod, waiting for something clearly disrespectful, watching for the proof of his complete madness.

Hod, for his part, took his time playing innocent. He was the picture of someone who would do all he could to assist the poor crocodiles in their distress—*That's Ektek?*

—Yeah. A frog. In an aeroplane. Wild, eh?

—So? Hod simply couldn't be more unconcerned—*What happened?*

—Doesn't matter what happened. What matters is you go and find them.

—You want me to go out into the world and find Ektek. A frog in a plane.

—Couldn't be more straightforward than that.

—Couldn't it?

—Right. We seem to have a deal. Better get on with it. As for us, this sanctuary isn't feeling so good. No place to hide. Shining Teeth got to her feet—*I'll go and ask these miserable creatures if they know anywhere else we can stay.*

—You could, said Hod.

—That's right. No doubt I will.

—Or I could.

—You could?

—I'm not sure your approach is very effective. Are you?

—You don't think my approach is very effective. My approach.

—You know what you want. I can get it for you. If you ask, they'll freeze. Seem petrified already to me. Do you really think you'll get much out of them?

—*Listen, wallaby. I don't know why, but I'm going to agree with you. I'm going to let you talk to them. But any sign of a trick and you're dinner. On toast. Understand?*

Hod looked her square in the eyes. He saw the flames of the dog he'd made go woof. The croc's eyes were the same colour and they burnt but Hod didn't flinch—*So? You need a place to stay. Anything else?*

—*Food. And then you'll go find Ektek for us. Right?*

Hod listened to the deep voice of Shining Teeth with his eyes on the increasing daylight and he nodded—*Whatever.* He moved to the terrified group of creatures and spoke—*She's asked me to speak on her behalf. I know we're all scared but...*

—*You're not.*

Hod acknowledged the possum with a nod. He was, of course, shit-scared, but there was no point in freaking out when he needed to concentrate on survival—*We're all scared. The crocs need some food. They need somewhere out of sight to rest. Any ideas?*

—*Then what?*

—*Then they'll leave us alone.*

The little slimed bandicoot honked and then spoke up—*This isn't where I sling me hook normally, see...*

Hod stared—*What're you doing here, then?*

—*Ah... bit delicate...*

—*Undercover?*

—*In a manner of speaking...*

—*Where do you live?*

—*Nearby. Close. Easy walk. Thing is, I can get them food and I can get them out of here but we can't muck around.*

Hod looked at the group and dismissed them—*You creatures got cages to go to?* All the animals dispersed, fast, leaving the bandicoot and the crocs facing Hod. The crocs flicked uncertain looks at each other but Shining Teeth had decided this Hod was capable enough. She nodded at the bandicoot—*Show us the food.*

The bandicoot led them to the food station, a brick building near the centre of the parkland. He broke in easily, climbing onto a wall to reach the door lock and using a key he found hidden in a flowerpot.

The crocodiles shifted restlessly. They were very, very hungry.

Hod entered the kitchen with the little bandicoot who pointed to the freezer—*Reckon you could get that opened?* Hod struggled for a bit before opening the lid. He surveyed the piles of food, unable to distinguish between the colourful wrappings—*What are you thinking?*

—*Croc lollipops.*

—*Huh?*

—*There. See? Frozen chickens all round? Ought to keep their mouths shut while we're on the road. See if you can roll 'em out.*

Hod and the bandicoot kept the crocs busy as they tipped out five frozen chickens and rolled them to the door. The crocodiles looked absurd, each holding a heavy frozen lump in their jaws. Hod looked over to the bandicoot as they shut the feed station door and left, quickly and quietly—*Like your style, honker.*

—*Right back at 'cha,* said the little bandicoot.

—*Name's Hod. You?*

—*FJ.*

—*FJ. All right, FJ. Got a plan?*

—*No. You?*

—*No.*

—*Room to move, then.* FJ spoke hopefully—*That's something, isn't it?*

—*Nup,* said Hod—*That's nothing. We've got nothing at all.*

—*They don't have to know that.*

—*Zed. Do you never give up?*

—*Never.*

Chapter Twenty-two

I

After the thrill of the tattoo, ants and beetles mingled together on the forecourt of the Ektek hangar area. The blended colours and shapes mixed into a brilliant moving mosaic. Behind the excited throng, three chimpanzees climbed the rope-ladder to the airship.

In the bridge, Helmut was a wreck; his neck unsteady, his eyes un-focussed, still gabbling—*... time to go, my darling one. I'll see you in heaven. I'll bring you a bouquet of comets. I'll find you. I'll recognise you at once and we'll come home to heaven. It will be beautiful in...*

The three chimpanzees lined up to watch him. Two of the chimps were bigger. Both of these were male and appeared to be restraining the smaller female. She studied Helmut. She recognised a snapped mind when she saw one.

The males conferred—*Don't think we're going to get anywhere with this guy.*

—Come on, Chimera. We got to go. Antenna's not here.

—But we only just got here. Chimera smiled at Helmut. She played cute and coy and moved toward him in a sashaying curtsey. The burly males moved after her. They held onto her arms.

—Take me with you, Granddad. You need someone to look after you, don't you, I can see that.

The guards tightened their hold and immediately she reacted, struggling pathetically, checking over her shoulder to see if Helmut had noticed her. He hadn't, of course.

She said, softly—*Ow, that hurt me, boys,* and then she cried, fetchingly. The tears filled up her eyes and ran down her face and dripped onto her fur.

The males were not impressed—*Come on, come on.*

—Not interested, sweetheart.

—Pull yourself together.

—We've seen your crap acting before.

Chimera gathered herself together with a big sniff and wiped her nose on the arm of a big, muscular hairy guard. He flinched and looked down at the snail trail in disgust. She looked up at her captors, flickering her eyelashes—*Can't we all sit down and talk to the nice bird for a little while? He seems lost. Don't you, Helmut? I've heard so much about you. Aren't you, like, the leader here?*

The cassowary appeared completely unaware of the chimpanzees. He continued blithering—*… Lonely… In trouble… Starving. Deep space… Cold. Up there by herself… All she wants… Get back to earth… Has to happen…*

—Well? What's stopping you? Why don't you go and see her? I'll come too. I can help. I could look after you. Hey, we could just go off together. You don't need her if I'm around to take care of you…

—That's it. The larger chimpanzee looked over to his partner and they nodded. It was time to leave. He turned to Helmut—*Sorry to disturb you, Helmut. We won't take any more of your time.*

The two guards took firm hold of Chimera and urged her on—*Come on, Chimera.*

—Let's find Antenna.

—We're leaving.

—Gee, that's such a shame. Be seeing ya, Helmut! See ya in heaven!

The two males dragged the female towards the door and pushed her down the rope ladder again, one guard in front and the other behind—*Get going. There's no sympathy for your act here,* said one guard.

—By Zed, you'd think you'd leave it alone now. You don't have to stir everyone you meet just for fun, said the other.

Chimera swayed on the ladder. She fluttered her eyelashes at no one in particular. It was just her way—*Why not?* She climbed down a few more rungs and looked out over the assembled Ektek creatures below her—*What have I got to lose?*

II

The hangar still bustled with creatures congratulating each other on a fantastic fly-past. The beetles were shiny with pride. The zoo creatures hadn't seen anything like it - ever. Ants rushed over to congratulate their friends. Tiny hands clapped tiny backs. It had been a great show. Well worth all that work; all those rehearsals. All judged the tattoo to be a triumph.

Spark, a young Christmas beetle and security apprentice, ran over to Antenna, closely followed by his master, Torque—*Antenna? Did you see me?*

—*I did, Spark, I did. I was up in the airship.* Antenna indicated the huge craft, tethered at the mouth of the cavern.

Spark looked up at the machine—*Did it look cool from up there?*

—*It did.*

—*Did Helmut like it?*

—*Yeah, Spark. I think so.*

—*Couldn't really tell, though, could you? I mean, he's not really all there, is he.*

—*That's enough of your lip, young collie.* Torque wheeled the young beetle out of the way—*Cheeky young larva. You hold your mandible unless spoken to, or else.*

—*That's okay, Torque,* said Antenna—*Well done. Please congratulate the stage management team for me.*

—*Who'll be giving the speech, Antenna? Is it to be Helmut?*

—*Helmut's not…*

—*Not quite up to it. No. No, of course not. Well then. Who else is there?* Torque studied Antenna carefully—*Who do all the creatures look up to? Who knows everything about everything that goes on?* Torque waited for Antenna to catch up. When she didn't he added—*What about you? You could do it.*

—*Me?*

—*That's right, Antenna.* Torque nodded—*You. Someone's got to bring everyone together and you are perfectly capable. You're the one.*

Spark agreed—*Yeah, Antenna, you could do it!*

This comment earned Spark a tap on the head from Torque's antennae—*Did I ask for your opinion, raw novice?*

—*No but…*

—*Well? Keep it to yourself, if you please. Honestly. You're more trouble than my job's worth.* Torque turned back to Antenna—*Antenna. The creatures need to hear some reassurances. They need to hear from you. You're their senior leader now.*

—*I am?*

—*You are.*

—*This is too much.* Antenna bowed her head, thought for a bit and then straightened. It was true. Someone had to speak to all these animals about the fallen ones, not just in the past, but the animals that continued to fall; and might fall, even yet. She sighed and then stood straighter.

She moved forward, carefully avoiding the ants still milling around underfoot and took up position on a rostrum usually used for fixing the small steam car. She waited and watched until the creatures realised she was there. Torque and Spark moved amongst the crowd, shushing and pointing her out. Other creatures hushed each other. She waited until she had their attention. This was a serious duty. Min's memory, Hod's desertion and Helmut's mental defection weighed deep in her. She looked at the strange mix of creatures in front of her and began— *Thank you, Ektek. Friends. Thank you all for being here today to remember Min. I'd like to thank the beetles for their extraordinary display. Ektek is proud to count such skilled piloting and loyal fellowship on our team. The ants, too, revealed their wonderful marching technique with precision and good humour. I am only glad that we can see those talents put to use in the name of celebration; celebrating a life lived among us. Today we are here because one of us, one of Ektek, one of our own, has fallen. Her name was Min.*

Antenna took a deep breath. Some of her listeners wondered if she was going to be able to finish… She straightened her spine and continued—*Min was our last Leadbeater's possum, Min was our fairy possum and Min was our head engineer. Min was my best friend. It is Min's life that we commemorate with all your dazzling skills in the dawn.*

Together with our beetle and ant ancestors, Ektek was founded by a group of animals in the Australian section of this zoo. Gradually, those original animals, our parents, have gone. We give thanks to all of them for their vision and their hard work in the beginning and their inspiration that keeps us fuelled and ready to help any animal in need. Now, far too early, we must also farewell Min. My friend Min was a delicate creature of the night and of the forest. She was the last known of her species, which was why she had become so valuable to humans.

—Who's going to be next? A voice came from the back of the crowd. Antenna didn't understand the question. In fact, she was amazed to have been interrupted at all. She squinted up over the group.

Torque lifted his head and tried to place the voice. Could he recognise it? Spark took off and flew around the group, trying to find who had spoken.

Antenna gazed at the animals, nonplussed. Many of the creatures turned, following her gaze, looking to see who had spoken.

—The next? The next what? asked Antenna—*Head engineer?* She couldn't imagine the speaker was asking who would be the next to die. Surely none of the creatures here wanted to think about that now? They all knew there would be a next to die. They were endangered, after all. Everyone would die; sooner rather than later, probably. But it wasn't something you brought up in the middle of a memorial speech, was it? Antenna stared at the animals blankly, confused.

Still unidentified, the voice shouted again—*Nah, nah, nah, nah; the faunal emblem?*

This, she wasn't expecting—*The faunal emblem?* repeated Antenna, none the wiser.

—*Yeah, nah, you know, how Leadbeater's possum was the faunal emblem? Well, they gotta get a new species, right? They won't want an extinct species as an emblem, will they?*

—*Yeah, too embarrassing for them, ain't it,* chimed in another voice.

—*Way, way too embarrassing... How could they have killed the last of their very own faunal emblem? How out of control are they?*

Antenna looked around desperately through the hubbub of agreement and derision and lifted her voice up a level—*It's nothing to do with us,* she said—*We're here today...*

—*Yes, it is.* The crowd shifted and still no one in particular could be identified as the speaker.

Antenna was beginning to get annoyed. She felt that the dignity of the moment, the cherished memory of her friend, was besmirched—*It is for human governments to decide.*

—*It's on their website. Says so on the sign outside the nocturnal house. Have a look. It'll tell you. It's worth your while being the faunal emblem.*

Antenna looked for a way to end this debacle—*It's not the time or place to talk about this.*

—*When is?*

—*Let her finish,* shouted Torque.

Antenna glanced gratefully at him and then looked down at the crowd—*We can talk about it, of course, but this is a time for Min.*

—*Well, who would she want to take over, then?* came another interjection.

Antenna held up her forepaw and raised her voice yet again—*We can never know. We're supposed to be thinking of her and her achievements; how she came to know so much about engines and computers and how she was able to fix even the most complex systems, such as our satellite link, which keeps us connected to the rest of the world. I don't know what we'll do without her.*

—*What about the tiger quoll?*

—*What?*

—*The tiger quoll'd make a great faunal emblem.*

—*Yeah! You would say that, Carney!* another voice interrupted—*You are a tiger quoll!*

A titter of general amusement arose and then, another, deeper, voice was heard—*I reckon diamond pythons are better suited to represent the state...*

—*Everyone knows it's going to be the corroboree frog.*

—*It is?*

—*Antenna?* One of the large male chimpanzees spoke from the very edge of the crowd, nearest to the rostrum where Antenna stood. She looked around anxiously at the sound of the commanding tone.

—*Yes?* said Antenna, almost glad for an interruption that didn't concern faunal emblems.

The three chimpanzees stood together to one side of the crowd. Chimera was posing and smiling at various creatures. Her guards watched her, nonplussed. She was incorrigible, really she was.

One of the males said—*We've got a problem.*

—*Yes?*

—*We're sorry, but we've waited long enough.*

The other male stepped forward and added—*We need to talk with you, privately.*

—*Okay, wait.* Antenna turned back to the crowd and raised her voice again—*Well, thank you, to all our beetles and to our ant squadrons…*

Her erstwhile audience had by now broken into individuals and each clump of creatures was absorbed in their separate discussions. They paid Antenna no heed at all as she finished—*… and thanks to you, Min, wherever you are. We will never forget. Thanks, everyone.* Antenna got down from the rostrum and the hum of conversation closed over where she had been, like bubbles in a creek.

—*There's a lot to recommend being a faunal emblem,* the sooty owl, Sweep, hooted as Antenna finished speaking.

Thumper the long-footed potoroo, agreed—*Good publicity…*

—*You get to be on stamps…*

—*… tea towels…*

—*… official government greeting cards…*

—*Yeah, and you get,* said Rick, the Orbost spiny crayfish—*… a breeding program.*

The crowd found this most amusing.

—*Why're you interested in that?* Carney was laughing with the rest of them—*Ya dreaming if ya reckon anyone would want to breed with you.*

—*I heard they'll be making a new state-of-the-art enclosure to try to save the species after they stuffed up the Leadbeater's possum,* said Spill, the diamond python.

—*Yeah! I heard that, too,* said another.

—*It's more than that, ain't it. You get a chance to become an icon.*

—*What's an icon?*

—*Why, iconic, of course.*

—*Iconic?*

—*Is that good?*

—Iconic is very, very good. Everyone wants to be iconic. Trust me. If corroboree frogs get to be the emblem, all we'll hear about is corroboree frogs. Everything is going to go black and yellow and froggy. You just wait and see.

As the hubbub of faunal emblem discussion continued amongst the creatures of Ektek, Antenna approached the chimpanzees who were waiting patiently. She sighed when she recognised Chimera. She had guessed the deputation might be about this particular beast—*Hi, guys. What's happening?*

—Thanks for your time, Antenna. We've got to talk to you about...

—... her. The larger chimpanzee moved his head to indicate Chimera. The two males drew Chimera away from the tempting faunal emblem discussions and pushed her towards Antenna—*We've just had enough, Antenna. Something's got to give.*

Chimera, whose attention had drifted to the iconic arguments in the background, sucked in an affronted gasp—*Oh, at least you could speak to me personally! It's so rude talking about creatures in front of them. I am here, after all! There's no need to be impolite, is there?*

The two burly chimpanzees stood on either side of her and held her arms. Chimera was smiling like a beauty queen but then, Antenna had met her before and had never been impressed. The male chimpanzees were well over Chimera and shook her—*Oh, will you just be quiet for once in your life?*

One of the males said to Antenna—*She's got to go.*

—We all met and decided. She can't stay with us any more.

—There's been that many arguments. She just creates divisions and conflict...

—She's been trouble from the very beginning.

Antenna nodded. She'd heard. She looked at the three chimps and took a breath as she wondered what to do.

But she didn't have the time to wonder long.

—Antenna! Antenna! Zip shouted as she ran—*Antenna!*

—What now? Antenna muttered under her breath.

—It's Helmut! Zip shouted—*Look! No! Look up! Up!*

Antenna stepped back and looked up. Outside the hangar, up in the air, the airship was moving. Helmut seemed to have cast off the craft and was leaving the hangar area.

Zip said—*He's loosed the ropes from the ship rather than untying from the ground.*

Antenna shouted back at Zip—*How will he be able to tie up anywhere?*

—There's rope on board. At least, there was when I last looked. He'll be able to land, wherever he goes.

—But where's that? He's got no supplies. He's got no food! He can't go off by himself! He's confused! We've got to stop him! Antenna ran behind Zip who jumped up and took to the air. She watched as Zip caught up with the airship. Zip tapped on the bridge window as the airship continued on its relentless way. She shouted and flapped her wings loudly. She fluttered around the airship. She tried getting into the lower entrance as well as the normal door way but Helmut had apparently had enough foresight to bar the entry points and would not meet Zip's eye as she fluttered around the airship.

Scattered across the Ektek grounds, Antenna and the other creatures looked up, shading their eyes with their paws or their tails. Some of the beetles had also taken to their wings, giving the airship a tinsel trail, but they could not catch up. The air was filled with much calling and shouting and calamity.

The airship floated further away. Zip followed for some distance, swooping around and over the craft, to no avail. She flew back down to Antenna and landed breathlessly—*He ignored me. It was as if he couldn't see me or hear me. He's focussed on something, I don't know what. I couldn't stop him. I couldn't get on board. I had to let him go.*

—*He's on a mission,* said Chimera—*A mission from Zed.*

Antenna looked from the airship to Chimera and then at the male chimpanzees. They shrugged and one of them said—*He was in a pretty bad way when we went up looking for you.*

—*Yeah,* said the other—*It's amazing he managed to get going at all.*

Antenna turned to Zip—*Get Bash and Crawf. We'll have to use the wingship.*

—*Right away, Antenna.* Zip took off in search of the flying team.

Antenna turned back to the trio of chimps—*As for you, Chimera, I'm sorry. It'll have to be the machine cage.*

—*What? A cage? Can this be true? My fellow animal is about to imprison me?*

—*It's safe. It's a lockable area where we keep heavy machines used for metal work.*

—*I can't believe it. You, of all creatures, putting me in prison? Prison. Do you understand what that means?*

—*Chimera. We live in a zoo. We are all incarcerated.* Antenna smiled at her—*After all, in what sense is any of us free?*

The two males looked at each other and nodded—*Ought to be prison.*

—*Too right.*

—*Best place for her.*

—*Bleeding drama queen.*

—*I'm sorry, Chimera.* Antenna looked at the chimpanzee—*I have to hear the complaint against you. I'll let you out as soon as I can.*

—*You better keep an eye on her, Antenna.* The two males spoke *sotto voce*; warning her—*I wouldn't let her out, ever. Throw away the key.*

—*You don't want to take any chances.*

Antenna acknowledged their fears with a small nod. She knew. She turned to Chimera—*This way.* Antenna led the way to a part of the hangar off where there was a gate in a metal grid wall. At her eye level, Antenna found the key hanging on the wall by the door and, with some difficulty, unlocked a padlock. The door opened with an underused screech. The two male chimps marched Chimera in and peeled her off their arms. She started to cry, glimpsing out from her damp lashes to see if she was having any effect.

The two guards slid out of the cage and Chimera was left inside. She crumpled into a dramatic, sodden heap. She sniffed and sobbed.

Antenna snapped the lock over the doorway and hung the key back on its hook. Antenna and the two guards left Chimera without a backward glance.

Chimera continued to sniff but she lifted her head to check the coast was clear. When her shrewd eyes judged the others had gone, she stopped sniffing and looked around her new home. What she saw there did not impress her; just machines, tools and other stuff for fixing machines. She got up and walked around the small enclosure, her hands trailing over containers of connectors, tins of paint and oil, and hard metal surfaces. Then she looked at the door. She moved along the fence line. Her long thin fingers reached through the bars and down to where she supposed the key hung on the wall. It was just beyond her grasp.

—*Blatta?* Chimera whispered to no one in particular—*You there?*

—*Yip,* came a little beetle-ish reply.

—*Give us a hand.*

Two antennae waved through Chimera's hair and rose up to reveal a small brown cockroach standing to attention—*'Sup, boss?*

—*Swing us over the key, would you?*

—*Key?*

—*Over there. Come on. What're ya waiting for? Hurry up.* Chimera raised her hand and Blatta jumped onto her waiting palm. Chimera transferred the cockroach carefully onto the wall near the key. Blatta took one look and gave a quiet whistle. This caused Chimera's hair to shimmy until the rest of her roach family was revealed. About twenty cockroaches of all ages and sizes watched as Chimera raised her hand again and they were all transported to the wall. They formed a chain gang and heaved against the key—*Yip, yip, yip,* said the cockroaches as they worked together—*Yip, yip, yip.*

Chimera reached and finally found purchase with her fingertips. She swung the key into her cell—*Thanks, guys.*

The cockroaches busied themselves, unscrewing the hook out of the wall and moving it closer for Chimera's convenience. They replaced the hook and smoothed over the wall. With a little bit of cockroach spit and polish, no one would ever notice that the small but crucial change had been made.

Chimera unlocked the padlock, opened the door and shuddered as the rusty screech sounded out. She spun around and, looking through the items on the shelf, found a small container of machine oil. She oiled the hinges on the door and swung the door to and fro. Silently. Smoothly. Mission accomplished.

Quietly she put the oilcan back on its shelf. She locked the padlock again and found she could easily hang the key back on the wall. Well, well, well. She held out her hand for the cockroach family to return to her warm and comfortable fur.

After they had trooped back on board and everyone was comfy again, she leaned back against the machine table and looked at her fingernails. How annoying. Her left little finger showed a tiny crack. She nibbled at it. She was in no hurry. No hurry at all.

Chapter Twenty-three

I

—*It's not that I'm impatient, bandicoot. It's just that we haven't got all day.* Shining Teeth was lying. She was impatient. Even her best friends would tell you she was always impatient, even on a good day. Just now, she was frothing keen to be leaving, which made her doubly impatient. She was raging against her confinement. She was the most impatient she'd ever been.

The sun was well up. Shining Teeth had no desire for her family to be found in the middle of a sanctuary enclosure by people with experience trapping crocodiles. She had a responsibility to the harem. They had to keep moving.

Just this one little bandicoot holding them up. She would have breathed fire if she could. Her breath was so bad that Hod imagined it could well have been flammable. He thought momentarily about the matches in his messenger bag and shrugged that off as a really bad idea. Luckily the bag was on the other side of the fence, out of temptation's way.

FJ, the Eastern barred bandicoot, struggled with the wire lacing— *Crikey!* he honked under his breath.

The five crocodiles and Hod waited by the fence. It was the same place Hod had used to break into the sanctuary. Hod made his way as close to the wire as the spikey plants would allow—*Do you want me to have a go? It was me that wired it up like that.*

FJ flashed him a doubtful look—*Um, this is how I always get in. I'll be right, ta.*

—*We found it useful, too,* said Shining Teeth.

The crocodiles were crowding FJ. He was feeling claustrophobic. He honked again but that didn't stop them asking him stupid questions.

—*So? Where do you live?*

—*Hang on a tick...*

—*And there'll be room there?*

—For all of us?

—Um... With a breath of relief, FJ finally cracked open the wire macramé—*Too right.* It seemed to take an incredibly long time as he carefully let everyone out and re-laced the fence after them.

Hod retrieved his messenger bag and joined the strange team as they journeyed across the carpark; five crocs, a yellow-footed rock wallaby and an Eastern barred bandicoot. They moved through the bush for some distance before they came to another long line of high fence.

FJ glanced round at Hod and nodded. This was it. A rotting miasma hung over the area. FJ didn't seem to notice and the crocs almost perked up when they smelled it but Hod could hardly breathe. He bent lower and choked on swells of nausea.

FJ stopped by the fence and looked around. The coast was clear. He bent down to work again. They continued into the area through a similar lacing of fence wires.

—I've got a place where I think you'll be safe. FJ led them into a maze of laneways through the wasteland. It was piled high with knotted together rubbish of all descriptions. The sun shed further light on heaps of plastic bags, furnishings smashed together with twine, broken cars and mattresses. It was a nightmare township, a sordid human rubbish tip.

Somewhere near the middle of this heap of waste was an expanse of concrete walls. It too was fenced off but the bandicoot paused momentarily before pointing to a gap in the fence. He looked at Shining Teeth and the other crocs—*There you go. Home sweet home away from home.*

The crocs looked at each other. There certainly looked to be space. Bare, cold, concrete space. It wasn't inviting, by any means, but it looked safe.

—What's the catch? Jata looked at Shining Teeth.

—Is it a trap? Damura started to move backwards.

—Who lives here? said Shining Teeth and looked around at her reptile family.

FJ shook his head in response.

The crocs didn't believe him—*No one?* said Jata.

—Nup.

—Why not? said Grater.

—Not a clue, said FJ—*We've always lived near here. Our family did. Way back before this was built. We liked where we were.*

—Maybe it's the Feng Shui? said Hod.

—*Feng what?*

—*Never mind.*

—*There's water inside,* added FJ.

—*Really?* said Grater as if this was the best news she'd had all day, which may have been the truth.

—*Not my scene,* said FJ.

—*I'm sold. Nice swim sounds perfect. I'm in.* Jata went into the building, closely followed by Damura.

Grater looked askance at FJ—*So, what's with the no swimming?*

—*Bandicoots don't like swimming.*

—*Weird.* Grater and Asunder proceeded to enter the concrete bunker area to join Jata and Damura. Soon the four crocs stood in a line looking at FJ, Hod and Shining Teeth through the fence.

Unsurprisingly, FJ seemed to want to leave them there as soon as he could—*Righto. Glad it suits. Don't think you'll get any unwanted visitors here. Toodle-oo.* When FJ turned to go, the croc grabbed hold of his bent little leg in her great big teeth—*Crikey!*

—*Not so fast, sonny,* said Shining Teeth—*Don't think you're getting away that easy. The girls can have a bit of a rest, but you and me, we're stuck together. Can't wait to meet the rest of the family. Couldn't come all this way without saying hullo, could we?*

—*Excuse me, Shining Teeth?*

Shining Teeth was annoyed at the interruption. She swung round to sneer at Hod—*What?*

—*Thought you were going to leave this to me?* said Hod.

—*Oh, we are. We are,* said Shining Teeth as she gently released FJ—*But, you know, events have made me cautious. Only reasonable, don't you think?* She turned to the harem—*You girls stay. Relax. Have a swim. I'll be back soon,* and then she smiled at FJ and Hod—*On we go.*

FJ and Hod shared a look. Nothing for it.

—*Right you are. Follow me.* FJ continued his trek through the stinking rubbish with Hod and Shining Teeth close behind.

II

The sun was overhead by the time the small parade marched through the rubbish tip; FJ in the lead, then Hod and finally Shining Teeth marched unsteadily through the refuse. They were tired to the point of stumbling. It had been a long morning for all of them. FJ stopped by a rusty old car, waited until the croc was close and said to her—*You can't come in.*

—*Oh,* Shining Teeth looked at him—*I think I can.*

—*You can't.* Having worked out he was more use to the croc alive had given FJ some guts—*Just the look of you will kill her and where will that leave you?*

—*I won't kill anything.*

—*You're a crocodile. You'll scare the crap out of them.*

—*You'd better get them used to the idea because there's five of us and we're not going anywhere until we've solved our little problem.*

FJ nodded quickly and called out—*Hooroo? Ma! Ma? You in there?*

—*Course I am.* A muffled voice came from underground—*Where else do you expect me to be?*

—*Ma. Stay where you are. Got visitors. No need to give them any food because I couldn't get any today so we're all going hungry.*

—*Oh, FJ.*

—*Yeah, sorry, Ma. Ran into a bit of trouble.*

Shining Teeth snarled—*Careful, sonny.*

Hod looked down at her—*Look, you stay here, I'll go in and talk to them. I'll let you know exactly how many are there and no one need have a heart attack.*

—*You try anything…*

—*Dead meat. Take it as read.*

—*I'll be right here*, said Shining Teeth—*Hurry. On my account.*

FJ led the way into the car that acted as an entrance into a tunnel leading down under the ground.

Hod found it a tight squeeze but he'd been brought up in the Ektek passageways under the zoo. As they squeezed round the corners, FJ asked Hod—*What the hell are we going to do? Tell me? What? How can we get away from her?*

—*We'll think of something.*

—*Oh, we really, really, have to do that sometime. Soon.*

—*You have my word as a wallaby.*

—*Hi, Ma.* They had arrived in a cave. FJ and Hod peered around the dim space. The family shifted and squawked in the gloom. FJ's mother bounded over and honked with delight—*Where have you been? I've been worried…*

—*So that's where you get that cute honking from…* Hod whispered—*Runs in the family…*

FJ decided to ignore him and speak only to his mother—*We've been a bit worried ourselves, Ma, believe me. This is Hod. We're on a reccie. He needs to meet everyone. Hey, Hod, Ma's name is Seebeck.*

—*Hi, Seebeck.*

—*Hod. You need to meet everyone?* asked Seebeck.

—*Yeah.*

—*Because…?*

—*You don't want to know the details.* FJ shook his head—*Not right now, anyway.*

Seebeck looked confused—*Well, your brother's not here. He's with your Dad and Chamley.*

—*Rightoh*, said FJ, then to Hod—*My brother's called Duffy and Dad is Rylah. Chamley is my sister's bloke.*

—*Your sister's here*, said Seebeck and indicated a small barred bandicoot curled around a group of children.

—*Serena.*

—*Hi, Serena*, nodded Hod.

—*Serena's kids. There's three from a couple of litters ago. Last one, what? Serena?*

—*What?*

—*How many kids in your last litter? I mean, you know…*

—*You mean born alive. These are them. Just the three.*

Hod smiled and nodded at the kids but he couldn't help staring at their disfigurements. Each young bandicoot had either a limb missing or twisted in some way; one was obviously blind…

—*'Course. So that's about everyone living here. The other kids have got their own cars now.*

—*Thanks, Seebeck. Nice to meet you.*

—*Thanks, Hod. I think it's nice to meet you too, only, I'm not sure.*

FJ opened his mouth to explain but Hod interrupted him.

—*We'd best report*, said Hod—*FJ'll explain everything when he gets back. But you'd better all stay here.*

—*I'll be home in a tick. Hod's right, Ma, don't let anyone go out tonight. Get Dad and Duffy to stay in when they get back, too.*

—*FJ, I don't know what's going on and I don't think I like it. But be careful. Whatever it is.*

—*We will, Ma.*

Hod watched the elderly female and tipped her a small nod as he turned to leave.

FJ and Hod clambered back into the tunnel, leaving the Eastern barred bandicoot family flummoxed and not very comforted.

III

Shining Teeth was tired. She was standing on her hind legs, trying to see into the car—*About time*, she murmured when Hod and FJ made their appearance at the car windows.

Hod didn't waste any time with his report—*Rylah is Dad, Seebeck is Mum. Serena's his sister, her bloke is Chamley and they've got three kids living here.*

—*And me,* said FJ.

—*No show without FJ. Wouldn't forget you, don't worry. That seems to be all that's required, thank you. Five adults, three kids. Nice. Reasonable meal. Have to make sure you're all fed up, though. Don't like a skinny dinner. Too many bones between the teeth.* Then she smacked her crusty lips together for emphasis.

A shiver ran down FJ's spine.

Hod made no sign that he had any reaction to Shining Teeth's enthusiasm.

Shining Teeth looked at him. Ooh, he was a cool customer, that Hod. She would love to know what was going on in his head. She could see she would have to watch him very carefully indeed.

Chapter Twenty-four

The hangar underneath Bedlam Zoo was littered by spots of light like some kind of moody nightclub; light poured onto work surfaces, trained into the space by solar reflecting tubes in place high above the caverns, beamed and bounced from mirror to mirror in a cylinder pushed through hard rock. The surrounding stonewalls were smooth and rounded. The place was vast. It was filled with activity on this day; noises of building, refuelling and ticking of beetle mental 'to-do' lists buzzed through the cavern. Ants and beetles crawled over various craft, maintaining and checking systems.

A pre-flight check was almost complete on the wingship and its tiny accompanying plane. The beetles played verbal tennis with their inspection processes—*Throttles?*

—*Primed.*

—*Mixture?*

—*Bio.*

—*Propellers?*

—*Primed and set to maximum.*

—*Fuel?*

—*Master cocks on.*

The wingship was a graceful vehicle with gently down-curving wings and an ability to travel long distances using battery power once optimum cruising altitude was reached. The smaller plane perched on top of the wingship, ready to be launched at high altitude if required.

—*Oi! Crawf?* Manifold, a bombardier beetle, stepped off the little plane balanced on top of the wingship—*Right to go, if you are?*

—*Hullo, said* Crawf, a large palm cockatoo. He looked up at her from checking the tyres on the landing wheels—*Thanks, Manifold. You've done a great job, as usual.*

—*Hope you find him.*

—*So do I.* Crawf's hair feathers were held back and perky. His red face marking was bright. This rare example of the largest cockatoo in the world was waiting, somewhat impatiently, for his mini co-pilot to turn up—*Now all I need is a navigator.*

—*There you go,* Manifold spotted some action down the hallway— *Think your wait is over,* she chuckled—*Check it out.*

Crawf looked up across the hangar to see Spark flying directly at him and shouting—*He's on his way.*

—*Hullo?* said Crawf—*About time.*

A strange miniature parade made its way down the hangar towards the wingship. Spark was the leader; because he was young and energetic he could continually fly to Crawf and then back again to Bash. Bash, the missing navigator, was a corroboree frog; small, shiny, black and yellow; lolloping along in his small frog kind of way, towing something. Then, bringing up the rear, Torque flustered and flew and nagged—*Hurry, hurry, they're waiting. As if I don't have enough to do without having to chase you all over the zoo. You're big enough and ugly enough to remember where you're supposed to be by yourself, aren't you? When do you kids grow up, I ask you?*

—*It's okay, Torque. I'm here now. Thanks for looking after me. You won't have to any more. Okay? Is that a deal?*

—*It's going to have to be, young frog, because it's simply more than my job's worth to have to run your life as well as mine…*

—*Great. Deal then.* Bash swung away to the wingship—*See ya, Spark. Ta, Torque.*

Spark waited until Torque, seeing that Crawf was ready to take charge, peeled off. The two beetles headed back towards the control room and a slight altercation could be heard as they flew—*I could have done that, Torque.*

—*Oh, you could, could you?*

—*You didn't need to. I'm perfectly capable of organising Bash…*

—*When you can blow that fancy shiny beetle nose by yourself, it'll be time enough for you to handle some of these reprobates by yourself, you young ingrate…*

As Bash neared the wingship, Crawf could see he was towing a little red wagon. The wagon contained a rolled-up yellow ribbon—*Yo! Crawf!*

Crawf leaned on the pilot's door as Bash struggled with the bulk of the fabric, getting it out of the wagon and heaving it up to the wingship. It was black and yellow, the same colour scheme as the frog—*Hullo, Bash.*

Bash managed to manoeuvre the rolled ribbon up to the top of the wingship—*Come on, Crawf. Lend us a wing.*

—*Hullo? What for?*

Bash proceeded to hop and clamber onto the roof and attach the banner to the tail of the little plane, like an infant nesting on the roof of the wingship—*My banner.*

Crawf eyed all this effort cautiously. The ribbon was bigger than Bash by a large margin. He tilted his grey head and his long head feathers sloped to one side - giving him a floppy emo look—*Your, what-say?*

—*Banner.*

—*Hullo?*

—*I've made this banner to fly out behind the plane to let people know the corroboree frog should be the new faunal emblem.*

—*You can't do that.*

—*Yes, I can.*

—*You can't. That's not what Ektek is about, is it?*

—*Isn't it? Why not?* Bash, determined nothing would stop his advertising campaign, continued to tie the banner's straps round the base of the plane by himself.

—*Bash? Hullo?* Crawf continued to watch with growing concern—*How's that going to affect the balance of the plane?*

—*It won't.*

—*You don't know that.*

—*Neither do you.*

—*You just can't do it.*

—*Watch me.* Bash finished fastening and straightened up—*Come on, we've got to stop Helmut.* The tiny yellow-and-black frog clambered into his little plane, perched like a dragonfly on top of the wingship.

Crawf watched, aghast, before he reluctantly climbed in the window of the wingship. He clambered to his own perch in the cockpit where he made himself ready, placed the communication headphones over his ears and fastened his safety harness muttering—*Oh, Bash, I swear you'll be the death of me…*

The small plane was best launched when the wingship was airborne. Bash would release the plane from the wingship's roof and guide it off in his own distinct flight path. Bash could communicate with his co-pilot through an intercom system between the two craft that, together with the airship, served as Uptek—*Do we know where we're going?*

—*You mean, do we have a plan?* Crawf prepared to get the wingship moving out of the hangar—*Other than Zip's initial direction, no, we've got absolutely no idea where Helmut's gone. He could be anywhere. Let's get radio contact.* Crawf leaned forward to the mic—*Hullo? Ektek come in, please? Over.*

—*We could find him straight away,* Bash said through the inter plane coms.

—*We could,* said Crawf—*Let's hope so, Bash. Let's hope so. Ektek? Hullo? Come in, please. Over.*

—*We are refuelled and all that stuff?* asked Bash.

—*Come in, Ektek. This is Uptek preparing for take-off. Over.*

—*Crawf? Sorry I missed the pre-flight.*

—*Don't worry your tiny little amphibian brain about that, Bash. Both wing-ship and plane are ready for hours of flying.*

Bash considered the 'tiny little amphibian brain' remark. On any other day he'd take offence but he decided he'd already pushed his luck by being late, dealing with his banner and not knowing the pre-flight details. He should probably stay quiet for a bit. Only, that was not his way and he pushed on—*If we did find him straight away, then seeing as we're refuelled and all that, we could go on a flypast through some busy streets on the way back home so that people could see my banner...* Interrupting Bash's happy forward planning, the radio sizzled and Antenna said—*Uptek, we read you loud and clear. Over.*

—*Any radio contact? Over.*

—*Helmut not in communication at all. Good luck finding him. Over.*

—*We're going to need it.* Crawf bent toward the mic—*Check Ektek, this is Uptek requesting taxi clearance, over.*

—*You got it, Crawf. Over,* said Antenna's tinny radio voice through the speaker.

—*Temperatures suitable for slipping,* said Bash, as he monitored the dials and equipment on the dashboard of the little plane.

Crawf surveyed his own series of flashing lights, dials and buttons. All systems were go. He flicked forward a series of switches and shifted more comfortably on his perch.

Outside the wingship Manifold could be heard shouting—*All clear above and astern.*

—*Contact,* said Crawf.

—*Roger,* said Bash.

Manifold shouted again—*Take-off clearance.*

Crawf began to taxi towards the hangar entrance. The radio fizzed again. Antenna's fuzzy voice echoed through the pilot's cabin—*Bring him home. However you find him. Over and out.*

Crawf nodded. He knew what she meant. Alive or dead.

Chapter Twenty-five

Hod and FJ accompanied Shining Teeth, through the maze of crushed multi-coloured stinky rubbish, back to her bunker. As they approached the fence from the different angle, Hod caught sight of some strange circular symbols posted around the perimeter. Yellow-and-black triangles arranged around a central circle in the colours of the corroboree frog: yellow and black. What could it mean?

Hod looked to FJ who completely ignored him as they marched along. Hod decided silence was the better part of this current tactic and kept walking. Soon back at the bunker, they were at the grim concrete entrance when Shining Teeth looked up at the two furry creatures—*You. Wallaby. With me.*

—*You know what?* said Hod, with all the nonchalance he could muster.

—*I know what I just said and you're annoying me by this hesitation. You don't want to annoy me, do you?*

—*If it's all the same to you, I'll bunk in with FJ and see you in the morning.*

—*Do you really think I'd let you do that?*

—*I'll be there.*

Shining Teeth stood and stared at them. She lowered her head and drilled them with her burning-eye energy—*You'd better.*

The wallaby and the bandicoot nodded and moved away.

Shining Teeth turned and entered the building. She paused in the doorway and then she turned to watch the two creatures leave. After a respectable time she started out after them, very quietly, as only the great ambush hunters can creep.

Hod and FJ moved like sleep walkers until they thought they were out of sight. Then they both ran and jumped and shook their mammal bodies like shorn lambs. By the time they'd calmed down, they had come back to the symbols around the fence line. Hod stopped and looked at FJ—*What do these mean?*

—*Those patterns mean something? I thought they were just decoration.*

—*Oh, I doubt that very much. Look at this sign.* Hod sounded out a word printed boldly on a nearby sign—*D...A...N...G...E...R... Danger. Tell us something we don't know.*

FJ looked confused—*Danger? What does that mean?*

—*You know; warning, we could die, be frightened, let terror rule your life,* said Hod.

—*I don't need a sign to tell me that. We're all endangered, all the time and do you know, those crocs aren't making me feel any safer.*

—*Funny that. We'd better get you back to your family,* said Hod.

—*They'll be so every-way which-way, what with you asking Ma all those questions before.*

As they walked on, Hod appeared to struggle with himself in some kind of internal debate. After a while he looked at the smaller creature—*Hey, FJ, do you mind me asking a personal question?*

—*No worries, mate. Can't be much more personal than you saving my life, can it.*

—*What's with your hand?*

FJ shrugged and looked at him—*Dunno. How I was born.*

—*And your sister's kids? Did one of them have a leg missing?*

—*Yeah. No one's fault. Just born that way.*

—*Any others?*

—*Guess most of the kids got some kind of problem, one way or another. I'm one of the lucky ones. I get to go out hunting for food. Because I can.*

—*Your parents don't have any problems?*

—*My sister always has trouble with her litters. Some are born dead. The ones that are born alive, well, sometimes nature goes a different way.*

—*Nature.*

—*Why are you asking?*

—*Just thinking.*

They travelled on in silence. Apart from the oppressive smell, the day had turned out beautifully. A bright blue sky was smeared with fluffs of cloud. Shrieking seagulls wheeled over the rubbish tip and the sun glinted from their wings.

Near the bandicoot's car, Hod paused and looked over at FJ—*Did you ever think there might be something in your tip?*

—*What you on about? There's heaps of 'something' in the tip. Tons. There's meant to be. It's a tip. For rubbish.*

—*I mean, some particular kind of rubbish, something that might have caused this...* And he gently touched FJ's hand with his paw.

FJ moved his hand away—*Like what?*

—*Some kind of chemical maybe? Something in the water?*

—We don't drink water.

—Really? Right. In the air then?

—There's laws against that stuff now. No one can just dump anything any-where.

—Right. FJ?

—Yeah?

—You ever had kids?

—Nah. Never seems to come to much. You?

—Not a great idea to bring kids into this world.

—You're not answering the question.

—You ever think your family should move?

—Ma would never leave. You're still not answering the question.

—Even if staying meant her grandkids weren't healthy?

—It may not be healthy, but at least it's safe. No cats in here. No foxes.

—Just five crocodiles and some kind of pollution that's causing birth defects in your family.

—Birth defects?

—Maybe, I don't know. I'm not sure. What about we give Ektek a call and speed this whole thing up?

FJ looked nervous—*Ya don't reckon that's bringing them into a trap?*

—Maybe. But then again it could just give us some control back.

—We could look like we're so keen to help those bad old crocs they'll relax and let us run rings around them.

—Zed, when you put it like that, I hope we're not underestimating them.

Hod turned and looked around him - checking to see if Shining Teeth had followed them.

FJ followed his lead and they both retraced their steps - looking down the nearest corridors of rubbish. FJ relaxed soonest—*Mate, those crocs are bone tired. Stuffed, like me. They'll be snoring like volcanoes.*

Hod was still *en garde*—*Hope so.* Hod lifted his head, took a deep breath and cried out to the sky—*Ektek! Ektek! Ektek! Hey? Any beetles around? Come on. Get going. Tell Ektek we got some crocs in trouble here. Be sure to mention the crocs. Tell them to be on high alert. Be alarmed and alert.*

A dozy beetle sauntered out to the end of a screwed-up chip packet and started bouncing. By the time he'd taken four or five decent bounces he was awake and his final leap turned into a wonderful swan dive up into the air and then down again until he found a pleasing cruising altitude. He squeaked—*One*—as he sailed off into the distance.

—That's done. Hod turned to FJ—*We'd better get some rest.*

The beetle beetled on.

Shining Teeth, parked just behind a smashed Chevrolet car just one corridor away from where Hod and FJ had left off their search, smiled to herself. This was proceeding even better than she had hoped. She waddled to a vantage point overlooking the entrance point to FJ's family tunnel and settled in to rest—*Be sure to mention the crocs. Hmmm.* As far as Shining Teeth's philosophy could be stated, she certainly believed that might was right, but she also considered that, since information was power, there was nothing wrong with a nice quiet surveillance on a pleasant summer's evening.

Chapter Twenty-six

Antenna turned away from the mic and turned to face Chimera.

Zip sat on the other side of the chimpanzee in an apparently friendly manner but really guarding the chimp from making a quick exit. Zip and Antenna had no illusions about Chimera's ethics. They didn't trust her. Not one iota.

—I really don't know anything about work, Antenna. Chimera crossed her hairy legs, battered her eyelashes and simpered at Antenna—*It's just not what I'm used to. I've never had to do any kind of job before. I've just never needed to. No one's ever asked me. It simply isn't in my nature.*

—So, you're saying you're helpless, Zip couldn't help herself, she snapped—*...and you like it that way?*

Antenna agreed with Zip's exasperation. She shared a sympathetic look with Zip before turning her attention back to the chimp—*Really, Chimera, it's not that difficult. Have a good, long, hard think. What do you imagine you might be able to learn?*

When Chimera seemed at a loss, Zip said encouragingly—*It's just that you're taking up all this space, we've got beetles running after you and your cockroaches, fetching you bananas and cool drinks...*

Chimera interrupted—*... and you still haven't heard my side of the story. You just went right on ahead and believed those nasty chimps without even asking me. Why didn't you at least give me a chance? What sort of justice is that? Is that your 'Ektek way'?*

—I'm sorry, Chimera, I really am but you can see what it's like here. We've got creatures missing, we simply don't have time to call a full court... said Antenna.

—Well, let me out, then. I'm innocent until proven guilty, aren't I?

—Sure. In a perfect world, but sorry, that's not here, said Zip.

—As Zip says, we live in a zoo, Chimera. A zoo. I can't take the risk...

—What? That I'd do what they said I did?

—Killing a baby isn't exactly..., said Antenna.

—You see? It's my word against theirs! That baby was dead already!

—*Chimera. All the chimpanzees, and I mean every single last one of them, explained to me how much trouble you've been causing ever since you arrived at Bedlam.*

—*I still have a right to be heard!*

—*I also spoke to Gumfluff,* continued Antenna—*She reminded me of your behaviour on board Ontek after your rescue from the Congo. Then, we decided to give you the benefit of the doubt and I can tell you right now, the rest of the chimpanzees wish we hadn't.*

—*Gumfluff. Bah.* Chimera spoke in tones of derision—*Why would you want to believe a koala over me?*

—*Because, Gumfluff's not only the highly responsible captain of Intek, she's also my friend.*

—*So you'd better watch what you say,* added Zip—*or you might cause offence.*

—*You're all against me.* Tears welled up in Chimera's charming eyes—*You're all pals and mates and cronies together.* She poked out her bottom lip and began to cry, rather prettily—*I don't stand a chance... I'm all alone. No one cares. No one understands me.*

Antenna took in a deep breath before speaking—*I do.* Such sentiments cut deep into her own feelings of loneliness and abandonment and she stared at Chimera, wondering if the poor creature was really suffering as much as she said—*I know what it's like, Chimera,* said Antenna with such sincerity that it even shut Chimera up for a moment.

Zip watched Antenna, aware how close this subject was, and reached out to touch the numbat with a tender wingtip. Antenna smiled at Zip and then focused back on the matter to hand—*Chimera. Pull yourself together, please. I've been hearing stories about how you set one group up against the other for your own personal gain. You did it in the Congo, you did it in our chimpanzee enclosure and I don't want you to do it again. It doesn't really matter if you're innocent or guilty. It matters to me that our chimps don't want you. They told me they would not live with you again. You cannot go back to the chimpanzee enclosure whether we have a full trial or not. You simply can't go back there. So I'm asking you now. What do you want to do instead?*

Zip thought she could explain it a slightly different way—*Either you learn to pitch in with Ektek and earn your keep or we're going to have to...*

—*Get me cleared!* Chimera screamed out, real terror on her face—*That's it, isn't it! You'll get me put down!*

—*No, Chimera, no, no, that's not it. Calm down...*

—*We wouldn't do that,* said Zip although the look she fired over to Antenna implied otherwise. Behind Chimera's back, Zip looked as

173

though she was filing 'Clearing Chimera' away as a very tangible possibility and she nodded intently as she listened closely to Chimera's next words. Antenna frowned and shook her head at Zip's grinning face as Chimera ranted on—*You would. That's what those chimps told me. They said they would do it. They were going to give me over to the vet with someone's x-rays, someone with like, advanced liver cancer, or something...*

Antenna tried to calm the chimpanzee—*Chimera. You must know we're not going to do anything like that to you. Ektek will protect you, you must believe that. Ektek exists to protect animals, if it can. The chimps are very angry with you and you can't really blame them, can you?*

—*They don't like me. They're jealous. They blamed me...*

—*Save it, Chimera,* said Zip.

—*As you said, it's your word against eighteen chimps. Who would you believe if you were me?*

Chimera stopped and fluttered her eyelashes at Antenna again—*Well, at least you're my friend, aren't you?*

—*We're both your friends, Zip and I; and the other Ekteks are your friends too.*

—*I tell you what. I've had an idea. You can teach me how to use all these...*

—*Computers?*

—*Important technical things. Yes,* Chimera indicated with a flourish of her long fingers—*I could be useful, you'll see, not just a waste of space...*

—*Okay, well. That sounds reasonable, don't you think, Zip?*

—*Too right,* Zip nodded—*Anything's better than being a waste of space.*

Antenna stifled a grin and decided to strike while Chimera's interest was apparent—*We could start by showing you the website. Can you read English?*

—*I suppose I could learn?*

—*We all had to.*

—*Come on, Chimera.* Antenna turned to the computer desk—*Check this out before we take you back to your enclosure.*

—*I don't want to go back there.*

—*Tough,* said Zip.

Chimera realised she had little choice, rolled her eyes and then moved in closer to the monitor.

Antenna opened the Ektek website. The front page was surrounded by ads displaying the logos of many environmental groups. Antenna turned to look at Chimera and gestured to the ads and links—*See? Here? All these different pictures and patterns? They represent our friends; Greenpeace, Wiser Earth, Earth's Endangered Creatures, Pachamama,*

Peta, Sea Shepherd, World Wildlife Foundation, Conservation International, The Jane Goodall Institute... You heard of any of them?

—They're... human?

—Absolutely.

—Do they know you're animals?

—Not relevant, said Zip—*Could be animals themselves for all we know.*

—Jane Goodall's an animal, Chimera nodded—*I know that for a fact.*

Antenna grinned at Zip before continuing to talk to Chimera—*We do know they're all active groups that work to help animals and conserve habitat. As you can see, Ektek is part of an enormous network. We help our friends and they help us.*

Chimera looked thoughtful and nodded respectfully as her eyes flicked over the information. She was taking it all in.

—Just like we're helping you. Okay?

—Okay. Chimera bent her head and looked up from under her brow at Antenna. The gesture made her lips pout and her eyes very liquid and she raised her hand in a gracious wave—*Thank you, Antenna. I know I'm very lucky. I'm a refugee, cast out from her homeland and family, with no one to love and no one to care about me. You're so kind to me. I don't know what I'd do if you weren't here to look after me.*

—That's the point, isn't it? We've all got to look after each other.

—Ooooh, couldn't have put that any better myself, Zip laughed—*Did you get that, Chimera? Nice place to end the first lesson, wouldn't you say, Antenna? Time to go. Come on, Chimera, back in your box.* Antenna and Zip shared a sympathetic look as they urged Chimera to her feet and out of the control room—*And, please, don't even think of complaining,* said Zip.

Unheeding, Chimera began to whinge about being hungry. Antenna and Zip turned their empathy into extreme eye rolling. Nothing was ever easy in Ektek.

Chapter Twenty-seven

Helmut flew the airship high above the suburbs. Tears ran down his beak and dripped onto the console. He was alone.

He muttered continually about Jupiter and asteroids and gaseous rings and Zed as he drove the airship ever onwards.

A bird, a pigeon, flew into the fabric side of the airship with a thud and bounced away. It shrieked in pain—*Hey! Watch where you're going, you bloody galah!*

In the cabin, Helmut's head snapped back and he fell forward in a whiplash. The steering wheel wrenched to the side. Helmut shook his head and tried to move the steering wheel but it did not respond. Helmut lay his head down on the control panel. His eyes went in and out of focus. He was drifting out of control. He slid down onto the floor.

The airship sailed on, over the rooftops, over the treetops and up, up, way up, into the backlit clouds.

In the tiny dent made from the pigeon's beak the fabric threads puffed out, into a rip. The hydrogen found the weakness and began to escape with an infinitesimal hiss.

Chapter Twenty-eight

I

A miniature aperture spilled a thread of light into a tunnel full of soft darkness. Antenna lay flat down with a tight scoop of light focussed on her face. She was peering from the dark of the tunnel into the light of an enclosure that used to be her home. Now it was bustling with human movement. Zoo workers in their khaki uniforms appeared to be enlarging the space and building new housing logs. Antenna could tell by the smell that new numbats had not yet arrived. She sighed and wriggled just that bit closer to the gap. Her nose was almost poking through and might even be visible to a keen eyed worker. Yet she knew she would never be able to go in there again and she stayed just far enough back to be safe from discovery.

A small cough behind her made her jump and pull her nose back into the darkness of the tunnel—*Who's that?*

—*Just me. Spark. Thought you'd like to know the wingship's just been sighted. No sign of Bash yet.*

—*Thanks, Spark. I would like to know that. I'm coming backwards. Watch out.*

—*Don't worry about me. I'll get out of your way.*

—*How did you know where I was?*

—*Guessed.*

—*Am I that obvious?*

—*In your place? I'd want to see them.*

—*You don't have any family here either, do you?*

—*Oh, I'm good. Beetles are beetles; mainly.*

By now Antenna was able to see the Christmas beetle and they turned to move back along the tunnels freely. She looked at Spark closely—*Is there a 'but'?*

—*Well…*

—*What?*

—*Don't like to speak out of turn…*

—*But?*

—Don't know if you'd noticed?

—Noticed? What?

—The cockroaches?

—Cockroaches? What cockroaches? There's always cockroaches. Everywhere.

—Not like Chimera's buddies.

—Really?

—Yup. Her gang.

—Chimera has a gang?

—You hadn't noticed. Yeah. Her own team.

—What's wrong with that?

—Can't actually give you specifics. Just the heebie jeebies.

—Can you keep me informed? Let me know if you do get specific?

—You can see them for yourself. In her hair.

—In her hair?

—Beats fleas, I suppose.

—Or ticks, added Antenna—*Or mites, come to that,*

—Still, said Spark.

—Yeah. Still, said Antenna—*Keep me informed.*

II

The interlaced process cries of beetles rang through the hangar once again as the wingship taxied in to the parking area. Inside the cockpit, pilot Crawf ran through his own parking ritual, this time without his errant co-pilot Bash. Inside and outside the wingship was a confluence of focus and action—*Flaps in and inverters off.*

—Inverter off.

—Temperatures good for running down.

—Roger. Running down.

—Lookout, start running.

Zip waited as the wingship pulled in to the parking space. Manifold waved her signalling leaves, indicating to Crawf how far back he could reverse. Crawf never lost concentration and the vehicle came to a halt, perfectly positioned—*Roger, temperatures good for cutting.*

The beetles scuttled around the stilled vehicle.

—Prepare bow.

—Roger. Standing by starboard drogue.

—Standing by port drogue.

—Starboard drogue away and holding.

—Port drogue away and holding.

—Roger, over and out.

Immediately beetles and ants swarmed over the down-turned wings. Manifold filed away her signalling leaves and turned to assist the mechanic beetles as they assessed any possible damage to the vehicle.

Crawf scrambled down the wingship's side, his head feather crest up, signalling anger.

Zip called out—*Anything?*

—*Hullo? Helmut? Gave us the slip.* Crawf looked around the hangar—*Where is he?*

—*Bash?*

—*Is he back?*

She shook her head and together they walked out to the entrance of the hangar to scan the sky. There in the distance the little plane could just be seen. Zip pointed—*There.*

—*Right,* said Crawf.

—*You don't sound too happy.*

—*You can see for yourself.*

—*What do you mean?* asked Zip.

—*The plane. Look. Trailing behind it.*

—*What? Oh, what's that…?*

—*A banner.*

—*A banner?*

—*Show Antenna. You might want to take your friend Bash with you when he lands. About time he had a little chat with Antenna.*

Zip was puzzled. She watched Crawf march away. Little chat? What the heck was that about? She looked up and shaded her eyes with her wing. The banner fluttered against the blue sky, a yellow kite string, as the miniature plane swung nearer to the landing area.

III

Bash, Antenna and Zip stared down at the banner unfurled across the floor in the control room. The yellow ribbon held black printing; 'Corroboree frog for Emblem!'

Antenna and Zip looked at each other and then Antenna turned to stare at the tiny frog for a long moment—*Let me get this straight. You used Ektek technology without permission and for personal glorification?* Antenna waited. She stared at Bash—*Is that how you'd see it?*

—*Not exactly personal. It's for my family; for my species.*

—*For his species, no less.* Zip looked over at Antenna before turning back to Bash—*You can't deny you'd benefit as well?*

—So what if I do? I'm entitled to a bit of comfort, aren't I? I'm part of the picture, aren't I? Frogs are bloody important in the scheme of things. How else are you going to tell if water is fit to drink?

—Where did you go? You were lucky to get home. The fuel tank was empty.

—Yeah, I know. I went a long way, I mean, after we couldn't find Helmut. He could be anywhere so I figured it didn't matter where I went. Couple of people waved, so I reckon us corroboree frogs are in with a good chance...

A computer chime signalled a new message had arrived in the Ektek in-tray. Antenna's attention drifted over to the screen, even as Bash continued his defence. It was an email from PulpAss—*Isn't PulpAss that timber company?* asked Antenna.

—The ones that sell wood pulp for paper? asked Zip—*What on earth do they want from us?*

Antenna jumped up for a closer look. The email was addressed to Bash—*Bash?*

—Yo.

—It's for you.

—Me? Are you sure?

—Yeah.

—Never had an email in my life.

—Who do you know at PulpAss?

—No idea. Never heard of them.

—It says: Then Antenna read the email out loud;

```
Dear Bash,
Thanks for letting us know about that
stand of old-growth forest. PulpAss was
previously unaware of this timber and,
thanks to you, it is all destined for
the wood chippers. We have made a large
donation to Ektek in your name. Please
let us know at once if you find any
more of these trees on private land.
Love your work!
```

Antenna and Zip stared at each other. Antenna shook her head in wonderment—*Old-growth forest?*

Zip stared at Bash—*Bash?*

—It wasn't me.

—What's going on, Bash? Antenna leaned forward and took a good look at the black-and-yellow amphibian—*What have you been up to?*

—Nothing!

—Who have you been talking to?

—No one.

—But you must have.

—But I didn't!

—You flew that banner out of the plane drawing attention to yourself and to corroboree frogs. You must have kept going and made some kind of deal with this timber company. You've said you flew a long way. Maybe you flew too far.

—Obviously, said Zip—*Way too far.*

The tiny frog frowned, giving an impression of a walnut; a shiny, lacquered walnut. For a moment, it looked as though he might cry or implode but suddenly he jumped up and shouted—*But I didn't and I wouldn't and I can't believe you'd ever imagine I possibly could! How dare you! I've given my whole life to Ektek: all my dreams; all my efforts; all my energies go into helping my fellow creatures and now you're saying I'd sell old growth forests down the river? Why? Why would I do that?*

—That's not what I'm saying. It's what this timber company, this Ass is saying, They say you located a stand of trees, perfect for their industry, that they didn't know about and made it possible for them to get in and pulp the lot. How did you do it? Did you use some new technology? Worse; did you use our technology? Or, no, did you take some beetles?

—I didn't. I couldn't. I wouldn't. It's so not true. You've got to believe me.

—I'm sorry, Bash. You're going to have to stay in your tank until we sort this out.

—I always do what I'm told.

Indicating the ribbon, Antenna said—*Not always.*

Bash just shook his head in frustration.

Antenna jumped up and went to the hallway calling—*Spark? Torque? You there?*

—Yes, Antenna, said Torque—*Ready and waiting.*

—And Spark?

—Yup.

—Spark, can you please escort Bash back to his frog-quarium? Torque, a word?

As Spark and Bash headed out, Bash turned back—*I'll co-operate. I'll stay where you put me. I'll do anything. But you have to believe me, I didn't do it.*

Antenna just looked at him. She really didn't know anymore. After Hod, she couldn't tell who to trust.

—Come on, Bash, said Spark.

Zip, Antenna and Torque watched them go. Then they turned to each other, all of them confused by this mystery.

181

—*Torque, I'm going to need surveillance on the frog-quarium at all times.*

—*You don't believe him?* asked Zip.

—*Can't take the chance. Whichever way, I need to know where he is at any moment of any day.*

—*Word'll get out. There'll be talk. There always is. This is a scandal waiting to happen,* said Torque—*I should know. I've seen enough scandals round here. Living in a Zoo. Shouldn't happen to a dog.*

—*They'll blame him.*

—*That's precisely why he's going to need guarding.*

Chapter Twenty-nine

Helmut was pressed up against the window. Outside, wisps of cloud wafted past at eye level. The sky was a searing blue. If he looked down he could see a kind of red-orange skin; folds and creases, warts and bulbous nodules, wrinkles and growths. He was flying over a desert, a land that looked like the lived-in skin on the belly of a creature. Sadly he was losing buoyancy and the skin was getting closer and closer…

No one steered the ship. Helmut wept—*Where are you? Tell me where? Tell me how to find you. Tell me where? Tell me what it's like? I only want to help you, you know that, I only want to see you. To be with you. You are my divine blessed one, my star amongst the stars, my dream against wakefulness…*

The airship engine slowly puttered and coughed. The floor of the bridge tilted and Helmut slid across to the other side of the space and smacked up against the wall. The engine stopped finally. The airship began to sink.

Helmut scrabbled to remain upright. When he realised he was certainly going to crash, he covered his head with his wings and held his breath.

The impact was huge.

The noise was explosive. A huge ball of flame billowed into the air from the remaining hydrogen in the balloon.

Jets of dust spurted into the still air and debris spilled crazily over metres of dirt.

The airship cockpit was designed as a safety escape pod but it detached from the hydrogen balloon and broke open like an egg. Helmut was thrown out of the cabin. He sprawled a little way from the machine, his beak half open in the dirt. He had a small cut on his head. He shook his head as he came to. He was alive.

Helmut stood. He seemed unhurt but he was dazed. He looked at the smashed airship and smelt the fire in the air. He shook his head and turned his back to it. He began to move. He was walking on sandy dirt. Scattered rocky outcrops grew out of a vast expanse of orange grit. The vegetation was sparse.

Helmut had crashed the airship into the desert. As this fact dawned on him he also realised how thirsty he was. The idea of not having any water began to haunt him. Taunt him. He had to have water. Immediately. He coughed. His throat tightened. The air rasped down his long neck. All he could think was—*Water. Water.*

He scoured the landscape. He walked. As he walked he leaned one way and then the other and then another as he tried to balance. The ground came closer and then faded into the distance again. His vision blurred. He persevered. He had to. He wanted to survive.

Finally he found some fat fleshy plants and ate some of their bitter leaves. They tasted cool. He swayed as he stood. He kept walking. The sun baked the dusty dirt. The surface of the ground shimmered in front of him. The rocks were weird shapes in the distance. The sun drove down into his back, into the bony plate on his head. Helmut's vision began to cloud. He tripped over a rock. He was clumsy but did not fall this time. He regained his balance and he kept moving forward. Then he misjudged a step and losing the fight to keep his balance, finally, he fell, and kept falling. He had toppled over the edge of a cliff. A precipice. As he fell through the air he felt as though he were flying but he knew that was wrong. Cassowaries are flightless. He could barely move his useless wings but still, he flew.

Down, down, down, he fell, seemingly endlessly until...

OOOOPH.

He met the ground.

He lay, bent strangely, at the bottom of the rock face. He lost consciousness. The shade moved to cover him. The day turned into darkness. Night enveloped him and the stars winked at his plight.

He grew cold.

He dreamed of asteroids.

Chapter Thirty

Crawf, Antenna and Zip were busy in the shadowy Ektek centre. Crawf was bent over the radio mic, his crest feathers lying calmly flat on his head as he repeated—*Come in, Helmut. Hullo? Over.* All three creatures listened to a slight hiss in reply. They hoped. They waited. Nothing broke through. Just more hiss.

—*Come in, Helmut.* Crawf tried again, as he had been trying, again and again, for some time—*Hullo? Helmut? Hullo? Over.*

Antenna was running all six monitors in the computer phalanx. One screen featured the PulpAss website. It was a torrent of forest, logs and woodchips in gaudy images. Another screen displayed a spread sheet listing endless screeds of numbers. She was typing at a keyboard designed specially for animal paws.

In front of another keyboard, Zip scrolled through a list of PulpAss employees—*Can we work out who actually put the money in our account?*

Antenna sighed—*I'm in our bank records now. I really don't know how to trace it…*

—*Hullo? Helmut?* Crawf tried again—*Hullo? Over.*

Antenna paused in her typing and looked over to Zip—*What on earth can we do with Bash?*

—*I always say you can't trust the small ones,* said Crawf—*Hullo? He's clearly a danger to everyone in Ektek.*

—*Not to mention all the creatures done out of a habitat when that forest's pulped,* said Zip.

—*You work with him, Crawf. Do you believe he had time to do it? And do you honestly believe he would actually do such a thing?*

—*PulpAss say he has,* said Crawf.

—*Do you really think so? Bash? Such a little frog?* Antenna continued down a list of figures, now on the PulpAss website.

—*I know,* said Zip—*Who would have thought? Suddenly we've got two creatures in lock up when we've never even needed a prison before.*

—*Probably should have locked up Hod,* said Crawf—*Might have taught him something.*

—*We're Ektek. We can't shut creatures up just because we don't agree with them*, said Antenna.

—*We have to if they're potentially harmful,* said Zip.

—*Chimera can't stay here indefinitely. She's already keeping her cockroaches busy running her food and drinks day and night and there's some problem now with the rest of the beetles. They're feeling invaded, I think.*

—*I heard that, too,* said Crawf—*The cockroaches just move in, take what they want and never speak to any one or ask permission for anything. They're not disruptive, but they're not...*

—*Friendly?*

—*Polite?*

—*I'll give her another internet lesson later,* said Zip—*She's a fast learner, I'll give her that.*

—*Maybe she's got some hidden talent we can use?* said Crawf and all three creatures sniggered before he bent to the mic again—*Hullo? Helmut? Hullo? Over.*

There was that hiss again.

As the three creatures listened intently for a voice that never came, Torque flew in to the computer bank and landed in front of Antenna. She acknowledged him—*Torque.*

He said—*I have news,* very quietly—*Just between you and me.*

Antenna said, also very quietly—*Okay.* She moved in closer to the old security guard. He looked around to see who was paying attention to them.

Crawf and Zip concentrated very hard on not listening and became completely absorbed in their tasks.

Antenna nodded and Torque went on—*They're being delivered...*

—*They?*

—*Your numbats.*

—*They're not mine. Today?*

—*Now.*

—*Oh. Thanks, Torque.*

—*Was it okay to, well, tell you like this?*

—*It was okay. See you, Torque.*

—*Antenna.* Torque flew out of the control centre again.

Crawf and Zip hardly heard a thing. They focussed on looking busy.

Antenna stood and stretched and went for a little jog around the perimeter of the control cave. She looked up, stretching her back. She rolled herself forward, looking down to the ground. She felt over-whelmed and kept shaking her head in disbelief as she paced around the control room. She was not going to let these new numbats get to her. She was senior Ektek now. She had work to do; animals to help. She needed to concentrate. She snapped into alert mode—*Okay. What we have here is mayhem; Helmut's lost, Hod's escaped, Bash has turned into some kind of traitor, Chimera's been kicked out of the chimps. What else could possibly go wrong?*

—*Don't say that! We've got to be constructive,* said Zip—*Let's think. What about the PulpAss employee who signed off on the payment?*

—*Okay, I can work with that,* said Antenna and she returned to the PulpAss website and began to search their accounts paid department.

—*Who could Bash have contacted? Can we find the sent email?* asked Crawf.

—*Should be able to see when it was sent, yes, yes, I'll look. Thanks.*

—*What about thanking PulpAss? If we do it in such a way they'll reply?* asked Zip.

—*Keep those ideas coming,* said Antenna as she typed and clicked. Then, as she realised what she was doing, she shook her head and slowed again—*How the hell could he do it?*

—*We'll just have to ask him,* said Zip—*...and keep asking until he can tell us something plausible.*

—*He'll just deny it,* said Crawf—*... again.*

—*What if he's telling the truth? What if he really doesn't know anything?* Antenna looked worried as she scanned the list of payments in the bank website—*Oh, I don't know, I don't know...*

Spark, followed closely by another beetle, rushed into the room, flying straight at Antenna. He landed on the control desk in front of her and flipped his shiny wing carapace over his delicate flight wings—*Sorry to interrupt, Antenna, but there's a new beetle alert come in and you need to hear this one straight from her own mandibles. Go ahead, Nellie.*

The new beetle fluttered down to the desk and arranged herself neatly. She was a seven spot ladybird. Antenna turned to the little beetle—*Thanks, you can proceed.*

—*Three hundred and twenty six. Wallaby says to be alert and alarmed. There's five crocs waiting for you.*

—*Five crocs?* Antenna thought for a moment and then looked over to Crawf—*Five? Isn't that...?*

— *No. What are the chances?*

Then Antenna thought again and said to the ladybird—*Wallaby? What sort of wallaby?*

—*Just a wallaby.*

—*Yellow feet?*

—Sorry, just a wallaby.

—Shall we...? The beetle, Crawf and Antenna went into the honey-bee direction dance, an ancient ritual taught to the founders by a series of trusted bees. Refined over the years, the honey-bee dance was how Ektek managed to navigate over huge distances.

—Thanks, said Antenna, bowing slightly to the beetle and Crawf—*... and thanks, Spark. Can you get this beetle some rest and sustenance?*

—No problemo. Come this way, Nellie. The two beetles flittered out of the cave.

Crawf looked nervous—*Different direction, different place, different problem...*

—Can't be, said Antenna—*Can it?*

—It would have to be the biggest co-incidence...

—Crocs are rather partial to a tasty wallaby. They aren't going to keep him on ice for long, said Zip—*Especially if it's Hod because, being Hod, he's going to piss them off sooner rather than later.*

—And then, cruncho.

Zip and Crawf chuckled together.

—Don't know why you should be sounding so happy about that. It's going to have to be you, Crawf, and you're going to have to keep your wits about you, said Antenna.

—Don't worry, if it's those same big croc girls, I'll be keeping my distance. With a megaphone.

Zip laughed—*Hey, what about telepathy?*

Crawf looked hopeful—*That could work...*

—I'm sorry there's no one to send with you, said Antenna—*While there's no-one looking for Helmut.*

—I can take that on, said Zip.

Crawf nodded, stood and stretched his wings, just a little bit, in the enclosed space of the control cave—*I'll be off then.*

—Good luck, Crawf.

—Can't see much good coming out of this...

Zip and Antenna shared a wry smile as Crawf left them. Zip moved to replace Crawf near the mic—*How much fuel do we think Helmut had on board when he took off?*

—That's the thing, no one can remember when it was last refuelled, said Antenna.

—He could go for miles.

—We just don't know.

—What on earth can we do?

—*No idea, Zip.* Antenna sighed—*I'm really at a loss. Starting to think we may not ever see Helmut again.*

—*Don't say that, Antenna. Don't even think it.* Zip bent over the radio mic—*Come in, Helmut. Hullo? Hullo? Helmut? Over.*

The two animals listened to the white noise fuzz from the speaker. Could there be some kind of hidden message amidst the hiss?

Chapter Thirty-one

Helmut opened his eyes. It was a bright new day. He was thirsty. His vision was blurred. It seemed like there was something impeding the bright blue sky. A great round shape blocked out the sun. An orange-and-black striped shape, made out of fur. A wild-smelling, hairy shape etched with white patches and wiry sides. Whiskers. Fur. Hot sour breath puffed onto Helmut's pointed bird face.

—*How are you feeling?* A big deep voice—*Do you need mouth-to-beak resuscitation? You ever done that before? Kissed a tiger?*

Helmut screamed.

Chapter Thirty-two

I

Spark and Nellie picked over some titbits dropped by human workers on their routine journeys to and from the rear of the zoo's food storage area. Nellie had just been explaining how she would head off as soon as she'd finished eating—*I have to fly away home to look after my children. I've already been away too long.*

As they chatted and munched, a line of grey cockroaches marched in from the direction of the bush boundary. Spark regarded the cockroach family with his head slightly to one side. Nellie was too hungry to notice anything amiss and continued to nibble. Spark, being a trained security officer, watched the roaches as they arrived and took up positions around the piles of scrap food.

—*Hi*, said Spark—*How's it going?* The cockroaches did not appear to have heard him and tucked in hungrily. He looked at them even more carefully. They were all dusty and footsore. They helped themselves to the food crumbs as though they hadn't eaten for days. Only a quiet 'yip' could be heard muttered under one or another's breath. It was if the spark had gone out of this team.

Spark wandered over and paused next to Blatta. He smiled at her in his whimsical Christmas beetle way—*What have you all been up to, then?*

Blatta just looked at him and continued to slurp from a drop of water on a bit of banana peel. Spark noticed that she appeared to be holding her front leg underneath her—*Are you hurt?*

—*It's nothing.*

—*Show me.*

—*I can cope.*

—*What have you been doing?*

—*Nothing.*

—*Come on.*

—*No, really. Please don't ask. I can't talk to you.*

—*Why not? We're just chatting, friendly like. Why, would you like to meet Nellie? She's a ladybird just flown in…*

—It's not for me. Friendly chatting. I can't do that. You mustn't expect it. I have work to do. Blatta left him, pushing past too hard, too hurriedly. He stared after her, confused. What had he said?

—Yip, said Blatta, and—*Yip, yip, yip,* the others replied. The cockroaches finished chewing and left, as downtrodden as they had been when they'd arrived.

Spark looked down at something he'd kicked. It was a grain of sand that must have dislodged from Blatta's carapace as she brushed past. It was unlike any sand he had seen before. It was the colour of blood. Mammalian blood.

Nellie slowed in her eating and looked up at him—*They're not very friendly.*

Spark shook his head—*No.* He stared at the red sand grain—*No. They're not friendly at all.*

II

Antenna shredded paperbark in her paws, adding to a large pile of shredded bark, twigs and leaves at her feet. She'd been shredding bark when she couldn't sleep, which was most of the night, because she was so worried. Nothing like this had ever happened at Ektek before. How could one of their number be so treacherous?

Bash jumped up onto the console in front of her—*What?*

—Yeah. Hi, Bash. She paused and when he said nothing she continued—*Good morning to you, too. I'm well. Nice of you to ask. How are you?* Antenna looked at the tiny little frog—*Okay?*

Bash sighed—*Shithouse, actually, Antenna. Really shithouse.*

—I'm glad Torque could bring you. I've got some news.

Bash looked at her without any animation in his demeanour—*Good or bad?*

—That depends on how you look at it.

—From the point of view of a wrongly accused victim; or...? Wait, is there another aspect I'm missing?

—Sci-poon.

—Sci-who-what?

—I've just received an email from Sci-poon, notifying you of their huge donation to Ektek. The money is already in our account and I've personally never seen so much wealth.

—Sci-come-again is, what exactly?

—Sci-poon is a fishing company. As if you didn't know.

—Antenna. I didn't know.

—You don't stop at anything, do you, Bash?

—Just tell me, Antenna. What exactly am I supposed to have done?

—You've given them the whereabouts of a pod of southern right whales, which was lucky, because that's exactly what they were looking for.

—Noooo... Bash shrank down and smacked his head on the hard surface of the console.

—Yes. Sci-poon tell me that southern right whales make very tasty eating. After they've been scientifically studied, of course. Then they'll boil the blubber down to make soap...

—Antenna...

—They'll make the soap into the shape of the corroboree frog...

—I can't take much more of this.

—As a celebration, a reward, for their nice friend, Bash.

—How do they know what I look like?

—You don't know?

—No, of course I don't.

—Well, apparently, you sent them a signed photo of yourself.

—I didn't. I didn't do it.

—I wish I could believe you, Bash.

—You have to believe me, Antenna. I couldn't, Antenna. I've never signed anything in my life. How can I? I can't even write. Who can? Can you?

Antenna didn't know what to think. She stared at Bash—*I don't know what to do, Bash. What do you imagine the other creatures will think? When they hear about the whales? What are the whales going to think as they get dragged up the ramp to the freezers?*

—Are you going to tell them?

—I can't keep it a secret.

—But I didn't do it...

—Someone did. You'd better keep a low profile, that's all I can say.

—I'll have to. Bash hopped down from the console, onto Antenna's rock and then, onto the ground. He hopped towards the door.

—You'd better wait for Torque or Spark, hadn't you?

—I'll go straight back to my tank and I'll stay there. Until you realise I'm innocent; or until I'm dead. Whichever happens first.

—Fine. Antenna swallowed but kept her grim exterior as she nodded that Bash was dismissed. After he'd gone, she shook her head. She stared at the screens in front of her with no comprehension. She threw the last shred of paper bark on top of the heap and paused. Then she stood up and left the control centre. Like an automaton, she headed down the tunnels towards her old home.

Once she'd made the decision to go, she broke into a run as fast as she'd ever run down those familiar tunnels. She paused as she got closer and sniffed, then sniffed again. Yes, there it was. The unmistakable smell of numbats. They were here. The new numbat family. Her kin. This would be her first look at the new family. What would they be like? How many were there? What ages would they be?

She could just see the crack of light at the end of the tunnel. She took one step forward, sniffing and smelling eagerly...

She stood still, tense, quivering, testing the air, leaning forward, savouring the idea of a numbat family, any numbat family, a group of creatures that spoke her language, that ate her kind of food, that liked the sorts of things she liked...

She bowed her head and breathed slowly in.

Then she stepped backwards and ran out the way she had come, ran fast, ran away, out past the control centre, past the hangar and out into the bushland surrounding the Ektek entrance. There, she ran to a paper bark tree and began to tear strips off it, ripping the great sheets that sounded like her heart breaking.

III

Bash kept moving through the tunnels towards his home. He had never felt so desperate. How could he prove he hadn't done it? Why was this happening to him anyway? It was like a morass, a great whirling hole and he was sinking and he couldn't see how to save himself.

—*Gidday, Bashy boy*, came a deep, greasy voice from the dim low shadows of the tunnel—*Long way from home, aren't you? All alone in the dark, poor little creature...* It was Spill, the diamond python. Spill was large for his size and Bash stared into his glittering eyes as though he'd been pinned to the ground. Bash wasn't scared of many things but pythons were up there with the most scary things of all. Well up there. Pythons were never conducive to a frog's feeling of good health, especially when that frog had recently been staring into a dark pit of despair. Suddenly Bash's pit seemed very deep and very dark and there was absolutely no way out—*Hi, Spill, didn't see you there, in the dark... How have you been? How's the family? Busy?*

—*Not as busy as you, Bash, from all accounts. I hear you've been very busy, Bashy boy. You've been up to some particularly interesting dealings, young Mr Frog, haven't you, hmmmmm?*

Bash nodded, following Spill's every head sway, every movement, gently hypnotised into staying put while Spill slid just that little bit closer... —*I admit, I did make a banner to encourage everyone to vote for the corroboree frog. We've got a lot of friends and I thought I could do my bit for the family but I haven't done anything else, I swear, just the banner and I know that wasn't right but corroboree frogs are in with a good chance, don't you...*

—What did I hear? Old growth forests, wasn't it? Pulped? Was that you, Bashy? Pulping habitat. Ummm... That's a naughty no-no, isn't it. I would have thought you'd know better... Spill moved closer to the little frog who, in turn, moved back hard into the wall of the cave. So hard he could feel grit cutting into his thin frog skin. Spill was so close, Bash could feel the breath puffing out of his mouth. He turned his mouth to the side to suck clean air into his froggy lungs—*Nothing to do with me, Spill. I swear...*

—Swearing's a nasty habit. Those poor little whales. I really feel for them. Gone for munchies. Makes me hungry just thinking about them. All I'd need would be one little morsel, maybe a little dorsal morsal, and I'd be satisfied...

—You were listening...

—Hey, froggie, the walls have ears around here. You should know that. Just happened to be passing. Fascinating the titbits that fall in one's path, ain't it.

Bash swallowed hard.

—The things you learn, continued Spill—*Makes you think, don't it. Makes me think; that's for sure, about all sorts of things; like, you. I've been thinking about you, Bash, ol'Basheola, Bashy boy; do you think you deserve to live? Or would you say I deserve a snack? A little Bashy-nashy snack?*

—Spill, I didn't do it, I really didn't do it, whatever you've heard, Spill, honestly, it's all lies. Bash became louder and louder as Spill got closer and closer. Bash was shouting for his life—*Really. I don't know what's going on. It's complete fabrication and I can't imagine why anyone would want to ruin me like this. I've never done anything to hurt anybody...*

Who is to say what might have happened if, suddenly, like super heroes, Torque and Spark had not flown down the tunnel towards Bash and Spill at that very moment with Bash stuck, hard and squealing, in Spill's hypnotising eye beam.

—Hi-ya there, Bash, all right, then? said Torque cheerfully—*Evening, Spill. How's it hanging?*

—Come to see you home, Bash, said Spark—*Need a lift?*

Without waiting for discussion, Torque and Spark flew down to either side of the little frog and lifted an arm of black and yellow each. They flapped their flight wings as hard as they could and, before the amphibian had any idea of what was happening, got purchase and winged that little black-and-yellow corroboree frog out of there as fast as they could carry him.

Spill slid round and watched the bizarre trio fly erratically down the hallway. He sneered and had a quiet little chuckle deep down in his long scaly throat before moving quietly on his way.

The two beetles flew so fast their antennae bent back over their heads. Tears came into Bash's eyes, though that could have been caused by something other than the wind, as they travelled around the bend. As soon as they figured they were past the danger zone, Torque and Spark glanced at each other and lowered their altitude. Together they let go of Bash and all came to the ground at the same time.

Spark looked at the shiny frog sympathetically—*All right, then?*

Bash stayed where he'd been dropped and another tear rolled down his cheek—*I wish you'd left me there.*

—*More than our job's worth, young tadpole.* Torque laughed, a brusque, jolly-up sort of growl—*How could we begin to explain your disappearance to Antenna?*

—*She'd be glad. She'd only think I'd got what was coming to me.*

—*Why do you think she's got us guarding you, Bash?*

—*To stop me getting out and making any more deals.*

—*She doesn't think you made any deals.*

—*She does.*

—*Nah. She's asked us to keep an eye on you for your own safety. Other creatures might take offence, like maybe old Spill there, without knowing all the facts, see? We're looking out for you. We're your friends, like. And don't forget it, young dribble features.*

—*Torque?* said Spark.

—*Young germ?*

—*Could I take him back? By myself? I'd look out for him. I would. He'd be right with me.*

—*Don't know about that, young grub. Think we'll stick together until he's home. Not sure danger's all over yet. That's if there was any to start with. You know old Spill, bit of a joker, that one. Come on, Bash, can you walk or do you fancy flying again?*

Bash hiccoughed, rubbed his wet face with his little frog hands and then said—*Can we fly? That was cool!*

Torque looked at Spark—*Now look what you've started.*

—*If it's too much for you?*

—*If it's too much for you. Why, you cheeky young embryo, it's not too much for me. I could carry twice as many frogs as you... Why, in my day... Come on, Bash. Up, up and away...*

Chapter Thirty-three

Helmut lay on the ground, panting painfully through what, if he could reason, he might have imagined was a broken rib. He wasn't thinking clearly. Dribble came out of his beak and stained the dirt beneath him. A shadow fell across his feathers and a large orange-and-white paw stepped into his vision. The claws were the colour of old ivory and clenched into the dirt. The tiger spat out a mouthful of juicy leaves and berries onto the pile already on the ground in front of the ailing bird— *You must eat.*

Helmut raised his head and looked at the offering—*I don't know that I can.*

The tiger growled slightly, deep in his throat—*You have to.*

—*What is your name?*

—*Gleam. And you?*

—*Helmut.* The cassowary looked up at Gleam with distrust and nervousness writ large on his face—*What about you, Gleam? When will you eat?*

Gleam shook his head slightly and indicated the leaves and berries on the ground—*I'm fine. This is all I need.*

Helmut sat up at this and stared at the assortment of fruits and leaves—*What? Flowers and fruit?*

—*Absolutely.*

—*You're joking?*

—*No joke.*

—*How can you digest this beetle food? Vegetation? Surely you need meat? To survive?*

—*Sometimes I might find a bit of road kill…*

—*Ah. You do eat meat.*

—*But I don't kill.*

—*A tiger that doesn't kill.*

—*That is so.*

—*Why should I trust you? You might be lying. You might kill me in my sleep.*

—You might just as easily kill me.

—I'm a cassowary. You're a tiger. I think we both know who the executioner is.

—What of those spur things on your legs?

—Excuse me? I'm the one lying on the ground. I can't get up.

—Soon you will be stronger.

—I'm not going to try to kick you to death.

—Fine. We've got a deal. I won't kill you either.

—Tell me—you must have killed? In the past?

—Of course. Like all tigers, I was raised to eat meat; chickens and legs of beasts thrown to us by our keeper. My brothers and sisters and I would play, argue, fight over the carcasses. Then we grew older and hunted on our own. Oh, yes, the taste of flesh with the warm blood rising into my mouth... Aaaaaaarrr... Gleam roared into the desert sky.

Helmut closed his eyes and shuddered. The roar was so loud in his head, in his bone cap, in his mind - it seemed to shake his already shaken frame - he felt as if he'd just endured an earthquake. After he managed to control his palpitations and his breathing he said—*Why not eat me?*

—Helmut. I don't want to offend you but you're a bit scrawny.

—I've still got a heart, warm blood...

—You're still alive. Consider yourself lucky.

Helmut nodded and began to peck at a berry—*How came you to be here? In the desert, like this? Wandering, lost?*

—I could ask you the same question, said Gleam.

—And I will tell you for sure. Helmut picked up a leaf, nuzzled it in his beak and then swallowed—*There. That's my part of the deal. Now your story.*

—More eating from you.

—Of course. Helmut pecked at more of the berries—*Where did you grow up, you and your brothers and sisters?*

—The Project Tiger, Gleam looked expectantly at the cassowary— *My grandmother was Tara.*

After a pause Helmut raised his head from his repast and looked curiously at the tiger—*Tara? Sorry, don't know... Should I recognise her?*

—She was given to the Project when she was only a cub. She was symbolically released into our reserve many years ago: a wonderful gift; a marvellous start to the continuation of tigers. Tara was a half-breed.

Helmut sighed, recognising the problem.

Gleam continued—*There was recently a purge in the Project. Half-breed tigers were caught. Half-breeds are no good any more. All us half-breeds were taken to a reserve where mixed breed tigers are kept for the viewing pleasure of tourists. Sometimes a rich tourist would buy a tiger to shoot.*

—*Oh, dear.*

—*Yes. They trapped me to release into the hunting area. Unfortunately for me the reserve was a desert and because of my Siberian background I carry a long shaggy fur coat. I'm always hot. As a result I have a short temper. When they trapped me and took me to be hunted down and shot by the fat pale hunter, I lost my temper and killed him...*

—*No-one could blame you for that!* cried Helmut.

Gleam shook his head and went on in a rush—*... and, more regrettably, I killed my own keeper who had looked after me since I was a cub. I do seriously regret this. It was a mistake. A bad mistake.*

—*But they were going to kill you.*

—*I should have died.*

—*You acted in self-defence.*

—*I should not have killed my keeper. I swore I would never kill again.*

—*It wasn't your fault.*

—*What do you know, scrawny bird? Aaaaaaarrr... I know how much damage I could do if I chose—eating animals—many of whom represent endangered species themselves. I want no part in granting tourist humans a thrill kill. I can't be responsible for another life. Too many creatures have died. Too many more will die, even today. Even this night. But not by my cause. Aaaaaaarrr...*

Helmut looked at the tiger, his majestic head back, his mouth open, enormous teeth gleaming and throat roaring and the bird shook nervously in his weakened jelly spine.

Gleam shook his head and slowed, remembering where he was and whom he was with. He focussed on the bird—*That reminds me. We have to get you home. There'll be some worried ones waiting for you?*

Helmut rubbed his face over his wings and winced as the movement jarred his rib—*I suppose so. Of course. They'll not know where I am. I should get back to the airship and try the radio. I can reassure them of my safety.*

—*Air... ship?*

—*You haven't seen it?*

—*No. There is no ship near here.*

—*It can't be far. I walked from it before I fell.*

—*You mean,* both cassowary and tiger looked up at the sheer wall of craggy rock beside them—*It's up there?*

—*I guess so.*

—*Better get your strength up, then.*

Chapter Thirty-four

—*Oh, no, no, no! I don't believe it!* Antenna shouted and jumped up from her seat—*This is beyond the limit!*

Zip leaned forward to read the email Antenna had left open on the screen. It was headed with a dramatic yellow and black logo featuring the letters CMC with black triangles surrounding a circle.

> Dear Mr Bash,
>
> Following your suggestions precisely, we are pleased to inform you we have located high-quality uranium just where you predicted. CMC will proceed with mining forthwith.
>
> Henceforth the lake will be known as Bash Lake and the works will be called the Corroboree Mine.
>
> Mr Bash, we are pleased to inform you that you, and your company Ektek, will receive a high percentage of the profits from overseas uranium sales. You will never need to work again. Congratulations and we look forward to a long and rewarding relationship.
>
> Caldicott Mining Co.

Zip looked around her, up and down, and back again, as her numbat friend paced the cave. Antenna sat down and then curled into her shredded paperbark nest momentarily before she jumped up and kept pacing.

Zip shook her head but kept watching for a while and then asked—*What do you think Bash's done to deserve all this?*

—*What?*

—*It's not Bash.*

—*You're sure.*

—*Of course. You must know that.*
—*That email says it is.*
—*You don't want to believe everything you read, Antenna.*
—*Uranium? I know he wants to be an emblem but, mining?*
—*Is that the reason?*
—*Must be. He must want money to campaign. I mean, what else?*
—*Antenna. Come on. He's being set up.*
—*What? Who would do that to a frog?*
—*Who else wants to be faunal emblem?*
—*Do you know, it's not something I've been giving a lot of thought. I mean, we've got Helmut missing, Hod… I don't know, there's just too much…*
—*Let me talk to him,* said Zip.
—*'Course. Be my guest. Can't do any worse than me.*

Zip headed off to the Frog Centre and Bash's frog-quarium. When she got there, the first thing she saw was Torque, curled up at the entrance. As Zip grew closer she could see that Torque was, in fact, asleep on the job. Zip looked at him, quietly snoring, raised a batty eyebrow and stepped over him. She flew up to the corroboree frog tank and peered into the glass. She breathed into the surface, creating a fog. She wrote 'BASH' in big letters with her big fat bat nose.

She landed and waited by Torque, who was evidently having a pleasing dream. Quiet chuckles crept out of the side of his old beetle mouth. She shook her head and looked with increasing annoyance for Bash.

Eventually Bash made an appearance down the side of the tank.
—*What do you want?*
—*Sssshhhh…* Zip indicated the sleeping beetle—*What took you so long?*
—*Didn't seem much point in rushing out of bed.*
—*Feeling sorry for yourself?*
—*Wouldn't you? You all think I betrayed Ektek. You think I gave away old-growth timber and, now, the latest, the whales…*
—*That's not the latest.*
—*Yes, it is.* He looked at her directly, realising there was more to her story—*Isn't it?*
—*No. Uranium is the latest.*
—*Uranium? Mining? Oh, for Zed's sake…*
—*Bash, it's obvious you didn't do it.*
—*It is?*
—*Of course it is.*

Bash closed his eyes and paused for a while. He seemed to be meditating.

Zip watched him warily. Then she reached out the tip of her wing—*Wake up. We've got work to do.*

Bash opened his eyes and shook himself—*You have no idea how wonderful it is to hear you say that.*

—*Probably not…but you can't just take this lying down. You've got to fight it. Someone's setting you up and you have to protect yourself. We have to find out what's going on and you have to help.*

—*I'm just a little frog…*

—*Not so small if the whole of Ektek think you're so powerful you can communicate with multinationals.*

—*But I didn't.*

—*They think you could have. So you must have some powers you don't know about. Get up. Get into the control room and start sending out some emails. Find out who's doing this to you.*

Bash flashed his black frog eyes at her, suddenly attentive— *…and give the money back.*

—*What?*

—*We got to give the money back.*

—*Do we have to?*

—*Of course we do. Come on, Zip. Let's get cracking. Come on, bend down.* Bash hopped up to Zip's back pocket—*Right you are. Go!*

Zip opened her mouth to comment but then shut it again with a quiet little smile. No need for words. Job done.

Torque snored on as Zip took off and flew down the hallway to the control centre.

Torque turned over and grunted.

After a little while, Spark flew into the Frog Centre from the opposite direction. He landed in front of Torque and snorted in derision. Then he went up to the tank. He could see the faint 'BASH' still lingering on the glass. He flew up and into the tank and shouted—*Bash! Where are you? Bash?*

Spark started to panic. He searched through the frog habitat, still calling Bash's name. On finding another corroboree frog, Spark asked what news of Bash? The other frog replied—*Got taken out.*

Spark stared as the implications of 'taken out' sank in. Bash had been assassinated? Surely not. This frog would be more upset, wouldn't he?—*What do you mean? Taken out?*

—*What's it sound like? He got removed.*

—*Removed? Who by?*

—*Dunno, mate. Do you mind? Got to get on, know what I mean? Got some tads here need educating, all right with you, then?*

—*Know what you mean. Thanks.* Spark flew out of the tank and balanced on the glass ledge looking down at Torque. He took a deep breath and flew down to wake his superior officer.

Chapter Thirty-five

Four crocodiles lay warm and comfortable in and beside a pool in a gloomy concrete cave. There were no windows in the brutal bunker. The entrance was distant, through twists and turns of tunnel. Yet light seemed to emanate from the green water. The glow was enough to see each other by and the crocs lounged, comfortable as humans in a spa.

—*Time to get going, girls!* Shining Teeth shouted through the doorway—*Rise and shine!*

The crocs rolled and stretched and groaned—*Must be morning*, said Grater.

Jata moaned—*How do you know?*

—*You got eyes, don't you?* said Asunder—*Look. Illumination.*

—*There's no window*, said Damura.

—*Shouldn't be light in here at all*, said Jata.

—*Probably some kind of algae*, said Damura.

—*Algae?* said Jata.

—*Whatever. Can't stay here all day. Have to get out and find us some food*, said Damura.

—*Can't we just eat the wallaby and the bandicoots?* asked Jata.

—*What about just the wallaby?* said Damura.

—*Come on, girls. Where the death are ya?* Shining Teeth shouted again.

It was loyal Grater who first came to attention and stood up. She moved, with difficulty, towards the door. The rest of the harem followed more slowly, groaning a little. They seemed to have developed all sorts of aches and pains overnight.

Outside, it had been raining. Things were wet and a blare of sunlight though the clouds forced them to strain to see—*Aaah, that's terrible*, said Asunder.

Shining Teeth had no sympathy—*Where the agony have you been?*

—*It's more than morning, we've missed half the day*, said Jata.

—*No wonder I'm starving*, said Grater.

—*All right, then*, said Jata. *What you want to do? Get round the tip and ambush a few seagulls?*

—*Too salty*, said Grater.

—*Make me thirsty*, said Damura.

—*Yeah, me too*, said Asunder.

The crocs stopped their casual amble through the tip and watched quietly as a vehicle, doofing with loud noise, drove into the carpark and stopped with a crunch of tyre against gravel.

— *Look*, said Grater—*That's a bit more like it.*

—*Yeah*, said Shining Teeth—*Meals on wheels.*

The doof-doof stopped. A plump, beared man with white skin got out and slammed the door behind him. He wore jeans, a red tartan shirt and a baseball cap. His greasy curling hair straggled down his collar. He strolled up to a small wooden building near the entrance to the tip, went inside and shut the door. Safe. For the moment.

—*What a shame*, said Damura.

—*Don't worry*, said Grater—*We'll get him when he comes out.*

—*Get into formation, girls*, said Shining Teeth—*Come on.*

—*Sometimes I get sick of you giving all the orders, Shining Teeth*, said Asunder—*I really do.*

Shining Teeth wasn't bothered but just to keep up appearances she added—*You don't have to be here.*

The five crocodiles spread out, slid into puddles and hiding places around the car park, and waited. After a while the man in the red tartan shirt meandered out and leaned his back on the wooden shed wall, crossed his booted feet and squinted into the sunshine while he lit a cigarette.

Shining Teeth started out towards him—*Doesn't he know those things will kill him?*

The crocs rushed across the carpark and the man, still shielding his match with a cupped hand, barely had time to register he was surrounded by reptiles before he felt the teeth sink into his leg. Soon he was splayed out across the gravel, there was a croc on each of his limbs and they were pulling as hard as they could go. His screams and yowls echoed off the rubbish, ricocheted into the gravel and bounced infinitely into the hard grey sky.

His arm was torn off first and Shining Teeth took hold of his gushing shoulder while Jata chewed on her prize. Slowly his coughs and groans subsided and his futile struggles ended.

—*Zed, I hate this peel*, said Grater as she ripped off a boot and spat it out—*It's too tough.* Quickly she grabbed higher over the man's meaty thigh.

With astounding strength the crocs dragged the man back to their bunker and forced the pieces into the tunnel. Shining Teeth watched as they picked up every bit of their prey and eventually the crocs made it back through the maze into the pool, the green water now warmly tinged with red. A piece of tartan fabric floated quietly by Damura. The crocs were happy now; warm and fed.

Just as Shining Teeth was about to enter the bunker she lifted her head and listened. Then she shouted to the harem—*What's that?*

—*What?*

—*That noise; I've heard it before. Hey... You've heard it too...*

—*Isn't that...?*

Shining Teeth sprinted out into the sunshine again. The drumming sound grew louder and louder until, sure enough, there was the Ektek wingship parked in the car park; elegant, spare and graceful in design.

—*That's a quick result.* The rest of the harem followed Shining Teeth as fast as their crocodile legs would carry them over the uneven patchwork of rubbish and dirt.

—*How would Ektek have known where to look for us?*

—*What do you think they're doing?*

—*Hurry up,* Shining Teeth kept moving on. She knew how Ektek had come to know about the rubbish tip, of course, but saw no need to share the information.

Soon enough Shining Teeth could see the pale black bird tapping out his mad rhythm onto the wing. (Even she knew that palm cockatoos were the best avian drummers in the world.) She shouted out—*Here! We're here!* And then she saw Hod leaping forward, just to her left, followed by the scurrying bandicoot.

—*What's going on?* Shining Teeth sprinted and grabbed, taking a fierce-sounding snap at Hod's leg and holding on. Hod fell face forward into the dirt. The bandicoot squarked in alarm and the palm cockatoo dropped his drum stick, lowered his head and began to growl, albeit from the safety of his wingship—*What the...?*

—*Why did you call them? I thought we had a deal?* Shining Teeth managed, even with her mouth full.

Jata breathlessly translated—*He called them?*

Shining Teeth spat out Hod's leg—*Thanks, Jata. I think I can talk for myself here.*

—*I don't think he understood. Did you?*

—*No, Jata, no, I didn't. But then, that might be because a crocodile had bitten me and I thought I was going to die and I was distracted by my ego. Listen,*

Shining Teeth, unless that was some kind of novel plan to prove to Ektek there's no relationship between us, then you're just going to have to trust me. Yes, I called them. I've got a plan and you've got a choice. Either you work with me, or against me. Your decision.

—*I didn't hurt you,* Shining Teeth glared at the yellow-footed rock wallaby.

Hod stood and brushed himself down—*Will you let me get on with this?*

—*Okay, have it your own way.* Shining Teeth looked at him, almost playfully—*I'll be waiting for you to stuff up. And when you do…*

—*I know, I know. Dead meat.*

—*You got it.*

A cavalcade of creatures marched out of the tip driveway to the wingship—the five crocodiles, lead by Shining Teeth, and then Hod and FJ. All came to a halt by the aircraft and Crawf surveyed them. He threw his chewed stick into the pilot's window and stood his ground. On the plane, that is. He hardly looked nervous at all. Of course, that's not how he felt inside—*Hullo…*

Interrupting him, Hod raised himself up to his tallest stance—*Hail, Ektek! Ektek creature that I do not know at all…*

Crawf watched him warily. Here was Hod, plucking himself out of a crocodile's mouth, apparently unharmed, shouting at him that he did not know him. Luckily the beetle's information had included the hint to stay alert because Crawf was feeling well out of his depth here. Crawf's head feathers rose in suspicion and his face patch paled—*Hullo?*

Hod continued his salutation—*Having never seen you before in my life, I have called for your help in regard to a family of bandicoots.*

—*Bandicoots?* Crawf was feeling very confused—*What are the crocs doing here? Is that Shining Teeth?*

—*It is I.* Shining Teeth lifted her snout—*We're all here. Where's your frog?*

—*Bit tied up, I'm afraid. Long way from home for you, isn't it?*

—*Lost. What can I say?*

—*It is the bandicoots that need your immediate help, oh, Ektek aviator.* Hod broke into these pleasantries—*They are sick, suffering in their home of many generations. We would like to travel with you to Ektek headquarters to research a particular symbol used here.*

—*Hullo? Civilians? Travelling in Ektek craft? That's… Never been heard of… Never been done before. Doesn't sound right. Doesn't sound safe.*

—*Just take this bandicoot, then. His name is FJ.*

FJ squawked—*Fair crack of the whip, Hod? Aren't you coming?*

Shining Teeth opened her jaw a crack, perhaps she might have thought of it as smiling, who knows—no one else did—*I think Hod is going to keep us company, isn't he? We can't let both of you go, can we? Then where would we be?*

Hod shouted—*Tell me, Ektek aviator, what other Ektek craft are there?*

Crawf looked askance at him but couldn't see the harm—*There's Uptek, Subtek, Intek and Ontek. Various ones.*

—*All with different pilots?*

—*Yeah*, said Crawf—*What do you want to know for?*

—*We don't believe you can help us.*

—*Well, we can give it a crack, get a plan cooking, then we'll bring up the best craft and personnel for the job and see what can be done getting you lost crocodiles home again. Not sure how many of you we can take at a time, but we'll give it our best shot.*

—*How long's all that going to take?* said FJ.

—*It's okay, FJ.* Hod nodded—*You'll be back in a couple of days and we can decide what's best.*

—*My family?*

—*FJ, I give you my word as a yellow-footed rock wallaby that no harm will come to your family while I am alive.*

—*You trying to reassure me, Hod?*

—*Best I can do right now.*

Crawf was not having a good time. He was trying to avoid imagining the response back at Ektek if he returned home without Hod. He twisted and mumbled at his beak and then clapped it together thoughtfully—*I could take both of you. It'd be a squeeze but it's possible. Haven't got a navigator today. Even though it's never been done. Even though it's probably far too dangerous.*

—*Thank you, Ektek creature, but I will stay. FJ knows what needs to be done.*

FJ clambered up into the wingship. He turned and looked at Hod—*Hoo roo, Hod. Stay alive.*

Crawf turned, too. With a slightly snide expression—*Good idea, 'Hod', do you call yourself? Humph.* Then Crawf climbed back into his pilot's seat and ignored the wallaby as he fastened FJ's safety belt and fussed over his civilian visitor.

Hod looked a little embarrassed. After a few splutters and coughs the wingship's engines hummed perfectly. Crawf was able to take off with only a small spray of gravel landing in Asunder's eye.

The wingship flew straight and disappeared into the clouds.

The crocs all turned to look at Hod.

Hod appeared to be fascinated in a streak of blood across the gravel. Did he only just notice it?

—*What's your game, then?* Shining Teeth took a step forward—*You just happened along, broke into a sanctuary and suddenly you want to do the right thing by a bandicoot?*

—*Maybe.*

—*Or maybe it's that you want to do the wrong thing by Ektek?* said Shining Teeth—*Like we agreed? I don't like creatures that don't keep bargains.*

—*I told you I had a plan.*

—*Hard to believe, Hod,* said Shining Teeth—*You just let our hostage go. What are we supposed to think?*

—*What have you got against them?* asked Hod—*Ektek, I mean.*

—*You don't need to know,* said Grater.

—*Ektek killed our mate,* said Jata.

—*Ektek did?*

—*Not them, not directly,* said Shining Teeth—*It was their negligence.*

—*Humans trapped him,* said Damura.

—*We could have got him out but Ektek stopped us,* said Asunder.

—*Them goody two shoes and their stupid little activities. I hate them,* said Jata.

—*All us harem hate them and we want to teach them a lesson,* said Asunder.

—*A big lesson they can't forget,* said Damura.

—*A lesson they can't ever come back from,* said Jata.

—*Only way to get things done, isn't it,* said Asunder.

—*Why did you let the bandicoot go?* said Grater.

Hod watched the crocodiles clamour questions at him with his arms folded in front of his fluffy pale chest. He took his time to reply—*I thought Ektek might come back with more of them to help us out. Then we'd be in a better position to work out how many of them there are and how to get them most effectively.*

Shining Teeth spoke first—*When Hardback got taken they said they had too much going on to help right at that moment.*

—*Couldn't spare the staff,* said Grater.

—*We trapped them. The bird and the frog I told you about but we got busy and couldn't see the point after a while and let them go,* said Shining Teeth.

—*Darn shame, too,* said Grater.

—*My thinking is there'll be some research and a meeting and then we'll get a mob of Ektek back here to help solve the problems,* said Hod.

Shining Teeth was not convinced—*What problems?*

—*You know FJ's bent arm?* Hod assumed they agreed—*Seems his entire family have defects like that...*

—*Defects?* said Jata.

—*Wouldn't stop me eating him,* said Asunder.

—*As well as deformities, many of their young have been stillborn. I believe there is some invisible danger here we do not understand.*

—*And you think Ektek'll turn out in force for an invisible danger?* asked Shining Teeth.

—*Maybe.*

—*If they come at all,* said Jata.

—*If not, then what?* said Asunder.

—*Then it'll be Plan B.*

—*What's Plan B?* asked Damura.

—*I'll let you know,* said Hod—*If we need it.*

—*You don't have one,* said Jata.

—*You're bluffing,* said Grater.

—*Let's just see if they swallow the bandicoot before we go rushing into hasty decisions.*

—*Nice one. Swallow the bandicoot,* said Damura.

—*Yeah. Good one. Sounds like a plan,* said Asunder.

Hod and Shining Teeth started to march towards the bunker. The rest of the harem fell in behind them, still giggling over a potentially swallowed bandicoot, looking forward to a nice siesta in their pool.

As they walked, Shining Teeth stole a glimpse at the wallaby. How could she ascertain where his loyalties lay; could she trust him?—*Why are you on the road?*

—*Nasty trail of blood there. Fresh, is it?* Hod went on conversationally, making relaxed little observations as though he didn't have a care in the world—*Bloody boot over there. Entrails. Something die here today? Some one?*

—*What business is it of yours?*

—*None. None at all. But you'd think there'd be some interest in this death sometime soon. Humans do like to find out what happened to their deceased. They're like ants; maybe organise punishment, retribution and even some retaliation...*

Shining Teeth couldn't believe the chutzpah of this wallaby—*You going to give us away?*

—*Of course not. I'm on your side. You're the ones who're going to make the changes on this planet.*

—*What changes?* said Shining Teeth.

—*What's he talking about?* asked Jata.

—*You,* said Hod—*You get to kill the humans. You're the apex predator.*

—*We're only interested in survival, mate,* said Shining Teeth. *We got to live. We're not interested in martyrdom, we just eat what's put in front of us.*

—*But, don't you think they deserve to die? They're destroying our habitats and overpopulating and...*

—*Yeah?* said Shining Teeth.

—*So?* said Grater.

—*What difference does that make to us?* said Jata.

—*Ektek destroyed our mate. We'll destroy them. An eye for an eye. A life for a life,* said Shining Teeth— *Maybe Hardback's worth a few lives, don't you think, girls? Only reason to eat people is to get fuel for our revenge.*

Hod held his composure on the outside. Had he been closely observed perhaps that twitch in his top lip might have given him away. Inside he was thinking that he might just be in a bit deeper than he ought to be.

Chapter Thirty-six

I

Spark flew fast down through the dug out corridors of Ektek Torque trying to keep up as best as he could. Torque shouted at his apprentice as they zinged around corners—*We should tell Antenna.*

—*Tell her what?* shouted back Spark—*That Bash has been frog-napped because you were catching up on some well-earned rest?*

Torque was angry with himself. He shouted back—*We don't know what's happened to him. He could have gone for a stroll!*

—*You should have let me do it. You can't keep pretending you can still do this job when you just go to sleep… You could use me more. You don't have to do it by yourself. You've got to let me have more responsibility, Torque.*

—*Listen, youngster. Once. Once I go to sleep. That's not enough for you to be laying down the law to me. Come on, let's head in to the control centre.*

—*But what will you say?*

—*Leave that to me, you preposterous young grub. I'm still the beetle in charge here and we're losing time trying to find him by ourselves. We need to get a search party organised…*

The two beetles flew into the control cave and immediately slowed and came to a rest by the doorway. They could see Zip and Antenna watching Bash as he arduously typed at the keyboard. The keyboard was more like a touch screen; the lightest tap of paw or amphibian foot would get a response from the keys. Bash was, of course, a skilled pilot and able to use technology without too much bother but he really didn't like typing—*I don't like computers. I really don't. See? I'm just not good at this stuff. There's no way I typed out all those emails. And I wouldn't use those words. I don't know what half of them mean.*

The two beetles watched from the doorway—*Ah*, said Spark as he turned to look at his senior beetle—*There he is. Helping them with their inquiries.*

—*No need for a search party then*, said Torque—*Why don't we go and inspect the boundaries?*

—*Good idea. Tell you what? Why don't you let me do that and you go and have a rest? Recover from the shock.*

—*Not a bad plan, Spark. You're in charge.*

—*Thanks, boss. I'll let you know if there are any developments.*

—*Over to you, Spark.* The two beetles made their way quietly out of the cave.

II

Antenna had been busy. She'd found the sent emails purporting to be from Bash. Not only regarding the trees but also the whales and the one regarding the uranium. She'd contacted the Ektek employees responsible for payment and arranged for the money to be returned. Apparently the trees on the edge of the forest designated for pulping had been marked with fluro paint. The whales' whereabouts and the uranium had merely been described in emails and that had been enough.

—*So, we're sure?* said Zip.

—*We agree it's not Bash,* said Antenna—*The next question is; who on earth would think this would possibly be a good idea?*

—*Has to be someone with access to the control centre...*

—*With the ability to turn on computers...*

—*Hang on, could they have sent those emails from any other computer? I mean, there's tons of computers around the zoo...* said Bash.

—*No, they were sent from here,* said Antenna.

—*They got out to tag those trees,* said Zip—*Maybe it's not even an Ektek animal? Did we think of that?*

The animals stared at each other in horror—*You mean a human?* said Bash—*Impossible.*

—*Can't discount it,* said Antenna—*They'd certainly have the ability to do all this. Most of our creatures simply couldn't.*

Zip stared at her—*That is so full on.*

—*We may as well give up,* said Bash—*How the hell can we solve this?*

—*We've got to,* said Zip—*What say they set up something else? We've got to stop them.*

—*Come on, guys,* said Antenna—*Let's concentrate. Started the same day as Min's memorial service, we know that. So most of the Ektek creatures were here and there, out milling around...*

Bash said—*Everyone was out. Could have been anyone...*

—*But not everyone wants to be a faunal emblem,* said Antenna.

—*You think it's tied up with that?* said Zip.

—*Could be. Yup,* said Antenna—*Could be anything, of course.*

—*We know Carney's keen. Who else?* said Zip.

—*Spill, Thumper and Sweep all talked about it,* said Bash—*No secrets there. I mean, who wouldn't want to be an emblem?*

Antenna and Zip smiled at each other—*Indeed,* said Antenna, who, as a numbat, was an emblem herself.

Zip thought for a moment—*What if it's someone who doesn't necessarily want it for themselves but doesn't think the corroboree frog should get it either? What do you think, Bash? Have you got any enemies? Do you think there's someone trying to stop you? Or can you think of someone who doesn't like frogs at all?*

—*Not that I can think of. I mean, Crawf didn't like the banner but then no one did and I can sort of see why. Maybe I've done something to someone unawares? I can't imagine. I can't tell you what it's like knowing that someone hates me this much. Thank Zed you two believe in me, at least.*

—*Huge effort, just to undermine someone,* said Zip.

—*Plus, as we've seen, it's got to be someone who can write; or at least turn on the computer,* said Antenna—*Not to mention picking up and posting the photo.*

—*That could have been sent electronically,* said Zip.

—*Better find out. Lot harder to physically pick up a postcard...* said Bash.

Antenna was thinking aloud—*... address it... post it... I know Spill talked about being the emblem but there's no way he could write. Pythons are useless at picking things up and I think that lets Rick out as well. Crayfish can hold things but they don't normally write... On the other claw, Sweep can hold things and owls are known for their quick learning...*

—*Needs to be someone with access to the boat,* said Bash.

—*To find the whales?* said Antenna—*Of course.*

—*Well? Who's that?* asked Bash.

Antenna thought—*Gumfluff and Carney have been working together on the illegal fishing traps up river. I honestly don't know anyone else who could start her up. The boat has a key and most creatures we know can't twist a key.*

—*Can't be Gumfluff. Koalas already are an emblem.*

—*Don't see her getting caught up in causing trouble for the corroborees either. Not her thing,* said Antenna.

—*I can't believe Carney would do it either,* said Zip—*But... looks like she's our only suspect, am I right?*

Bash sighed—*It could be anyone or simply coincidence or...*

—*I don't know, it's just spiteful,* said Antenna.

—*What about doing a handwriting comparison?* said Zip—*Can we get Scipoon to send the photo back?*

Antenna nodded—*If it was a postcard. Right. I'll do their email next. We also have to clear our name with the whales. This is bad for Ektek. In fact, it couldn't be worse.*

III

Bright lights snapped on to the tiger quoll's furry face. She blinked. Her spots stood out like chunks of ice in the glare. Her long thick tail wrapped around her hunched body for protection. She was cold and defensive. Her small ears flicked backwards and forwards in confusion. Her round black eyes watched Antenna as she paced between shredded paperbark and her desk—*This is ridiculous,* Carney spat—*You've been downloading too many cop shows. What a joke.*

—*We're deadly serious, Carney*, said Bash.

—*What on earth makes you think I'd want to destroy an old-growth forest?*

—*Exactly my point!* shouted Bash—*Now you know how I feel! Why won't you believe me?*

—*... and the whales? We couldn't even go near the open sea if it weren't for the whales helping us. How can you possibly imagine I'd want to something as dastardly as that? It's criminal. All I want is for us tiger quolls to be able to live in relative peace, not to be put upon and falsely accused of hurting other creatures when this stupid frog has stuck his unthinking selfish neck out far too far and needs a serious trim. Below the chin, preferably. You've got to punish him.*

—*But, Carney, seriously*, said Zip—*It's obviously a put up job. He's not that stupid. No one is.*

—*Who would frame him?* said Carney.

—*That's what we're trying to find out*, said Antenna.

—*So, are you asking everyone or just me?*

—*Well, everyone eventually. We just thought we'd start with you. I mean, it had to be someone with access to the boat...* said Antenna.

—*Here we go. You do think it's me...*

—*Hang on, hang on*, said Antenna—*We're just talking here! Have you noticed anyone hanging around that isn't normally there?*

Carney, although furious, was mollified enough to try to think about this until Zip interrupted—*What if it were more than one creature?*

—*That'd make sense*, said Antenna—*A team. Certainly a computer-minded animal working the strategies and the emails and then some other creature going out and about doing reccies...*

—*Just the fact you've accused me. How could you begin to see me as such a traitor?*

—*Same applies to you. How could I ever do anything like that? I'm only a little frog. I can't even start the boat. See? You don't know. I don't know. I couldn't have even dreamed these things much less have gone and done them.*

—*I suppose if I'd thought about that, it's obvious. Okay, Bash, if you say I didn't do it then I'll say you didn't...*

—*Then, maybe, we can turn our attention to whoever did do it?* said Zip.

Chapter Thirty-seven

The figure of the tiger climbing over rocks and around twisted pathways was the only thing moving in the afternoon light. The land bumped and tumbled with rocks and wisps of trees as the shimmering air cooled after the hot day. Gleam and Helmut had sheltered from the worst of the sun, resting and gaining strength through the heat. Now, as they made their way up the hill, the shadows lengthened and the desert crust stretched for kilometres into the horizon. Earlier they had walked around the cliff face looking for an easier gradient to make their way back up the hill. When they had found it Gleam put his feet carefully down onto uneven ground and climbed up the hill.

Helmut lolled on the tiger's back, his head resting near Gleam's head. They talked in whispers as Gleam continued to move as smoothly as he could. They whispered about Ektek and families and journeys and means of transport. They talked about loyalty and meteors and fruit.

—*Gleam? Perhaps we should rest. You have carried me very far. You must be weary.*

—*I'm happy to keep on. We can travel slowly. There is no need to race.*

It was rocky underfoot and the going was slow. The sinking sun picked out flashes of gold in the stripes of the tiger and highlighted the hints of gloss still left in the cassowary's black dusty feathers.

Helmut flopped on the tiger's back. His mind was hazy and he was almost sinking into unconsciousness. He began to mutter—*In space all the animals are free from time. Free with the asteroids and the meteors, light and giddy as feathers, floating without decisions. There is no need to think.*

Gleam had not heard him raving like this before. His tiger curiosity was piqued—*Helmut?*

—*Hmmm.*

—*How do you know? I mean, all this space stuff? That asteroids float and stars flicker?*

—*I just know.*

—*But how?*

Helmut became worried. He started to look in all directions, fraught, tense and bothered. He twitched, increasingly uncomfortable—*I think maybe I should try to walk for a while, Gleam. Give you a rest.*

—*If you would like,* Gleam slowed down—*I'm happy, however...*

Helmut got down and stumbled. He was able to lean on Gleam and catch his breath. His long neck shook when he tried to hold his head up. Each footstep was laborious.

Gleam watched him, doubting Helmut would be able to go much further by himself.

—*She's gone.* Helmut sighed and put his head down into the soft fur of the cat—*I haven't heard her for days.*

—*Who?*

—*She's like another presence... I don't know. My conscience, perhaps? My consciousness?*

—*Your consciousness? Isn't that you?*

—*I don't know what you would call her; my muse, my friend, my angel...*

—*You've been hearing a voice?*

—*A voice. Yes.*

—*Not yours? In your head?*

—*My heart.*

—*Do you hear the voice now?*

—*Gone. All gone. I'm alone.* Helmut lifted his head and cried out—if he could have roared perhaps that's what he would have sounded like—as it was, a thin reedy wail instantly dissipated into the infinite sunset.

They were near the top of the hill and the desert stretched out its red rainbow skin; stretched and wrinkled and gnarled over as far as the distant horizon. It was difficult now to say where the land finished and where the sky began. The sky, too, was contoured and shaped by endless colour and cloud; less skin, more depth.

Gleam watched the red distance as the bird snivelled into his back. The tiger's chest rumbled when he spoke to the crumbling bird—*You're not alone.*

—*I am.*

—*You're not. You've got me.*

Helmut gasped and lifted his head—*It's true. You are here. Yes. Thank you.*

Gleam smiled—*No need for thanks. We can help each other.*

—*You are better than she, though it is she who tells me what is happening in outer space. She describes the stars and the planets and the satellites and I feel lost without her...*

—When did you last hear her?

—I suppose… It must have been the airship.

—Can you walk? We should go further while there is still light.

—We must go further. Yes. Perhaps I can hold on to your fur while we walk?

—That would be fine, Helmut. Just fine.

The bird placed his huge feet, like the triangular trunks of a wiry tree, into the dirt one after another, and they kept travelling, the scaly prehistoric feet, next to the four great pads of orange and white. They reached the top of the hill and walked until they found the remains of the airship.

The smash site was a charcoal scar on the landscape, the cockpit snapped open like an egg. The tiger opened his mouth and very gently put his teeth around Helmut's neck as he lifted the sore, feathered body with his great furred paws. He guided Helmut into the passenger seat without harming a cell of Helmut's blue and red skin. Helmut slumped into the seat almost unknowing.

Gleam went around to the other side of the cockpit and sat, next to Helmut's dusty pile of feathers, in the pilot's seat. Both creatures were exhausted and sank further into their seats, letting their tiredness flood through them. They slept. The bright stars rose in the sky and turned inexorably in the immense wheel of the hemisphere.

Suddenly Gleam sat up. His hair stood on end—*Oh, Zed!* He had heard a voice. Where was she? Then he realised. It must have been the cassowary's angel. The tiger listened intently, his head tilted on one side, curiosity overtaking his need for sleep. As he listened, a snide guffaw snuck out from between his disapproving lips—*Some angel…*

He looked over at Helmut—*Let the poor bastard have a break.* He would tell him in the morning. In the meantime, Gleam got out of the seat and slid under a piece of cockpit wreckage in the sand. He lay, staring out into the enormous darkness, watching those same stars and thinking of the extraordinary voice he'd heard before his eyes closed and he slept again, the sleep of the completely whacked.

He woke to the strange mutterings of a cassowary in futile com-munication—*… I have been dreaming of the stars, sliding into the Milky Way. I've been following the drama of the darkness, the velvet black touched by gleams and shimmers, I want to see your world, show me, how can I see where you are?*

Sure enough, Helmut was poised in an earnest listening position in the pilot's seat silhouetted against a magic tinge of light in the east. The cassowary swayed as he was captured again by the siren song of space.

Gleam shook the sleep from his head, jumped up and ran to the cockpit. He grabbed Helmut in a bear hug with his two great paws and wrestled him out into the air—*I think not, my friend. I like you best in this time and place. Can you snap out of it? Do you know who I am? Let me listen again. Don't keep all the good stuff to yourself.*

Gleam bustled past the floppy bird and sat down again in the pilot's seat—*Sounds like one voice, doesn't it. Frustrated. Not happy. Trapped. Do you think you've been picking up this transmission for some time?*

—*Trans… mission?*

—*Some kind of vehicle stranded somewhere perhaps? Certainly sounds a long way away. Maybe under the ocean. She's not a whale?*

—*No, not a whale. She's no whale.*

—*Thanks, Helmut. Beginning to think you weren't coming back. You right?*

—*Thanks, yes, Gleam. Sorry.*

—*What? We're in this together. Better?*

—*Yes. I'm all right.*

—*Well. I think we get some rest and some food and then we head out and try to get you back to Bedlam.*

—*Ektek. Should contact them.*

—*Did you try to use the radio?*

—*No, I will now.*

—*Not sure that's such a great idea. We've got to keep you safe from your mysterious voices, don't we? Can you access the radio from the passenger's seat?*

—*I'll try.*

—*You do need to protect yourself, Helmut. That voice has convinced you to abandon your home and your organisation. She's too powerful. You do know that, don't you? Don't you?*

—*I know.*

—*I'll help you. Don't worry. You'll be fine.*

Helmut watched the tiger carefully. He was worried. What he really wanted was to sit enthralled in the pilot's seat and plug his mind in to the voice of dreams and be wafted into orbit.

He resisted.

Helmut sat in the passenger seat and switched the radio mic to 'on'. He leaned in to the mic—*Hullo? Come in, please? Uptek calling Ektek. Can you come in, please?*

There was no reply and, as the dawn seeped in to the new day, gorgeous, new, soft as a sonnet, the two creatures set out, slowly at first, to find food and to locate a beetle. As they moved along, Helmut called to the beetles—*Ektek! Ektek!* His thin voice drifted unheard into the air.

Maybe there were no beetles in this arid area. Maybe they could not hear Helmut's weak voice but something stopped Gleam from shouting too. Helmut's authority or Helmut's need to be useful, whatever the reason, Gleam was solicitous of his friend's role. Soon enough, they found a large cactus plant and feasted on the fruit, juicy and quenching. They set out again with renewed vigour.

—*It will be good, you'll see, Gleam. We'll get you into the zoo and you'll be able to eat meat. You'll never have to worry about scraping old mince meat off the roadside again. You're just the sort of creature we need in Ektek now. You have the same sort of concerns. Beliefs. Change through peace, non-violent activities, that's what...*

WHAP!

Helmut was hit.

He never heard it coming.

It was a ground shaking engine roar.

A huge, dusty off-road vehicle sped through the land.

Helmut soared into the air and flew, flopping like a rag doll over and over until he fell, smashed, into the dirt.

The four-wheel drive growled on, jumping over rocks and bounding into indentations in the dusty land, heedless.

Gleam stood in horror and watched the life drain from his friend's broken back. A trickle of blood dribbled out of Helmut's beak. His eyes rolled in his head, never to see again.

The tiger roared, too, as the machine tossed and leapt across the desert into the distant day—*Ektek! Ektek! Ektek!*

This time, he was heard. A melyrid beetle flipped its wings and leapt for the sky.

—*One.*

The tiger roared on, feeling useless, frustrated and alone.

Chapter Thirty-eight

I

—*Crikey,* FJ was staring out the window of the wingship—*Never, ever, not in my wildest dreams...*

—*What?*

—*I never imagined I'd fly. I mean, I'm a bandicoot, for fluff's sake! None of my family have ever seen this view. My ma and pa would just die... Thanks, Crawf. Really. It's awesome. You're awesome. How the heck did you find out how to fly a plane?*

—*Just doing my job. Anyone could do it. Better than me, too, I bet. Better hang on, we're landing soon.*

II

Antenna and Spark marched from the control centre towards the hangar. Antenna was expecting Crawf to return any moment. She wanted to be there to greet him and discover out how he'd got on with those crocs.

Spark had been looking for a chance to talk to Antenna privately. He looked around carefully to make sure the corridor was clear before he spoke—*I've seen them.*

Antenna knew right away what, or rather who, he was talking about—*Have you?*

—*Did you?*

—*No,* said Antenna—*I didn't.*

—*Not yet?*

—*I had no right.*

—*No,* Spark agreed. Then he paused and looked at her seriously—*Then again, maybe you do.*

—*Do I?*

—*Well. You know as much about the workings of the zoo as anyone else. Maybe more. Who better than one of their own kind...*

—*Own kind? What does that mean?*

—*You know what I mean...*

—I don't. Does it matter what our 'own kind' is?

—You don't think so?

—I don't know. I don't want it to be so. Is not every living creature my family?

—Maybe some family are more family than others.

—Maybe some families are entitled to their privacy?

—Maybe. There's seven of them all together.

—Seven?

—There might have been more sleeping but there's certainly a young mother with two babies...

—Already?

—A young male, another older couple and one more female.

—Three females, two males and two babies. Antenna shook her head. She had no business discussing the new numbats with a surveillance beetle—*Spark. Thanks, but please don't tell me any more.* She felt ashamed of herself—*Sounds like Crawf's back. Come on.*

Antenna moved into the hangar proper where the beetles were gathered to welcome the returning wingship.

Crawf piloted the craft in and parked as directed by the beetle crew.

Antenna could see Crawf had brought a small passenger with him. A long pointed nose and black bead eyes were peering out of the window. This was irregular; civilians were not normally carried in Ektek vehicles. She assumed Crawf would have good reason and watched as he disembarked and went to attend to his passenger.

Just as Crawf was helping the little round bandicoot out of the wingship; a visitor, a bright red cardinal beetle, fluttered into the cave.

Spark flew to greet the newcomer, communicated briefly and then turned back to find Antenna.

As Crawf brought the small hopping bandicoot over to meet her, Antenna could also see Spark approaching with the new beetle.

Crawf got there first, not seeing the beetles coming over from the other direction and spoke urgently—*Antenna. This is FJ, our bandicoot from the tip. You won't believe what he's got...*

—Wait a minute, Crawf, sorry, said Antenna, as she nodded and turned to attend to the beetles. Spark pointed at Antenna and encouraged the cardinal beetle—*This is Antenna. You can tell her.*

Crawf and FJ watched, taken aback by this blatant thunder stealing.

The cardinal bowed, waving his long serrated antennae—*Forty seven. Tiger in desert.*

—Tiger?

—Did you say, tiger?

—What sort of tiger?

—You know, national emblem, big, stripey, hairy, mammal. Calling to Ektek for help.

—Tiger? Antenna immediately began to calculate the whereabouts of her personnel—*I'm sorry, Crawf, it's happened again.* Antenna looked up at Crawf—*There's only you.*

—But... I've only just landed. They'll have to check the vehicle, refuel...

—You will also need feeding, I take it? Please tell Sunday I'm sorry...

—If I get time. It's really not fair on her.

—No. It's not. Do you want me to talk to her?

—That might help.

—We'll make it up to you as soon as we can.

Crawf nodded his reluctant assent and then added—*One question.*

—Go ahead.

—How am I going to deal with a tiger?

—Very carefully?

—Thanks, Antenna. You're a great help. What would I do without you? I'd better get going. Will you look after FJ?

—Of course, she said—*FJ, welcome to Ektek. Come on, everyone,* Antenna motioned to FJ and the beetles—*Let's go in and find you all some food.*

III

Later that day, Ektek creatures jammed into the control centre cave. Rick, Spill and Carney were there, by the door. Bash, Torque and Spark were ranged along the console, together with a gathering of ants. FJ was seated with Zip, Antenna and Chimera next to the computers.

Bash spent his time surveying the other animals. He checked out each one, weighing up their appearance, their character, their interest in the faunal emblem... He was still not convinced that Carney was innocent, though she seemed thoughtful as she, too, surreptitiously examined the company. Rick waved his long crayfish antennae and looked as if he might be drying out. Bash tried very hard not to catch Spill's eye. Even Zip and Antenna were not above his observations, though he wasn't sure he could reasonably suspect them.

Bash even contemplated Crawf, who was not with them, having left to find out what a tiger was doing calling Ektek from the middle of a desert. Crawf had been doing a heck of a lot of travel recently. He would have had plenty of opportunity to mark a few timber trees on that flight searching for Helmut. But what had Crawf to gain? Bash's thoughts travelled to Helmut. Would Helmut be capable of causing old growth forests to get pulped? Why would Helmut want to discredit him? Though, come to that, why would anyone want to discredit him? It was a mystery, that was plain, but it was causing him more grief than any mere puzzle.

—*Hod?* Torque couldn't quite believe the news—*Our Hod?*

Spark said—*Didn't think we'd heard the last of him.*

—*Yes, and who'd have thought he'd get involved with Hardback's harem?* Torque clicked his wings—*Of all the creatures in the world…*

—*Can we trust him?* Bash muttered quietly to himself.

Torque heard, though—*That's the question, ain't it. Hod and a bunch of crocs; that's some strong combination… That's more than my job's worth, that's for sure…*

—*Especially if Hod is playing some weird double-agent game*, said Spark with respect resonating in his tiny beetle voice for the bravery of an intelligence officer.

—*What makes you think that?*

—*Well, he's clever, ain't he.*

Bash, obsessed by his own concerns, let his thoughts bubble to the surface—*Not if he's busy trying to destroy me and make sure corroboree frogs don't get to be an emblem, he's not clever at all.*

Everyone stared at him.

Zip voiced the question on all their minds—*What are you on about?*

—*We're here to talk about Hod, if we can concentrate, please*, Antenna quietly reminded him—*FJ, could you clarify the situation for us all?*

FJ stood in front of Antenna and Zip and, as he talked, he was willing them to make a quick response—*There's no doubt, it's fair dinkum the crocodiles want to pay Ektek back. They want to destroy Ektek. They want to make you pay for Hardback's death and, well, Hod volunteered to help them.*

—*There! See!* said Torque—*That Hod, he always was a bad egg!*

—*He's a mammal*, said Spark and Torque gave him such a look.

—*But he volunteered first because of me. He saved my life. Too right, Shining Teeth was going to eat me. For sure, it was a close thing. I was right in her gob when Hod spoke up. Covered in her spit slime, I was. Crikey, if it hadn't been for Hod, I don't know, well, I wouldn't be here telling you this, that's for sure*, FJ's voice was clear and steady—*I'd've been a repast.*

—*Well, then. Hod is still one of us*, said Spark—*How's he holding up, do you think, FJ?*

FJ continued—*He's hunky dory, or he was when I last saw him but as you might imagine, things change pretty quick when you've got five crocs moved in down the street from your family.*

—*Threatening your family, he means,* explained Torque to Spark.

—*Got that,* said Spark.

Antenna rose to address the meeting—*We haven't been wasting our time since FJ arrived. We've researched the symbol that Hod noticed outside the bunker where the crocs were staying. It's a symbol humans use to indicate radioactive material.*

—*Radioactive?*

—*It's unsafe material that spontaneously disintegrates at an atomic level. Contact with radioactivity can cause defects in living organisms, even death.*

—*What good's that then? Do humans make it?*

—*It's generally naturally associated with particular minerals, like, for instance, uranium.*

—*Don't look at me!* cried Bash.

—*Don't worry, Bash,* said Antenna—*Humans dig it up with particular purposes in mind.*

—*Better off in the ground,* said Spark.

—*They use radioactivity for energy, medicine, security…*

—*Also in weapons,* said Zip.

—*There's a number of drawbacks with radioactivity, the main being a dangerous left-over substance that is difficult to store. It's known as nuclear waste. Apparently FJ's tip is being used as some kind of waste facility but we can't tell exactly what. All we know is that something with a level of radioactivity is being stored there. We also know that the wall of the building, where the radioactive material is being stored, has been weakened by water or some kind of fault, allowing the crocs access. There's now a lake in that bunker building and the crocs think it's purpose built for them.*

—*So, the crocs are okay amongst this radioactivity?* said Zip.

—*It was perfect for them. Nice swimming pool,* said FJ—*They love it. Think it's very comfortable.*

—*What's it going to do to them?*

—*They shouldn't touch it,* said Antenna—*According to the web, the actual hazardous stuff will be in some kind of protective covering, maybe concrete casing. I mean, could one of the containers be damaged or flawed in some way?*

—*Does that mean they could be affected?* said Zip—*Concrete doesn't necessarily stop radiation, does it?*

—*We just don't know. At least it's not enriched or military which could be stronger or even more unsafe. We think,* said Antenna, who then added after a pause—*We hope.*

—*What's the story about FJ's family?* said Zip—*Did you say they had problems?*

—*All my life, anyway,* said FJ. He raised his bent forearm to show the assembled creatures—*My sister's last litter were all born dead. We don't speak about it. We didn't ever look for what might be causing it. It was only Hod who connected this symbol with us. There still could be something else causing it or it could be drought or maybe we just don't get enough food...*

—*So, either the bandicoots have to move or the waste does.* said Rick.

—*Is it possible to move this stuff?* asked Zip.

—*We can't do that,* said Antenna.

—*Why not?* said Spill.

—*Because,* said Antenna—*Where would we put it?*

—*I guess anywhere it goes will have some effect on whoever lives nearby,* said Zip—*That's the problem for the bandicoots.*

—*That goes double for the crocs, of course,* said Antenna—*Because we'd have to move them as well as the bandicoots.*

—*Can't we just leave them? The crocs?* said Zip—*They could be full of radiation by now. Swimming in it. Won't they affect everyone they meet?*

—*That's assuming it is leaking. It still might be something else that's causing the bandicoots distress,* said Antenna—*It is a tip, after all. They're surrounded by waste products.*

—*If we just leave them without telling them what we suspect? The crocs, I mean. They could just die?* said Zip—*That'd solve it. They wouldn't cause anyone else any problems, just swim themselves quietly to death.*

—*What about Hod? Won't he be affected too?* asked Bash.

—*What if he's acting as a double agent? He could easily infiltrate and destroy Ektek to keep the crocs happy. How can we be certain?* said Carney.

—*We can't be certain of anything. Ever,* said Antenna.

—*I can,* shouted Bash and he jumped up and down as he continued shouting—*I can be certain that it's Chimera! It's been Chimera all along! She's the one that's been setting me up and I demand she be punished! Chimera's the one! She's a traitor!*

—*How dare you!* Chimera jumped to her feet and screamed at the miniscule frog—*Why you low-down, jumped-up, pip-squeak! What would you know about anything?*

—*Wait!* Zip shouted—*Stop!*

—*Bash, how do you know?* asked Antenna.

—*Look at her hands! Look at her finger-nails! She's got yellow fluoro paint on her hands! Look! Look for yourself!*

—*What's that?* asked Torque.

Spark muttered—*Fluoro paint was used to mark the trees that got pulped.*

—*And!* Bash jumped up and down again, agitated and elated to have caught his attacker—*And! And! Of course you know how to run the boat! They brought you all the way home from the Congo in it! You must be the one who's been causing all this trouble. There's no one else who could have done it! It has to be her. Who else?*

—*Why? Why did you want to trash a perfectly good forest?* said Carney.

—*I didn't!* screamed Chimera.

—*How dare you,* said Zip.

—*How dare YOU. There's nothing to link me to this,* Chimera was beside herself.

—*What about the paint?* said Antenna.

—*I painted a wall in the machine cage. You can see for yourself. Bit vivid but it brightens up the place. It had nothing to do with trees,* she eyed the group nervously but then decided it might be better to brazen out the accusation—*You did say trees, didn't you? What's the rest of it?*

—*You know perfectly well,* said Bash.

—*No, as a matter of fact, I don't. Why don't one of you explain exactly what is going on here? If I were a male you would not treat me so. But, no, I'm alone, far from my family, far from my homeland, lost, with no friends; and you attack me unmercifully.*

Spark stood up and waved for his turn to speak. Antenna nodded and Spark faced Chimera and squeaked in his little beetle voice—*Chimera? Can you explain where your cockroaches were last week?*

—*What?*

—*Your cockroach team went out to a place with red sand. Could your cockroaches have been on a uranium exploration exercise?*

After a pause where the assembled creatures looked at each other in disbelief, pandemonium burst forth in the cave as everyone shouted over everyone else. It was loud and tense and fraught. It was Bedlam.

—*Chimera, what do you want?* asked Antenna.

—*It must have been you,* said Bash.

—*How did you get out of your cage?* asked Zip.

—*I'm sure she did,* said Bash.

—*She must have,* agreed Carney.

—*You knew of this forest previously! You sent your cockroach team to discover uranium deposits and I suppose when you went out in the boat you were contacted by a whale, Smacker, was it? That's how you knew where they were. My only question is, why?* said Zip.

—*That's my question too,* said Carney.

—*And mine!* said Rick.

—*She's got to be punished!* said Bash.

—*She should be locked up!* said Carney.

—*Forever!* said Rick.

—*She should be cleared!* said Carney.

—*No!* said Antenna.

—*Kill her!* said Rick.

—*She's too dangerous to keep,* said Zip.

—*There's got to be a way to make her pay!* said Bash.

—*She should have to work to protect the whales,* said Zip.

—*She's got to learn you can't destroy animals and get away with it!* said Bash.

Tempers were high and eyeballs bulged with fury.

Antenna looked around at them all and sighed. Where was this going to end?

IV

Then, stepping into the eye of the storm, Crawf brought Gleam into the space. Suddenly there was no room in the control centre. All the creatures flattened themselves against the wall. All eyes were on the tiger, monstrous and hairy and breathing and filling the cave. He was dirty, smelly and gaunt.

Crawf's crest was flat and his pink face patch was so pale it was almost white. He was downcast and spoke softly. Everyone had to sit forward to hear him—*This is Gleam. He has brought us a report about Helmut. I warn you, it is not good news. If it is acceptable to everyone, I'd like him to tell us all together to save him repeating his story.*

Antenna leaned forward with an involuntary gulp - an intake of air that sounded like a sob.

Gleam had his head bowed as he entered the cave but now he raised his noble face and looked at every creature in turn as he spoke. Aware of the high emotion in the space, his voice was a deep glorious rumble and there was great sincerity in his words—*Thank you, Crawf. I cannot tell you how sorry I am to arrive at Ektek's door with such news. I want to say first that I admired Helmut more than I can say. He was filled with wisdom, compassion and love for you all. He particularly spoke of Crawf and Antenna, Zip and Bash as the four who should lead Ektek into the future. He remembered working with your parents and felt enormous affection and admiration for you all.*

—*Where is Helmut?* said Bash.

—*He cannot be here. He is...*

—*Not dead?* said Carney.

—*No!* said Zip.

—*Is he...?* said Rick.

Antenna said nothing and looked down at the ground.

—*Helmut is dead.* Gleam and Crawf both bowed their heads and waited for this dreadful information to sink in.

—*What happened to him?* asked Zip.

—*He was hit by a car.*

—*In the desert?* asked Rick.

—*One of those off-road SUVs.*

—*How do we know he's telling the truth?* asked Carney.

—*Oh, he's telling the truth,* said Crawf.

—*But how do we know? For certain?* said Rick.

—*You don't want to know,* said Crawf, looking over to Antenna who still looked to the ground and offered no help.

—*I do,* said Zip.

—*Yes, me too,* said Bash.

—*He's brought Helmut's remains home.*

—*What?* said Rick.

—*Show us,* said Zip.

Crawf stood his ground—*You really don't want to…*

The animals moved, shifted in their places, uncertain, wanting to speak…

—*I will show them.* Gleam shook a black necklace from his neck and over his head. Now that it wasn't hidden amongst his fur, the animals could see the cord was made of Helmut's black feathers, rolled and woven together. At the bottom, the feathers had been fashioned into a vessel that had hung under Gleam's chin.

Gleam cracked the feathers of the vessel open with his frightful claws to reveal Helmut's head, still crowned by the bony chef's cap, still stained by a dribble of blood. The once fiercely intelligent eyes were now blank, clouded and unseeing. Gleam placed the head, with the neck neatly severed and blood free, nested in black feathers, in the centre of the cave. The animals gasped and shifted again, uneasy now, as they looked at the disconnected head of their most senior member.

—*But, where's the rest of him?*

—*He had been run over. He was roadkill.*

—*You…?* Slowly realisation dawned on Antenna and she finally looked up at the tiger—*You ate him?*

Gleam nodded—*But I didn't kill him. We had a deal.*

V

A bright yellow smiley face grimaced down from the sandstone wall of the machine cage. Anyone could see it had been sprayed in a rush.

Paint dribbled from the mouth, causing it to turn down, and the eyes seeped yellow custard tears.

Gleam curled up on one side of the machine cage. Exhausted, he lay his majestic head down on his forepaws with a sigh and closed his weary eyes. He did not rest easy, however.

Inside the same cage, as far from Gleam as she could get, Chimera was furious. She stood and shouted, rattling a rectangle of metal across the bars, trying to make as much noise as she could—*What does that say about me, hey? You can't keep me in here with a tiger! What does that make me? I'll tell you! Bait!*

Antenna, Zip and Crawf stood with their backs to the hangar opening. They watched Chimera's antics impassively. Her cries did not register with them.

—*We have to get Hod out,* said Antenna.

—*That also means extricating an entire bandicoot family,* said Zip.

—*What can we do about the crocs?* asked Crawf.

— *We can't just leave them there to fry,* said Antenna—*Sorry, Crawf. Get some rest before you go.*

—*You'll be right, Crawf,* said Zip—*It's all in a day's work for Ektek.*

Gleam raised his head and stared at Chimera, still clamouring and clattering in their shared cage. He took in a deep breath and roared— *Aaaaaaarrr…*

That made Antenna, Zip and Crawf pay attention and it turned Chimera into jelly. She screamed and then began to sob as they approached the cage—*Oh, you've got to get me out, he's going to kill me, can't you see? Why are you leaving me here to die? It's inhumane, it's inanimalane, it's diabolical, you're murdering me…*

Antenna looked at Gleam, who nodded at her, and then she glanced back to Chimera—*Chimera? Shut up.*

As Chimera gasped in surprise, Gleam said—*Just one more thing…* Antenna nodded.

Gleam asked her—*Helmut had been haunted by a strange voice in his head recently, telling him what to do?*

—*That's true. We were worried about him.*

—*With good reason. Turns out, his mysterious siren was actually a transmission from somewhere else. The pilot of the airship worked as a kind of receiver, getting the sounds and words directly from another creature. If you sat in the pilot's seat, you could hear the signals quite clearly. I did. I don't know how it worked. Perhaps the pilot sitting in the seat and touching the controls acts as a conductor, who knows. Whatever it is, this animal is still trapped somewhere and very unhappy. Helmut was tormented by thoughts of finding her.*

—*Did he? Find her?*

—*He couldn't have. No one could. Not in this lifetime. Not on this planet.* Gleam had everyone's attention by now and he looked at his listeners carefully before he next spoke—*I think she's in space.*

—*Space?* echoed Antenna.

Chimera dropped her metal noisemaker with a clang.

—*What do you mean, space?* asked Zip.

—*The sort of space that's not on earth. Beyond-our-atmosphere space.*

—*Orbiting space?* said Crawf.

—*You mean, a satellite space?* said Zip.

—*You think there's a live creature on our satellite? Transmitting to our airship?* said Antenna.

—*That's what I think.*

If anyone had been watching Chimera, which they were not, they would have noticed a quiver and a shiver as a change was wrought within her. At each repetition of the word 'space' in the preceding conversation, Chimera altered. She straightened up. She became serious. Her face focussed. Her eyes undimmed to reveal a flare of intense intelligence.

Chimera's time had come. She did indeed have hidden talents and, it would have been obvious to any observer, they were to do with 'space'.

Chapter Thirty-nine

The orbiting satellite hummed with very little life at all. Only the most basic systems were operational. Stillness and lack of expectancy haunted corridors of neatly organised purpose. The internal fixtures and fittings managed only to gather dust. Only one living thing roamed the orderly hallways and currently she was resting on the bridge.

Her long, furry, striped body drifted in solitary comfort over a couch facing a bank of buttons. She did not touch the couch. She did not touch anything. She floated, weightless, in zero gravity. Everything about her was long. She had a long face, long limbs and a long tail. She had a long, thin body and breathed in long, lonely sighs.

With one long, languid arm she reached over to a bank of faders and curling out one long claw, lifted a button gently. The air filled with the gentle sound of whale mothers playing with their young, milling in the warm waters of their breeding grounds. The whales sang and screeched and communicated their love for one another in tousled eddies.

She lay back, hummed to herself and twisted slightly in the lethargic air until she could stare out of her porthole. She could see for kilometres. Infinitely. One side of her view was black velvet strewn with generous vomits of glittering gem stars and the other side was taken up with a huge, blue-green orb she called Earth. Her parents had called it Earth and her grandparents had called it Earth and so it had ever been called: Earth. It had always been there, filling half her vision and she had always been in orbit around it.

She screeched, loud and long, joining in the whale song, singing along.

Or she could have been screaming.

Out of her porthole, Earth's blue-green pattern was wreathed in smoky cloud swirls. Never was a sphere so round. Never was a planet so unreachable. Never was there a creature so out of touch with the world.

Chapter Forty

I

In the Ektek control centre, Gleam and Zip drew in close to the communications centre deck, offering little more than moral support as Antenna set up the communications relay system.

They could all hear the unspoken words, 'If only Min were here... ' and they all decided to leave them unspoken.

Zip busied herself on the other keyboard, picking out the way to the Ektek website—*Gleam?*

—*Ah ha?*

—*Do you think... I just wondered... Do you think this voice... this siren... Could she be... I mean, I know about the story and all but...*

—*Yes?* said Gleam, patiently.

—*Would it be at all possible that it's an...*

—*Yes?*

—*Well, you know, like, an... um...alien?*

—*An alien?* snorted Antenna.

—*Sounded like a real animal to me,* said Gleam.

—*Come on, Zip, you don't really believe in aliens?*

—*We're talking about a voice from space. That's all we know.* Typing arduously, Zip's bat fingers checked the Ektek email inbox—*You think it's normal to have a creature from Earth in orbit?*

—*I can't honestly say I'm surprised,* said Antenna—*There's always been rumours, haven't there.*

—*Legends,* said Zip—*Which don't discount aliens. What if the aliens had overrun the animals? Imagine if they've interbred?*

—*Zip. Really. Shut up.*

—*Hmmmm,* Gleam examined the complex equipment: bones, plant roots and shells wound though with cables and metal *object trouvés*. Gleam was overwhelmed. He'd never imagined that animals could control this much technology. Full of awe, he watched Antenna as she opened websites and turned everything on. He asked—*Why are there so many computer screens here?*

—We can't ever really know what was in their minds when the founders set it up. Sometimes it can be helpful, said Antenna—*We seem to use them all. We might be broadcasting live material from several sources and editing on the fly. We might still need to check up on other sites and keep incoming channels open in case of an emergency from one of the actives out in the field.*

—You must be very proud.

—Proud?

—Of your parents? The founders.

—Yes, of course. Antenna continued with her connections, explaining everything as simply as she could to the newest, and largest, member of Ektek. She also noted, privately, that he had the biggest, most yellow teeth of any creature that she'd had the pleasure of working with.

—What if they'd want to kill us and collect us for their museums? Zip shook her head—*We'd be stuffed.*

—Didn't sound like an alien to me, said Gleam—*Really, Zip. I wouldn't worry about aliens.*

—Yeah. But what do aliens sound like?

—Forget about aliens. It's not aliens, okay? Antenna was beginning to sound annoyed—*Aliens. Zed. If it were aliens the airforce would have killed them by now. Or put them in their zoos. Can you imagine? People would pay big money to see aliens, wouldn't they?* Antenna turned her attention to the computer screen in front of her. She typed away, thinking on her paws—*You think Helmut was picking up a real creature? Broadcasting direct from the satellite?*

—Yes, I think so, said Gleam—*I believe so.*

—Could be anywhere, couldn't it? said Zip—*We don't know this…*

—Don't say it…

—This… voice… really is in space. I mean, space is a bloody big place, isn't it.

—Got to start somewhere, said Antenna—*It's just we've never connected with the satellite directly before. It's always been a means to an end. I mean, it was a joke, right? Who thought that scientist-making-an-ark thing was for real?*

Zip, still doubtful, turned to Gleam yet again—*Do you think Helmut was really talking with her? Like, you know; to and fro, give and take, listen and comment type conversation?*

The tiger considered before answering—*I think he thought he was, to-ing and fro-ing, as you put it. Presumably she'd answer something in a pertinent way and then he'd believe they'd connected. If enough serendipitous remarks interlaced, then, hey presto, they'd be communicating.*

—But, only in his head.

—*Well, here goes our first space contact.* Antenna, Ektek radio numbatham, attempted to find the channel of communication for the fabled satellite. Suddenly, through the speakers, and the magic of digital radio, they were in a pod of whales, dancing in motes of mottled sea-sun, singing their hearts out.

—*That's weird.*

—*What's that?*

—*Sounds like Smacker's family having a party!*

—*Sounds alien to me.*

—*It's not aliens. It's whales, Zip, whales. I told you, forget the aliens.*

—*Though, why are whales transmitting? They don't need radio to communicate with us.*

—Antenna turned to Gleam to explain—*Helmut was one; an understander. Whales can use extra-sensory perception to connect. Smacker will miss him.*

—*Whatever we're listening to,* said Zip—*We're not in space any more.*

—*Unless there's whales out there swimming through the stars.* Antenna altered the frequency and the animals leaned in to listen to a new world—*This isn't right either...* Their cave filled with human sounds patting little word shapes with their gravely voices—*Maybe that's truck drivers or police or...*

—*Amateur astrologers?*

—*Who knows? Aliens, maybe?*

—*Zip, can you please drop...*

—*You want me to search this freq?*

—*No time.*

The discussion was so intent on their radio exploration that no one noticed Chimera enter the office. The chimpanzee stood to attention, surveying the scrum of creatures around the cacophony of human sounds crackling through the system. She decided that actions were louder than words and she knew what needed to be done. Time was a-wasting.

Chimera's long, dark, hairy arm reached out over Antenna's shoulder and her long, dark, hairy hand adjusted the frequency on the stations. Chimera's hairy, dark face moved in to the mic and said in a businesslike voice—*Zee One One, come in please, Zee One One? Can you read me? Over.*

Gleam, Zip and Antenna looked at each other in alarm and then stared, completely taken aback, at this new version of what, or who, Chimera was. Their concern was not tempered when the sound of whales blasted back into the room. Without turning a hair, or a cockroach, Chimera turned down the volume and repeated herself—*Zee One One, can you copy? Over.*

The sound of whales came abruptly to a halt. A howl of feedback flared through the cave. A hiss of static and then a rusty old voice sawed out of the speaker—*Helloooo, Houston! Is that really you?*

—*That's her!* said Gleam—*That's the voice!*

—*Hey, I'm here to help*, said Chimera. With her yellow oblong teeth, Chimera stretched back her lips and grinned at everyone staring at her before bending back to the mic—*Zee One One, welcome aboard. Sorry to say, my Houston days are over, we're Bedlam calling here. Pleased to meet you. Over.*

Zip, Gleam and Antenna were non the wiser. What did she mean her Houston days were over? And who let Chimera out of her cage?

Up in orbit, the long lean, creature floated closer to the mic embedded into the control deck—*Bedlam? What happened to Woomera? Nah, I don't care. Just get me out of here. When are you coming to get me?* All four of her paws were clinging onto the deck as though she could squeeze herself into the comm system and she pushed her face desperately into the mic. Finally. She'd been contacted. Finally, her mission would be over. She was finding it hard to breathe. Her jaw jutted out…

The speakers blared—*Can't say yet, Zee One One. We've only just worked out where you are after all this time but you can be darn tootin' we're keen as to meet you. Can you tell us a bit about yourself, please? What's your situation? Over.*

Her long limbs pulled towards the radio. She was frantic. Tears came out of her eyes; she started to shout, her limbs were shaking— *Get me out of here!*

—*Can you tell us a bit about yourself, Zee One One? Over.*

She jammed her foot down on the communications button—*I am the walrus, goo goo a joob…* Then she lifted her foot again.

Chimera's strange business like voice echoed her with the question—*You're a walrus? Over.*

Down went the red communications button—*'Course not. I'm Big Taz. When am I coming home?*

—*Right you are, Big Taz. Soon as we can get organised we'll have you back on Earth. We've got a bit of homework to do here and we'll be there as soon as we can. Can you let us know what you're seeing out your window, there, Big Taz? Over.*

—*Metal sculpture forest. Shards of burnt-out smashed satellites. Never hit us, though. Not hard, anyway. Tinkle, tinkle little sat, up above the world you're at…*

—Us? Who else is up there with you, Big Taz? Over.

—All my family. All the creatures. Great and small. We're all here.

—But only you speak? Over.

—Yis. That's right. I'm the only one doing talking now. Talking. To you. I'm the only one doing anything. I'm the only one who can move. I'm the only one with flesh on her bones; hair on her skin. I'm the only one who can breathe. I'm the only one who can eat... Oh, food! Give me something decent to eat, will you, for the love of Zed, please, you've got to get me out of here, come on, please, get me out of here...

—You're the only one left alive? Over.

—I'm the only one. That's right. Are you coming today? I'm ready.

—Where are you, Big Taz? Over.

—I told you that. Up, way up high. Higher than you, little Bed Lamb. Much, much higher...

—Can you see any land at all? Over.

—Dark. Stars. Rocks. Planets. Satellites. Earth.

—Earth? Can you tell us what Earth looks like? Over.

—Round. Big. Clouds. Blue. There's a green hook curving through it.

—How long have you been out, Big Taz? Over.

—Out? Never been out. Only in.

—You were born in space? Over.

—Yis, yis, yis, born in space. Parents born in space. Their parents pups when sat shot out.

—Who shot the sat? Over.

—Don't you know nothing? Zed, of course. Zed made everything in the beginning. You know that. Enough talking. Get me out. Get me out now.

—No worries, Big Taz. We're on our way. Hang on in there. Over and out. Chimera pushed back from the mic and settled in close to the keyboard—*Let me search this sat and we'll see if we can find its launch and orbit range.* She began typing efficiently, searching her way through a complicated series of databases—*Ah, ha, yup, thought so... hmmm,* she muttered to herself as she linked through various sites.

Antenna, Gleam and Zip all watched Chimera in complete amazement before they came to their senses and spoke at once—*How?*

—How did you get through? said Gleam.

—How did you get out of the machine cage? said Zip.

—How did you know what to say? said Gleam.

—Why did you tell me you couldn't use a computer? said Antenna.

—How on earth are we going to get her down? said Zip.

Chimera looked up at her audience with knowing amusement burning in her eyes. She smiled. She appeared to be brimming with confidence and knowledge about this business. It was as though she were an old horse, back in harness and she certainly knew her way home. She spoke as though the answer should be obvious to all—*Build a rocket,* she said, smiling a broad chimpanzee grin.

—*Build a rocket? How do you propose we do that?*

—*It's only a sat. All we have to do is get out of the Earth's first layer of atmos, dock, break in, rescue the Big Taz and get back down to Earth without burning up. Shouldn't take more than a week all up.*

The three earthbound creatures watched her, speechless. Gradually each one came back to life, shaking their head a little or blinking as the strange ideas filtered through their impossibility gauges.

—*A week?* echoed Antenna.

—*But...* said Zip.

—*You're talking space travel...* said Gleam.

—*Orbiting the planet?* said Antenna.

—*How the heck are we going to do that?* said Zip.

Again, Chimera seemed to take charge. She seemed confident. She appeared calm. It was as though everything were possible—*You must have some sort of craft we can adapt? All we have to do is attach rockets, fuel tanks... Some kind of airtight, watertight, flameproof cockpit?*

—*The airship cockpit...*

—*... is in the middle of the desert...*

—*The plane...*

—*... isn't waterproof...*

—*Subtek?*

—*Subtek. Oh, yeah.*

—*Subtek might just work...*

—*Flameproof?*

—*Certainly treated for a wide temperature range and has its own oxygenation systems,* said Antenna thoughtfully—*Might be able to reinforce the outer surface...*

—*There we are then. I knew you could do it,* said Chimera.

—*Hang on,* said Antenna—*We're a long way a way from finalising this yet. What about fuel? We can't use biodiesel to get out of the atmosphere. We need real rocket fuel. Where can we get that?*

—*Ah, I may just have a solution,* said Chimera—*Or rather, you might.*

II

Minutes later, in the hangar, Chimera, Gleam, Zip and Antenna were gathered around Manifold. With a strong arch of her abdomen, Manifold demonstrated the ejection of her defence system: a hot, fast and powerful jet spray out of her rear end. Chimera had seen the explosions the flying bombardier beetles had performed at the entomological tattoo memorial service for Min and filed them away for reference.

—*That's just great!* Chimera was fascinated and bombarded the bombardier with questions—*Can you just release the spray without the chemical reaction? Like, just the actual liquid? How much of this stuff do you generate every* day? *How long do you need to recharge before you can go again?* Without waiting for the answers, Chimera turned to the assembled creatures. She seemed to be speeding up before their eyes and they watched her, bemused—*We can use this fuel. It's obviously some kind of hydrogen peroxide. We might be able to boost its efficiency by adding polyethylene residues collected from rubbish left at the zoo. We just need to collect enough chemical from the beetles. If we could emulate the method whereby this energy is transformed, this will certainly be enough to get us into orbit. Not to mention the fact it's not going to affect Ektek's carbon footprint.*

—*Chimera?* said Antenna—*What is going on here? You're talking like you think Ektek really could go into space.*

—*That's true. That's what I believe.*

—*Chimera. We don't have the resources. None of us has any experience...*

—*I've got plenty enough for all of us.*

—*What are you talking about?*

—*You got to relax. Trust me. I'm an astronaut. NASA born and bred. I mean to make it happen. You guys just hang on and enjoy the ride.*

—*But what ride? Where are we going?*

—*We're going to rescue a Big Taz from the satellite that Zed built. Of course.*

Zip and Antenna stared at each other and then back to Chimera. She just grinned—*Hey, don't worry, guys. Nothing can go wrong if I'm in charge.*

Zip stared at Antenna—*She's trying to reassure us, right?* asked Zip—*She thinks this is a good thing? To risk our lives rescuing who-knows-what that has already caused Helmut's death? A creature that up till now we thought was a joke, a part of a mythological ark from the mists of ancient history?* Their shared smile was more like a grimace.

Chapter Forty-one

High up in the air, all Crawf could think was how Ektek never seemed to get involved in anything nice and easy. Space? Get real. Just because this new-arrival tiger said outer space they had to take it seriously and jump. And what if Gleam had killed Helmut? Who knew? Antenna and Zip seemed to think Gleam was *bona fide* but Crawf wasn't convinced at all. He hoped they didn't make contact with any creature out in space. He didn't think Ektek needed to get caught up in aliens. What if the aliens liked to eat animals? As far as he could see, whatever was decided was bound to be difficult and there would be more work for everyone, particularly the ones who didn't need any more work, like him for a start, with his partner alone back in their enclosure, trying to have an egg, her heart breaking because she couldn't seem to and him getting sad and miserable because he knew he should spend more time with her but he certainly hadn't said any of this because he'd learned to keep his beak shut when young, hopeful creatures were curious and passionate and wouldn't listen to common sense. He grunted and looked over to his fluffy passenger—*Nearly there.*

—*So soon?*

—*Sooner you tell them, sooner we can start moving them out.*

—*They're not going to go, Crawf.*

—*But they've got to. There's no choice. They can't survive there.*

—*They'll never leave. This is the only home, the only safe home, they've… we've ever known.*

—*But it's not safe.*

—*I know that. You know that. They know that.*

—*They know?*

—*Well, it's about risk management, isn't it. They've seen the problems; we all have, of course. They knew it wasn't right when Serena's last litter were all born dead. But they've learned to live with it. The risks are far greater outside the tip. It's just when Hod comes in, all bouncy and fresh, he can see the problems with his outsider's eyes and he's all keen for me to go and tell Ektek all our problems but it's still not going to get Ma and Pa out of their comfort car. Nothing's ever going to* do that. They like it there. If it wasn't for the crocs we'd still be there, not knowing the extent of the danger but…

—Even though it probably means the end of the line?

—They don't like change.

—Could you go? By yourself?

FJ hummed for a little bit. Then he said in a small voice—In one way I'd like to.

—You could come and work with Ektek and live in Bedlam…

—It'd be great, wouldn't it? But I couldn't leave my family.

—What will you'll tell them? You'll still try to get them out?

—Yup. I'll try. But don't hold your breath.

—We'll all try. I don't know what good I can do but maybe Hod will have better…

—Hod. How am I…?

—I don't know, FJ. He's got himself into this. He's going to have to get himself out. If you drop him in it, well, it's not your responsibility. He's a big wally now.

Back on earth's hard gravel car park, Shining Teeth finished laughing.

—You mammals, you kill me, you really do. She gave one last snort and drew breath—Don't know why you're making such a fuss. There's bloody radioactivity everywhere. Her fellow harem members began nodding their heads as if they knew what she was talking about—In all the dirt, all the rocks, all the air. Radioactivity's all around us all the bloody time.

Crawf and FJ stood to one side and Hod on the other. Everyone nodded their heads, as agreement was entirely the best way to deal with Shining Teeth, just as with any large rogue croc, and they'd survived so far, so they knew they were doing something right—Especially now there's all those goddamn radio waves and mobile phone towers everywhere. My ancestors put up with more radioactivity than you've had back scratches and look at me; I turned out just bonza.

—Yes, well, Crawf was not exactly sure how bonza Shining Teeth really was—… we're simply not sure how more or less radioactive this particular area might be, Crawf kept nodding his head—… and we're not sure what levels might be safe for you or for anyone else for that matter. So we're offering you a chance to transport you somewhere. Somewhere else. Somewhere safer. If we can find such a place…

—Let me get this straight. You're telling me that Ektek wants to rescue us.

—Well, yes.

—That's not turned out too well in the past, has it? said Shining Teeth.

—Well, no. It hasn't, said Crawf.

—How do you propose getting the five of us out of here?

—We've got a vehicle, we call it the tank, which could transport two or perhaps three at a time. Trouble is, it's slow and it's parked up in the Ektek garage. It's going to take time to drive it over here. I've got to get to the fallen airship - see if we can bring a crew out to fix that up - and then I'll be heading out.

—What's wrong with the airship? asked Hod.

—Crashed it.

—Anyone hurt?

Shining Teeth suddenly swirled around to face Hod—*You seem mighty interested in Ektek business, young flat-footed wallaby. What's got into you all of a sudden?*

Hod opened and shut his mouth, speechless. Had he given himself away?

Crawf sighed and looked up to the heavens. He looked at Hod and sighed again—*No one you'd know. Anyway, I'm going to need a driver. Any ideas?* He looked out over the sea of crocodiles and sighed once more.

Shining Teeth looked in turn at FJ and Hod and then back to Crawf.

—I'm your mammal, Hod said, adding quickly—*If it's not too tough to learn.*

—Thanks, Crawf nodded—*You'll cope. About the right size. I suggest the crocs move out of the bunker - can you find them somewhere, FJ? I'll head out with my volunteer here. We'll be back in a couple of days. Perhaps if you source your food away from the tip you might avoid any more serious contamination. We'll get you all out as soon as we can. If we can. Barring disasters.*

The two animals climbed on board the plane and got into the cockpit. Crawf spoke loudly for the sake of the crocodiles and his voice was sharp, too. He was plainly annoyed with Hod—*Come on, 'Hod', is it? 'Hod'. You sit there. Do up your seat belt. Never been on a plane before, then? Just do what I tell you and we'll try to make you as comfortable as possible.*

FJ waved as the plane took off into a grey cloudy sky and flew out of sight. He turned around to see the crocs watching him very carefully. He willed himself to remain calm though nothing could hide the shivers of fear shaking his little bent limbs—*Rightyho. I reckon maybe the Italian job with the real leather seats? Or perhaps you'd prefer something more roomy and American?*

Hod and Crawf flew along in silence for a while and then headed out over the desert. Hod was watching the changes in the landscape out of the window—*It's not so much a line in the sand, is it? It's a gradual shift. When you fly over it, I mean.* When he spoke it was almost to himself, a kind of meditation. He was almost unaware of Crawf, certainly of Crawf's suspicions, and meant him no harm. He would have been surprised if he'd known the struggle that was going on in Crawf's mind. He continued his meditation on the landscape—*The plants change, the soils change and then, without noticing the change itself has happened, everywhere you look, you're in the desert when you weren't there before.*

Crawf flicked Hod a glance. He shook off some of his disapproval and decided to join his ex-friend in making pleasant chat. Not that he'd forgiven him, mind, no, Hod wasn't forgiven just yet—*I picked up Gleam from just about here, yes, you can see it now...*

—*Gleam?*

—*Gleam is Helmut's... friend. Tiger. Helping Ektek.*

—*Tiger? Big, bloody, hairy, roaring thing? Excellent. Tiger's not going to muck around with namby pamby peaceful little actions, is it?* Then Hod was still as he saw the extent of the airship wreckage—*Oh, Zed. He was lucky to get out alive.*

—*Who?*

—*Helmut.*

—*Hod...*

Hod looked over at the palm cockatoo—*What?*

—*Helmut didn't make it.*

—*But you said...*

—*Did you want me to tell you in front of the crocodiles?* Crawf concentrated as he guided the wingship through some turbulence—*Hullo? I'm not completely stupid, though you might think I am.*

Hod stared hard at the grey cockatoo. After a little while his anger turned to understanding and then sorrow and he hastily wiped his eyes—*Right. How did you find...?*

—*Gleam found him. And ate him.*

—*Ate him?*

—*He's a tiger.*

Hod struggled with understanding—*That's what tigers do, I guess.*

—*He brought Helmut's head back to Ektek. He says he didn't kill him. He says he doesn't kill. He only eats roadkill. He's the one who asked to be put in safe custody...*

—*Crawf?*

—*Yup? You might consider bringing the crocs here, to the desert. How long can they survive without water? Maybe we can find a river for them...*

—*Crawf?*

—Maybe see if they've got any radiation sickness before bringing them back to Bedlam. Like a quarantine. Though what good that's going to do us in the long run, I don't know. Germs, radioactivity, bacteria, insecticides, poisons, bird-flu, swine flu, human flu; all out to get us; if we don't go from one then we'll go from the mutation. Next time…

—Crawf. Listen. I just want to apologise. I'm sorry. I shouldn't have run away.

—Let's just see what we can salvage, shall we? Crawf brought the plane down on a flat area near the wreck. He and Hod got out and began sifting through the debris. The mess was scattered over a considerable distance - most of it from the fuel framework. Crawf and Hod loaded up the wingship with as much of the computer assembly and the engine systems as they could safely carry. Then they stood quietly surveying the litter. Hod wasn't sure any overtures would be welcome so he just looked at the wreck.

It was Crawf who spoke first—*You'll have plenty of time to think about things; long drive back in the tank.*

—Better get going, then. Hod looked around the smash site and then over at Crawf—*I really liked Helmut.*

—Bullshit. You were always arguing with him. There was never a moment's peace with you two in the same place.

—But I liked him for all that. At least he died quick.

—Maybe. Hope so. We don't know. It's not very likely, is it? I mean, hullo?

—I would have liked him to be proud of me, one day.

—He'd be proud now. I'm proud of you. I'm glad you apologised. Makes a hard job a bit more do-able. Thank you.

—Really? Even though I'm working for a bunch of crocs?

Crawf looked at him seriously—*Are you?*

Hod bounced back into the plane—*Let's get this stuff back to Ektek. It's time to face the music.*

Crawf followed more thoughtfully. He was still not certain if he could trust this wallaby. What was Hod up to?

Chapter Forty-two

I

The call went out across the world. Bombardier beetles on every landform lined up to donate their precious fuel to one unknown but endangered creature, up in space. The bombardier beetles would be making history and it was not an entirely unpleasant experience. A fuel donation was a safe process, carried out among friends and relatives and rewarded with an invigorating massage, before and after, from the stag beetles, their large pronged mandibles proving to be excellent equipment for getting deep into pressure points and relieving the stress of fuel release.

Huge tanks were filled, lashed together and swallowed by a whale, much as though the enormous mammals were swallowing a tiny vitamin pill, and then brought to Bedlam. Some of the whales needed to be persuaded of Bash's innocence before assisting Ektek, of course, but once they had heard the extraordinary tale of a Big Taz, whatever that was, who had been stuck out in orbit for all of her life, all of her parents' lives, most creatures were only too happy to help.

Finally, the beetles ran over the surface of their newly fuelled and provisioned rocket, ready to proclaim it finished. They had taken the submarine, coated it with highly protective cells from the backs of giant tortoises, attached colossal disposable fuel tanks and made ready the detachable capsule, which would once again become the bare submarine by the time it splashed back into the ocean on Earth (if everything went according to plan, and that was a very big IF).

There could be no test flight. The rocket fuel was so precious, so difficult to gather, there could only be one execution of this plan and it would be led by Chimera, Ektek's first astronaut.

II

Spark sighed, watching the cockroaches follow Chimera's brusque orders as they worked in the hangar—*She never lets them rest.*

Faint yips echoed around the hangar as the roaches worked.

—*Who?* said Torque.

—*The cockroaches. She's always got them slaving away on some task, carrying things far too heavy, fitting machinery together…*

—*Just between you and me, Spark my friend, can you tell them apart? They all look the same to me.*

Spark looked across the hangar to the hard-working team. He could see Blatta straining under the weight of the main fuel tank together with about a hundred of her colleagues. Blatta worried him. She was not free. He did not believe that she was ever happy.

—*Not to me.*

—*I got to tell you, I'm having trouble. I mean, does that make me old?*

—*No, Torque. Just beetl-ist.*

III

Chimera told everyone who would listen that she had been training for this event all her life. Gleam was particularly interested in her history. He was prepared to listen to her for hours, all the stories about her experience flying in the space shuttle and her involvement in experiments in space labs. It was apparently on her re-entry to Earth's atmosphere that her capsule had smashed open and she'd been swallowed by a whale. Then she'd been spat out onto the shores of the Congo where she'd caused a civil war between two chimpanzee tribes and from where she'd been rescued by Ektek during the heat of battle. Gleam shook his head with amazement.

It was true, though, that she knew exactly what was required to get the rocket to the satellite. She and Antenna had spent hours plotting the precise course the rocket would need to take in order to intersect with the satellite's path.

Chimera and Zip worked through the re-entry protocol and it was with Mandible that Chimera went through every eventuality on board the ship. Together with Blatta and her team of cockroaches, Chimera and her Heads of Departments calculated food requirements, waste storage and how best to contain a creature, they knew not what, who had very probably grown into never-before-seen shapes in zero gravity. Chimera seemed to have boundless energy. She was able to think of everything—every contingency, every possibility. She had revealed her hidden talents and they were formidable.

IV

Blatta and her team were returning to work in the hangar after a food break. They were all exhausted and marched slowly back to their duties.

—*How you doing?* Spark greeted the cockroach and then walked beside Blatta when she did not stop. He was not sure what he should say to her. After a little moment he asked—*Can I get you anything?*

Blatta said—*We're fine.*

—*I meant you. You, particularly, Blatta.* Spark stood in front of her and Blatta had no choice but to stop—*Can I do anything to help you? You all look so tired. Why do you help her so much?*

—*She's my friend.*

—*Chimera?*

—*Yes. I've been with her since…*

—*Yes?*

—*I was there, at the space lab. She looked after me.*

—*Saved your life?*

She glanced at him. He understood this was the case and also understood that it wasn't a subject for casual comment—*You don't have to say anything…*

—*I shouldn't… too much to do before we go.*

—*You're going? All of you?*

—*Just me. She needs me.*

—*What will you be doing?*

—*Anything that needs doing.*

—*Like always,* said Spark.

—*She looks after me.*

—*She's the lucky one.*

—*Have to go.* She stood and waved at the rest of the team to get back to work. Then she turned back to Spark—*Thanks, Spark.*

—*Good luck,* he said—*I'll see you when you get back.*

She paused, looked down, then looked up at him again and then, surprisingly, fleetingly, smiled—*Yes. I'd like that.* She quickly returned to the chain gang, handing up supplies to the rocket frame.

Spark stood and watched her work and then, with a fresh spring in his step, flew up into the air.

V

Crawf taxied the wingship into a parking space in the hangar and came to a standstill. As they unclipped their safety harnesses, he looked over to Hod—*Good luck, Hod.*

—*Thanks, Crawf,* Hod nodded—*Going to need it.* He knew he had a lot more than just plain cold humble pie on his menu this day. It felt like years that Hod had been away from Ektek, when really it was only a couple of months. He looked around him as he disembarked from the wingship. Everything seemed familiar yet strange and small to him.

Hod met Antenna as he strode down the corridor away from the hangar. They looked at each other for a considerable time before Antenna said—*Welcome home, Hod.*

Hod stared at her. Then he looked to the floor. Then he looked up and came closer in order to give her an embarrassed hug—*You have no idea.* He released her and stepped back. Then he leaned down towards her again and Antenna could see that he wanted to touch foreheads. Since childhood the two old friends had been close in so many ways. They had evolved a system of commingling their breath; a touch of their forehead and a bringing together of their noses gave them a sense of togetherness and community. The touching of foreheads was almost a meeting of minds. It was a sign of trust. Hod obviously wanted to rekindle their friendship and to pick up where they had left it just weeks before.

Antenna was not ready for that. She moved out of reach and clenched her jaw. Her mind was ready to forgive him but she was finding it difficult all the same. She found it difficult to look at him and turned away to look into the hangar.

When Zip, however, came down the corridor, she had no such inhibitions—*You working for the crocs or for us, buddy Hod, old wally shit head?*

Antenna gasped but Hod just stared at the bat—*Zip. Give me a break. I've only just found out about Helmut.*

—*Is that right? Poor thing. If you're part of Ektek you'll suck it up, won't you. If you're working with the crocs, then you're lying. So, either way, I don't trust you, Hod. Remember that. I just don't trust you.* Zip turned and left him, slumping now against the wall. She turned and just before marching out of sight, spat over her shoulder—*I never trusted you, wally shit-head.*

Hod bowed his head and took a deep breath in before looking at Antenna. She returned his gaze as he asked—*Is that what you think, too?*

—*I wish I didn't, Hod. I want to forgive you...*

—*I'd better get going, then. I've got some bandicoots to rescue.*

—*Stay for the launch first.*

—*I want to come home, Antenna. It's not easy out there. I'm on the run the entire time. I thought there'd be a wilderness and I could catch up with all the other rock wallabies and go tribal but I couldn't... There just isn't... It's not like I thought.*

—*No.*

—*I'll take the tank and get the bandicoots and do something about the crocs and then I'll be back; as soon as I can.*

—*Hod?*

—*Yup?*

—*I do trust you.*

—*Thanks, Antenna. That makes it easier.*

—*At least come and take a look at our rocket.*

Hod nodded and turned to walk with her through the hangar, back through the forecourt, through bushland and into a disused part of the zoo. Designated for a new elephant enclosure in five years' time, it was an abandoned concrete area once used as a home for polar bears. As they rounded the corner Hod could see the extensive rocket building works. A new tunnel had been excavated specifically to make way for the body of the fuel tanks. These were stored partly outside, in what was once a rudimentary swimming pool, for access and ventilation. An army of beetles and cockroaches were loading in fuel from the drums, still slimy from whale spit. Chimera was siting cross-legged on the concrete ground, holding a meeting with a group of earnest grey cockroaches—*Yip,* they said—*Yip, yip, yip.*

Antenna explained the set up to Hod who was gob-smacked by the breadth of the operation—*But, Chimera? Of all creatures? Who knew?*

—*She's familiar with the language and I do believe she's had some training somewhere. NASA certainly used chimpanzees. A lot of scientific laboratories still do research into HIV AIDS and Hepatitis with chimpanzee labour. Gleam has taken it on himself to double-check her stories when she's not around. He's found some reasonable accounts that might back her up, even though she does spin some incredible yarns. There's no doubt she's had an adventurous life. I mean, she's scarred, isn't she; inside and out.*

—*What if something goes wrong?*

—*Chimera seems happy with her odds.*

—*What are the chances of missing the intercept?*

—*High.*

—*What happens then?*

—*She goes sailing off into outer space and is never heard of again.*

—She can't turn back?

—She's got enough power to make an attempt but if she misses by much, she won't be back.

—Does she have the right co-ordinates to get back to Bedlam?

—They'll get pretty near.

—If everything goes according to plan.

—Yes. If everything goes right.

Hod had something else on his mind. He tore his eyes away from the rocket ship and turned back to face Antenna—*About… Helmut?*

—Hod. I couldn't stop him going. I wanted him to go to the vet. I thought he was depressed. Hearing voices. I didn't imagine they could be real.

—It was his choice, said Hod—*To leave.*

—Was it your choice, too? asked Antenna.

—Of course. You have to make your own decisions.

—I do trust you, Hod.

—Thanks, Antenna. You know, I am sorry. For deserting…

Hod and Antenna were embarrassed. They had been friends and now they were finding it difficult to speak at all. Hod drew in a deep breath and forced himself to look directly at Antenna—*I was wondering about Helmut.*

—You know about Gleam?

—Yes, Crawf told me about the road kill. I was wondering if you'd buried him. I mean…

—His head. No. It's still in the control centre.

—What about taking him up in the rocket, too? Get him up to the stars? Maybe leave him in the satellite. Where he wanted…

—… to go. Yes. Antenna looked at the wallaby in wonder. He would never cease to surprise her. Imagine Hod of all creatures, thinking of Helmut so kindly—*Thanks, Hod.*

—No worries. Better get going. Pong's already over by the tank.

Antenna watched him lope over in his rock-wallaby way and saw him give the tank a once-over, check the fuel was topped up, and talk with Pong, the dung beetle, about the latest report from the mechanics. Hod looked over to Antenna and gave her a smart little salute before hopping into the cabin and firing up the engine.

The tank roared into life. Beetles ran over the hangar, shouting, clearing the way and waving him through.

Antenna lifted a paw in response. She didn't know if she would ever see him again—*All clear above and astern,* she whispered, echoing the business of the beetles. Then she turned back to the control centre, ready to find Helmut's remains, ready to give him the send-off of his life.

VI

For once, soft darkness enveloped all the caves and tunnels under Bedlam Zoo except one place. The light concentrated in only one area. The glow-worms and the fireflies had been enticed into the control centre by their avid interest in the take-off. All Ektek creatures were enamoured by the idea of space travel. It had once seemed so remote, so impossible, and now everyone had strange imaginings of living in orbit and habitats on the Moon... Never before had the Ektek passageways reverberated with so many discussions about air supply, solar power and hydroponic farming. Exciting mutterings about aliens as well - but quietly, between only the closest of friends.

The launch had to be at night to avoid detection by zoo staff. Antenna was fairly certain some amateur astrologers might be a bit confused by an unofficial rocket launch from the middle of the CBD but that was their problem.

The rocket was primed and ready in the disused enclosure, pointing at the sky, surrounded by beetles performing last minute checks. It was shiny and stood incredibly tall, considering a team of ants and beetles in an old polar bear pool had assembled it. The two fuel tanks were massive and decorated boldly in blue and red, the colours of bombardier beetles. The mixing tank was large and shiny and coloured black in honour of the ants.

Chimera was lying in place, locked into the former submarine, earphones on, talking to Antenna. Her cockroach team had been left behind, all except Blatta, who was able to brace herself in a corner of Chimera's suit, able to breathe the same air mixture as Chimera. She would assist Chimera, mainly by keeping out of her way until required. It had been so forever, it seemed.

Antenna was in the control centre and nearly every animal ever seen in an Ektek tunnel was in there with her - or trying to be. Crawf, Gleam, Zip and Bash were next to her, all with roles of their own: Zip was in charge of communications and research, Bash was monitoring the co-ordinates of the trajectory, Gleam was observing Chimera's physical status (and when he had time, continuing his research into her past). Gleam was most interested in Chimera's age. Since chimpanzees were long-lived Gleam suspected that Chimera was older than she was letting them think. Vanity? Gleam thought so and he worried about her physical ability to withstand the forces she would encounter on the journey out of the atmosphere.

Crawf was keeping a close eye on the exterior of the rocket. He would be responsible for seeing the fuel tanks disconnected at the right time and the docking system operated smoothly.

Ektek creatures, large and small, packed into the central cave, stuffed out along the hallway and jammed into the hangar. They were all trying to hear what was going on and watching everything they could see out of the hangar entrance.

Antenna had contact, not only with Chimera, but also with Big Taz, who was trying impatiently to come to terms with her imminent release, unable to say anything useful or sensible. Antenna spoke clearly and slowly to Chimera knowing full well she was actually speaking to the multitudes gathered around her—*After the tattoo in honour of Min I knew Ektek to be an extraordinary team but I did not imagine then that we would soon take off into space. I am deeply proud of each and every one who has worked on this endeavour, as I am sure both Helmut and Min would also have been.*

Zip started the countdown when they were a minute-and-a-half away from launch time, which then built to a chorus with every creature shouting—*5 - 4 - 3 - 2 - 1…*

And then…

Then…

No-body breathed…

Nothing…

… happened…

Animals looked at each other…

Uh oh…

Just as the pause was beginning to turn…

… into a sense of failure…

… instead…

… a loud hiss, a whoosh and a flare of flame!

—*BLAST OFF!*

The jets burst into action, a blare of roaring blasted everyone's ears, a cushion of fumes and fog accumulated under the rocket and filled the concrete enclosure, making made everyone splutter and cough as the rocket took off. Bombardier fuel was concocted of a series of chemicals that, after mixing, turned into water vapour. It was quite harmless, despite the intense force.

Everyone screamed and yelled and applauded in their different creature way and the rocket shivered up into the sky, roaring and

fizzing and blasting out into space—*Zed*, said Manifold to Torque—
Reminds me of my crazy old grandfather. He used to fly like that. Used to smell like that, too.

When the safety beetles gave them the all clear, the creatures ran out into the darkness and watched the silver stream of the rocket as it straightened out and flew up and out into the clear black night like an arrow.

Spark said—*Who's that like, then?*

—*That's more like me.* Manifold said—*Obviously.*

The three watching beetles laughed. Then Torque said—*What if we hit some of that space junk?*

Manifold said—*If that's the only thing that goes wrong, we'll have done well.*

—*What if, what if… If we only ever worried about risks then nothing would ever get done,* said Spark—*Risks, risks, risks; just breathing is a risk.*

—*Of course, we could hit something,* said Manifold.

—*We're about to make some more junk of our own,* said Torque—*When those fuel tanks are dropped.*

—*… but wouldn't it be great if it worked? First time? No problems?* said Spark—*Ektek's first flight into space, how awesome!*

—*What's the likelihood of that, young greenhorn, eh?* said Torque as they watched the thin thread of the rocket fumes winding up into the sky.

VII

The rocket raced onwards, up, up, up, towards the stars, up through the troposphere, up through the stratosphere, up into the mesosphere and on into the thermosphere where the sub would go into orbit in less than an hour. With her face plastered back into the submarine chair, Chimera whispered with the effort of speaking against the G forces working against her small frame—*Destiny.*

Blatta curled in behind Chimera's neck and waited. She could sense she was off duty now and could take the opportunity for some rest. It would not last long. It never did.

VIII

Back down in the forecourt of the hangar, creatures watched the rocket trail lengthen out across the sky.

—*What about that Big Taz, then?* Spark asked Torque—*Do we have any idea of what kind of creature she is?*

—*She still says she's a walrus. What do you think?*

—*Probably not,* said Spark.

—*No.*

—*Still, hard to believe there's any creatures up there at all.*

—*Guess it's wait and see.*

—*Wonder how she'll cope when she gets back down to Earth?*

—*How do any of us cope?*

IX

Antenna was jostled in the control centre. Creatures spilled into the corridors and the beetles relayed the news. The crowd buzzed with discussions and comments.

The beetles flew down the corridors shouting as they went—*The fuel tanks have been jettisoned!*

—*Meeting point is half an hour away!*

—*Interception in five minutes…*

—*Counting down to docking…*

—*Intercept has been missed!*

—*Oh, no!*

—*Fly by is repeated…*

—*Back on track.*

—*Docking complete!*

—*Chimera is having trouble getting the door opened.*

—*She's done it.*

—*Chimera has entered the satellite!*

Everyone cheered at that!

—*She's taken Helmut's head with her!*

Torque nodded at Spark—*Helmut would be so pleased to know that.*

—*Such a lovely gesture,* Spark agreed.

X

Still in full astronaut gear, Chimera floated through the corridors of the satellite's zero gravity, thoroughly enjoying her return to weightlessness. She held the woven bag containing Helmut's head as she examined the dusty metal of unused cupboards and machinery lining the walls. She shook her helmeted head sadly. Her radio contact buzzed as she spoke to Antenna—*Reminds me of the space lab. Only this one's more like a ghost ship. All fitted up and no one to visit. Nothing's going on here at all. What a waste.*

Antenna's voice fizzed through the sat's hallways—*Any sign of Big Taz?*

—*I'll head up to the bridge. She said she'd be there,* Chimera took a gigantic leap and pirouetted thrillingly—*That's where she was when I last spoke with her.*

—*Here you are at last! Let's go!* Big Taz leapt out of a doorway and hugged Chimera so hard her helmet fell off—*Don't worry, you won't need that her,* said Big Taz.

With the force of the helmet's flight, Blatta was flung out of her comfortable nook from within Chimera's space suit. She curved through the stale air and crashed into a wall. She slid down and lay still. Chimera did not notice and Big Taz was too busy bounding to see the now comatose insect.

Immediately Chimera got a whiff of Big Taz's intense personal smell, she bent down, retrieved and put her helmet back on, firmly—*Big Taz! Pleased to meet you. You all ready to go?*

Blatta stayed where she was, motionless, quiet, cockroach antennae akimbo. Disregarded. Comatose. Forgotten.

The two larger, bouncing creatures looked at each other, or rather, Chimera tried to look at her, but Big Taz was leaping and floating and bounding all around her and, when not leaping, she was trying to jump up and hug her. Chimera found she was warding the larger, thinner creature off, albeit in a friendly kind of way—*Calm down, Big Taz. Got a job to do.* She indicated Helmut's head in the bag. Once Big Taz understood what it was she thought it best to leave it on the bridge, where it could float, overseeing the endless orbiting journey of the empty satellite. Chimera had hardly known Helmut so it was with little ceremony that she tied the bag to the control panel—*Anything you want to bring with us, Big Taz?*

—*No, no, let's go. Got anything fresh to eat? Something to chew? Apple, maybe? Let's go.*

Chimera laughed as much as she could, given that Big Taz had a firm hold of her round the shoulders—*Big Taz certainly seems to enjoy bouncing. She's leaping all around the sat now...*

Antenna chuckled—*One small leap for the chimpanzees, one giant leap for... Any idea what species she is?*

—*Mammal. Long tail, almost like a kangaroo. Long thin body, like a dog but striped. She's got a long, thin face with stripey eyes. She could be a relative of yours, Antenna, only smooth and ten times bigger. And stinky, phee-heew, is she stinky.*

XI

Antenna glanced around the cave and met blank faces. No one had ever heard of a creature that sounded like Big Taz—*Maybe that's the zero gravity? Bones could grow any direction, couldn't they?* Antenna got back on the radio to Chimera—*Totally confused here, Chimera. Can you run through that description again with Zip and we'll get an identikit thing going?*

Zip jumped onto the other keyboard and, showing up on one of the six monitors, worked up a picture that had all the animals puzzled. They agreed there was nothing that looked like Big Taz in the zoo, or any other zoo in the world, for that matter.

—*Hang on,* said Antenna as she opened yet another web site called Extinct Australian Mammals. Antenna indicated a picture and asked Zip—*Do you think she's one of those?*

—*Can't be. Her whole family would have been extinct for fifty years before sats were ever invented.*

—*Maybe Zed had some kind of supernatural powers after all?*

The beetle news-criers flew down the Ektek corridors again, relaying the bizarre information that it seemed Big Taz was suspected to be an extinct thylacine; a Tasmanian tiger. More news was soon to follow:

—*The sat's been locked up again.*

—*Chimera has loaded Big Taz into position in the sub.*

—*Both are strapped in and ready to commence re-entry.*

—*The space-sub has disconnected from the sat without a hitch.*

—*They're heading home!*

—*It'll take less than an hour to get back down to the Pacific ocean.*

—*We're going to lose contact with them as they re-enter the atmosphere.*

—*The whales will pick them up. We'll have them soon.*

XII

Thin slivers of dark clouds lanced across the dawn sky. Looking east as the sun rose, under the atmospheric flying javelins of clouds, whale plumes erupted high up out of the sea, geysers of greeting. A crew of motley creatures lined the coast and their cheers were quickly stifled. They had a job to do and it was not to be noticed by any human tourist. The animals stood, waiting to welcome home the first Ektek explorers of space; their own hero and their first ever star-dweller.

With a mighty flip and splash of Smacker's tail, the submarine drove hard up on to the beach. Gleam silently acknowledged the work of Smacker's family. Strangely, Gleam had found that he too could communicate with whales without sounds, just as Helmut had. Sometimes, he wondered privately, and of course the whales knew by default, if eating Helmut's heart could have imparted those skills within his tiger's digestion. However it had occurred, both Gleam and Smacker acknowledged it was a wonderful inheritance. Tiger and whale found they had much to discuss.

On Gleam's head, almost invisible amongst the fur and stripes, stood a small, dignified, black-and-yellow pebble. It was Bash. He shouted out—*I, Bash, member of Ektek, thank you from the bottom of my heart for all you have done for us and our fellow creatures here today. I solemnly swear I have had nothing to do with any fishing company, now and forever. I have never, and never will have, anything to do with any kind of fishing. Please believe me.*

The waves continued to roll carelessly onto the shore and then Gleam chuckled.

—*What?* said Bash—*What's so funny? What?*

—*They didn't think you'd be so small.*

—*Tell them I haven't been well.*

—*Don't worry. Whales like small things. Krill for example.*

—*They eat krill!*

—*Don't worry. They're not going to eat you. Not today, anyway.*

Bash shook his head, trying to shake out his disgruntle. He watched the spray plumes in the distance, revealing the whales were on their way out of the bay.

Still chuckling, Gleam turned to see what was happening around the sub. It was surrounded by creatures, among them Zip, Antenna and Crawf, trying to open the hatch. The submarine itself had sustained considerable fire damage on re-entry into the atmosphere. It was burnt and scorched in places and the doorway was stuck shut. They banged on the outside and soon enough a muffled bang was heard in response.

—*They're alive then,* said Zip.

With some hefty jolting, the hatch opened and out sprang Ektek's first astronaut, Chimera. She wrenched off her space helmet, her eyes beaming with victory. She leapt onto the submarine and posed with her hands triumphantly clasped over her head. She stood like a mighty warrior on a dead beast as her feet rested on the body of her craft. She had survived another trip into space and she wanted to let everyone see her glory.

Gleam, Antenna and Zip watched her for a moment while Crawf entered the sub. When he stuck his feathery head out of the vehicle and said—*Hullo? I'm going to need you lot to lend a paw here...* All three glanced at each other and without further conference, ran to help. As they drew closer they could hear the inhabitant and, closer still, they could smell her, too.

—*Oh, for ark's sake, you're killing me, aaaaargh, oh, I can't stand up, this is a disaster, I can't breathe this crap… what do you call it? Air? Disgusting. Revolting. Get me to Tasmania at once! Why are you pulling at me? Zed, I hate this life, oh crap, I'm in agony!*

Antenna entered the submarine and approached carefully—*Big Taz? It's an honour to have you on* terra firma.

—*Terra firma? I'll give you* terra firma! *I'm terrified! This is terrible! If this is land then I don't want to have anything to do with it!*

—*I think we'd better get you back to Ektek and try to make you comfortable. Can you stand at all?* Crawf and Gleam, squashed in the doorway, tried to help her stand. Big Taz was almost as long as the tiger but skinny, stretched out like a rubber version of a dog, and floppy. Her limbs went everywhere as the group managed to pull her out of the submarine and land her on the beach.

—*Ah, ark, what are you trying to do to me? Break my legs, you bastards?* Big Taz sucked in a deep breath and then all the fight went out of her and she slumped onto the sand, long legs akimbo.

—*What's wrong with her?* asked Bash, panicked.

—*She's fainted, I think. We'll need the stretcher and the hovercraft. Let's get her into the control centre. Can we find her some food and water, please?* said Antenna.

—*How the hell are we going to look after her?* said Crawf.

—*Maybe deliver her to the vet and see what they make of her? The zoo'd be pleased to see her,* said Zip—*Get them a bit of notoriety and a few paying customers through the turnstiles. Can you imagine?*

—*That's got to be her call. Let's get her safe and then she can decide when she wakes up,* said Antenna.

Creatures ran off in all directions, beetles and birds took to the air. Everyone had a purpose.

Except Chimera, who watched all the activity with apparent dismay. Everyone focussed their attention on rescuing the faint and weak Big Taz and seemed to have forgotten her. She stood, still in her astronaut suit, with her helmet under her arm, posing as if for celebratory photographs. Only, there was no photographer.

Antenna nodded to her as she went past.

—*Well?* said Chimera—*Don't I get any attention?*

—*Thanks, Chimera. Good job.*

—*Good? Good? Is that all? Just 'good' job? No photos? No paparazzi? No interviews? After all I've been through?*

Antenna did stop and look at her—*We can't tell the world what we've been up to, can we?* Antenna said—*Don't you think that would be counter-productive?*

—*But I did all that work! I was so clever!* Chimera was more than dis-appointed. She was devastated—*I rescued an extinct creature from certain death. Don't you think I deserve some kind of recognition? Some kind of accolade? I've worked all my life towards this moment and it's not fair I get nothing at all!*

—*What did you have in mind, Chimera?*

—*It's not supposed to be up to me! You're supposed to think of something! Ektek are supposed to give me a gift, a wonderful and surprising acknowledgement of all that I've been through! Like, unconditionally! I've given all my expertise and my knowledge and almost died in space! Like, you know, the keys to the city or a life membership of something…*

—*Just tell me what you want, Chimera.*

With a rush Chimera admitted—*I want to be the new faunal emblem.*

—*That's why you did it? Chimera, can you please explain to me how you thought pulping old-growth forests, selling out whales and organising uranium sales could help you to become the faunal emblem?*

—*It was going to the corroboree frog, wasn't it? I had to discredit him. You told me who Ektek's friends were. All I had to do was hook up with the opposition and I could bring him down. It was easy.*

—*But, Chimera, so much suffering?*

—*That's how it works, isn't it? Collateral damage. That's how you get what you want. Everyone knows that.*

Her eyes blazed out and, for a moment there, Chimera looked every millimetre what she was; the closest relative of homo sapiens.

Chapter Forty-three

—Mate, I am so glad to be out of that tank. I've been cooped up in there... Hod stretched out his little furry arms and swung his head to his left shoulder and then to his right and back again. His ears flickered to all angles—*Waaay too long.*

FJ and Hod were outside FJ's family car, back at the tip. Hod had driven the tank as fast as he knew how to reach the Eastern barred bandicoots and was now preparing himself to get right back into the tank and keep driving. Driving his friends to safety.

—You've come a long way today, mate. I know. We all know. FJ looked at him and controlled a smirk—*All you ever think of is helping us poor little endangered creatures. Bringing us to a world where we can survive. Just plain old survive. That'd be nice wouldn't it? Wouldn't have to run anywhere, wouldn't have to see the sky any more, wouldn't have to sit and watch the wind blow through the gum trees any more...*

—Nice to see you too, FJ. You all packed?

—We're not going.

—Don't argue, FJ. I don't have the patience.

—Not arguing. Just the way it is.

—Don't believe you.

—You'll have to talk to them for yourself.

—I will happily do that. Hod hopped impatiently and waited for FJ to take him into the tunnels under the car—*Come on, then.*

—Watch yourself. No need to push, FJ led the way through to the cramped living tunnels of the Eastern barred bandicoot family, with Hod puffing and cramped behind him—*Hi, Ma. Hi, Pa.*

Seebeck and Rylah were delighted to see Hod but FJ cut short their welcomes—*Hod's pretty serious about all this, Ma, Pa. He wants us to go through it all again. He reckons we don't understand the issues.* FJ started to describe the Ektek rescue plan to Seebeck and Rylah but, of course, Hod couldn't hold his tongue for long—*You've got no choice.*

—*You're a great kid, Hod, but we 'aint moving.* Rylah tipped his head to one side and considered Hod—*We know you've had a big journey and all but we're just not ones for changing.*

—*If you don't adapt, you'll die.*

—*So be it. Can't see why anyone would want to live in a world of concrete and potted plants and measured meals that arrive from the sky in plastic plates. It's just not our scene, Hod.*

—*We like it out here.* Seekbeck smiled at Hod—*No one bothers us...*

—*Apart from a bunch of crocs...*

—*Don't worry about them,* said Rylah—*They'll be moving on soon. Not the types to hang around a tip.*

—*We've got all we need...* Seebeck continued.

—*But you don't. You have to steal food from the sanctuary to survive.*

—*Guess that's what sanctuaries are for, eh,* said Rylah—*Looking after all us creatures. Leastways, our sanctuary is, anyhow.*

—*We'll do that as long as we can,* said Seebeck.

—*See, Hod, if I could change,* said Rylah—*I'd be a mynah or a rat or one of them possums or something. One of those families who can get on with humans; likes a bit of noise and mess and who can change to fit in with what's available. Nice bit of scavenging, that's all good for some creatures. Not our way. Am I right, Mum?*

—*Course you are, Dad. Everyone ready for a nice root salad?*

—*Too right, Mum. Hod? You're staying, of course?*

—*Thanks, Rylah, Seebeck, but I already had something on the way over. You're too kind and I can't stay. And, really, neither should you.*

—*Good luck, mate.*

—*If you change your mind?*

—*We'll give you a shout. FJ, you see him out, darl. Toodle-ooh.*

—*Come on, Hod.* FJ started up the tunnel. Hod followed, his paws getting tangled up with roots and buried rubbish. FJ had no sympathy for him—*I hate to say it, but I just can't help it and I know it's going to feel so good. You ready? Here goes: I flaming told you so.*

—*FJ.*

—*Yup?*

—*Shut up.*

FJ smiled to himself and kept on climbing up the tunnel.

When Hod and FJ emerged in the car interior, Hod turned to FJ, put one of his paws on the smaller creature's shoulder and spoke in a low insistent voice—*You've got to change their minds, FJ. They're going to die, worse, they're going to get sick, their grandchildren are going to mutate and it's not fair to you or your kids...*

—I won't be having kids, Hod.

—What? You mean, you're coming with me?

—No, mate. I'm staying put. You've got kids, don't you? I thought you would. Just don't like talking about them, am I right? Maybe it's all a bit too complicated? Too many promises to the ladies? No need to dwell. But we do need to think of the kiddies. You make 'em, you try and look after 'em, that's what I think. Look at my ma and pa. Couldn't have done more for our family if they'd tried. But they're tired now. I don't mind being the end of the line. Makes no difference to me. Unless...

—What?

—You want to have my babies?

Hod choked back a laugh and grinned at the smaller creature—*No offence, but you're not my type.*

—None taken, said FJ—*But, can you take the crocs with you? You know where they are? I'd be grateful if you got them out of here.*

—Next stop. You know you can change your mind at any time.

—Thanks, Hod. For everything.

—Ah, shut up, FJ. It's what I do. I am Ektek, after all.

It was at that point that Shining Teeth decided to reveal herself. She had heard enough and ran forward fast enough to show the wallaby and the bandicoot her full power, and her self control—*Is that so?* She snarled at Hod, just close enough for discomfort—*You're Ektek through and through, are you?*

FJ let out a honk of alarm—*Crikey!*

—Oh, for Zed's sake! Hod sighed—*You have to creep up on animals like that?*

—What the death do you expect? I am a crocodile after all! Ambush is what I do. Got some news for you. Been thinking as I've listened to your little tales of woe. Come up with a new plan. We're not leaving.

—You can't stay here, said Hod.

—We can stay here. We've got a nice family of bandicoots to play with and all these nice cars to live in. They keep sending us juicy, tender humans to eat. What more can we desire?

—I thought you wanted to destroy Ektek?

—Well, yeah, that's right, said Shining Teeth, still smiling—*You're going to love this, Hod. Really love it.*

—I am? said Hod, with just a tiny note of disbelief in his voice. He knew sarcasm when he heard it. And he also knew that whatever made Shining Teeth so happy was bound to be bad for him. Bad for him and bad for Ektek.

Chapter Forty-four

I

Chimera snored in a corner of the machine cage. The door was left open these days in honour of her valiant space travel efforts but otherwise not much had changed. She was still restricted from travel. Gleam had made some progress researching her past but, as Chimera was *animal non grata* in Ektek, no one else expressed any interest in her at all. Bash would have liked to see her punished but he accepted that, as an organisation that purported to protect animals, Ektek could hardly be seen to hurt a chimpanzee. Chimera was avoided and ignored when she did venture out of her cage, so she stayed where she was. She made a soft bed for herself in one corner and brought in some small comforts.

Spark, sparkling Christmas beetle, flew into the cage and settled beside the chimpanzee on her bedside table. She snored on. He coughed, cleared his throat and then whispered—*Blatta? You there?* He watched Chimera's hair but there was no movement—*Blatta?* He watched the hairy giant snore and then, coughed again. He looked around the cage. What could he put to use? He said—*Chimera? Are you awake?* Nothing. She continued to snore even louder. He shouted even louder—*Chimera? Wake up!* He sighed. He looked at her cup beside him and, putting his shoulder to it, edged it, bit by bit, to the side of the table. Before he could manage to shove it over the edge of the precipice he heard her voice and it was chilling—*What are you doing?*

He turned to find Chimera awake, with one eye open, watching him. He had concentrated for so long on pushing the cup he had not noticed her stop snoring—*I didn't know how else to wake you, sorry, Chimera.*

—*Well? What do you want?*

—*I was just looking for Blatta. None of the other cockroaches seem to know where she is. They've searched the rocket and all through your suit but...*

—*Hmph. Haven't seen her...* Chimera rolled over, dismissing him. Spark jumped in fury—*What?*

But she was thinking and after a time she rolled back and propped herself on one arm—*Haven't seen her since we went...*

—*What?*

—*No. Haven't seen her since we got back.*

—*What do you mean? Where is she?*

—*I don't know. What's it matter?*

—*What do you mean, 'what's it matter?'*

—*She's just a cockroach, for Zed's sake.*

—*Just a cockroach?* Spark stared at Chimera, unbelieving. He took a moment to compose himself before speaking—*She's your friend!*

—*I wouldn't say 'friend'...*

—*She did. That's exactly what she said. She thought you were her friend and you know what, it's a two-way thing, this friendship lark.*

—*Kept me amused on the space lab, I'll give her that. Like a pet, she was. Taught her all sorts of tricks.*

—*Well? Where is she? When did you last see her?*

—*I don't know.*

—*What?*

—*Haven't you got better things to worry about? She was there, now she's not. Who cares?*

Spark did.

Seems he was the only one.

II

Big Taz lay in Antenna's torn paperbark nest at the back of the control centre like a long stretchy baby. She was weak, confused and dribbling. Her fur was patchy, with a number of tufty, scabby bare bits and she was very, very stinky.

Gleam crouched in front of her, speaking softly, trying to get her to eat. After a time, seeing he was making no impression, he turned back to his position at the keyboard. The sound of tapping seemed to annoy the thylacine - she moaned, turned her head and slumped into exhaustion.

Antenna and Zip watched from the doorway on their way out to the hangar. Ektek had agreed each creature would keep watch over Big Taz in turn.

Zip wondered—*Could we get her up to the vet?*

—*Gleam still thinks we have to give her the choice but it's like she can't hear at the moment.*

—*Sort of a sensory overload?* asked Zip.

—Don't know. Obviously she's affected by gravity for the first time in her life...

—What's Gleam got there? said Zip.

—Couple of rats from the reptiles and a hunk of lamb from the big cats.

—You think she'd love sheep meat, considering thylacine history.

—... but she doesn't. She doesn't love anything. When she wakes up all she does is complain and whinge and moan and carry on like some pathetic, unhappy, dreary monster from a horror lab. She hates that she can't walk, she can't bounce, she can't do anything...

—Aren't we the lucky ones? said Zip—*We get to listen to her.*

III

Crawf stood, drumming on the side of the control desk with one of those ubiquitous little sticks he chewed. He had a faraway look in his eye and his dreamy little rhythm had all but hypnotised him. He was shaken out of his pleasant reverie by a screech from the nest in the corner—*Aaaaargh. What is that incessant noise? Aaaaargh! My mind is beaten! I can't think! I can't breathe!*

—Hullo, I know, it's dreadful, I'm sorry. Crawf dropped the stick and moved carefully closer to the Tasmanian tiger. It wasn't that he was afraid she might bite. He was afraid he might smell her—*Big Taz? Is there anything I can get for you?*

—Can you get me the hell away from here? I'm dying!

—I don't know. I really don't. We could take you up to the vet?

—What is this 'vet'? Why do you all keep on talking about 'vet'? All you keep saying is vet vet vet like vet is Zed or something.

Crawf considered—*You know, there is a chance that Zed might have been some kind of vet.*

—Really?

—Well. Zed made the sat and stuffed it with creatures...

—Never seen your kind before. What are you?

—Cockatoo. When Big Taz remained blank Crawf added—*Palm cockatoo?* Big Taz still showed no sign of recognition. Crawf continued—*Bird?*

Big Taz shook her head, uncomprehending—*Not sure. Bird?*

—Feathers? Flight? Eggs?

—Think my parents must have eaten all the 'birds' before I was born.

—Right. Crawf drew further away, this time not only because of her smell but also because of her omnivorous status—*Anyway, the vet might be able to help you. I don't know. Never seemed to do much for me. Just pecks at you and prods and pokes...*

—*Nothing can help me. It's all over for me. I want to be buried in Tasmania.*

—*We could get you there. If you like. Not to get buried. Just to see it. Do you know where you want to go?*

—*Tasmania. That's all.*

—*I could ask Antenna to search where your family were last seen, perhaps? I'll go find her.*

As Crawf left the cave, Big Taz shook her head and sank into the nest. Soon, she dribbled and moaned in her troubled sleep once more.

When Big Taz next woke, she became aware of Antenna, working at the keyboard. One monitor was open on an extinct animal site and another to a site entitled Tasmanian Tiger Sightings. Antenna was so absorbed in her task she nearly jumped high enough to touch the sleeping glow-worms when Big Taz shouted out—*What is that noise? Always tapping, tipping, tapping... It's driving me mad! I tell you, arking mad!*

—*I'm just having a look for you, to see where...*

—*Well, don't. Why don't you just leave me alone? I can't stand it, I really can't.*

—*I'll come back when you're feeling better. Though I did wonder if you've thought any more about the vet?*

—*Aaaargh, the vet sounds like a torturer; what sort of hocus pocus rubbish is that? Get away from me, you vile creature...*

—*Anything you say, Big Taz. Only too pleased to oblige...*

Big Taz gradually calmed down enough to doze again or perhaps she lapsed out of consciousness. A stream of drool landed into the slop of the paperbark nest.

When she woke again it was to the industrious sounds of Zip sanding down a small section of the smashed airship's engine.

Big Taz rolled her eyes and her head—*What is this? Am I never to be left by myself? What price privacy, I ask you? This is killing me, really killing me. I want to go hooooome.*

—*To Tasmania?*

—*Don't be stupid you big bat thing, you. I want to go back to the sat.*

—*You need to eat something and you need to be able to stand before we can get you back in the rocket, don't you think? You've been lying around feeling sorry for yourself long enough. Get up and try. Maybe then we'd be willing to help you. Come on, hurry up. Get up now.*

Big Taz was so surprised that she did try to stand up. Her feet gripped the filthy shreds of the nesting material and she managed to arrange her limbs in some sort of order. She wobbled and struggled and finally pulled herself back up to standing on all four feet, until, swaying and dipping, she slowly sank again—*Aaaargh! My back! Aaargh! I can't stand! It's all your fault, you interfering bastards! If only you'd left me alone! If only I could be weightless again!*

—*You're the one who called for help. You're the one who drove our pilot to despair. You're the one…*

Big Taz released a huge stream of yellow urine. It washed through the shredded paperbark bed and down the middle of the control cave in a stinking steaming river—*Get out! Get out of here and leave me alone! How dare you, you fat-nosed bastard! Get out get out get out get out get out get out get out…*

Zip got out.

Even the glow-worms were making an arduous getaway, their slimy bodies creeping along their strings high in the crevices of the cave. It seemed that no one wanted to be near one who should be extinct.

Big Taz burst into hot shouty sobs and slumped even further into her bed of shred, burying her nose and trying to hide. Perhaps she was trying to die.

IV

Antenna was out in the bush with a pile of bark strips. She nosed them up until they leaned against a tree and came in against them sideways, pushing up close enough to have the pile topple over onto her back. She was able to carry a reasonable load if they didn't over balance onto one side. Big Taz was making a foul mess of her nest. It needed replenishing. Fully laden, she was heading off towards the Ektek cave when Torque flew up beside her. He looked around to see if anyone was in earshot before saying—*Antenna? Got a minute?*

Antenna paused—*Torque. 'Sup?*

—*Just wanted to let you know there's seven of them. They got a whole lot of cameras and stuff in there.*

—*I know.*

—*You've seen them?*

—*No, Spark told me.*

—*Already? He's quick, that grub, mighty quick,* said Torque—*Suppose I should be proud. I trained him, after all. I taught him everything he knows, the pipsqueak.*

—*Thanks, though.*

—*When are you going?*

—*Thought I might leave them alone.*

—*Give them time to get settled.*

—They got a right to their privacy.

—Not with all those cameras snooping on them the whole time, they don't have any privacy at all. Like a bloomin' faunal emblem they are.

—They are.

—Are they? Well, there you go.

Then, Antenna and Torque heard the tank's unmistakable roar in the distance. They looked at each other as they listened to the big engine revved up high and crashing down the path towards them.

Torque shook his head—*Hod's driving.*

—Don't make me laugh, said Antenna—*I've got to carry this stuff.* She adjusted her load of paper bark and, as the two animals made their slow way back though the scrub, she muttered—*Hod's driving us all around the bend.*

V

In the hangar, Bash and Gleam looked up from working on the rocket ship as they heard Zip approach.

—Impossible, said Zip—*She's impossible.* Zip kept marching through the hangar, spitting out words—*She's her own worst enemy. Bitch.*

—Do you want me to take over? said Bash.

—I don't mind sitting with her—said Gleam, lifting his huge head from the mysteries of engineering—*I've still got a few leads to follow up and she might let something slip.*

—I wouldn't bother if I were you. Zip looked at them both with a faint sneer on her bat lip—*Leave her to stew. Either she'll wake up to herself or she'll die and we can just leave her body on the vet's doorstep and cause a furore in the human world as to the mysterious arrival of a freshly dead thylacine at Bedlam Zoo. Revolting bitch.*

Gleam and Bash exchanged glances—*You don't really think that,* said Gleam.

—Yes, said Zip—*I do think that.*

Bash sighed—*I'll go,* and he lolloped towards the control room. But he did not get very far because, with a crash of burly engine, Hod roared the tank into the forecourt area. The beast of a vehicle howled as he hauled down through the gears. He parked as close as he could next to the rocket. He didn't even see Bash, Zip or Gleam standing behind the burnt submarine and they watched him with curiosity as he bounded past them in the direction of the control centre.

When Hod crashed into the control cave he splashed through the urine puddle and tripped over Big Taz—*Where's Antenna?*

—Get me out of here! I've got to get back! I can't even stand up! It's an ark-ing nightmare! Zed, Zed, Zed! Damn and blast it!

Hod backed straight out and leapt down the hallways until he made it back into the hangar where he found Crawf working at the wingship—*Crawf, mate...*

—Hullo, didn't expect to see you so...

Hod interrupted him—*Crawf. Got a problem. An urgent problem. Can you find Antenna? Get her here. I'll go looking for some beetles.*

Hod ran through the hangar and, after dashing to and fro and seeking around corners and crying out, he found Mandible and Spark, alerted them and rushed back to join the others.

In contrast, without moving one step, Crawf looked up and saw Bash, Zip and Gleam standing impassively by the rocket. He also saw Antenna, carrying her bark, and Torque coming in the entrance to the hangar. He indicated Hod with a simple tilt of his head.

Bash, Zip, Gleam, Antenna and Torque all shared a look and shrugged. After dropping her bark, Antenna and the others made their way across the hangar. They were joined by Crawf and various other creatures as they gathered together.

—Tank's full, Hod explained—*We're going to have to shift it. Immediately.*

—What stuff? asked Antenna.

—Don't know. Maybe radioactive. Maybe some kind of nuclear waste.

—Nuclear waste? Here?

—Yup and we need to load it onto your rocket and blast it into space.

—What's new clear waste?

—Here? Did he say here?

—What the...? The small crowd erupted into confusion, shouting at Hod and muttering with each other—*What are you talking about?*

—Take it slower, Hod. What exactly is going on?

Hod took an impatient breath, looked around and started again—*You know how the crocs hate Ektek?*

—What? said Bash.

—They blame us for Hardback, said Zip.

—But that's not our fault, said Bash.

—Doesn't matter what the truth is, you have to see it their way. They still hate us. So, their plan is to keep a load of radioactivity sitting in the hangar... Hod continued.

—You mean that stuff that was buried in the tip with the bandicoots? said Crawf.

—We could all get sick... said Bash.

—*It's here. Now. In the tank.*
—*Why didn't you get rid of it somewhere else?* said Zip.
—*Where?*
—*Ah, pff, I don't know...* said Zip.
—*That's the problem. Anywhere you put it, it's going to cause someone a problem sooner or later. So, I thought, we could just stick it in a rocket and quickly get rid of it...*
—*Give the aliens a problem...* said Zip.

Antenna glanced at Zip, almost amused by her alien remark, but not quite—*We can't quickly get rid of a rocket load of anything, Hod,* she said.
—*What do you mean?*
—*The rocket's been damaged,* said Gleam.
—*We can fix that.*
—*Hod. It's the fuel. We don't have the fuel,* said Antenna.
—*What?*
—*The rocket fuel. We used it up. Every last drop,* said Antenna.
—*That fuel doesn't come easy, Hod,* said Bash.
—*We had bombardier beetles all over the world donating their personal assets. They won't be able to discharge again for months,* said Gleam.
—*It was a massive effort, involving half the world's marine life as well as the beetles. We can't just whip that one up again,* said Antenna.
—*Well, now what? How do you suggest we shift a tank load of nuclear waste from out of the Ektek hangar? With no time to lose?*

The animals were silent, coming to terms with Shining Teeth's dastardly ploy. Everyone was so quiet they could plainly hear the confident voice that spoke out from the back of the group—*I might just be able to help you with that,* said Chimera—*That's if you could see your way clear to helping me.*

Antenna and Gleam exchanged a look. Chimera. Not exactly the kind of help they could have wished for.

Chapter Forty-five

I

Antenna peered over Gleam's shoulder at a loading symbol circling around the centre of the screen. He had been researching female chimpanzees born in the southern United States and their history in experimental science and the space program over the last sixty years— *I think this might interest you...* The website took a long time to appear— *I'm only guessing how old she is but from her stories I'm putting her around forty...*

—Forty! Are you sure?

—Maybe older.

—Really? She acts like a teenager.

—Acts is right. I think she may even have been in the movies. No, for real, wait, you've got to see this chimp who looks so much like her...

The website loaded and Gleam and Antenna stared at the photo of a much younger Chimera. It had to be her. The mascara was a flattering touch. The white lace mini dress was not.

—See what I mean? said Gleam.

—Doesn't that explain a lot?

—Yeah, doesn't it.

II

Meanwhile, Chimera was throwing a tantrum. She was outside the feeding station where the cockroaches had taken up permanent residence. They were cowed and clustered together near the bottom of the drain. Chimera took in another breath of air and shouted—*You stupid, selfish, ninnies! You think you can just get up and go whenever you like? What do you think you're doing, lazing around, stuffing your faces all day? There's work to be done and just looking at you slothful, indolent slobs make me sick.*

Torque came up beside Spark who had been standing watching the proceedings from a healthy distance—*What's with her?*

—Chimera's annoyed the cockroaches won't help her.

—Annoyed? I'd hate to see her angry. She can be heard all over Ektek. We'll get zoo workers breaking into the tunnels soon. She's like a foghorn!

—Come on! We've got work to do! Chimera raged on—*You have got to snap out of this egotistical sulking. How dare you think only of yourselves!*

—Don't look at me, Spark shrugged—*I wouldn't have the first idea how to stop her.*

—What's the cockroaches' issue? said Torque.

—Blatta. Seems Chimera lost her in space. Just left her. Up in orbit. Forgot about her. Not sure if she's dead or alive. Doesn't seem to care. So the cockroaches have stopped work.

—They can't! said Torque.

—Don't blame them, do you? asked Spark—*Chimera was taking advantage of Blatta. All Blatta wanted was friendship. The cockroaches are upset. They are all related to Blatta, after all.*

—Does this mean we're stuck with this radioactive stuff?

—Appears so.

Chimera was still bellowing—*I expect you by the rocket in ten minutes. Don't keep me waiting, you self-serving creeps!*

—We have to do something, said Torque—*We've got to get rid of it. They're the only ones qualified to move it.*

Chimera, still carrying on, picked up a piece of melon and threw it at the cockroaches. They easily dodged the missile and went back to their quiet contemplation of food. Chimera gave up and stamped off towards the control centre.

Torque looked at Spark—*Go on. Talk to them. You'll think of something. You've got to.*

—Thanks for the vote of confidence, boss, Spark sighed—*It's impossible.*

—Give it a try. If you talk to the cockroaches, I'll go tell Antenna what's going on.

Spark simply nodded his shiny head and proceeded over to talk to Blatta's family. They had multiplied since moving in with Ektek and they now numbered in the hundreds. Before leaving, Torque watched as the crowd surrounded Spark and gave him a sense of their mood—*Yip!*

—We're not going to do it.

—Yip!

—Not going to do anything to help that fat, hairy humanoid, shouted out some cockroach voices—*Finished with her.*

—Yip, yip, yip.

—Fair enough, said Spark.

—What? said the cockroaches.

—Blatta was my friend.

—It's true, I saw them talking, shouted out a female.

—*Yip, yip.*

—*I couldn't believe her when she brushed Blatta off so easily. It's not fair and I've told her that myself,* said Spark—*I think Chimera should be held accountable.*

—*Not going to bring Blatta back, though, is it,* said a gruff male cockroach.

—*Yip.*

—*Yip, yip.*

—*No, it's not. I don't think we'll ever find out what happened to Blatta.*

—*Because that fat bitch didn't care,* said a cockroach voice.

—*That's truth,* said another.

—*Yip, yip.*

—*So I respect you not wanting to move the radioactive material for Chimera,* said Spark.

—*Thank you,* said one of the cockroaches.

—*S'okay.* Spark sighed again—*I wondered what you had planned for your future.*

—*Not sure. We're still shocked by Chimera.*

—*Yeah. How could she?*

—*These things do take time, of course,* said Spark—*But I wondered if you were thinking about moving into the human city; great place, rich pickings, full of waste with plenty of dropped food?*

—*I heard that too!* squeaked a young cockroach.

—*You're right. But,* said an elder—*We do have to take some time to work things out.*

—*Yip, yip.*

—*So,* said Spark—*You'll be here?*

—*Probably.*

—*Got some things to sort, you know…*

Torque scurried across the area, leading Antenna, Gleam and Zip to witness the confrontation. They arrived just in time to hear Spark say—*What do you think about helping Ektek anyway? Seeing as you're here already? It's not helping her—she just happens to be here—for the time being. There's plenty of others to consider.*

—*It is a good cause,* said the elder cockroach—*Ektek, I mean.*

—*I ask myself, what would Blatta have done?*

—*That's truth.*

—*Okay, Spark. We'll do it for you.*

—*Don't you worry about me,* Spark smiled—*Let's do it for Blatta.*

—*Yip, yip, yip.*

Antenna closed her eyes and took a deep breath in before she too heaved a sigh of relief.

III

Blatta woke up. She shook her cockroach head. It took her a while to realise where she was. She stood and looked around her, at the cold metal corridors of the satellite. Then she began to walk. She walked for a long time. Then she began to run. She ran until she tired. Then she took to her wings. She flew all over the satellite. She became exhausted. She realised she was alone. Chimera had left her behind. Blatta had to think about that. She did not know how long she had been unconscious. She knew there was no way off the satellite. Unless Chimera would come back for her…

A taste of hope rose in the cockroach, just for a moment. She chewed that idea for a little while until the flavour grew sour.

Until Blatta realised that Chimera was not coming back for her.

She began to take more notice of her surroundings. She saw the bones of all the animals that had been collected into one place. She saw how the corrals had been too flimsy and the aviary had been eaten away at the base. She noticed that she could crawl into the dried food and recycled water storage and help herself at any time. She saw there was a good system to keep her going for her entire lifetime and maybe some extra should she get any surprise visitors. She refreshed herself and then she slept.

When she woke she continued her reconnaissance. She found herself at the control desk and flew up to look out of the window. She sat at the lip of the window and stared out. There, a round, cloud-wreathed, blue-green bauble hung in a dark, starry sky. Blatta stared at the planet and then beyond it, into the depth of space, and the infinity of stars scattered beyond her imaginings.

Then, Blatta started to hum, just quietly, under her breath. She had always loved cockroach music—*La cucaracha, la cucaracha…* She hummed and she relaxed, gazing at the majesty in front of her, tapping her toes. With a little smile, Blatta enjoyed uninterrupted, infinite peace, at last.

IV

Later, after Chimera had started the countdown, Gleam, Antenna and Zip stood together and watched the cockroach teamwork in amazement. Hundreds of cockroaches bustled over the rocket, now back in the defunct polar bear bunker. Not only Blatta's relations but also thousands more had been called in to assist. Cockroaches were, of course, able to withstand much higher levels of radioactivity than other creatures, as well as possessing the ability to work together as cohesive units to achieve enormous tasks. The tank had already been emptied and the cockroaches had been deployed fitting re-invigorated fuel rods to the altered submarine.

Antenna shook her head at the sheer risk of it all happening in the Ektek facilities.

—*Explain to me*, said Gleam—*how she can make nuclear waste a power source?*

—*Yeah*, said Zip—*Isn't it depleted? Doesn't that mean it won't work?*

—*Apparently the technology has been around for some time. Luckily Chimera knows how to squeeze the last drops of energy out of these fuel rods and she says it's safe. All we can do is hope.*

Gleam said—*You know, I'm going to be beyond relieved to have the waste disappear but I can't help feeling this journey is… well… hazardous?*

—*When the waste makes it into orbit it'll be out of reach of any living thing. Even if it is unstable, it can't affect life on Earth.*

—*Hullo? We hope*, said Crawf.

Zip agreed—*Yes, I heard Chimera explain it's heading into a higher orbit than the sat but things can still go wrong and the closer we are to that rocket the wronger things can go. For us.*

—*None of it makes me reassured, I have to admit*, said Antenna—*I don't like the daytime launch timetable, I don't like any of it.*

—*Anyone been checking what Chimera's been doing?*

—*She's confounded me with science whenever I've asked. I still don't know if they're working on fission or fusion or what*, said Antenna—*I'm just waiting for the chance to hack in and check up on her.*

The three Ektek workers watched as the cockroaches parted ranks to respond to Chimera's arrival from the direction of the control centre.

—*Yip, yip, yip.*

She stood and discussed matters before hopping into the rocket for her last inspection.

Antenna and Gleam looked at each other. Antenna raised one of her darkened eyebrows—*Good timing?*

—*At least we know where she is…*

—*What say we go and visit Big Taz? No harm in that?*

—*No harm at all…*

They entered Antenna's office area and greeted Big Taz who was busy practising her exercises. Her long legs could barely keep her standing and she tottered around the room swaying dangerously. Ants had been working around the clock to keep her fed and cleaned and eucalyptus had been sprinkled around her to keep her smell bearable.

Zip ran to Big Taz's side and helped her to keep her balance—*You have so improved, Big Taz. Oooops! Take it easy there…*

—*Arking hell, this Earth's a bitch! Is the Tasmania the same? The same as this? Arking hell.*

Gleam and Antenna moved to the keyboards and appeared to forget Zip and Big Taz as they became absorbed in their tasks. Antenna concentrated on checking over the workings Chimera had set up for the rocket's journey while Gleam continued his search through the NASA chimpanzee archive.

Big Taz redoubled her efforts and wobbled out of the doorway. She headed back towards the hangar, followed closely by Zip.

In the control room, scanning the settings for the rocket's trajectory, Antenna gasped as she began to understand the scope of Chimera's constructs. She looked over at Gleam to see if he'd noticed. He hadn't.

—*Gleam*, said Antenna.

—*What?* said Gleam, barely lifting his head, busy with his own screen and emails.

—*Have you see what she's done?*

—*No, no, no, busy for the minute…*

—*With what?*

—*Tracing her family. Got a new lead. What? What is it? Explain.*

—*She's set landing co-ordinates.*

Gleam was still engrossed in his own research. It took him a while to focus and then understand what Antenna was telling him. He looked at her and frowned—*There isn't going to be a landing.*

—*That was our plan. Not Chimera's.*

—*But isn't that the idea? Get it into as high an orbit as possible? That's what I understood.*

—*… but that's not what she's done.* Antenna shook her head—*We have to stop the countdown.*

—*… and why would you want to do something like that, Antenna?* Chimera's dulcet tones washed over the two animals working at their computers. Both froze and then looked at Chimera, leaning comfortably in the doorway to the cave.

— *Chimera.* Antenna stared at the chimpanzee coldly—*Either you shut it down or I'll have to.*

—*No can do, Antenna. You will have seen the system is locked. Can't have any interference, can I? That would be unsafe, wouldn't it? Got to keep everyone safe, haven't we? After all, we've managed to shift the waste from the tip to the rocket without any disturbance so far. Wouldn't it be a tragedy if anything were to happen now, right in the middle of Bedlam Zoo?*

—*Chimera, not only must your plan be interfered with but you will be damn glad of it. You won't be able to live with yourself if this is carried out.*

—*What?* said Gleam—*What do you mean? What's she done, Antenna?*

—*Oh, you can tell him, Antenna. You've got to admit, there's an element of genius in it, isn't there? Anyone would have to be impressed.*

—*No way I'm impressed, Chimera,* said Antenna, turning to Gleam— *She's got the rocket aimed at the most densely human populated city in the United States of America. It would be a catastrophe if it were to hit…*

Chimera turned and headed out down the corridor.

—*Stop!* Antenna yelled—*She's trying to run! We need her here!*

—*Aaaaaaarr…* Gleam bounded explosively out of the control room and within a split second faced Chimera—*What are you thinking?*

Chimera dodged him and kept on running, following the twists and turns of the thin tunnel system.

Spill, woken by the shouting, stretched himself out across the hallway. Chimera tripped and fell headlong. Gleam, roaring profoundly, pounced and cornered Chimera as she lay, face pressed into the ground. He caught her stringy arm in his huge teeth and bent it up behind her.

Chimera started shrieking and screaming and crying like a strange hairy fountain.

—*You okay?* muttered Gleam to Spill.

—*I'll live. Don't talk with your mouth full.*

—*You've got to change those co-ordinates, Chimera,* Antenna ran up behind them—*You can't be responsible! We can't be responsible!*

—*What have you ever done for me?* Chimera thrashed her head from side to side and wailed—*What has anyone ever done for me? I worked for the whole of the USA when I was up in Space Lab. I worked for all the people of the world and what did they do for me? I'll tell you what they did for me, they abandoned me to be swallowed whole by a whale and then spat out into the arms of illiterate jungle creatures with no idea of culture. That's how much they cared for me. To them, I'm just an animal. Not even sentient…*

—*Like a cockroach,* muttered Zip.

—*… Not even worth a little retirement condo in Florida.*

—That's what you wanted? said Antenna—*A retirement resort in Florida?*

—Why not? I served my country to the best of my ability. I deserved better.

—You did, said Gleam.

—No-one understands and no-one tries to.

—We might be able to help you, said Gleam.

—Florida? said Antenna.

—Well, said Gleam—*We might.*

—Damn sight easier than making her a faunal emblem; that's for sure, said Antenna.

—You'll all see how clever I am when there's a huge gaping crater in the middle of the USA, then they'll be interested in me, won't they? Everyone will know I'm a genius.

Gleam loosened off his hold on her hairy arm—*We're already interested in you, Chimera. Did you know, I've been researching your life? You have had quite a time of it, haven't you?*

Chimera sat up, suddenly interested and gratified—*If only you knew...*

—I do know some of it and I can tell you now, I've got a surprise for you. I've made contact with your family. They're going to come and get you. They should be here any day now.

—Mbazi? Mbazi will come for me? My lovely husband Mbazi?

—Mbazi? Isn't he the one who wanted you executed in Zaire? No. Not Mbazi.

—Then who? Who is coming for me?

—Fix those co-ordinates, Chimera. Antenna was cold—*Then we'll talk.*

V

Back in the hangar, a cockroach marched away from the rocket. She was the last cockroach mechanic to leave the safety zone, wiping her tiny feet on an oily rag. The rocket now stood, empty, quiet, pulsating with radioactive energy; waiting for its departure, its journey into space, the computerised countdown continuing inexorably in the background. Safety concerns meant a wide cordoned no-go area surrounded the vehicle. No living thing was to go near the potentially lethal cargo and power-pack of this machine while it still held the potential threat of destroying an entire city.

Big Taz tottered her long-limbed way down the tunnels and into the hangar, closely followed by Zip—*Good job. That's the way.* Zip kept up her friendly, interested support—*Hey, Big Taz you're surpassing all my expectations. You really are.* Big Taz made it all the way out into the bushland surrounding the zoo and across to the polar bear enclosure—*Great work,* said Zip—*You've been working hard.* But Big Taz was not only inspecting the rocket from a distance, she was intent on ploughing through the safety barrier and getting to the rocket—*Wait, Big Taz, we're not supposed to be here. We're too close. Big Taz, we need to stop now. I think we've come far enough. Big Taz? Can you hear me? It's time to head back...* Big Taz continued her laborious journey by climbing the ladder up to the sub—*Hey, no, we don't need to go up there, Big Taz.* The hatchway had been left open like an invitation—*Come on down, Big Taz.*

Big Taz put all her effort into climbing the ladder. After some wobbling and swaying she made her way up the slender steps, one foot trembling into the air and then landing almost by chance onto the next level. By this laborious method, Big Taz eventually made it up to the doorway of the rocket.

Zip was frantic with worry. Should she run back and fetch help? Should she physically pull the decrepit old carcass down from the steps? Would Big Taz fall if she left her? Which way to turn? As these thoughts zipped through her bat-mind circuitry she was saying—*I think we'd better head on back, now. Big Taz. I think you've seen enough. No, Big Taz. Don't go in there.*

—*Of course I'm arking well going in there. Don't you think I've had enough of this shit heap? I'm leaving Earth and you can't stop me.* And so, Big Taz entered the ex-submarine and clambered down the internal stairs.

Zip stood outside and shook her head. She looked down into the rocket as Big Taz made her torturous way down to the driver's seat—*Phew. It's hot in here. Get me some water.*

Zip looked around the concrete enclosure. There were beetles everywhere, checking and double-checking pre-flight systems. She could hear ping-pong questions and responses played out in strict sequence but they were too great a distance away for effective shouting and it seemed there was no one to see any kind of signal. Everyone was too busy, engrossed in their jobs. There were orders and rattles and rumbles as tests and procedures were followed. No one was looking her way; not a beetle, not an ant, not a cockroach turned to see her. At a loss, Zip stepped into the rocket. She made her way down the stairway, close enough to speak to Big Taz without shouting—*Okay, Big Taz. You've had your fun. Get up. We're leaving.*

—*Off you go, then.*

—*You're coming with me.*

—*I'm arking not.*

—*You do know this rocket is not going to your sat?*

—*Yes, I arking know that. It's going to the stars. That's all I need. Except maybe some water, bat face.*
—*If you want water, get out of here and go and get it yourself.*
—*Ark off.*
—*Then you'd better load up some supplies. There's no provision on board for any animals, just the fuel rods; you can see that for yourself.* It was true that the entire sub was loaded with nuclear waste. The two seats, that had been designed for chimpanzee and for what they had originally thought might be an elongated walrus, had been left in place surrounded by spent fuel rods in concrete casings.

—*Still going somewhere, isn't it?* said Big Taz as she nestled further into the pilot's seat. The two creatures were locked so intently into their argument they didn't hear the sudden increase in activity outside the rocket-sub. Suddenly, with a crunch and a grind, the hatchway slammed shut, locking them in with a terrible sound of finality.

—*Oh, no!* Zip gasped. Then she yelled out—*Wait! We're in here!* Big Taz started to laugh.

—*What are you laughing at? You'll never get your water now!*

Still Big Taz laughed.

—*Hey! Wait!* Zip rushed up the stairs to the exit and began pounding on the door—*Help! You've got to let us out!*

She looked around for something to use to make more noise. She found a small metal spanner someone had left and began to bang on the door.

Big Taz groaned and held her head—*Always, always, tapping, tap-ping, I can't stand this arking noise… Ah, bastard…* With a wibble and a wobble and a lurch and a sway she drove herself to her feet and climbed up the stairs behind Zip.

As Zip kept up her urgent banging on the door, Big Taz managed to claw her way up to her. She clung onto the railings and lifted her forepaw… With one blow she pushed Zip off the stairs and then paused, panting against the door…

Unprepared and off balance from her beating Zip soared down into the body of the renovated submarine without even attempting to fly. When she landed, she banged her head hard on the back of the pilot's chair. Her limp body flopped down, broken and unconscious.

At the top of the stairway, Big Taz listened to the silence and breathed in—*That's better.* She leaned against the doorway for a while to get her breath back and then made her way down the stairway again. Still breathing hard, she looked at the bedraggled bat's body. Then she grabbed Zip's head in her huge maw. She flicked the head up, twisting and breaking Zip's neck in the process. Then she dragged Zip down to the passenger seat and tucked her in—*Ha. We'll be right.* Big Taz settled in to the driver's seat and fastened up the seat belts—*Bring her on, Chimera. Let's get the hell out of here! Yee haaaaaaaaa!!!!*

Zip's eyes were open, unseeing. Her wings were spread akimbo, crushed over the seating area. Her neck was twisted back into an impossible angle and a thin trail of blood ran down her chin. The blood dropped like red tears down her chest.

She was not breathing. She never would again.

Chapter Forty-six

I

Gleam, Bash, Hod, Crawf and Antenna focussed on the bank of flickering computer screens. As the shifting light played across their different faces, everyone felt the dread simmering in the cave.

Working at the keyboard and switching between screens, Antenna tried to untangle the protective layers Chimera had built to prevent interference in her diabolical plan. There seemed to be no way through the defences and the red countdown numbers clicked over ever downwards at the bottom of the screen.

Gleam worked industriously at another keyboard. At one point, after reading an email quietly to himself, he gasped, looked round at Chimera, turned back to the screen and shook his head.

Hod happened to see this and said—*What?*

—*You wouldn't believe it,* said Gleam.

Bash shook his head. He was furious. He had agreed to let bygones be bygones with Spill, Rick, Thumper and Carney who had all decided that faunal emblems weren't worth fighting over. It was a human decision anyway and the position might even be best left empty as a memorial to the Leadbeater's possum. But Chimera was another matter and Bash stared at Chimera with hatred burning in his black frog eyes.

Chimera sat in the corner, surrounded by stained and smelly shredded paperbark. Both her hands were open, palm up, on her knees. A parade of concerned cockroaches marched through the cave, visiting her, checking their final orders…

—*Yip, yip, yip.*

She had nothing for them. No word, no gesture, no sign that she even knew they were there. The cockroaches stopped and tapped her hands with their long feelers, willing her to move or respond in some way but she seemed to have shut down.

Spark nodded to the cockroaches as they left—*Thanks for trying. I know you did your best.*

Antenna turned back from the screen to face Chimera. She moved over and crouched down in front of her—*What can we do to change your mind?*

Chimera stared into the distance in front of her.

Antenna came back to the computer screen—*I don't know. It's like her mind has slipped a cog or something. I'm going to have to alert the human defence forces.*

—*No, wait.* Gleam was reading an email—*It's going to be all right.* Gleam stood, left the computer and went over to Chimera. He lowered his head until he was looking directly into the lost chimp's eyes. With his deep voice he spoke clearly to her—*Chimera? Your mother's here.*

When he made this announcement everyone gasped. Everyone looked at everyone else. Who was this old female chimp who had given birth to Chimera? What had Gleam been up to?

Chimera looked up at the tiger. Her eyes seemed to come into focus and she tilted her head in disbelief—*Mommy? Here?* Her voice was little and she seemed to move like a doll. She was slow, as if hypnotised. She had regressed to her childhood.

—*Yes. You're going home.*

—*I'm going home? To Mommy?*

—*Yes. Your mother is looking forward to seeing you. We're going to get you out of here just as soon as...*

Chimera stood and moved rapidly towards the door but Gleam was quicker. He barred her way—*Not so fast, Chimera.*

—*Can't keep Mommy waiting.*

—*Just for a moment. You've got to clean up all your mess before you go, don't you?*

Chimera looked down in distaste at the messy paperbark, stained with urine and faeces—*That's not fair. I didn't do that!*

—*Not that mess, Chimera.* Antenna indicated the screen containing the calculations for the rocket's flight plan—*This mess.*

Chimera smiled—*Oh, that. Easy fixed.* Chimera skipped to the computer and started typing. Then she slowed and stopped and stared at the screen.

—*Why have you stopped?* asked Bash.

—*You play a trick on Chimera?*

—*Chimera?* said Gleam—*You don't really want us to bring your mother in here? To this cave? Do you?*

Chimera looked around the cave and then back at Gleam.

Gleam stared at her—*You want your... mother... to see what you've been up to?*

—*No. Mommy not like. I want my Mommy!*

—*Right. You'll see her as soon as you've unlocked the rocket system. Come on now, focus.*

Chimera stared at Gleam and then seemed to shake off her worries again. She returned to the keyboard and typed with a flurry until she finished and shyly looked up at him—*All done!* She fluttered her eyelashes.

—*You haven't quite finished, have you?* Gleam was still stern—*Correct all the flight details, please, Chimera. Then we'll escort you out.*

—*The countdown's still going,* said Antenna—*Six minutes.*

—*Zip could drive her,* said Bash—*Where-ever she needs to go.*

—*Where is Zip?* asked Hod.

—*Don't know. Haven't seen her...* said Bash.

—*Wasn't she with Big Taz? Doing her walking practice?* said Antenna—*Spark, could you go find her? Tell her to get her car ready straight away, please.*

—*Immediately, Antenna.* Spark flew out of the control centre.

Chimera thought for a moment and then continued typing—*I thought mommy had left me for good. I thought she'd forgotten me.*

—*Chimera,* said Gleam—*Your mother loves you very much. She doesn't think threatening millions of people is very nice. She's disappointed in her baby.*

Chimera moved like a sleepwalker away from the computer.

—*We good?* Gleam asked Antenna as she moved in to check the chimpanzee's work.

—*Seem to be...* Antenna examined the systems and then the analytical spreadsheets, comparing them to GPS and mapping data—*Okay, yes... It's now aimed out past the space telescope as originally planned. Can't see any problems. Just as soon as it's out of here, of course.*

—*I am ready now.* Chimera stood in the middle of the stinky cave. The paperbark shreds were everywhere—*Where's my mommy?*

Antenna turned to ask Crawf—*No sign of Zip?*

—*Not so far...*

—*I'll go see what's happening,* said Bash.

—*I might take a look for her, as well,* said Hod—*If that's okay?*

—*You asking my permission?*

Hod looked a bit sheepish. Antenna laughed and said—*You've got it.* As Hod and Bash made their way out towards the hangar, Antenna added—*Can't imagine where she is.*

—*Okay, we'll walk you out,* said Gleam—*Crawf?*

—*Hullo?* Crawf led the slow-moving chimpanzee out—*Hope you're going to a better place, Chimera.*

As soon as Chimera had left the room, Antenna said—*Do you think we can get a cleaning team in here? The place stinks.* Antenna looked around the cave and at Gleam—*Where is Big Taz?*

—*No idea. Here we go. Last two minutes of countdown...*

—*Gleam, is her mother really here?*

—*Oh, yes. I made contact a couple of days ago. She got on a plane as soon as she could.*

—*A chimpanzee? On a plane? How's that work?*

—*Well, Chimera's mother... She's not exactly... Well, put it this way, she's not quite what you'd expect...*

II

Out in the hangar, two columns of cockroaches marching in battalions flanked Chimera as she strode towards the entrance of the Ektek cave system. All the other Ektek creatures joined her as the countdown drew to a close. They watched this countdown in silence, with none of the excitement or anticipation of the first launch. This was a dark and necessary launch, a dire experiment to save themselves, with unknown consequences.

Still surrounded by cockroaches, Chimera watched with glittering tears in her eyes as the power packs kicked into action and the old polar bear pool filled with steam. The rocket was propelled with an enormous blast of energy, firing the former submarine into the sky once more. This time the power-up didn't create so much wobble in the craft. The steam produced turned into a mist and the creatures stopped coughing and instead enjoyed the sensation of cooling rain on their upturned faces. The rocket travelled upwards in a smooth straight line.

—*It's out of here, anyway,* said Antenna.

—*A long way out,* said Gleam.

—*Still exists,* said Bash.

—*But we don't have to worry about it,* said Hod.

After the launch area had cooled down and the safety beetles had given the okay, Crawf shoved the chimpanzee in her back with his beak. Chimera continued her march through the creatures in silence. Most of the Ektek animals still had their heads in the sky, watching the ribbon of vapour, imagining the radioactive rubbish speeding away from them. Chimera and Crawf kept walking up towards the surrounding bushland.

—*Stop*, said Chimera, turning and looking down at her cockroach companions. She had morphed into her superior astronaut dignity once again. She spoke with eloquence and grandeur—*Don't come any further. All of you, I must thank you for your tireless loyalty. Thank you for your remarkable work. You have managed to do what many scientists and physicists could not even imagine. You have managed to power a rocket with nuclear waste and remove the stuff safely from our own atmosphere. We hope, of course, it will do no harm to any other life form in the future but at least we have removed the immediate danger from our Earth's environment for the time being. I'm incredibly proud of you and I know Blatta would be too. Perhaps you could continue that calling with other dangerous substances around the world? Whatever you choose to do, I wish you well in your future endeavours and now I must go.* Chimera raised her hand in generous salute before she turned away and began to walk. Then, with an afterthought, she turned back again and said, as though it explained everything—*My mother is waiting for me.*

Then Chimera walked away and kept walking. She did not turn back again.

Crawf nodded to himself and waited at the back of the crowd respectfully until she had turned and walked out of sight. Then he jumped and flew up into the sky, still misty from the vapour released from the rocket, and followed her. He became a great dark silhouette in a cloudy sky.

The cockroaches milled around in a swirling dance—*Yip, yip, yip.* They farewelled each other before they scattered in all directions.

Crawf watched as he flew. Chimera marched to the nearby Zoo railway station. She was quiet and unobtrusive in her movements and was able to pass among the humans unnoticed. She went all the way up to the platform and without hesitating walked directly towards a small elderly woman. The woman, with soft white hair and dressed in a red woollen suit, looked anxiously in all directions until she saw Chimera. Then she stopped, put down the small bag she was holding and, throwing her arms open wide, smiled at the chimp.

Chimera flung herself forward at a run, shouting something indistinguishable at the woman. The woman also gave vent to an emotional cry, perhaps some meaningful word but Crawf could not hear from his flying height. The woman bent down and caught Chimera as she ran full pelt into her. She picked up the chimpanzee who wrapped herself around the human being. Chimera's legs went around the woman's waist and they stood together like this for a long while, holding each other tightly, until the train came.

Then they separated and the woman picked up her bag and took hold of Chimera's hand. They got onto the train and then the train clattered away from the station.

Crawf circled in the air above the station and watched light-glints refract from the train's roof snaking through the landscape. He flew back down to the safety of Ektek. He was completely bewildered.

III

—Her mother was human? said Bash—*Her real mother?*

—A female human person? said Crawf—*How's that work?*

—You mean her adoptive mother? said Hod—*Was homo sapiens?*

All the animals were shaking their heads in wonder and revulsion.

—Surrogate. Gleam corrected him—*There's no doubt that Chimera was of woman born.*

—'Spose they're animals, too… said Bash.

—Though you wouldn't know it, would you, said Hod.

Gleam took up the explanation —*You know that scientists around the world were going through chimpanzees at an alarming rate by the end of the last century?*

—I've heard of some of the experiments… said Antenna—*They'd been infected with serious diseases, hadn't they, like hepatitis and HIV AIDS and malaria…*

—Everything humans could imagine. And the chimps died. In their hundreds, said Gleam—*In addition to disease and deliberate maiming in the name of experimentation, there were accidents. Some chimpanzees were overheated, some starved, some were poisoned; all sorts of terrible incidents. Anyway, chimpanzees became almost impossible to get from the wild and became too expensive for scientists to even consider for their myriad of tests. So, when reproductive science evolved beyond merely helping humans to become parents they tried using different species to grow endangered creatures…*

—Didn't the Bedlam vet get involved with using antelopes to carry bongo calves? asked Antenna.

—Scientists and vets have also used feral cats to carry wildcat kittens. And of course, the closest relative of the chimpanzee is…

—Disgusting, said Hod.

—But she hated humans so much. She was going to blow them up! said Bash.

—Doesn't make sense, does it, said Gleam.

—Hullo? said Crawf—*Nothing about Chimera ever made sense.*

—Apparently, the woman gave birth to Chimera and bought her up for the first four years as a human child. Then she handed her over to NASA for her training. That must have been a terrible shock. Not the last shock Chimera ever received either. She was renowned in NASA for her ability to withstand electric shocks. They called her the chimp electric. She's regarded as a wonder of modern science.

—She's a bloody criminal, that's what she is, said Hod.

—*Well, she's out of our hair,* said Gleam—*Now she's someone else's problem.*

—*We don't have to be responsible,* said Antenna—*She was her own creature.*

—*No, we're so, so lucky,* said Hod—*We're shot of her, got rid of the waste and now all we've got to do is decide what to do with the one who ought to be extinct.*

—Still no sign of Zip, either, said Bash.

—*Well. We'd better go find them,* said Antenna—*Who knows what sort of trouble that thylacine can find.*

IV

Antenna stood in the middle of the hangar. She was completely baffled. What could have happened to Zip? Where on earth could she be? Torque flew in to land beside her and shook his darkling beetle head, accidentally whipping his antennae against Antenna's leg.

—*She hasn't been anywhere near her enclosure. She's not been seen. Big Taz neither.*

Antenna nodded and stepped out of the way of his antennae.

Spark flew in from searching near the feeding buildings. He too shook his head—*The cockroaches have gone. I can't find any of them anywhere. Nobody.*

Bash had been down to the water and found—*Nothing.*

Hod had been up to the roadside and found—*Nothing.*

Crawf had retraced his flight from the railway station. He said—*They seem to have vanished off the face of the earth.*

Antenna listened as Manifold reported that her team had been focussed on checking off the rocket and disconnecting the electrics—*Oh, there was something,* said Manifold—*One of the grubs thought perhaps there might have been a funny noise coming from the hatch...*

Antenna stared—*From the rocket?*

The mechanic beetle continued—*He said the rocket but it could have been from anywhere. Lot of sound ricocheting round that pool today. Tough place to work. Must have driven the polar bears mad.*

—Did you ask what sort of funny noise?

—He did say… um… sort of tapping? Yeah, we thought it might have been a loose nut but it wasn't.

—Like a knocking? Antenna made no further comment but ran back in the direction of the control cave.

Hod gasped—*Oh, no.*

—What? asked Crawf.

—You're the one who said it, Hod looked at Crawf before he too turned to follow Antenna—*She thinks they really have vanished off the face of the earth.*

V

Antenna's face was contorted as she ran into the control room and switched on the communication system. As the ground computers made contact with the satellite, she attempted to find the bandwidth they'd used previously to contact the rocket—*Should have seen this coming,* she muttered bitterly to herself—*Should have noticed. Should have known. My fault…*

With the rest of their friends, Gleam entered the cave and spoke to her—*It's not your fault, Antenna. It's no one's fault.*

She ignored him and spoke forcefully into the mic—*Outtek, come in please. Outtek? Can you hear me please, Outtek? Are you there, Zip? Over.*

With a rattle and a hiss, the radio fizzed to life and the Ektek team was privy to the bizarre and awful sound of Big Taz laughing; a horrendous rusty and maniacal cackle. Across the now hundreds of kilometres of air between them, Big Taz crowed. The creatures in the control cave could see the horror from the awful screech reflected in each others' faces.

—What can we do? said Antenna. She looked down and tried to pull herself together. Her breathing shuddered and her ribs hurt her.

—There's got to be some way to get them back, said Hod.

—What? said Bash.

—I don't know, said Hod—*Something. We can think of something. We can always think of something…*

Antenna shouted into the mic—*Big Taz. Can we speak to Zip, please? Zip? Can you hear me? Over.*

Crawf looked from creature to creature—*Can we get Zip to… I don't know… What?*

—There's nothing we can do, said Gleam.

Antenna kept trying at the mic—*Outtek, outtek, come in, please. Over.*

—But it's Zip… said Hod—*Zip.*

—*I know,* said Gleam.

—*You don't. You can't. Not Zip. I've known her all my life. You haven't. We can't just leave her out there. Not Zip.*

—*We have to, Hod,* said Crawf.

—*We can't,* said Hod as he ran out of the control room. Gleam followed him with Bash and Crawf.

Antenna just stood and stared. Her black eyes shone bright in the line of dark fur etched across her face. Another friend lost. Tears trembled in her eyes but did not overflow. Antenna stared at the mic, blinked hard several times and then, rising to her feet, stepped out of the control centre.

VI

Together with a group of mechanic beetles, the Ektek animals—Bash, Antenna, Hod, Crawf and Gleam, stood in the forecourt of the Ektek caves and strained upwards to watch the rocket's now distant trail.

—*If we could fly the plane...*

—*Hod,* said Crawf—*She's gone. It's out of our control.*

—*She's my friend. We've got to go after her...*

—*She was a friend to all Ektek and she's gone because she wanted to help a hideous old monster who should have died eighty years ago...* said Bash.

—*If it wasn't for that mad vet called Zed and his ark,* said Antenna.

—*His arking ark,* said Crawf.

—*She did it all out of spite,* said Gleam.

—*She was out of her mind,* said Crawf.

—*Out of spite, out of mind,* echoed Bash—*Just like Chimera.*

—*It should have been me,* said Hod—*I'm the one who deserted. Zip didn't. Zip was always there. Zip was always looking out for everyone. It's not right. It's just not right.*

—*Hod, you have to calm down,* said Gleam—*We can't bring her back.*

—*Who asked you? How can you, some freak of a wild cat, come in here and make pronouncements about things you know nothing about?*

—*Hey, Hod. Gleam's right. There's nothing we can do,* said Crawf.

—*I wish I'd never left. It's obvious, isn't it? We've got to stay together. It's when we go off by ourselves that we get trapped. That's why Ektek exists. To help animals help each other. Together. We've got to stay together.*

As they stood in the forecourt, staring at the sky, a rustling came from the bushland surrounding them. Someone was approaching from the coast. Someone had heard Hod's shouts and was crawling through the bush. That someone broke cover from a tough clump of straggly shrubs and dragged the heavy menace of her prehistoric body across the forecourt—*Well, well, well, isn't this cosy? This must be the famous Ektek headquarters. How nice. What great good fortune to find you here after all this time, Froggy, Bird and good old Wally. And, look at you, there, a big, fuzzy cat thing. Aren't you going to introduce me to all your friends, Hod?* Shining Teeth pressed further into the cave.

—*Shining Teeth.*

—*I think I've been cooling my heels long enough, don't you? I think it's time to put our little plan into action.*

—*No. I have to ask you to leave. You don't need to come in to Ektek. I want you to go away and leave us alone.*

Antenna looked at Hod in amazement—*You brought her here?*

—*Either that,* Gleam interrupted, speaking to Shining Teeth—*Or you could stay and join us.*

—*Wait,* said Antenna.

—*Me?* Shining Teeth laughed, flashing her teeth. It was a nasty, nasty laugh—*Join Ektek?* She went on pealing with laughter, her huge teeth glinting in the sun.

Gleam did not seem at all fazed by her colossal reptile strength. He had his own resources—*We're in the same boat, Shining Teeth; all of us. It's not you against Ektek. That's not the point.*

Antenna persisted—*Hod?*

—*Yes. What exactly is the point?* asked Shining Teeth, grinning all the while—*Hod? Can you explain it to me?*

Hod looked at Gleam and then flicked his gaze back to Shining Teeth. He said—*It's all of us, together, trying to make a place in the world for animals. Somewhere safe. Somewhere away from humans…*

—*… and their waste,* added Antenna.

—*I'm like you, Shining Teeth,* said Gleam—*I'm a killer. I'm a tiger; a creature to strike fear into the heart of any living beast. But I've made choices so that I am no longer responsible for fear and death. I choose to work for peace.*

—*Oh, shut the death up before I vomit.*

—*Where's the rest of the harem, Shining Teeth?* asked Crawf.

Shining Teeth drew in a deep breath before speaking again—*The girls couldn't come. They're too sick. There was just me surfing on the tank, must say I enjoyed that.*

—*Surfing?* said Antenna—*You weren't in the tank?*

—*I hitched a ride,* said Shining Teeth—*Hod was up the front in his little protected pod. We stacked all the waste in the back, away from him.*

Suddenly, way up in the sky, there was a flash. The rocket, which the Ektek creatures now understood contained Zip and Big Taz, transformed, in the daylight sky, into a star; a very bright star. It flared and then guttered and, finally, fluttered out. Star no more.

The group of watching creatures gasped in shock. The sound from the explosion was much later than the flash, just a tiny woof, if they heard it at all, much, much later.

—*No way. Just no way,* said Hod—*We just can't win!*

—*Oh, for death's sake,* said Shining Teeth—*Pull yourself together. I can't stand your feeble whingeing.*

Without warning and without thought, Hod jumped into the air. He flew as though leaping over rocks was something he had done all his life, which it was, and he landed hard on Shining Teeth's head, crushing her lower mandible into the grit. Blood started almost immediately.

Hod continued his trajectory after his energetic leap and was several metres away before he stopped. He turned and stared at Shining Teeth as if he could not quite believe what he had done. In fact, no one could believe what he had done, least of all, Shining Teeth. She spun wildly through the dirt and barked loudly.

Terrified, all the animals ran to what might be a safe distance as fast as they could. Some beetles are still running today.

Shining Teeth scrabbled for purchase and swung back round. She lunged desperately at the nearest shape. It was Gleam but he was immovable. He lowered his great head and he roared in her face—*Aaaaaaarrr…*

That stopped her, at least for a moment, and the two of them stayed still, panting, staring at each other, a magnum standoff. Shining Teeth lowered her head and backed out a step or two. She nursed her jaw. She was still shaken and a bit dizzy.

Gleam stood in front of Shining Teeth, with his front paw raised and his mouth gaping, watching her.

Antenna marched up close to Hod and spat through clenched teeth—*With me.* She turned and abruptly strode away, expecting Hod to follow, which he did, and they trooped in single file until she stood in among the paper bark trees where she harvested bark for her nest.

—*Did you? Bring that crocodile into Ektek?*

—*I didn't have a choice, Antenna.*

—*Did you or did you not?*

—*I did but I didn't know she was there until we stopped.*

—*I trusted you.*

—*You still can.*

—*Hod. You defect, and then you arrive back with some pathetic sob story about bandicoots and, instead of a lovely rescue, we get half a tonne of nuclear waste and a rogue croc. None of this exactly endears you in my eyes.*

—*What can I say?*

—*Say you'll take her back.*

—*I can't do that.*

—*Because?*

—*Her family are probably dead. Her mate is gone. She has nothing.*

—*And? What the hell do you think we are we going to do with another roving magnum? We've already got a tiger to deal with in the tunnels. How are we going to cope with a crocodile? Especially now you've jumped on her head. What was that? Peace talks? You are some negotiator, that's for sure. Can't you understand that you, yourself, one crazy wally, is more than enough of a wild card for Ektek? We never know what you're going to do next. Then we've had Chimera to contend with and now, to top it all off, you've brought in something, a loose cannon if ever I saw one, that has promised to finish Ektek. She's more than a threat. Why should I trust you, ever, again?*

—*She needs sanctuary.*

—*She can just take her chances with all the rest of the wildlife in the world.*

—*Who is to say which animal should live and which should die? Who is right? You? Shining Teeth? Gleam? The zoo? All I can see is, if we don't all work together, we're all gone.*

—*The big question for me is, Hod, how can we work together after this? You and I? Because, apart from Bash and Crawf, you and I are the only ones left. It's up to us. We're the elders now.*

This gave Hod pause. He stopped and looked around, trying to gather his thoughts, pull himself together, before staring at her—*Bloody hell, Antenna. What chance have we got?*

Suddenly, a crashing and pounding plunged through the bush. A numbat blasted through the undergrowth, colliding full pelt into Antenna and Hod. He fell back, confused, staring at both creatures. Then, recognising Antenna as one of his own, he said—*Hey, you're a numbat! You from around here?*

Antenna and Hod exchanged glances and watched him warily. They were speechless. The male numbat stared at both creatures and then turned to Antenna—*Sorry. Didn't mean to crash into you. I've got to get out. Which way to the wild lands?*

Hod and Antenna looked at each other and burst into laughter.

The new young numbat glanced between Hod and Antenna, mystified. His gaze fixed on Antenna and the two numbats stared at each other, transfixed.

Hod also looked from Antenna to this new numbat. He was glossy, healthy and his colours were vibrant. There was no denying they looked good together although Antenna was somewhat ruffled and dusty these days.

—*Aaaah. Would you look at you two*, said Hod, coming up with a new idea—*'Ain't you sweet together? You know, if I was a matchmaking kind of wallaby…*

—*Shut up, Hod*, said Antenna—*Or Shining Teeth won't need to kill you.*

EKTEK003

Kill the Pandas

Chapter Forty-seven

I

Knife-shadows scattered across the numbat enclosure. Eucalypt leaves trembled in the breeze. The sun tipped sharp new growth with gold. Three adult females and one senior male stretched out in the gritty sand enjoying the lazy pleasure of sunbaking in the late afternoon. The strips of light and dark shifted on their banded coats. So clever was their striped camouflage, it was difficult to see where beast and sand separated.

They were surrounded by the sounds of inexorable rituals in the closing zoo. It happened every day: just the same, day after day, reversing morning openings into afternoon closings. Human workers, dressed in crumpled khaki, squawked to each other as they puttered in their re-purposed golf carts from enclosure to feeding station to rubbish area. Doors clanged, buckets clattered, hoses swished and animals shouted their particular evening cries to each other. On thin legs, calling to their neighbours, birds high-stepped their way to their night perches. Gaggles of human visitors straggled through the shop on their way out, bleating to their children and barking at the shop assistants, clad in bright plumage and marked with sticky ice-cream drips.

In their striped enclosure, two young numbats laughed, jumped and scampered in play, at times even daring to crash carelessly over their elders. They raced around the logs, laughing, chasing and dodging away from Antenna. She pretended to be a bird of prey, flying and dashing at them, using her long thin face as a sort of beak-mask. She wasn't very frightening but she kept those scallywags moving, for which their parents were endlessly grateful. During their cheerful exertion, one of the youngsters fell over and began to cry. Antenna stopped running, caught the other kid easily and moved to comfort the fallen one. Pulling the two infants to her, she cradled the snivelling youngster in her forelimbs, the other child leaning into her side and watching solemnly. Antenna was gentle with the wounded child. Both trusted her.

This was the touching scene that greeted Spark, Christmas beetle, as he flew into the numbat enclosure. The sun reflected from his multi-coloured wing case as he communicated—*Do you want to see them before they go?*

—*Of course,* Antenna barely looked at him, her attention taken by the still sniffling youngster—*We have to go through all the arrangements again. Can you let them know?*

—*What about Eid?*

—*Eid doesn't need to know anything. He just gets back on duty and behaves himself like a good numbat should.*

—*Yeah, right. Good luck with that.*

—*Come on, Spark, round 'em up. No time to waste.*

With a heavy metal clash, the door to the numbat's sleeping quarters opened and the boots of the human keeper crunched over the granitic sand. As the man counted the numbats and checked they were where they were supposed to be, Spark, still flittering nearby, couldn't help remarking to Antenna—*You should think about having some of your own.*

—*Babies?* Antenna was astonished—*I don't think so.* When Spark sniggered she added—*What are you doing, hanging around here? Buzz off, you annoying collie!*

Spark flew a farewell Christmas beetle arc around her head. When she snapped at him, he did as he was told and buzzed off. Then she turned back to the young numbats, just toddlers really, and looked at them anew, wondering. She closed her eyes and thought for as long as… Ooooh, half a tick… What it might be like to be a mother… Then she laughed to herself and opened her eyes. Her? Have kids? Not likely. At least she could give these back before she headed out to work and that's exactly what was going to happen next—*Come on, you kittens! Race you home!*

II

In a different enclosure entirely, one piled with rocks and boulders in a landscaped effort to look natural, Hod leaned back on his tail and surveyed the setting sun with bleary half-shut eyes. He had just arrived at his customary spot at the summit of the yellow-footed rock wallaby area. He surreptitiously checked his family were all around him before commencing a personal grooming session. His ears flicked as he heard a little voice shouting—*Dad! Dad! Watch me!* He ignored it. That didn't stop the childish voice, however—*Dad! Dad! Hey! Dad! Look at this!*

On the path outside the enclosure, a small truck pulled up with a shriek of brakes and disgorged two humans, dressed in their Bedlam Zoo branded khaki, showing their hairy knees, prepared to do a last minute job for the day.

Three of the more daring joeys raced down to get closer to the people. —*Dad! Dad! Hey! Dad! Who are these guys?* They knew these particular humans had nothing to do with them. Although they were young they could smell a vet from a considerable distance and they knew these guys weren't vets. The joeys braced to rush off in pretend terror and they relished every second of the frisson.

The two humans went around to the back of the truck and, with an enormous effort, untied a large sign. They dug two holes for rear support, stuck in two large braces, hammered the sign up to the fence and reinforced the struts.

The joeys rushed around, pretending to be hunted, pretending to be petrified and shouting all the while—*Dad! Hey, Dad! Check it out, Dad!*

Hod only had eyes for the workers and the sign. As they swung it from the truck he'd not been able to read it and now it was hammered up he couldn't see the front. It annoyed him. What might it say? Stuck up on his own home and he had no way of telling what the blasted thing said. It had to be about them. Didn't it? The two humans seemed keen to finish work for the day and packed up. As they drove away, the joeys laughed at the tools they'd left to rust in the weather—*Dad! Dad! Hey! Dad!* But all Hod could think was: What could it mean for the yellow-footed rock wallaby community? More space? More funding? Had they been selected for some kind of honour? How could he find out?

Another, slightly smaller, wallaby bounced effortlessly up the rocks and came to rest beside, though slightly below him, on the rock pile, raising her short arms wide to balance her position. Before she had even stopped he said—*Did you see what it said?*

—*What?*

—*What. She asks me what. The sign, of course. Are you blind?*

—*Oh. No. Sorry.*

—*What is it? How can I find out?*

—*Hod.*

—*What?*

—*Don't you hear them?*

—What?

—Calling you.

—I hear them.

—Would it kill you to talk to them? They're your kids…

—Don't start.

—You know they look up to you.

—They can come up here, anytime. I'm not stopping them.

—If you're even here.

—I can't help that. I've got more important things to worry about.

—What can be more important than the next generation? She looked at him. She really did have the most beautiful eyes—*Hod?*

Hod just looked at her. Didn't she know anything? Didn't she have any idea what his work entailed? Did she never listen to a word he said? He was saving lives and all she worried about was her selfish little joeys. Some of them didn't even look like him. Did she think he was a fool? Playing dad to a bunch of joeys that weren't even his kids?

The annoying little voice came again—*Dad!*

And then there was another—*Hey, Dad, look at me!*

Christmas beetle Spark didn't even need to open his mouth as he flittered up to see Hod but he did anyway—*Hey, Hod. Right to go?* The wallaby didn't bother to stop and chat; just shot away down the hill, as soon as he'd seen the glittering beetle, and shouted at him—*Over here!*

—What? Spark flew, following Hod to the fence and the rear of the fresh sign.

—Can you get round the front; tell me what it says?

—What's it worth?

—Cut it out, Spark!

Spark understood it wasn't time to be joking and took off with a whiz and a whirr to hover over the sign.

Hod waited attentively, his joeys racing around him.

Spark whizzed back and said—*The pandas are coming.*

—What's that?

—Beats me. See you at the meeting. Got to get going, and Spark slipped away in a gentle flurry.

—Dad! Dad!

—Dad!

—Sorry, children, places to go, creatures to see…

—Aw, Dad…

And Hod leapt away and over the fence.

On top of the rock pile, she looked over to another female, this one with a tiny joey in her pouch, and shrugged. She'd done her best. They knew nothing would ever hold Hod for long.

III

—Pardon me? Could you tell me, please, how much longer I am to be waiting? A young female beetle with a red lozenge-shaped body, black abdomen and black head nosed up to Torque. She had cute trim antennae that curled round in a shapely way behind her head. Torque turned to her and worried. He was feeling harassed. What on earth could he say?

The beetles were under the feeding centre of the zoo, a wooden structure where human Bedlam Zoo staff prepared a continual stream of meals and treats for creatures of every size from all around the world. The slats around the edge of the building splintered the remaining sunlight from outside into slivers inside, revealing the many different shaped and coloured elytra bustling about on the ground. A large group of beetles tucked into scraps and they were from everywhere, albeit within flight range from the zoo centre.

Torque, a darkling beetle with a long black body, was still nominally in charge of Ektek's security, even though these days he seemed to spend all his time acting as provisioning officer for this disparate group of beetles who just kept on arriving at Ektek's door. There was no stopping them. They seemed to come across the sea, across the land and across the city nearly every day now. The Ektek team wasn't able to keep up with the demand. It was impossible to see even half of them, much less follow their directions to rescue the endangered animal that had requested assistance. Some stayed, waiting in the queue. Others left with their missions unfulfilled.

Torque found it more than frustrating keeping up. He sighed and said—*Look, mate. You got a name?*

—Lewis, thank you, please.

—Lewis. Yeah. Lewis, well, I'm sorry, I don't know when they'll see you. I don't even know if they ever will. It's more than my job's worth to tell you a day and time because it'd just be made up. I've got no idea. You know as much as I do and if you think that's fair, well I don't because I've been working here all my life and you'd think the least they could do is let me know what's going on and do you think they do? No. They don't. Torque shook his head as he watched the crowd. What was he to do with them? What was he to do with Lewis?

Lewis, with the red elytra snapped into place over her wings, wasn't unhappy, she just wanted clarification—*Do you think it is time I*

*have waited long enough? Maybe I should leave you? I have delivered the message.
You are clear about it?*

—*Nah, hang on, wait a bit; you the one with the Iberian lynx? Was that
you?* Torque struggled to remember as he gazed at her—*They're getting
run over all the time? Was that it? No? No, don't tell me, it was the beleaguered
beluga whales?*

—*Wolverines.*

—*Oh, Lewis. I said not to tell me. Okay, wolverines. Though what Ektek
can do about melting icepacks, I don't know.*

—*I am also in trepidation about this, Mr Torque. Wolverine seems in trouble in many areas of life and death, not just in ice; but, if no ice, no den, no babies,
no more wolverines. So they say.*

—*No ice, no dice.*

—*Beg pardon?*

—*No worries, Lewis. Look, it's up to you, mate. More than my job's worth
to try and guess what your chances are but it won't be today, I can tell you that for
nothing because they're already off on an action, and it won't be tomorrow because
they'll have to process their findings and publicise it. So at least three days and
you're not even first in line, are you?*

—*Not sure but... No. Not first, no.*

Spark, the Christmas beetle, appeared through the darkness and
landed by the entrance near the tap. He waved to Torque in a relaxed
manner as he found a little flower to gnaw upon.

Torque nodded back and started walking toward him even as he
continued talking to Lewis—*We'll just have to hope the others know where
they are in the line. Go chew on those flowers there and let me have a think. Let me
know if you want to head out, okay?*

As Torque moved toward Spark he travelled through the group,
most of them happily munching on flowers, melon-peel and rotting
grape stalks. The visiting beetles called to him or waved their antennae.
Torque would have liked to stop and chat to each of them but he was
tired and had no answers. When he got to Spark he was hoping for
some good news—*Hi, Sparky.*

—*Hi, Torque. I was a bit hungry. Thought I'd drop in.*

—*Good, there's a few things...*

—*Got to crack on... The meeting's about to start.*

Torque nodded—*Be there as soon as I can.*

—*Oh, no worries. You don't need to be there. I can handle it.* Spark
looked round at the throng—*Wow. This is getting more than just a queue,
isn't it?*

—Tell me about it. Queue? Hardly. I can't even seem to hear the messages any more.

—I'll mention it at the meeting. Maybe someone might come up with an idea.

—Like what?

—Don't ask me! It hasn't been had yet, has it? See you.

As Spark left him standing in the midst of the crowd, something happened in Torque. He made up his mind. Something had to change right here and right now and he was the beetle for the job. After all, he was supposed to be head of security, even though that young Spark seemed to think he could take over all the work by himself.

Torque moved to the middle of the group and stood on a piece of pineapple stalk to get a little bit above the crowd and shouted—*Oi! Collies! Over here!* Once he had their attention, he went on—*Thank you, all you coleopties, for waiting so patiently. Listen, I don't want to waste your time. If you want to stay at Bedlam and wait for Ektek to see you, you're welcome. I would ask, however, that you don't go wandering off by yourselves. This zoo's got more vehicles and machinery than you can poke a stick at and they've got a habit of materialising and running creatures over just when you least expect. As for getting to see the Ektek team, well, it's more than my job's worth to guess when that's going to happen. You have important messages, I know you do, all of you are holding stories of life and death in your thoraxes. Ektek can only do what it can do. Please be patient. I'm off to find out what's happening. While you're waiting, please relax, get to know each other and stay safe. I'll be back as soon as I can.*

A friendly muttering of agreement rose above the group. They mostly had no rush to be anywhere else; they'd all had reasonably long journeys to get there and were happy to rest for a while. No reason to give Torque any problems. But still, something needed to be done. Where was he going to put them all? He nodded grimly and headed out toward the Ektek hangar.

IV

The aviaries at Bedlam Zoo consisted of rows of small sheds connected by a walkway for human access, covered in bold and bright signage for human understanding. They were planted inside and out with an attractive array of greenery, depending on the type of bird and the country of origin. It was all very educational and alluring. From the front, that is. From the point of view of the paying public, it was designer and gorgeous. The back, however, was just a series of wire cages with locks and bolts and double access doors. There, it was all practical. Feeding, watering and cleaning had to be done effectively without any troublesome escapes. Which is not to say there were never any escapes. Of course there were, nearly every day. The Ektek team needed to get in and out of their cages without any bother from their human carers and did so, with frequent regularity. Of course, they always came home again, before any alarm was raised.

The various birds housed in these aviaries raised their voices to the great sky in evensong and there was general ruckus as everyone tucked in for the night. Except for one very quiet cage.

Palm cockatoos, from Far North Queensland, one of the largest birds in the world, were accommodated in a luxury of fronds and leafiness. This evening found one Palm cockatoo, Crawf, alone in his small shed. His normally perky headdress was slumped and flat; his grey feathers dark and lifeless. His usually pink cheek patches were pale, almost white. He was still, his head bowed.

Spark beetled in to the cage and shouted—*Hey! Crawf! Time to go!* and without looking or waiting for a reply, he zoomed away again yelling as he went—*See ya there!*

Anyone who had cared to look at Crawf closely would have seen a tear rise out of his round, dark eye, flood out over the reddened rim and trickle down his face and over his feathered front.

Only, no one did look.

Chapter Forty-eight

I

In the gloom of the tunnel system that ran under Bedlam Zoo, Gleam, tiger, stalked toward the control centre of Ektek. Although he was thin and unkempt, Gleam filled the tunnel almost completely. This was an excavation designed by beetles and ants working with small community-minded animals. They could never have imagined that large prowling predators turned vegetarian would use the tunnel but there he was. He squeezed himself through the thin burrow in order to meet the other Ektek creatures in preparation for an action that was due to commence in a matter of minutes.

Gleam and the others had been researching the local teaching hospital laboratory online for some time now and they had learned enough to believe that many live animals were suffering for science. The Ektek team had decided they needed to see the experiments for themselves. There'd been many questions raised, even by the scientists involved, in the motivation behind using these creatures to improve human health. Hardly any clear answers had been provided, especially in these days of advanced molecular and genetic chemistry, when it would seem using livestock would be obsolete. Instead, millions of different animal experiments continued all over the world and breeding facilities made constant healthy profits.

Gleam's mind was full of scientific developments, as well as opposing excuses, as to why some of the data resulting from experiments on rats and mice could not be accepted by various companies and authorities. After all, everyone knew that although non-human species had much in common with humans, there was enough of a difference in physiology to disqualify findings that ran contrary to the desired views. Gleam was hoping his own experience might help him to understand what the experiments entailed. They also intended to broadcast proceedings on the Ektek website, exposing the experiments without interfering in them.

As he made his way through the tunnel he became aware of another creature approaching. Another large creature, lower to the ground than Gleam, dragged her heavy carcass along the floor. Gleam drifted into a slow-motion walk, lifting his feet and carefully replacing them onto the ground, crouching even more than the corridor had forced him to do previously. He sniffed the air and knew exactly who was approaching. He gauged her mood: bad, as usual. As he rounded a corner to the doorway of the control centre, he could see the low crocodile shadow in the darkness. She knew he knew she was there and they both stopped equidistant from the door in a croc-tiger standoff. Light glinted from the croc's marble eye. A hint of flame flickered in the tiger's. Here was trouble and it was not just a physical puzzle as to which creature should enter the doorway first. It was a psychological dilemma of dominance. Both reptile and feline were unmoving and mute in the darkness as they weighed up their options. These were the large, dangerous animals; these were the magnums.

Gleam spoke first—*After you, Shining Teeth.*

Shining Teeth snorted, a horrible sound that could have been clearing her catarrh, or it might have been laughter, and then she said—*Oh, no, no, no; I insist! After you…*

Gleam sighed—*Please don't be like this.*

—*Like what?*

—*You know perfectly well.*

—*I don't have the faintest idea what you're talking about.*

—*Shining Teeth.*

—*Gleam, oh, please, do explain what you mean?*

—*Your sarcasm. Your forced etiquette. It doesn't suit you.*

—*It doesn't suit you, you mean.*

Gleam sighed again—*We have to make an effort here.*

—*Do we?* said Shining Teeth—*Do we really? An effort? To work together? To 'get on'? I'm sure I'm not the one with the forced politeness, hiding behind a mask of civility when all I want is to eat…*

—*How do you manage, then…?*

—*Oh, I manage fine.*

—*… not to eat me?*

—*All that fur? No. I've cut a deal with Hod. To stay here in Ektek, means, well, picking my dinnertime…*

—*So, you've controlled your instincts.*

—*Only just, fuzz features. Ektek is just going to have to take me as they find me.*

—*Shall we go in? They must be waiting for us.*

—I really do insist…

Gleam bowed to Shining Teeth's greater nastiness and entered the control room where hundreds of glow-worms lit the cave with their inimitable blue blush. Over in the computer section a screen threw multi-coloured light patterns over Bash's tiny black-and-yellow-frog face. He was engrossed in an activity showing on the monitor and paid no attention when the other Ektek creatures started to arrive for the planning meeting. He'd turned down the sound so that, apart from the flickering light of his monitor, no one would notice the corroboree frog or what he was doing and no one did.

Gleam took up as little space as he could, which was still a lot of the small area in the control centre. Upon her arrival, Shining Teeth filled considerable legroom herself. The two large predators gave no indication of noticing each other but both were exquisitely alert to the other. They lay on opposite sides of the floor, croc closer to the door, tiger squashed up against the wall, apparently ready to doze. No matter what they looked like, in reality, both were more than ready to spring at each other's throats.

In direct contrast, Eid, the young male numbat, was sitting up on his hindquarters twitching with excitement. His erect fur made him appear much bigger than his normal size. Antenna barely glanced at him as she marched in with Hod following close behind and brushed past the earnest numbat, saying—*What're you doing here?*

—*This time I could help*, said Eid—*I really could.* He made no effort to hide his admiration for her; he gazed at her, enthralled with her.

—*You could be where you're supposed to be.* Antenna went straight to a computer and, with Hod looking over her shoulder, started typing in a website address—*Go home, Eid.*

—*Please, Antenna*, said Eid—*Give me a break. Let me see the plan. I'm capable. You know I am…*

—*No.* Antenna looked to Gleam for backup. They'd had this argument so many times before she almost had to admire Eid's perseverance. Almost. Her eyes narrowed in frustration and she turned her back to him. She focused on the website downloading on the monitor in front of her.

—*Eid, we've been through this*, said Gleam. He spoke as though explaining basic road rules to a kid poised to cross a freeway—*You've got your responsibilities. You have to get back to the enclosure. Antenna took your duties earlier today. Now you're on duty. You know this.*

—*They wouldn't miss me!*

—*Go away*, repeated Antenna, intent on her monitor.

—*Eid,* said Gleam—*We understand you were bred in captivity. Of course you're itching for the wild and a chance to prove yourself. What normal young numbat wouldn't? But…*

Eid had escaped from his enclosure a few weeks ago and run straight into Antenna, a numbat with misfortune of her own, just outside the zoo. Luckily, she'd been able to persuade him, by the sheer force of her presence, it was better to remain in the vicinity of the Zoo, even if she'd had to parlay her own liberty to do it. This had been shattering for Eid, life changing. His dreams of wilderness, his ideas of freedom and his very concept of what he was had been shaken to the core. Every day, he was still being shaken to the core and the name of his own personal earthquake was Antenna. He could not take his eyes off her and he thought of little else. How could he get her to notice him? How could he get her to respect him? How could he impress her? At the moment, these were insurmountable questions and he watched her glare at him, again, as usual, as though she found him the most annoying creature in the entire world. Maybe she did.

—*Eid, stop arguing.* Directing what seemed her most fierce stare at him, Antenna reiterated the threat—*It's a risk we can't afford. If the humans should find you missing…*

—*Come on, it's been ages…*

—*Not in human terms. You know they'd dig the whole place up looking for you. We can't risk that. They'd find Ektek and that would be the end, of everything.*

Eid felt his chance slipping away, again, and he just couldn't bear it—*I know I could be useful,* he tried, one more time—*I'd pay attention, I'd be obedient…*

Gleam had been suffering quietly. He'd kept his head down and he'd counted mentally to ten but his patience was tested and he'd only got to five before he snapped and jumped up with a roar— *Aaaaaaaaaaaaaargh…*

Shining Teeth would have raised an eyebrow, if she'd had one. Instead a slight twitch appeared above her flame-coloured reptile eyes as she sneered in a sing-song voice—*Hmmmm. Temper…*

Hod looked over to the croc and shook his head.

—*What?* Shining Teeth noticed the subtle admonishment and looked as innocent as she possibly could, widening her eyes and blinking flamboyantly. She looked at Hod—*We all know the tiger doesn't go in for killing anything. He won't even scratch. His roar is the only scary thing about him and even that's not so bad, is it, Eid?*

Hod sighed and turned back to Gleam. There was no way he wanted to bait Gleam. He didn't want to encourage Shining Teeth either. He knew only too well she loved a fight. Her eyes shone and she almost wagged her crocodile tail as she looked over at Gleam and Eid and silently egged them on.

Eid and Gleam were now nose to nose simply because of the limited space. When the tiger stood up he filled the room. The fact that Eid had no fear of the enormous tiger should have been astounding, but everyone knew that Gleam had made a solemn oath never to kill another living thing. The worst he would do was roar, and, although that was fairly imposing and had been known to bring down small rocks from the dug-out ceilings under the zoo from time to time, it posed no real danger, except to hearing.

—*Sit down,* said Gleam and Eid, deciding he was better off proving his obedience right now, sat. Gleam also returned to sitting and then lay, squashing himself back against the wall with a slight look of guilt at losing his temper yet again.

—*Eid.* Antenna took up the argument with an air of weariness— *You have to believe us and you have to be patient. You're still too new. The numbat breeding program is one of the most expensive projects Bedlam has ever undertaken. You're worth a lot to them in terms of credibility. There will come a time when your absence won't be noticed but, seriously, Eid, it's not now.*

Eid watched Antenna, judging how far he could push her. The last thing he wanted was to piss her off but he couldn't help it. He needed to be involved with this work. He needed action. He couldn't go back and moulder behind bars. It was sheer luck - their coats were so similar (tones of sandy red by their shoulders) and they were alike in size - that she'd thought of the exchange program. Eid was a little bigger than Antenna, but as they would never be seen in the same place at the same time, that didn't matter. This meant the two numbats could swap without arousing interest from the human keepers. He knew he was being unfair to Antenna but he suspected she found certain benefits from her time with the numbat family. He also knew that if the keepers took a closer look, due to the boy-girl thing, they would be found out. He decided he'd probably pushed her as far as he could at the moment but he couldn't help going in for one last attempt—*At least could you…*

—*No,* said Antenna—*No.* She turned to rebuke him further but before she could get her mouth open Torque flew in from the corridor outside, straight toward her, landed on the console and said—*Antenna. We've got a problem.*

—I know, we're just looking them up…

—What?

—The pandas…

—Pandas? What? No. Beetles. Far too many of them, more than my job's…

—Beetles? What? No. Can we deal with these pandas first? Hod's reported a sign over his enclosure…

—Look, said Hod, pointing at the monitor—*Here we go. Told you.* And he was staring at a newsflash across the Bedlam Zoo website announcing the arrival of their very own pandas; a potential breeding couple named Zui Hou and Xia Shi—*Oh, no.* Hod was shaking his head. He banged his paw on the desk.

—Antenna. There are so many beetles I can't even count them any more much less listen to their numbers, Torque carried on—*Do you think you could see even one today? Two would be better, of course…*

—Not today, Torque, said Antenna—*Come on, we're late as it is. You know we're supposed to get organised for this action…*

—Then when? When can you see them? Should I tell them to go?

—Can we transfer them electronically? said Hod.

—The beetles? said Antenna.

—No, the pandas, said Hod.

—Why? said Gleam—*They might be worth something to us.*

Antenna was not impressed—*To us?*

Gleam continued—*Pandas are the biggest marquee animals…*

—Marquee? said Hod quietly to Shining Teeth—*What's that mean?*

— Why's he's talking about tents at a time like this? Shining Teeth muttered—*Pointless.*

—Our last zoo had pandas and they raised enough turnstile money to run all sorts of conservation programs, said Eid—*They're a good thing, really, for the bank.*

—We don't need them, said Hod—*Pandas just hog all the money and attention. What about all the other suffering species?*

—Stop them coming, said Shining Teeth—*Be a lot easier than getting rid of them.*

—Eid, asked Antenna—*What's turnstile money?*

Eid perked up then. This was something new. Antenna had actually heard something he'd said!—*The marquee is the hoarding over the door where you put the name of the stars to get public attention. Pandas bring the public. Humans love pandas…*

—Oh, disgusting… said Shining Teeth.

—And they bring in money. Lots of money.

—Humans fawn over them because they're like cute fluffy toys, said Hod— *All the other creatures in the zoo will fade into the background and disappear.*

—You don't need pandas, said Shining Teeth.

—Think about it, said Antenna—*Like, Eid said... Perhaps the extra money would be used to protect habitat for other creatures?*

—As if... muttered Shining Teeth.

—There's a lot to be gained, said Gleam—*from having such a drawcard.*

—Oh, no, here we go... said Shining Teeth to Hod who just rolled his eyes.

—I think we should welcome them, continued Gleam—*They too are endangered; and a flagship species; like the website says; a high profile exotic species. Could help to bring the spotlight to us all.*

—You're talking like they're some kind of emblem for threatened wildlife, said Hod.

—Which they are, said Antenna.

—Well, they're doing a useless job so far, aren't they, said Hod—*Plus, what about us rock wallabies? They're shoving us right down the end of the zoo in a tiny enclosure next to the waste disposal centre.*

—Okay, Hod, we're not going to solve this now, we need to be preparing for the university. Where's Crawf?

—Coming, said Spark—*At least, I thought he was.*

—What's keeping him? You're supposed to be leaving now. Is everyone else here? Where's Bash?

—Here. Antenna and Gleam looked over to the source of the little frog voice and then looked at each other. That young corroboree frog had been playing computer games for as long as he could stay away from water for some time now. Should they worry about him? Just as Antenna was about to say something Eid piped up yet again—*Please? Can I go?*

—No, you can't. Torque, will you please take Eid back to his enclosure and make sure he stays put? Spark, can you get over to Crawf and put a cracker under him?

—Sure. Spark flew up and whizzed past Eid's head. He came back round and clipped Eid's ear. Eid reached up and spat out his long worm tongue but Spark was ready and zipped out of reach - a considerable distance - Eid's tongue was long.

—I can't believe you animals! This is no time for mucking about! We've got an action to get to. Now!

Eid followed Torque and Spark out of the cave.

As the other creatures got to their feet and stretched in preparation to leave—*There is one more thing,* said Shining Teeth—*I'm not taking orders from anyone; not even a tiger. Especially a tiger as piss weak as this one.*

Gleam just laughed. Weakness was in the eye of the beholder as far as he could judge—*I don't feel weak, Shining Teeth.*

Shining Teeth sneered at him—*It's not for you to decide. If I'm on an 'action' with you busy bodies then what I do is my business.*

Antenna flung Hod a look that asked 'What are we going to do with her?'

Hod saw that look and said—*Shining Teeth's just joking, aren't you, Shining Teeth? You agreed to help us, didn't you? I mean, we're helping you, giving you sanctuary and all that, right? Remember?*

—*Yeah. Giving me a place to live when you're all in hiding underground. Right. Big deal. I'm still my own boss.*

—*We'll work it out,* said Hod, pouring on reassurance as fast as he could—*Don't worry, Antenna. Nice, simple surveillance, back before breakfast. You'll see. We'll work together like a well-oiled machine, won't we? Gleam? Shining Teeth? Bash?*

Gleam agreed with Hod but couldn't help flicking Shining Teeth a worried look. Bash didn't look up from his computer game. Shining Teeth snickered.

Antenna sighed and then caught sight of the computer screen in front of her. Pandas. Friend or foe?

II

Torque flew and Eid walked through the hangar to get to the numbat enclosure. Eid sniffed the air, looked at everything and just couldn't help his paws from reaching out to touch. Torque kept having to fly back to keep him on track—*Come on, Eid,* which worked for a moment. At least, until the next time Torque was forced to remind Eid to—*Put that down, you don't know where it's been,* and get moving again.

After all this time, his whole working life, in fact, even Torque wasn't immune from the fascination of the working Ektek hangar. It was a huge cave, carved out and enhanced over the years by an army of beetles and ants. Here mechanic beetles tended to vehicles used in actions to rescue endangered animals all over the world. The Ektek fleet covered everything from boats to steam powered cars and, in theory at least, each vehicle would be ready at a moment's notice. The hovercraft and five-legged remote controlled stalkers were parked in dimly-lit recesses.

The noise was intense; the business of vehicle maintenance flourished with the attendant shouting and clashing of metal on metal produced by skilled beetle mechanics.

Sculpted skylights captured daylight up on the surface of the zoo landscape, some incorporated into human buildings and some cleverly camouflaged in animal enclosures. Sunlight entered the skylight, was captured and funnelled by tubes containing mirrors; the light, bouncing down the tube mirror to mirror, could be directed to where it was most needed. Currently, half of the light tubes were focused on a small group of beetles working on the tank, an armoured vehicle capable of moving through and over most obstacles. The rest of the light was beamed onto a team working on the wingship, an elegant plane with curving wings.

After a little time spent observing her, Torque approached Manifold, a red-and-blue bombardier beetle. She was the chief mechanic and she looked worried.

—*Manifold?* said Torque.

—*Yup?*

—*Got a moment?*

—*Nup. Up against it. Got to get the tank and wingship out.*

—*We've just come in from the control centre. They'll be a while yet.*

—*No one told us.*

—*They're a bit behind. It's just, I've had an idea.*

—*Quick then. You know what it's like. When they're tired, that's when accidents happen,* and she watched her team even as she bolted the side of the fuel lid back on the wingship.

—*Am I right in thinking you could use some extra hands?*

—*Could I, what.*

—*I've got some.*

—*What?* She looked him up and down as if expecting to see his extra hands sprouting from under his elytra.

Torque didn't notice—*If you want some extra workers, I've got them.*

—*Where from?*

—*Everywhere. The numbers. There's no time for the team to hear them so they're just waiting around. Eating. They've got nothing to do.*

—*Haven't got time to teach them anything.*

—*What do they need to know? To start with, I mean?*

—*Safety protocol, cleaning, I don't know, everything…*

—*I'll train them.*

—*You?*

—Well, if I don't know about safety, what do I know, eh? That's my job, Manifold. Security. I can give them the occupational health and safety drills and teach them what goes where. If you let me know anything else you need, well, you got some extra workers.

Manifold stared at him, thinking, that just might work, when another voice broke in—*What about me?*

Torque and Manifold both looked up at Eid, who stood roughly a hundred times bigger than both of them put together. They looked back at each other and before they could say no, Eid continued—*I could help. I know I could. I'm a fast learner and I...*

—Already have a job, said Torque—*You're supposed to be on duty in the numbat enclosure right now. It's more than my job's worth to have you hanging around...*

—When I'm not on duty, I could be here. I could clean. I can listen...

—We'd have to ask Antenna. Let's go...

—Actually, Manifold broke in—*Could use someone with a bit of height. Got a new skin for the airship coming out of the spiders even as we speak. Previous skin got blasted into a million pieces and we need it reassembled to get a pattern. You could do that.*

Eid could have hugged her but he didn't know how to hug a beetle without squashing her. He grinned instead and said—*Thanks, Manifold. See? Torque? Antenna doesn't have to know, does she? After I've been counted I can just come here and what she doesn't know, she doesn't have to worry about.*

—More than my job's worth to make a call on that, said Torque.

—Don't say no...

—I'll think about it. Sorry, Manifold. We'd better get him back to work.

—Listen, Torque, if you can help, that'd be great, said Manifold—*And I meant what I said: I could use the numbat.*

—I'll bring them round for an orientation...

—After the action's gone.

—Looks like you've got yourself an extended workforce.

Manifold watched them leave the hangar; Eid moped behind, his tail down between his legs, as he followed Torque like a bizarre giant pet. She shook her head and turned back just in time to see a young stag beetle drop a shifting spanner right on an unsuspecting rose chafer's head. The rose chafer shook his head and continued without even a pause but even so, Mandible reckoned it was time to trot out her safety-with-tools lecture and it was worth seeing the look on those two beetles faces when she started forward, shouting—*Whoa! That's the sort of negligence I'm talking about right there!*

III

Spark watched Crawf from the edge of Crawf's cage. He could see how the bird was slumped and realised he'd been remiss. He hadn't actually heard the cockatoo speak when he'd been through the aviaries before. Spark watched for a while and then looked further into the cage. He hesitated for a moment before he jumped into the air and flew toward the grey cockatoo. He landed on a stick that grew out from Crawf's perch and cleared his throat.

Crawf gave no indication of being aware of his beetle visitor.

—*Crawf?* Spark said quietly—*Where's Sunday?*

After a miserable silence, Crawf gave a sigh and then said—*Gone.*

—*Cleared?*

—*No.*

—*What then?*

—*My fault.*

—*Crawf?* Crawf stayed silent but Spark pressed on—*How can it be? Tell me.*

—*She was lying on the floor.*

—*When?*

—*This morning.* Crawf looked up through his net ceiling at the darkening sky. If he'd been thinking he might have noticed the first stars were visible but he didn't see. He couldn't see anything except the vision of his dead partner on the floor at the break of dawn. He opened and shut his beak silently before he could continue—*An ant walked out of her beak.*

Spark needed to confirm what Crawf was telling him—*Dead?*

Crawf was in pain and could only spit words out like shrapnel—*Dusty. Cold.*

—*It's not your fault, Crawf.*

—*She died of a broken heart.*

—*Crawf.*

—*Because her eggs never hatched. Did you know that? It was my fault. She tried and tried, always sitting on cold dead eggs. Because of me.*

—*Crawf. You don't know that.*

—*Hullo? I know. I know what I did in my own life. I left her alone. I was always out on Ektek business; more and more, far more than she wanted me to. You know how much I've been away. She never wanted me to go but I left her and she was always alone and then she died.*

—*Crawf. You can't take this on by yourself.*

—I have to. I'm the only one; the last Palm cockatoo in the world. I can't leave this place again. I've got a responsibility to educate the human public.

—What about Ektek?

—What about them?

—You're supposed to be flying the wingship? For the action? Starting now?

—None of that matters any more.

—But it does.

—Go away.

—What will I tell them?

—Tell them I'm not doing it any more. Tell them that. Tell them I quit.

—What?

—I'm done. Do you hear me? That's it. Finished. I quit Ektek.

—You can't.

—I can. I just have.

Spark stared at Crawf from his perch next to the giant bird. Could Crawf quit? Spark decided he needed some help with this one. He'd never heard of anyone quitting before. He shook his head and left Crawf to his lonely perch.

Crawf raised his claw to stamp but he did not have the energy. He placed his foot back on the perch and curved again into stillness.

IV

A tall masculine human figure in a long leather overcoat, heavily armed and begrimed, ran over a smashed landscape. The world was in sepia, in ruins, all colour bleached from the sky and soil. Trees were oddly stunted trunk memories. Plant life was grey, pale and the sort of tough stuff that clung to life on the mere promise of water. The man ran past a ruined building, the remnant walls pitted by a history of explosions.

A ball of flame appeared in front of the man and he raised an enormous gun and shot repeatedly at a figure now running fast directly toward him. The figure blasted apart, the head atomised and the chest exploded in a spray of bloody gore. The crumpled remains fell apart, lumped onto the pallid sand. Leather-coat man stood above the mess and was suddenly blocked out by a rectangle of black. A grid of green letters glowed on the screen; a menu of weapons and medicines the crushed victim had been carrying.

Bash tilted his head to one side, narrowed his eyes, selected a stimpack, a wrench and a minigun from the list before clicking the instructions for his leather coat character to run on through the post-apocalyptic landscape. It was definitely kill or be killed in this arena and Bash needed to concentrate in order to survive. He tightened his lips in determination and his character forged on in a loping run.

Spark flew into the control room and joined Antenna at the console where she and Hod continued to read about pandas. Spark looked up at the numbat and frowned. She wasn't going to like what he had to say but he had to say it anyway—*Crawf's not coming.*

Antenna said—*What?*

—*He quit.*

—*He what?*

—*He's quitting Ektek.*

—*He can't do that.*

—*He has.*

—*Okay. They'll have to go without him. Oi!* Antenna stood and waved her paw in front of Bash's screen—*Quit the game.*

—*But I've just found a munitions factory!*

—*Now.*

—*If you say so.* Bash ran over the trackball and leapt onto the drawing tablet to save his game and quit. He turned to look at the team and quickly looked down again.

Gleam, Antenna, Hod and Shining Teeth waited for him and none of them looked happy.

—*Let's go,* Antenna left first, followed in the air by Spark.

Gleam said—*Come on, Bash. What are you waiting for?*

Bash jumped from the console to the top of Gleam's head and then squished himself down by the big cat's ear as they scraped under the door and into the corridor.

Hod and Shining Teeth brought up the rear and, as they travelled smartly through the tunnel toward the hangar, he said—*You got to leave the tiger alone, Shining Teeth. It's not a joke.*

—*Not to you.*

—*Not to any of us. Just because he's made himself a promise, doesn't mean you have to rile him up. We've got work to do.*

—*Okay, I'll be good. Don't you worry about a thing.*

Hod shook his head as they hurried down the hallway. Shining Teeth couldn't have said anything more disturbing. There was no way he'd not be worrying now and there was no way he'd be able to stop her doing whatever she thought was 'good'.

They arrived in the hangar to find the beetles had built a tiny palanquin for Gleam to wear and a group of them were affixing it from a platform about tiger head height. Gleam did not look at all pleased about this new headgear.

Hod sent Shining Teeth a silent plea to keep her trap shut about it. Shining Teeth flashed him an innocent smile. Then again, given her large row of visible teeth, it always looked as though she was smiling anyway. It was doubtful she ever was. Hod hoped she kept her opinions to herself and worked as part of the team.

Antenna and Manifold were in hurried conference about which vehicle to take now they were one pilot down. It seemed best that the activists all travel in the tank together. The ant and beetle ground crew swarmed to work over the land vehicle.

Hod moved round to the front of the tank, observed the team's efforts and then jumped into the driver's seat, which had been adapted to his wallaby size and shape after the death of the previous driver. Bash already sat on the dashboard like a shiny black-and-yellow ornament.

Shining Teeth and Gleam arrived at the tank's rear door about the same time. Shining Teeth took a long hard look at Gleam wearing the strange new contraption on his head and snorted her careless snort of snotty laughter again.

Gleam watched her cautiously.

Shining Teeth said—*After you... I insist...*

Gleam snarled, just a little bit, more of a turn of the lip, and climbed up the ramp without giving in to the strong urge to bite her head off.

Shining Teeth swept her large body up into the tank and, as far away from Gleam as she could, made herself as comfortable as possible in these trying conditions.

Antenna looked in at them. Both tiger and croc looked uncomfortable, such large beasts squashed into the small passenger space. Given their difficult relationship, Antenna didn't imagine they'd be playing 'I Spy' on the journey—*Okay?* she asked.

—*What's it look like?* said Shining Teeth, staring at her, staring anywhere at all except at the tiger in the tank.

—*Fine,* said Gleam who was also avoiding looking in the direction of the crocodile.

Antenna nodded and said—*Good luck,* into the almost palpable apprehension. She went to join Manifold who had just finished delivering her report about the roadworthiness of the tank to Hod. He sat separate from the passengers in his own protected driver's pod. The plan meant Hod would stay with the vehicle as the nominated getaway driver while the others inspected the lab. When Antenna appeared, the small bombardier beetle said to her—*Sound's still a problem.*

Antenna sighed and rolled her eyes—*Wasn't that fixed?*

—*Can't*, said Manifold—*Wiring's stuffed.*

—*Is there no way we can…?*

—*Not without using the wingship as relay station. And we can't do that…*

—*We don't have a wingship. Right.* Antenna turned to Spark who was hovering nearby—*And you're certain about Crawf?*

—*Crawf 'ain't going nowhere.*

—*We're on limited AV as it is,* said Bash—*We've only got the one camera for me.*

Antenna nodded—*We'll need footage of whatever creatures you see. Remember to get shots of labels on the cages and any other paperwork you find. If there are any charts, descriptions of the experiments, anything at all to go on, get some vision, right?*

—*I'll try,* said Bash.

—*Be careful,* said Antenna.

Hod grinned—*Aren't we always?*

Knowing the answer, for him at least, was a clear and resounding 'no', Antenna shook her head at him—*You could at least pretend to be reassuring.* She raised her front paw in farewell and backed off to stand by Manifold and the team of disparate mechanic beetles.

Doors slammed shut, were cross-checked and made fast. Hod gunned the engine and the tank roared out of the Ektek cavern in a cloud of burning recycled chip oil redirected from the zoo's kiosk. Antenna couldn't help coughing at the pungent smell of old chips and dim sims. As she wiped tears from her eyes, Torque flew up to her—*Antenna? Can we speak?*

Gasping for air, she managed—*You might,* and she continued to cough.

Taking that as permission, Torque pursed his little darkling lips—*It's all these beetles. We've got a crisis. Some of them have been waiting for weeks now. Is there any way we can forward them to other zoos to deal with?*

Antenna gathered enough air to speak—*I can ask but I suspect that everyone's got the same sort of pressures as us. Like, for instance, we're just not going to be able to get to those gorillas. It's not possible to save them. We've got to be real about this. We have a limited crew. We need a way to hear the numbers and decide, rapidly, if the job's too far or too difficult. Could you do that? Sort them, I mean? Make the decisions? What's that called? Triage, isn't it?*

—*I'll give it a go. What do you think if Manifold finds work for some of the ones that're waiting?*

—*Torque. Ask Manifold. It's up to her. If she can use them…*

—*Any of them?* interrupted Torque, thinking of Eid, but not wanting to mention him by name or by species. Seemed reasonable to expect that what went for the collies would apply to the numbats. Why not?

—*Do with them what you will for I have no answers. It's all too much for me. What can I do?*

—*A lot.*

—*It's never enough, though, is it.* Antenna turned and left.

Torque looked around the hangar and found Manifold—*Oi!* He shouted—*We're on!*

Manifold looked up from the airship's engine block where she was about to start work and stared at him—*Please remember, I can't deal with a bunch of beginners, Torque.*

—*Leave them to me. It'd be more than my job's worth to let you down…*

V

Crawf curved even further into his sad question mark shape when Antenna arrived at the aviaries. It was getting dark and cold and Antenna had to work hard to discern his silhouette in the shadows—*Crawf? They've gone. Without you.*

Crawf said nothing and Antenna sighed. She wasn't going to give up just yet—*Crawf, I'm sorry about Sunday.* Crawf remained silent.

After an impatient wait on Antenna's part she continued, with a voice much sharper than usual—*I don't believe you.*

Crawf looked up in the dimness and sought her out—*What?*

—*Spark told me you quit.*

—*What's not to believe about that? I do. I quit. End of story.*

—*Oh, I believe that. It's the rest I don't believe.*

—*Antenna? What are you talking about?*

—*I don't believe you're the last of your kind.*

—*Why not? My partner's dead and we didn't have any eggs. Why wouldn't I be the last in the world?*

—*You might be the only one in this zoo but not the world, Crawf. The whole world's a big, big place and you, my friend, are an attractive parrot.*

—*Not a parrot.*

This was more like the old Crawf. Antenna felt quite pleased she'd managed to rouse him—*When did you last see your siblings?*

—*How can that help?*

—*Don't know. Just tell me.*

—*When I was taken from the nest to come here I saw Budge. Budge was my brother. I saw them squash him into a tube.*

—*You what?* said Antenna.

—*He got taped into a tube and a man put him under his shirt and went away. That was the last I saw of Budge.*

—*You saw that?*

—*You calling me a liar?*

—*No, no, not at all, I'm just thinking there'll be records where you came from and if they're involved in smuggling... We should be able to find them. Come on, let's get out of here. We've got work to do.*

—*You think you can find Budge?*

—*We can only try. That's all Ektek can ever do, isn't it?*

Chapter Forty-nine

I

The crocodile made no secret of her scrabble under the fence. She wasn't careful and she wasn't quiet. She made it through her shallow tunnel and rose to her reptile feet on the other side when a large dog arrived to shout at her. He proceeded to yell and scream. Right in her face.

She'd been expecting him, or someone like him, earlier and so flared one nostril at his appearance—*What kept you?*

He had a dark pointed face, large fluffy ears and enormous teeth. He ranged in colour from darkest black to palest fawn. He was gloriously huge and his luxurious fur coat made him look bigger. He was furious at the discovery of this blatant intrusion. He was on duty and it was his job to kill the invader. He pawed the ground and leaned forward into her as he blasted her with his biggest shout and showed her his awful teeth. He almost lost his reason in this flood of righteous rage and the croc stood and watched, acting just a little bit bored, as he shouted again and again—*Piss off! Get out! You stupid idiot! I have to kill you!*

The croc smiled and the wave in her jaw, fenced with teeth, was formidable even though it could have done with a good scrub.

The dog didn't understand the crocodile. She was such a completely different species from his own, he could not have realised who he was dealing with.

Shining Teeth did not back down.

Lucy, patrolling at the far side of the university building, hated the weight of hunger in her guts. She would not be fed until morning, after her work was done. She was sick of the metres and metres of chain-link fence. All she had done since starting work, years ago as an adolescent, was to march up and down this same fence line every night and she was cold and she was over it. But then she heard Mack barking like the devil itself was trying to break in to the grounds. It was unusual to get intruders this early in the night. Sometimes there were pathetic attempts by drunken humans that never lasted long after the dogs had showed them their teeth. Oh, now, Lucy could hear the dogs in the lab start up. Barking, panic, bellowing, it was infectious. There, the monkeys and the sheep were joining in. Contagious—*What's going on?* The trapped creatures all shouted. Lucy lifted her beautiful head to listen to Mack. A note of urgency in his bark told her she'd better see what was happening and she turned to go. That's when she heard the gentle pads of very big feet treading toward her. She swung around to see the largest creature she'd ever seen looking right at her and on her side of the fence, too. Lucy stared into eyes coloured with darkest caramel flames and she growled with exceeding menace—*What the hell do you think you're doing here?*

II

In the Ektek control room, Antenna and Crawf concentrated on separate monitors. Five out of the six available screens were on; two for the lab action and two for their Palm cockatoo research. The other active monitor still showed the panda newsflash. Antenna had not yet decided how she felt about pandas. They were a distant problem, however. Right now, Antenna had more immediate concerns.

Both Antenna and Crawf controlled different types of keypads. The evolution of Ektek meant that all sorts of creatures with diverse skills and attributes had worked in front of these monitors. Antenna worked with a touch-sensitive flat input mat on which she could type or draw with a light touch of her paw, or even her nose, come to that. Crawf operated the track ball and click system, still warm from Bash's warfare, using beak, feet and his chewed-up stick.

Antenna had prepared one screen to receive footage from the ex-perimental lab. She'd already set up a story based on Gleam's research. They'd investigated animal experiments after they'd had contact with a chimpanzee that, in the course of her working life had been observed after being infected with HIV AIDS and Hepatitis B plus she had served her country in an orbiting space lab. It had come as a surprise to all of them that the local university hospital still used live animals and that the various research studies were paid for by such a wide range of industry. Education had a price and for some animals it was about as high as a price could get.

The Ektek page was open and read: 'Who will save the animals?' If a viewer were to click on the question, the answer, 'They will' would take its place on the screen. An updated link encouraged visitors to check out the vivisection page for refreshed information.

On another monitor, Crawf checked to see if any Palm cockatoos were listed in the official international studbook registry. As soon as the studbook page downloaded he gasped with surprise—*Hullo?*

—*What?* said Antenna, coming up to look over his shoulder.

—*There is a Palm cockatoo studbook...*

—*Still operating?*

—*What about that?*

—*So, I was right? You're not the only one?*

—*You can say 'I told you so' if you like.*

—*That's okay. Even if I did tell you so.*

The two creatures grinned at each other and then turned to look at the pages of birds: names and numbers from all over the world. Crawf took in a huge breath of air in relief—*I'm not the only one. I truly am not. Wow. It's hard to believe.*

The pink colour was already darker in his face patches. His crest rose and flounced back, an improvement on the Emo dripping look he'd been sporting earlier. Antenna watched him recover. She leaned over and gently snuffed into his feathers—*Better now?*

—*Hullo? Antenna? Thank you. I can't...*

—*Well, don't. Just see if you can work out where Budge might be.*

—*Oh, I will. Don't you worry about that. Hel-lo, Budgie boy. Come out, come out, wherever you are...* Crawf set to reading the list in more detail. He muttered to himself—*I've got family. How about that? That's something, isn't it?*

—*That most certainly is...* Antenna spoke faintly. Her concentration was taken up with the search through pet shops and online bird fanciers. Out of the corner of her eye she noticed that Bash had switched on his camera. She looked up to see the feed from the university was now alive on the other monitor—*We're on,* she said as she adjusted the colours and prepared to send the footage to the web page. She watched as a large dog glared, focusing just below the camera's lens—*Hmmm, guard dog...* From the angle of its head she realised it must be looking directly at Gleam. The dog was obviously surprised by Gleam's appearance and, of course, was *en garde*; ready to strike at any moment. Antenna wasn't worried. She knew Gleam could put on the charm and make the dog understand their reasons for breaking into the university grounds. She was incredibly frustrated that she couldn't hear anything—*What are they doing?*

III

—We come in peace, friend, said Gleam*—We mean you no harm.* He spoke rapidly with an obvious and clear intention to calm the dog*—Let us find your colleague. He's in danger. You must not underestimate how important this is. Please, lead on. Immediately. Unfortunately, my associate is capable of great mischief unless we find her, right now.*

Hesitating, Lucy heard Mack's voice strangle into a desperate yelp she had never heard before and wished henceforth to never hear again. Immediately she turned and raced across the compound to where she suspected Mack was at bay. The tiger ran behind her shouting*—Shining Teeth, we're in! Shining Teeth, hold your combat!*

They were too late. Shining Teeth stood over the ripped remains of Mack, once handsome creature, now irrevocably crushed. She lifted her long heavy head from the still warm, furry body and smiled at the tiger. Her crocodile muzzle was decorated with gore.

Lucy rushed to Mack's side and then anchored, barking with all her might, teeth bared at Shining Teeth, barking, barking, as if she were a hound from hell.

Gleam stood, breathing heavily after their desperate run. He growled*—There was no need, Shining Teeth.*

—What's need got to do with it? Shining Teeth looked up at him, ignoring Lucy's fraught shouts*—What would you know, you great hairy marauder? It was kill or be killed. It's the natural order, after all.*

Gleam shook his head*—There is another way.*

Shining Teeth nodded, her head signalling the heaviest sarcasm— *Of course there is, Gleam. You'd know best, Gleam. Whatever you say, Gleam.* Then, as she'd had enough of everyone bewailing a dead creature she had no interest in, she considered it was time to move on*—Let's get away from this shit, shall we?* The croc swung aside from the corpse and strode, as deliberately as her short legs would carry her, toward the main university building*—This way, I believe?*

Bash, tiny frog, rode a jerky trip in the palanquin tied to the top of Gleam's head like a little hat. He could not believe his eyes as they stood beside the dead dog. He was silent as he watched Lucy cry. The camera he held continued to record.

IV

In the control room, Antenna watched the screen as Shining Teeth left the bloody scene. Slowly, from her place in the Ektek control cave, the numbat got to her feet. She was not aware of any conscious decision to move. Antenna could not believe what she was seeing; the bloodied crocodile leaving a mangled dog spread out on the grass. This was no Ektek action. This was disgusting. She let out a small sound of revulsion but could not drag her eyes from the screen.

Crawf urgently searched through a list of numbers. He glanced up when he sensed Antenna's movement but, unseeing, went straight back to his task. As it soaked into his birdbrain that something had changed, that Antenna was standing, staring in shock at the video monitor, he came out of his hopeful reveries of family reunions and, in double take, looked again at Antenna. She was in shock. She continued to stare in horror at the screen.

—*Hullo?* Crawf also stood and came to stand beside her to look at her monitor—*What happened?*

—*Shining Teeth happened,* said Antenna. Both stared at the dead dog with alarm.

—*She's too dangerous,* said Crawf.

Antenna swallowed—*I know.*

—*What are they saying? Why can't we hear?*

—*No sound. If we'd had the wingship…*

—*We could relay it. Of course. I'm sorry, Antenna.*

—*You had your own problems.*

—*Yes, but this…*

Antenna stamped her foot in frustration—*I've never felt so helpless!*

They watched the screen as the living guard dog flung back her head and howled over the body of her mate.

Antenna and Crawf could only imagine what that howl, mute to their ears, must have sounded like.

V

Hod stared at the small screen in front of the tank's driver's seat. He leaned forward. When he finally took in air he realised he must have been holding his breath. It wasn't because he couldn't believe his eyes. He knew Shining Teeth better than the others. He knew she was capable of killing randomly, without need or compassion. He'd been dreading it or something like it. He'd known it would come sooner or later but he'd been hoping for later. Now she'd done it he didn't know what his response should be. He tried to clear his mind and quell his rising panic.

He sat in the tank parked outside the teaching part of the hospital, where the university and the hospital met. Here were research facilities and lecture theatres, tutorial rooms and a car park with a boom gate across the entrance to the car park. He'd not bothered taking the tank inside in case there were video cameras surveying the car park. He waited, hopefully unobserved by university security, just outside the campus grounds.

Bash's footage relayed into the tank's system and from there bounced up to the satellite. It played out on the small screen in the cockpit of the tank and, here also, the sound could not be fixed. Hod could only see those dreadful pictures. He could not hear what Bash heard, he was unable to contact Ektek and they could not contact him.

The others knew where he was, of course, and he was supposed to wait there for them. That was his job: getaway driver. Only, now, Hod was overcome. He started to shake. He felt hot and cold and shivery all over. He'd had his share of confrontations with dogs, but in his case it had been self-defence; they'd been feral, unwilling to negotiate and trying to eat him when he was on the run in unfamiliar country. He felt responsible for Shining Teeth's behaviour; that was it. There was a sort of inevitability about her going amok and killing a guard dog with no reason. Of course she would. Was she trying to draw attention to Ektek? What would she do next? And Hod had to ask himself; what would he do next? Oh, what indeed?

Hod sat in the driver's seat of the tank and reached for the key to turn on the engine. He moved slowly. He let his paw rest on the key. He turned on the engine and let the revs ride up and down. He listened to the sound of the machine. He took off the handbrake and drove around the cul-de-sac past the car park entrance, past the boom gate, past the university, past the hospital. As he entered the main road he picked up speed.

Hod was running away.

Chapter Fifty

I

Lucy could not contain her grief. She was overpowered by her sense of loss. She howled to the black, clouded sky and her eyes were filled with wet.

—*I am sorry,* said Gleam—*I would have prevented her if I could.*

When she could speak again Lucy stared at the tiger, numb. She swayed on her feet as she stared back down again at Mack's remains. When she had recovered she looked at Gleam and said—*Go away, now!*

—*We wish to examine the laboratories.*

—*What laboratories?*

—*You need not deny their existence. We can hear them.*

It was true. The animals locked up in the lab were still calling. Dogs, pigs, even cats could be heard; shouting, calling out, wondering still what Mack had been on about.

—*I can't let you in there.*

—*We just want to see. Nothing more.*

—*Then you'll leave?*

—*Then we'll leave.*

—*What about her?*

—*She'll be with us.*

—*And you will prevent her from...?*

—*Yes.*

—*Arguing is useless?*

—*Yes.*

Lucy turned away from Mack and marched, stiffly, to the entrance of the great mausoleum behind them. When she saw Shining Teeth standing to one side she could not go further. Gleam saw her hesitation and moved to stand between them. The dog rose onto her hind legs and pressed the large button requesting admission. The doors slid open and Shining Teeth slithered inside.

Lucy said—*I will not go in with you. I will not be near… her. I cannot say how long before a human gets here. There are random checks. And they are, random.*

—*Thank you,* said Gleam and he and Bash entered the doorway— *We will be quick.*

Lucy said nothing and moved back in the direction of her fallen comrade.

Gleam, Bash and Shining Teeth now stood in the foyer of a large public building. The tension between them was palpable. Shining Teeth seemed to have no fear but even she was worried what would happen if a human should find them in a place of vivisection. Each creature looked about them with trepidation as they entered. They could easily be entering a trap.

Gleam shook his head and whispered up to the litter on his head—*Bash?*

—*Yes?*

—*Any reason my head's wet?*

—*Won't happen again.*

—*Good.*

They kept walking, nervously checking as they went through a series of swing doors. Did the doors operate the same way when coming back? (They did.) Who would be there, round the next corner, waiting for them? What would they do to them? It was not a question of IF they would die. They knew that. It was more a question of HOW they would die.

The floor was a pale lino that might have been green once but had been bleached over the years into a grey white. They breathed a smell of chemicals; perhaps bleach and other, stronger, synthesised cleaners. After they had passed, the path from the swinging door to the sterile facility was streaked by a long, red, bloody wave, swirled into being by a dragging crocodile tail.

Outside, Lucy stayed for a moment by her dead partner. After a time she realised she could do no good for Mack sitting still beside him. She reached over and kissed his nose, her tongue lingering over the salty blood tang. She would miss him. They had grown up together. Had children together. She lay down beside him, head to head. He was still warm. She whispered—*She will pay, Machiavelli. She will pay dearly.*

She returned to the shadows by the university main entrance. She picked her position strategically and sat down outside the door of the facility where she had last seen the aggressor. She lay down and put her head between her front paws. She would wait for them. Revenge was necessary. She would see what damage a dog could do to a crocodile when surprised.

II

Bash's camera footage beamed brightly into the computer screen. The change in lighting surprised Antenna and Crawf. From grim, dark and shadowy outside, the live interior footage became luminous. The fluro lights of the university corridors painted a too-white picture in a square, distant perspective with white walls, white ceiling and pale, almost white floor. Antenna and Crawf could see Shining Teeth on the ground, slightly ahead, still leaving bloody streaks in her wake. Occasionally Gleam's paw or ear or nose came into frame as they strode through the barren corridors, Bash recording from his chair in the palanquin tied to the tiger's head.

Antenna snapped to attention and began working. She loaded the video stream into the live web broadcast. She pushed 'send' on the waiting email addressed to media, activist groups and politicians. The video captured the march of the long hallway as it went on and on.

The camera pushed through the swinging doors until it came to a corridor lined with windows. Each window looked into a small room containing lines of cages. Each was lit brightly, each was vibrantly clean and each cage was clearly labelled with a long twisted word; perhaps the name of a drug or chemical of some sort. Each had a series of numbers on it.

Antenna took a screen shot of each of the cages with clear labels. On the other screen she enlarged the label enough to read the chemical name and then copied those to a folder for further research. She shook her head. There were so many cages.

Bash's camera revealed the contents of each cage; mice, rats, birds, guinea pigs…

—*Guinea pigs*, Antenna spoke without thinking.

—*Hullo?*

—*Every living thing in this lab is a guinea pig.*

—*Sorry?*

—*You know guinea pigs? Furry round beings? Used in cooking and for experiments? But they don't stop there, do they. Is there a species they don't use?*

Room after room was filled with cages. Corridors led to further rooms. Different animal faces either turned to the camera or turned away.

—There's more animals in there than in this zoo. Crawf had had enough. He was overwhelmed by the enormity of it. He went back to his own monitor and became engrossed in his studbook research.

Antenna watched him for a moment and then turned back to the screen in front of her. Bash's camera was collecting faces. Some appeared drugged, who knew with what or why. The creatures behaved erratically, some jerkily running from one side of their cage to the other and some lying still, spreadeagled. Some seemed in such pain they seemed insensible, almost blinded by weary anguish. Some literally could not see their visitors for their eyes were closed by infection or bandages. Some could not hear them because they were not conscious. Most could not smell them because they were behind glass. Antenna shook her head and said, even though she knew Bash could not hear her—*That's enough. Get out of there. I can't watch this any more.*

Antenna turned back to the list of pet shops on the other monitor next to her. She had to concentrate on something else. Just watching the long litany of experiments was turning her blood cold. She turned to look at Crawf, busily pecking letters with his beak and chewed stick, and said—*Okay, Crawf. Let's get you a family.*

III

The barking and shouting died down as the strange trio approached and they were watched, smelled and heard by a multitude of eyes, noses and ears. It was unbearable being the focus of attention like this and Bash said—*Can we do nothing?*

—*We are doing something,* said Gleam—*We're informing.*

After more of this white, clean, gruesome tour and his careful filming, Bash spoke again—*We must help them.*

— *We cannot interfere,* said Gleam—*Our priority is to get out safely so we can explain to the world what we have seen.*

—*I've seen enough,* said Shining Teeth—*We should leave, now.*

—*It seems so wrong,* said Bash.

—*You know these creatures may well be assisting scientists to save hundreds of lives,* said Gleam.

—*Not animal lives.*

—*We don't know, do we. It might be so. We'll find out when we get back to Ektek and research our findings. We must not jump to conclusions. Veterinary science has saved many of our friends. Perhaps even those who suffer here…*

A strange, bold voice cried out to them—*Oi! You! Over here!*

—*What?* said Gleam, looking to see where the voice had come from.

—Get over here, come on, I'm not going to eat you.

—As if, sneered Shining Teeth. The Ektek team looked at each other and then approached the voice. Shining Teeth, Gleam and Bash's camera peered into a cage sitting on the ground containing a straggly shaved creature with wires inserted into its skin. Although it seemed to have aspects of a common cat about the face, it was being uncommonly treated. It seemed to have a large hook projecting from its spine—*About time! I thought you were ruddy deaf.*

—Hullo, friend, said Gleam.

—Just tourists? Or is this a hands-on eco-adventure?

—Tourists, I'm afraid, trying to find out what happens in here.

—And we've seen enough, said Shining Teeth. She looked around vigilantly. She was in no hurry to meet pro-active scientists on their turf.

The shaved animal spoke urgently—*You'd be doing me a big favour if you could just unlock that little latch there and unhook, see that wire there? That'd help me out of here. I've got a feeling you might just be saving my life.*

—We've been here too long, said Shining Teeth—*We need to get going.*

—Know how you feel, darlin', said the shaven stranger.

—We want to save everyone, of course, said Gleam—*But this is just a reconnaissance mission. We're running out of time.*

—Reconnaissance is useless, replied the shaved one—*You could save me right now. Be doing us all a great service.*

—What if your service is to others? What if the tests they are running on you help many to avoid suffering?

—Listen, mate, do you honestly believe that even if I was saving thousands of lives I'd choose to do this? Nah. I wouldn't. I'd choose to be lying in the sun with a fat belly and some gorgeous minx giving me the come on. Know what I mean? Why me with the wires? Why not you? Do you really think you'd give a rat's arse about the others? What about a rat, come to that? Here, why don't we swap and you could find out?

—I'm sorry, we just can't, said Bash.

—We've got to go, said Shining Teeth—*Come on!*

Gleam looked at her and nodded. He turned back to the caged creature—*I'm sorry, please don't take this the wrong way but you do seem to be... a cat?*

—What's that got to do with the price of fish?

—It's just that we're Ektek...

—Ooooooooooh, get you! Ektek is it? Marvellous. Hey, did you hear that? The cat-like creature shouted to the world in general, all those ears that could hear nearby—*Youse guys? Did you hear? These here tourists ogling at us? They're 'Ektek'! Isn't that something?*

A general yowling and bawling of hilarity ensued and Bash said to Gleam—*Why does everyone have to be so sarcastic?*

—*Gleam*, said Shining Teeth—*Humans.*

—*What? Where?*

—*Here. Any minute. We need to move. Now.*

—*Now, do tell,* said the shaved creature—*What's an Ektek when it's at home?*

—*Ektek helps endangered animals.*

—*Well, you've come to the right place. We're all endangered. No one lasts long here. You can bet your sweet crocodile handbag on that, darlin'.*

—*Come on*, said Shining Teeth—*We can't help a cat.*

—*Why not?*

—*It's called assisting the enemy*, said Bash.

—*Enemy? I'm not the enemy here, son. I'm not a cat. Really. What a suggestion. Look at me. Don't I look like him? What's your name?*

—*Gleam.*

—*Look at cha. You'd be the biggest moggy I've clapped eyes on this week, wouldn't cha? You telling me you're not a cat?*

—*I'm a tiger, friend.*

—*Tiger, tiger, burning bright, still a cat, 'ain't 'cha. 'O'right, if you're a tiger, then I'm a quokka. I am. Can't you tell a quokka when you're looking at one? Us poor quokkas are so endangered, if I go we'll all be extinct so you'd better save us.*

Bash filmed the sign outside the quokka's cage and muttered to Gleam—*Nothing, no name or species on his sign. Just numbers.*

—*We've got to go*, said Shining Teeth. She moved restlessly across the floor. She was becoming impatient and Gleam was aware that an impatient Shining Teeth was not a generous soul.

The poor shaved creature, literally hooked up and wired into his cage said—*Call me Quokka. All me friends do. Don' cha?* He shouted again—*You all call me Quokka, right?* The other creatures cried out over each other in reply, things like: save me, forget the quokka, of course he's a cat, are you blind, listen to me, I'm the one, help me, save me…

—*Ah, don't listen to them. It's true, I'm a quokka. They all want to be saved too, you got to understand that, can't you? Come on, undo the latch, it's easy and then we can scarper…*

—*Enough*, said Shining Teeth—*I'm out.*

Gleam called after her—*Shining Teeth! Wait!*

She didn't wait. She kept on going—*Wait!* called Gleam again and then sighed and said in a normal voice—*We're right behind you.* Shining

Teeth slammed through the first of the doors but, as Gleam turned to go, Bash tapped him on the head.

—*What?* said Gleam, already walking down the hall.

—*This is a nightmare,* Bash sighed and then banged his head on the side of his little carriage—*How can they live like this? Please, Gleam, let's take him, let's just save one, we can, we've got room...*

—*Bash, you must quell your sentimentality. This is a mere fact-finding expedition. We can't rescue anybody. We've got to make plans, be strategic, and we have to get out after Shining Teeth, you know what she's like, I don't want to leave her alone...*

—*He's not very big...* said Bash.

—*Does it have to be the cat?*

—*But what if he's telling the truth? What if he is a quokka?*

—*I am a quokka,* he shouted from his cage—*There's no doubt at all.*

—*We can't stand around here arguing while Shining Teeth...*

—*No. Right. Let's just get him out.*

—*Yeah, come on,* said the quokka—*Get him out.*

The volume rose, the creatures that were able to call out, shouted: save me, save me first, no, not him, save me... The desperation was sticky, the noise was guilt-inducing and the pressure to do something, anything to relieve some of this suffering became unbearable.

Gleam sighed—*Okay. Let's go.*

Bash was elated and babbled instructions as Gleam reached out his paw to open the cage—*You could just unlatch the door and he could jump on your back and we could carry him...*

IV

In the cool blue of the control room, Antenna focussed on the website now displayed on Crawf's screen. He'd found a chain of pet shops that took orders for any bird the customer might like—*Any bird at all? You sure?*

—*Read for yourself. There. That's what it says. "We have connections with a wide range of bird breeders and are able to find whatever bird takes your fancy. Name your feathered fantasy!" Huh.*

As well as filling orders on demand, the chain had a number of popular shops where you could get puppies and kittens and guinea pigs and all manner of fluffy little living things, wherever they came from, and there was an address for a warehouse - Pet Met - a building down near the wharf.

—*Okay, you're right,* said Antenna—*May be worth a look. Let's get them under surveillance.*

—*I'll go*, said Crawf—*I could get the wingship ready in half an hour.*

—*You can't go by yourself.*

—*Hullo? Antenna? Please? I've got to do something. I need to move. I can't sit here and wait to die for one more minute. I need to find my tribe.*

Antenna stared at him for a moment and then said—*Okay. Try this. Email the shop and ask if they've got any palmys.*

—*What if they say no?*

Antenna thought again and said—*What if they say 'yes'? We'll think of something.*

Crawf began typing, using his much-chewed stick to press the letters on the keypad. He looked around surreptitiously to make sure Antenna wasn't reading over his shoulder—*I'm just asking if they've got any Palm cockatoos and how much they'd be, okay?*

If Antenna had been looking over his shoulder she might have seen that what he was typing did not exactly square with what he was saying. Crawf made no outward sign of his subterfuge. Outwardly he was calm. He had made up his mind. He was in complete control of his future. Instead she said—*Maybe ask how long they expect you'd have to wait?*

Even as she spoke, the other monitor feeding Bash's footage in to the control cave caught her attention. She watched the screen to see Gleam flick his huge claw under a latch on a cage containing a...

—*Isn't that a cat?* She asked and Crawf, quickly pushing 'send' with his chewed-up stick and glad to have an excuse to change the subject, came to look over her shoulder. He said—*Hard to tell with no fur but...*

—*Why would they help a cat?*

The numbat and the cockatoo watched as the shaved creature had a quick sip of water from its bubbler bottle and then stretched out to reach the doorway. The wires in his spine pulled at him. He swayed and his eyes went out of focus. Carefully, with his huge yellow claws, Gleam detached the wire from the hook in the quokka-creature's back. The vertebrae were visible.

—*Antenna?* said Crawf—*Why would scientists need to put a hook through a spine?*

—*See how much it weighs? See what happens when you put a hook through a spine? I don't know. Poor bastard.*

—*Antenna?* Crawf had returned to focus back on his own screen—*They've replied already.*

—*That was quick.*

—*They want to talk about it. Face to face.*

—*That's not going to work, is it?*

—I'm going.
—Crawf, you can't…
—I can. And I will.
Crawf stood. He walked out of the control centre.
Antenna watched him go, speechless.

V

—Stay with us, now, Bash called out*—Or we can't help you.*
The shaved creature shook itself and arduously clambered onto Gleam's back. It wobbled along the sharp edge of Gleam's spine and then lay down inelegantly, draped over the peak of the tiger's back like shaved fleshy saddlebags. Wires and tubes dripped from it like council street decorations.

The trio would have made an odd sight if anyone had seen them as they proceeded through the hallways of the large university building. They were expecting human intervention at every turn, every footfall, every passing window. Watching intently for signs of doors opening, listening for any squeaking chairs or tapping of keyboards, the tiger marched through the corridors of higher learning as rapidly as possible without dropping the shaved thing. As soon as they were out of the main building and into the entranceway, Gleam looked in every direction for Shining Teeth. He did not see her so he called softly into the night*—Shining Teeth.* When she did arrive out of the darkness she stayed back in the shadows and drawled*—You took your time.*

Gleam growled*—Where's the dog?*

Shining Teeth still did not come forward*—Probably staying out of our way, if it's got any sense.*

Gleam waited but Shining Teeth said no more*—Wanted to thank her for trusting us.*

—Oh, don't worry about her. She said not to hang around here any longer than was absolutely necessary so we'd better get going. Hod will be wondering what's happened to us.

Gleam considered what Shining Teeth was not saying before he agreed with what she did utter*—Of course.*

—Let's get out of here, Shining Teeth turned to lead the way to the nearest exit*—Come on.*

—Wait. Gleam was sure the dog Lucy would have stayed to see them off the premises. She'd have wanted to know they were gone, doing her duty, wouldn't she?*—No. No, Shining Teeth. Where is she?*

—What do you mean?

—You know exactly what I mean.

338

—*Sure I do. She's tucked up in bed holding her breath until she can relax knowing we're out of here.*

—*Holding her breath?* Gleam watched the croc—*Would that have had anything to do with you?*

Shining Teeth may have smiled but no one could see her in the dark. She said—*Come on, we're wasting time.*

—*You've killed her.*

—*I haven't, you know.*

—*We could have negotiated with them. They didn't need to die.*

Shining Teeth swirled round and came into the light from the doorway. They could all see the fresh blood around her snout. She hissed vengeance at the tiger—*You are so naïve. They'd seen us. They could identify us. Of course they had to be silenced.*

—*Who were they going to tell? Humans don't listen to dogs.*

—*You are putting us in danger every second you stand here mouthing your petty little philosophical theories. I'm leaving even if you want to stay and get experimented on.*

—*Bloodshed makes you as bad as them.*

—*For agony's sake. We're all part of the same life force, right? It's called a force because it's forceful. It always ends in death; one hundred per cent of the time. Survival is the only way forward and all your namby-pamby compassion for others won't change a damn thing for anyone.*

—*Force of nature and survival of the fittest is one strand in the multiple entirety of life. Obviously any living being will fight against their own death. All living creatures will choose a gentle evolution if they can.*

—*Shut up, you boring old fart*, said the crocodile, dangerously impatient again—*It's time to go!*

—*Or what? You'll kill me?*

—*Might.*

—*I feel sorry for you, Shining Teeth. You must live the loneliest of lives. Always seeking death. One day it will come for you and you cannot win.*

—*You're a fool, Gleam. An agonised fool. I'm going to laugh when you die. Just laugh.*

—*Can you take me back to the lab, please?* said the quokka-creature—*I don't think I much like this freedom of yours.*

—*Show me the dog*, said Gleam, standing his ground, determined to find out what the crocodile had done.

—*Feeling a bit peckish, are we?*

—*What have you done with the dog?*

—*Oh, talk about stubborn. You're never going to give up, are you? Over there, if you must know.*

Gleam lifted his head and smelled in that direction. His ears flickered. He was suddenly alert to a sound. He flashed a glance back to the crocodile and then he ran. Bash was bumped and crashed in his palanquin and the quokka-creature shouted out in alarm as it tried to cling to Gleam's bony back.

Soon they could all hear it; a dreadful gargle of pain. Lucy was still alive. When Lucy had ambushed her, Shining Teeth had retaliated. It had been a dreadful fight and she had left the dog for dead. Intestines spread out over the grass in a bloody lace curtain. Lucy whimpered and cried. She could not help it. Her throat was severely lacerated and one of her back legs was broken, bent out behind her at a ghastly angle.

Gleam rushed to her side, Bash bumping along awkwardly in his little hut on the tiger's head. The shaved creature slid that way and this but managed to hold on. All three animals stared at the partially dismembered dog. It was difficult to assess if a vet could be brought in time and how one could possibly be alerted. Gleam bent down and looked into her wet face—*Can you talk? What's your name?*

She stopped squealing enough to breath—*Lucretia.* Every breath hurt. Every beat of her pulse splintered her mind. She whimpered again—*Please, help me.*

—*You've got to do something,* said Bash.

—*I can't,* said Gleam.

—*You have to,* said Bash.

Gleam crept as close as he could to her ear—*You got kids?*

—*Yes,* she whispered and panted for air.

—*Where are they?* Gleam cared for her. He bent his great face to hers.

—*Don't know,* she gasped—*The youngest... Training... Now...*

Gleam almost smiled—*Going to be a guard, like Mum?*

—*Please...* gasped the dog.

—*You could do something,* said Bash.

—*But she might live, for her kids...* said Gleam.

—*Give her some dignity!* cried the shaved creature—*Quickly!*

—*Please...* said Bash.

—*Please...* whispered the dog.

Gleam closed his eyes and tried to think. All he could hear was the air sucking in and out of the dog's shredded lungs. Gleam heard 'life' on the in breath and 'death' as the air whistled out. Life and death; death or life, why was it up to him to choose?

Chapter Fifty-one

I

The electronic information beamed from Bash's little carriage up to the tank and then to the satellite. It powered back down to Ektek's centre onto the video display. Antenna and Crawf watched the screen; watched the dying dog in wretched pain; watched the creature twitching and shuddering; watched her bleeding uncontrollably.

Sometimes the camera caught glimpses of Gleam's ear or paw but mainly Bash kept the camera on the dog; her restless pain, her beautiful face contorted.

They watched as Gleam took her up with his long-clawed paws and his powerful forearms. He held her in an embrace, the camera moving in closer to her broken face. He held her tight and her head lolled back and he nuzzled in even closer to her, closer to her neck and he opened his great mouth in a lover's overwhelming.

The camera's image blurred into a great lashing movement… the image swung, flashed, away and around like a whip…

Then it refocussed.

They watched as Gleam held Lucy in his fatal embrace. It was as if he could not let her go.

II

This was the second time Hod had gone AWOL. He'd disobeyed direct orders, left his team; and yet, in his beating heart, his flawed vacillating heart, the only home, the only family, the only friends he'd ever known, were Ektek. They forgave him when he returned from his previous childish escapade and they'd allowed him to bring a crocodile into their midst, a crocodile apparently bent on destroying Ektek for some perceived fault in the past; she'd tricked him.

Of course this was all about keeping Ektek's enemy where they could see her. Only this particular enemy was completely unpredictable. Now the worst had happened and she had killed horribly for no reason at all. Hod was driving aimlessly through the city in the middle of the night because he couldn't handle the thought of her unnecessary cruelty. He was shocked and dismayed and running out of steam.

He brought the tank to a halt and parked on the side of a busy road. He leaned his head onto the steering wheel. He knew there was no wilderness for him to run to. He understood it was time for him to grow up. He had to take part in this debacle. He had to attempt to be part of the solution. If things were going to change and Ektek was going to survive, he wanted to be part of the winning team. He reasoned all this to himself and understood that he had no choice.

He turned the video screen back on and what he saw there, Gleam cradling the lifeless dog (no, was this even a different dog?) and a grinning bloody crocodile, made him take in a deep, stern breath. Then he sat up and turned on the engine. He gunned the machine, making it roar like a tiger and spun the tank across eight lanes of highway, which luckily, given the early hours of the morning, was not busy, and then he roared back the way he came. He had to get back to his post before they saw he'd gone. Maybe, he thought, just maybe he'd even get a chance to run over that flaming croc.

III

Bash, who had been clinging to the edge of the palanquin on Gleam's head, whispered—*Gleam. Come on, Gleam. We have to go. We've got to leave her.*

Shining Teeth, standing a distance away, was also restless, but with agitated glee, shifting with an edgy dance from claw to reptilian claw. She cackled and cackled again.

Her cackling ricocheted high between the tall concrete buildings of the research facility and Gleam felt violated by her reality. He very gently released the destroyed dog and Lucy slid back to the ground like the contents of a cracked egg. Then he rose to stand, majestic. He could not muster himself to confront the crocodile as he would have liked. He tried. He tried to lift his heavy head and he tried to snarl at her but he could not. He was bowed; he couldn't help the tears overflowing down his magnificent face. He stood, watching Shining Teeth twitching in her malevolent little dance and his wet tears streamed from his dull flame eyes.

—*I always knew you had it in you,* sniggered Shining Teeth—*Once a killer, always a killer.*

Gleam moved away from her. He muttered—*Bash, I'll drop you in with Hod? And this, quokka, or whatever you call it?*

—*Oi,* said the shaved creature—*I'm a quokka, I tell you!*

Gleam ignored him. He shook his head and continued to murmur to Bash—*I can't travel in the tank. I'll find my own way back.*

—*Hey! Fuzz Face! Psycho Killer!* Shining Teeth had followed them and, still snickering like some drug-crazed human, said—*I'll see ya back at the zoo whenever! I need some down time - away from you stupid Ektek freaks!* She let out a guffaw and she slid away down a drain in the gutter with a cheerful flick of her reptile tail.

Her disappearance seemed to release something in the tiger and he stumbled and slowed to a halt and said with his great shaking head—*I can't go on.* As he spoke his head movement extended further into a kind of sway—*I'm no good. I'm a liability.* He was swaying his head from side to side as if he were trying to shake some sense into himself. He droned on and his voice became deeper and deeper as he seemed to reach down further and further inside himself—*You have to leave me. I'm no good to myself. I'm no good for Ektek. I can't do anything any more.* He sank to the ground and the others couldn't have been more horrified when he started, gut wrenchingly, to sob.

The shaved creature slid from the tiger's back and stood watching the emotion roll from the great beast. He let out a blast of air in a silent whistle and turned to Bash. He said—*Now what?*

Bash, still sitting in the palanquin on Gleam's head, even now shaking with the distress of the tiger, put down his camera at last—*I'll go get Hod. You wait here.*

—*No, don't...* said the shaved one but Bash had hopped out of his little carriage, jumped down the side of the tiger, and leapt out of sight in the night gloom before the so-called quokka could even think what to say. That he didn't want to be left with a sobbing tiger? That he couldn't walk anyway? That he didn't know what was going on and he didn't like it? That he wanted out? What was a Hod anyway? He glared at the crying tiger. What sort of feline behaviour was that?

The strange shaved being, still with wires and tubes hanging out of it, crawled and dragged itself over to the tiger and leapt at him. He shouted—*Get up! Get up, you great pathetic thing!* He lifted his scrawny shaved arm and struck Gleam on the nose. He unsheathed his claws and scratched him until tiger blood popped out of the sliced skin like tiny red balloons—*What the hell are you complaining about? You're still alive! You did the right thing by her. You don't give up because you did the right thing! Don't let that croc beat you without even touching you! Get some spine! And would you look at me? I'm the one with the spine problems here.* The shaved creature jumped on Gleam's head and bit his ear, hard, before whispering—

Don't give up the fight! You've got enough power for all of us here. We need you. Please, Gleam or Beam or whoever you are. Don't give up. Not like this. Get up.

Then the shaved creature, who was not at all well himself, slid down from Gleam's leg and, exhausted, lay down on the ground next to the tiger and sighed feeling weak and dreadful. After a while he realised the tiger had stopped sobbing and what's more, when he looked up, the tiger was staring right at him.

—*Wha'choo lookin' at?* said the shaved creature.

—*A cat,* said Gleam.

—*No cat here, tiger.*

—*What's your name?*

—*Told you. Quokka.*

—*Your real name.*

—*Bluey.*

—*Bluey, the cat.*

—*That's Bluey the quokka, to you, cobber!*

—*Bluey,* said Gleam—*I owe you for waking me up here.*

—*Ah, forget it.*

—*I know I've been weak. I know that. But I also know you to be a cat and I know we're taking you into a place where there are hundreds of creatures that you will want to eat. You've seen that crocodile. You know what uncontrolled instincts are like. I know you do, I recognise you. The difference between us is that I made a promise not to kill and now I've broken it.*

—*You can remake it.*

—*Doesn't make it any better.*

—*That's just it, isn't it. You can make a decision to start again. Right now. Accept you've made mistakes and then agree you'll not make them again.*

—*Here's the deal, Bluey. I know you're a cat and I can see you want a chance to survive.*

—*Of course I do.*

—*Right. And you'll get that chance. But it's only one chance, Bluey. One chance. If I find you've been eating small, endangered creatures in our zoo, then all bets are off. All my promises might just get broken again. I'll tell Ektek you're a cat and you'll have to take the consequences. All I ask is that you curb your most basic animal instincts and find something to eat that isn't potentially one of the last of its kind on the planet. Do we have a deal?*

Bluey looked at the tiger, still wet around his eyes and sighing in that jagged exhausted way with spent tears. He narrowed his eyes and calculated how likely the tiger was to carry through the threat—*What's the big deal about endangered animals anyway?*

—*Do you want to come with us or not?*

—*No, tell me. Who cares what lives or dies? What does it matter?*

—*Maybe it doesn't. Maybe a planet populated by human beings and their pets and their farmed animals is enough life.* They looked at each other for a feline moment before Gleam added—*Doesn't seem fair to me, though.*

Engine noise roared and suddenly the tank smashed through the fence. Gleam lifted his head and rolled his eyes—*Hod always takes it just that little bit too far.* He stood and looked at Bluey—*Okay? Shall we go?*

—*That's our ride? Okay. I'll take your chance.* Bluey stood and hauled himself toward the tank where Hod had activated the rear ramp so that the injured animals could easily enter the passenger compartment.

From the direction of the car park where he'd been waiting, Bash came leaping around the corner and jumped through the driver's door and then up to the console. He shouted at Hod—*Where have you been? I went to the stop and you weren't there.*

—*I'm here now,* said Hod.

—*You telling me you left us in the lurch again?*

—*I came back, didn't I?*

Bash understood that Hod had no more to say on the subject but Bash hadn't finished yet. This was very useful information. Bash filed it into his mental filing cabinet under Things To Remember Just in Case.

As he walked toward the tank, Gleam turned back and looked at Lucy's remains one more time. He bowed his head and moved toward the tank. His head hung heavy as he stepped forward, the fur around his feet painting a trail of blood.

Chapter Fifty-two

I

Manifold and her team of beetles leaned heavily on a slender metal bar—*Heave,* shouted Manifold and the team heaved. The bar was part of a cutting implement that was currently biting into a metal ring around a scaly leg. The ring featured Bedlam Zoo's logo and a series of numbers and letters. It was Crawf's identity band and he wanted it off.

The beetles pressed down, levering their combined energy along the length of the handle to the sharp edge. Antenna's paw was keeping the pliers in place and the jaw of cutting teeth edged through the thin band of red-and-silver metal. Finally, the plier jaws clenched together, the handles turned over and, as the beetles jumped to safety, they all cheered with relief. The band was severed. Crawf was free.

Crawf used the claws on his other foot to stretch and widen the gap in the band. Together, he and Antenna, with the beetles, managed to manoeuvre the ring away from his leg. It clattered to the ground by the workstation in the hangar. He was now officially a wild bird. He was not aware of any other markings on his body, although some animals had brands or tattoos with their owner's mark or number, it did not appear that Crawf had suffered the sting of inked needles in his lifetime. He could not remember any and not one little mite on his body could see anything.

Crawf jumped up and did a little dance. The beetles scattered away from his capers, laughing. They dodged his mad ballet and watched him kicking out his legs in front of him to admire their bare beauty—*You have no idea how good this feels!*

—*I hope you know what you're doing,* said Antenna.

—*Never been more certain of anything my entire life.*

The beetles picked up the pliers and dragged them back to their spot in the tool rack. Manifold followed Crawf and Antenna as they commenced the wingship's pre-flight check.

Although Crawf had to bend as he examined the vehicle's sub-structure, his feather headdress was up and perky. He moved with purpose and strength, checking gauges, tyres and fuel. Every now and then he would look down at his newly bare leg and the sight of it would give him a shiver of joy. He was determined to get going as soon as it grew lighter and he could see to fly. The colour was back to deep pink in his face patches and he marched tall, with excited energy in his clawed step, that is, until he had to bend under the wing of the plane to check the struts.

Antenna followed him with much less fervour and considerably more anxiety—*Crawf, please,* she said—*Can you wait 'til they get here?*

They were both very tired. It was so late in the night it had become morning.

—*Hullo? You just saw what happened,* said Crawf—*You think they'll be in any condition to go anywhere? They'll need to recover.*

—*It's just surveillance.*

Crawf gasped—*Hullo?*

Manifold scurried after them, prepared to assist should there be something practical she could do but when she noticed the temperature rise between them she dodged out of the way. Crawf turned back to face Antenna—*Spying's something best done awake, don't you think?*

—*You've waited this long, Crawf.*

—*Hullo? Can't you see? That's why. That's exactly the reason I can't wait any longer. I have to go. Right now.*

As Crawf climbed up onto the landing gear preparing to enter the wingship's cockpit, Antenna tried yet another tack, anything to slow him down, to get him to reconsider—*What if something goes wrong?*

—*With what?*

—*You've been on enough actions. Anything could go wrong. What about the wingship? What then?*

—*Oh, if it'll keep you happy, I'll fly there under my own steam. I've got my own wings. I can use them for once.*

—*There's no need for that!*

With an exasperated sigh, Crawf hopped down from checking the landing gear under the wingship and said to Antenna—*Come to that, forget it, I'll just head out now. See ya.* Crawf turned away from Antenna, away from the wingship and made his way to the mouth of the hangar, stretching out his huge wings, testing them and warming up. His wingspan measured almost the entire mouth of the cave.

—*Crawf!* Antenna had to break into a run to catch up with him— *Take someone with you!* The numbat spun round to check who was handy. Couldn't be Manifold 'cause she was needed there—*Manifold? Can you please send for Spark?*

—*Yup*, at once, Manifold buzzed off.

Crawf stopped and turned back—*You'll let me have the wingship?*

Antenna nodded and continued—*But this is only surveillance, right? We're just gathering intelligence. We're not going to rush into any hasty actions, like rescuing a cat or anything, right?*

—*Even if there's an opportunity?*

Antenna's voice rose as she tried to explain the need for caution, which seemed so obvious to her—*Every rushed thing gets us into trouble and we're in enough trouble already, don't you think? We have to take the time to research.*

—*What if we don't have time?*

—*Crawf. You saw that stuff on the internet; we're talking about people who move material through illegal channels here: drugs, pornography, weapons, slaves, wildlife - it's all the same to them. They're just smugglers dealing with the contraband of the day. Such large sums of money are involved; such an essential need for secrecy, it's a matter of life and death. Crawf*, she spoke clearly now, emphasising the words—*I don't want to lose you.*

Crawf stared at Antenna for a moment before he spoke—*What do you mean? Obviously, it's a matter of life and death for the smuggled birds...*

—*As well as birds; it's lives, liberty and in the case of humans, fortunes. They're different from us. They're prepared to risk their freedom for the sake of their bank accounts.*

—*I've got to go, Antenna.* Crawf made his way back to the wingship and climbed up into the cockpit, Antenna still shouting instructions as he went—*Remember, this is only basic reconnaissance, Crawf. I want you and the wingship back here, safe, before noon, okay? They'll notice if you're not here for the whole day. When Bash gets back, I'll get him to rest and then you can both go out again tonight.* Antenna tailed off, aware that Crawf was going and there was nothing she could do to stop him—*I wish I could come with you.*

In the wingship, Crawf was now busy with the control panel and getting comfortable on his perch—*But you can't*, he muttered.

—*What?* said Antenna.

—*Hi Crawf*, said Spark as he flew through the window shining like a spangly bullet specially designed for use in nightclubs.

—*Hullo*, said Crawf.

Outside, down on the Ektek version of tarmac, Manifold commenced taxiing procedures—*All clear above and astern...*

The wingship headed out of the hangar and proceeded along toward the road where they would get to a reasonable speed in order to lift into the air. Soon, uneventfully, the wingship was airborne and they were travelling over the city lights toward the wharf.

—*What's everyone staring at?* Antenna turned to Manifold and the beetle crew and shouted—*We've got work to do!*

II

A chunky black beetle flew into the hangar and shouted—*They're coming!* The waiting collection of animals assembled by the entry, waiting for the tank to arrive. This group was prepared to take care of the Ektek activist team when they arrived back on Bedlam soil. As well as the team of beetles, a koala and a tiger quoll waited beside Antenna as the tank rolled into the parking place in the hangar. Gumfluff was captain of the Ektek boat, *Intek.* Carney, a tiger quoll, was her ship's mate. Both were onshore now to help Antenna when the activists, shocked and exhausted, climbed out of the tank.

Gumfluff and Carney took hold of Gleam, slumped in the rear of the tank, and guided him gently to his cage. He lived in a space off the hangar, the machine cage, purpose built to keep machinery work away from dust, now his own private bedroom stocked with food and water. He sank into his bedding, slumped his head back and lay still. Gumfluff and Carney looked at each other and went quietly away.

A team of beetles lifted and carried Bash away to the frog-quarium. Antenna directed Bluey to lie on the mini hovercraft, which she and Hod moved to the control centre and her own nest. Once they had made sure he was comfortable they left him to rest. He fell asleep almost immediately.

Antenna walked Hod outside to the tunnel leading to his enclosure and said—*As for that cat, he puts one paw wrong…*

—*Isn't he a quokka?*

—*He's having you on.*

—*He's too sick to do anything…*

—*He'll get better. They've got nine lives.*

—*Unless he's a quokka?*

—*If he's a quokka I'll eat Gleam's hat.*

—*Only going on what he said.*

—*You can't believe what they say, Hod.*

—*I'll be careful.*

—*Good. What about her? Where is she?*

—*Gone.*

—*For good?*

Hod didn't know how to answer. He swallowed and waved his arms around helplessly.

—What if she comes back? Antenna stared at him—*What then? How are you going to control her?*

—Me?

—Who else? You brought her here, Hod.

—I thought she was coping…

—She can't stay.

—She's not here now.

—If she comes back I want to know everything she does. Everything. And I want you to tell her she's not welcome.

—Me?

—You're not that obtuse. We can't work with her.

—Anti. What can I do? She's a croc!

—Should have thought of that before you brought her here, then, shouldn't you.

III

Crawf pushed one of his feet forward and lifted a lever in the cockpit of the wingship. He pointed his claw, pushed a yellow button and the wingship levelled out. He established radio contact with Antenna and heard her report on the tank's safe return. She mentioned there was no sign of Shining Teeth. There was nothing he could do from here, on his way to the wharf area, so he said—*All clear above and astern. Over.*

—Roger. Stay safe, Crawf. Spark, keep your eyes open. Over.

Listening to the strange tone in Antenna's voice, Spark wondered what he'd got himself into. He looked over to Crawf, grimly operating the controls and staring hard through the windscreen, looking ahead at something Spark couldn't quite see.

—Crawf? After a while of waiting for a reply that never came, Spark realised Crawf wasn't in the mood for small talk, well, any talk really, and instead, he crawled up to stare ahead out of the windscreen as the wingship approached the main city wharf area. It was not difficult to find the large Pet Met Warehouse in the docklands and they circled it, flying in closer and closer as they went around. Crawf noticed the two entrances and then came in closer still over the roof.

—What now? asked Spark, but Crawf had no reply. Spark shook his head and couldn't help but feel frustrated—*Crawf? You going to ignore me the whole way?*

—I'm thinking.

With that, and Spark didn't think it was nearly enough but knew it would have to do, Crawf began to bring the wingship down onto the roof.

—You have to be kidding? No? You're not kidding. Well, at least tell Antenna you're landing. Crawf? Come on. You have to let Antenna know what you're doing. Don't you?

Crawf didn't even seem to hear Spark. He turned off the engine and started to climb out of the window. Spark really did begin to panic—*Crawf! What are you doing? Crawf! You can't!*

Crawf had.

Spark flew out of the window and down to follow Crawf, as he explored the roof, looking for surveillance vantage points. An overhanging veranda above the doorway blocked his view and Crawf became increasingly frustrated that he couldn't see into the building from this angle. There appeared to be a shop front there with billboards advertising pet-food and bones and toys and bedding… Pet Met was a barn of a place.

—Crawf? As he followed the Palm cockatoo, the beetle kept trying to establish a connection, any connection—*Crawf? You got to tell Antenna what you're doing. Crawf? Talk to me?*

After some exasperated mutterings under his beak, Crawf lost his patience and snapped—*Shut up and let me get on with it.*

Spark stepped back and watched as Crawf continued his exploration across the roof. Eventually Crawf found a loose covering over the air-conditioning system and crawled into the ducting. Spark followed him and, in bizarre single-file, they crept into the building itself.

When Crawf came to a grate overlooking the shopping barn, he looked down and noticed a man pacing up and down in the aisle of the shop. From above, through the grid, Crawf watched him walk. The man's head was bald, he had a downward-pointing half-moon of bushy brown hair over his top lip and he wore a shiny blue tracksuit that made him look like a bluebottle jellyfish.

Presumably this was the man that Crawf had emailed. Presumably this was the man that expected to buy and sell a Palm cockatoo for a large profit. This was the man that Crawf had set up to meet.

Crawf watched him, pacing, up and down, waiting for someone who would never show up. Well, that was if he was expecting a human. Crawf knew the man could hardly expect a Palm cockatoo by himself and yet that was exactly the bird's plan.

Spark did his own pacing, up and down in the duct, beside the still silent grey cockatoo, every now and then flicking the bird a look. What the hell was going on? Why wasn't Crawf talking to him? He was supposed to be his partner after all. How could he best help Crawf and keep out of trouble? Should he be here at all?

Crawf let fly a poop through the grate. It landed on top of a cage some metres below and not very far from the man. Spark looked at the cockatoo. Did he know what would happen if that had landed on the bald man's pate? Not only that, but now (oh, what now?) Crawf was busy unscrewing the grate from the duct with his claws. It was an arduous business. The screws were positioned all around the grate. He took out each screw separately. When each screw was nearly out, Crawf carefully grasped it in his beak and spun around it as though he were taking it for a dance. He turned and lifted until the screw came out in his beak and he quietly laid it to one side. Then he unscrewed the next one.

At one stage the hairy-lipped man glanced upwards - did he hear the turning of the screw? Spark held up his front leg in the international sign to HALT but Crawf took no heed, just kept walking around the screw with his head tilted over to one side and the Philip's head screw firmly in his beak. Luckily the man appeared not to notice anything amiss from the ground. He lost interest and wandered off to check on the front door.

Spark sighed with relief. He settled back to watch Crawf's circles with resignation. This was not teamwork. There was no point to him being here. It didn't seem to matter what he said or did, Crawf was going to do precisely what he wanted. All Spark could do was wait for the plan to be revealed. He could see it would be too late for him to do anything about it, of course.

When Crawf had seen the rows of cages in the warehouse, he couldn't help himself. He had to get down and examine each one to see if they contained a Palm cockatoo. He couldn't take the time to explain to the beetle because, right now, he was a bird of action and he was sick of talking and he didn't want to argue with anyone and he had to concentrate because he had a hollow beak and it needed to be treated with respect when being used as a screwdriver. The last screw twisted out and Crawf shook himself into a less dizzy state of mind before he managed to pry up the grate using his own claws and fragile beak.

—*Watch out, Crawf,* Spark sprang forwards and hissed—*Watch for the man.*

Crawf tilted his head and considered the Christmas beetle with one black, beady, shiny eye. Wasn't it obvious? He was already watching the man and when the human blue bottle had progressed in his pacing to the other side of the barn, Crawf managed to lift the grate away from the opening and drop into the store itself.

He flew through the shop checking out each cage. None held a Palm cockatoo although there were almost as many birds there as back in the zoo aviary. Over in the next aisles there were dogs, cats, rabbits, mice and guinea pigs - where ever did they all came from, he wondered, some kind of pet breeding centre? Along the wall fish tanks glowed in unnatural colours, as though from acid plumes deep under the ocean. A line of reptile tanks smouldered under red heat lamps.

Crawf's huge wings stirred the muggy air as he fluttered up and down in the glare of the fluros and the garish colour of the animal toys and the hard steel of the cages; feathered, real, alive and free.

The bald human bluebottle with the hairy top lip felt the air shift over his head and he looked up like a startled fur seal. He yipped some of that strange human gibberish out loud and moved to follow the bird. He grabbed a handful of seed out of an open packet and eventually, inevitably, Crawf appeared to succumb to temptation and land on the man's outstretched arm like a pet budgie. Crawf was well and truly caught. The man handled him gently but it was firm management. It was a matter of moments before the cage door clanged behind him. The man in the shiny tracksuit looked perturbed, shook his head and stared at Crawf making some smooth talking and admiring guttural sounds with his big hairy mouth. Then he left and turned out the lights on his way out.

Spark waited until the outside door was locked before he flew down to Crawf's cage. He landed on the latch, saw there was no way he could open it by himself and flew over to speak to Crawf from the outside of the wire—*Why did you let him catch you?* Crawf was still in his ignoring-the-beetle frame of mind, obviously. Spark heaved a sigh of frustration and climbed right inside the cage to whisper in the bird's ear—*You let him catch you. I saw you. What are you playing at?*

—*Have to find my brother or someone of my family or even just one other of my species before I die.*

—*How do you expect to get the wingship back to Ektek?*

—*It'll be all right where it is.*

—*I'll have to go back and tell them.*

—*Yes, tell them. And, Spark, tell them not to worry.*

—*Oh, that will make all the difference, Crawf. Good luck. Hope you know what you're doing.*

—*Never been more certain.*

Spark climbed out of the cage and flew up to the vent. He turned back to look over the edge of the duct at Crawf, stuck in a cage far too small for him. His headdress was still perky as he dipped his beak into some birdseed. He looked up at Spark and nodded, as if to say, 'it's all going to be all right, Sparkie. Don't fret.' He even opened and shut one eyelid in a gesture that made him look revolting, like a jolly feathered human being. What was that? Winking? Disgusting.

Spark shook his head, tut tutted and crawled through the duct. He climbed out onto the roof and took a fluttering jump or two. He felt duped, as though Crawf had made a joker out of him. He glanced over at the parked wingship in the shade of the lift-well and sighed. He turned and looked out over the enormous expanse of fading city lights. The electric lights were dimming in the face of a red dawn in the east. The sun was rising yet again.

Then Spark jumped off the roof.

Chapter Fifty-three

I

The shaved creature called Bluey slept. He lay curled in Antenna's nest of bark. He was a messy, motley scruffy thing. His shaved hair had started to grow back and the scar on his spine was starting to fade to pale pink. He slept with one eye open and appeared to be watching everything but in fact it was a strange kind of war wound, a slash across his face that had caused damage to his eyelid. However, there was nothing to watch in the control room when he did eventually wake. The shaved creature was alone.

He stood, shook himself and tried to stretch, began to arch his sore spine upwards but, finding it uncomfortable, growled a little bit under his breath with the pain. He looked around at his surroundings to distract himself. Gleam had offered to share the food 'borrowed' from the zoo's resident big cats so a small heap of raw red flesh had been provided next to the paper bark nest, together with a curved leaf full of water.

The creature stepped out of the nest placing each paw deliberately. He tested himself as he moved. He was stiff but he could feel his strength returning. He could feel the muscles in his forelimbs and those in his haunches. When he had four paws on the floor of the cave he stretched again. He arched carefully, testing for twinges as he moved. He pushed his weight evenly onto each paw and delighted in aligning his bones, tendons and cartilages to the very tip of his scabby tail. This he shook as if he were a rattle snake, shimmering and delicate, reminding him of the concentration of the hunt, his innate hunter. Oops, get down, there, boy. Then he attended to the meat and ate until he was full.

The creature was in no rush and he sat, thrusting one leg sky high for his toilet. There was plenty of time for inspection and grooming and his tongue set to work, soothing and patting down those bruises from needles, and scars from clamps. There was no denying it, the shaved creature was thrilled to be out of that lab; he was finding his way back into his body and was about to resume normal operations. He sat back on his haunches and considered his options. First, he'd have to work out how best to repay the kindness of his rescuers, of course. What could Bluey do for Ektek on this day, he wondered. The shaved creature got to his feet. It was time to do a little exploring.

II

Around the corner from the main hangar, Gleam lay unmoving in the machine cage. His head was still and heavy on his paws. His exotic striped fur made strange contrast with the surrounding dull rock and metal.

Antenna was cautious as she approached him. She had left him to rest for a good long while, hoping he would be able to regain his strength and assuming he would need time to process what had happened to him. She looked at him. Was he asleep? She could not see him breathing. She whispered—*Gleam?* She stood and watched him. She was scared he might be dead. She didn't want to do or say anything in case her fears were true. She held her own breath until she was almost overwhelmed by relief when she saw his ribs moving. She could not imagine how he must be feeling.

With his great head immobile, Gleam stared with hard eyes at the rock wall. He struggled with the memory of Shining Teeth's power and her awful disregard for life. He struggled with his need to forgive her. He couldn't yet find the strength to do that. He was filled with anguish for the wasted lives of those two dogs. He considered them to have been proud warriors, lost at the peak of their powers, killed by a monster who did not care for any other living creature great or small, other than what they could offer her; food, shelter, entertainment, it was all the same to that damned croc.

Antenna coughed.

Gleam shifted and she cleared her throat—*Gleam? It's me, Antenna.*

Gleam sighed. He was reluctant to communicate with anyone but he made an exception for Antenna. He said—*You know what the worst thing was?*

—*What?*

—*The blood.* Gleam seemed to be in the grip of a nightmare. He spoke as if under a spell—*Her blood.* He appeared captivated by memory—*The smell.* Like any hunter he relived the kill—*Flesh. Her flesh. Her meat.* Only, in his mind, he was no hunter, but murderer. Guilt pulsed through his being like the very blood that had so compelled him.

—Yes, of course.

—So fresh. I could taste it, and Gleam was overwhelmed by a sensory flashback. He could see it; he could feel it and he savoured that blood in his recollection. He focused on what it looked like in his mind and his taste buds ran rampant and the remembered red-velvet warmth poured clots through his gullet. His thoughts were far away from the machine cage where he huddled now—*The sensation of her leaving the body; I could feel her departure, once vibrant creature. Then she was just empty; still, empty meat. Bloody, fresh meat and I could not... eat it... Her, I mean. I could not eat her. How could I?* The tiger's deep-set eyes filled with tears and, as he struggled to bring his emotions under control, he tilted his head so the tears would not run down his face and betray him. In vain.

Antenna sat up on her hindquarters and watched him curiously. His surge of instinct did not surprise her. Why should it? She too ate the zoo's pre-prepared anteater custard to avoid eating the very creatures (ants and termites) that built the foundations of Ektek. Ants were literally the life-blood of Ektek and Antenna could not eat them. It would be beyond the pale. It had always been a struggle, and there had been unfortunate incidents, notably when she and her best friend, Min, had been young and foolish but, mostly, she was in control. It was a matter of self-knowledge, after all.

Neither Gleam nor Antenna was an inmate of Bedlam Zoo. They were both outlaws hiding out in the tunnels beneath it. They stole food - or rather the ants and beetles 'borrowed' food for them - as they worked for an animal organisation that extended all over the world; Ektek.

Antenna saw Gleam's sacrifice as entirely matter-of-fact and said so—*You wanted to eat her. There's nothing wrong with that. In fact, thinking about it, it might have been sensible to bring both dogs back with you.*

—What? said Gleam—*That's deplorable.*

—Gleam, be practical. You don't get much fresh meat. You're probably malnourished. That's partly why you're so overcome with emotion now.

—I promised.

—Who?

—My keeper.

—After you'd killed him?

—Yes. Yes. See? I was ashamed. I promised him I would never kill again and I have never...

—Would you have had that dog suffer more?

—I couldn't bear it. It was selfish.

—Selfish?

—Because of my own distress, I chose the easy way out. Who knows how much longer she would have lived?

—From what Bash told me, and from what we saw here, she had no chance at all.

—I can't stay here.

Antenna looked at the larger beast and considered her words before she spoke. She felt they needed to be said, however, so she proceeded—*I never took you for the self-pitying kind, Gleam. If anyone had asked me I would have said, Gleam? Selfish? No way. He always thinks of others before himself. Now, we need to know more about this particular lab, for instance. We've got all this footage and information to research. There's also the small matter of Bluey. What about him? I'm still waiting for Crawf and Spark to return - they're both late - and I need your help. I can't do this by myself.*

—I can't work with…

—Did you ever think she set you up?

—What?

—Perhaps she wanted to make you kill. So, having broken your oath, you would feel compromised.

—Shining Teeth? Do you really think she would be so heinous?

—You're the only one who can stop her.

—No. I can't.

—Maybe now you've broken the promise it wouldn't seem so bad?

—Antenna. You ask too much…

—I was just thinking out loud but, when you think about it, after what she did to you…

—Antenna, you can't possibly agree with your own suggestion. If she's judged by her peers to be so evil that she must be removed from society then that is what must happen. We can imprison her; try to rehabilitate her. But Antenna, I will not kill her. She's part of the fabric of this planet's life. Every part of the web is necessary, even we large predators…

—Hard to manage sometimes.

—Yes.

—No one can cope alone. We need to get everyone together so we can work out what to do. Come on. Get up. Don't give up. There's work to do.

Gleam looked at Antenna. She waited, not willing to let him go. He nodded in agreement. There would be no more thoughts of leaving Ektek. He was part of the organisation. He was not alone any more. He raised himself to his feet. Together they strode out of the control room.

III

In the computer control centre, Bash ran on a small track-ball, staring, deep in his own obsession, at a computer screen. As he ran, he was manipulating a virtual beetle running in long grass trying to avoid a spider. The beetle was able to spit some kind of foul poison at various flying insects attacking it. When it hit the flying insects the poison caused them to explode in an entirely satisfactory, bloody kind of way, across the screen. Splatter followed splatter after splatter and Bash was spellbound as he ran and dodged and clicked and spasmed with the splatters in the game.

Antenna entered the control cave, closely followed by Gleam. When Gleam saw what Bash was doing he straightened his tiger frame. He could not believe his eyes. No sooner had they returned from cruel devastation in the university grounds than Bash had lost his sense of reality in the dream world of violent video games. He could do nothing about Shining Teeth but he could deal with a teeny little frog all right.

—*How could you?* roared Gleam—*Have you no compassion?*

Bash ignored him and continued to run, oblivious to the tiger's howl.

—*We've come straight from murder and you choose more death?* Gleam came close to Bash now, incensed by the frog's indifference—*How can you keep pulling that trigger when so many deaths are surrounding you in real life?*

Bash glanced at him but returned his attention to the screen almost immediately—*Not the same.*

—*It is the same.*

Antenna watched the exchange in increasing discomfort—*Gleam, perhaps Bash is trying to escape the pain of what he's witnessed.*

—*By more killing?* said Gleam, hardly looking at her as he tried to follow Bash's on-screen activity.

—*Don't worry, Gleam,* said Bash—*'s'not real. They're just computer simulations.*

—*Are they not shaped as live beings?*

—*Guess so.*

—*Do they not bleed?*

—*Aw, well, red pixels come out of them...*

—*Are you not inflamed by excitement; intent on further bloodshed?*

—*It's a game, Gleam. I pull the trigger and I get a result. That's what games are for...*

—*But you happen to like the games where the life form explodes.*

—*Chill, Gleam. It's just a game.*

—*It's so much more than a game. How would you like to play a game where the response to your action is something other than red splatter? Perhaps little stars or a puff of smoke comes from imaginary broken bottles. Not the same, is it?*

—*Ah... S'pose not.*

—*So it is the idea of blood, of death, that stirs you up and gets you going, doesn't it. Here, I'll get you going...* and Gleam grabbed the little frog up in his mouth.

Bash screamed!

Gleam picked him up and carried him away, Bash yelling the whole time.

Antenna was taken by surprise and could only watch as Gleam carried Bash out of the control centre. She scrambled to her feet and followed.

— *No!* Bash clung to the tiger's slimy teeth, screaming—*Put me down! You big bully! You'll crush me!*

Gleam kept marching until they got to the hangar. He spat the tiny frog out onto the ground next to the little plane jettisoned by Crawf earlier—*You were there. You saw the disgusting mess that Shining Teeth made of that dog...*

—*That's not fair! I hated that!*

—*I hate what you're doing.*

Antenna followed Gleam into the hangar, worried that he might hurt Bash and, seeing that Bash was still holding his own, kept her own counsel.

Those already in the hangar were astounded to see the tiger spit out the noisy frog. Manifold and Torque were in the midst of talking to a large group of number beetles about potential work as mechanics. Manifold's trained team of worker beetles let their tools rest as they all stared, their little beetle mouths open at the confrontation.

Eid, who had been piecing together the airship's skin in another area of the hangar, faded back into the shadows, not wanting to be noticed by Antenna. He was supposed to be on duty in the numbat enclosure and he didn't want to have to undergo another lecture. He watched her, though. He rarely got a chance to observe her unnoticed and he scrutinised her as though she were the only creature there.

Antenna must have somehow felt his attention because she swung round to look in his direction but he managed to dodge back unseen. She didn't know what had caused her to look in that corner and made a mental note to check there later. Right now, her attention was taken up by Bash and Gleam.

Whoever was in that hangar was stunned by this unlikely argument between the tiger and the frog. Everyone watched to see what would happen next, which was, simply, that the frog went hopping mad.

Bash leapt and bounded around Gleam, shouting at him—*You're as bad as Shining Teeth! How could you! Would you look at the size of you? There was no need to get physical!*

Gleam's eyes suddenly lost their ardour as he realised what he'd done—*You're right. I'm sorry, Bash. I acted like a bully.*

—*You did!*

Gleam was on the threshold of an epiphany and lowered his eyes. He was deep in thought. He was no longer paying any attention to the frog or even to his surroundings—*I do have something in common with Shining Teeth after all.*

—*I'm just a little frog!*

Antenna did step forward then and said to Bash—*Gleam has apologised, Bash.*

—*Apologies aren't enough,* stamped the little frog.

—*No. What would be enough, I wonder?* said Gleam as he thought about reparation for his impulsive aggression toward Bash. Gleam looked around at all the beetles now standing with Torque and Manifold, waiting to become mechanics and selected one—*You, beetle, yes, you, small one with the orange-and-black elytra. What's your name?*

—*You mean me, sir?*

—*Yes, you sir.*

—*Niti. I'm Niti, sir.* Niti had short legs and little bulbs on the end of his squat antennae. He was suddenly removed from the patient waiting to which he had become rather accustomed and thrust into the full glare of the limelight. He looked around at all the other beetles, swallowed his nerves and stood up straight as Gleam questioned him—*Niti, eh. Are you from around here?*

—*No, I'm a number. I'm 472. Waiting, with everyone else* (he indicated all the other beetles standing with Torque) *to tell my story. If I get a chance, that is.*

—*What? All of you are numbers?*

—*Yes, sir. We're waiting to see someone from Ektek.*

—*Well, today's your lucky day. Go on. Tell him. Tell Bash here.*

Niti looked to Bash and then back up at Gleam—*Now, sir?*

—*Yes, now and stop calling me sir.*

—*But, sir, I don't think it's my turn…*

—*Never mind that now. Get on with it.*

Niti bowed, moved closer to Bash and began his honey-bee adapted dance of fact and direction. Bash moved to join him and copied every move faithfully. Soon they were moving in a graceful *pas de deux*, creating a figure of eight with tremulous bows in the directions of sun and north and west. Bash, with his shiny black-and-gold frog skin, and Niti, with his black-and-red beetle elytra, together made a striking couple dancing gravely on the hangar floor.

Gleam watched them impassively. Antenna also watched in silence as Bash bowed to Niti and turned back to Gleam to report—*It's feral camels. They're worried. They've got no water. They're forced into human villages by their thirst and can't help blundering into human property as they search. Most of them can't read, poor things. They wish no harm. They don't mean to be destructive. It's just that they're so thirsty. They need to find a better place to live.*

Gleam nodded and said—*Get on with it, then.*

—*What?* said Bash—*You want me to head out there? Into the desert? By myself? What can I do about it?*

—*You can reconnoitre, can't you? Report back. Get going.*

—*I can't! I need Crawf to fire off the mini plane from the air...*

—*Crawf? Well? Where's he? Get him organised.*

Antenna stepped up to Gleam and muttered that Crawf was still out on an action. She hoped he'd be back any minute but she hadn't heard a word since they'd gone. She didn't elaborate to Gleam and the others just how worried she was about Crawf. Eid saw it though. He wished he could help her but he knew she must never begin to suspect he was even there.

Gleam sighed with irritation and turned to the bombardier beetle—*Manifold? Any way we can launch this plane from the ground?*

Manifold thought for a moment—*We could, maybe, set the plane at the mouth of the hangar and launch it using the maglev tracks we salvaged from the airship.*

—*Do it. Let's go.*

The beetle mechanics, the ones that knew what they were supposed to be doing, ran to the small plane and commenced their preflight inspections. The new beetles ran around in circles for a bit until Torque quietened them down and they settled, lining the walls of the hangar, watching to see if they could learn anything.

Bash tightened his lips. He looked over to Antenna—*Do I have to?*

—*No,* she said.

Bash let a little smile grow in the corner of his mouth before he glanced over at Gleam but Antenna hadn't quite finished—*But what else are you going to do? You can't live your entire life through video games, Bash. Go ahead, get on board. You might be able to help someone.*

Bash looked at her, hoping the argument might have another loophole but before he could think of something Gleam broke into the conversation.

—*Time to get out in the real world, Taddy. See what's really going on*— Gleam thought for a moment, shook his head and continued—*Let me put that a bit more succinctly, shall I, Bash? Time for you to grow up.*

As Bash made himself ready, sullen and silent in his little cockpit, Manifold took over directing operations with her beetle crew. The little plane lined up on the maglev track and commenced lift-off procedure.

Antenna watched Bash roll out to the launching area before she turned and, apparently without purpose, wandered back into the shadows of the hangar. She looked at the airship skin and sniffed the air. She could have sworn she saw... No, perhaps not. She turned away and went back toward the control centre. When he was sure she'd gone, Eid stepped forward from the darkness where he'd been hiding. He looked after her and sighed, just a little sigh that, had she heard it, might have melted the sternest numbat's heart. Antenna did not hear anything except the clash of metal on metal and the squeak of mechanic beetle lift-off jargon—*All clear above and astern...*

—*All right then, now he's gone,* Gleam turned to the number beetles and said—*Torque? Do you want to introduce me to your friends?*

—*What? Oh, them.* Torque snapped to attention and shouted— *Collies! Attention! Form an orderly queue, in number order, please. This is it, your big opportunity. You'll all get a chance to talk,* Torque flashed Gleam a questioning look, hoping this was the case. The tiger nodded; he would hear them all no matter how long it took.

A great excitement rose in the beetle ranks. They did know their order and managed to scramble into position ready to speak in honest turn to Gleam.

Gleam watched this operation with growing concern. No wonder Torque had been pestering them. How many beetles were here? How on earth could Ektek deal with this many problems?

IV

The shaved creature had been busy wandering through the Ektek world; exploring tunnels and hallways that led from the hangar and to the different enclosures in the Bedlam Zoo. Knowing no different, he strolled from the hangar out into the surrounding bushland. This was freedom and he walked with stiff legs, happy to be outside, breathing the warm air. He found a patch of slanting sunshine and sat upright, his ears flicking around him. He relaxed and, with some spine discomfort, lay down in the dappled sunshine. His tail twitched as an ant ran over him. He melted into the ground, feeling his cells healing and the stench of laboratory chemicals being cleaned from his nostrils.

Lazily he began again to clean himself with his pale pink tongue, initially as he lay, working down his shoulder. Then he carefully sat up and worked down his front. Suddenly he caught a flicker of movement through the eye that could never close and he looked up and froze like a statue.

A small lizard edged out into the sunny aspect and lifted its head to see what the world offered that morning. Quick as a wink, the shaved creature pounced, jumping a curving metre with no trouble at all. The lizard hung from the shaved creature's mouth and shrieked as it felt teeth.

Torque, halfway up a small gum tree above the sunny clearing, shook his head and signed to the beetles behind him to be silent.

Niti didn't hear him—*So, Mr Torque? I am worried, now that I have imparted my number's message, that I must leave?*

—*Shhh*, said Torque. Then, as he processed the question, Torque looked at Niti and wondered what he meant—*Sorry?*

—*Am I to be allowed to stay with you and learn to work with Ektek?* said Niti.

—*Ah*, said Torque—*I don't see why not. But now is not the time to chat about that. Can you see what I'm looking at here?*

Niti smiled with relief, bowed and fell back into line with the others. The beetles that had indicated their interest in staying to train as mechanics had seen the work, listened to an introductory talk from Manifold, given their story to Gleam and were now hanging on Torque's every word as he gave them a tour; showing them everything that Ektek had managed to create in order to assist animals over the last few years.

The talk had been interrupted however, when Torque saw Bluey attack a smaller creature. Torque had heard about the rescue of the 'quokka'. He knew what he'd just witnessed and he knew he'd have to warn Ektek. That shaved creature lounging in the sun just by the entrance to the hangar was dangerous. Seriously dangerous. He turned back to his beetle class—*You see that animal there? Eating a poor little lizard? That's a cat, my friends, and it's more than my job's worth to have a cat anywhere near any of us. You stay well away from it. We'd best go and report it. Come along, stick together, look lively there!*

Chapter Fifty-four

I

Comfortable and concentrating hard in his little plane, Bash flew out in great curves across the desert land. He knew exactly where to go, thanks to Niti's danced instructions, and Bash played the horizon like one of his games. Colours ranging from dust beige through ochre, orange, yellow and pink grew into mounds and outcrops dusted with puffy green trees on thin line stalks.

The skin of the land was criss-crossed by etched lines, roads shimmering in the sun. He squinted his eyes into the sun searching for those so-called ships of the desert: camels. Where were they?

Then he saw movement among the shadows and trees. Was it a rock? No, it did move and there, there was his first camel. It walked on long thin legs between the stems of stick trees. The creature seemed gigantic to Bash who was a mere frog in a miniscule plane, zitting around like a robot insect in the air.

He became aware of a change in atmosphere. A rackety roaring noise thundered some distance away. Could he be flying into a storm? He cast his eyes to the sky and saw no clouds. He continued to search the ground, concerned with the origin of the sound.

Then he saw the rest of them; a host of camels strutting out across the land. They were proud beasts the colour of desert and the size of trees, even the young ones. They moved with a swaying grace that seemed to power them forwards - each easy leaning footfall as deliberate and equally weighted as the next. They were hypnotic in their smooth, continual tread onwards, onwards through the trees.

They had enormous heads that bounced when they hit the ground. Dust rose up around them as they crashed into the dirt. What? Another fell? Those that could move broke into loping runs. They were running, running, into the dust and bodies of other camels and toppling, collapsing, dropping...

Why were the camels falling like this? Bash realised that, as far as he could see and everywhere he looked camels plummeted to the dirt and they could not get up. The ground became red with blood and the survivors were running, running, pell mell, this way and that...

He was not the only thing flying in the air that afternoon. An occasional bird and perhaps those bushflies counted, but the real objects of interest to him were two roaring helicopters and everywhere the helicopters went travelled too the sound of death.

Loud reports cracked again and again from the whirling dervishes. Mostly the helicopters seemed to target the camels and hit them cleanly. Bash flew over the killing field and could even imagine he was hearing moans as the creatures the colour of sand fell and died. Perhaps it was him that moaned with distress and disbelief as he flew around the killing field in his tiny little plane.

He could not understand what was happening. He stayed away from the helicopters. Once he felt he'd attracted interest and he dodged away into a line of trees like a pigeon escaping from a hawk but the helicopters did not swoop him nor did they even seem to care.

The camels did not escape. They fell. One by one. They fell. In the tens, twenties, fifties... Many, many camels fell that day.

Bash was silent as he made his way back to Ektek base. What on earth could it mean, this mass slaughter of camels, he wondered. Why were they to be obliterated when all they had done was turn to humans to ask for water?

II

Spark flew up and down, over Bedlam Zoo's high wall. He gasped for air, flapped his underwings and desperately found one last pinch of energy to drive him to Ektek's door. He was completely exhausted. He had pushed himself to the limit. He could not go another millimetre. He lay on the ground, just outside the hangar mouth, gasping for air.

Concerned beetles surrounded him and the word spread through the hangar that Spark was back and that he was hurt.

—*Clear the way. Get out of my way, now. Please.* On his way back from touring with the trainee beetles, Torque marched through the crowd—*Come on, come on, what's going on here? Sparkie? What's happened? Are you all right?*

The sparkly beetle gathered himself together and spoke—*I'm okay, Torque. Don't fuss.*

A small green beetle squeezed a flower into Spark's mouth, letting tiny atoms of watery nectar quench his thirst. Torque pushed her away—*If you're so okay, what are you doing lying on the ground, then?*

—*Bit tired, that's all.* Spark reached out for the nectar again but Torque prevented him from drinking.

—*Tired? Where's Crawf?*

—*Tell Antenna. They got him. They got Crawf. Can't move. Must rest. Tell Antenna.*

—*Crawf?* said Torque—*Our Crawf?*

—*S'true. I swear it.*

Torque shook his head and indicated to the watching beetles they could get back to looking after his young assistant and Spark gratefully gulped nectar from the offered flower. He sent the trainee beetles back to the feeding centre. He would tell Antenna the bad news. Although he was finding it hard to believe that Crawf, of all creatures (Crawf!) would get himself captured. Torque never thought he'd live to see that.

III

Crawf dozed. He was reasonably comfortable on his perch but he was getting cold. Some vague light permeated into his cage but it was difficult to see. He knew he was in a small enclosure wedged between the outside wall of a ship; the wall beside the sea, and the inside wall of the cabin; the wall beside the humans. Constant noise kept him awake. Just as he fell asleep, a noise on either side of him, a thump or a bump or a wallop would startle him back to his dark surroundings.

He couldn't say how long he'd been there but even in this short time Crawf had come to like the press of water beside him. There was something familiar about it. Perhaps it reminded him of being close to a loving parent while still in an egg. The wall of the vessel was thin and the water sounded as a heartbeat kerplunking next to him: continual, rhythmic and powerful. He knew the great oceans were unforgiving and enormous, and that, at least, was predictable. Crawf knew he did not matter to the deep and would drown in a matter of moments should that wall be breached.

It was not the same fear he felt about the human beings on the other side of him. Humans could just as easily decide to eat him, torture him, free him or sell him depending on their nature and their whim. Who knew which way these humans might choose to go? It was obvious that the sea would go its own way, no matter what occurred but humans were risky, very, very risky.

The egg feeling gradually became less comfortable as time went on. Still cold, Crawf was increasingly thirsty. He could see there was water and even seed in the cage but he could not reach it. How long could he last like this?

His beak was taped. Clearly the humans wanted him silent. He still had his feet free, however, but he could not get good purchase on the tape. After a lengthy silent debate with himself he decided to lift one foot up and tap it down onto his perch in a light tip tap tip tap… If any living creature were nearby (beside the huffing humans) hopefully, they would hear him and take a look. Perhaps they might be able to let him know what was going on? Perhaps they would agree to help him. He tapped on, uncertain whether it would result in a visit from an inquisitive Customs officer, a defensive smuggler or a lusty deathwatch beetle in search of a mate.

Suddenly he became aware of a quick scrabbling coming up from beneath him. Incredibly, a wizened old rat managed to squeeze through the bars of his cage and get inside with him. Without a by-your-leave it proceeded to help itself to the birdseed waiting there, apparently just to torment Crawf. In the dim light seeping though the seams in the cabin walls, each creature could just make out the glittering eyes of the other—*Ahoy, mate,* said the rat, casually.

Crawf tilted his head to one side and tried to say, Hullo? but of course his beak was taped and he could not make anything like a normal sound. Instead he uttered a muffled groaning. The rat sat back on his haunches and nibbled a piece of dry corn watching Crawf's bird features with intense interest—*What's your story, then? Can't talk, can you, 'cos of that there beak being all tied up. Well, I could maybe have a bit of a go at peelin' it off ya. What you reckon? Bit invasive when we haven't been introduced, eh? You might think I was trying to chew your beak off. I wouldn't of course, but you might think it all the same. You couldn't be sure, could you. You wouldn't be able to help wondering. You might even decide to spike me with that great big beak once I got it free. See? Can't be sure, can we. Either of us. Don't want to walk into a big sharp beaky trap, do I? Tell you what. I'll give you my name, which is Salty, by the way, and in my mind you can be Big Grey and that'll stand as a formal introduction until we can have a proper conversation. Now, the thing is, they'll think you've had help unless we make it look like the tape came loose by itself. Can you cope with waiting 'til I make it look good, then? Right. Can you manage to jump on the ground and I'll get up on the perch and that'd be about the right height to do the job. Coping all right in this stuffy air? Okay? You must be worth a pretty penny if they're doing this trip with just the three of you. No, you'll have to wait to speak but I can tell you there's a big old snake in the cage under you and a lizard up above you. There's always some special creatures stashed away in this section of the wall. Must have built it 'specially for the purpose, I always think. Never the best way to enjoy a sea going voyage but then, you're prisoners, aren't you. Let's see. I think that's got most of it loose. I'll leave the other side attached.*

—*Hullo?* said Crawf—*Thank you…*

—*Well, you can talk then.*

Crawf filled his beak with water and nodded as he swallowed, trying to regain his composure. He looked at the rat—*Who are you?*

—*Told you, Salty. You?*

—*Crawf.*

—*Pleasure to un-tape ya, Crawf, though I have to say, I kind of liked Big Grey, had a certain gravitas…*

—*Salty. Thank you. I don't know what…*

—*No worries, mate. Look, we've got to get you away before we cast off…*

—*It's okay, I'm not after any help at the moment, thanks. I need to join up with some other cockatoos. Hopefully, this is my ticket to see my family.*

—*Really? The lengths you youngsters will go, I don't know. Anything you need, then?*

—*Can you tell me, are we at sea yet?*

—*Cripes, no! Waiting for the tide. Can't you tell? Be rocking a fair bit more if we were out in open water! Never been to sea before? Shiver me timbers, you've got a journey ahead of you, haven't you!*

—*Will you be on board?*

—*Too right. Did you want to get a message out? Do your creatures know where you are?*

—*That might be useful. Yeah, thanks. I'm with Ektek. You just contact any beetle and…*

—*Don't you worry about that, matey. We know all about Ektek. I'll get your message off in a jiffy.*

—*You do need to tell them I don't want rescuing. Tell them I'm safe. I'm fine. I just want to let them know where I am. I have to find my family. They'll understand that.*

He hoped.

Salty the rat picked up another corn kernel and gave him what might have been a cheery wave if Crawf had been able to see him properly in the dark before squeezing back between the bars and climbing back down the wall gap.

Crawf was alone again. The walls began to press in on him.

Chapter Fifty-five

I

A meeting gathered under the glow-worm lights of the control centre. Antenna was there, of course, as was Gleam, folded up, by the wall, just as small as he could manage.

Manifold and Spark were on the console desk. Spark was tucked up in a leaf to keep warm. Goodness knows how he'd managed to fly all that way on his own. He was still feeling overwrought but he was determined to be on hand to talk about Crawf. He just kept seeing him tucked into that tiny cage. Why had he done it and where was he now?

Manifold didn't want to be there, feeling there were far too many beetles running around her hangar and she was responsible for them all. So many were completely ignorant and the hangar was fraught with dangers. Fraught. She just hoped they kept their extremities out of sharp edges and stood away from falling objects. She was hoping this meeting wouldn't take long. Goodness knows what disasters she'd have to sort out when she got back to work.

Hod was there, keeping his head down. He didn't want to be questioned too much about absconding from duty on the uni lab action. So far no one had noticed, apart from Bash, and he was hoping he might just get away with that particular lapse in judgement.

The shaved creature who called himself a quokka was there, also keeping a low profile for his own reasons and, of course, Eid was there, front and centre, ready to leap into action at the merest beginning of a signal. He was so ready. He had eyes only for Antenna.

—*I should have been paying more attention but it was when you were in the uni lab,* said Antenna. She was bowed in front of the computer screen, which was open to the sent email folder—*I knew he'd sent the pet shop an email but I didn't realise what it meant. I didn't read it. I should have read it. I can't believe I didn't read it. I should have known what he was doing...*

—*It's not your fault, Antenna,* said Hod—*Crawf was going to do what he needed no matter what you thought.*

—*There was too much else going on...*

—He never intended it to be just surveillance, said Spark.

—No, said Antenna. She couldn't understand what Crawf had been thinking. She shook her head and said in absolute amazement— *He sold himself.*

—He gave himself away, you mean, said Spark.

—There's a difference, said Manifold.

—Many thousands of dollars difference, agreed Antenna—*We're going to have to doctor his cage in the aviary section - make it look like he broke out. Can you fix that, Manifold?*

Manifold opened her mouth to speak when she was interrupted.

—This is impossible, said Gleam—*We can't go off chasing after Crawf! We've got a line of number beetles out there with issues ranging from puppy mills to a bonneted bat. Crawf is exactly where he wanted to be. That beetle messenger said so. She said there'd been a rat and they'd talked and Crawf wanted to be left to find his family in peace.*

—You're not saying we should leave Crawf on a yacht going who knows where with a gang of dangerous smugglers doing who knows what, are you?

—There's something else! Torque flew into the middle of the meeting to report the cat's presence outside—*I would have been here before but...* When he saw Bluey lounging in the space before him, he did a classic double take and his voice faltered. What was the cat doing here?—*I had to take the beetles back to the feeding station...*

—What is it, Torque?

—Him. Torque pointed to the rescued shaven beast that lounged, wound over his spine still showing, in the middle of the cave.

—The quokka? asked Hod.

—That ain't no quokka, said Torque.

—What are you talking about? said Bluey, sitting up very straight and snapping into defensive mode—*How dare you?*

—That, said Torque in his best announcement voice—*...is a cat.*

—Who are you calling 'cat', you bastard? I'm a quokka! What would you know, you buzzing, jumped-up fly!

—Look at him, said Torque—*Anyone can see he's a lying scoundrel.*

Of course, anyone could see Bluey's lip tremble and they noticed that instead of spots on his fur, which was by now a gentle flocculation all over his scrawny rabbit like body, there were in fact, distinct ginger-esque stripes.

Torque shook his head and turned back to the group—*He's a damned feral cat and he shouldn't be here.*

—Feral? I'll have you know I've eaten out of tins in my time. I came from a good family. Once.

—See? He's a cat; a murdering, jumped-up cat. Even he admits it.

—This is unbearable. Everyone stared at Bluey who continued to rant—*I've just been racking my brains about how I can possibly thank Ektek for rescuing me and now you're accusing me of being a murderer.*

Gleam said—*Now, hang on…*

—Well, you're accusing me of something… I won't stand for it.

—He is a murderer, said Torque—*I saw him eat a lizard.*

—We can't live with a cat! said Hod.

—Sorry, Bluey, but you're going to have to go, said Gleam—*We agreed. You had one chance. Just one. And you blew it.*

—Okay, okay, I'm hearing you, and no matter what, I am still grateful you pulled me out of that hellhole. So, I've got an offer in mind to prove how grateful I am. Here's the deal. I'm prepared to go undercover for you.

—You don't need to do anything… said Antenna.

—No, really, I used to live on the wharves. Hear me out here, said Bluey—*I've known many a fat sea-bodied rat - slightly too salty for my taste - entirely edible when you're hungry. I could get on board that yacht and be useful.*

—A spy?

—A cat looking after a smuggled bird, said Hod—*What could possibly go wrong with that?*

—Look, I swear I mean you guys no harm. I love Ektek. I owe you. I can easily survive on rats - they weren't endangered last time I looked…

—What about the wingship?

—We can't just leave it to rot on the roof of Pet Met.

—Someone will have to go and get it. Hopefully, it'll be Crawf.

—That's not going to happen any time soon, is it.

—Who else?

—I'm too big, said Hod.

—I could.

—Eid, said Antenna and they all swung round to look at him.

—You can't fly.

—I could learn.

—Could you? How? By flying off the edge of a building and seeing how long it takes to smash into the ground? Antenna was so over arguing with this stubborn numbat—*Can't you see how difficult that's going to be? And then we're back to the same old problem. They'll spend all their time looking for their valuable breeding stud and Ektek will be exposed.*

Manifold had been watching Eid work for her in the hangar. She liked what she'd seen. He worked efficiently and only needed to be told things once—*He's a quick learner.*

—How do you know? asked Antenna.

Manifold and Eid exchanged a quick glance. Antenna saw it and wondered what it meant. She watched them. Manifold decided that ignoring that question was the quickest way through the discussion. She was on Eid's side, now. She continued, hoping Antenna would forget all about it—*If we could take a team of beetles with us we can make some alterations to the perch...*

—*Crawf's coming back*, said Spark.

—*Not necessarily permanent alterations...*

—*Temporary adjustments*, said Manifold.

—*Hod, you could take us in the tank*, said Eid.

—*Have to wait 'til dark*, said Hod.

Antenna nodded to Manifold, not sure why she was making this rash statement—*Go teach him*. She studiously avoided looking at Eid.

Manifold looked at him, though, when his jubilation broke through his striped face. Eid had been given his chance. Manifold allowed one tiny degree of lift in the corner of her mouth. That was a big smile for her. No need to get carried away about it.

—*It's unlike Crawf to cause us trouble*, said Spark—*He's always been so reliable.*

—*He wants a family*, said Antenna—*He's desperate.*

—*We should have known*, said Spark.

—*Is there enough fuel?* asked Manifold.

—*Only went as far as the wharf*, said Spark—*Should be plenty.*

—*Eid. I'm counting on you.*

Eid nodded. He knew this was his big chance and if she'd had any other option at all she would not have chosen him. It was as if there were only the two of them in the cramped control centre—*I know, Antenna. I'll do my best.*

Antenna knew he would. She also knew then as she looked into his intense eyes that he did mean his very best and that there'd been an unspoken addendum. For her. He wanted to please her. Somehow he'd cracked through a layer of defence and struck home somewhere in her and she had seen him, really seen him, for the first time. Now she knew he was more than just an irritating young numbat out to cause her trouble. Now she knew he was a male, a young male numbat who was out to cause her trouble, trouble as a young female numbat and she started to feel just a teensy bit troubled somewhere close to her heart and somewhere further down, somewhere hormonal, some-where that had never felt this way before, somewhere closer to her tail.

II

Bash flew over the wall into Bedlam Zoo and round into the valley that hid the entrance to the hangar cave. Because he was so tired, he misjudged the landing spot. The plane slid and bounced and skidded into the bush and came to rest against a rock. When he realised he was still alive and he'd calmed down, Bash let out a sigh of relief that he had made it home in one piece. He was despondent about those camels. More than despondent, he was shattered. He needed to see a friendly face and debrief. He leaned forward onto the cockpit control panel and rested for a moment. He knew he'd have to go in and find Manifold or someone to tell them where the little plane was. He expected to get into trouble and he wasn't quite ready to face the music yet.

Suddenly the rock began to move and the little plane joggled and jolted and then bumped to the ground. Bash shouted out—*Oi!* He unbuckled his safety harness, thinking some idiot was playing stupid games. He clambered out the cockpit window muttering to himself and hit the ground prepared for a fight. Only, it wasn't a rock that the plane had hit. It was Shining Teeth. She stood smiling down at him. The fight drained out of him and he looked into her furnace-red eyes and said—*What are you doing here?*

Shining Teeth raised where her eyebrows might have been and said—*I live here; and you?*

Bash stared at her with loathing and rising fear. He opened and shut his mouth like a fish.

Having heard the plane land, a team of beetles, headed up by Manifold ran out of the cave. Some of the newer members tried out—*Hup, hup, hup* as they ran and some of the older members of the gang looked at each other and sneered. Hup, hup, hup was a bit over the top, wasn't it? They managed to put their differences behind them when they saw Shining Teeth near the little plane's awkward position. The beetles checked the craft and realised they'd have to get it up to the hangar to check it out in better proximity to their tools. A pair of runners took off back to Ektek and shortly returned with Hod and Gleam, ready to help Bash if need be.

Ignoring Shining Teeth, Hod went directly to the beetle team and helped lift the little plane following Manifold's shouted orders. He took it in his little wallaby arms and held it carefully to carry it back to the hangar. Many of the beetles followed but some of the newer ones stayed to watch Shining Teeth in action. They'd heard about her but never seen her. Oh, she looked a lot worse than they'd heard. They kept a good distance away.

Shining Teeth targeted Gleam with her firey eyes and grinned from ear to ear—*Goody goody, a welcoming committee. Is there cake?*

Gleam ignored her, which took some doing, and spoke to Bash—*What did you see? With the camels.*

—*Horror, the horror...* Bash stared into the past and smoothed his little frog hand over his shining head. He looked up at Gleam and whispered—*Just horror, plain and simple. I blamed you for sending me out there. I couldn't believe it. I didn't want to see that but now I know what the world is like. Now I know.*

—*Can we rescue them?*

—*There are none left to rescue.*

—*I thought they wanted to be guided to water?*

—*The helicopters. Helicopters rounded them up and shot at them and they all...*

Shining Teeth decided she'd been silent long enough—*Died?*

—*Yes, yes. There were hundreds of them and they were driving them into a sort of canyon and they herded them and then they fell and the blood ran...*

—*Sounds like your sort of picnic, Gleam. Can we go back and get the meat?*

Gleam lowered his head and burst forth in a huge roar of frustration right in Shining Teeth's long thin face. She never moved a muscle. Never even twitched but then she said in that sing song voice—*Ngnair, ngnair, ngnair, ngnair, ngnair,* and, for good measure, added a whispered—*Whachoo gonna do about it?*

Gleam stared at her, fighting his anger. Luckily Hod had returned from delivering the little plane back to the hangar. Sensing there might be trouble between the magnums, although he knew he could do little should a crocodile and a tiger chose to fight, he decided he needed to be there. Even though he preferred to be anywhere else he knew he had a responsibility and he'd had enough of running away. He stepped down beside Gleam and whispered—*She's not worth it. She'll go away if we ignore her.*

Gleam recovered his dignity. He managed to step away and ignore her again. He stared at the surrounding bush and looked at the beetles around them - anywhere but at that blasted crocodile.

—*Shining Teeth, have you ever considered taking a holiday?* Hod stepped up to the croc and said—*Perhaps a trip up the coast? You could catch some waves, chill out on the beach, eat some tourists...*

Shining Teeth stared at him. She could do belligerent extremely well.

—*You've got nothing to lose, here, you know.* Hod covered his confusion by some more words. He realised he was blathering—*We do. Ektek, I mean. Ektek's got a lot to lose if you stay here. Shining Teeth?*

—*Yes, Wally-woo-woo?*

—*Why are you here?*

—*You know, Hoddy, to be perfectly honest, I'm not sure.*

—*Why don't you go away until you are sure?*

Gleam had been chatting to the beetle team and located one of the numbers. He turned to Bash and said—*Listen, Bash, all these numbers have extraordinary tales to tell. Like this one, what's your story again, little one?*

The beetle puffed out its thorax and squeaked—*Number 247* and then added—*Kangaroos.*

—*Kangaroos?* said Bash—*What's wrong with them?*

—*Ah,* said the beetle—*Let me show you,* and, under Gleam's watchful eye, they proceeded to dance around the belligerent crocodile. Shining Teeth rolled her eyes and sashayed her long tail as she left beetle and Bash to their beautiful and informative *pas de deux.*

III

A team of beetles jogged in to the hangar from the bushland—*Hop, hop, hop...*

Manifold looked up from her task at the sticks-and-grass-woven instrument panel to watch them coming in. She wasn't sure about the hip-hop thing but they'd certainly managed to form a cohesive unit and were getting the jobs done. She'd put them to work building the flight simulator to train Eid and it was looking very close to how she remembered the original. Of course, this one would never fly but, as a facsimile, it was a reasonable teaching tool.

Eid was already in place in the makeshift cockpit with Torque sitting on the control panel as coach. They hadn't bothered with walls or niceties; just the dirt floor to sit on and the cockpit with a basic frame of whittled sticks for the windshield. Eid, sitting up on his hindquarters, was not much bigger than Crawf. He was managing to remember most of the controls, what they did and where they were, even with Manifold barking at him. He'd lost count of the times he'd 'crashed' the wingship but aside from his dignity, nothing had really suffered.

The beetles placed their sticks and leaves in an orderly manner in neat little piles around the workspace and then waited for their next instruction. Manifold nodded at them and looked to Torque—*Don't have anything else for them right now.*

Torque shouted through the stick frame at the beetle team—*Well done, everyone. See you back here after your break.*

The learning beetles looked at each other. Strangely, most were disappointed not to have been given their next task but off they went to the feeding station. Probably because they'd been idle for such a long time they were happy to feel like they were doing something with a purpose instead of sitting round twiddling their antennae in a queue.

—*Ow,* said Eid as a small branch hit him on the head during a difficult manoeuvre where Torque explained how to fly during a rainsquall. As she looked at the makeshift cockpit, falling down and completely inadequate, Manifold was less and less confident this bizarre plan would work. She sighed as she had to explain the landing gear system yet again but, after they'd picked up after one of their biggest crashes, Eid finally seemed to have got the hang of the thing. He relaxed into it. Why, he even started making zooming noises. Manifold saw no need to smile.

IV

After dark, Hod drove the tank to the wharf. On board were Bluey, a team of mechanics and Eid. Once they'd dropped Bluey off at the waterfront they headed straight to Pet Met.

Hod shouted back to Eid, the pilot who had never flown—*You'd better listen to Manifold. She's the only thing standing between you and oblivion. We'd rather have the wingship, okay? Don't be reckless.*

Manifold, who was sitting up on the dashboard, snorted tellingly.

Hod flashed her a glance and then had the grace to laugh—*If I can't warn him away from recklessness, then who can?*

They had arrived and Hod roared off leaving Eid and the beetles standing on the path next to the warehouse. Eid's heart was beating like a kettle drum but he was determined to make this work. There was no way he could let Ektek down. No way he would let Antenna down. He would be a proper fully-fledged pilot before this night was out. Or dead.

Eid, Manifold and a team of mechanics climbed up to the roof of Pet Met. It was a tough climb and all of them were exhausted when they made it to the top.

The wingship was still parked by the lift housing. It looked to be still in good condition after spending a few nights in the weather. The beetles, together with Eid's brute strength, made quick work of the simple modifications to the cockpit, removing Crawf's perch and making room for Eid's feathery tail. Once seated in front of the instrument panel Eid was able to run through the basics confidently with Manifold. She started to think he might just be able to pull it off. Crawf had mainly operated the vehicle with his beak and feet while Eid would work with his hands, the occasional foot and, in emergencies, he had the luxury of utilising his very long tongue.

Eid had a reasonably good grasp of the theory. Manifold had impressed upon him that she was the pilot brains and he was her mere puppet. It was imperative he follow her instructions to the letter. Eid replied to her lecture with a swift—*Yes, sir!* And he was not joking. She looked at him to be sure. He seemed sincere and he was. He was clear about following her orders. He had no problem with that. He would much rather be alive and flying than squashed into a can for pet food which could well be the alternative if they were discovered near here.

After the final pre-flight check, which seemed to take forever to Eid and not long enough for Manifold, the group fastened their safety harnesses and prepared for take off. For real. There was plenty of fuel on board and Eid kept his eyes open and his concentration on full alert.

The time came when there was nothing left to check, double or even triple check and they had to make a move.

Manifold and Eid got into position, started the engines and proceeded to taxi out of the parking spot. All clear above and astern and Eid managed to reverse the wingship following the leaf wavers on either side. When the wingship was in position for a safe launch, the two beetles clambered on board and made themselves safe. They were extremely nervous and, without consultation, made sure their personal escape hatches were ready.

—*Moment of truth,* said Manifold and told him what to do. They managed to lift off, albeit a little bit jerkily. Eid was concentrating so hard he barely noticed they were off the ground and flying. They rose above the city. He didn't give himself time to gloat but he did sneak a look out of the window. He could admire the buildings and the cars and the tiny humans looking just like ants crawling on the ground. Suddenly they were losing altitude. The city skyline got closer and closer. Manifold screamed at him—*Lift up! Lift up!*

For a moment Eid froze. He couldn't work out what to do. Then, as the wingship flew close to a billboard with a polar bear standing on the very edge of a tiny icefloe in the middle of a huge expanse of ocean, he managed to galvanise his wits and pull the wingship back up into the sky. Manifold kept quiet and thereafter Eid kept his concentration tight inside the plane. The two beetles in the passenger compartment clicked their seat belts back and shut the safety windows from where they'd been preparing to bail.

Eid kept hold and managed to fly the wingship back to the hangar. They made it home and it seemed to him it had been easy - he'd come through on some kind of autopilot. However, he also felt extremely tired so he knew he must have done something.

With care and precision he put it into the correct parking spot, bang on straight and even. Manifold was impressed with his work but being Manifold, didn't get too carried away with ridiculous exaggerations or grateful exclamations. She patted him on the back and said softly—*We didn't die.* The other beetles let out an exuberant cheer from the back seats.

Eid was exhausted. Sweat dripped down his face, though it was hard to tell with the dark bar across his eyes—*You were worried.*

—*Slightly,* said Manifold—*You were sweaty.*

—*Slightly,* said Eid, wiping his face with his forepaws.

—*You know,* said Manifold—*You keep this up, you could learn to fly the airship, when we get it back together, that is.*

—*Really?* said Eid—*Only…*

—*Yup?* said Manifold.

—*Do you, I mean, is it possible, can we not mention that to Antenna, just for the moment?*

Manifold knew what he meant. She could see Antenna wasn't making Eid's life all that easy but then, she also knew Eid wasn't entirely beyond reproach—*Sure.* She'd keep quiet for the moment.

Torque was waiting for them on their return. He flew up to the cockpit and admired Eid's safe return—*You did good, Eid. I'm sure Antenna will be proud of you. But what she does have to say right now is; get back to the enclosure. Immediately.*

—*She would.*

—*Don't worry, Eid. She'll come round.*

—*Yeah. When I'm a hundred and six.*

—*Hey, there's nothing wrong with being old, you cheeky bugger!*

Eid smiled at the elderly beetle but he held to his melting insides. When would Antenna take him seriously? When? When?

Torque knew what he was thinking. He'd been young once. He'd seen the way Eid looked at Antenna. He wasn't heartless.

—*I feel for you, kid.* Torque was a bit gruff. He wanted to see Eid happy—*Listen, more than my job's worth to tell you what to do but…*

—*What?*

—*Well, I may just have an idea…*

—Any idea's worth a try, Torque.

—Well. Now, I'm not saying it's a sure thing, mind, but… Look, I'll tell you what I'll do. I'll have a bit of a think and get back to you. I want to make sure this'll work before I stick my neck out, and yours. More 'n my job's worth…

Eid looked at the little beetle—*You're a good friend, Torque. You really are.*

Torque was a bit embarrassed but he said—*No more than my job. Come on, hop it.*

Eid rolled his eyes but did. Hopped it, back to his enclosure but this time with a straight spine and a shine in his eye.

V

Bluey managed to find the yacht in question; at least he hoped it was. After examining the lines of boats tied up at the marina, he'd narrowed it down to two that were pretty close to the beetle's description. He made a hurried decision. He prepared to observe one named the *MsTree*, and make some sort of plan. He found part of the wharf buildings that overlooked an area leading up to the yacht in question. He needed to discover which vessel held the smuggled animals because, once boarded, the risk of being taken out to sea while he was searching was too great. He hated swimming. So, he took his time. He made himself comfortable on an old bit of sacking squashed in next to the wall of a barn-like building, perhaps to keep the metal door from rattling in the off shore breeze. He kneaded and pounded the sack until he'd made a tolerable bed. There he would lie and keep that one eye open on the *MsTree*, a sparkling yacht with wooden trim. He was still a bit sore and glad of the opportunity for a snooze. Even though it was night, humans came and went, up the gangplank and down the wharf, carrying supplies and luggage. Bluey supposed the smugglers had the same kind of requirements as did Ektek. They didn't want to advertise their real purpose in life so working under cover of darkness was a necessity. He watched and judged each individual, putting pieces into a plan. Patience, perseverance and positivity, his old mum had always said and although Bluey had run through a few lives, he was still here, and he had no immediate intentions of doing anything but surviving. His patience was rewarded by a flash of a rat, crawling along the rope tethering the boat to the shore. It was a youngster, without highly developed survival skills, so busy concentrating on hanging onto the rope upside down that Bluey was able to pick him off like a ripe plum from a tree. Bluey hugged the rat tightly around the neck with his teeth and trotted around the corner to his bit of sack out of the wind.

—*Now then*, said Bluey, when he'd been able to place his foot firmly on to the captive—*This yacht; the MsTree. Any smugglers on board?*

—*Let me go!* squirmed the rat.

—*You idiot*, said Bluey—*I'll let you go as soon as you talk. Tell me if that's a smuggler's yacht. I need to find a grey cockatoo.*

—*What's a cockatoo?*

—*Just tell me. Are there any prisoners on board?*

The young rat had no reason not to tell Bluey about the three caged creatures stuffed into the wall cavity. So he did. Bluey acknowledged the information but kept his shaven foot heavily on the rat's guts to keep him from wriggling away. He looked out over the yacht, judged distances, timing and calculated for a while, all the while watching the comings and goings.

—*You said you'd let me go*, said the plaintive rat.

—*So I did*, said Bluey. Still that paw weighed heavy on the pinned rat until one group of humans approached the ship. Bluey had already taken note of a particular man and he'd been waiting for his return. This homo sapien was dressed in white, with a hat. His shoulders were decorated with bars of gold trim. Bluey waited until the humans were heading up the gangplank before he let the rat go free. Just as predicted, the youngster bolted. Instead of wasting time and confidence running up the rope, he took the easy option of running up the human's walkway and the humans didn't like it. They jumped away from the rat, snarling and growling at it and that's when Bluey chose to make his move. Just as fast as the rat, Bluey streaked up the gangplank. He let the rat lead him a speedy chase around the foredeck, giving Bluey the chance to show off; leaping and pouncing in such a balletic way he managed to attract the attention of all the humans on board. He came to a dramatic rest in front of the man in white, with the rat clenched firmly in his jaws and a pleasing attitude.

The rat murmured—*You broke your promise*, just before it died.

The people all laughed and praised the cat, who sidled and slid around the legs of all, but most pointedly, the man in white. All were enchanted with the peculiar shaven cat and the humans gabbled and blabbed in their bizarre manner. All this resulted in the dead rat disappearing (eventually to the snake in the wall cavity next to Crawf) and Bluey tucking into a large plateful of shredded fish. Everything was most satisfactory and Bluey curled up and kept his one eye open as the humans prepared to cast off the yacht and leave for open waters. As he slept, or pretended to sleep, he heard a voice. He looked around with his one eye but could see no creature. The voice seemed to be coming from right next to him; from the very wall itself.

—*It's luck, ain't it. Got to make your own luck, I say. In our case, us rats are luckier than most because we eat anything. We're not reliant on a plant that grows on the eastern side of a particular hill that only gets one night of frost every four years. No, that's not the way for us rats. We're adaptable. Flexible. Just like human beings, ain't we. That's why we all get along so nicely. Everywhere they go, we go too. You cats are the same, 'en'cha. Like to eat whatever you can and ingratiate yourselves in deep with the people. Wind them round your little paws, give them a purr and they think you like them - oh I know - I've seen ya - you're already in good with the captain there, 'ain't cha. You suck up to them and they'll fall for yer every time. Give you a tasty bit of fish - after you've caught the rats. Well, you ain't catching me, see. I'm cleverer than that. I've got my reasons for wanting to live, and so have you, I'm guessing. Ever need anything, the name's Salty. Give us a call, sometime.* And then, silence. The rat had gone.

Bluey got up and kneaded his cushion. He'd done enough for one day. He was content having heard from Salty and did not feel the need to contact Crawf. He knew he was near by. That would be enough for the moment.

In his wall cavity, Crawf, however, was desolate. The cage seemed to be shrinking. It was dark. It was cold. The bravado that had driven him this far was sinking as fast as his heart. He was lonely and scared and could hear the bumping and scrapes as the *MsTree* left safe harbour and headed out to open sea and to his future. Whatever that might be.

Chapter Fifty-six

I

This time, the land Bash flew over in his little plane was not arid orange. It was grey, grey green, and it was smooth. Although trees and stunted shrubs dotted here and there, the landscape was barren, except for the rows of sticks like toothpicks that stuck into the surface of the olive grey skin in long intersecting lines. Bash knew these toothpicks to be fencing, enclosing areas designated for farming livestock. This stock was the sort of thing destined to be eaten or drunk or worn by humans. The fence lines stretched as far as he could see over the smooth grey surface of the land. Then, not far from a clump of buildings, he saw an enclosure markedly different from the straight-line paddock surrounds. This fence was much higher, for a start, and the area it enclosed was round, round as Bash's eyes, which stared uncomprehending at the circle. It reminded him of footage he'd seen on a website about circus animals where Ektek had once worked to help save an aging elephant.

The circus-ring fence line was covered in something opaque; a brown sacking material. Some humans marched from the building to the enclosure. Inside the barrier were kangaroos. Their grey brown fur almost blended into the grey of the land. Were they to perform tricks in the circus ring?

As Bash flew the little plane around the curved fence line he saw some of the kangaroos in silhouette and even as he saw them and noted their tall ears and their little arms and their round haunches, these shadows did do tricks. One did a flip and lay still. Then another did a crazy jerky dance and also, fell. The next jumped and flopped its head backwards at an unearthly angle before it too slid to the ground. None of the acrobats got up again. These macabre dances reminded Bash of nothing so much as those camels he had seen cracked down by gunning helicopters.

Bash could not understand what these kangaroos had done to deserve this. Why were they falling? The question pounded in his tiny frog brain as he flew around the enclosure and then, not able to bear the weight of fallen beasts any further, he flew straight across the olive green skin of the land, heading for home. As he flew and looked down from his cockpit, he saw livestock, sheep and cattle grazing in their allotted rectangles. Then he saw more kangaroos almost flying across the ground as they ran and leaped away from the humans that were herding them, racing and jumping, to their circular death tent.

Bash could not understand. Wet lines streamed down his face as he wept salty frog tears, terrible for his skin. He was overwhelmed. What could he do? He had to do something. He could not stand to see this slaughter. Everything was out of kilter, the balance too far gone. It was up to him. He could no longer be a silent witness. He had to become involved. He must make a stronger protest than mere observations. He needed to be effective. As he flew back down and into the Ektek hangar, this time without getting tangled in a crocodile, he seemed to shut down into himself even as he shut off the engines to the little plane. He needed time to process what he'd seen. He would have to formulate a plan, he needed strength and he would need some help. He unplugged his safety harness and lay down on the cockpit floor and went to sleep.

II

The sea welcomed the yacht. It stretched out in front of the wood-trimmed vessel with open arms and inviting sea breezes constant enough to keep the sails trim. The *MsTree's* engines had been cut long ago. Plenty of wind kept them moving and conserved fuel. At least, that's what Bluey surmised. He looked out at the ocean with his one eye open and felt rocked, soothingly. He was calm for the first time since he'd been incarcerated in the lab. He could feel his spine healing with every lungful of sea air. He'd been fed again when he had rewarded his carers with another fat rat from the kitchen. At least, that's what cook was given to believe by Bluey's careful orchestration. Bluey had had further congress with Salty - not seeing him of course - but they understood each other. Bluey had not mentioned Ektek and Salty had not mentioned Crawf. There was no need to speak further at this time. Just at the moment, Bluey could think of nothing better than to lie on deck with a fat belly and contemplate the tiny white tips to the deep blue waves that dimpled the water around them. The sun shone and really, seagoing life was picture-postcard glorious and suited a convalescent cat very well. Bluey turned and slept some more, his one eye open now turned down to the cushion giving any who should care to examine him an impression of extreme relaxation.

The roar as the engines revived woke Bluey again. The water was now flat all around them; greasy and grey. The surface undulated with smooth muscular energy. The smell of fuel was in his nostrils once more. He picked himself up and twisted and turned in his efforts to straighten his poor spine. Then with his feet stretching and pounding, he kneaded his bed again and prepared to make himself comfortable. Idly, he noted another vessel on the horizon. Other objects, of course, all around them, bobbed and dipped in the calm. Plastic buoys, bottles and bits of nylon rope were easily identified floating on the surface nearby but this particular vessel was not flotsam, it was a speedboat, and it was getting closer, fast.

The noise of the engine now moving the *MsTree* through the flat water drowned out the other approaching and it was getting near surprisingly fast. Bluey was startled to see the vessel, instead of zooming past, stop just beside them and edge in even closer until the other boat was beside them. A group of men stood on board, watching the yacht get nearer. It must have been feline imagination that made him think he saw the glint of greed in their eyes.

Bluey stood up. None of the humans on board the *MsTree* had noticed the boat approach. They were all seated around a table eating food. Bluey went in to them and told them about the boat moving alongside but was not rewarded by their attention. They assumed he was chasing tidbits from their plates and they pushed him away with growls. Bluey's urgent shouts only made them more protective of their plates. How could he make them look to their own security?

He then went up to the bridge, where the man in white was looking out to sea, and not having eyes in the back of his head, did not notice the visitors now almost close enough to touch. Again, when Bluey spoke and wound around the man's legs, the man just kicked him aside. As a recent arrival on board, there was no way Bluey could risk further antagonism. He went back toward the side of the boat, calling out as he went—*Salty. You there? We got company. Not friendly. Our human smugglers are unco-operative. We have to fend off the visitors ourselves.*

Bluey was annoyed when he didn't get any response from the walls. He reasoned with himself; what did he expect talking to walls? But he was hoping, almost beyond hope, that those walls literally had ears and might even have some brains between those ears. Was it too unrealistic to expect those rats to make an appearance and not think it a trick to get them to walk into his mouth on cue? But he understood their reticence—*Just come and take a look, will ya?*

By the time he'd made it back to the side of the yacht, two human hands were clinging to the railing - from the outside. He knew he would only have one chance at this so before he leapt he shouted out as loudly as he could to Salty to get on board! Then the man hoisted himself over the side and landed heavily where he fell. Bluey ceased to think rationally. He just launched himself at the man's throat. The sounds that man made were awful, guttural yowls that didn't stop because Bluey was scratching his face, biting his neck and even as the man stood and tried to pull him off, tried to strangle him, tried to push him aside, Bluey dug his claws in, held on and fought for all he was worth. He was gratified at one point to hear a shout from Salty— *Pirates! Keep 'em off, everyone!* Bluey could see he'd been joined by a number of rats who ranged alongside his fight and bit and scratched every human hand that laid onto the side of the *MsTree*.

By now the smugglers on board had heard the commotion and felt the bump from the invading boat. At last they made their way on deck with their weapons and what a screeching and squarking those humans made as they fought to protect the smugglers' yacht. Rats stood aside as heads knocked together with thuds and reports cracked as metal tubes spat fire at the humans. Both pirate and smuggler pointed long cylinders at each other and kept bellowing for good measure. The rats were singing their own battle hymn as they faded into the ship's crevices but Bluey remained silent. He was not at full strength after his brush with science and he needed every ounce of energy to keep attacking this man. He was fighting for his life and the two creatures, man and beast swung together on the very edge of the yacht before the man sagged and toppled into the water.

Bluey went too; dropped into the drink while still clawing at the man's fleshy face. The pirate's compatriots, loud and shrieking the entire time, soon scooped the injured buccaneer out of the water, dripping a stream of red blood. They turned on their speedboat's engine and roared away from the smuggler's yacht, defeated, at least this time. The yacht's engines also blasted full steam ahead and powered away leaving a white foam wake and Bluey bobbing around in the water, floating like a cork.

Bluey, soaked to the skin, having little fur to protect him, trod water miserably. He took another mouthful of brine as the wake smashed up against his face. He loathed swimming. He detested being wet. He spat out water and felt himself sinking. He struggled back up to the surface and kicked hard to stay there. He watched the *MsTree* recede into the calm flat water and could only just hear Salty's parting shout— *Watch out for the sharks, mate!*

III

It was twilight and the humans had left the zoo; all except the security guards who were tucked into their cabin watching football on the television and belching while they ate hamburgers.

The creatures left their cages and stealthily came to the Ektek hangar to watch the floating of the airship and to pay their respects to Helmut. Helmut had been the previous pilot of the airship who had died in the explosion in the desert.

As the airship filled and began to rise into the air outside the Ektek hangar, everyone watching remembered the cassowary, one of the founding members of Ektek, and a wise and thoughtful counsellor to most.

The glow-worms had been enticed outside for once. It was a beautiful night, still and warm. They lined up on the oval balloon as it started to take shape and they spelled out, 'Helmut' with their radiant blue beams.

Eid had never seen the airship inflated before and he was amazed at the size of the craft. To him it appeared to be one of the wonders of the world. It would soon be painted with gaudy signs and ads for the zoo - the animals believed the best camouflage for the airship was something bold and asking for money - but the ongoing argument about whether the advertisement had to be about the pandas or generic Bedlam fundraising had held the painting up. Debate raged around equality; was it unfair to have a figurehead animal taking all the attention away from 'lesser' animals? Who were the lesser animals? While recently-extinct Christmas Island pipistrelle bats faded into the caves of memory, what right did any animal have to attract major funding and focus when other species would certainly disappear for want of attention? Hod, particularly, was vehemently against any image of pandas and fought bitterly to prevent black-and-white fluffy pictures going anywhere near it.

Eid looked up at the airship skin. This was a big test for him. He'd been able to fit the pieces of the jigsaw together, he hoped, without any holes or too much stretching, tacking them in place with careful stitches. The ants and beetles then finalised the seams with their immaculate needlecraft. Frogs had supplied the final layer of glue and weatherproofing - the slime from the back of a burrowing frog was extremely hardy stuff. The spider web had been spun and the fabric woven from three different species of spiders to give the best of elasticity and strength.

The new beetle team had made short work of reassembling the airship engine. Each piece had been cleaned, oiled and polished as part of the education of the disparate beetles. Mandible was impressed with their progress. She had expected the airship restoration project to take much longer. She had, by now, accepted the newbies as part of her team. She'd even found some of them more reliable than her senior workers. She didn't have much to say about it - she always found it difficult to offer praise - but she'd been seen to smile every now and then. The new beetles understood themselves blessed by the head mechanic of Ektek. This was no small honour and the hope of being bestowed with that loveliness made her interminable orders, reminders and chivvying-along much easier to bear.

Rebuilding the cockpit and the rest of the gondola had proven to be an enormous learning curve. If it hadn't been for Eid's height, the ants and beetles would have taken three times as long to get it back together. The gondola held the bridge and a passenger area. Then there was the cargo hold, which was capable of storing the tank and the red steam car. On board emergency gear included water and dried food, and surveillance equipment together with a small satellite dish, which relayed data from other vehicles up to the satellite in orbit. This satellite was still working, dedicated to animals' use by a visionary vet who had gone by the name of Zed.

A conga line of mechanics, both ant and beetle, held the hose pipe steady as it pumped hydrogen gas into the balloon, filling the skin taut up against the frame shaping the airship and lifting the ship into the air once more. It seemed to be holding. Eid breathed a sigh of relief.

Hydrogen was sourced during power generation. Ektek utilised solar panel arrays on the zoo's buildings. The power generated fed into a bank of batteries stored to the rear of the hangar - in a well-ventilated area, of course. Once recharged, those batteries were ready for use in any Ektek vehicle. The build up of hydrogen around the batteries was collected for the airship. The hydrogen had been stored in large tanks waiting for this moment and was now feeding into the airship very effectively. The great ship rose into the air.

—*Check moorings!* shouted Mandible. She ran toward the ropes curled in loops on the hangar floor and sure enough, no one had thought to tether the airship to the ground. It had been so long since their airship had been a useful part of the Ektek fleet; the creatures had become lax in their attitude toward it. A charge of beetles made the airship fast. No floating away on the twilight evening for this vehicle. Mandible shook her head. She didn't like to micromanage, but when it came to beetles there was sometimes no choice. Someone had to think of everything.

The airship was airborne. It looked as if the skin was working just as intended. Eid was stoked when Antenna appeared beside him. He was outwardly calm, of course, when she congratulated him on the work he'd done to get the airship back in service again, although she couldn't help asking—*When did you get a chance to do all this work?*

—*When you were with the family, of course*, said Eid, hardly lying at all. In fact, sometimes when he was supposed to be on duty at night, he had snuck out and worked on the skin but he felt confident that no one would dob him in and no harm had been done. He smiled radiantly at her and turned back to look at his handiwork. Just standing beside her, that was enough, looking in the same direction. When she moved away from him he felt just a touch colder.

Manifold and Eid didn't mention Eid's continued flying practice, both on the wingship and in the cockpit of the airship; and Antenna was none the wiser as she left the hangar. Both Eid and Manifold felt guilty about this omission. Not lying exactly. Just not telling her the full story. Both numbat and bombardier were fully aware that Antenna would think it lying - had she been told. Which she hadn't. And she wouldn't.

Eid looked over to the bombardier beetle—*Thanks, Manifold. I owe you.*

Manifold pulled one of her dried up smiles and said—*Debt repaid.*

Then she strode away to get those beetles moving the gas line out of the way, shouting—*Do you want everyone tripping and breaking their necks?*

As Eid stared up at the finished floating airship, watching the glow-worms take their slow sticky path down the tethering rope, Torque arrived to see Eid—*I think I may have something for you. For you-know-what-and-you-know-who? You interested?*

—*You mean…?* Eid couldn't even say her name. His thin pointy face brightened. As far as he was concerned - bring it on!

—*Yes*, said Torque—*I reckon this has to work. She's got to love it.* He turned slightly to reveal that he was accompanied by a small metallic looking beetle. Her dark green elytra had striking red tips. She had thick bold antenna and an unusual flat thorax. Torque looked around cautiously to make sure they weren't going to be overheard and, even though there wasn't anyone remotely close, he grabbed a hair from Eid's hairy leg and tugged him away to a more quiet spot in the hangar—*Come here. We've got work to do.* Eid barely felt the follicle encouragement but went along with the two beetles to be obliging.

—*This is Mala,* said Torque—*If you follow her dance, you'll learn everything you need to know. Make sure you pay close attention, and copy everything she does, down to the last detail. Understood?*

Eid nodded, without the faintest idea of what Torque had in mind. Still, he followed Mala's direction in the honey-bee dance and shook and shimmied her directions with all his heart and soul.

When Eid had finished he knew the plan and it was ambitious to say the least. As the huge reality of it dawned on his consciousness he slowed the dance down and saw that Torque had joined in. Mala made sure Torque was just as confident in the steps and shakes as Eid had been. Eid was puzzled—*Why are you learning it?*

—*Because,* Torque growled at him—*I'm coming too, of course.*

Eid said—*But…*

Torque ignored him and looked to Mala. He said—*Thank you, Mala.*

—*Yes,* added Eid, remembering his manners—*Thanks, Mala.*

—*You move beautifully for a* bipunctatus. *Tell me,* said Torque—*What are your plans now?*

Mala bowed gracefully to the elder statesman and said—*I think I'd best be moving home. I've enjoyed working on those plugs but I've got family and I've been getting a bit homesick.*

—*I wish you all the best, my dear. Please give my regards to Mandible and tell her I'll speak with her soon. I'm sure she'll be more than amenable to your wishes. Happy journey.*

—*Thank you so much, Torque,* said Mala. She turned to Eid and added—*I hope things go well with… you know. If it's any help, if I were a numbat… I wouldn't hesitate.* She smiled a cute little smile and skipped off back to the mechanics who leaned on their work bench watching the airship reach the end of its tether and float gracefully in the air. The re-floated airship was a real source of pride for these beetles who'd been without aim or purpose such a short time ago.

Eid couldn't help but feel more positive after this encouragement and drifted away on a little dream of his own involving the numbat of his hopes, and celebrations with a large family… Torque brought him back to earth—*So. When are we off?*

—*Torque. This is a long journey. A really, really, long journey. I had no idea you were going to come up with something like this and I do agree, it's a good plan. Big, but good. She might even like it. But if I do it, I think I should do it on my own, don't you?*

—*'If' you do it? You are going to, aren't you?*

—I'd like to, Torque, but…

—I'm an old coot, Eid. I don't know how much longer I've got. Spark's well on top of the job here. He doesn't need me. You do. Life's too short. Let's get cracking.

Eid was going to argue that no, he didn't need an aging darkling beetle on a trip over many seas but figured it was more than his job's worth. Looked like he had a travel partner whatever happened—*I guess we're a team, then. So. Do we have a plan? How do you propose we get there?*

Torque looked up. Eid followed his gaze and stared even harder— *Oh, no…*

—Yup. We'll borrow it and, if we hurry, no one will even notice it's gone.

—'Borrow it'… I see. Eid nodded thoughtfully—*One question.*

—Ask away.

—Just exactly how are we going to 'borrow' the airship without anyone noticing?

All around the hangar, under the airship, over the airship and up the rope ladder to the airship, the beetles and the ants continued their feasting party; cups of nectar clinked, whistles blew and streamers were flung through the air. All around the airship were crowds of insects and animals celebrating the airship's refloating; it was the centre of attention.

IV

Hod concentrated on turning a small metal tube in his hands. He held it up to his eye. It looked smooth enough to him but he put it back to the grinding machine again to make sure. Sparks flew around the space in a fire waterfall. He was wearing a protective apron to prevent his fur catching. He lifted the tube away from the machine and a small voice piped up—*Looking good, Hod.*

The voice belonged to Bash, tiny frog, who was hiding behind a pair of welding goggles lying on the bench. Frogs didn't normally have any place in a machine shop but these were desperate days and called for extreme measures - at least in Bash's eyes - so he sheltered from the spark storm and watched his dastardly plan come into fruition.

Gleam entered the machine cage and lay down in the corner. He had every right to do that because this was where Gleam slept. As he was not a bone fide member of the zoo community, Ektek had to house him. The machine cage was the most suitable place and had been since the first day he'd arrived. He was exhausted and laid his head down on his paws.

It was only the sound of metal grinding that made him lift his head again and look at the wallaby working in the other corner. After a while Gleam couldn't help his curiosity—*What are you doing?*

Hod continued grinding as though he hadn't heard. During a pause in the metal work, Bash replied in his tiny frog voice—*It's for me. For the little plane.*

From under the bench came another voice; a deeper, more sardonic reptilian voice—*We invented it. We like to call it 'machine gun'.*

Gleam stood up and stared through the gloom and around Hod to see that Shining Teeth was also sheltered away from the sparking machine.

Bash, thinking that Gleam was about to give them one of those boring peace and love lectures jumped out from behind the goggles and leapt up to stand on a vice. Hod downed tools because he didn't want to get the frog fried with an accidental spark and Shining Teeth also came out from her cover. The three of them stood staring at the tiger - the frog almost at confronting eye height—*I just have to, Gleam. You didn't see. You don't know.*

—*With the camels. Yes, you told me.*

—*With the kangaroos! They were harvested and thrown away. They were laid waste! I can't bear it, Gleam. I can't sit by in my comfy little cabin and do nothing any more.*

—*What's your plan?*

—*I'm gonna get 'em.*

Gleam let that roll through the cage—*And?*

Bash saw immediately it wasn't enough but he had no more to say.

On the other hand, Hod and Shining Teeth were happy with 'get 'em'. It seemed to work. Punchy. To the point. They nodded to each other and turned back to watch Gleam's reaction.

—*Glad to see you've thought it through,* said Gleam. He indicated Shining Teeth and Hod—*With a little help from your friends.*

—*He's right, Gleam,* Hod insisted —*From that lab to those killing fields, you must have known what he'd witness. You can only see so much before it starts to get to you. I'm glad to help him. Something has to be done; you have to admit that. I admire him. At least he's got guts.*

—*Yes,* said Gleam—*But what's he going to do?*

—*I've got a plan,* said Bash.

—*Glad to hear it. However, Bash, there's action and there's...*

—*... and there's action, yes,* said Shining Teeth—*But come on, realistically, Gleamster, he's just a little frog. What do you honestly believe he's going to be able to achieve?*

—His own demise, without a doubt.

—That's comforting, isn't it, Bash? said Shining Teeth, ever conciliatory. She might even have been trying to goad the frog.

—Shows how much faith you have in me, said Bash. He was feeling goaded.

—Nothing to do with you, little frog, said Gleam. He didn't mean to be patronising, it just came out that way—*It's all about firepower, isn't it? Biggest wins. You're putting yourself in the firing line, don't you understand that?*

—You see, that's just where it doesn't matter to me any more, said Bash—*If I go down after hitting some clumsy thoughtless bastard who's doing the wrong thing because they're ignorant or maybe even because they don't care, then I've achieved something. Maybe they might take a minute to work out what I was doing. Maybe they might start thinking.*

—If they're clumsy and thoughtless why would they even notice you?

—I don't know, Gleam, but I do know I can't just bear witness any more. I have to do something! It's too much… It was wrong. Those kangaroos… They'd done nothing I could see except be in the wrong place at the wrong time. It always comes down to humans. Whatever they want they get. Wherever they want to go - well, off they go - and I'm sick of it. I want to teach them a lesson they'll remember.

—Bash, said Gleam—*I'm worried.*

—Don't be.

—I'm worried for your life.

—It's my life.

Gleam stared at him in disbelief. How could he get through to him?—*I don't see how you're going to make that much of an impression.*

—That's my job, interrupted Hod—*…and I think we can make it work.* He revealed the two guns he'd been working on. They were gleaming, mean looking, a perfect fit for either side of the little plane—*The plane will essentially become a gun turret on the wing. Bash is going to be effective.*

—Until he gets hit.

—He can fly out of the way.

—For how long?

There was no answer to that, and Gleam turned and went back to his bedding. He lay back down, put his head on his forepaws and closed his eyes in unhappy resignation. The other three looked at each other and shrugged. When Hod got back to work, Bash and Shining Teeth took cover again. Hod clenched his teeth and worked the metal against the grinder. Sparks flew and reflected in the little frog's black eyes. Everything was going to plan.

Chapter Fifty-seven

I

Antenna looked up into the sky—*What do you mean, it's gone?* She sat down on her haunches, straightened her spine and looked up. She searched the clouds for any sign of the airship—*It can't have.* Was it possible it might just materialise? Return right there and then? A raven called out, up high against the ceiling of the sky, but no airship could be seen anywhere.

Beside her just outside the hangar, stood Mandible, looking anywhere but up. She was extremely uncomfortable—*Thought you knew.*

—*Of course I didn't know. With Eid gone... That means I'm in the exhibit.* Then, another realisation struck Antenna—*More than just part of the family, I'm part of the breeding program... Oh... Where did he go?*

—*Sorry, Antenna, I don't know. They'll be back...*

—*They? Who else?*

—*Torque.*

—*Torque? What the...? He's too old to head out on actions! Anyone else?*

—*Just Torque.*

—*Torque. Why didn't he tell me? Hang on.* Antenna thought this through—*Oh, no.* She stood up, horrified, as she realised that Torque must be a hostage—*Eid must have threatened him...*

—*Torque wasn't threatened, Antenna.*

—*Why else would he have betrayed me like this? He's the head of security!*

Manifold was very apologetic. She knew it wasn't enough but she hung her beetle head just a little bit—*I thought it was a normal action.*

—*You helped them?*

—*We did the pre-flight and loaded their supplies.*

—*No one thought to mention it to me?*

—*You weren't here.*

—*No, I was doing what I'm supposed to be doing. Okay, where's that number now?*

—*Gone.*

—*Gone?*

—*Buzzed off after she'd passed on the details. She'd been here for weeks, you know. Helped with the spark plugs. Needed to get home to her larvae.*

Antenna sat down again and looked at Mandible. Then she rubbed her paws over her face—*Right. Of course. Any idea when they might get back?*

—*Don't know.*

—*Mandible. I thought more of you. I really did. I'm going to attempt a radio link...*

—*Er, not fixed yet.*

Antenna stabbed the head mechanic with a look that said 'that'd be right' before she said—*I'm trying anyway, on the off chance. If anyone remembers something, anything, please, let me know.*

—*I will. Sorry, Antenna.*

Without acknowledging her, Antenna marched back inside the hangar, filled with worries on a number of fronts. If anyone had asked her she would have said she was concerned for the airship itself. It could already be seriously damaged. It had only just been repaired! It was the prize of the Ektek fleet, it was fragile and it was needed to run rescues. It was an extremely useful vehicle and not to be used foolishly by a beginner numbat who could easily get himself killed. She might also admit to worrying about Torque whom she had known for all of his life. As head of security she had always been able to rely on him and she had no idea why he wouldn't have told her about going off on some bizarre action with no research at all, taking with him a disobedient numbat that needed to be where Antenna could see him because she was supposed to be his doppelganger and if he didn't get back from this childish running away nonsense they'd be found out and she'd have to stay in the enclosure and they'd think she'd changed sex and she'd have to undergo invasive scientific tests and her keeper might recognise her from the old days and it would cause all sorts of troubles and she'd probably get dissected in the name of further studies and she wouldn't have him there to blame and he could have just thought for one moment about leaving her like this. If he were in front of her right now wouldn't she have some things to say to his pointed stripy face! How dare he go anywhere without telling her? Did he have no respect for her as an Ektek colleague? As a fellow numbat? As a friend? As... Anything? Did she mean so little to him? Did he not think of her at all? How could he endanger himself like this? What would she do if anything happened to him? Why couldn't he have come to talk to her himself? Why didn't he say goodbye?

She brushed the tears away. She was beyond angry and she muttered all the way to the control centre and found as she entered the cave that her foul temper was more than matched by Hod. He was shouting at a computer screen open at the Bedlam Zoo website. He was on the yellow-footed rock wallaby page and he was very angry—*I just knew it. I knew it.*

—*What?* said Antenna, wishing she didn't have to. She stared at the screen trying to work out what had made him so upset—*Is it the pandas?*

—*Oh, well, it's more than just zedding pandas now, isn't it. I was checking to find out when they're landing on us…*

—*When?*

—*Soon but that's not the main thing…*

—*You're moving?*

—*Yeah we're moving, oh, yeah, they've got us a most salubrious position, you'll be jealous, you will, of all the yellow-footed rock wallabies now; down next to the waste transfer station, isn't that a step up in the world and get this: we're part of a 'Special Program' so I guess you could say that's a blessing because at least that means they're not getting rid of us. Treating us like dirt but still feeding us; ain't that a blast?*

— *What 'Special program'?*

—*Turns out, us yellow-footed rock wallabies are playing surrogate parents. I was right all along! Some of those joeys I thought weren't mine really aren't mine. The zoo's been putting stolen embryonic joeys from wild brush tail wallabies into my wives' pouches and, by the way, what's happened to my children? That's what I'd like to know. How dare the zoo treat me like some kind of guinea pig? It's a violation of my personal rights, that's what it is. My right to be a parent has been stolen from me. I don't mind helping another species in trouble, of course I don't but, come on, stealing a fellow's kids and plonking a cuckoo in the nest, how'm I supposed to take that lying down?*

Antenna sat at the computer and prepared to use the radio to call the airship—*I don't know.* Antenna was so glum by now - Hod's fiery indignation had somehow cancelled out her own anger - all she was left with was bare misery. She didn't know where they were or how to get hold of them and she was worried sick she'd not see either Eid or Torque again. Particularly Eid and she hadn't even known she'd cared that much about that annoying numbat and that shocked her. She wanted him back at Ektek safe and sound so she could throttle him. Or at least be near him. She was shaken and she was sad and after a considerable time of venting his selfish spleen, even Hod noticed she had nothing to say for herself—*What's up with you?*

—Nothing.

—Don't give me that. Give.

—Oh. It's ludicrous.

—What?

—Eid…

—Oh, yeah?

Antenna didn't hear the taunt. She continued her report in a business-like manner. She had no time for frivolous chitchat—*… and Torque. They've stolen the airship and gone off to do some stupid secret activity on their own.*

—Stolen the airship? Even Hod was taken aback by the audacity of this—*Torque and Eid? Where did they go?*

—No one knows. Manifold hasn't fixed the sound on the airship so, this is a long shot but; she spoke into the mic—*Uptek? Uptek? Come in please. Over.*

Both Antenna and Hod waited for a moment and listened to the white noise coming through the computer speaker. They looked at each other and then she tried again—*Uptek? Can you hear me? Eid? Torque? Come in please? Over.*

—At least they're doing something, said Hod—*Got to give them that.*

Antenna sat back on her haunches again, giving up on the radio for the time being. She sighed—*I don't know, if they're not dead or mangled in an exploded mess then I suppose, maybe, they just might be able to help someone. There's huge queues of beetle numbers waiting with emergencies we can't ever seem to get to. Then again, we're talking about Eid. He's never been on an action before and Torque's not getting any younger…*

—Bash has taken on another one.

—Another beetle? Where's he gone?

—You don't want to know.

—I don't?

—He's going to defend wild ducks.

—Defend? A frog in a plane?

—An armed plane.

—He's armed? Hod?

Hod felt a rush of guilt and he didn't like it. He hoped she wouldn't ask who helped Bash. Right now, Hod didn't want to lie to her because he knew full well she wouldn't like the truth and he didn't want to see any more disappointment in Antenna than he could see already. Deciding attack was the best form of defence he said abruptly—*What you looking at me for?*

—I can't believe this. I thought Ektek'd agreed what was right for us…

—You agreed.

—*No.*

—*Yes, you did. You thought everyone was like you. At one stage, I thought I was too but, news flash, Antenna, not everyone is like you.*

—*We're all working for the same thing, aren't we?*

Hod felt another wave of guilt and cast around for another subject—*Yes, yes, yes and in order to do that we have to stay together, work smarter and work stronger but we've got a problem; we're running out of resources. We're losing our trained workers. We need Crawf back. We need to rescue Crawf.*

—*Crawf? But he wanted...*

—*Crawf's my brother, Ant. My Ektek brother.*

—*I know.*

—*I was thinking of Smacker. If they're still at sea...*

—*... we could ask...*

—*Yeah, Gumfluff to go out...*

Antenna had to think for a moment before she remembered what *Intek* was doing at the moment—*They're out in the marine park...*

—*Illegal fishing again?*

—*How did we get into this mess, Hod?*

—*I don't know.*

—*I don't either. I can't see how Ektek can come back from this... It's like all of us, Ektek itself, is endangered. There's these threats surrounding us, threatening creatures all over the world and our own organization is so fraught with troubles inside we can't answer or protect any one.*

—*It's going to be all right.*

—*You hope.*

—*What else have we got, Ant?*

Hod and Antenna looked at each other for a moment. Neither knew the answer, neither knew what could possibly lie ahead. Antenna sighed and looked back to the mic.

Hod also sighed. He looked back to the pandas on the Bedlam website. Oh, those zedding pandas. If Bash were here, the way he felt now, he'd point that little gun turret right at those blinking fluffy bears himself.

II

Eid and Torque were happily floating along in the airship. Eid possessed a natural talent for flying which was unusual in a numbat. He seemed to be able to predict the best of the air currents but, he insisted, he was just lucky. The weather was beautiful, the clouds were white and sculptural, and the landscapes were dramatic and magnificent. Eid was transfixed with everything he saw out of the window—*This is the life, isn't it, Torque?*

The airship was on cruise control as they shared a bite of the special zoo custard anteaters enjoy so much. Torque munched and said with his mouth full—*Wonder if they've missed us?*

—*Nothing they can do about it*, said Eid—*We'll just keep on, get the job done and head home all safe and sound.*

—*If everything goes according to plan.*

—*By the way*, Eid turned to Torque—*What is the plan?*

—*We've got a plan?*

—*We know what has to be done*, said Eid.

—*That's half of it.*

—*What's the other half?*

—*'How', my friend, 'how' we do what has to be done*, said Torque—*That's more than my job's worth, I'd say.*

—*Wait, there it is. Okay. Let's see if we can fly over the farm, take a little shufti, without anyone seeing us.*

Eid flew steadily over the bizarre place. The two creatures looked down on the ground to see the entire farm was fenced with dark brick walls. Inside the walls were two small human sized buildings surrounded by a series of rectangular metal wire boxes. The boxes filled the space neatly, like containers on a ship, which meant there was nowhere to land and nowhere for the airship to hide. Neither he nor Torque liked what they saw. They were going to have to act, and quickly.

III

The extra weight of the guns mounted on the wings made the little plane difficult to fly. Bash was frightened by how long it had taken him to gain altitude. He'd spent more time and fuel than he'd expected on the journey. He'd needed to practice turning, banking slowly in a much wider curve than he was used to take. He knew he hadn't thought this armament plan through properly but he was determined to carry on with it. For the first time he felt powerful and he meant to make the most of it.

He managed to catch a small breeze and used it as if he were a glider to help him slide through the air as he came closer to the coast. He started to sing to himself - a little war song - a frog hymn of might and supremacy. He was a frog warrior and he was going to fight and he was going to win. Din, din, din; din, din…

He flew into wetlands smooth as a mirror surrounded by grasses and reeds soft as fur. The scattered trees were silent sentinels raising their arms in supplication, into the warm embrace of the soft galah coloured sky.

Over the hum of his engine he imagined he could just hear the dawn chorus of wild frogs. Perhaps they were particularly raucous this morning in support of his new power; his battle hymn was rousing them too. The little plane swooped down over the shallow lakes - a place where sea met shore and lakes met sea - and seeped and spilled - and made land wet. This was the place where fish came to breed and mosquitos ruled the airwaves. Waterfowl travelled enormous distances in their annual migrations across the planet to find their ancestral wetlands, to bring up their families and to travel forth yet again. How did they know where to go? Only the birds themselves could tell.

Bash's plane was about the same size as a large duck and he tagged along with a flock as they flew across the watercolour land-scape. Their calls were audible over the purr of his engine and for once the frog felt truly like a bird. Being off the ground and away from water seemed just as natural to his amphibian world as he flew among these beings of grace.

The waterfowl stretched their necks further through the air and turned into the breeze. Bash, having learned from his early morning experience with his newly weighted wings, took his time to bank around and when he was relaxed enough to look ahead again he saw that the flock had been depleted and there, there was a bird falling even as he looked. Falling, turning with wings useless, flapping open as if an umbrella in a storm, dropping into a straight down plunge.

Now he could hear the pops, cracks and their echoes across the water and across the sky. A clap followed by another clap grew into applause scattering across the dawn.

So this was the duck hunt. The birds fell from the sky like boul-ders. This time Bash did not have to stand by helplessly and bear witness. Now was his moment, when his blood pumped and he remembered the satisfaction of computer game carnage. He was filled with energy and a determination to put things to rights. Now he'd levelled up from mere pathetic games. Now Hod had given him control over life and death for real and it felt wonderful and he felt commanding and the need for retaliation welled up in him. It was a solid feeling. He was clear in his purpose and he took hold of the plane's controls and surveyed his options.

As Bash took another turn over the water's edge, he noted small islands and inlets where clumps of strange looking plant material bunched unnaturally. Then, out of the corner of his eye, he noted movement. He saw a bulky human silhouette lift the metal tube to his shoulder and looked up to see another duck fall almost immediately as a result and then he saw the dog pouncing out of the shadows. Bash took his plane closer into the clump and let loose a round of ammo from one weapon. The force spun back into the plane and he rocked unnervingly before he could get control and fly level again.

Bash rolled around and flew back over the camouflage. He was so angry he could not think evasively. He could hardly think at all. He rose too late as that man took aim and shot. Like a duck, the small plane plummeted also.

The plane swan dived into a flat stretch of idyllic water with a genteel splash. Then silence. The dawn streaked the sky with watery blood and the lake's surface tension reflected all those rosy hues while the indigenous frogs continued their endless glottal conversations.

Chapter Fifty-eight

I

Crawf was still stuck in solitary confinement. Although he was physically in his little cage in the wall cavity of the *MsTree*, he had entered a kind of dark zone. His mind floated in and out, through all sorts of memories and dreams, even dating from the time of his egg days. Although he was cold, sometimes he felt hot; burning with the memory of sun reflected from the airship, broken in the desert, as he navigated the plane over it, ignorant of the whereabouts of the pilot. Sometimes he felt the despair he'd felt when he'd been held captive by crocodiles on the banks of a far off muddy river. Then his mind would shift again and he would find himself at home with his partner Sunday by his side and then he would remember that she had died and then he would mourn her all over again.

Into the mist of all these reminiscences and sensations swirling in his brain came an impression of Ektek but it was not a sight familiar to Crawf. It was a view from the sea. It was not Crawf's normal aspect, as a creature of the sky, and Crawf understood that a whale was communicating with him and that he did not have to do anything but let his mind open. Since he was thirsty for communication of any kind, Crawf let himself remember Gleam, Gumfluff and, from them, his mind pictured Antenna, Hod and Bash. All the Ektek crew were remembered and shared in this most pleasant of understandings.

Crawf was not sure why he was able to communicate with the whale - this had previously been beyond his capabilities - and he imagined it must be Smacker himself, a friend to Ektek. Crawf felt such an uplifting of his spirits as a result of knowing this he sent a rush of gratitude to the huge beast that must be drifting just underneath the yacht. It felt wonderful to be in contact with Ektek, even as strangely as this.

Smacker wondered if Crawf was looked after and Crawf was able to communicate the image of his seed tray and recently replenished water bubbler. However, he was less happy about the fact his beak had also been retaped while they were filling his food dish. Smacker informed him the yacht was nearly at their journey's end. They were already in a harbour approaching a busy port. This must surely be his destination. That explained why the humans wanted him silent.

Smacker wondered why Crawf had chosen to make this journey. Crawf send images showing that he'd worked all his life for other creatures and serving the disadvantaged. Now he believed it was his turn to seek fulfilment, among his own tribe. Crawf painted a wonderful picture of living among the Palm cockatoos in dream family existence. If only...

Smacker sympathised and hoped all would go well for Crawf. He was able to reassure him he was nearing his destination - Philavian. Smacker communicated that most of Philavian's work was above board and very visible. Human tourists could visit the haven of bird life, and have their photos taken as they fed colourful birds. They could buy colourful feathers and even birds to take home as living pets. Philavian was a commercial world of colourful, feathered friends. However, behind the colourful tourist façade operated another, more determined, moneymaking venture; a breeding centre for secret bird collectors, and Smacker feared that that was where Crawf was destined to be taken.

Crawf shaped the thought that he was impressed by Smacker's knowledge. Smacker replied that whales knew many things but that was their sorrow. To know is not the same thing as to have an effect. Smacker imparted wistful feelings; if only the waters were theirs to roam freely as in ancient days. So many interests and so many points of view crowded the world now that it was difficult for whales to live in such a teeming soup. Who knew what would join them in the brew next. A submarine? An island of shredded plastic? A ton of poison effluent? A fishing net over a mile long? A great missile fired from a factory ship sailing in formation with a team of other ships (ironically these were the very strategies learned from the tactics of killer whales). Smacker and his family were hard pressed keeping their heads open to approaching danger from all angles, evolving exit plans at all times.

Smacker could not stay long in port, he was in danger even now. His parting thoughts were about saying hullo to the cat and then Smacker's presence faded from Crawf's head. Crawf wondered out-loud—*Cat? What cat?* But of course his beak was taped and all that came out was a gurgle.

II

Bash returned to consciousness in a rush. He was cooking. He was stinking hot. He was drying out. He could smell water nearby. He was still strapped into the plane and it appeared to be above the water somehow. Bash didn't think about this. His only thought was that he had to get wet, urgently. He could only think of water. Water was essential. Nothing else mattered. He was panting and clumsy as he snapped out of his safety harness, clambered out of the window and climbed out onto the wing, all the time, water, insistent, water, throbbing, water, yearning, water, flooding his mind, his soul, his guts... Get wet, get wet, absorb water, now, now, now, and he leapt as far as he could off the wing, flew over the mud and plunged into blessed water.

The water was fresh and cool and his skin returned to froglike and he swam through the water effortlessly and it was whole-heartedly, skin-full, marvellous. He was in no particular rush to get back into that heat again and he stayed where he was, relieved to be swimming, even chewing some delicious silage just to top off his satisfaction.

As he swam, recollections of flight and of fighting solidified in his mind. He remembered aiming at the hunter and he remembered seeing the shooter's eyes, the whites of his eyes, and then he remembered an impact and tumult and then... Nothing. What had happened to him? Of course, this was no game. He'd been shot. He realised how lucky he was to be alive. He'd been shot down by real pellets and he had real consequences to face.

As his memories clarified he realised he'd best return to the little plane and assess the damage. He knew he was far from Bedlam and he'd have to contact a beetle. Of course, the beetle might not get heard when it returned to the crowded hangar but it was the only thing a frog in the wilderness could do to get rescued. Bash knew it was time to get out of the pond and get serious.

As he came closer to the edge of his puddle of lake he realised that what he had taken for a boulder on the shore was moving. The boulder moved to where Bash was going to climb out of the water. The boulder lowered its head to the very edge of the water and Bash stared at it from under the surface. Bash then understood, at the same moment, that the boulder was in fact a large ginger cat, easily within reach and that Bash was about to become lunch. Strangely, though, as Bash backwatered frantically, the boulder cat made no effort to swipe at him. The cat sat as if it were waiting for him. Waiting for Bash? A cat?

Bash cautiously rose to the surface again, took another, closer, look at that cat and wondered. Then he broke the meniscus and, bizarrely, his hunch proved true. He swam to the water's edge and said to the ginger cat—*How many lives have you got left?*

—*Could ask you the same question, cobber.*

Bash climbed out of the water and sat in the shade of a coolibah tree—*Your whiskers have grown.*

—*Ta, mate.* Bluey stretched out in the sun nearby, close enough to chat if need be. They sat together companionably for a time before Bash asked—*What happened to me?*

—*You got taken for target practice. At least, the plane was. Downed into the lake. I just happened...*

—*Just happened?*

—*Too right, mate. I fished you out. No problem,* said Bluey. Then he changed his mind—*Oh, I tell a lie; it was a bit of a problem. Had to get wet, didn't I. I resent getting wet, seriously hate it, but seeing as it was you, I got over it.*

—*Did I say thank you?*

—*Bit drowned, you were. Hung you out to dry, over there, see?*

Bash looked over at the little plane, which was hanging to dry in the sun in a small shrub, tilted so any water could run out. No wonder he'd been hot.

—*Thank you.*

—*No worries, mate. I owed you one. Though I'd say me debt's all clear. That's twice I've taken a bath for you Ektek lot. Even though, hey, don't get me wrong, I'm acutely grateful to you for not being hooked in that bastard cage any more.*

Bash thoughtfully wiped the last of the juicy mosquito he'd nabbed out of the air off his chin—*The other?*

—*Crawf.*

—*Crawf?*

—*Yeah, you know, your cockatoo? Out on a yacht in the middle of the sea? Had a pirate infestation, the rats and me had to take it all a bit serious and I got meself dropped overboard in all the drama.*

—*Crawf?*

—*Don't think he even knew about it. We got rid of them and the smugglers sailed on.*

—*Leaving you behind...*

—*In the drink. But I climbed up onto a bit of some plastic drum or something quick smart, well, given the large fin that cruised past, I shot out like a rocket, I don't mind telling you I don't think I've ever moved so expeditiously and, anyway, after a bit of time in the hot sun, chewing on a fish or two that wandered by, that brought me over here.*

—Lucky. For me, as well.

—Don't go on about it, mate. Could get embarrassing.

So Bash didn't and the two companions dozed again for a moment or two. The lake water lapped at the edges of the reeds, the air was mild in the shade and Bash snapped awake with a guilty jump— *Bluey? I've got to get back.*

—Yeah, of course, look, I don't think you'll be flying that… She's onkus.

They both looked over at the little plane. It was riddled with tiny holes from shot pellets - some embedded still in the surface of the wings - some holes you could see sky right through the entire workings.

—No, said Bash—*Guess not.*

—I reckon I can carry you.

—No need, said Bash—*I'll call a beetle.*

—What about them number queues they were all jabbering about? Don't they take them in order? When do you think they'd get to your beetle?

—It was a long flight to get here.

—It'll be a longer walk then.

—I could still call a beetle.

—Nah, let's crack on. Though, I do have a slight complication…

—What? said Bash, dreading the answer.

—You mean; 'who?' Me girlfriend.

—You old dog, said Bash.

—Hardly, said Bluey.

III

Antenna lay asleep in the numbat enclosure. She appeared completely dead to the world. She'd been working around the clock for what seemed days on end and even her dreams were full of Ektek business. The numbat children were talking to their mother - who knew the stress that Antenna was under - asking when Antenna would be up, ready to play. The mother shushed the kids saying—*Leave the poor creature alone. She needs her rest, children.*

When Antenna did turn over and twitch awake, it was not due to youngsters wanting to play. She had a beetle whispering in her ear. It was Spark and he hissed—*Have you seen it?*

—What?

—Get up. Look.

Groggily, Antenna got to her feet and came to the front edge of the numbat enclosure as guided by the Christmas beetle.

—*Look up.*

Antenna did as she was told and when she'd wiped the sleep out of her dark striped eyes she gasped in surprise. For there, hovering in full view above the zoo, was the airship—*What are they doing?*

Spark was too busy staring up to reply.

As they watched, the cargo hold opened and something began to be lowered to the ground. It was rectangular in shape and lowered jerkily down to the enclosure outside the vet's building. As it came down lower, Antenna and Spark could see there was a creature inside - bigger than both of them but smaller than Gleam. It had dark coloured fur and filled the cage almost completely. The cage was built of heavy iron bars. The bars were thick and rusty. Up in the airship something snagged on the winch and one of the ropes held too short. The cage jolted and tilted at a frightening angle. The creature trapped in the cage moaned as it slid to one corner. It was a piteous sound.

Antenna sighed. This was too dreadful. The living creature was squashed into that cage and when it moved even Spark let out a surprised squeak - and that was saying something because nothing much had surprised Spark lately - both numbat and Christmas beetle saw the snout and the eye of a bear. The cage continued its uneven descent and, finally, clonked onto the ground. Then, from their vantage points all around the vet's building, hundreds of beetles, Spark among them, flew to unlatch the catches holding the ropes to the rusty cage. The airship winch wound up the ropes and floated away, presumably to the Ektek hangar.

Antenna waited impatiently, surrounded now by the other numbats, staring after the airship. They all knew that Eid had decided to run his own action and they were just a little proud of his initiative but they didn't like to rub Antenna's nose in it. There was something about that Eid, they thought. He was destined for great things.

When Spark returned to the numbat enclosure and alighted on a rock near Antenna, she almost spat in her eagerness to hear his report—*What?*

—*A bear. Doesn't look well.*

—*What were they thinking?*

—*The human vet is already in attendance and not looking up at all. They're only concerned for the bear.*

—*One of those humans is bound to look up.*

—*I don't think they're interested. They only care about her.*

—*What about security?*

—*I've asked a couple of pals to keep an eye on them and so far they just seem to think it was a normal zoo delivery.*

—*You're saying they could get away with it?*

—*Amazing though it seems, they just might.*

—*Oh, what would I give to be there now. Would I give them a piece of my mind...*

—*I'll go see what's happening?*

—*You'd better tell them to expect me. I'll be there as soon as we get shut down.*

—*I'll tell them.*

—*Come back and let me know what's going on...*

Antenna was anxious to get down to the hangar and see Eid, and Torque of course, for herself. Why did she have to be on display now? This was awful. The mother numbat shooed her two children away from Antenna, fearing her frustration might get taken out on them. She stood beside the jumpy numbat and, after a time, laughed at her irritation—*I told you he'd be back.*

—*You didn't mention the bear.*

—*Anything Eid does is to impress you, Antenna. He thinks very highly of you, you must know that. And I can tell you, Eid isn't one to play with anyone's affections lightly. Think about that before you chew his ear off.*

Antenna was certainly thinking of him. That was for sure. She had no idea what she was going to say to Eid but she knew it was going to be important. She had a feeling that what ever happened with Eid next would change her life. Absolutely.

IV

Bluey's girlfriend returned from her hunting session in the wetlands to find Bluey and Bash sitting in the shade of a coolibah tree stripping reeds. She was a large bulbous cat. Her muscles had outgrown normal cat parameters. To Bash she looked more like one of the jaguars back at Bedlam and he decided he would give her the same respect he reserved for any other big cat; distance and plenty of it.

They had assembled a small pile of reeds around the little plane, which lay next to them on the ground. The reed bending and stripping was difficult work for untutored cat's paws and Bash was not any help at all, save being a good companion. They had not got very far in their plans. When they explained they intended to make a kind of backpack or harness which Bluey would wear while they walked back to Bedlam Zoo, she just laughed in their faces.

—Leave it to me, she said and left their shady spot with much the same kind of spring as that jaguar.

Bash and Bluey looked at each other.

—What's she up to? asked Bash.

—Ah, she's got a mind of her own, that one, said Bluey admiringly— *We'd better follow her.*

They dropped their reeds, pleased to be rid of them, and followed the path of the she-cat. Bash rode on Bluey's neck and they made good time after her fleet steps.

After a short journey through the bush, Bluey cautiously approached what smelled like a human campsite. In a clearing, they could see his girlfriend, busy making friends. Bash could hardly believe his eyes—*There she is!*

Bash and Bluey nestled in close and peered out from behind a leafy shrub.

—But what's she doing? Bash was astounded to see her standing on a dog's back as though she stood on dogs' backs every day. The dog did not seem to be upset, in fact, what Bash was about to witness was nothing at all like an upset dog.

Bluey whispered—*Poor bastard can't groom himself through all the mud and he's getting annoyed by all those mozzies so, what's a creature to do?*

Get a back scratch, it seemed and there she was, that giantess of a cat, scratching the big brown dog's hindquarters. She must have partially sheathed her pin-like claws because she was briskly scratching the bird dog as though she were digging a hole in his back in which to do her business. After a bit of this he lay down - or rather he kind of flopped down - and she moved acrobatically to keep balance with him, as if she were a circus lion running on a large coloured ball, as he hit the ground. She was now able to work on his side and she did so with aplomb. When she hit 'that' nerve, his leg went into an automatic running reflex and his face dissolved into an incredibly silly grin. The dog seemed to have lost all reason and became what Bash could only describe as 'ga ga doglally'.

—How can she do that? said Bash.

Bluey thought for a moment—*She grew up on a farm.*

Without too much further fuss, the she-cat, with the help of the grateful dog, was able to sneak them on board a huge four-wheel drive - grey, shining, new, stuffed with muddy men dressed in bulky camouflage, together with their guns and carrying on like a flock of galahs. They kept their dog in the front of the vehicle with them, and every now and then he'd look back through the little rear window and stare at them. The agreement between cats, frog and the dog was simple. If they kept out of sight, he'd bark when it was safe for them to leave the truck when they arrived in a built up area. If they let themselves be seen by a human all bets were off and he'd have to chase them. Bluey and Bash had agreed this was fair enough and hoped like billy-oh they wouldn't get seen.

In the back of the vehicle, the blokes had piled tents, cold storage bins, camouflage and their booty, all covered with a flapping blue tarpaulin. Bluey had been able to pass the little plane up to his girl-friend into the back of the truck unnoticed. She stacked it beside the feathered payload. Bash clung to Bluey's neck and they jumped up into the tray and buried themselves. Then they lay, two cats and a frog, hidden under a heap of dead ducks. The flopping birds were all the colours of the rainbow, their feathers incandescent. Their blood served as moisturiser for a sore frog. All they could hope was that the humans were going somewhere near their zoo and that no human looked back. They were in for a ride anyway, wherever they went.

As the engine started up and the four-wheel drive hit the dirt road, the two cats made no bones about feasting on a waterfowl each, and Bash, figuring the birds were already dead after all, just moved away from the cats while they ripped and gnawed at the flesh until they were full and tried not to think about them. Then they lay back, made themselves comfortable and, eventually, snored. Bash must have slept for a while too. He woke again when the dirt road changed to a smoother faster journey and the wheels changed cadence, humming along. He watched the cats for a while until he realised that Bluey was also awake - watching him with that bizarre one eye.

They looked at each other for a moment before Bluey asked— *What do you reckon me chances are?*

—*What for?* asked Bash.

—*Getting back in to Ektek.*

Bash didn't know how to tell him he thought his chances were nil. He crumpled up his little frog forehead and worried before he said— *Um, it's difficult, isn't it. I mean, the facts are... Well, to put it bluntly... No one likes cats, Bluey. You know that.*

—*I know, I know. It's, well, it's just such a hard life on the street, you know?*

—*You're not on the street.*

—*Out here? Pedant, are ya? I'm telling ya, still nasty in woop woop, mate. Got to keep out of them foxes' way, there's goats and pigs and all these sharp shooters gunning fer yer. Never get a moment's peace. Not to mention hunting all the time. You wouldn't believe how exhausting it is trying to get tucker. What I wouldn't give for the sound of a tin opener and a spoon hitting the side of an easy feed. Saw a fox cracking into a duck egg, easy as, so that's been a blessing...*

—Not for the ducks.

—No, well, they got their own problems, don't they, but Bash, you know, the main thing is, look at her. She's going to have kittens...

—Yours?

—Who else? Cheeky blighter...

Bash didn't think the cats should stay at Ektek. He knew full well no one else would either so he watched the cats in silence. Maybe they might be able to find them a home of sorts. At least they were travelling in the right direction at the moment. They'd see when they got there. Where ever that was...

The she-cat groaned as she re-settled herself. She was huge, bulging and a green fire flashed in her eyes that screamed at Bash—*You're a snack! Tasty nibblet! One day, you're going to be all mine! Crunch, crunch, lunch...*

Bash turned away, made sure Bluey was between him and her and he sincerely hoped that heap of ducks would last till they got somewhere where they could work out where they needed to be. He studiously avoided looking at the great she-cat and made himself think good happy thoughts.

The truck droned on and on and on, but to where? They'd find out soon enough. The corroboree frog settled down to an uneasy snooze, slimy and damp with blood from the dead.

V

Antenna ran down the tunnel to the control cave. There was no one there. If she'd been thinking clearly she might have noticed there was no one in the tunnels either. All she knew was she could feel something was wrong. The hangar was silent. Everything was still. She raced to the airship and climbed the rope ladder up into the body of the craft. There she found a group of beetles standing in the cargo hold. They were all very serious. Antenna looked at each of them and saw Mandible was among them. She asked her—*What?*

Mandible replied—*Torque.*

—Where? said Antenna.

—In the cockpit.

Antenna ran to the cockpit to find Gleam and Hod already there, standing with Eid. They were looking at the console where Torque was lying on a makeshift cot. He must have slept there for the duration of their long journey. He was looking frail and weak. It was clear this was the end of his pilgrimage.

Beside him was Spark. He was trying to stop himself from weeping. He was unsuccessful. He continually sniffed and gasped for each tearful breath.

Torque looked up at the young beetle who had worked beside him for so long and whispered—*More than my job's worth to see all you... Glum bum. Take care... Of each other, won't you?*

—*Don't you dare, Torque.* Spark said, choking within his crying— *You're getting better, do you hear me? Who else is going to tell me what to do?*

Torque sighed and turned in his little bed as though in some pain. When he regained his composure he cleared his throat and said— *You've been telling yourself what to do for long enough now.* After a further bout of strength gathering he started again—*We all have our time, young flibberty gibbet. Make sure...* His voice faded and his eyes dulled. He seemed to be slipping away...

Spark caught his own breath and leaned forward as if to will Torque to keep living. Slowly Torque inhaled and focussed on Spark again—*You're a good beetle, my little friend. You've got first-rate grit.* Then, before his breath gave out again, he added in a rush—*Look after Antenna.*

Antenna stepped forward and with a game effort at rallying humour said—*I don't need looking after.* She didn't feel very funny and no one laughed.

Spark looked up at her, a tiny jewel of tear welling in his eye and admonished her—*We'll do what he wants.*

—*Of course,* concurred Antenna.

Torque coughed violently, obviously in pain. Everyone leaned in to him, as if to tend him and when they all realised they could do nothing to help him, like a wave they all moved back again. Torque called up his last strength from the bottoms of his tiny toes and said, very quietly, with enormous effort—*You're all smart enough,* and then he muttered something else. After he'd spent this final effort it seemed he was empty for he lay down his head and sighed. His body slumped to one side, the shine went from his elytron and he was gone.

Spark leaned his head forward and then, taking a huge breath in, he leapt to his feet and flew. He flew directly at Eid, hovered in front of the now alarmed numbat and shouted—*It's all your fault. He was too old. He should never have gone on your abortive action. You killed him. You should be ashamed of yourself! You used him up and sucked him dry!* Then, shockingly, Spark hoicked up some spit and gobbed, right in Eid's face. Then the Christmas beetle raced away through the airship, out into the warm evening air, leaving Eid wiping a teeny tiny drop of spit off his face.

Antenna was watching Eid. She was surprised when he returned her look. They held the shared gaze, solemnly looking at each other with no titivations, judgements, or expectations, just clear understanding and knowledge. This was no time to play games, no time for niceties. It was as if they were the only two in the airship, the only two numbats in the world and they too, with unspoken agreement, turned and left the airship. Together.

Gleam and Hod watched as the couple walked past the assorted beetles, climbed down the rope ladder and went into the Ektek caves together. They seemed to grow closer as they travelled. As they entered the hangar their shoulders touched by chance and they turned to look at each other with some surprise. Perhaps the electricity had stunned them. They stayed together, looking, just for a moment. It was as if they drank each other in. Then they disappeared into the shadows.

Mandible flew up to sit beside Torque's body—*What did he say at the end? We heard him say: 'You're all smart enough…' but not the next bit. What was that?*

Hod stared out of the cockpit windscreen at the hangar, now still again—*He said, 'We're all vulnerable'.*

—*Really?* said Gleam—*I thought he said, 'Behave honourably'.*

Mandible looked down at the loyal old darkling beetle and sighed—*Goodbye, old collie jobs-worth. We're going to miss you. Never could work out what you were talking about half the time.* She looked up at the group of beetles standing by, indicated the darkling beetle with a flick of her antenna, and said—*Come on, let's get him out of here.*

As the beetles tended to their dead elder, Gleam turned to Hod—*I rather think Torque would have been more likely to exhort us to honour, don't you?*

—*He was on his deathbed.* Hod stared at the tiger—*What greater reminder of vulnerability do you want?*

They were going to have to agree to disagree and, as it was doubtful these two would ever agree on anything much, perhaps they would simply continue to disagree.

Gleam and Hod both started to move through the cargo hold. Gleam looked over to the exit to the rope ladder—*After you,* he said with just a trace of sarcasm. He didn't mean it in a nasty way, it was an accident; it just came out like that.

Hod stared at him—*We can always ask Antenna. What she heard, I mean.*

Gleam paused for a while, then raised one of his eyebrows—*Later.*

—*Oh, yes,* said Hod, understanding him completely—*Much later.*

Now, both creatures smiled.

Only, they both knew there was more to come in the story and it was highly unlikely the ending could ever be happy.

Chapter Fifty-nine

I

Seated at the computer desk, Antenna stared wistfully into space.

Gumfluff entered the control centre and greeted her—*Ahoy, Antenna!* But the numbat didn't even look up. The screens in front of her were blank. She was in a profound daydream. This behaviour was unlike the normally ever-present Antenna and sent shivers of worry through those observing her.

The large koala lumbered over to stand next to Gleam and they both watched the dozy numbat while she did nothing at all—*What's up with her?*

Gleam said—*Missing Eid.*

—*Eid?*

—*Haven't you heard?* said Hod, who, in contrast to Antenna, sat in front of an active monitor, clicking away on a control system for all he was worth. He was checking the Bedlam Zoo website for news about pandas and shaking his head over the incredible amounts of money being used to landscape the pandas' new enclosure—*It's the only thing anyone talks about these days. Have you seen how much money these pandas are costing?*

—*Been at sea, Hod,* said Gumfluff—*Out of the loop when you're looking into the deep.*

—*They can't be seen in the same place together,* Gleam attempted to clarify Antenna's problem for the koala—*Eid and Antenna. They share the display work. When he's on, she's off. Means they can't have much time. Very difficult when you're young...*

—*Oh well. Can't do anything about that right now. Got some news, Antenna, from Crawf.*

—*Antenna!* said Gleam, loudly—*Gumfluff's heard from... Smacker is it?*

—*Yup. Smacker's come through once again. Crawf's heading to a bird-breeding farm. We know where he is...*

Hod jumped up and hopped toward her—*Can you get us there?*

—... *and we can get you there.*

—*Thanks, Gumfluff,* managed Antenna. This news was enough to bring her attention back to business—*Did Smacker say how Crawf was?*

—*When can we go?* asked Hod—*How long would it take to launch Intek?* Ignoring his determination, the others kept on with what he obviously thought was extraneous discussion.

—*Reasonable spirits. Kept in the dark. Lonely. Much as you'd expect from a prisoner.*

—*He wants to find his family,* said Antenna—*I didn't understand what he was on about at first but now...*

—*He's part of Ektek,* said Hod—*We can't afford families.*

—*That's easy for you to say. You've got at least three families of your own plus surrogates...*

—*There's no need to go into my personal life.*

—*It is relevant,* said Antenna.

—*Can we not give him some time?* asked Gleam—*We might be able to get beetle surveillance into the facility.*

—*He'll have had plenty of time,* said Hod—*We'll rescue any other Palm cockatoos we see, how's that?*

Gumfluff looked up at the ceiling of the cave where the glow-worms clustered so helpfully and sighed. Ektek. Always discussions. Always consensus. Took far too much time out of her life. This was why she preferred being at sea, onboard the Ektek vessel, *Intek*, doing something, going somewhere. She said—*Can we agree that you may at some point require the use of Intek?*

—*It's not certain,* said Antenna.

—*You know how I hate last minute decisions,* said Gumfluff. She turned to march back into her marine world—*Let me know.*

Antenna waited until Gumfluff had left before she spoke again—*Hod, you're going to have to cool down. There are many creatures that need help right now.*

—*Yes, yes, but they're not Crawf,* said Hod—*They're not part of Ektek. We need him. And he very probably needs us.*

—*What about Bash?* said Gleam—*He was due back hours ago. What's happened to him, Hod? With his machine guns? That you made for him?*

Antenna focussed on the wallaby—*Hod? You made guns?*

Hod looked from Gleam to Antenna and back again before he looked down at the ground—*I was helping him.*

—*With that kind of help...* Gleam shook his head.

—*Any idea where to start looking for him?* asked Antenna—*Can we find the number?*

—I'll go ask Manifold.
—And Hod?
—Yes.
—Before you help anyone else, can you stop and think for a moment?
—I'm sure Bash will be fine.
—Are you?

II

The truck clunked to a stop. The engine turned off. Silence. Bash looked over at Bluey. Suddenly both cats were wide-awake and both instantly pressed into the darkest corners of the truck. The tarp flicked back and a wave of daylight and another wave of carousing man cackles hit them. The shooters were out of the truck and grabbing stuff from the luggage tray. Bash shivered underneath a bloody duck wing as the blokes heaved out a cold storage bin and another bag. They lifted a couple of ducks off the pile and then flicked the tarp back down.

The dog started to bark and the humans joined in too, bawling and carrying on as if they were a pack. The noise faded away.

—Go! said Bluey and almost immediately the she-cat leapt down and Bluey was heaving the little plane out of the truck and down to the ground. Bash clung to Bluey's neck, getting spiked in his delicate frog skin with that short ginger hair, and they were out and dashing along hard concrete.

They headed for a small line of little shrubs up near a wall. They sheltered in among the rubbish that littered the little strip. While they recovered, breathing hard and rubbing bruises, they took stock of their situation. They appeared to be at a refuelling station. The blokes had gone inside the building, except for one who was holding the dog on the end of a piece of string and walking him around the withered plant life at the boundaries of the refuelling place. The dog kept sending them glances but appeared to be leading its human off in the opposite direction. Bash eyed the she-cat with admiration. That must have been one exceptional back scratch.

—Are we there yet? said the she-cat.

—We're closer, said Bluey, utilising his extra-sensory cat sense of direction and distance—*Much closer.*

Bash wasn't satisfied with that—*But not close enough.* He was still nowhere near home as far as he was concerned.

—Okay. What about that one?

Before Bash or Bluey could give her an answer, she was out in the open, sprinting toward a van, which happened to be pointing in the right direction. She was full of tricks, this one, thought Bash. She jumped at the rear doors of the white van, performing some kind of twisting action as she did so and the doors flew open. She looked over to Bash and Bluey and they ran, Bluey dragging the little plane along with him. She ran back over to help him and between them they managed to throw the plane into the van, wait until Bash climbed up Bluey's neck, and jump in. Then, as she left the ground, she swung the van door to. It did not click closed - hopefully it would as they went around a corner or something - or everything would fall out of the van and they would be doomed.

They had barely got inside when the van started. It swerved out of the refuelling station, around the corner to the exit and as it veered the door swung wide open. The terrified animals clung on to whatever they could reach, staring helplessly out at the row of cars parked at the refuelling station shop. Then, as the van moved out into the traffic, the door flapped a couple of times, swung back and slammed shut with a bang. They breathed a sigh of relief. They were safe. They sat back and relaxed.

That was, until Bash found himself shivering. Where he was sitting was hard. It had felt refreshingly cool before the door slammed shut. Now, almost immediately, it felt like a winter's day, a very cold winter's day, in a very cold climate, and a chilly drowsiness started to come over him. He crawled over to Bluey and up the cat's back to his neck. The little frog nestled into the soft fur under the cat's chin and shivered some more. Then he said—*Bluey? You cold?*

—*Cold? I'm freezing.* Bluey spoke slowly. It sounded as though he too was drowsy.

—*We've got to get out!* shouted the she-cat and she rushed at the door. It had no handle. She scrabbled round the edges of the door and at the hinges. She turned and stared at them—*We're in a refrigerated truck! We're going to freeze to death!*

III

At the back of the vet's building was a secure and private enclosure for the use of sick animals in recovery. It currently housed the bear rescued by Eid and Torque; the airship bear. Although the bear was out of her cage, in the fresh air, on dirt surrounded by leafy greenery, she slumped in a curved mound, hardly moving, eyes closed.

Shining Teeth had taken it upon herself to go where no crocodile had been before, certainly not voluntarily. Always adventurous, she'd heard about the airship bear and thought she'd like a close up look to see what all the fuss had been about. She sidled through the Ektek tunnels and up to the vet's compound. It was only a matter of minutes before she dug through the rock garden into the enclosure. She paused, gathered her breath, wiped the clay out from between her claws and strode out into the enclosure. She wandered up to the curved mound of bear as if she were perusing an interesting exhibit in a sculpture garden.

The moon bear did not move as the reptile with very big teeth approached. She did see the crocodile but she didn't feel the need to move. She'd never seen one before. She could see it was a dangerous animal, the bear wasn't stupid, but she was depressed. They stared at each other for a good long while before they were interrupted by shouting—*What are you doing here, Shining Teeth?* It was Eid and he was flustered—*Get out of there, she's in quarantine! Who knows what germs she's brought with her! This is the vet's compound, didn't you know?*

Shining Teeth looked at the numbat with something like amused distain—*It's going to take more than a little germ to get me.*

—*Still, no need for unnecessary risks,* said Eid, dodging back out of her way as she turned toward the tunnel she'd dug out—*I mean, I've already had contact with her, so, I might be developing something right now; a disease never before seen in these parts. You've got to be careful.*

—*Bear flu,* said Shining Teeth—*Hope you get it bad.*

Eid's heart sank when he saw what a mess the croc had made with her digging. He'd have to try to cover that up too.

Shining Teeth didn't bother with any further chitchat. She swept out of his way and disappeared down the tunnel with a flick of her serrated tail. After he was sure she'd gone, Eid shook his head to clear it of terror and tried to meditate his heart rate down. He started picking up the clay chunks and rocks littered around Shining Teeth's tunnel. He'd have to rebuild it as best he could and notify the beetles about the breach. Even the most stupid of humans would easily see these diggings and Ektek was vulnerable enough already without a big glaring signpost pointing straight into the tunnel system. As he tidied up Shining Teeth's mess, he tried to make conversation with the bear—*You're in quarantine. I didn't make that up. That's why you're so far away from everyone else. But at least you can get up and go for a stroll if you want to. I mean, you don't have to or anything but it might be nice, feeling the ground under your feet, not iron bars, sun on your back, fresh air…* Eid tailed off. Conversation was generally regarded as a two way kind of thing but the bear didn't seem to be interested in him at all. Eid was not yet ready to give up—*They treating you all right?* He saw her uneaten food lying on the ground nearby—*Getting enough to eat?*

Once he'd patched up the ground again, Eid put himself inside the tunnel and, before he sealed up the gap, continued his attempts at communication. He felt responsible for this little bear. Antenna was on duty in the numbat enclosure so he was at a loose end, ready for a chat, but he couldn't seem to get through to the moon bear at all. When they'd been on the airship it had been the same. He had stared into her eyes of deepest pain and not known what to say then. Now he tried all the normal gambits: names, weather, how are yous, but they all fell unanswered; inadequate, futile and irrelevant. After some time of sitting in the tunnel in silence he mentally slapped himself, he was the healthy one after all, and said—*You must feel better now, though? They got that thing out of your side? I know it was a bad trip but I couldn't work out how to save you otherwise. I just had to winch you up and fly you away, cage 'n' all. Depends how you look at it, doesn't it. I mean, we're all in cages of one sort or another, aren't we, but that was some awful crate you were in. Wasn't it?* The bear said nothing except a little grunt. It wasn't clear if she grunted at him or maybe she just felt a twinge of pain. Assuming it was a response he went on—*You can talk to me, you know.* The bear flashed him a miserable look and Eid thought perhaps that was encouraging. Maybe he was getting through to her. He went on—*Look, I know this isn't perfect; it's not your family or anything like what you're used to but you're safe and you'll heal in no time. Then you'll be able to move around comfortably and no one will make demands from you. Hey, at least you're not dead.*

Still she said nothing. Eid sighed again before he eventually continued—*Torque is. Dead, I mean. My friend who helped rescue you? I don't know if you had much to do with him on the trip. He was getting pretty weak by the time we got to you. Old age I think. He was still active right to the end, though. Always interested, knew all the answers, found them out if he didn't, tried to look out for everyone. Now he's gone and I think he was a bit, well, undervalued? He helped me, though. Really helped me. I don't know if I ever said 'Thank you'. Helped me get the best female in the world. I'm so lucky. Have you met her yet? Looks a lot like me. She knows all about you. We've been following the vet's records. We know they removed that valve from your gall bladder. We know you got put on antibiotics for the infection. We know you won't eat much. They're trying to find out where you came from. This zoo doesn't keep moon bears; just the brown. They probably told you, but who can understand those humans, eh? They're trying to find you a new home, some kind of sanctuary or zoo that already has your family. So you can join a community. Other bears to look out for.*

The bear stood up. Eid was so surprised he jumped and hit himself on the wall of the tunnel. He knocked down some rocks and had to fix up the breach again. By the time he looked back at her she was moving away from him. It was arduous work for her, standing, and she wobbled a bit. She was in pain, that much was obvious, and she couldn't balance very well. As she walked, or rather, stumbled, to her night quarters at the back of the vet's area Eid felt a jolt of shock. She was missing a paw. Her right forepaw had been amputated. It was an old injury - completely healed over now - but still, Eid found it dreadful to see. She limped away from him, looking as if she might fall at any moment. She went to the doorway and began to pace in front of the window next to it; a horrible tortured lumbering over a space of a few metres. Back and forth she went, over and over again, past the window, signalling to those inside, obviously desperate to get in to the vet's rooms.

Eid stood, watching her, filled with useless pity.

Finally the door unlocked with a click and swung open. She was allowed inside. Just before she went in she looked over to the crevice where he had sealed himself into the tunnel and stared hard. Did she see him? She said in a voice rusty with neglect—*What am I doing here?*

—*Nothing,* said Eid in his most reassuring tones—*You don't have to do anything...*

—*I'm just one big problem.* She went on as if he hadn't spoken— *Before, I had a purpose.* As she entered the doorway she called back to him in a voice hard as little pebbles raining on corrugated iron—*Thanks for nothing.*

Eid stared at the closed door for a hard moment and then bowed his head. He was rocked by shame and a kind of unspeakable epiphany. He realised he'd gone to follow that beetle's dance injunction out of selfishness: because he was thinking of his own personal happiness; his desire to be with Antenna. And it had worked, there was no denying that. Antenna was the love of his life, his numbat mate and because of that trip, she saw him now, really saw him. She had admitted him into her heart and her life in every way and Eid couldn't be happier. Until now.

He'd wanted to be useful to Ektek. He'd wanted to save this bear from her suffering and he'd wanted to give her some kind of life. Only now, it seemed, that's not what this particular bear wanted at all. He imagined that Torque might have said 'Did you get the wrong bear?' and Eid thought he might have because there had been so many; each in their heavy iron cage, each with their streams of bile dripping into little pots...

Eid shook his head. Surely she would have a better life now? In time she'd get used to it? She'd been rescued. She was free. Wasn't she?

IV

Crawf was wakened by a great banging and clanging. He was still in the dark, trying to doze in his usual timeless state of caged reverie. A real wallop hit the side of the yacht, right next to Crawf's head. He was startled then, wide-awake and, as he had done every time he'd woken in this dark hole in the wall, he tried to remember where he was. Once his beating heart had slowed and his mind had caught up to what he was doing once again, he sat on his perch and listened to the thuds and booms of action topside. Things had changed. They were no longer rolling from side to side. These sounds of action and movement were different. What was going on?

Salty squeezed into the cage and ran up the side to talk to the bird.

—*We've arrived. They're just making her fast,* said Salty—*Hop down and I'll loosen off your beak for you. Make you a bit more comfortable while they get sorted out there.*

The large cockatoo wearily stepped down onto the floor of his cage. It was too tight for him to move easily. He was stiff and sore but hearing the continual wacks and smashes coming from above gave him renewed energy. He'd arrived. Soon he'd be able to see his family. Soon, he'd be at home.

Salty skittered up to the perch and set about chewing the tape from Crawf's head artfully—*Not too long now. You'll be right as rain, matey.*

Once free, Crawf bent his head up to the water bubbler and took in a large gobble with his blunt tongue nuzzling the drops down his gullet.

Salty sat on the perch on his hindquarters watching the bird—*Not just you disembarking, mate. Me as well. Time to settle down after all me seafaring years. I've got a girl in this port I reckon might take me in. She's got a nice little nest not too far from the docks, still be able to sniff the sea for breakfast. That last run-in with the pirates did it for me.*

—*Pirates?* said Crawf—*What pirates?*

—*There you go. We saw them off, your cat and us…*

—*What cat?*

Something slammed hard into the deck above them and Salty's answer was lost in the reverberations.

—*Whillickers, they're careless up there!*

—*What cat?* repeated Crawf, remembering Smacker's mysterious image of a ginger cat somehow connected to Ektek.

—*That's right*, said Salty—*The whale knew. The cat got chucked in the drink helping to protect you. That Ektek mob, they're persistent, I'll give them that.*

—*I'm retired from Ektek. I've got to meet my family. Make a new life. I don't want to see Ektek again. Not a cat anyway. Not in the foreseeable future, anyway.*

—*Know what you mean, mate. Anyway, sounds like this old bucket's tied up properly now. I'm off. Just popped in to wish you well. Hope it all works out for you, the dream, I mean.*

—*Same to you, Salty.*

—*Thanks, Big Grey, but somehow, matey, I think you're going to need a lot more luck than me. Bon voyage, eh.*

The rat slithered down to Crawf's seed tray and grabbed a few sunflower seeds before disappearing through the bars. Crawf was alone again. He stared at the tiny strip of light coming in through the cabin wall and dreamed about his new family, the eggs they would have and how he'd look after everyone in their enormous nest in the empty tree in the verdant forest and how happy all his family would be together, at last.

V

Hod lay sleeping in the sun in the new yellow-footed rock wallaby enclosure. He was pleasantly dreaming about bounding to the top of a mountain with a magnificent view across the tops of high forest trees when through his dream state he could hear a kind of rise in the voices of his children that he'd not heard before. It was a new note of hysteria he did not like at all.

—*Dad! Dad! Dad!*

—*Dad! Look!*

—*Hey, Dad!* They were almost screaming. In fact, yes, one of them was literally screaming. Screaming as if terrified.

Reluctantly he opened his eyes and thought, if these joeys are playing some kind of dumb game I'm going to give them trouble like they've never had it before…

—*Hod,* called his first wife and he heard her very clearly—*You have to deal with this… Right now.* She had a particular tone of voice that brooked no argument. She only ever spoke when it was completely necessary. Hod understood it was necessary for him to move immediately. He stood, turned to face the hysteria and saw all his children and wives clustered over to one side of the new and, as far as he could see, totally inadequate enclosure. The rocks had been piled up by an earth mover and they'd all felt dumped by the time the zoo's landscape staff had spent a couple of hours raking it over. You could almost hear the workers saying 'That'll do' but as no animal could ever understand the mad gibberish that came out of human's mouths, well, it may or may not have been.

Hod, already feeling dumped and belittled, was in no mood to discover his new yellow-footed rock wallaby enclosure had an uninvited guest but sadly, it was so. Shining Teeth, of all unwelcome beings, had invited herself for a visit. She'd crawled in from the Ektek tunnel system, and Hod understood from the looks he was getting from his wives, that he'd better move her out and quick smart. He jumped in front of his family and confronted her. To his family, he looked like a super-wallaby. But they had no idea of his travels and adventures with Ektek; no idea that he knew this crocodile and was, unfortunately, 'friends' with her. He figured what they didn't know wouldn't worry them and he liked the sense of having a completely separate life away from the petty concerns of children and food.

Shining Teeth, however, greeted him cheerfully—*Wondered where they were hiding you!*

Hod replied in a cold voice—*Don't ever come here again.*

—*Oh,* said Shining Teeth—*Worried, are you? Scared for your tasty little family?*

Hod was completely terrified, but there was no way he'd let her see that. He said—*Come on,* and led her to the disguised exit to the tunnel system. He noted that she'd made a mess of her entry into his enclosure. He'd have to get the ants and beetles around to repair it. He thought, everywhere she goes this croc causes trouble. As they walked into the tunnel he said—*What are you doing here?*

—*What's wrong with catching up with an old mate?*

Hod looked at the croc—*You're bored.*

—*Could say that.*

—*Okay.* Hod kept moving down the tunnel—*This is good.*

—*It's good I'm bored?*

—*Well, I'm thinking you might be ready to be useful.*

—*Me? Useful? I don't get used, Hoddy. I use you, remember.*

—*Oh well, if you'd rather stay here and do nothing…*

—*What have you got in mind?*

—*A little sea voyage.*

—*Ah, lovely. Nothing like a cruise.*

—*That's right. Nothing like it. We're heading out to rescue Crawf.*

Shining Teeth stopped in her tracks. Walking over land was an ungainly task for a crocodile. She was getting tired and more than a bit annoyed.

—Crawf? That bird that caused me so much trouble?

—Crawf. The Palm cockatoo, Crawf. Hod looked back at her. He was willing Shining Teeth away from his family. He could see them all there, watching him; particularly her, his long-suffering wife with her beautiful eyes. He'd fix that tunnel entrance to make it more difficult for the crocodile that was for sure. He may have been many things, but careless of the safety of his family, no, he was not that.

The crocodile continued—*Should have eaten him when I had the chance. And that frog.*

—See, there we go. Problem is, no one trusts you.

—Look, attack dogs are a menace. I was doing everyone a favour getting rid of them.

—You can't do that if you come with us. You have to follow the team's decisions.

—You want me to toe the line?

—Just follow common sense. Consensus.

—Oh, for agony's sake. Consensus. I can tell you right here and now I won't be listening to that pathetic tiger.

—Okay, then I guess you get to stay here and wander round the zoo making trouble for everyone until Ektek decide they've had enough of you and you'll have to go.

—Really? Who's going to make me?

—You'll make a lovely pair of shoes one day.

Shining Teeth almost laughed. She hung her head and thought for a moment before she continued walking down the tunnel to the hangar— *I don't think I'm much of a team player.*

—What about the harem? Weren't you a team?

—Don't mention the harem. She stopped again and sniffed. Hod was astonished to see a large tear plop on the tunnel floor. Was she crying crocodile tears over her harem? They were presumably long dead of radiation sickness by now. He didn't think she had it in her.

—Come and talk to them. You'd be useful getting out of certain situations. Humans find it difficult to argue with an unexpected croc.

—Yeah. It's all very well for you lot but what about me? What do I get out of it?

—I just told you. Variety. Interest. Keep your brain active.

Hod didn't care what he said to her but he knew he couldn't be more relieved he'd moved her out of his enclosure and away from the joeys. He had her in check now but he knew sooner or later he was going to have to finish this game. His mind raced. Just how was he going to keep a rogue croc out of the way?

VI

Spark lay by Torque's grave. It was just a little mound in the dirt, outside the hangar area, in the bush. Torque had been rather fond of banksias so that's where the beetle team buried him, under an old banksia bush. Spark was still and quiet, apparently thinking about his old mentor, when Eid marched up to him and shouted—*Are you or are you not in charge of Ektek security? Could you please tell me why Shining Teeth broke in to the vet's enclosure and terrified the wits out of Gingseng?*

—*Who?*

—*Gingseng. You know, that poor moon bear we brought home? Should you not be aware where Shining Teeth is at any given moment? Have you not got her under surveillance? If you haven't, then, could you please tell me, why not?*

Spark looked up at Eid miserably. He was filled with sorrow and guilt that he had treated Torque in such a cavalier manner when he was still alive. He was not interested in Shining Teeth or in any of Eid's accusations—*Go away,* he said to Eid—*It's all your fault.*

—*It's no one's fault, Spark.* Eid could see that Spark was grieving for Torque. He crouched down beside the beetle. He didn't have time for this but he did want to befriend Spark, knowing that as head of security, Spark was going to have to deal with Shining Teeth in the future—*Torque was an old beetle. He died. He died doing what he wanted to do. It had nothing to do with me and it had nothing to do with you. But now you're treating his memory like rubbish. You've got to maintain the standards that he set for this place. Otherwise what is left? Get up. Keep fighting. Keep up the energy. Don't give up. Do you understand me? Get up and get going.*

Eid left Spark then and Spark wiped the tears from his eyes. He looked down at the little grave and then he stood up. Maybe Eid was right. He wasn't being fair to Torque. He couldn't give up. There was plenty of work to do around here. There were standards to maintain. More than his job's worth to see the place go to rack and ruin.

VII

Hod and Shining Teeth stood looking at Antenna and Gleam in the control centre. The backdrop of flashing computer screens gave them a kind of halo. Hod was trying to convince them it was time to make Crawf's rescue a reality—*I know this is no time to leave my family, what with the new enclosure and the pandas, but I have to go. We need Crawf. I'm sorry about Bash. The number has moved on. I have no idea where to start looking for him. At least with Crawf, we know where he is.*

Anyone could see Antenna and Gleam were not convinced. Then Eid walked in.

—*What are you doing here?* said Antenna, knowing it was Eid's turn to be on display.

—*I just want you to know that Shining Teeth is a menace.*

Shining Teeth smiled—*Little old me?*

—*Ri-ght…* said Antenna, looking cautiously at Eid and then back to Shining Teeth.

—*That's just what I've been saying,* said Hod.

Shining Teeth wasn't so pleased—*You should listen to yourselves.*

—*Okay. If we do go, Gleam has to go too. He can communicate with whales,* said Antenna—*… and he has a good sense of strategy.*

—*… and,* said Gleam—*I won't work with Shining Teeth.*

—*You know what,* said Shining Teeth—*I'm out of here. Let me know what you decide.*

—*Wait a minute,* said Hod—*How will we find you?*

—*Oh, I'll be in touch.* Shining Teeth departed with alacrity while Hod stood looking after her. He was vibrating with trepidation. When he was sure she'd gone, he said to Gleam and Antenna—*That's what I'm worried about. We need to know where she is.*

—*I agree,* said Eid—*She was hassling Ginseng, the airship bear, from inside the vet's compound. She had no business being there and she'd made a serious mess getting in. She has to be controlled.*

—*So we get her out of the zoo,* said Hod.

Eid looked from Hod to Gleam and then to Antenna—*What's going on?*

Antenna said—*Hod wants to take her out to rescue Crawf.*

—*She'd be good,* said Hod—*She knows how to frighten humans.*

—*She knows how to frighten everyone,* said Eid—*She has no place here. I've got to go.* He turned to Antenna and smiled—*See you later.* They shared a quiet look and he departed.

Hod watched Antenna's face as Eid left the cave and then said—*He could come too. Give him something useful to do.*

—*He's got something useful to do. Hod,* continued Antenna—*We can't trust her.*

—*Isn't that strange. That's what you used to say about me.*

—*What do you mean, 'used to'?*

—*You can trust me, Antenna.*

—*What's loyalty mean to you, Hod?*

Antenna and Hod looked at each other. In their shared history lay childish games at their parents' feet, awkward political lessons and lost

427

comrades. There was also that stinging burr of having left the team in the university car-park still surviving just under Hod's skin and he wasn't sure who knew about that. Hod sighed before he tried to explain—*At least if Shining Teeth is with us, we know what she's doing.*

—*Keep your enemies where you can see them,* agreed Gleam.

—*She'll be out of the zoo…*

—*I don't know if that's enough,* said Antenna—*You're going to have to get her to agree to follow orders. We can't afford to let her go on another killing spree.*

—*I'll talk to her.*

—*And she'll listen? No, Hod. We can't be sure that crocodile will ever change,* said Gleam—*Not ever. We have to get rid of her.*

—*How?*

—*Betray her to the authorities?* said Antenna—*It feels wrong.*

—*Feels right to me,* said Gleam.

—*I can't believe you, of all creatures, want to sacrifice a living being to humans,* said Hod, his voice rising in tone—*After all your namby-pamby peace-and-love talk. You're no better than them.*

—*Hod, she's the one who goes round killing other creatures for no reason,* said Antenna—*She'd probably be sent up to a farm. We're not suggesting putting her down. How else can we get her under control?*

—*Let me try before you make up your minds.*

Gleam and Antenna looked at each other. Gleam could only see a mental image of the crocodile decorated with far too much blood and gore standing over a keening dog and Antenna could only imagine what the tiger was feeling. She drew in a large breath and said—*Talk to her but get her to understand. She can't go if she's going to cause trouble and she can't stay here if she's going to cause trouble. It's up to her.*

Instead of replying, Hod hopped out into the hallway before they could put up any further objections. Gleam sighed and looked over at Antenna—*How are you going to stop her?*

—*She might not want to go.*

—*Sea voyage, promise of carnage to rescue one of ours, what's for her not to like?*

Chapter Sixty

I

Crawf looked around him in dismay. He had arrived in Philavian but he hadn't been taken to the colourful bird fair. After farewelling Salty he'd spent what seemed hours, days, ages in suspense; probably because he thought they'd come for him any minute and they hadn't. This last time of expectant waiting was by far the worst part of his trip. Finally, after all his patience, he had been 'emptied' out in the pitch of night, stuffed into a tube and carted uncomfortably to this place. He had no idea what had happened to his travel companions, the reptiles. They'd not had much to do with each other, locked in their separate isolation chambers. But now Crawf had no time for the past. He looked forward to the future, filled with anticipation and hope.

The dark side of Philavian was a huge place of interwoven wires, locks and bars; a place of heavy avian stench: feathers, guano, illness and chemicals. Thick bars on the outer wall boundaries - open to the air and the dawn light - and corridors upon corridors of thinner mesh cages. It felt as if it were raining but it was not. It was hot. Hot and wet and sultry and Crawf could feel the sauna air doing him good almost as soon as he was tipped out of the tube and into what must have been a holding cage.

From this cage, which was mercifully much larger than his hole in the yacht wall had been, Crawf could hear other birds, and, more to the point, other cockatoos. He could see the different birds through the wires of his side of the corridor of cages and he could see opposite him and along their side for some distance in both directions. Almost straight away he saw what he had been dreaming about for so long; the reason he had suffered the indignity of capture and discomfort in the wall of a yacht. He saw her.

Diagonally across from him was another Palm cockatoo, one of his own species. She was standing on a large branch stabbed through and across her cage. He sprang to the edge of his allotted space (rather awkwardly because he'd not had any exercise aboard the *MsTree*) and hooked his beak between the wires to enable him to climb the wall of the cage and get a better view. He opened his beak to shout at her but the shout did not eventuate. She was absorbed in what she was doing. She was dancing. Or so it seemed to begin with. It was a slow sinuous sort of sway, executed with a bow and a dainty bob at the end of the swing before the return along the branch. It was a regular dance and, as Crawf watched, never altered in rhythm or pace. She seemed hypnotised by the movement. Or was the movement a result of her hypnosis? Crawf watched her for ages and the dance was always the same. He drew in a deep breath and waved at her. She didn't notice. He called—*Hullo? Hullo?* And she did not hear. He could see this Palm cockatoo had been incarcerated for a very long time and, as a result, she had decided to leave. At least, mentally, she was somewhere else. Crawf could see he would have to work very hard to reach her. He had no choice but to try. He was determined she would be his friend, his mate, his kin and he said—*Don't worry. I'll help you, no matter what. I'll be here for you.*

She kept right on dancing, far off in a world of her own.

Crawf leaned his head on the netting wall of his cage and tried not to cry. He'd find a way in time. That's all it would take. Time. Well. He wasn't going anywhere.

II

It was getting late. The white van waited for the boom gate to rise. The boom gate was always down after hours. The driver waved at the security guard as he drove through the gate. The security guard made a cheerful, and possibly rude, gesture in return. Keeping carefully to the speed limit the driver made his way to the kiosk and parked by the delivery bay. He got out of the van and stretched his back. It had been a long drive and his back was never good. He felt that ergonomic beaded seat cover was making a difference, just a little bit. He scratched at his grey beard, went round to the van's back door and pulled out the trolley. He loaded out the normal delivery for this kiosk and stacked the boxes one by one onto the little carrier. He tipped the weighty pile of cardboard boxes back onto the wheelie and rolled the load over to the back door. He parked the trolley and went round to the front to announce his arrival.

The driver left his load standing in those last shards of afternoon sun by the delivery door. Well, he'd only popped in to the kiosk for a tick, just to let them know he was there and they'd need to unlock the loading bay. Still, not really the best thing to do for frozen goods, was it. But for these particular frozen goods, it turned out to be just perfect.

Inside the top box were a couple of cat popsicles. In the panic to keep warm in the refrigerated van the frog had stayed clinging to Bluey's chin as Bluey had clawed his way inside a half-full cardboard box. In her turn, the solid female had clung to Bluey. This had meant, though, she'd got the worst of the chill as she'd been closer to the outside. Now, she was almost frozen through.

Bash had remained tucked into Bluey's soft neck fur in the centre of the popsicle. Being an alpine frog, Bash probably had the best chance of recovery from the extreme cold. The insipid warmth from the afternoon sun managed to permeate the cardboard and somehow got Bash to start moving - prodding and shoving at Bluey's throat - until he heard a gasp. The frog was too exhausted to make any noise but he became more strenuous in his endeavours to wake the cat wrapped around him. He may have been cold but he was dry and this was not a good thing for a frog. Bash needed to get out, get wet and quickly. He was desperate.

Their box was placed on top of the pile loaded onto the trolley, possibly because the weight was so uneven in the package. As Bluey started to cough and move, so too did the box. When Bluey realised he was getting hit in the throat by a frog, he also realised he was thawing and therefore they must be out of the van. He started to shove at his girlfriend. The box rocked and shifted and teetered…

Finally, the box toppled over the edge of the pile and hit the ground. The box fell open and split, revealing a scatter of small tubs of ice-cream plus two cold cats now split asunder. The fall had not done the she-cat much good. Near frozen, she lay on the pathway, dazed and immobile. Bluey was able to move, stiffly, and he was up on his paws and checking out his girlfriend before you could say Cat Frost. Bash swung from a tuft of chin hair and spun around dangerously like a strange black-and-gold necklace. The she-cat did not look too well but she was all in one piece. Bash coughed and said—*Bluey. We've got to go. Humans approaching.* Bluey looked up and saw the driver was walking toward them. His long beard was tucked in behind his clipboard where he was engrossed in checking off the invoice and making sure all his orders were present and correct. He still hadn't looked up as Bluey scarpered down a side path and skittered round under a shrub, still with Bash clinging to his neck.

—*Hullo, hullo, hullo,* said Spark, newly appointed Ektek Head of Security, who just happened to be waiting in that particular shrub to oversee a used chip-oil pick up—*What have we here, then?*

—*Spark!* said Bluey—*We've got to help her!*

—*No can do, mate. She's already under arrest. Look.*

Bluey, Bash and Spark peered out from under their cover to see the driver pick up the she-cat. He stood for a moment watching her defrost and then he looked around him in all directions. Then he opened the van and had a good look inside. He pulled out the little plane. He stood, cold cat over one arm and small plane in the other hand, nonplussed. The watching creatures ducked back into hiding.

—*What'll happen to her?* said Bluey.

—*Anyone's guess.*

—*Spark?*

—*Yes, Bash?*

—*Can you get me to a puddle? Please?*

—*Birdbath do?*

—*Too right, mate and make it snappy.*

III

Intek was finally ready to go. There had been a false start earlier when the previous tide had proved not quite up to full depth. Gumfluff and Carney had miscalculated: *Intek* was not used to such large passengers or their provisions; the magnums had unfortunately kept the craft aground with the inadequate tidal swell. However, this incoming tide was predicted to float the boat. Captain Gumfluff was in control of her vehicle. She knew the vagaries of *Intek* better than her own weary frame. She just didn't understand magnums.

Intek was nestled in a small cove near Bedlam waiting for conditions to reach optimum levels. The mangrove mud popped as little crabs scuttled across the surface. Tendrils of roots wove fabulous patterns in the air. A family of ducks tut-tutted as they marched along their path. They kept to themselves but they watched the Etkek preparations with an air of disapproval. No doubt their first concern lay with the large crocodile. What was she doing there and how could the ducklings best avoid her? The ducks probably did not even see the tiger - too far above their eye line - but it seemed certain they would not have approved of him either, no matter how laudable his objective.

Gleam had every intention to be cautious. He regarded himself as the brakes in this squad and he knew he had Antenna's backing. Both Hod and Shining Teeth had proven themselves to be reckless, careless and dangerous. He had no desire to be caught up in their disregard for the living. He stayed by the bridge where the Captain worked. He trusted Gumfluff; the Captain oozed reliability and, as they were about to embark upon this long journey, Gleam knew he was going to need every bit of her reassuring authority.

Antenna also stood on board and watched the tide come in over the mangrove mud. Soon it would be time for her to go ashore and watch *Intek* head out to sea without her. She could see little good coming from this trip. Of course she wanted Crawf back but not at the expense of his free will. What good would he be to Ektek, to anyone, if all he did was bemoan his return? Antenna did not trust Shining Teeth and could not imagine Gleam would be able to prevent her from the worst - if it came to that - his own promise prevented him from hurting her. Or, if Gleam did rise up against the crocodile, what would that do to Gleam's fragile sanity?

Intek was a curious looking vessel. Mainly sail driven, it was able to run both on solar or run the engine on used chip oil if the wind was not up to it. As the journey to Crawf's port would be a long one *Intek* carried a large amount of biodiesel - another weight to be factored into the tidal calculations.

Intek was designed to slice through substantial waves with very little deviation. It was made of a patchwork of burnished metal parts welded together with solar panels giving it a variety of textures. The burnt metal collage shone as the craft chopped through the sea.

In full sail, *Intek* could cut like a knife, jutting out of the water at an acute angle. It sat low like an iceberg and was therefore much larger than it looked. Almost submarine in spirit, there was room and food on board, in addition to the current crew of Gumfluff, Carney, Hod, Shining Teeth and Gleam, for two or three large birds on the return voyage. Hod insisted Crawf and any of his family as could fit would be joining them. Gleam was unconvinced and, when Hod passed him on board, Gleam said—*Crawf has to be free to follow his dream.*

Hod turned to look at the tiger—*Even if that means he's not free?*

—*It's his choice, Hod. You've been allowed to make your own strange choices from time to time…*

They were interrupted by Gumfluff's whistle heralding the start of their voyage. She busily attended to the computers on the bridge, making her final calculations. Carney called out from the front of the boat where she was coiling a rope on deck—*Sailing immediately! All visitors ashore, please. See ya, Ant.*

—*Bye, Carney. Good-bye, Captain. Safe trip.*

Gumfluff was too busy to acknowledge Antenna's departure with more than a brief nod.

Both Hod and Gleam turned to follow Antenna to the gangway. Antenna looked at them both but could find no more words before heading down the plank and wading through the mud. When she landed on the firm ground, she turned back to look at them and found she still had no words. What could she say? She'd already wished them good luck and asked them to be careful. And all those caring words of caution to Shining Teeth had run off the side of her armoured skin like confetti.

Carney pulled up the plank and latched it to the side of *Intek*. Hod, Gleam and Shining Teeth watched the numbat standing in the mangroves. Antenna, uncertain if she would see any of the crew again, sat up on her hindquarters and stared at them as they moved on the deck above her. Gumfluff let loose a farewell blast from her seagoing foghorn. Then they were off, the propellers churning and the smell of burnt chips taking *Intek* out into the harbour where, in good time, she would try to catch the wind.

Antenna raised her forepaw in a salute. Gleam nodded and disappeared, presumably to stand with Gumfluff on the bridge. Shining Teeth got down from the railing and also disappeared from Antenna's view.

When he saw he was alone, Hod, too, lifted his front paw. Numbat and wallaby recognised they were separated by more than just a stretch of water but they also knew they were inseparable. They were part of Ektek and that had to be bigger than any of their differences.

IV

Spark balanced on the side of the frog-quarium, looking down into an arrangement of moss and rocks. Just below him, a new delivery of tadpoles found their legs; jumped, hopped and scampered in the damp greenery. The black-and-yellow stripy babies were tiny and Spark couldn't help but be amused by their antics. The display frog-quarium was carefully landscaped to offer no place for frogs to hide. Even so, corroboree frogs often managed invisibility. This was why Bash was able to come and go so readily; it was difficult to count the inhabitants of this particular glass container. Bash clambered up the walls and, by flying behind him and pushing, Spark gave him a shove over the final distance.

—*Thanks for that*, said Bash, when they were safely on the ground.

—Sorry I can't fly you... Previously Spark and Torque had been able to take hold of Bash and take to the air with him fluttering between them like an irregularly shaped black-and-yellow flag. The memory gave rise to recollections of Torque. Frog and beetle walked on toward the tunnels and the control centre in contemplation of their late darkling beetle friend.

Bash said—*You'll have to find an assistant.*

—Me?

—Torque found you. You'll need to train a successor after all and then...

—You'd be able to travel in style...

—The style to which I've become accustomed. Hey, it's not all about me.

—It is today, Bash. What were you thinking? Bringing two cats into Ektek. One was bad enough; but two?

—He saved my life and so did she, come to that.

—You better hope it was worth it.

Bash opened his mouth to ask what the zed the beetle meant by that but realised he wasn't sure he'd like the answer. He knew cats were murdering bastards. He knew that and yet, as he was grateful to be alive, so he believed Bluey and the she-cat deserved to live too. If they wanted to live in Ektek then he'd try to help that happen for them - up to a point. They walked the rest of the way through the dark tunnels in silence.

They arrived at the control centre to find Antenna, Eid and Bluey already there. Antenna had asked Spark to escort the frog to see her first thing in the morning. She wanted to hear from Bash himself exactly what had happened in those wetlands.

Bluey had spent the night in the machine cage in Gleam's place. He looked refreshed and well fed. His ginger hair had grown out to such an extent there was now no mistaking him for anything other than what he was; a large, ginger tomcat.

Bash jumped up onto the console desk. He looked longingly at the computer, remembering all those happy hours shooting pixels, shook himself free from the siren call of killing games and asked— *How is she?*

—She's survived, said Eid.

—At the vet's, said Antenna—*Here.* Antenna gestured toward an open page on the Bedlam Zoo website designed for the human public to get a bird's eye view; Bedlam's Vetcam.

Bluey was glued to a grainy picture streaming from a camera mounted on a wall in the room. There was no mistaking the fat she-cat standing in a cage on the opposite side of the treatment centre. It was one of many cages lining the walls. The she-cat had her eyes fixed to the staff moving around the room and every time a human came anywhere near her she arched her back, hissed and let them have a good look at her teeth.

—*They haven't examined her yet,* said Antenna—*They've just left her to rest and recover. I expect they'll give her the once over today.*

—*Have you seen her sit down?* asked Bash.

Antenna said—*She's been standing or pacing…*

—*In that cage?* said Bash.

—*All the time,* said Eid.

—*She's got a lot of energy,* said Bluey with a sigh in his voice.

—*You're worried about her,* Antenna was sympathetic.

Bash opened his mouth to speak then looked over at the cat. Bluey shrugged and silently agreed with the frog he was the one who should explain all—*Antenna. She's expecting.*

—*Who?* Antenna's attention flashed back to Eid. She felt him prepare to stand up. She didn't want him to go but she knew he had to head back to the numbat enclosure. The zoo would open soon and, as agreed, one of them had to be on display. This morning it was Eid. They both stood up together. Standing with her partner, Antenna looked back at Bash. She needed to have some serious conversations with both Bash and Bluey about Bash's appalling behaviour. They could also see the little plane, damaged on the surface but still apparently structurally sound, in the vet's office. It leant on the wall next to a desk. They had to get that plane out of the way of zoo management. But right now she didn't want to let Eid out of her sight. Her head was teeming with thoughts and her heart was full of Eid. She was abuzz, hardly knowing which way to turn, what to think and who to talk to first.

In contrast, Bluey only had one thing on his mind—*Her.*

They all turned to watch the she-cat, hissing and caterwauling as the vet nurse picked up her entire cage and placed it onto the scales on the floor near the exit. The nurse made a note of the red electronic numbers that flashed up on the screen next to the scales, then the nurse carried the cage full of erect fur and violent feline over to the vet's examining table.

—*The cat with no name,* said Bash.

—*Why doesn't she have a name?* said Eid.

—*She doesn't need one,* said Bluey.

—*What do you mean, expecting?* said Antenna—*What's she expecting?*

—*Kittens, of course. What else would she be expecting?*

—*Breakfast?* said Bash—*She hasn't had anything to eat, has she?*
Antenna realised—*She's pregnant?*

—*She got us here,* said Bash—*We can't abandon her.*

—*No one's talking about abandoning anyone. But kittens? That's a problem. I don't know what the vet will do with them.*

Bluey thought for a moment before he said—*What do you mean? What could the vet do with them?*

Antenna weighed up the vet's choices—*She could go several ways, I suppose. Sell them to a pet shop...*

—*What?*

—*Euthanase them...* said Eid.

—*Huh?*

—*Feed them to the snakes...* said Bash.

—*These are my children you're talking about!*

—*You asked! I don't know what they'll do. Maybe they'll go to a good home.*

—*Or maybe not,* said Eid.

—*All we can do is monitor the records and make sure she gets de-sexed after she's had them,* said Antenna.

—*What do you mean, de-sexed?*

—*They'll remove her uterus so she can't have any more children.*

—*What?* Bluey was devastated—*Without even asking?*

—*You don't think there's enough cats on the planet?* asked Eid.

—*You want to get de-sexed?*

—*They're never going to de-sex me. I'm from an endangered species on a special breeding program.*

—*Yes,* laughed Antenna—*If they knew about me I can tell you I bet I'd be pregnant right now.*

There was a small pause. Bluey's gaze lingered on Antenna—*I thought you were,* he said.

—*What?* said Antenna.

—*Pregnant.*

—*What?* said Eid.

—*She looks pregnant.*

—*I do?*

—*You've put on weight.*

—*It's true Antenna,* said Bash—*You have.*

—*I have?*

Eid looked at her with glistening eyes and said, with wonder in his voice—*You have.*

—*Oh,* said Antenna.

—Believe me, I've seen plenty of pregnant females before today. Cats are very good at this whole pregnancy thing. Take it from me; you've got the look. Don't you feel any different?

—I thought… maybe… worms?

—Ha. Numbat worms. Well. Congratulations. How's it feel to be telling me your babies are worth more than mine?

—I'm not even sure…

—They're not! Bluey exclaimed*—Every life is equal, cobber. I've got a right to have as many children as I like!*

—I'm sorry, Bluey but what on earth gives you that right? said Eid.

—Me! Because I can! It's my survival and my genetic survival into the future. It's what I've got to do. It's my main purpose in life. It's my drive, for zed's sake.

—We're responsible for saving our species! said Eid*—From extinction!*

—So am I!

—As if! Eid let out a bitter laugh*—There's no danger of cats becoming extinct. You just want to replicate yourself and add to the thousands of cats eating mammals, eating fish, eating birds, eating reptiles all over the world.*

—Isn't it a basic right; for every life to reproduce?

Eid turned back to look at Bluey*—You surely can't think we need more humans?*

—Oh, of course not…

—Well, then, said Eid*—Some lives are clearly more necessary than others.*

—It's called biodiversity, added Antenna*—It's what makes us all strong.*

—If only a few species succeed then the limited variety of life forms become vulnerable to germs or climate or geological danger that could theoretically take out the whole spectrum of life, said Eid.

—You got to look at the bigger picture, Bluey, said Antenna.

Bash tried to help Bluey understand*—Told you no one likes cats.*

—Thanks, Bash.

—Bluey. I couldn't be more serious. I like you. I owe you my life. I want you to know, I'm on your side. However. I don't think the world needs more cats. Okay?

Bluey looked at the frog sadly. He looked over at Vetcam and then sighed*—That's my girlfriend in that cage. Pacing, hissing, scratching… She's a wild one, for sure.*

Antenna watched the trapped cat in the vet's office with new compassion. So. Kittens. New life. Breeding. How would it feel to be locked in a cage with no way out knowing you needed to provide for your young? She looked around her at Eid and at Bash and Bluey as they all stood in the dim blue glow of the control cave. Who was she kidding? Antenna had no choice in the matter either. She may have a bigger cage but she was still a prisoner.

Eid stood next to Antenna and breathed her in. He could not find a way to leave her today. He looked at her face, her fur and felt the warmth from her. She smiled up at him. Pregnant. Wow. He said— *Now you'll come into the enclosure for good.*

—*I will?* she said, sharply.

—*Of course,* he said, in surprise. Why wouldn't she? It was obvious it would be better for her. The vet could look after her and the babies and she'd have the support of the other numbats but before he could explain, she finished the discussion—*No.* As far as Antenna was concerned there was no further need for debate—*That won't be necessary.*

Eid just looked at her in disbelief.

V

It had been a long voyage. Tempers were winding up into a grim level of tension. To alleviate her nagging boredom, Shining Teeth started to snap at passing sea birds, once even diving dramatically overboard in an over-enthusiastic reach into the air. On her return on board *Intek* she insisted she was just playing and enjoyed the swim but still... Gumfluff reminded her she didn't need to be murdering any passing albatross just for fun. Another time Shining Teeth slid into the drink, for a swim alongside, Gumfluff looked over at Gleam just for a fleeting moment. If they changed direction and piled on another sail, they'd pick up speed and then, that croc'd have to swim mighty fast... Gleam looked back at the koala and there was a pleasant frisson between them. But they knew that, even though they could do it, they would not. After bathing Shining Teeth was usually tired and she would sleep long into the day.

Gleam spent most of his time in meditation. Apparently calm on the outside, inside he struggled with his magnum instincts. On the one paw he had his responsibilities to Ektek; should he, if it was warranted, physically prevent the crocodile from attacking again? On the other paw lay his vows of passivism and refusal to cause death. Gleam knew he was the only creature on board capable of overpowering the croc but he did not wish to ever use that power. More than that, he felt he must not. He could not speak of these fears to anyone but often found himself on the bridge with the Captain. Somehow Gumfluff had an empathetic air and, although he never broached his personal dilemma, the tiger was happy to while away the hours discussing strategies, stories of the sea and sailing techniques with the koala.

Hod's behaviour was in direct contrast to the stillness of the tiger. He energetically joined Carney in all the chores of shipboard life. He was happy to swab and sluice the decks and enjoyed nothing more than climbing to the top of the bridge to scan the horizon for any sign of trouble. Often he'd spy the distant plumes of water that signified the presence of whales. Gleam, as an interpreter, was able to reassure everyone that *Intek* was on the correct route and Smacker was monitoring their course.

Gumfluff appeared nonchalant on board her ship. She chewed a eucalyptus leaf continually. Her sleepy demeanour belied her alert reactions. Carney needed little instruction and took care of the running of most of the activities on board. The five creatures passed the days uneventfully.

Through night and day, sun and cloud, smooth seas and rough, the journey went on and on. They were able to dodge pirates and avoid flotsam due to Hod's eagle eye of protection. They avoided storms with Smacker's navigation skills and their provisions showed no sign of running out too early.

One morning Hod, as compelling as any ship's crewmember had ever been, cried out—*Land ho!* And there, in the distance, was the faint fringe of green along the horizon. This was the country they had come to see. It grew larger and more definite as the day grew brighter. Following Smacker's advice they avoided the busy port where Crawf was held captive and tied up in a sanctuary designed to protect migrating birds. There they met a black beetle with red legs recently come from the breeding facility behind Philavian. His name was Trogo and he was keen to help in any way he could. Armed with this new beetle information the group could make a plan to rescue Crawf.

Gumfluff and Carney would stay with *Intek*, reprovisioning and replenishing water stores with the help of local zoo animals. The rescue party would make their way on foot, following the beetle.

The trio of animals, guided by Trogo, at last judged it safe to set out from the sanctuary. Even though there was no moon, the stars blazed out, lighting their way brighter than all the Ektek glow-worms back in those dim blue caves in their distant home.

Hod went first, then Shining Teeth, followed by Gleam. He had insisted on being last, mainly because he wanted to keep an eye on Shining Teeth every step of the way. The plan was simple. Gleam, as the most stealthy one, would creep into the bird facility, find Crawf, open his cage with his large tiger claws and bring Crawf and any Palm cockatoo relatives out. If need be, Gleam would ascertain any difficulties, bring in the others to assist if required and then lead Crawf and any other palmys back to the road to the sanctuary. There would be no need for sudden decisions. No need to jump into rash violence. Trogo assured them their beetle surveillance team had been watching Philavian for days. They had studied the security systems and, if the Ektek animals followed the local advice, the rescue would be a straightforward operation. Trogo was personally prepared to do anything to make their trip a pleasant and easy one.

The three animals and their guide were quiet and careful as they proceeded through the streets. They managed to reach the facility undetected. Shining Teeth and Hod planted themselves by the exit and Gleam slunk in under the bolted gateway, low to the ground, dreading to disturb any bird that had not been warned of his approach. Trogo and his team of beetles assured him they had already alerted the birds of a visitor that night and that his interest lay only in one particular bird. No one wanted a whole aviary of birds to start up a hue and cry as if he were a fox in the henhouse! So far, the birds had been informed of his purpose and were nervously pretending to sleep as Gleam slunk along the corridors of cages, his stripy fur acting as camouflage against the bars of the walls. He came eventually to the cockatoos. They were all a bit sleepy and soon Gleam found Crawf. Unlike the others, Crawf was standing bolt upright on his perch, wide-awake, tapping his foot impatiently. He had been waiting for him. Gleam looked up at the latch he must undo and said—*Are you ready?*

Crawf said—*I'm not coming with you.*

Gleam sat down on his haunches and stared at the cockatoo, grey in the shadows—*Now, Crawf…*

—*Did anyone ask me? No. Did that beetle wait to find out what I thought when they told us you were coming? No. Did everyone assume I got myself captured by mistake? I have to suppose so. Well, they were wrong. This is no mistake, Gleam. I know what I'm doing. I wanted to be caught. I wanted to be sent to a place where I might find family. And I have. And I want to stay here.* Crawf looked over at his friend, the swaying Palm cockatoo who, mercifully, was asleep. He knew she would never survive a trip out of the institution. He would not sacrifice the chance to make a family now.

Gleam followed his eye-line and looked back at Crawf—*We can take her with us.*

—*No,* said Crawf—*We'll be fine. Really. Thanks for coming all this way…*

—*We won't be back; you know that. The distance is too great.*

—*I never wanted you here in the first place,* whispered Crawf. Every word felt like a chip of glass spitting out of his beak. How could they put him in this situation?—*Look, maybe there are birds here who would like to be rescued but I'd need time to ask them. When do you have to return?*

—*As soon as possible. The longer we're in port the greater the danger. We'll be in the sanctuary until we have reprovisioned. Then we must leave. One more night. That's all you've got. We'll be out on the next dawn tide.*

—*I'll send word. Leave a beetle with me.*

At a glance from Gleam, Trogo flew to land beside Crawf. Crawf acknowledged him and then raised his head-feathers to farewell the tiger. The tiger bowed and said—*Good bye, Crawf. You have a day to change your mind.*

—*I've had a lifetime, Gleam. I've worked out what I want. Have you?*

Gleam stared at him for a moment. He realised they had made a huge blunder. He was sorry for Crawf but more sorry that he'd been swept up in this mad journey. He bowed to Crawf, believing that nothing more needed to be said. He silently made his way back along the lines of cages and slunk out to meet Hod and Shining Teeth in the shadows outside.

Hod looked past him and then said—*Where is he?*

—*Not coming.*

—*What?*

—*Let's get him,* said Shining Teeth.

—*No,* said Gleam—*Not this time. Let's go. After you...*

For once, Shining Teeth didn't protest and set out at once. Gleam waited to follow them both. Hod reluctantly set out along the path, turning back to speak but Gleam's determination silenced him until they were nearly at the sanctuary. Hod was livid—*We need him at Ektek.*

—*We can train someone else,* said Gleam.

—*He knows things we don't know to teach someone else. He can't abandon Ektek.*

—*He has. We must leave him.*

—*We can't.*

—*We have. Perhaps, in time, he can do Ektek's work from here but he will not come with us.*

—*We've come all this way!*

—*No one asked him,* said Gleam—*It's not the fault of the beetles. It's our fault for not listening to him at the outset. We've made assumptions; gross assumptions about who is best, who is right and who is wrong. We need to take stock.*

By this time they were back at the boat and Gleam boarded *Intek* with a heavy heart. He went straight to the bridge to report to Gumfluff and Carney.

Hod and Shining Teeth stayed ashore and looked out over the swaying reeds to the little wharf where *Intek* floated gently in the soft starlit night. Hod said—*That's not a good outcome.*

—*No*, said Shining Teeth thoughtfully—*It's not.*

Chapter Sixty-one

I

The vet arrived in the clinic. She went over to a side desk and fiddled with something (the watching creatures could not see what it could be from their Vetcam monitor) and then went over to the examining table. The cage took up much of the space. The tabletop surface was one of those easily wiped materials suitable for using with animals. It featured a mechanism that enabled it to be adjusted up or down according to the size of beast to be examined. The table was currently adjusted so the cage was at the vet's hip height. It also appeared the cage itself could be altered.

The vet waited while the nurse hefted a lever on the side of the she-cat's cage. Part of the cage wall closed down closer to the cat, crushing her into a smaller and smaller space, leaving the she-cat no option but to back up. Hissing and spitting, she soon found she had nowhere to turn.

Bluey sighed again. He was uneasy for his girlfriend—*She does herself no favours.*

The vet was waiting with a hypodermic syringe. She plunged the injection though the wire webbing of the cage into the cat's backside. The she-cat's humour did not improve; her hissing and back arching became even more vehement. The vet disposed of the used sharp, turned away to the computer, logged in and began to type.

Antenna hacked into the vet's account and opened the link. They were able to watch what the vet was typing as she hit the keys. Antenna read it and translated out loud for the benefit of Bluey whom she suspected could not read—*She's sedated her.*

—*Hope she's used a double dose*, said Bluey, worried for his girlfriend's peace of mind—*She doesn't trust humans.*

—*And why should she?* asked Bash.

There was an unspoken shiver of agreement in the control centre.

—*If the vet's on duty, you'd better get going,* said Antenna to Eid even though she didn't want him to leave. The zoo would be opening. Duty called.

—*Wish I didn't have to...* Eid prepared to leave the control centre but he was easily distracted by Bluey's next comment and stayed, poised by the door, to hear what happened next.

—*Now what?* Although Bluey was focussed on the plight of his girlfriend he was also aware he himself was in a uncertain situation—*I mean, she's in there and I'm here... What's going to happen to me? How long can I stay with Ektek?*

—*That's up to you, Bluey. You don't have to go, yet,* said Antenna—*I suppose the ants can keep bringing you Gleam's food - or a part of it anyway - and you can stay until we see what happens with the children. But, Bluey, you can't kill anyone...*

—*Thank you, Antenna. I promise I won't be any trouble. It's just that, life's so difficult on the outside, you've no idea. I don't want to be free any more.*

—*Feral, you mean,* said Bash.

—*Yeah, well, there's a fine line between feral and free, ain't there.*

—*Antenna, I have to go but I want to...* Eid couldn't bring himself to talk to Antenna about the future and their children. Not here. Not now. He was thrilled she might be pregnant but he worried she wasn't so enthusiastic.

—*We'll talk about it,* she said—*Don't worry.* Eid leaned down close to her and they touched the sides of their heads together. With their eyes closed, they stood, cheek to cheek for a short time. Then Eid stepped back and left the cave.

Acknowledging Eid's departure, Antenna, Bluey and Bash turned back to Vetcam on their monitor and stared at the cat in the crush cage. She was no longer showing any signs of aggression. Instead, she slumped between the cage walls. There was absolutely no fight left in her now—*What's wrong with her?* said Bluey.

—*The sedative,* said Antenna, used to Zoo veterinary examinations.

The vet nurse dragged the limp she-cat out of the cage and laid her on her side on the examination table.

—*There, now, the vet will be able to get a good look at her,* said Antenna. Bluey added—*If she can just stay still and not attack the good doctor.*

But the vet took a cursory look at the animal and the cat did not move again. Instead, the good doctor took another hypodermic syringe, stuck the needle into the she-cat's heart - from just behind the feline's elbow - and depressed the plunger. Still the she-cat did not move. At all. The vet withdrew the needle and watched the cat. The vet's face was impassive.

The vet turned away again and typed at her computer. According to the screen the cat was a de-sexed female weighing 10.3kg. The required dose of Lethobarb had been given at this time and this place. Then the vet closed the cat's page. Forever.

—*Lethobarb?* said Bash—*What's that?*

—*A medicine of some kind,* said Antenna—*Maybe she's got to be unconscious to do the examination.*

The she-cat lay on the table. Still. Very still.

In a while the nurse came back and picked up the she-cat. The heavy feline lolled in the nurse's arms as she put her into a plastic rubbish bag, rolled the plastic down her muscular form and twisted a strip of wire tie around the top. The she-cat would not be able to breathe. That was supposing she'd been able to breathe before she went into the bag, which the watching animals had come to realise she probably had not. Then the nurse carried the bag away to the cool room. The vet sprayed the bench top with a chemical preparation in a green plastic misting bottle and gave it all a good wipe.

The Ektek control cave remained silent. On their monitor, the vet moved to open another cage. She turned and brought a small monkey to the examining table.

Antenna took in a deep breath and turned to face Bluey—*She's been cleared.*

Bash stared at the numbat. It was unbelievable. They had thought the cat would be assisted to give birth and be found a good home and then...

They both looked at Bluey— *But that's not fair.* His eyes were confused as he stared back at Bash and Antenna—*What about my kittens?*

—*Bluey. There were no kittens.*

—*There were...*

—*You saw what the vet typed,* said Antenna—*She was already de-sexed. There must have been a scar. She lied to you.*

—*Can't trust a feral.*

—*Bash!* Antenna was shocked at his lack of tact.

—*Sorry.*

Bluey stared at them. She'd saved his life. She had so many survival skills. He didn't know how he'd cope without her. It didn't matter what she was. It didn't even matter that she'd lied to him. She had been a force and he wanted her the way she was. He turned to stare at Vetcam and then his eyes filled with tears—*Can we get her back?*

II

Silent in his cage in Philavian, Crawf was resting on his perch when he heard a clanging kerfuffle from the doorway. The birds seemed to be calling too early and from only one direction. It was not yet dawn but even so the birds seemed to be shouting louder and louder until they were calling near him too, and there, suddenly, right in front of him was Hod.

Hod reached up and flicked open the latch holding his cage door shut. The door swung open and Hod grinned at him—*Pleased to see me?*

—*No, Hod, I really am not.* Crawf stayed where he was and stared at Hod—*Go away. I told Gleam, I don't want to go.*

—*Nonsense,* said Hod—*Come on.* He looked around the cages, some as yet unopened—*Let's see. Who else? Tell you what, I'll go get the other palmys. Where are they? Well, actually, don't worry, we're letting everyone out anyway,* and he hopped away to the next cage and flicked that door lock open too.

Crawf was immediately alarmed—*Everyone? No!*

The beetle Trogo flew criss cross up Crawf's cage to sit beside him on his perch and said—*What should I do?*

—*I don't know.* Crawf looked round and saw the doors along the corridor were hanging open. Hod had flipped all the latches. The air was filling with panicking birds, shouting and yelling for all they were worth. A large black-and-white bird with a dazzling red crest crashed headlong into another gigantic bird with a proud white head, a yellow, hooked beak and brown plumage. Each bounced backwards, scrabbling with their wings as they fought to find equilibrium; then both rose into the air again. They shook the potential concussion from their heads and rushed madly to the exit where they might manage to climb over or under the gate. Another enormous dark-brown to grey bird with a bald head and a looping neck hurried past. A brown pelican dashed overhead while a whooping crane shouted out, ecstatic with freedom, visible now above the roof of wire.

Colours blurred in the air: a large red bird with a long-laddered tail zipped by, seeking an exit in vain; a huge, intensely green parrot with yellow nostrils crawled past remarkably quickly on the floor while a blue-and-gold macaw blasted through in the other direction, just missing a circling dove with a distinctive splash of red on her front that looked for all the world like a bleeding heart. It was a madhouse: a flood of feathers, a barrage of wings and a surge of birdshit. And in the middle of it all, laughing, stood Shining Teeth, menacing and malevolent.

Crawf's heart plummeted. He'd seen Shining Teeth at work in the university lab footage. His heart started to beat faster. He knew her capabilities and he shouted to Hod, losing control of his voice, panicking—*What's she doing here? Get her out!*

Trogo thought he was shouting to him and immediately flew down to see Shining Teeth. He danced in front of her - he had sensed Crawf's rage - and shouted as loudly as he could in his teeny tiny beetle voice—*You have to leave! Please go!*

Shining Teeth barely even registered he was there. She knew there was something annoying happening around her head so she snapped at it. Trogo disappeared down her gullet with hardly an interruption to her oesophagus.

Crawf jumped to the edge of his cage, trembling with rage and impotence.

Hod was now on the other side of the corridor of cages, flicking open the doors, laughing too, as he saw the various and sometimes extreme reaction of the birds to their liberty and the ensuing crazy bombardment of other birds. Shining Teeth ambled over to see how he was doing, enjoying every minute of this destructive aerial ballet. She flicked Crawf a glance and then she spotted his girlfriend; she checked back and forth to make sure the Palm cockatoos were in fact part of the same species. Right. Same feather colour. Same cheek patch. Same hair crest. Same, same, same. Only one, the scrawny one, was a girl and the other one was Crawf. She laughed back at Crawf—*This is the family you came all this way to find?* Sniggering, the croc turned back to examine the poor excuse for a female palmy. The palmy pressed hard against the back of her cage to get away from the reptile's snout and Hod called to her—*We've come to take you away from all this.*

Crawf's heart increased in tempo yet again. He hopped to the open door of his cage and called to Hod—*Shut her in, leave her alone, we don't want to come with you*, but Shining Teeth didn't hear him or she ignored him if she did. She jumped up on her hind legs and poked her nose into the female's cage—*Come on, out of there*, she cooed, soothingly. Only the sound of a crocodile was not the sound an emotionally unhinged cockatoo needs to hear and the poor bird fell away in a dead faint. Shining Teeth thought no more and grabbed her up in her great teeth-filled mouth, heaved her out of the cage and spat her out onto the ground. Perhaps the croc imagined she might fly once she felt the air around her wings. Her teeth did not mark the cockatoo but Crawf flew out of his cage and rushed at Shining Teeth. He flew into pande-monium. Other birds also flew this way and that in the corridors and Hod, having just released every single one all along the line of cages, was so full of himself, so gleeful, that he was bounding along, jumping and leaping in the air thick with feathers. They all met with a crash; Crawf, Hod and Shining Teeth. Several other birds barely missed them as they swung around them in the mêlée.

Crawf landed with his claws out, into Shining Teeth's head. He missed her eyes and he wished he could have hurt her more but he stood forcing his talons into her shoe-leather flesh as hard as he could and flapped, trying to lift her out. He screamed at them—*Get out! Get out now!*

Shining Teeth, with a heavy bird digging himself into her head, started, awfully, shamefully, to giggle—*Oooh. This is a bit much, isn't it?* Madly, Hod joined in. The giggling progressed to belly laughing altogether far too fast. It was unseemly. Their laughter was dreadful.

Feathers of all sizes and colours floated around them and landed on their bodies. They were overexcited, energetic, but underlying that heightened buzz was a gnawing undertow; a pulse of nausea. On some level they understood that things had got way too far out of their control. Hysterical birds zoomed around them.

Crawf could not bear it. He stabbed Shining Teeth harder with his claws before he released and flew back up to the now empty female's cage. He went into the cage and paced, paced up and down. What could he do? How could he cope? He had brought them there by his own carelessness. He should be able to stop them. His mind's voice berated him. It was his fault. He had only himself to blame and while he could still draw breath, he would never stop blaming himself.

On the ground in the corridor nearby, Hod and Shining Teeth had shining eyes and grinning mouths. But even as they were hurdy-gurdy swept up into exhilaration they could feel an ember of guilt starting to flicker in their guts. They knew they'd done wrong even though they still believed they'd been justified at the outset. They also knew they had to get out before the cacophony of bird noises and the fountain of fowls in flight from the aviary brought humans to investi-gate. They raced down to the exit and disappeared.

Birds still flew, chicks tumbled onto the ground, fledglings made wild dashes into the air to try to reach some safety; all helter skelter in the aviary. Crawf judged when it was safe to enter the air stream and as soon as he could, he flew down to land beside the female palmy. His female. He'd never even spoken to her. She was lying prone on the ground. A little bit of blood seeped out of her beak and spilled onto the damp concrete. A panicked bird flying overhead let loose a juicy white crap. It plopped onto her head and splattered over Crawf beside her. She did not move.

Crawf could not move either. At first. Then, he started to sway where he was. Just a little bit; just rock, rock, rocking himself into some small comfort; over and over again.

III

Hod bounded up *Intek*'s gangplank, ignoring all other activities, comings and goings and other creatures industriously working there, and rushed up to the bridge. There he found Gumfluff, chewing her ubiquitous eucalyptus leaf, checking the weather forecast and tide movements on her computer screen. Hod said—*We should be off.* There was urgency in his voice that made Gumfluff turn to look at him hard. She twisted her head to a slightly skewed angle. Her eye was quizzical and shrewd as she examined him—*What's your hurry?*

—*Might have attracted human interest. Sorry.* All Hod was interested in was getting the boat to sail at once. He didn't care what he said as long as it worked. He figured humans would be the last thing Gumfluff would want to see and he was right.

Gumfluff moved out of the bridge and went on deck to see where Carney was. As she moved she spat back to Hod—*Check with Gleam.* She swayed off in that strange loping koala walk to negotiate their departure with Carney. Her sharp claws scraped on the deck, turned her feet and made her legs bend out as she walked.

Hod sought out Gleam. He found him helping a deer with a tawny brown coat and three pronged antlers load provisions into the cargo hold. The local zoo inhabitants were also part of the extended Ektek family and prepared to share their foods with the rescue party. A lizard with a large fin extending along the length of his body delivered a small package into the hold and then left again. The storage areas were redolent with the smell of eucalyptus - Gumfluff refused to go short of her favourite sustenance - which covered a multitude of sins because both croc and tiger had to be fed meat. The smells of stored road-kill and other creatures less fortunate than themselves rose into the air. Gleam looked up when he saw Hod. An intense feeling of uncertainty and danger drilled into his guts. He became more alert and crouched, ready to spring if need be.

Hod was panting. He was trying to cover his jittery excitement (bordering on manic) with a thin veneer of civility but had some trouble. He said—*Time to go.*

—*Really?* said Gleam. He examined Hod's dishevelled appearance and calculated likely disasters as he asked—*Where is she?*

Hod knew the tiger was talking about Shining Teeth and he also knew he was expecting him to report that something frightful had occurred. Hod would not give him satisfaction—*Right behind me. We have to leave.*

—*We said we'd wait for Trogo. Crawf was going to check what birds might need…*

—*Look, I know you told us; I know everything that ought to have happened, you can save the lecture, but we went to Crawf to see for ourselves.*

Gleam could not help but remember those two dogs. He could not help but imagine the worst but he so dreaded hearing what a crocodile might have accomplished, among hundreds of birds just for fun on this bright and sunny morning, that he swung his mind out on an angle and said to the wallaby—*He really doesn't want to come, does he?*

—*He really doesn't want to come,* said Hod in all honesty—*… but I think some humans might have followed us so we have to get out of here. Now!*

—*I see.* Gleam still looked at him, holding his attention, waiting. He had no idea what he was waiting for but he dreaded that Hod knew more than he was saying and the tiger could not countenance hearing grim news about Crawf. His hesitation was rewarded by the appearance of Shining Teeth in the hold doorway. She was backlit by the morning sun. Chips of gold light glittered on her back like shining armour. Gleam studied her. She said—*See something you like?*

Gleam said—*Fetching.*

—*What?*

—*Feather by your eye, there.*

—*I told him,* Hod interrupted—*How Crawf told us it was okay to go. How we might have attracted too much attention - how it was getting light…*

—*There's no doubt,* Shining Teeth nodded—*We have to go right now.*

Gleam turned to a compact heavyset buffalo laden with packages for the hold and asked him if there was much more. The dwarf buffalo said—*Nearly there,* and left the hold again. Gleam looked up at Hod and Shining Teeth—*Well? Don't just stand there. Help.*

Hod found it easy enough to get back ashore and find something suitable to carry up to the hold but Shining Teeth was only able to convey things in her mouth. Unfortunately a container of water burst as she lowered her jaws over it and punctured the plastic with her teeth. She was allowed off duty. She slunk back on board and landed heavily near the railing. She sprawled.

Gleam flicked her a glance every now and then. He didn't trust her. He could feel something was off - more than just the odd bit of road-kill steaming in the hold - something was very wrong and he had no idea how to find out what it might be. He could only hope Crawf had survived and some word might come from him before they departed. His eye searched the air for an approaching beetle. There was still no sign of Trogo.

Gumfluff and Carney rushed to make sure the hold was fast and all their visitors were ashore before commencing procedures to untie the boat from the little wharf. Gleam and Carney thanked the helping creatures who stood ashore and raised a paw or inclined an antler in farewell.

Carney went below to start the engines. The smell of twice-cooked deep-fried chips filled the sanctuary and *Intek* belched into action. Gumfluff swung the wheel and the little boat turned away from the wharf and made her way out of the safe harbour. It was broad daylight but both Hod and Gumfluff felt it safer to be on their way if humans had decided to investigate.

The smell of brine soon overtook the biodiesel fumes waving behind them. Back on the ocean, back into the wind and back to their journey home to Ektek.

Gleam knew they'd failed in their mission. More than that, he knew Hod and Shining Teeth were keeping something from him. He was determined to find out what that was. He began to think of Smacker. Whales could communicate with everyone; from beetles to crocodiles, if they only put their mind to it. Where was that whale when you needed him?

Several birds flew overhead, different sized and shaped silhouettes in the bright blue sky. Where had they come from? Where were they going?

IV

Bluey lay in Gleam's old bed in the machine cage. He was a smaller and paler version of the tiger. He didn't look like he could do much damage to anyone. He hadn't eaten. He was curled up in a knot with his bad eye turned inwards. His breathing was shallow.

Antenna and Bash watched him for a little while and then they turned away. As they walked through the corridors Antenna said—*We have to do something, Bash. He can't stay here.*

—I know.

—We have to think of something.

Bash said—*We have to get the little plane anyway, so, can we find her body and bring it out?*

—Give her a decent burial?

—A feral burial.

V

Intek bit into the water and sent a white wake out behind her. A straight line led from the sanctuary to their boat travelling now in the deep blue ocean. A salt breeze in the warm air ruffled tiger and koala fur alike as Gleam stood beside Gumfluff on the bridge and surveyed the horizon sliced in two by that straight white wake—*Still nothing*, he said.

—Can't say I'm surprised, said Gumfluff.

—No.

—Should we have stayed?

—If they did nothing, as they say, then what good would have come from our intervention? If they had caused mayhem and we rushed in…

—We might have made it worse.

—We could have been caught; we could have exacerbated the problem; could we have improved the situation…? Gleam shrugged.

—Which do you think?

Gleam looked at her before he spoke. He was reluctant but in a way he needed to speak, needed to communicate his fears to her— *Mayhem. You?*

—Also, mayhem.

—I wish I'd known what they were thinking. Maybe I could have…

—Stopped them? You think?

—No, Gleam didn't have any idea what would be best—*I don't know.*

—Should I have given them an order? As captain of the ship, Gumfluff was in charge and what she said went.

Gleam knew better—*Shining Teeth takes orders from no one.*

—Then, as she is on board my boat, next time she goes swimming she will no longer be my responsibility. We find that strong wind and… She let the words trail off.

Gleam did not answer. He left the bridge and stood on deck. He scanned the horizon - before and aft - watching various craft go about their glittering business. *Intek* was not being followed. They had made good their escape. They were safe. The sun shone, the whitecaps rose pointed in the deep blue around them and the ocean tang flared his nostrils. He came back onto the bridge and stood beside the captain. She indicated a small pile of gumleaves—*Want one?*

—*No, thanks.*

—*You think they lied?*

Again, Gleam said nothing. His eyeline slid over to look at her. Gumfluff took a sidelong glance at him and they shared a look that said: Of course they lied but what are we to do with the truth?

Gleam broke their gaze first. He looked down and left the bridge. He went to see where Shining Teeth and Hod had put themselves on this homeward bound voyage. He watched them, standing in the sharp midday shadow of the cabin structure. Shining Teeth was sunbaking. She lay as if dead to the world. In contrast, Hod looked as though he could not get comfortable. He twisted into one resting position and almost immediately turned into another. Gleam watched his contortions for a while before leaving the deck. As he did so he passed by Hod and said under his breath—*No rest for the wicked, eh, Hod?*

Hod wasn't even sure what he'd heard, the tiger had passed him by so swiftly. His guilt was making him nervous and a little bit paranoid. He stared after Gleam as he strode on those big soft cat paws and the wallaby wondered if the tiger was on to him. How could he have found out? The beetle couldn't have told his story to another before Shining Teeth chomped him and there hadn't been a whale sighting since they left the sanctuary. Nah. He was imagining things. Still, it was darned near impossible to get comfortable on this blasted deck.

Days turned into nights and nights into days and still the journey was as before; the weather held for them, the pirates kept away and the provisions were ample. Their greatest concern was there had been no word from Smacker.

It was not until the voyage was nearing completion that they had any sign of whales. As they came closer to journey's end, more and more vessels were sighted on the horizon. Gumfluff was adept at steering around the different craft so usually there was no need to examine them closely. This time though, with the alert given for whale spouts—*Whales, Ahoy!* the entire crew turned out along the railings to watch for Smacker and his pod. Their pleasure at sighting the whales again turned to impotent rage within moments. The ships seemed to come fast and they came from three different directions and those aboard *Intek* watched as they closed in on the pod's position. Gleam's relief at connecting with Smacker's mind grated into shards of fear as he was overcome by the whales' desperation as they raced away from their pursuers. Gleam felt the impact when the harpoon hit Smacker. When it detonated, the explosion missed his brain. Instead Smacker was dragged backwards through the water and up the ramp of the factory ship. Gleam felt him choking as he drowned. Then Gleam was released from Smacker's mind, forever.

Gleam, Shining Teeth and Hod saw Smacker's blood run down the ramp in the distance as *Intek* wallowed in the waves, directionless. With that loss of hope, there was a sudden burst of energy on board *Intek*. All three watching creatures moved. Hod yelled with fury—*Board them!*

Shining Teeth ran to the small dingy and examined it—*How can we untie this thing?*

—*Ram them!* cried Hod.

Gumfluff stood by on the bridge, unable to move, transfixed by the whaling boats. Gleam walked in to stand beside her. He said urgently—*Go. Go now.*

Gumfluff turned to look at him. Her eyes were full of tears and she said—*Yes. I know.*

Hod also came to the door and shouted—*Let's get them!*

Then Gumfluff snapped back into the disciplined naval officer that Gleam expected to see at the wheel of *Intek*—*Full steam ahead,* cried Gumfluff and Carney ran below decks to look after the engine. The smell of burnt chips rose around them, Gumfluff spun the wheel and *Intek* turned tail and ran.

Gleam looked down at Hod—*We're leaving.* He left the crew to their work and came back to stand with Shining Teeth; looking back at the whaling fleet and the red waters boiling around them. Hod bounded back to them—*We should do something!*

—*He's right. We have to show them,* agreed Shining Teeth.

Gleam watched the crocodile with suspicion and something else in his face; something approaching pity. Shining Teeth paid him no attention at all. Why should she? He sympathised with her anger and frustration but she had no understanding of him—*There is nothing to be done here.*

—*I don't believe in your nothing.* Shining Teeth did not know what to do with her hatred and rage. She marched up and down the deck, swinging her tail dangerously as she turned. She could not stop moving—*I've been foolish. It was humans that killed my husband and my harem. It was humans that have delivered our lands into filth and bondage. It is humans that cause us all great harm and yet I've been misled by Ektek. I've been wasting my time.*

Hod watched her. He was thinking hard.

—*You want to take them on?* asked Gleam—*You want to kill those humans? How long do you think you'd last? How many do you think you'd get? They utilise sophisticated weaponry. If one should fall, many, many more, will rise in their place.*

—*If we must die for the cause then so be it,* said Shining Teeth—*We must take out as many as we can on the way.*

Gleam looked at the crocodile—*They will not be taken out by anything animals might be able to do to them.*

—*Even a few would do.*

—*They are their own worst enemy,* said Gleam—*They will pass in time.*

—*But what of the creatures they take out with them?* There was no answer to that question. They all knew that. In the silence that followed, even Shining Teeth became resigned to the enormity of their problem.

Gleam could see the initial reaction to Smacker's death had lost its impetus and there was little danger of impulsive reaction from the crocodile now. He left Hod and Shining Teeth and went to stare back over the churning wake. The whaling fleet was still there and Gleam's heart was broken. He stood on board with the sea wind whipping his hair and whiskers around his face. He knew that whatever Shining Teeth and Hod might prepare, humanity would be ready for it and would put them down. Forcibly.

At their side of the railings, Hod watched Shining Teeth. He saw a hardened reptile, a warrior, a returning soldier who had fought many battles—*You made me turn against Ektek. You said it was a waste of time.*

—*Ah, grow up, Wally. You made your choices.*

He understood that she was only one and the humans were many but it was an attractive idea, dying for the cause. He could taste the glory when he imagined dying as retribution for the whales that had died; for all the creatures that had suffered at the hands of humans. He stood with Shining Teeth and they watched the whalers recede into the distance; the grey of the sky almost the same as the grey of the water.

—*We will avenge him,* said Hod.

—*Yes,* said Shining Teeth—*The time is coming when we will avenge them all.*

VI

In the shiver of a raining night, Spark, Bash and Bluey were in hiding under a hardy shrub. They were in the area of the zoo that demonstrated butterfly-attracting plants for the home garden. Bash was nestled in a fork between the main trunk and a low branch of the shrub. Spark was clinging to a stalk just above him. Bluey was lying damp and miserable on the ground. Their cover was a thin leaved specimen and did not offer much protection from the rain. Not only was it raining, it was dark. The only light source near them came from the security shack. The light glistened on the falling raindrops between them and the shack window.

They were near the rear of the zoo, past the yellow-footed rock wallaby's new enclosure. Two Bedlam golf carts were parked outside the security shack. A pair of yellow headlights cut through the rain and flashed over the watching creatures. A car stopped briefly and then proceeded through the boom gate. It parked nearby, turned out the headlights and one of the guards got out and slammed the door. He hurried through the drizzle as though he didn't like being wet. Bluey knew how he felt. The man carried a brown paper bag. He went inside the shack. The door was left ajar and a cheery electronic drone of massed humans spilled into the yellow slice of light reflecting in the wet footpath outside.

Bash and Spark looked keenly at Bluey. Water dripped through their shrub. All three were cold. Bash didn't mind but the other two preferred more comfortable habitats.

—*Right, mate?* said Bash.

Bluey was unenthusiastic especially now he was wet to the skin. His head lay down on his front paws. He was as wet from the drizzle as though he'd been swimming and he hated swimming. He was despondent. He didn't understand why Bash and Spark were so excited for him. Even Antenna, though she was too tired to join them in this outing, wished him all the best.

They were putting a brave face on a terrible situation. Spark had overseen an Ektek team that been able to extricate the little plane from the vet's clinic overnight but when it had come to the she-cat, they found the cool room was filled with plastic bags. There had been too many for them to untie and sort through. Spark had made the call. He reported back to Antenna that they could bring just one of them back. It might have been the feral cat or it might have been any number of other animals cleared from the zoo that week. They might have pretended it was the cat but what if Bluey had wanted to look at her and discovered instead some part of another creature? It could scar an animal for life. Instead of lying to Bluey, they'd explained that all the bodies were going to landfill. She would have her burial, only it would be in a mass grave.

All this had not made Bluey feel any better. He missed his girlfriend. He couldn't understand what was required of him. What job? Why did he have to leave Ektek? He couldn't even be bothered asking the questions. He was just wet and that was all too much.

—*You got the idea?* said Spark. He was trying to be helpful and sounded very enthusiastic. It was difficult to keep this perky energy up in the face of Bluey's lack of response but he felt sorry for the cat. This was a good chance for him—*It's all because of the pandas, yeah? Antenna reckons we'll be getting hundreds more people through, at least at the start. There's been all sorts of ceremonies and parties so far, landscaping and plumbers and chippies and sparkies and comings and goings. More than my job's worth to list everything but the point is, with all the extra eyeballs peering round the place, some stickybeak might notice something about Ektek and we need to know the moment someone gets suspicious about anything, anything at all. So, this is your mission.*

—*Can you read?* said Bash.

Bluey sighed—*Not really.*

—*Shame,* said Spark—*Antenna seemed to think you might be able to understand some of their noise?*

—*Only a tiny bit.*

—*Really? You can?*

—*I'd never be able to talk to them but sometimes I can make a bit of sense out of it. I could always tell when they wanted to give me some food, come here, stop that, you know, that sort of thing.*

—*Amazing.*

—*Not really. They brought me up. They trained me. I used to be a pet.* He said 'pet' much as though he meant 'an evil virus'. Nevertheless, Bluey started to feel wistful about being a pet. A nice, dry, fat, pet.

—*Anything you can find out, brilliant,* droned Spark enthusiastically—*I'll station a beetle up with you every day - let them know what's going on - and I'll pop in for a visit when I can.*

—*What do you think, Sparkie? How are we going to get him in?*

—*I was thinking they'd love to rescue him. How do you feel about getting stuck in a drain?* Bluey made no response—*Up a tree?* suggested Spark.

Bluey flicked Spark an unimpressed glance and slumped his head back on his paws again.

—*Spark!* said Bash—*Don't you think he's been through enough? He's been vivisected, cast out of the zoo, fought with pirates, nearly drowned and then, watched his girlfriend put down. Of all creatures alive today, Bluey really doesn't need any more pressure.*

Spark agreed. He tried a different angle—*Bluey, you're valuable to me, mate. If you can read, that's one thing, but if you can understand any of that horrible noise they make, well, that's brilliant. I'd like your help with security matters. You'd be like, a spy.*

—But you have to make an effort, Bluey, said Bash—*Ektek can't support you. You're displaced, friendless and a danger to wildlife. You have to make your own way. We can't help you any more. Do you understand?*

Bluey turned his head further away to avoid the continual hectoring and, as his neck twisted, his nostrils caught a whiff of a most attractive scent. Bluey sat up. His natural feline curiosity got the better of him. He analysed the smell. It appeared to be a gorgeous amalgam of meat, cheese, salad and bread bun. Bluey had not eaten for days, not since the she-cat was destroyed in front of him. He began to dribble. Bash's voice echoed in his head, resonated in his heart: displaced, friendless and a danger to wildlife, and those feelings of worthlessness began to mix in with the fragrant feeling of what could only be… hamburger.

As though hypnotised, Bluey stood up and rose to his four paws. He arched his back high into the air. He stretched this way and that and felt the blood flowing through him and the scent of greasy minced meat twined round his stomach and gave a mighty tug. The idea that he might be able to change his cat status from unwanted waif to spy was thrilling but the aromatic tease coming from that security shed was irresistible.

He began walking. His nose was elevated and traced scattered atoms of cooked animal fats. His feet followed where his nose led. He continued tracking on that path as if in a trance and soon reached the door of the security hut. He didn't even pause but went straight in.

Spark and Bash rushed out of cover and ran to stare around the corner into the warm shed at this shocking transgression. Bluey was wet to the skin which accentuated his thin frame. He had a desperate demeanour. He did not hesitate. He jumped straight onto the largest man's lap and began kneading his leg; not in a bad dig-in-the-claw way but in a comfortable, reassuring, friendly way. The man got a bit of a fright but nothing much would loosen this particular man's hold on a hamburger so there was no danger of him dropping it. Bluey made himself comfortable and sat down as if he'd known this man all his life. The man held his hamburger aloft and stared at the other two security guards, then back down to Bluey as if to ask if they too saw this outrage. The three humans gabbled on for a moment, squarking and clucking but, the astounding thing to Spark and Bash watching from outside, the man made no move to shift Bluey away from his lap. Bluey had chosen well, it seemed. This man must be a cat lover. How could he have known? Spark and Bash looked on half in amazement and half in horror as Bluey did the best cute acting they'd ever seen in their life—*He looks just like a pet*, said Bash in tones of quiet awe.

—*Pet, spy, what's the difference?* More than anything else, Spark was Ektek's head of security and a practical kind of beetle—*As long as he stays on our side.*

The humans had an array of screens in front of them, not dissimilar to the Ektek display, showing black-and-white images of zones around the zoo. One square of glass was set apart from the others, the one making that buzzing, raucous sound. It showed a green background with humans, dressed in white, all standing around, waiting for something.

Once the hubbub of human braying - the reaction to this bold feline trespass - had died down, the man was left staring at Bluey with something that might have been respect in his eye. Then he reached over with his free hand and patted Bluey gently on the head. Spark and Bash were agog. They stared at this astounding behaviour and then back to each other again with their mouths hanging open. They looked back into the cosy shed to see the man break off a piece of mince patty from his burger and wave it in front of Bluey. Bluey ate it politely and pushed his head up against the man's hand as if in gratitude. It was such endearing behaviour that the man could not resist. He broke off another piece of meat and gave that to Bluey. Then one of the other men found a circular ceramic dish of some kind, filled it with cow's milk from a carton and set it down on the floor. Bluey jumped down and started to drink. As he drank the other man grabbed a towel and rubbed the feline all over until his fur stood up. Bluey lapped the milk up and jumped back to his 'favourite' man again. The men all cackled together for a moment and eventually turned their attention back to the green-and-white television set. While he watched the screen, the man absent-mindedly patted the cat. Bluey shut his eye and gave a great sigh. Everyone relaxed and Spark and Bash imagined they might even be able to hear... Could it be? It was. Bluey was purring. Purring like a fat kitten! At his age!

—*He's in!* said Spark.

—*You got to hand it to him,* said Bash—*That's one class cat.*

Bash and Spark turned away from the yellow light, the smell of hamburgers and the babble of humans. They returned to the dark, the rain and their duties as members of Ektek.

VIII

Hod ran into the control centre. He was desperate to see Antenna. He stopped in the doorway. *Intek* had moored moments before and some urgent instinct had driven Hod inside to see Antenna first. The others were still making *Intek* fast and offloading spare provisions. Hod stood in the doorway and watched Antenna. He had not seen her large with child before. He was taken aback. Antenna had not yet seen him. He paused, observed her and then came in slower. He understood that life would be different for Antenna now. Life would probably be different for them all.

—*Anti?* he said quietly so as not to disturb her too much.

She looked around dreamily, and when she saw who it was, jumped up. She ran to him and they touched foreheads and breathed together, mingling their thoughts and their air. Only after this initial welcome calmed did she think of the many different things that might have happened on their voyage and she stepped back to see him better— *Crawf?*

—*He will have nothing to do with Ektek.*

—*What happened?*

Hod could not answer her. Shame pumped through him and she could tell; she knew something was wrong. He could not face her and he could not hide it.

—*What, Hod? Tell me. What happened? What did she do?*

—*I can't.*

—*Hod, she will destroy us. She will destroy Ektek.*

—*She won't.*

—*Hod*, said Antenna, panting—*I think she already has.* With that Antenna gasped at a pain in her belly. She became still and listened to herself, then she doubled over as though she'd been punched and struggled to breathe. She couldn't balance properly and slid to the ground. Hod stood looking at her - poised to help or run for help or… He knew not what. He was terrified. She rolled onto her side and, sucking in air for power, said on the exhalation—*Get Eid.* Hod did not wait to hear more. He leapt out of the control centre and ran to the hangar to alert every single creature he could find. Antenna lay on the ground in terrible pain. Before she lost consciousness, she sighed—*Eid, where are you?*

Chapter Sixty-two

I

The control centre became a centre of pain. The epicentre was Antenna's nest of shredded bark. Antenna lay there, or rather could not lie but shifted constantly. She could only concentrate on her core. All around her was a whirl of concern. She was not aware of anything outside her.

The glow-worms tried to shed as much light as they could. Eid had brought the older mother numbat in for support and she murmured words of love and encouragement. No one knew what Antenna could hear. She had shut down to that inner place, close to the edge of the world, where only she could urge her babies to enter life and where she could find herself and focus on existence. She could not help uttering small yelps and groans in reaction to her body's changes.

Eid felt slashed every time he heard her.

Bash, Gleam, Hod, Shining Teeth, Gumfluff and Carney waited in the hangar with all the other Ektek animals. Eid rushed past every now and then, frantic with worry and keen on some purpose or other that the mother numbat had set him to keep him doing meaningful work. One, he must fetch water. Two, he must fetch fresh bedding bark. Three, he must discard waste bedding materials. Four, he must take a message to mother numbat's own children. Five, he must stay put in the numbat enclosure. Six, no really, he had to stay visible to the keepers. Seven, no, she really meant it or she would have to leave Antenna by herself. Eight, would he please get out of here?

At each meeting of Eid and the mother numbat he insisted that Antenna be taken to the numbat enclosure, for her own safety; and that of the as yet unborn children. He insisted that her keeper would forgive everything once it was realised she was with child. Then she would receive the medical attention she so obviously needed. Then she would be safe and the babies would have a better chance of survival.

Mother numbat knew that Antenna could not be moved now. She also knew that nature would take its own course; and she knew that sometimes nature took the long way round just for the journey. Mother numbat tried her best to reassure Eid but she knew Antenna was in difficulty. None of her own progeny had been birthed with such trouble. Mother numbat was almost as worried as Eid himself. What could they do but carry on? He insisted, she reassured, and so it went, for a long time.

The animals out in the hangar fretted and worried and teased and blamed each other. Bash sat up on the red steam car and demanded Hod tell him everything about Crawf. Gradually the whole Philavian story came out and gradually Gleam, listening in, came closer and closer to the wallaby. When Smacker was killed Gleam's suspicions had been stilled by his concerns over Shining Teeth and Hod's anger. Now Gleam's worst fears were realised. He blamed himself and worried for Crawf.

Bash wanted to know why on earth Hod could have thought it was a good idea to release all the birds and Gleam wanted to know if he imagined they all got out of the aviary unscathed? Both wanted to know how Crawf had reacted and given all their worries and given they were all tired after their different travels and given they were all hungry too, there was a rising tide of anger and frustration developing among them all.

Voices grew louder and more strident. Barbs grew sharper and struck targets more forcefully. Just at the utmost of the mounting reproaches and recriminations, in walked a ginger cat, already tamer and better fed, but still Bluey. He jumped to the top of the wingship and landed thud, thud. He stalked over the wings like an actor taking control of his stage. He strode downstage centre and loomed over the crowd. He piped a shrill whistle (an old farm trick his girlfriend had taught him out on the wetlands) and called the rabble to attention—*Oi!* he yelled—*Pull yourselves together! I've got some news, yeah? The pandas have arrived. They're still in crates on the back of two large trucks waiting to be unloaded. There's media, there's dignitaries, there's a heck of a lot of people all watching, all snooping, all around. It's a blooming circus at Bedlam today. I suggest everyone needs to get back on duty immediately. We all need to be front and centre and normal - at once. And keep the noise down. The last thing we need is nosy parkers sticking their big fat hooters in where we don't want 'em.*

Creatures swallowed their pride and left the hangar abashed. They went away to their respective enclosures. Bluey jumped down from the wingship and, intending a brief word with Spark about security issues, said—*What are they on about; all their selfish concerns running away with them?*

Obviously Antenna needs peace and quiet and all they're doing is unleashing a tempest! I could hear the noise outside! What're they thinking? How dare they?

Spark could see these were rhetorical questions and agreed with every drop of indignation—*I know, mate, I know.*

Then Spark, Bluey and Manifold went back to their duties leaving Gleam on guard outside the control centre. He lay like a sphinx, belly to ground, forepaws parallel outstretched in front, tail wrapped around his haunch. His ears flipped to attention, listening into the quiet, breathing in the calm, wondering when the next storm would hit.

Into that fragile peace came a tiny plaintive numbat cry.

Gleam breathed in a great slow breath. He was overcome. He blinked. He found it hard to see. His vision blurred. His eyes were full. One tear balanced, overflowed and rolled slowly down his great sphinx face.

II

Bash and Hod were seated in the driver's pod of the tank. Shining Teeth could not fit in so she was draped over the edge of the trap door, peering down at the computer screen, which was dark and fuzzy. Panda Cam. All three creatures were tired and dirty. They had been digging, fruitlessly. The animals had made an abortive attempt to dig their way into the new panda area. They failed. The tunnel no longer fed into what used to be the yellow-footed rock wallaby enclosure. Ektek collapsed the tunnel in case landscape workers noticed something untoward and decided to investigate. Then, during the construction of the new panda area, walls had been dug down deep, creating foolproof fortification for the precious icons.

The pandas were extremely well protected. After their attempted break in, Bash, Hod and Shining Teeth agreed they would see more on-line and, as Antenna was still recovering in the control centre, they came to the tank to watch the media fawning over the latest arrivals at Bedlam Zoo.

A stream of painted human faces filled the screen and opened and shut their mouths. Pictures of the pandas lying in their new home did not impress Hod, Shining Teeth or Bash but the humans seemed to explode with joy every time footage of one of them doing something was shown; anything at all. Eating was just fantastic. Sitting down was awesome. Having a big old wee was thrilling. They didn't see a bowel movement but presumably the humans would go ape over that. People prattle seemed to be on every link, every page, except Panda Cam, so the three Ektek creatures did without the bleating commentary and expert interviews and watched the black-and-white fluff balls in colour and in silence.

—*Are they going to do anything?*

—*Jet-lagged. Poor buggers.*

It was boring watching the slow moving creatures get acclimatised to their cages and, after a time, Bash looked around the tank as though he were on a historical tour—*So, tell us, Hod. Is this the very screen you were watching when you ran away?* Bash smiled at Hod, feeling superior and not a little smug.

Shining Teeth perked up as soon as she heard Bash's tone and turned to Hod. She was just on the edge of jeering when she said to him—*You ran away? From what?*

Hod shook his head at Bash, daring him to say more but before the little frog could open his mouth, which he had every intention of doing, Hod threw caution out the window and turned to face Shining Teeth—*It was you.*

—*Little old me?* said Shining Teeth, loving it—*Surely, you're not scared of me?*

—*It was when you killed those dogs.*

—*Those pets, you mean?*

—*Those animals, yes; the guard dogs.*

—*Trained attack lap dogs. They were slaves; unquestioning, slavering, obedient, adoring puppets in the service of human masters. They were nothing more than extensions of their controller's brain, doing their human dirty work like robots. What sort of life is that for an animal? Worse than a performing seal clapping for a fish. How demeaning. I set them free! I was the one who made them independent! They're not slaves anymore and they can thank me for that. I didn't kill them, I recognised them. They'd be grateful if we could ask them. There's nothing better than dying for such a just cause. The liberty and honour of animals is surely and absolutely the highest reward a creature can aspire to.*

Bash nodded thoughtfully.

Hod looked as if he had a bitter taste in his mouth—*Bit revisionist?*

Shining Teeth carried on—*What else can we do in these days of human power? They have all the cards. They're literally all over the world with their agricultural poisons and their residential developments. Everywhere I've travelled I've seen human beings and their detritus. Not only is their waste scattered over every part of the land, it's all over the ocean as well! There's no room left for animals! We have to make a stand. This would be a good start, don't you think?*

She looked at Hod and Bash. They were taken aback, not knowing what she meant. She continued—*They'd surely take notice then.*

—*When?* said Bash in a small voice.

—*When we do it.*

—*What?*

—*This,* Shining Teeth indicated the computer screens with her head—*Them. The pandas.*

Hod felt nauseous—*What are you talking about, Shining Teeth?*

—*Think about it,* said Shining Teeth.

—*You want to set them free?* asked Hod. He was nervous—*Like the birds?*

—*That's it. That's it exactly. I want to give those cute fluffy pandas their liberty. And what's more, you two are going to help me do it.*

Hod and Bash looked at each other. They certainly had a desire to do something to help the cause but there was risk involved when dealing with Shining Teeth. She had the power, she had the energy, she had the rage but she also had that unpredictable inclination to go too far. Hod and Bash could see that if they followed this particular crocodile unthinkingly they might not like what happened next.

—*By the way,* Shining Teeth watched them with interest—*If you don't help me I'll tell your little friend Antenna the story of the wally woo woo who ran away from the university laboratory. I don't think she'd like that story very much. I don't think she'd ever trust you again, would she. I can't see you've got much choice. It's all or nothing, now.*

There was no need to convince Bash. He was won over and he sat up straight, listening to Shining Teeth with sincerity and hope in his eyes. He needed no persuasion. He'd felt the power of the gun out in the wetlands. He could not live with himself if he was destined to be a helpless bystander. He was ready to follow Shining Teeth. He was ready for action. He was ready to do whatever it took.

Hod was not converted. He could not rid himself of a deep sense of guilt and that undertow of fear.

Shining Teeth looked at Bash and nodded. Then she turned to Hod and said—*Well?*

Hod said—*Don't tell Antenna.*

—*We've got work to do,* said Shining Teeth, bustling to be off—*Let's get on with it.*

III

Eid and Antenna walked very slowly down a corridor. Eid had his mouth full. He carried a tiny scrap of numbat gently at the back of her neck. Antenna bumped into the wall. She leaned for a moment and Eid tried to support her. She broke free and tried to stagger on but, like the bursting of a dam, pent up words bubbled up from her body

466

and spilled out to him—*I don't want you to hate me, please don't hate me, I know I should have gone to the vet. I know, I know, I'm so sorry. I'm sorry. It's all my fault they died. I didn't know I was trying to work I was trying to do everything and you told me, I know you did, you said I should go back to the enclosure but I wanted to wait and I wanted… and I wanted…*

Eid put the tiny scrap down on the ground and turned to Antenna. She was melting with distress. His heart went out to her and he said—*Antenna. I love you. Nothing will change that. Ever. Tell me.*

She tried to pull herself together and Eid waited for her. He repeated very softly—*Tell me what you wanted.*

—*I wanted…*

—*Yes?*

She looked at him and spoke clearly—*I wanted our babies to be born free; to exist without having to know humans; not to have to rely on them. I hardly knew that then, I couldn't have said that in words before but that's the reason I didn't want to go back to the enclosure.*

Eid stood with her for a moment and leaned in to her. He whispered—*You're doing the right thing.* Then he picked up the rusty ball of fluff in his mouth again and waited for Antenna to move. She could not. She remained propped against the wall. She said—*What if I get cleared?*

Eid breathed in and then gently set the little one down again—*You're not going to get cleared.*

—*They cleared Bluey's girlfriend.*

—*Bluey's girlfriend was a feral cat with diseases, parasites and an uncontrollable habit of eating wildlife; probably numbats if she'd been given half a chance. They're going to love you. You know that. I'm with you. Okay? You ready?*

Antenna nodded and Eid carried their baby all the way to the numbat enclosure. The other numbats clustered around them and made her feel part of the family right away. Mother numbat saw Antenna was comfortable and nestled into her neck for a moment. She whispered—*It takes a village to raise a child. You're doing the right thing.*

Antenna stared at her and nodded. Then she lay back with her baby nursing comfortably and waited for the keeper to arrive. She was home again.

Chapter Sixty-three

I

Eid had taken to popping in to visit the moon-bear whenever he could. She was still housed in the vet's enclosure and there was no word of how much longer she would be there. He didn't have much of a relationship with her but he thought it was worth persevering. Seeing as he was the one who had rescued her, he felt responsible for her welfare and he didn't know if she talked with anyone else. He suspected not. He'd been sneaking closer and closer to her each visit until now he was able to sit almost right beside her without her limping away or begging to be let into her night quarters. There had even been a couple of times when she'd taken a swipe at him. She seemed to have accepted him now and they would sit quietly and exchange a few words relatively peacefully. Well, he did most of the talking but she had told him one or two things about herself.

Over time he'd discovered her name was Ginseng and, one day, she had agreed with him, yes, after all, it was better to be out of a cage. She was gaining in strength and looked glossy and almost fat. But she felt in limbo. She didn't know how long she would stay here. She didn't know where she might go. She only knew what was happening day-to-day, hour-to-hour, minute-to-minute. She was living in uncertainty and that couldn't help but make her feel frustrated. Eid empathised. That was as far as their conversation had gone, at least on her side.

Eid, on the other paw, told her everything about his family; how Antenna had found it difficult giving birth; how from the outset he'd wanted her to go back to the numbat's enclosure but she hadn't wanted to go; how two of the babies had died but the one survivor was as tough as her mum and they'd called her Zip Too after another Zip that Eid hadn't known. When the keeper had found mother and child snug in the enclosure, in the same time and place as Eid, he'd brought the in vet to examine her but the vet had done nothing more than observe them from the edge of the enclosure. What theories they'd come up with for her reappearance in the zoo, Eid couldn't imagine but so far they'd kept her out of the limelight and there'd been none of those flashy media stunts that Antenna had been dreading. Antenna had even been able to pop back to visit Gleam in the control centre a couple of times but in the main she was happy to stay put in the enclosure, look after Zip Too and recover.

On one of these visits, as Eid poured out his thoughts to Ginseng in the vet's enclosure, a strange high buzz came through the air. It was late afternoon, after closing time and the zoo was clear of all but those humans who thought they were essential; mainly Bluey's hard-working team of hamburger-eating security guards. Most of the animals and birds were in their night housing. The high hum sliced through the sky and seemed to centre over the panda enclosure. Eid looked up and saw it was the little plane circling over the zoo. Both Eid and Ginseng watched as the plane looped the loop and tilted into some wild and crazy acrobatics. It was a chipper demonstration, one that straightened the backs of the watchers as they stared up into the sky. It made them glad they were alive to witness such death defying antics, such devilry in the heavens. It was after one particularly spectacular loop that the pilot, and Eid assumed it must have been Bash, pointed his nose to the ground and plummeted straight down with full power. There was no last minute U turn. The plane screeched as it directly, headfirst, nosedived down.

Eid saw the puff of smoke before he heard the muffled crash.

Almost at the same time he heard the screams, both human and animal, and he rose to his feet, fighting the urge to be sick. What was happening? What was going on? A siren started up and Eid could hear engines and running feet around the zoo.

Suddenly, awfully, the crocodile Shining Teeth was upon him. She had burst through his carefully disguised tunnel entrance. He stood, stunned at her appearance. She was covered in blood and was threshing around wildly. She made straight for Ginseng. Eid ran between them crying—*Stop!*

Shining Teeth grabbed his leg, jerked him off balance and whipped him out of her way. Ginseng heard the bone crack as his front leg broke. However, Eid's effort had bought Ginseng some time to prepare for Shining Teeth's deranged assault and the bear was able to find stability on her three feet before the croc came hurtling at her. Shining Teeth was put off balance herself by attempting to attack what she expected would be a front paw but grabbed instead on something that was not there.

In her turn, Ginseng rose up on her hind legs and dropped her full weight on the reptile before attempting to grab some part of the attacker with her teeth. The croc spun away, thrashing and squirming to get free of the bear's weight. As Shining Teeth spun out of reach, Eid tried to get between them again, perhaps to reason with the magnums, not having any clear idea or thought in his head, not knowing what was wrong with Shining Teeth and he hardly even knew when Shining Teeth reached up and grabbed him by the head and pulled him to the ground. Ginseng heard his neck snap as Shining Teeth twisted him down.

When Ginseng saw that Eid was destroyed, desperation flooded through her, giving her strength she might only have imagined as a young cub in far-off wilds. Again she rose up on her hind legs. She managed to scoop the crocodile up with her front stump, using her sharp claws on the other paw to pin the reptile in a bear hug. Energised by rage and by sadness Ginseng bit into the soft pale neck in front of her and tore backwards, letting the blood spurt. Shining Teeth's madness was hardly abated and she fought for her life, kicking and scrabbling with her legs and thrashing with the full length of her enormous body. The magnums, bear and crocodile, twisted and strained together in a concentrated battle. Finally, Shining Teeth managed to wrench herself free and ran to the tunnel where she disappeared with an armoured flick of her bloodied tail.

Ginseng lowered herself down to Eid's body and wept for the waste of a life and for the loss of her only friend. Then she looked around and saw the mess that the crocodile had left by the tunnel. Ginseng bowed her head, thought for a moment and then picked up the broken numbat. She carried him over to the entrance and pushed him into the tunnel. She lay on her side and pushed him in as far as her good arm would allow. Then she began scooping and smoothing to obliterate any sign of the diggings. When she finished she went to sit down in her normal spot. She was numb. She stared into space in front of her for a while. Then she called, softly—*Ektek? Ektek?* and a longicorn beetle appeared beside her. This beetle had the longest antenna Ginseng had ever seen but she did not consider the beauty of the creature. She only knew Ektek had to be informed of Eid's whereabouts and most importantly, warned that finally, dangerously, Shining Teeth had gone completely mad.

II

High panic reigned in the tunnels and byways of Ektek. Creatures ran through the gloom this way and insects flittered another. A lorikeet flew desperately through the hangar. A spiny crayfish hid in a crevice. A whirlygig beetle cried for its mother. All was movement and cacophony, worry and chaos. Sirens could still be heard from the zoo above. Into all this alarm flew a beautiful longicorn beetle. She sought someone in charge in vain. Then she sought someone stationary, someone who might be able to listen to her tale. Eventually, she found Manifold who agreed to listen—*Don't you know there's an emergency on?*

Longicorn beetle said—*Number One.*

Manifold looked her up and down and said—*Well, you haven't come far, have you.*

—*No. Not far.*

—*Haven't you heard? The pandas are dead,* said Manifold.

The longicorn nodded and said—*There's more…*

As Manifold listened with growing horror and the longicorn danced out her information, Bluey ran past, heading for the control centre. There, he burst into a gathering consisting of Spark, Gleam, Antenna, Gumfluff and Carney. They moved to make space for him and watched him speak. Tears welled up in his eyes and his voice cracked—*He was my friend! I saved his life! What a joke. He goes and throws it away. How dare he! What is a life worth? I had imagined kittens and I was shattered for them and they didn't even exist! He was alive and he saved my life and yet he killed a panda for the sake of what? Doing something? Because he felt frustrated?*

Antenna stepped forward and lifted a paw to pat him on his arm. He stopped speaking and let her soothe him. Then, in a calmer voice, he gave them the latest security update, as he'd understood it from the human security guards. It was true. The pandas had both been killed. The humans believed the nosediving plane was some kind of incendiary device. Both pandas had been strafed and then, the humans believed, some kind of small bomb had directly hit one of the pandas. Bluey looked around the group and took a deep breath—*It was Bash, deliberately flying into the poor beast. The other panda, suffering from bullet wounds, was then slashed by some kind of wild animal. This could only have been Shining Teeth. I just can't believe it, Antenna. Not Bash. How could he? What must have he been thinking when the panda looked up at him falling to earth, what must he have thought when he drilled into an innocent creature?*

Spark confirmed that both Shining Teeth and Hod were nowhere to be found. The group of animals still looked at each other in shock, still unable to find words to express feelings or thoughts, when Manifold stalked into the room accompanied by the longicorn. That's when Antenna's world shifted yet again.

Gumfluff and Carney left immediately to take Eid's body back to the numbat enclosure while Bluey and Spark went to interview the moon bear. Antenna crumpled into a heap. Mother numbat back at the enclosure was tending her baby while Antenna helped Ektek work out what was to be done about the pandas. In behind her fallen form the computer screens carried online news and grabs coming from free-to air-networks. Human faces revealed revulsion and shock. All was sorrow and anger that anything so inhumane could be done; to deliberately maul and kill pandas, that iconic species, was inconceivable. Subtitles rolled across the screen as interviews with police, zoo officials and government representatives repeated that whomsoever was to blame would be held accountable and would pay.

Antenna lay quiet, insensible, at the news of Eid's death. She was fallen and sunken and limp. Gleam sent Manifold to fetch the mother numbat and then, once alone with her, he said to Antenna—*You have to get up. You must not give up. You must go to your child.* Antenna moaned and said—*The keepers can bottle feed the baby. I cannot.*

Gleam said—*You must. You have no choice. That baby needs her mother more than anyone else in the world. Would you sentence your child, Eid's child, to be an orphan?*

—*Eid's child. I can't…*

—*She needs her mother and you have to get up right now.*

Antenna tried to stand but she could not. She looked up helplessly at Gleam and said—*Give me some time.*

Gleam said—*There is no time. You must get up. You must go to your family.*

—*She's done it, hasn't she,* said Antenna—*She's destroyed Ektek. She said she would and she has.*

—*I don't know that she can…* said Gleam, thoughtful—*How can you destroy something that exists all over the world, that is beyond animals and insects and fish… Isn't Ektek in all life?*

—*I think she has.*

—*Well, in that case, we can't give up, Antenna. We can't let Ektek go like that. She mustn't win. We have to keep fighting. You have to stay safe and you have to keep going.*

The Mother numbat was near and came to support Antenna. Together they walked out of the control centre. Antenna leaned against Mother numbat and her eyes were filled with tears. It was difficult to move but she did and Gleam watched them go. Then Gleam went to the computer. He typed out an email. He addressed it to the zoo's vets and copied in global veterinary organisations. In the subject line he put; 'Universal Euthanasia' and it said:

```
After the panda atrocity, it is time
that all the animals of the zoo were
put down. The zoo has served its pur-
pose. Trapped animals do not enjoy
their limited lives. Humans do not, as
a rule, enjoy seeing them incarcerated
in small cages. Zoos are holding up the
process of extinction, which most hu-
mans seem to desire, and they are
little more than freak shows wrapped in
designer so-called educational packag-
ing. If a creature is extinct in the
wild, then it should be gone from cap-
tivity too. Let extinction be
extinction. All this inbreeding into
bottleneck generations can hardly be
expected to garner strong stock for fu-
ture biodiversity. Let every soul be
free. Let evolution have full reign. If
humans are to win the competition, then
let it be so. The victors take the hab-
itat. The losers die.
```

Gleam sat and pondered over his message for a very long time. His great claw hovered over 'send' but in the end he did not press send. He pressed 'cancel' and then 'don't save' and the email disappeared, never to be seen again. He logged out of the computer system and turned everything off.

Then he went into the machine cage and stood at the workbench. He assembled some tools in front of him: a wrench, some pliers and a machete. He looked around the workspace and saw the grinder that Hod had used when first making the guns to fit on Bash's plane. After looking at the machine for some time from different angles, Gleam managed to turn it on. It hummed away, the grinding barrel turning, turning, turning...

Gleam opened his mouth and attempted to bite the spinning rock. His teeth bounced away from the force. His head jerked backwards. He had to take a step to balance himself. Then he tried again, holding his lips back from his teeth in case he might catch flesh when bringing his teeth against the spin. He could not hold his teeth against the grinder. His head flicked back again.

This would not do. He turned off the machine and, in the pleasant silence, went back to the tools lying in a line on the workbench. He found he was able to manipulate the pliers with two paws together. He sat up on his haunches and applied the pliers to one of his big canine teeth. He managed to get a firm grip. He bent his head forward until his spine curved and then he pulled down on the pliers and pulled back with his head and dragged the tooth forcefully out of his gum. The pain caused his eyes to water and he blinked to keep the tears away so he could see what he was doing. He carried on, grabbing the next tooth with the jaws of the pliers. His mouth was swollen by the time all the teeth were collected, bloody and wet with spit on the bench. Then he turned to his claws. He could do one paw with the pliers but he could not manage the other. He put the next claw into the vice and wound around to keep it firm. He could not help gasping as he accidentally brushed against the bleeding paw pushing the handle of the vice around. Then, holding the machete in his bleeding mouth, he dropped the blade through the pad containing the claw. With great difficulty he undid the vice and moved to the next claw. Every now and then he would stumble. He cried out once or twice. Once he even fell. It was impossible to staunch the flow of blood. His breathing became harsh and difficult. Then he finished. Gleam had ripped out all his own teeth and claws.

III

Shining Teeth and Hod had come to rest. They were in hiding in the sewer system under the city. They sat in a large echoing cylinder of drips and stench and giggled hysterically. The smell may have been rank but they were safe, at least for the moment. Eventually they calmed down enough to speak. Hod, seeking grounding, said—*We can't go back, can we?*

Shining Teeth looked at him—*What do you mean, we? I never could go back any which way.*

—*No, but my family?*

—*You can kiss them all goodbye, can't you.*

Hod stared at her as if she had started to speak human gobblede-gook. Her assumptions about him had been difficult to accept previously but now it was impossible. No, he couldn't. He could not leave his family. Not finally. Not forever. Kiss them goodbye? What? He watched the croc as she spoke, with determined certainty growing in his mind. He couldn't be forced to choose between his family and a crocodile. She banged on some more, not recognising that his loyalty had suddenly slipped and gone from her—*We're animals non-grata my little wally woo woo. You killed those pandas sure as...*

—*It was Bash! And you!*

—*Who stole the little plane from the hangar? Who armed and prepared it for flight? Who broke into the panda's enclosure to start with? Who has blood all down their front? There's no use backing away now, Wally boy, you're at war.*

—*War? But... who are we fighting?*

—*Who do you think?*

—*I didn't...*

At his hesitation, something snapped in the rogue crocodile and she seemed to double in size. She began to spew forth long-held philosophies powered with the sudden release of long-held vehemence and the certain knowledge that might is always right—*Aren't you sick of running, hiding, cowering and slithering into corners that knives, nets and poisons can't reach? Why must we be creatures of the shadows and drains, running always from the pets of men who delight in killing for blood lust; those ferals that humans have bred for sport and profit; dogs, foxes, pigs and goats, who steal our food and our homes?*

In his turn, Hod felt himself shrinking, appalled, reaching for the kinder thoughts that he'd grown up with—*That's not the way Ektek thinks...*

—*Ektek? Who cares what Ektek thinks!* Shining Teeth almost laughed—*We have to go back to the old ways; animals should kill other creatures if they invade their territory, and that includes humans. Don't you feel invaded?*

—*But we can't keep fighting all our lives!*

—*That's all we can do. Finish them before they finish us.*

—*But...*

—*But what, wally?* Shining Teeth had thought he was with her and his indecision made her angry. She looked at him and she did not like what she saw there—*What exactly is your problem?*

—*Ektek believe killing for the sake of killing is vile.*

—*Ektek, Ektek, Ektek is a waste of time, a pathetic helpless band of do-gooders who have absolutely no idea. Tell me. When is it right to kill? No, don't tell me. Surely it's right to kill them before they kill us? Don't we have a right to live? Weren't we created before men?*

—What about dignity and honour?

—What about it? What about living? You're starting to sound like that agonised tiger...

—But aren't we as bad as them, if we go round killing them? Besides, in a battle, who would win? Who holds all the weapons?

—If we are, if any animal is, to stand upon an earth with no humans left, then we must seek them everywhere. Not one human can be allowed to survive, not in a cave, not in a sliver of space between forest trees, not in a submarine in the depths of the ocean, not in a space ship sailing between the stars. We will find them and we will finish them and we will never let the great apes rise again. For they spell death and destruction. Their daily activities despoil the land, the air above and the sea below. They clog the very pores of the earth itself as they mine the ground for their short-lived riches. The rule of humanity is all-pervasive. Our brethren who survive in large numbers only do so because humans see them as useful. But we can't be jealous of a cow or a sheep or a racehorse or even a bright fish selected to swim before nervous dental patients. Imagine their lives, hemmed in by fences, continual performance demands and stale monochromatic food...

—How do you know all this stuff?

—Come on. I've seen their billboards, their television and their internet. So have you. So, tell me, how is it that humans have the power to destroy our home many times over and can choose to select and reproduce the species they think are worthy? Not only a species, but the very DNA itself is chosen, and finally, fatefully, they let the rest go to extinction in a hand basket? Tell me this, wally woo woo; when did humans rise so far above their animal stature they can no longer see their own navels? Humans have changed the course of evolution. Now, it's time for the animals to do our own choosing.

—But, the first strike was against us! The pandas hadn't done anything to you...

—Do you think the humans will be hurting? Aren't the pandas the prettiest of the icons?

—Yes...

—Now we go and finish the job.

—What?

—We let loose the magnums, all of them, and the snakes and the venomous creatures of the world. We've got hundreds of years of retribution to score. For all their sins against us, humans are going to pay. With their lives. Shining Teeth stood and prepared to go—*Which way to the reptile house? Hey, which way to Justice?*

476

Any giggle remaining in Hod had long gone. When he'd trespassed and let Shining Teeth into the panda enclosure he'd had no idea he was fighting any more than one little battle. He'd always imagined he'd be able to go right back to his family and live in the inadequate enclosure and carry on just as before but now he understood that he had been playing a treacherous game. He clearly had not understood the rules. Here at endgame, he really did not want to play any more. He stared at the expectant crocodile and hope died within him. He suddenly saw what Shining Teeth was and he could not stand the sight of her. She was filled with a sort of self-importance, a weird animal royalty; she was pumped up with her speech and high-flying words. It was as though she had been speaking to all the animals in the world but really it had just been him, little old Hod, wally woo woo, sitting in a sewer. He felt as if he'd looked into a distorting mirror only he suddenly understood that the distortion was the real beast and he'd been trapped by his desire for action, any action, without imagining what that meant, what it could look like. He felt horribly cold and he knew, with a kind of gross nauseating epiphany, he had strayed onto the wrong path—*Shining Teeth?*

—*Yeah?*

—*I don't want to be at war.*

—*Bit late now.*

—*Maybe, but I have to go.*

Shining Teeth turned to look back at him and he hesitated no more. He ran, he bounded, he flew away from her; he knew she must not catch him for she would kill him easily.

She watched him go with little emotion clouding her view—*Bye, bye, Hoddy woo woo. Don't worry. I can find the reptiles by myself. I can find the Ektek crew, too. Then, I'll come to find you. Guess you're endangered in all sorts of ways.*

Chapter Sixty-four

I

Drips of bloody paw prints splashed the dirt floor of the hangar. Shining Teeth followed the trail to the machine cage where she found Gleam lying in his bed. He was bloody. He was misshapen and swollen. His paws were red raw and his mouth was sunken and smeared with blood and dribble. She swaggered up to him and smiled, as only a crocodile can. She said—*What happened to you?*

Gleam had trouble forming words with his toothless mouth. The letters were slurred and pain confused him. He had to resort to a whisper—*Took your time.*

Shining Teeth leaned in close to hear him. She could hardly control her giggling as he struggled to make himself understood. She longed to mock him yet didn't want to engage her victim in humour. She wanted to kill him, pure and simple but she had one more question for him—*Why didn't you stop me?*

—*Can't take responsibility for your actions.*

—*What if I don't care what I do?*

—*Then you won't mind when you're hunted down and made into a pair of shoes with matching handbag.*

—*I make that an 'if'.*

The whisper came with added hurt—*Nothing is more certain.*

—*Nothing?* she sneered.

—*I am disarmed.*

—*Disarmed!* Shining Teeth laughed or barked or she might have cleared her throat of catarrh; it was a sound of such ugliness—*I could have killed you any time I liked.*

—*What are you waiting for?*

—*Your last words.*

Gleam could barely turn his head to see her properly but he made his eyes focus on her and he made her connect with his empathy and he made her hear him as he whispered—*I forgive you.*

Shining Teeth stared at him, his watery eyes, his dishevelled coat, his bloodied paws and his dribbling mouth. She closed her eyes and took in a deep breath. How dare he forgive her? Then she attacked.

Gleam relaxed at last and found his roaring instinct, found his deep urge to kill, to rend, to unleash and he let loose and he was free, flying into infinite, deep, crimson pain.

II

Antenna sat in the numbat enclosure where she could see the entrance to the Ektek tunnels. She could see when Gumfluff and Carney arrived with Eid's body and she waited where she was when the numbats helped to carry him in and lie him down beside her. Antenna could not take her eyes from him. Shining Teeth had not broken his skin and Eid lay as if sleeping. Antenna came closer and sniffed at him. She nuzzled her nose into the fluff of his stripes and the rust of his shoulders. She ran her face through his luxurious tail and breathed in his armpit. Then she lay down with him, nestled into him and sighed.

The other numbats stood away from the couple, the elderly mother numbat keeping baby Zip Too warm and quiet. The baby was far too young to understand what had happened to her father. Antenna embraced Eid and whispered to him. No one could hear the soft thoughts she shared with his body. They turned away and left her to her privacy and her farewells.

Spark flew into the enclosure and, before anyone could stop him, went straight to Antenna. He hardly noticed Eid. He had to report that Shining Teeth had continued her rampage. She had released all the magnums in the zoo. Gorillas stormed through the public, causing panic and broken bones. The elephants had broken out of the zoo entirely and were responsible for a number of bad car crashes and trampling incidents. The big cats were also prowling around the local suburbs causing mayhem and killing children.

Antenna slowly rose to her feet. She breathed in the smell of Eid for the last time. She looked at Spark sadly—*It won't take them long to recapture them.*

—*Maybe not,* said Spark—*The venomous snakes might be more of a problem. I understand Shining Teeth is encouraging all animals; rats, birds and dogs, everyone, to attack humans in whatever way they can and they are. The word is spreading fast. Humans have begun to retaliate.*

—*Oh,* said Antenna—*Then we truly are at war.*

—*Yes,* said Spark—*War.*

—*Hod?*

—We don't know. There is no word of him.

—Could she have killed him?

—Yes.

—But we don't know.

—No.

Antenna looked at the beetle with wide eyes before she turned round to see the numbats staring at her. She looked down at Eid who could not be helped further. Then she looked back to her living faux family, who trusted her and had looked after her when all she had wanted was to give up. Mother numbat too looked around at their group and then back to Antenna. She said—*What should we do?*

—I don't know, said Antenna—*I can't advise you. It might be safer to stay here, in the enclosure. You could collapse the tunnel and bar the way but Shining Teeth can go where she wants in the end. It might be safer to run away but you might cross the path of some other rogue magnum caught in bloodlust.* Her eyes filled with tears and she embraced the mother numbat for some time—*Thank you for all you've done for me.*

Mother numbat nodded, her own eyes wet—*You won't stay with us?*

—I think you will be safer without me. I'm sorry. Then Antenna picked up her only baby in her mouth and left the numbat enclosure for the last time. Spark flew beside her—*Antenna?* asked Spark—*Shall I come with you?*

Antenna put down her baby again and reassured her before she spoke to Spark once more—*No, Spark. You will fly away from here. You will stay safe and find a mate and have many larvae. You will be happy, Spark.*

—But... Listen. I can fly ahead and scout for you. I can let you know where is safe to travel. I can help you. Let me.

Antenna looked at him for a while, torn between wanting to keep him away and safe and wanting to continue with some form of Ektek, her family. It was too much to ask, yet, looking into the beetle's eyes, she knew what she had to do.

—I'll meet you outside the hangar, Sparkie. Got something to do first. She bent down to pick up Zip Too again and continued on her way.

—All clear above and astern, Antenna. Spark flew ahead of her out of numbat enclosure and into the air.

Leaving Eid lying with his family and carrying her baby in her mouth, she went through into the tunnel and looked both ways, her eyes scratching through the gloom. Was that movement ahead? She stood, staring, her heart beating and, when she was certain there was nothing in front of her, she tiptoed forward. So began the longest journey she had ever made down that familiar path to the hangar and the control centre; a path she had taken at least twice a day every day of her life. This time she held her child and she feared for her future. Quietly she crept to the next corner, carefully she observed and listened and smelt the air before moving on; and finally, she made it to the hangar. There she too saw the trail of blood and she followed it to the machine cage. It was clear what had happened. Shining Teeth had been to see Gleam. The pleasure had been all hers.

Antenna put her baby down on a piece of sacking and soothed her. Then she turned back to the red splatter that was Gleam's remains. She moved forward and found him, with dulled eye and twisted legs, slowly bleeding out.

Antenna knelt beside him and placed her head on his fading heart—*Please don't go, Gleam. Stay, here with me.*

Now little more than breathing, and little enough of that, his whisper was so faint, she almost had to stop breathing herself to hear him—*You must survive.*

—*And you*, she retorted—*Don't give up. You told me that. You told me I had to keep going. You told me I had to keep fighting. It's not just for your own life. It's for all the different creatures. All the animals you've helped… You told me that…*

—*For the children,* whispered Gleam. His breathing was arduous, his fight no longer on this earth—*I am already gone.*

Antenna turned her head into his neck regardless of the blood, sticky and puddling everywhere around him. His heart stopped pumping and his lungs stopped circulating air. He was no longer in pain.

Antenna, lying in the bloody arms of a dead tiger, closed her eyes and then her mind turned to dread. All was downturn and fear. Where would she go? What could she do? She would meet Spark at the hangar and they would find somewhere. They would make a start and they would not give up. She thought of Eid and then she thought of Gleam and as she said her farewells to them both she heard her little baby squeal.

She looked up to see Hod standing in the doorway.

She did not think. She jumped up and ran to protect her child. She crouched down and nestled around the baby. She looked up at the yellow-footed rock wallaby.

Hod almost laughed but it was all too serious for that—*I wouldn't hurt her.*

—*How do I know?*

—*You know me.*

—*Not any more.*

Hod looked over at Gleam—*Is he...?*

—*Gone.*

Hod nodded. He looked around the cage, seeing the blood and seemed overcome by the extent of Shining Teeth's carnage—*Antenna, you must come away.*

—*With you?*

—*With me. I will guide you and we will go together, up into the hills and far away. She will never find us.*

—*Why, Hod? Why are you leaving her?*

—*She is filled with hate.*

—*She has done it, Hod. She has destroyed Ektek.*

—*She has not destroyed us. We won't let her.*

Hod bent down and picked up Zip Too. He placed her carefully into his messenger bag. Already there was a tiny joey inside and the babies cuddled together for warmth and for comfort.

Antenna saw the baby rock wallaby and looked at him then back at the two babies nestled together.

—*Yes,* he said—*He's all that's left.*

—*Shining Teeth?*

—*Encouraged the lions to visit my family.* He went close to Antenna and touched her forehead with his own. They mingled breath and rested there, their foreheads pressing together for a moment—*Come on,* said Antenna—*Spark's waiting.*

Numbat and wallaby turned and left the control centre.

The glow-worms flickered at the top of the cave and then, slowly, one by one, the blue glimmering lights went out.

Fin

www.ingramcontent.com/pod-product-compliance
Lightning Source LLC
Chambersburg PA
CBHW022236020726
47496CB00004B/934